MICHAEL CRICHTON
STATE OF FEAR

"Crichton has written a book that deserves to be taken seriously."

The New Yorker

"You have to hand it to Michael Crichton; he knows how to tell a story. From *The Andromeda Strain* to *Jurassic Park*, Crichton has managed to excite readers' imaginations to such an extent that his novels actually change how people think. . . . In *State of Fear*, Crichton takes on global warming—and he finds the scientific evidence lacking even as he finds the storytelling possibilities intriguing. . . . It's a good story . . . hair-raising . . . And, if you don't read it, you won't be much fun at cocktail parties."

Wisconsin State Journal

"Gripping . . . Nothing short of spellbinding, with a series of wild twists and turns, numerous and engaging subplots, and the introduction of countless characters, most of whom resonate."

Pittsburgh Post-Gazette

"[Crichton] succeeds quite well. . . . A thriller in which the perils faced by the leading characters would put Pauline of 'The Perils of Pauline' to shame."

Washington Times

"Be sure to read Michael Crichton's novel *State of Fear*. . . . A great read . . . a genuine page-turner . . . [Crichton] is a master storyteller and this is one of his best. . . . It's hugely entertaining."

Anchorage Daily News

"Incendiary . . . revolutionary . . . fascinating . . . *State of Fear* is the first thriller in history whose goals are to convince you that there's really nothing to be afraid of, and then to scare you to death about it."

San Francisco Chronicle

"The sort of page-turner that will induce beads of sweat from even the coolest armchair detective."

Milwaukee Journal-Sentinel

"Provocative and controversial . . . He marries compelling subject matter with edge-of-your-seat storytelling. . . . [Crichton] can thrill readers who love the heart-pounding chase. . . . He can impress techno-geeks eager to analyze the scientific data he weaves through his stories."

USA Today

"Crichton knows how to craft a tale, one that keeps the reader turning the pages."

Houston Chronicle

"[A] page-turner that people will want to read in one gulp."

Washington Post

"Thought-provoking . . . definitely page-turning . . . You can't miss it. . . . You'll want to read *State of Fear* for the excitement first, of course. But promise yourself that you won't stop until you've read everything Crichton has to say through the end."

Detroit Free Press

BY MICHAEL CRICHTON

MICHAEL CRICHTON

STATE OF FEAR

A Novel

HARPER

An Imprint of HarperCollinsPublishers

A hardcover edition of this title was published by HarperCollins December 2004 and a special edition and mass market edition by Avon Books, an Imprint of HarperCollins Publishers, August and November 2005, respectively.

Grateful acknowledgment is made for permission to reprint from "You May Be Right" by Billy Joel, © 1980, Impulsive Music. All rights reserved; used by permission.

HARPER

An Imprint of HarperCollins*Publishers*
10 East 53rd Street
New York, New York 10022-5299

Copyright © 2004 by Michael Crichton
Excerpt from *Next* copyright © 2006 by Michael Crichton
ISBN 978-0-06-178266-4

First Harper paperback printing: May 2009
First Avon Books paperback printing: November 2005
First Avon Books international printing: August 2005
First Harper hardcover printing: December 2004

Printed in the United States of America

Visit Harper paperbacks on the World Wide Web at
www.harpercollins.com

10   9   8   7   6   5

There is something fascinating about science. One gets such wholesale returns of conjecture out of such a trifling investment of fact.

—MARK TWAIN

Within any important issue, there are always aspects no one wishes to discuss.

—GEORGE ORWELL

INTRODUCTION

In late 2003, at the Sustainable Earth Summit conference in Johannesburg, the Pacific island nation of Vanutu announced that it was preparing a lawsuit against the Environmental Protection Agency of the United States over global warming. Vanutu stood only a few feet above sea level, and the island's eight thousand inhabitants were in danger of having to evacuate their country because of rising sea levels caused by global warming. The United States, the largest economy in the world, was also the largest emitter of carbon dioxide and therefore the largest contributor to global warming.

The National Environmental Resource Fund, an American activist group, announced that it would join forces with Vanutu in the lawsuit, which was expected to be filed in the summer of 2004. It was rumored that wealthy philanthropist George Morton, who frequently backed environmental causes, would personally finance the suit, expected to cost more than $8 million. Since the suit would ultimately be heard by the sympathetic Ninth Circuit in San Francisco, the litigation was awaited with some anticipation.

But the lawsuit was never filed.

No official explanation for the failure to file has ever been given either by Vanutu or NERF. Even after the sudden disappearance of George Morton, an inexplicable lack of interest by the media has left the circumstances surrounding this lawsuit unexamined. Not until the end of 2004 did several former NERF board members begin to speak publicly about what had happened within that organization. Further revelations by Morton's staff, as well as by former members of the Los Angeles law firm of Hassle and Black, have added further detail to the story.

Thus it is now clear what happened to the progress of the Vanutu litigation between May and October of 2004, and why so many people died in remote parts of the world as a result.

MC
Los Angeles, 2004

From the Internal Report to the National Security Council (NSC) from the AASBC (Classified). Redacted portions from AASBC. Obtained FOIA 03/04/04.

In retrospect the ███████ conspiracy was extremely well-planned. Preparations were under way for more than a year before the events themselves took place. There were preliminary ██████ as early as March ███ 2003, and reports to the British ████ ██████ and the German ███ ██████.

The first incident took place in Paris, in May of 2004. It is ████ ██████████ ████████ that the authorities ████████████████████ But there now can be no doubt that what happened in Paris ██████████, and the serious consequences that followed.

I

AKAMAI

In the darkness, he touched her arm and said, "Stay here." She did not move, just waited. The smell of salt water was strong. She heard the faint gurgle of water.

Then the lights came on, reflecting off the surface of a large open tank, perhaps fifty meters long and twenty meters wide. It might have been an indoor swimming pool, except for all the electronic equipment that surrounded it.

And the very strange device at the far end of the pool.

Jonathan Marshall came back to her, grinning like an idiot. *"Qu'est-ce que tu penses?"* he said, though he knew his pronunciation was terrible. "What do you think?"

"It is magnificent," the girl said. When she spoke English, her accent sounded exotic. In fact, everything about her was exotic, Jonathan thought. With her dark skin, high cheekbones, and black hair, she might have been a model. And she strutted like a model in her short skirt and spike heels. She was half Vietnamese, and her name was Marisa. "But no one else is here?" she said, looking around.

"No, no," he said. "It's Sunday. No one is coming."

Jonathan Marshall was twenty-four, a graduate student in physics from London, working for the summer at the ultra-modern Laboratoire Ondulatoire—the wave mechanics laboratory—of the French Marine Institute in Vissy, just north of Paris. But the suburb was mostly the residence of young families, and it had been a lonely summer for Marshall. Which was why he could not believe his good fortune at meeting this girl. This extraordinarily beautiful and sexy girl.

"Show me what it does, this machine," Marisa said. Her eyes were shining. "Show me what it is you do."

"My pleasure," Marshall said. He moved to the large control panel and began to switch on the pumps and sensors. The thirty panels of the wave machine at the far end of the tank clicked, one after another.

He glanced back at her, and she smiled at him. "It is so complicated," she said. She came and stood beside him at the control panel. "Your research is recorded on cameras?"

"Yes, we have cameras in the ceiling, and on the sides of the tank. They make a visual record of the waves that are generated. We also have pressure sensors in the tanks that record pressure parameters of the passing wave."

"These cameras are on now?"

"No, no," he said. "We don't need them; we're not doing an experiment."

"Perhaps we are," she said, resting her hand on

his shoulder. Her fingers were long and delicate. She had beautiful fingers.

She watched for a minute, then said, "This room, everything is so expensive. You must have great security, no?"

"Not really," he said. "Just cards to get in. And only one security camera." He gestured over his shoulder. "That one back in the corner."

She turned to look. "And that is turned on?" she said.

"Oh yes," he said. "That's always on."

She slid her hand to caress his neck lightly. "So is someone watching us now?"

"Afraid so."

"Then we should behave."

"Probably. Anyway, what about your boy-friend?"

"Him." She gave a derisive snort. "I have had enough of him."

Earlier that day, Marshall had gone from his small apartment to the café on rue Montaigne, the café he went to every morning, taking a journal article with him to read as usual. Then this girl had sat down at the next table, with her boyfriend. The couple had promptly fallen into an argument.

In truth, Marshall felt that Marisa and the boyfriend didn't seem to belong together. He was American, a beefy, red-faced fellow built like a footballer, with longish hair and wire-frame glasses that did not suit his thick features. He looked like a pig trying to appear scholarly.

His name was Jim, and he was angry with Marisa, apparently because she had spent the previous night away from him. "I don't know why you won't tell me where you were," he kept repeating.

"It is none of your business, that's why."

"But I thought we were going to have dinner together."

"Jimmy, I told you we were not."

"No, you told me you were. And I was waiting at the hotel for you. All night."

"So? No one made you. You could go out. Enjoy yourself."

"But I was waiting for you."

"Jimmy, you do not own me." She was exasperated by him, sighing, throwing up her hands, or slapping her bare knees. Her legs were crossed, and the short skirt rode up high. "I do as I please."

"That's clear."

"Yes," she said, and at that moment she turned to Marshall and said, "What is that you are reading? It looks very complicated."

At first Marshall was alarmed. She was clearly talking to him to taunt the boyfriend. He did not want to be drawn into the couple's dispute.

"It's physics," he said briefly, and turned slightly away. He tried to ignore her beauty.

"What kind of physics?" she persisted.

"Wave mechanics. Ocean waves."

"So, you are a student?"

"Graduate student."

"Ah. And clearly intelligent. You are English? Why are you in France?"

And before he knew it, he was talking to her, and she introduced the boyfriend, who gave Marshall a smirk and a limp handshake. It was still very uncomfortable, but the girl behaved as if it were not.

"So you work around here? What sort of work? A tank with a machine? Really, I can't imagine what you say. Will you show me?"

And now they were here, in the wave mechanics laboratory. And Jimmy, the boyfriend, was sulking in the parking lot outside, smoking a cigarette.

"What shall we do about Jimmy?" she said, standing beside Marshall while he worked at the control panel.

"He can't smoke in here."

"I will see that he does not. But I don't want to make him more angry. Can I let him in, do you think?"

Marshall felt disappointment flood through him. "Sure. I guess."

Then she squeezed his shoulder. "Don't worry, he is busy later with other business of his."

She went and opened the door at the back of the lab, and Jimmy came in. Marshall glanced back and saw him hanging back, hands in his pockets. Marisa came up to stand beside Marshall again, at the control panel.

"He's all right," she said. "Now show me."

The electric motors at the far end of the tank whirred, and the wave paddles generated the first wave. It was a small wave, and it rippled smoothly down the length of the tank, to splash on a slanted panel at the near end.

"So, this is a tidal wave?" she said.

"It is a simulation of a tsunami, yes," Marshall said, his fingers tapping the keyboard. On the control panel, displays showed temperature and pressure, generated false-color images of the wave.

"A simulation," she said. "Meaning what?"

"We can make waves up to one meter high in this tank," Marshall said. "But the real tsunamis are four, eight, ten meters high. Occasionally even more."

"A wave in the ocean that is ten meters?" Her eyes widened. "Really?" She was looking toward the ceiling, trying to imagine it.

Marshall nodded. That would be over thirty feet high, the height of a three-story building. And it would be moving at eight hundred kilometers an hour, roaring up to the shore.

"And when it comes to the shore?" she said. "Is that the slope at this end? It looks like a pebble texture on it. Is that the shore?"

"That's right," Marshall said. "How high the wave goes up the shore is a function of the angle of the slope. We can adjust the slope to any angle."

The boyfriend came forward, moving closer to the tank, but still he hung back. He never said a word.

Marisa was excited. "You can adjust it? How?"

"It is motorized."

"To any angle?" She giggled. "Show me *vingt-sept* degrees. Twenty-seven."

"Coming up." Marshall typed at the keyboard. With a slight grinding sound, the slope of the shore angled higher.

The American boyfriend went closer to the tank to look, drawn by the activity. It *was* fascinating, Marshall thought. Anybody would be interested. But the guy never spoke. He just stood and watched the pebbled surface tilt. Soon it stopped.

"So that is the slope?" she said.

"Yes," Marshall said. "Although in point of fact, twenty-seven degrees is fairly steep, more than the average shoreline in the real world. Maybe I should set it to—"

Her dark hand closed over his. "No, no," she said. Her skin was soft. "Leave it. Show me a wave. I want to see a wave."

Small waves were being generated every thirty seconds. They rippled along the length of the tank, with a slight whoosh. "Well, I first have to know the shape of the shoreline. Right now, it's flat beach, but if it was an inlet of some kind . . ."

"Will it change to make an inlet?"

"Of course."

"Really? Show me."

"What kind of inlet do you want? A harbor, a river, a bay . . ."

"Oh," she said, shrugging, "make a bay."

He smiled. "Fine. How big?"

With the whir of electric motors, the shoreline began to sink into a curve, the slope indenting into a bowl.

"Fantastic," she said. "Come on, Jonathan, show me the wave."

"Not yet. How big is the bay?"

"Oh . . ." She gestured in the air. "One mile. A bay of one mile. Now will you show me?" She leaned toward him. "I do not like to wait. You should know this."

He smelled her perfume. He typed quickly. "Here it comes," he said. "A big wave, coming into a one-mile bay, with a twenty-seven-degree slope."

There was a much louder whoosh as the next wave was generated at the far end of the tank, and then it rippled smoothly toward them, a raised line of water about six inches high.

"Oh!" Marisa pouted. "You promised me it would be *big*."

"Just wait," he said.

"It will grow?" she said, giggling. She put her hand on his shoulder again. Then the American glanced back, and gave her a dirty look. She jerked her chin in the air, defiant. But when he looked back at the tank, she took her hand away.

Marshall felt despondent again. She was just using him, he was a pawn in this game between them.

"You said it will grow?" she said.

"Yes," Marshall said, "the wave will grow as it comes to the shore. In deep water a tsunami is small, but in shallow water it builds. And the inlet will concentrate its power, so it goes higher."

The wave rose higher, and then smashed against the curved shore at the near end. It foamed white, and sloshed up the sides of the shore. It came up about five feet, he guessed.

"So it comes high," she said. "In the real world?"

"That's about forty, fifty feet," he said. "Fifteen meters."

"Ooh la la," she said, pursing her lips. "So a person cannot run away from this."

"Oh no," Marshall said. "You can't outrun a tidal wave. There was a wave in Hilo, Hawaii, in 1960, came right down the streets of the town, tall as the buildings, people ran from it but—"

"So that's it?" the American said. "That's all it does?" His voice was growly, like he needed to clear his throat.

"Don't mind him," she said quietly.

"Yes, that's what we do here," Marshall said. "We generate waves—"

"Jesus fucking A," the American said. "I could do that in my bathtub when I was six months old."

"Well," Marshall said, gesturing to the control panel, and the monitors displaying data, "we generate a lot of databases for researchers around the world who are—"

"Yeah, yeah. That's enough. Boring as whale shit. I'm leaving. You coming, Marisa, or not?" He stood and glared at her.

Marshall heard her suck in her breath.

"No," she said. "I am not."

The American turned and walked off, slamming the door loudly as he left.

Her apartment was just across the river from Notre Dame, and from the balcony in the bedroom he had a beautiful view of the cathedral, which was lighted at night. It was ten o'clock, but there was still a deep blue in the sky. He looked down at the street below, the lights of the cafés, the crowds walking on the streets. It was a busy and glamorous scene.

"Don't worry," she said, behind him. "If you're looking for Jimmy, he won't come here."

Actually, the thought hadn't occurred to him, until she mentioned it. "No?"

"No," she said. "He will go elsewhere. Jimmy has many women." She took a sip of red wine, then set the glass down on the bedside table. Unceremoniously, she pulled her top over her head and dropped her skirt. She was wearing nothing beneath.

Still in her high heels, she walked toward him. He must have seemed surprised, because she said, "I told you: I do not like to wait," and threw her arms around him and kissed him hard, fiercely, almost angrily. The next moments were awkward, trying to kiss while she tore off his clothes. She was breathing hard, almost panting. She never spoke. She was so passionate she seemed almost angry, and her beauty, the physical perfection of her dark body, intimidated him, but not for long.

Afterward she lay against him, her skin soft but her body taut beneath the surface. The bedroom ceiling had a soft glow from the church façade opposite. He was relaxed, but she seemed, if anything, to be energized, restless after making love. He wondered if she had really come, despite her moans and her final cries. And then abruptly, she got up.

"Anything wrong?"

She took a sip of wine. "To the toilet," she said, and turned away, passing through a door. She had left her wineglass. He sat up and took a sip, seeing the delicate pattern of her lipstick on the rim.

He looked at the bed and saw the dark streaks on the sheets from her heels. She had not taken them off until midway through their lovemaking. Now the heels were tossed away, coming to a stop beneath the window. Signs of their passion. He still felt, even now, as if he were in a dream. He had never been with a woman like this. Beautiful like this, living in a place like this. He wondered how much this apartment cost, the wood paneling, the perfect location . . .

He took another sip of wine. He could get used to this, he thought.

He heard water running in the bathroom. A humming sound, a tuneless song.

With a *bang!* the front door slammed open and three men burst into the bedroom. They were wearing dark raincoats and hats. Terrified, Marshall set the wineglass on the table—it fell—and dived for his clothes beside the bed to cover himself, but in an instant the men were on him, grabbing him with gloved hands. He yelled in alarm and panic as they threw him over, shoving him facedown on the bed. He was still yelling as they pushed his face into a pillow. He thought they were going to suffocate him, but they didn't. One man hissed, "Be quiet. Nothing will happen if you are quiet."

He didn't believe him, so he struggled, calling out again. Where was Marisa? What was she doing? It was happening so fast. One man was sitting on his back, knees digging into his spine, his cold shoes on Marshall's bare buttocks. He felt the man's hand on his neck, shoving him into the bed.

"Be quiet!" the man hissed again.

The other men had each taken one of his wrists, and they were pulling his arms wide, spread-eagling him on the bed. *They were getting ready to do something to him.* He felt terrified and vulnerable. He moaned, and somebody hit him on the back of the head. "Quiet!"

Everything was happening quickly, it was all impressionistic. Where was Marisa? Probably hiding in the bathroom, and he couldn't blame her. He heard a sloshing sound and saw a plastic baggie and something white in it, like a golf ball. They were placing the baggie under his armpit, on the fleshy part of his arm.

What the hell were they doing? He felt the water cold against his underarm, and he struggled but they held him tight, and then inside the water, something soft pressed against the arm, and he had a *sticky* sensation, like sticky chewing gum, something sticky and tugging against the flesh of his arm, and then he felt a little pinch. Nothing, hardly noticeable, a momentary sting.

The men were moving quickly, the baggie was removed, and at that moment he heard two surprisingly loud gunshots and Marisa was screaming in rapid French—*"Salaud! Salopard! Bouge-toi le cul!"*—and the third man had tumbled off Marshall's back and fallen to the ground, then scrambled up, and Marisa was still screaming, there were more shots, and he could smell powder in the air, and the men fled. The door slammed, and she came back, stark naked, babbling in French he could not understand, something about *vacherie,* which he thought was a cow but he wasn't thinking straight. He was starting to tremble on the bed.

She came over and threw her arms around him. The barrel of the gun was hot and he yelled, and she set it aside. "Oh Jonathan, I am so sorry, so sorry." She cradled his head against her shoulder. "Please, you must forgive me, it is all right now, I promise you."

Gradually his trembling stopped, and she looked at him. "Did they hurt you?"

He shook his head, no.

"Good. I did not think so. Idiots! Friends of Jimmy, they think they make a joke, to scare you. And me I am sure. But you are not hurt?"

He shook his head again. He coughed. "Perhaps," he said, finding his voice at last. "Perhaps I should be going."

"Oh, no," she said. "No, no, you cannot do this to me."

"I don't feel—"

"Absolutely no," she said. She pushed closer to him, so her body was touching his. "You must stay a while."

"Should we call the police?"

"*Mais non.* The police will do nothing. A quarrel of lovers. In France we do not do this, call the police."

"But they broke in . . ."

"They are gone now," she said, whispering in

his ear. He felt her breath. "There is only us, now. Only us, Jonathan." Her dark body slid down his chest.

It was after midnight when he was finally dressed and standing at the window, looking out at Notre Dame. The streets were still crowded.

"Why will you not stay?" she said, pouting prettily. "I want you to stay. Don't you want to please me?"

"I'm sorry," he said. "I have to go. I don't feel very well."

"I will make you feel better."

He shook his head. In truth, he really did not feel well. He was experiencing waves of dizziness, and his legs felt oddly weak. His hands were trembling as he gripped the balcony.

"I'm sorry," he said again. "I have to leave."

"All right, then I will drive you."

Her car, he knew, was parked on the other side of the Seine. It seemed far to walk. But he just nodded numbly. "All right," he said.

She was in no rush. They strolled arm in arm, like lovers, along the embankment. They passed the houseboat restaurants tied up to the side, brightly lit, still busy with guests. Above them, on the other side of the river, rose Notre Dame, brilliantly lit. For a while, this slow walk, with her head on his shoulder, the soft words she spoke to him, made him feel better.

But soon he stumbled, feeling a kind of clumsy weakness coursing through his body. His mouth was very dry. His jaw felt stiff. It was difficult to speak.

She did not seem to notice. They had moved past the bright lights now, under one of the bridges, and he stumbled again. This time he fell on the stone embankment.

"My darling," she said, worried and solicitous, and helped him to his feet.

He said, "I think . . . I think . . ."

"Darling, are you all right?" She helped him to a bench, away from the river. "Here, just sit here for a moment. You will feel better in a moment."

But he did not feel better. He tried to protest, but he could not speak. In horror he realized he could not even shake his head. *Something was very wrong.* His whole body was growing weak, swiftly and astonishingly weak, and he tried to push up from the bench, but he could not move his limbs, he could not move his head. He looked at her, sitting beside him.

"Jonathan, what is wrong? Do you need a doctor?"

Yes, I need a doctor, he thought.

"Jonathan, this is not right . . ."

His chest was heavy. He was having trouble breathing. He looked away, staring straight ahead. He thought in horror: *I am paralyzed.*

"Jonathan?"

He tried to look at her. But now he could not even move his eyes. He could only look straight forward. His breathing was shallow.

"Jonathan?"

I need a doctor.

"Jonathan, can you look at me? Can you? No? You cannot turn your head?"

Somehow, her voice did not sound concerned. She sounded detached, clinical. Perhaps his hearing was affected. There was a rushing sound in his ears. It was harder and harder to breathe.

"All right, Jonathan, let's get you away from here."

She ducked her head under his arm and with surprising strength got him to his feet. His body was loose and floppy, sagging around her. He could not control where he looked. He heard the clicking of footsteps approaching and thought, *Thank God.* He heard a man's voice say in French, "Mademoiselle, do you need help?"

"Thank you, but no," she said. "Just too much to drink."

"Are you sure?"

"He does this all the time."

"Yes?"

"I can manage."

"Ah. Then I wish you *bonne nuit.*"

"Bonne nuit," she said.

She continued on her way, carrying him. The footsteps became fainter. Then she paused, turned to look in all directions. And now . . . *she was moving him toward the river.*

"You are heavier than I thought," she said, in a conversational tone.

He felt a deep and profound terror. He was completely paralyzed. He could do nothing. His own feet were scraping over the stone.

Toward the river.

"I am sorry," she said, and she dropped him into the water.

It was a short fall, and a stunning sense of cold. He plunged beneath the surface, surrounded by bubbles and green, then black. He could not move, even in the water. He could not believe this was happening to him, he could not believe that he was dying this way.

Then slowly, he felt his body rise. Green water again, and then he broke the surface, on his back, turning slowly.

He could see the bridge, and the black sky, and Marisa, standing on the embankment. She lit a cigarette and stared at him. She had one hand on her hip, one leg thrust forward, a model's pose. She exhaled, smoke rising in the night.

Then he sank beneath the surface again, and he felt the cold and the blackness close in around him.

At three o'clock in the morning the lights snapped on in the Laboratoire Ondulatoire of the French Marine Institute, in Vissy. The control panel came to life. The wave machine began to generate waves that rolled down the tank, one after another, and crashed against the artificial shore. The control screens flashed three-dimensional images, scrolled columns of data. The data was transmitted to an unknown location somewhere in France.

At four o'clock, the control panel went dark, and the lights went out, and the hard drives erased any record of what had been done.

The twisting jungle road lay in shadow beneath the canopy of the Malay rain forest. The paved road was very narrow, and the Land Cruiser careened around the corners, tires squealing. In the passenger seat, a bearded man of forty glanced at his watch. "How much farther?"

"Just a few minutes," the driver said, not slowing. "We're almost there."

The driver was Chinese but he spoke with a British accent. His name was Charles Ling and he had flown over from Hong Kong to Kuala Lumpur the night before. He had met his passenger at the airport that morning, and they had been driving at breakneck speed ever since.

The passenger had given Ling a card that read "Allan Peterson, Seismic Services, Calgary." Ling didn't believe it. He knew perfectly well that there was a company in Alberta, ELS Engineering, that sold this equipment. It wasn't necessary to come all the way to Malaysia to see it.

Not only that, but Ling had checked the passenger manifest on the incoming flight, and there was no Allan Peterson listed. So this guy had come in on a different name.

Furthermore, he told Ling he was a field geologist doing independent consulting for energy companies in Canada, mostly evaluating potential oil sites. But Ling didn't believe that, either. You could spot those petroleum engineers a mile off. This guy wasn't one.

So Ling didn't know who the guy was. It didn't bother him. Mr. Peterson's credit was good; the rest was none of Ling's business. He had only one interest today, and that was to sell cavitation machines. And this looked like a big sale: Peterson was talking about three units, more than a million dollars in total.

He turned off the road abruptly, onto a muddy rut. They bounced through the jungle beneath huge trees, and suddenly came out into sunlight and a large opening. There was a huge semicircular gash in the ground, exposing a cliff of gray earth. A green lake lay below.

"What's this?" Peterson said, wincing.

"It was open-face mine, abandoned now. Kaolin."

"Which is . . . ?"

Ling thought, this is no geologist. He explained that kaolin was a mineral in clay. "It's used in paper and ceramics. Lot of industrial ceramics now. They make ceramic knives, incredibly sharp. They'll make ceramic auto engines soon. But the quality here was too low. It was abandoned four years ago."

Peterson nodded. "And where is the cavitator?"

Ling pointed toward a large truck parked at the edge of the cliff. "There." He drove toward it. "Russians make it?"

"The vehicle and the carbon-matrix frame are Russian made. The electronics come from Taiwan. We assemble ourselves, in Kuala Lumpur."

"And is this your biggest model?"

"No, this is the intermediate. We don't have the largest one to show you."

They pulled alongside the truck. It was the size of a large earthmover; the cab of the Land Cruiser barely reached above the huge tires. In the center, hanging above the ground, was a large rectangular cavitation generator, looking like an oversize diesel generator, a boxy mass of pipes and wires. The curved cavitation plate was slung underneath, a few feet above the ground.

They climbed out of the car into sweltering heat. Ling's eyeglasses clouded over. He wiped them on his shirt. Peterson walked around the truck. "Can I get the unit without the truck?"

"Yes, we make transportable units. Seagoing containers. But usually clients want them mounted on vehicles eventually."

"I just want the units," Peterson said. "Are you going to demonstrate?"

"Right away," Ling said. He gestured to the operator, high up in the cab. "Perhaps we should step away."

"Wait a minute," Peterson said, suddenly alarmed. "I thought we were going to be alone. Who is that?"

"That's my brother," Ling said smoothly. "He's very trustworthy."

"Well . . ."

"Let's step away," Ling said. "We can see better from a distance."

The cavitation generator fired up, chugging loudly. Soon the noise blended with another sound, a deep humming that Ling always seemed to feel in his chest, in his bones.

Peterson must have felt it, too, because he moved back hastily.

"These cavitation generators are hypersonic," Ling explained, "producing a radially symmetric cavitation field that can be adjusted for focal point, rather like an optical lens, except we are using sound. In other words, we can focus the sound beam, and control how deep the cavitation will occur."

He waved to the operator, who nodded. The cavitation plate came down, until it was just above the ground. The sound changed, becoming deeper and much quieter. The earth vibrated slightly where they were standing.

"Jesus," Peterson said, stepping back.

"Not to worry," Ling said. "This is just low-grade reflection. The main energy vector is orthogonal, directed straight down."

About forty feet below the truck, the walls of the canyon suddenly seemed to blur, to become indistinct. Small clouds of gray smoke obscured the surface for a moment, and then a whole section of cliff gave way, and rumbled down into the lake below, like a gray avalanche. The whole area filled with smoke and dust.

As it began to clear, Ling said, "Now we will show how the beam is focused." The rumbling began again, and this time the cliff blurred much farther down, two hundred feet or more. Once again the gray sand gave way, this time sliding rather quietly into the lake.

"And it can focus laterally as well?" Peterson said.

Ling said it could. A hundred yards north of the truck, the cliff was shaken free, and again tumbled down.

"We can aim it in any direction, and any depth."

"Any depth?"

"Our big unit will focus at a thousand meters. Although no client has any use for such depths."

"No, no," Peterson said. "We don't need anything like that. But we want beam power." He wiped his hands on his trousers. "I've seen enough."

"Really? We have quite a few other techniques to demon—"

"I'm ready to go back." Behind his sunglasses, his eyes were unreadable.

"Very well," Ling said. "If you are sure—"

"I'm sure."

Driving back, Peterson said, "You ship from KL or Hong Kong?"

"From KL."

"With what restrictions?"

Ling said, "How do you mean?"

"Hypersonic cavitation technology in the US is restricted. It can't be exported without a license."

"As I said, we use Taiwanese electronics."

"Is it as reliable as the US technology?"

Ling said, "Virtually identical." If Peterson knew his business, he would know that the US had long ago lost the capacity to manufacture such advanced chipsets. The US cavitation chipsets were manufactured in Taiwan. "Why do you ask? Are you planning to export to the US?"

"No."

"Then there is no difficulty."

"What's your lead time?" Peterson said.

"We need seven months."

"I was thinking of five."

"It can be done. There will be a premium. For how many units?"

"Three," Peterson said.

Ling wondered why anyone would need three cavitation units. No geological survey company in the world owned more than one.

"I can fill that order," Ling said, "upon receipt of your deposit."

"You will have it wired to you tomorrow."

"And we are shipping where? Canada?"

"You will receive shipping instructions," Peterson said, "in five months."

Directly ahead, the curved spans of the ultramodern airport designed by Kurokawa rose into the sky. Peterson had lapsed into silence. Driving up the ramp, Ling said, "I hope we are in time for your flight."

"What? Oh yes. We're fine."

"You're heading back to Canada?"

"Yes."

Ling pulled up at the international terminal,

got out, and shook Peterson's hand. Peterson shouldered his day bag. It was his only luggage. "Well," Peterson said. "I'd better go."

"Safe flight."

"Thank you. You, too. Back to Hong Kong?"

"No," Ling said. "I have to go to the factory, and get them started."

"It's nearby?"

"Yes, in Pudu Raya. Just a few kilometers."

"All right, then." Peterson disappeared inside the terminal, giving a final wave. Ling got back in the car and drove away. But as he was heading down the ramp, he saw that Peterson had left behind his cell phone on the car seat. He pulled over to the curb, glancing back over his shoulder. But Peterson was gone. And the cell phone in his hand was lightweight, made of cheap plastic. It was one of those prepaid-card phones, the disposable ones. It couldn't be Peterson's main phone.

It occurred to Ling that he had a friend who might be able to trace the phone and the card inside it. Find out more about the purchaser. And Ling would like to know more. So he slipped the phone into his pocket and drove north, to the factory.

Richard Mallory looked up from his desk and said, "Yes?"

The man standing in the doorway was pale-complected, slender, and American-looking, with a blond crew cut. His manner was casual, his dress nondescript: dirty Adidas running shoes and a faded navy tracksuit. He looked as if he might be out for a jog and had stopped by the office for a moment.

And since this was Design/Quest, a hot graphics shop located on Butler's Wharf, a refurbished warehouse district below London's Tower Bridge, most of the employees in the office were casually dressed. Mallory was the exception. Since he was the boss, he wore slacks and a white shirt. And wingtip shoes that hurt his feet. But they were hip.

Mallory said, "Can I help you?"

"I've come for the package," the American said.

"I'm sorry. What package?" Mallory said. "If it's a DHL pickup, the secretary has it up front."

The American looked annoyed. "Don't you

think you're overdoing it?" he said. "Just give me the fucking package."

"Okay, fine," Mallory said, getting up from behind the desk.

Apparently the American felt he had been too harsh, because in a quieter tone he said, "Nice posters," and pointed to the wall behind Mallory. "You do 'em?"

"We did," Mallory said. "Our firm."

There were two posters, side by side on the wall, both stark black with a hanging globe of the Earth in space, differing only in the tag line. One said "Save the Earth" and beneath it, "It's the Only Home We Have." The other said "Save the Earth" and beneath that, "There's Nowhere Else to Go."

Then off to one side was a framed photograph of a blond model in a T-shirt: "Save the Earth" and the copy line was "And Look Good Doing It."

"That was our 'Save the Earth' campaign," Mallory said. "But they didn't buy it."

"Who didn't?"

"International Conservation Fund."

He went past the American and headed down the back stairs to the garage. The American followed.

"Why not? They didn't like it?"

"No, they liked it," Mallory said. "But they got Leo as a spokesman, and used him instead. Campaign went to video spots."

At the bottom of the stairs, he swiped his card, and the door unlocked with a click. They stepped into the small garage beneath the building. It was dark except for the glare of daylight from the ramp leading to the street. Mallory noticed with annoyance that a van partly blocked the ramp. They always had trouble with delivery vans parking there.

He turned to the American. "You have a car?"

"Yes. A van." He pointed.

"Oh good, so that's yours. And somebody to help you?"

"No. Just me. Why?"

"It's bloody heavy," Mallory said. "It may just be wire, but it's half a million feet of it. Weighs seven hundred pounds, mate."

"I can handle it."

Mallory went to his Rover and unlocked the boot. The American whistled, and the van rumbled down the ramp. It was driven by a tough-looking woman with spiked hair, dark makeup.

Mallory said, "I thought you were alone."

"She doesn't know anything," the American said. "Forget her. She brought the van. She just drives."

Mallory turned to the open boot. There were stacked white boxes marked "Ethernet Cable (Unshielded)." And printed specifications.

"Let's see one," the American said.

Mallory opened a box. Inside was a jumble of fist-sized coils of very thin wire, each in shrink-wrap plastic. "As you see," he said, "it's guide wire. For anti-tank missiles."

"Is it?"

"That's what they told me. That's why it's wrapped that way. One coil of wire for each missile."

"I wouldn't know," the American said. "I'm

just the delivery man." He went and opened the back of his van. Then he began to transfer the boxes, one at a time. Mallory helped.

The American said, "This guy tell you anything else?"

"Actually, he did," Mallory said. "He said somebody bought five hundred surplus Warsaw Pact rockets. Called Hotfire or Hotwire or something. No warheads or anything. Just the rocket bodies. The story is they were sold with defective guide wire."

"I haven't heard that."

"That's what he said. Missiles were bought in Sweden. Gothenburg, I think. Shipped out from there."

"Sounds like you're worried."

"I'm not worried," Mallory said.

"Like you're afraid you're mixed up in something."

"Not me."

"Sure about that?" the American said.

"Yes, of course I'm sure."

Most of the boxes were transferred to the van. Mallory started to sweat. The American seemed to be glancing at him out of the corner of his eye. Openly skeptical. He said, "So, tell me. What'd he look like, this guy?"

Mallory knew better than to answer that. He shrugged. "Just a guy."

"American?"

"I don't know."

"You don't know whether he was American or not?"

"I couldn't be sure of his accent."

"Why is that?" the American said.

"He might have been Canadian."

"Alone?"

"Yeah."

"Because I hear talk about some gorgeous woman. Sexy woman in high heels, tight skirt."

"I would have noticed a woman like that," Mallory said.

"You wouldn't be . . . leaving her out?" Another skeptical glance. "Keeping her to yourself?" Mallory noticed a bulge on the American's hip. Was it a gun? It might be.

"No. He was alone."

"Whoever the guy was."

"Yes."

"You ask me," the American said, "I'd be wondering why anybody needed half a million feet of wire for anti-tank missiles in the first place. I mean, for what?"

Mallory said, "He didn't say."

"And you just said, 'Right, mate, half a million feet of wire, leave it to me,' with never a question?"

"Seems like you're asking all the questions," Mallory said. Still sweating.

"And I have a reason," the American said. His tone turned ominous. "I got to tell you, pal. I don't like what I am hearing."

The last of the boxes were stacked in the van. Mallory stepped back. The American slammed the first door shut, then the second. As the second door closed, Mallory saw the driver standing there. The woman. She had been standing behind the door.

"I don't like it either," she said. She was wearing fatigues, army surplus stuff. Baggy trousers and high-laced boots. A bulky green jacket. Heavy gloves. Dark glasses.

"Now wait a minute," the American said.

"Give me your cell phone," she said. Holding out her hand for it. Her other hand was behind her back. As if she had a gun.

"Why?"

"Give it to me."

"Why?"

"I want to look at it, that's why."

"There's nothing unusual—"

"Give it to me."

The American pulled the cell phone out of his pocket and handed it to her. Instead of taking it, she grabbed his wrist and pulled him toward her. The cell phone clattered to the ground. She brought her other hand from around her back and quickly gripped the side of his neck with her gloved hand. She held him with both hands around his neck, as if she were strangling him.

For a moment he was stunned; then he began to struggle. "What the fuck are you doing?" he said. "What are you—hey!" He knocked her hands away and jumped back as if he had been burned. "What was that? What did you *do?*"

He touched his neck. A tiny trickle of blood ran down, just a few drops. There was red on his fingertips. Almost nothing.

"What did you do?" he said.

"Nothing." She was stripping off her gloves. Mallory could see she was doing it carefully. As if something were in the glove. Something she did not want to touch.

"Nothing?" the American said. *"Nothing?* Son of a bitch!" Abruptly, he turned and began to run up the ramp toward the street outside.

Calmly, she watched him go. She bent over, picked up the cell phone, and put it in her pocket. Then she turned to Mallory. "Go back to work."

He hesitated.

"You did a good job. I never saw you. You never saw me. Now go."

Mallory turned and walked to the back-stairs door. Behind him, he heard the woman slam the van door, and when he glanced back, he saw the van racing up the ramp into the glare of the street. The van turned right, and was gone.

Back in his office, his assistant, Elizabeth, came in with a mockup for the new ultralight computer ads for Toshiba. The shoot was tomorrow. These were the finals to go over. He shuffled through the boards quickly; Mallory had trouble concentrating.

Elizabeth said, "You don't like them?"

"No, no, they're fine."

"You look a little pale."

"I just, um . . . my stomach."

"Ginger tea," she said. "That's best. Shall I make some?"

He nodded, to get her out of the office. He looked out the window. Mallory's office had a spectacular view of the Thames, and the Tower Bridge off to the left. The bridge had been

repainted baby blue and white (was that traditional or just a bad idea?), but to see it always
made him feel good. Secure somehow.

He walked closer to the window, and stood
looking at the bridge. He was thinking that when
his best friend had asked if he would lend a hand
in a radical environmental cause, it had sounded
like something fun. A bit of secrecy, a bit of dash
and derring-do. He had been promised that it
would not involve anything violent. Mallory had
never imagined he would be frightened.

But he was frightened now. His hands were
shaking. He stuck them in his pockets as he stared
out the window. Five hundred rockets? he
thought. *Five hundred rockets.* What had he gotten
himself into? Then, slowly, he realized that he
was hearing sirens, and there were red lights
flashing on the bridge railings.

There had been an accident on the bridge. And
judging from the number of police and rescue
vehicles, it was a serious accident.

One in which someone had died.

He couldn't help himself. Feeling a sense of
panic, he left the office, went outside to the quay,
and with his heart in his throat, hurried toward
the bridge.

From the upper level of the red double-decker
bus, the tourists were staring down, covering
their mouths in horror. Mallory pushed through
the crowd clustered near the front of the bus. He
got close enough to see a half-dozen paramedics
and police crouched around a body lying in the
street. Above them stood the burly bus driver, in

tears. He was saying that there was nothing he could have done, the man had stepped in front of the bus at the last moment. He must have been drunk, the driver said, because he was wobbling. It was almost as if he fell off the curb.

Mallory could not see the body; the policemen blocked his view. The crowd was nearly silent, just watching. Then one of the policemen stood, holding a red passport in his hands—a German passport. Thank God, Mallory thought, feeling a flood of relief that lasted until a moment later, when one of the paramedics stepped away and Mallory saw one leg of the victim—a faded navy tracksuit and a dirty Adidas running shoe, now soaked with blood.

He felt a wave of nausea, and turned away, pushing back through the crowd. The faces stared past him, impassive or annoyed. But nobody even glanced at him. They were all looking at the body.

Except for one man, dressed like an executive in a dark suit and tie. He was looking directly at Mallory. Mallory met his eyes. The man nodded slightly. Mallory made no response. He just pushed through the last of the crowd and fled, hurrying back down the stairs to his office, and realizing that somehow, in some way that he did not understand, his life had changed forever.

IDEC, the International Data Environmental Consortium, was located in a small brick building adjacent to the campus of Keio Mita University. To the casual observer, IDEC was part of the university, and even showed the coat of arms (*"Calamus Gladio Fortior"*), but in fact it was independent. The center of the building consisted of a small conference room with a podium and two rows of five chairs facing a screen at the front.

At ten in the morning, IDEC director Akira Hitomi stood at the podium and watched as the American came in and took a seat. The American was a large man, not so tall but thick in the shoulders and chest, like an athlete. For such a large man he moved easily, quietly. The Nepali officer entered right behind him, dark-skinned and watchful. He took a seat behind the American and off to one side. At the podium, Hitomi nodded to them and said nothing.

The wood-paneled room darkened slowly, to allow eyes to adjust. On all sides, the wood panels slid silently away, exposing huge flat-panel screens. Some of the screens moved smoothly out from the walls.

At last, the main door closed and locked with a click. Only then did Hitomi speak.

"Good morning, Kenner-san." On the main screen it said "Hitomi Akira" in English and Japanese. "And good morning, Thapa-san." Hitomi flipped open a very small, very thin silver laptop. "Today I will present data from the last twenty-one days, correct up to twenty minutes ago. These will be findings from our joint project, Akamai Tree."

The two visitors nodded. Kenner smiled in anticipation. As well he should, Hitomi thought. Nowhere else in the world could he see such a presentation, for Hitomi's agency was the world leader in the accumulation and manipulation of electronic data. Now images on the screens came up, glowing one after another. They showed what appeared to be a corporate logo: a green tree on a white background, and the lettering AKAMAI TREE DIGITAL NETWORK SOLUTIONS.

This name and image had been chosen for their similarity to actual Internet companies and their logos. For the last two years, Akamai Tree's network of servers actually consisted of carefully designed traps. They incorporated multilevel quad-check honeynets established in both business and academic domains. This enabled them to track backward from servers to user with an 87 percent success rate. They had baited the net starting last year, first with ordinary feed and then with increasingly juicy morsels.

"Our sites mirrored established geology, applied physics, ecology, civil engineering, and biogeography sites," Hitomi said. "To attract deep divers, typical data included information on the use of explosives in seismic recordings, the tests of the stability of structures to vibration and earthquake damage, and in our oceanographic sites, data on hurricanes, rogue waves, tsunamis, and so forth. All this is familiar to you."

Kenner nodded.

Hitomi continued: "We knew we had a disseminated enemy, and a clever one. Users often operate behind netnanny firewalls, or used AOL accounts with teen ratings, to imply they are juvenile pranksters or kiddie scripters. But they are nothing of the sort. They are well organized, patient, and unrelenting. In recent weeks, we have begun to understand more."

The screen changed, showing a list.

"Out of a mix of sites and discussion groups, our sys progs found the deep divers clustered on the following category topics:

> Aarhus, Denmark
> Argon/Oxygen Drives
> Australian Military History
> Caisson Seawalls
> Cavitation (Solid)
> Cellular Encryption
> Controlled Demolition
> Flood Mitigation
> High-Voltage Insulators
> Hilo, Hawaii
> Mid-Ocean Relay Network (MORN)
> Missionary Diaries of the Pacific
> National Earthquake Information Center (NEIC)
> National Environmental Resource Fund (NERF)

Network Data Encryption
Potassium Hydroxide
Prescott, Arizona
Rain Forest Disease Foundation (RFDF)
Seismic Signatures, Geological
Shaped Explosives (Timed)
Shinkai 2000
Solid Rocket Propellant Mixtures
Toxins and Neurotoxins
Wire-guided Projectiles

"An impressive, if mysterious list," Hitomi said. "However, we have filters to identify smees and high-performance clients. These are individuals attacking firewalls, setting trojans, wild spiders, and so forth. Many of them are looking for credit card lists. But not all." He tapped his little computer, and the images changed.

"We added each of these topics into the honey net with increasing stickiness, finally including hints of forthcoming research data, which we exposed as e-mail exchanges among scientists in Australia, Germany, Canada, and Russia. We drew a crowd and watched the traffic. We eventually sorted a complex nodal North America—Toronto, Chicago, Ann Arbor, Montreal—with spines to both American coasts, as well as England, France, and Germany. This is a serious Alpha extremist group. They may already have killed a researcher in Paris. We're awaiting data. But the French authorities can be . . . slow."

Kenner spoke for the first time. "And what's the current delta cellular?"

"Cellular traffic is accelerating. E-mail is heavily

encrypted. STF rate is up. It is clear there is a project under way—global in scope, immensely complicated, extremely expensive."

"But we don't know what it is."

"Not yet."

"Then you'd better follow the money."

"We are doing it. Everywhere." Hitomi smiled grimly. "It is only a matter of time before one of these fishes takes the hook."

Nat Damon signed the paper with a flourish. "I've never been asked to sign a nondisclosure agreement before."

"I'm surprised," the man in the shiny suit said, taking the paper back. "I would have thought it was standard procedure. We don't want our proprietary information to be disclosed." He was a lawyer accompanying his client, a bearded man with glasses, wearing jeans and a work shirt. This bearded man said he was a petroleum geologist, and Damon believed him. He certainly looked like the other petroleum geologists he had dealt with.

Damon's company was called Canada Marine RS Technologies; from a tiny, cramped office outside Vancouver, Damon leased research submarines and remote submersibles to clients around the world. Damon didn't own these subs; he just leased them. The subs were located all over the world—in Yokohama, Dubai, Melbourne, San Diego. They ranged from fully operational fifty-foot submersibles with crews of six, capable of traveling around the globe, to tiny one-man

diving machines and even smaller remote ro-
botic vehicles that operated from a tender ship
on the surface.

Damon's clients were energy and mining companies who used the subs for undersea prospecting or to check the condition of offshore rigs and
platforms. His was a specialized business, and his
little office at the back of a boat repair yard did
not receive many visitors.

Yet these two men had come through his door
just before closing time. The lawyer had done all
of the talking; the client merely gave Damon a
business card that said Seismic Services, with a
Calgary address. That made sense; Calgary was
a big city for hydrocarbon companies. Petro-
Canada, Shell, and Suncor were all there, and
many more. And dozens of small private consulting firms had sprung up there to do prospecting
and research.

Damon took a small model down from the
shelf behind him. It was a tiny white snub-nosed
submarine with a bubble top. He set it on the table in front of the men.

"This is the vehicle I would recommend for your
needs," he said. "The RS Scorpion, built in England just four years ago. Two-man crew. Diesel
and electric power with closed cycle argon drive.
Submerged, it runs on twenty percent oxygen,
eighty percent argon. Solid, proven technology:
potassium hydroxide scrubber, two-hundred-volt
electrical, operational depth of two thousand
feet, and 3.8 hours dive time. It's the equivalent
of the Japanese Shinkai 2000, if you know that
one, or the DownStar 80, of which there are four

in the world, but they're all on long leases. The Scorpion is an excellent submarine."

The men nodded, and looked at each other. "And what kind of external manipulators are there?" the bearded man said.

"That's depth dependent," Damon said. "At lesser depths—"

"Let's say at two thousand feet. What external manipulators are there?"

"You want to collect samples at two thousand feet?"

"Actually, we're placing monitoring devices on the bottom."

"I see. Like radio devices? Sending data to the surface?"

"Something like that."

"How large are these devices?"

The bearded man held his hands two feet apart. "About so big."

"And they weigh what?"

"Oh, I don't know exactly. Maybe two hundred pounds."

Damon concealed his surprise. Usually petroleum geologists knew precisely what they were going to place. Exact dimensions, exact weight, exact specific gravity, all that. This guy was vague. But perhaps Damon was just being paranoid. He continued. "And these sensors are for geological work?"

"Ultimately. First we need information on ocean currents, flow rates, bottom temperatures. That kind of thing."

Damon thought: *For what?* Why did they need to know about currents? Of course, they might be sinking a tower, but nobody would do that in two thousand feet of water.

What were these guys intending to do?

"Well," he said, "if you want to place external devices, you have to secure them to the exterior of the hull prior to the dive. There are lateral shelves on each side—" he pointed to the model "—for that purpose. Once you're at depth, you have a choice of two remote arms to place the devices. How many devices are you talking about?"

"Quite a few."

"More than eight?"

"Oh yes. Probably."

"Well, then you're talking about multiple dives. You can only take eight, maybe ten external devices on any given dive." He talked on for a while, scanning their faces, trying to understand what lay behind the bland looks. They wanted to lease the sub for four months, starting in August of that year. They wanted the sub and the tender ship transported to Port Moresby, New Guinea. They would pick it up there.

"Depending on where you go, there are some required marine licenses—"

"We'll worry about that later," the lawyer said.

"Now, the crew—"

"We'll worry about that later, too."

"It's part of the contract."

"Then just write it in. However you do it."

"You'll return the tender to Moresby at the end of the lease period?"

"Yes."

Damon sat down in front of the desktop computer and began to fill in the estimate forms. There were, all in all, forty-three categories (not including insurance) that had to be filled out. At last he had the final number. "Five hundred and eighty three thousand dollars," he said.

The men didn't blink. They just nodded.

"Half in advance."

They nodded again.

"Second half in escrow account prior to your taking delivery in Port Moresby." He never required that with his regular customers. But for some reason, these two made him uneasy.

"That will be fine," the lawyer said.

"Plus twenty percent contingency, payable in advance."

That was simply unnecessary. But now he was trying to make these guys go away. It didn't work.

"That will be fine."

"Okay," Damon said. "Now, if you need to talk to your contracting company before you sign—"

"No. We're prepared to proceed now."

And then one of them pulled out an envelope and handed it to Damon.

"Tell me if this is satisfactory."

It was a check for $250,000. From Seismic Services, payable to Canada Marine. Damon nodded, and said it was. He put the check and the envelope on his desk, next to the submarine model.

Then one of the men said, "Do you mind if I make a couple of notes?" and picked up the envelope and scribbled on it. And it was only after they were gone that Damon realized they had given him the check and taken back the envelope. So there would be no fingerprints.

Or was he just being paranoid? The following morning, he was inclined to think so. When he went to Scotiabank to deposit the check, he stopped by to see John Kim, the bank manager, and asked him to find out if there were sufficient funds in the Seismic Services account to cover the check.

John Kim said he would check right away.

Christ, it was cold, George Morton thought, climbing out of the Land Cruiser. The millionaire philanthropist stamped his feet and pulled on gloves, trying to warm himself. It was three o'clock in the morning, and the sky glowed red, with streaks of yellow from the still-visible sun. A bitter wind blew across the *Sprengisandur*, the rugged, dark plain in the interior of Iceland. Flat gray clouds hung low over the lava that stretched away for miles. The Icelanders loved this place. Morton couldn't see why.

In any case, they had reached their destination: directly ahead lay a huge, crumpled wall of dirt-covered snow and rock, stretching up to the mountains behind. This was Snorrajökul, one tongue of the huge Vatnajökull glacier, the largest ice cap in Europe.

The driver, a graduate student, climbed out and clapped his hands with delight. "Not bad at all! Quite warm! You are lucky, it's a pleasant August night." He was wearing a T-shirt, hiking shorts, and a light vest. Morton was wearing a down vest, a quilted windbreaker, and heavy pants. And he was still cold.

He looked back as the others got out of the backseat. Nicholas Drake, thin and frowning, wearing a shirt and tie and a tweed sport coat beneath his windbreaker, winced as the cold air hit him. With his thinning hair, wire-frame glasses, and pinched, disapproving manner, Drake conveyed a scholarly quality that in fact he cultivated. He did not want to be taken for what he was, a highly successful litigator who had retired to become the director of the National Environmental Resource Fund, a major American activist group. He had held the job at NERF for the last ten years.

Next, young Peter Evans bounced out of the car. Evans was the youngest of Morton's attorneys, and the one he liked best. Evans was twenty-eight and a junior associate of the Los Angeles firm of Hassle and Black. Now, even late at night, he remained cheerful and enthusiastic. He pulled on a Patagonia fleece and stuck his hands in his pockets, but otherwise gave no sign that the weather bothered him.

Morton had flown all of them in from Los Angeles on his Gulfstream G5 jet, arriving in Keflavík airport at nine yesterday morning. None of them had slept, but nobody was tired. Not even Morton, and he was sixty-five years old. He didn't feel the slightest sense of fatigue.

Just cold.

Morton zipped up his jacket and followed the graduate student down the rocky hill from the car. "The light at night gives you energy," the kid said. "Dr. Einarsson never sleeps more than four hours a night in the summer. None of us does."

"And where is Dr. Einarsson?" Morton asked.

"Down there." The kid pointed off to the left.

At first, Morton could see nothing at all. Finally he saw a red dot, and realized it was a vehicle. That was when he grasped the enormous size of the glacier.

Drake fell into step with Morton as they went down the hill. "George," he said, "you and Evans should feel free to go on a tour of the site, and let me talk to Per Einarsson alone."

"Why?"

"I expect Einarsson would be more comfortable if there weren't a lot of people standing around."

"But isn't the point that I'm the one who funds his research?"

"Of course," Drake said, "but I don't want to hammer that fact too hard. I don't want Per to feel compromised."

"I don't see how you can avoid it."

"I'll just point out the stakes," Drake said. "Help him to see the big picture."

"Frankly, I was looking forward to hearing this discussion," Morton said.

"I know," Drake said. "But it's delicate."

As they came closer to the glacier, Morton felt a distinct chill in the wind. The temperature dropped several degrees. They could see now the series of four large, tan tents arranged near the red Land Cruiser. From a distance, the tents had blended into the plain.

From one of the tents a very tall, blond man appeared. Per Einarsson threw up his hands and shouted, "Nicholas!"

"Per!" Drake raced forward.

Morton continued down the hill, feeling distinctly grouchy about being dismissed by Drake. Evans came up to walk alongside him. "I don't want to take any damn tour," Morton said.

"Oh, I don't know," Evans said, looking ahead. "It might be more interesting than we think." Coming out of one of the other tents were three young women in khakis, all blond and beautiful. They waved to the newcomers.

"Maybe you're right," Morton said.

Peter Evans knew that his client George Morton, despite his intense interest in all things environmental, had an even more intense interest in pretty women. And indeed, after a quick introduction to Einarsson, Morton happily allowed himself to be led away by Eva Jónsdóttir, who was tall and athletic, with short-cropped white blond hair and a radiant smile. She was Morton's type, Evans thought. She looked rather like Morton's beautiful assistant, Sarah Jones. He heard Morton say, "I had no idea so many women were interested in geology," and Morton and Eva drifted away, heading toward the glacier.

Evans knew he should accompany Morton. But perhaps Morton wanted to take this tour alone. And more important, Evans's firm also represented Nicholas Drake, and Evans had a nagging concern about what Drake was up to. Not that it was illegal or unethical, exactly. But Drake could be imperious, and what he was going to do might cause embarrassment later on. So for a moment Evans stood there, wondering which way to go, which man to follow.

It was Drake who made the decision for him, giving Evans a slight, dismissive wave of his hand as he disappeared into the big tent with Einarsson. Evans took the hint, and ambled off toward Morton and the girl. Eva was chattering on about how 12 percent of Iceland was covered in glaciers, and how some of the glaciers had active volcanoes poking out from the ice.

This particular glacier, she said, pointing upward, was of the type called a surge glacier, because it had a history of rapid advances and retreats. At the moment, she said, the glacier was pushing forward at the rate of one hundred meters a day—the length of a football field, every twenty-four hours. Sometimes, when the wind died, you could actually hear it grinding forward. This glacier had surged more than ten kilometers in the last few years.

Soon they were joined by Ásdís Sveinsdóttir, who could have been Eva's younger sister. She paid flattering attention to Evans, asking him how his trip over had been, how he liked Iceland, how long he was staying in the country. Eventually, she mentioned that she usually worked in the office at Reykjavík, and had only come out for the day. Evans realized then that she was here doing her job. The sponsors were visiting Einarsson, and Einarsson had arranged for the visit to be memorable.

Eva was explaining that although surge-type glaciers were very common—there were several hundred of them in Alaska—the mechanism of the surges was not known. Nor was the mechanism behind the periodic advances and retreats, which differed for each glacier. "There is still so much to study, to learn," she said, smiling at Morton.

That was when they heard shouts coming from the big tent, and considerable swearing. Evans excused himself, and headed back to the tent. Somewhat reluctantly, Morton trailed after him.

Per Einarsson was shaking with anger. He raised his fists. "I tell you, no!" he yelled, and pounded the table.

Standing opposite him, Drake was very red in the face, clenching his teeth. "Per," he said, "I am asking you to consider the realities."

"You are not!" Einarsson said, pounding the table again. "The reality is what you do *not* want me to publish!"

"Now, Per—"

"The *reality*," he said, "is that in Iceland the first half of the twentieth century was warmer than the second half, as in Greenland.* The *reality* is that in Iceland, most glaciers lost mass after 1930 because summers warmed by .6 degrees Celsius, but since then the climate has become colder. The *reality* is that since 1970 these glaciers have been steadily advancing. They have regained half the ground that was lost earlier. Right now, eleven are surging. That is *the reality*, Nicholas! And I will not lie about it."

"No one has suggested you do," Drake said,

---

* P. Chylek, et al. 2004, "Global warming and the Greenland ice sheet," *Climatic Change* 63, 201–21. "Since 1940 . . . data have undergone predominantly a cooling trend. . . . The Greenland ice sheet and coastal regions are not following the current global warming trend."

lowering his voice and glancing at his newly arrived audience. "I am merely discussing how you word your paper, Per."

Einarsson raised a sheet of paper. "Yes, and you have *suggested* some wording—"

"Merely a suggestion—"

"That twists truth!"

"Per, with due respect, I feel you are exaggerating—"

"Am I?" Einarsson turned to the others and began to read. "This is what he wants me to say: 'The threat of global warming has melted glaciers throughout the world, and in Iceland as well. Many glaciers are shrinking dramatically, although paradoxically others are growing. However, in all cases recent extremes in climate variability seem to be the cause . . . blah . . . blah . . . blah . . . *og svo framvegis.*'" He threw the paper down. "That is simply not true."

"It's just the opening paragraph. The rest of your paper will amplify."

"The opening paragraph is not true."

"Of course it is. It refers to 'extremes in climate variability.' No one can object to such vague wording."

"*Recent* extremes. But in Iceland these effects are not recent."

"Then take out 'recent.'"

"That is not adequate," Einarsson said, "because the implication of this paragraph is that we are observing the effects of global warming from greenhouse gases. Whereas in fact we are observing local climate patterns that are rather specific to Iceland and are unlikely to be related to any global pattern."

"And you can say so in your conclusion."

"But this opening paragraph will be a big joke among Arctic researchers. You think Motoyama or Sigurosson will not see through this paragraph? Or Hicks? Watanabe? Ísaksson? They will laugh and call me compromised. They will say I did it for grants."

"But there are other considerations," Drake said soothingly. "We must all be aware there are disinformation groups funded by industry—petroleum, automotive—who will seize on the report that some glaciers are growing, and use it to argue against global warming. That is what they always do. They snatch at anything to paint a false picture."

"How the information is used is not my concern. My concern is to report the truth as best I can."

"Very noble," Drake said. "Perhaps not so practical."

"I see. And you have brought the source of funding right here, in the form of Mr. Morton, so I do not miss the point?"

"No, no, Per," Drake said hastily. "Please, don't misunderstand—"

"I understand only too well. What is he doing here?" Einarsson was furious. "Mr. Morton? Do you approve of what I am being asked to do by Mr. Drake?"

It was at that point that Morton's cell phone rang, and with ill-concealed relief, he flipped it open. "Morton. Yes? Yes, John. Where are you? Vancouver? What time is it there?" He put his hand over the mouthpiece. "John Kim, in Vancouver. Scotiabank."

Evans nodded, though he had no idea who that was. Morton's financial operations were complex; he knew bankers all over the world. Morton turned and walked to the far side of the tent.

An awkward silence fell over the others as they waited. Einarsson stared at the floor, sucking in his breath, still furious. The blond women pretended to work, giving great attention to the papers they shuffled through. Drake stuck his hands in his pockets, looked at the roof of the tent.

Meanwhile, Morton was laughing. "Really? I hadn't heard that one," he said, chuckling. He glanced back at the others, and turned away again.

Drake said, "Look, Per, I feel we have gotten off on the wrong foot."

"Not at all," Einarsson said coldly. "We understand each other only too well. If you withdraw your support, you withdraw your support."

"Nobody is talking about withdrawing support . . ."

"Time will tell," he said.

And then Morton said, "*What? They did what? Deposited to what?* How much money are we—? Jesus Christ, John. This is *unbelievable!*" And still talking, he turned and walked out of the tent.

Evans hurried after him.

It was brighter, the sun now higher in the sky, trying to break through low clouds. Morton was scrambling up the slope, still talking on the phone.

He was shouting, but his words were lost in the wind as Evans followed him.

They came to the Land Cruiser. Morton ducked down, using it as a shield against the wind. "Christ, John, do I have legal liability there? I mean—no, I didn't know a thing about it. What was the organization? Friends of the Planet Fund?"

Morton looked questioningly at Evans. Evans shook his head. He'd never heard of Friends of the Planet. And he knew most of the environmental organizations.

"Based where?" Morton was saying. "San Jose? California? Oh. Jesus. What the hell is based in Costa Rica?" He cupped his hand over the phone. "Friends of the Planet Fund, San José, Costa Rica."

Evans shook his head.

"I never heard of them," Morton said, "and neither has my lawyer. And I don't remember— no, John, if it was a quarter of a million dollars, I'd remember. The check was issued where? I see. And my name was where? I see. Okay, thanks. Yeah. I will. Bye." He flipped the phone shut.

He turned to Evans.

"Peter," he said. "Get a pad and make notes."

Morton spoke quickly. Evans scribbled, trying to keep up. It was a complicated story that he took down as best he could.

John Kim, the manager of Scotiabank, Vancouver, had been called by a customer named Nat Damon, a local marine operator. Damon had deposited a check from a company called Seismic Services, in Calgary, and the check had bounced.

It was for $250,000. Damon was nervous about whoever had written the check, and asked Kim to look into it.

John Kim could not legally make inquiries in the US, but the issuing bank was in Calgary, and he had a friend who worked there. He learned that Seismic Services was an account with a postal box for an address. The account was modestly active, receiving deposits every few weeks from only one source: The Friends of the Planet Foundation, based in San José, Costa Rica.

Kim placed a call down there. Then, about that time, it came up on his screen that the check had cleared. Kim called Damon and asked him if he wanted to drop the inquiry. Damon said no, check it out.

Kim had a brief conversation with Miguel Chavez at the Banco Credito Agricola in San José. Chavez said he had gotten an electronic deposit from the Moriah Wind Power Associates via Ansbach (Cayman) Ltd., a private bank on Grand Cayman island. That was all he knew.

Chavez called Kim back ten minutes later to say he had made inquiries at Ansbach and had obtained a record of a wire transfer that was paid into the Moriah account by the International Wilderness Preservation Society three days before that. And the IWPS transfer noted in the comment field, "G. Morton Research Fund."

John Kim called his Vancouver client, Nat Damon, to ask what the check was for. Damon said it was for the lease of a small two-man research submarine.

Kim thought that was pretty interesting, so he

telephoned his friend George Morton to kid him a bit, and ask why he was leasing a submarine. And to his surprise, Morton knew absolutely nothing about it.

Evans finished taking down notes on the pad. He said, "This is what some bank manager in Vancouver told you?"

"Yes. A good friend of mine. Why are you looking at me that way?"

"Because it's a lot of information," Evans said. He didn't know the banking rules in Canada, to say nothing of Costa Rica, but he knew it was unlikely that any banks would freely exchange information in the way Morton had described. If the Vancouver manager's story was true, there was more to it that he wasn't telling. Evans made a note to check into it. "And do you know the International Wilderness Preservation Society, which has your check for a quarter of a million dollars?"

Morton shook his head. "Never heard of them."

"So you never gave them two hundred and fifty thousand dollars?"

Morton shook his head. "I'll tell you what I did do, in the last week," he said. "I gave two hundred and fifty grand to Nicholas Drake to cover a monthly operating shortfall. He told me he had some problem about a big contributor from Seattle not coming through for a week. Drake's asked me to help him out before like that, once or twice."

"You think that money ended up in Vancouver?"

Morton nodded.

"You better ask Drake about it," Evans said.

"I have no idea at all," Drake said, looking mystified. "Costa Rica? International Wilderness Preservation? My goodness, I can't imagine."

Evans said, "You know the International Wilderness Preservation Society?"

"Very well," Drake said. "They're excellent. We've worked closely with them on any number of projects around the world—the Everglades, Tiger Tops in Nepal, the Lake Toba preserve in Sumatra. The only thing I can think is that somehow George's check was mistakenly deposited in the wrong account. Or . . . I just don't know. I have to call the office. But it's late in California. It'll have to wait until morning."

Morton was staring at Drake, not speaking.

"George," Drake said, turning to him. "I'm sure this must make you feel very strange. Even if it's an honest mistake—as I am almost certain it is— it's still a lot of money to be mishandled. I feel terrible. But mistakes happen, especially if you use a lot of unpaid volunteers, as we do. But you and I have been friends for a long time. I want you to know that I will get to the bottom of this. And of course I will see that the money is recovered at once. You have my word, George."

"Thank you," Morton said.

They all climbed into the Land Cruiser.

The vehicle bounced over the barren plain. "Damn, those Icelanders are stubborn," Drake said, staring out the window. "They may be the most stubborn researchers in the world."

"He never saw your point?" Evans said.

"No," Drake said, "I couldn't make him understand. Scientists can't adopt that lofty attitude anymore. They can't say, 'I do the research, and I don't care how it is used.' That's out of date. It's irresponsible. Even in a seemingly obscure field like glacier geology. Because, like it or not, we're in the middle of a war—a global war of information versus disinformation. The war is fought on many battlegrounds. Newspaper op-eds. Television reports. Scientific journals. Websites, conferences, classrooms—and courtrooms, too, if it comes to that." Drake shook his head. "We have truth on our side, but we're outnumbered and out-funded. Today, the environmental movement is David battling Goliath. And Goliath is Aventis and Alcatel, Humana and GE, BP and Bayer, Shell and Glaxo-Wellcome—huge, global, corporate. These people are the implacable enemies of our planet, and Per Einarsson, out there on his glacier, is irresponsible to pretend it isn't happening."

Sitting beside Drake, Peter Evans nodded sympathetically, though in fact he took everything Drake was saying with a large grain of salt. The head of NERF was famously melodramatic. And Drake was pointedly ignoring the fact that several of the corporations he had named made substantial contributions to NERF every year, and three executives from those companies actually sat on Drake's board of advisors. That was true of many environmental organizations these days, although the reasons behind corporate involvement were much debated.

"Well," Morton said, "maybe Per will reconsider later on."

"I doubt it," Drake said gloomily. "He was angry. We've lost this battle, I'm sorry to say. But we do what we always do. Soldier on. Fight the good fight."

It was silent in the car for a while.

"The girls were damn good looking," Morton said. "Weren't they, Peter?"

"Yes," Evans said. "They were."

Evans knew that Morton was trying to lighten the mood in the car. But Drake would have none of it. The head of NERF stared morosely at the barren landscape, and shook his head mournfully at the snow-covered mountains in the distance.

Evans had traveled many times with Drake and Morton in the last couple of years. Usually, Morton could cheer everybody around him, even Drake, who was glum and fretful.

But lately Drake had become even more pessimistic than usual. Evans had first noticed it a few weeks ago, and had wondered at the time if there was illness in the family, or something else that was bothering him. But it seemed there was nothing amiss. At least, nothing that anyone would talk about. NERF was a beehive of activity; they had moved into a wonderful new building in Beverly Hills; fund-raising was at an all-time high; they were planning spectacular new events and conferences, including the Abrupt Climate

Change Conference that would begin in two months. Yet despite these successes—or because of them?—Drake seemed more miserable than ever.

Morton noticed it, too, but he shrugged it off. "He's a lawyer," he said. "What do you expect? Forget about it."

By the time they reached Reykjavík, the sunny day had turned wet and chilly. It was sleeting at Keflavík airport, obliging them to wait while the wings of the white Gulfstream jet were de-iced. Evans slipped away to a corner of the hangar and, since it was still the middle of the night in the US, placed a call to a friend in banking in Hong Kong. He asked about the Vancouver story.

"Absolutely impossible," was the immediate answer. "No bank would divulge such information, even to another bank. There's an STR in the chain somewhere."

"An STR?"

"Suspicious transfer report. If it looks like money for drug trafficking or terrorism, the account gets tagged. And from then on, it's tracked. There are ways to track electronic transfers, even with strong encryption. But none of that tracking is ever going to wind up on the desk of a bank manager."

"No?"

"Not a chance. You'd need international law-enforcement credentials to see that tracking report."

"So this bank manager didn't do all this himself?"

"I doubt it. There is somebody else involved in this story. A policeman of some kind. Somebody you're not being told about."

"Like a customs guy, or Interpol?"

"Or something."

"Why would my client be contacted at all?"

"I don't know. But it's not an accident. Does your client have any radical tendencies?"

Thinking of Morton, Evans wanted to laugh. "Absolutely not."

"You quite sure, Peter?"

"Well, yes . . ."

"Because sometimes these wealthy donors amuse themselves, or justify themselves, by supporting terrorist groups. That's what happened with the IRA. Rich Americans in Boston supported them for decades. But times have changed. No one is amused any longer. Your client should be careful. And if you're his attorney, you should be careful, too. Hate to visit you in prison, Peter."

And he hung up.

The flight attendant poured Morton's vodka into a cut-glass tumbler. "No more ice, sweetie," Morton said, raising his hand. They were flying west, over Greenland, a vast expanse of ice and cloud in pale sun beneath them.

Morton sat with Drake, who talked about how the Greenland ice cap was melting. And the rate at which the Arctic ice was melting. And Canadian glaciers were receding. Morton sipped his vodka and nodded. "So Iceland is an anomaly?"

"Oh yes," Drake said. "An anomaly. Everywhere else, glaciers are melting at an unprecedented rate."

"It's good we have you, Nick," Morton said, putting his hand on Drake's shoulder.

Drake smiled. "And it's good we have *you*, George," he said. "We wouldn't be able to accomplish anything without your generous support. You've made the Vanutu lawsuit possible—and that's extremely important for the publicity it will generate. And as for your other grants, well . . . words fail me."

"Words never fail you," Morton said, slapping him on the back.

Sitting across from them, Evans thought they really were the odd couple. Morton, big and hearty, dressed casually in jeans and a workshirt, always seeming to burst from his clothes. And Nicholas Drake, tall and painfully thin, wearing a coat and tie, with his scrawny neck rising from the collar of a shirt that never seemed to fit.

In their manner, too, they were complete opposites. Morton loved to be around as many people as possible, loved to eat, and laugh. He had a penchant for pretty girls, vintage sports cars, Asian art, and practical jokes. His parties drew most of Hollywood to his Holmby Hills mansion; his charity functions were always special, always written up the next day.

Of course, Drake attended those functions, but invariably left early, sometimes before dinner. Often he pleaded illness—his own or a friend's. In fact, Drake was a solitary, ascetic man, who detested parties and noise. Even when he stood at a podium giving a speech, he conveyed an air of isolation, as if he were alone in the room. And, being Drake, he made it work for him. He managed to suggest that he was a lone messenger in the wilderness, delivering the truth the audience needed to hear.

Despite their differences in temperament, the two men had built a durable friendship that had lasted the better part of a decade. Morton, the heir to a forklift fortune, had the congenital uneasiness of inherited wealth. Drake had a good use for that money, and in return provided Morton with a passion, and a cause, that informed and guided Morton's life. Morton's name appeared on the board of advisors of the Audubon Society, the Wilderness Society, the World Wildlife Fund, and the Sierra Club. He was a major contributor to Greenpeace and the Environmental Action League.

All this culminated in two enormous gifts by Morton to NERF. The first was a grant of $1 million, to finance the Vanutu lawsuit. The second was a grant of $9 million to NERF itself, to finance future research and litigation on behalf of the environment. Not surprisingly, the NERF board had voted Morton their Concerned Citizen of the Year. A banquet in his honor was scheduled for later that fall, in San Francisco.

Evans sat across from the two men, idly thumbing through a magazine. But he had been shaken by the Hong Kong call, and found himself observing Morton with some care.

Morton still had his hand on Drake's shoulder, and was telling him a joke—as usual, trying to get Drake to laugh—but it seemed to Evans that he detected a certain distance on Morton's part. Morton had withdrawn, but didn't want Drake to notice.

This suspicion was confirmed when Morton stood up abruptly and headed for the cockpit. "I want to know about this damn electronic thing," he said. Since takeoff, they had been experiencing the effects of a major solar flare that rendered satellite telephones erratic or unusable. The pilots said the effect was heightened near the poles, and would soon diminish as they headed south.

And Morton seemed eager to make some calls.

Evans wondered to whom. It was now four A.M. in New York, one A.M. in Los Angeles. Who was Morton calling? But of course it could concern any of his ongoing environmental projects—water purification in Cambodia, reforestation in Guinea, habitat preservation in Madagascar, medicinal plants in Peru. To say nothing of the German expedition to measure the thickness of the ice in Antarctica. Morton was personally involved in all these projects. He knew them in detail, knew the scientists involved, had visited the locations himself.

So it could be anything.

But somehow, Evans felt, it wasn't just anything.

Morton came back. "Pilots say it's okay now." He sat by himself in the front of the plane, reached for his headset, and pulled the sliding door shut for privacy.

Evans turned back to his magazine.

Drake said, "You think he's drinking more than usual?"

"Not really," Evans said.

"I worry."

"I wouldn't," Evans said.

"You realize," Drake said, "we are just five weeks from the banquet in his honor, in San Francisco. That's our biggest fund-raising event of the year. It will generate considerable publicity, and it'll help us launch the conference on Abrupt Climate Change."

"Uh-huh," Evans said.

"I'd like to ensure that the publicity focuses on

environmental issues, and not anything else. Of a personal nature, if you know what I mean."

Evans said, "Isn't this a conversation you should be having with George?"

"Oh, I have. I only mention it to you because you spend so much time with him."

"I don't, really."

"You know he likes you, Peter," Drake said. "You're the son he never had or—hell, I don't know. But he *does* like you. And I'm just asking you to help us, if you can."

"I don't think he'll embarrass you, Nick."

"Just . . . keep an eye on him."

"Okay. Sure."

At the front of the plane, the sliding door opened. Morton said, "Mr. Evans? If you please."

Peter got up and went forward.

He slid the door shut behind him.

"I have been on the phone to Sarah," Morton said. Sarah Jones was his assistant in LA.

"Isn't it late?"

"It's her job. She's well paid. Sit down." Evans sat in the chair opposite. "Have you ever heard of the NSIA?"

"No."

"The National Security Intelligence Agency?"

Evans shook his head. "No. But there are twenty security agencies."

"Ever heard of John Kenner?"

"No . . ."

"Apparently he's a professor at MIT."

"No," Evans said. "Sorry. Does he have something to do with the environment?"

"He may. See what you can find out."

Evans turned to the laptop by his seat, and flipped open the screen. It was connected to the Internet by satellite. He started to type.

In a few moments he was looking at a picture of a fit-looking man with prematurely gray hair and heavy horn-rim glasses. The attached biography was brief. Evans read it aloud. "Richard John Kenner, William T. Harding Professor of Geoenvironmental Engineering."

"Whatever that means," Morton said.

"He is thirty-nine. Doctorate in civil engineering from Caltech at age twenty. Did his thesis on soil erosion in Nepal. Barely missed qualifying for the Olympic ski team. A JD from Harvard Law School. Spent the next four years in government. Department of the Interior, Office of Policy Analysis. Scientific advisor to the Intergovernmental Negotiating Committee. Hobby is mountain climbing; he was reported dead on Naya Khanga peak in Nepal, but he wasn't. Tried to climb K2, driven back by weather."

"K2," Morton said. "Isn't that the most dangerous peak?"

"I think so. Looks like he's a serious climber. Anyway, he then went to MIT, where I'd say his rise has been spectacular. Associate professor in '93. Director of the MIT Center for Risk Analysis in '95. William T. Harding Professor in '96. Consultant to the EPA, the Department of the Interior, the Department of Defense, the government of Nepal, God knows who else. Looks like a lot of corporations. And since 2002, on faculty leave."

"Meaning what?"

"It just says he's on leave."

"For the last two years?" Morton came and looked over Evans's shoulder. "I don't like it. The guy burns up the track at MIT, goes on leave, and never comes back. You think he got into trouble?"

"I don't know. But . . ." Evans was calculating the dates. "Professor Kenner got a doctorate from Caltech at twenty. Got his law degree from Harvard in two years instead of three. Professor at MIT when he's twenty-eight . . ."

"Okay, okay, so he's smart," Morton said. "I still want to know why he's on leave. And why he's in Vancouver."

Evans said, "He's in Vancouver?"

"He's been calling Sarah from Vancouver."

"Why?"

"He wants to meet with me."

"Well," Evans said, "I guess you'd better meet with him."

"I will," Morton said. "But what do you think he wants?"

"I have no idea. Funding? A project?"

"Sarah says he wants the meeting to be confidential. He doesn't want anybody to be told."

"Well, that's not hard. You're on an airplane."

"No," Morton said, jerking his thumb. "He specifically doesn't want Drake to be told."

"Maybe I'd better attend this meeting," Evans said.

"Yes," Morton said. "Maybe you should."

The iron gates swung open, and the car drove up the shaded driveway to the house that slowly came into view. This was Holmby Hills, the wealthiest area of Beverly Hills. The billionaires lived here, in residences hidden from the street by high gates and dense foliage. In this part of town, security cameras were all painted green, and tucked back unobtrusively.

The house came into view. It was a Mediterranean-style villa, cream colored, and large enough for a family of ten. Evans, who had been speaking to his office, flipped his cell phone shut and got out as the car came to a stop.

Birds chirped in the ficus trees. The air smelled of the gardenia and jasmine that bordered the driveway. A hummingbird hung near the purple bougainvillea at the garage. It was, Evans thought, a typical California moment. Evans had been raised in Connecticut and schooled in Boston; even after five years in California, the place still seemed exotic to him.

He saw that another car was parked in front of the house: a dark gray sedan. It had government license plates.

From out of the front door came Morton's assistant, Sarah Jones, a tall blond woman of thirty, as glamorous as any movie star. Sarah was dressed in a white tennis skirt and pink top, her hair pulled back in a pony tail. Morton kissed her lightly on the cheek. "You playing today?"

"I was. My boss came back early." She shook Evans's hand and turned back to Morton. "Good trip?"

"Fine. Drake is morose. And he won't drink. It gets tiresome."

As Morton started toward the door, Sarah said, "I think I ought to tell you, they're here right now."

"Who is?"

"Professor Kenner. And another guy with him. Foreign guy."

"Really? But didn't you tell them they had to—"

"Make an appointment? Yes, I did. They seem to think that doesn't apply to them. They just sat down and said they'd wait."

"You should have called me—"

"They got here five minutes ago."

"Huh. Okay." He turned to Evans. "Let's go, Peter."

They went inside. Morton's living room looked out on the garden in back of the house. The room was decorated with Asian antiques, including a large stone head from Cambodia. Sitting erectly on the couch were two men. One was an American of middle height, with short gray hair and glasses. The other was very dark, compact, and very handsome despite the thin scar that ran down the left side of his face in front of his ear. They were dressed in cotton slacks and lightweight sport coats. Both men sat on the edge of the couch, very alert, as if they might spring up at any moment.

"Look military, don't they?" Morton muttered, as they went into the room.

The two men stood. "Mr. Morton, I'm John Kenner from MIT, and this is my colleague, Sanjong Thapa. A graduate student from Mustang. In Nepal."

Morton said, "And this is *my* colleague, Peter Evans."

They shook hands all around. Kenner's grip was firm. Sanjong Thapa gave a very slight bow as he shook hands. He spoke softly, with a British accent. "How do you do."

"I didn't expect you," Morton said, "so soon."

"We work quickly."

"So I see. What's this about?"

"I'm afraid we need your help, Mr. Morton." Kenner smiled pleasantly at Evans and Sarah. "And unfortunately, our discussion is confidential."

"Mr. Evans is my attorney," Morton said, "and I have no secrets from my assistant—"

"I'm sure," Kenner said. "You may take them into your confidence whenever you choose. But we must speak to you alone."

Evans said, "If you don't mind, I'd like to see some identification."

"Of course," Kenner said. Both men reached

for wallets. Evans was shown Massachusetts driver's licenses, MIT faculty cards, and passports. Then they handed out business cards.

> John Kenner, PhD
> Center for Risk Analysis
> Massachusetts Institute of Technology
> 454 Massachusetts Avenue
> Cambridge, MA 02138

> Sanjong Thapa, PhD
> Research Associate
> Department of Geoenvironmental Engineering
> Building 4-C 323
> Massachusetts Institute of Technology
> Cambridge, MA 02138

There were telephone numbers, fax, e-mail. Evans turned the cards over. It all looked straightforward.

Kenner said, "Now, if you and Miss Jones will excuse us . . ."

They were outside, in the hallway, looking into the living room through the large glass doors. Morton was sitting on one couch. Kenner and Sanjong were on the other. The discussion was quiet. In fact, it looked to Evans just like one more of the endless investment meetings that Morton endured.

Evans picked up the hall phone and dialed a number. "Center for Risk Analysis," a woman said.

"Professor Kenner's office, please."

"One moment." Clicking. Another voice. "Center for Risk Analysis, Professor Kenner's office."

"Good afternoon," Evans said. "My name is Peter Evans, and I'm calling for Professor Kenner."

"I'm sorry, he is not in the office."

"Do you know where he is?"

"Professor Kenner is on extended leave."

"It is important that I reach him," Evans said. "Do you know how I could do that?"

"Well, it shouldn't be hard, since you are in Los Angeles and so is he."

So she had seen the caller ID, Evans thought. He would have imagined Morton had a blocked ID. But evidently not. Or perhaps the secretary in Massachusetts had a way to unblock it.

"Well," Evans said, "can you tell me—"

"I'm sorry, Mr. Evans," she said, "but I'm not able to help you further."

Click.

Sarah said, "What was that about?"

Before Evans could answer, a cell phone rang in the living room. He saw Kenner reach into his pocket, and answer briefly. Then he turned, looked at Evans, and waved.

Sarah said, "His office called him?"

"Looks like it."

"So I guess that's Professor Kenner."

"I guess it is," Evans said. "And we're dismissed."

"Come on," Sarah said. "I'll give you a ride home."

They walked past the open garage, the row of Ferraris glinting in the sun. Morton owned nine vintage Ferraris, which he kept in various garages.

These included a 1947 Spyder Corsa, a 1956 Testa Rossa, and a 1959 California Spyder, each worth more than a million dollars. Evans knew this because he reviewed the insurance every time Morton bought another one. At the far end of the line was Sarah's black Porsche convertible. She backed it out, and he climbed in beside her.

Even by Los Angeles standards, Sarah Jones was an extremely beautiful woman. She was tall, with a honey-colored tan, shoulder-length blond hair, blue eyes, perfect features, very white teeth. She was athletic in the casual way that California people were athletic, generally showing up for work in a jogging suit or short tennis skirt. She played golf and tennis, scuba dived, mountain biked, skied, snowboarded, and God knew what else. Evans felt tired whenever he thought about it.

But he also knew that she had "issues," to use the California word. Sarah was the youngest child of a wealthy San Francisco family; her father was a powerful attorney who had held political office; her mother was a former high fashion model. Sarah's older brothers and sisters were all happily married, all successful, and all waiting for her to follow in their footsteps. She found her family's collective success a burden.

Evans had always wondered why she chose to work for Morton, another powerful and wealthy man. Or why she had come to Los Angeles at all, since her family regarded any address south of the Bay Bridge to be hopelessly tawdry. But she was good at her job, and devoted to Morton. And as George often said, her presence was aesthetically pleasing. And the actors and celebrities who attended Morton's parties agreed; she had dated several of them. Which further displeased her family.

Sometimes Evans wondered if everything she did was rebellion. Like her driving—she drove quickly, almost recklessly, shooting down Benedict Canyon, heading into Beverly Hills. "Do you want to go to the office, or your apartment?"

"My apartment," he said. "I have to pick up my car."

She nodded, swerved around a slow-moving Mercedes, then cut left down a side street. Evans took a deep breath.

"Listen," she said. "Do you know what netwar is?"

"What?" He wasn't sure he had heard her over the sound of the wind.

"Netwar."

"No," he said. "Why?"

"I heard them talking about it, before you showed up. Kenner and that Sanjong guy."

Evans shook his head. "Doesn't ring a bell. You sure it wasn't net*ware?*"

"Might have been." She sped across Sunset, running a yellow light, and then downshifted as she came to Beverly. "You still on Roxbury?"

He said he was. He looked at her long legs, protruding from the short white skirt. "Who were you going to play tennis with?"

"I don't think you know him."

"It's not, uh . . ."

"No. That's over."

"I see."

"I'm serious, it's *over.*"

"Okay, Sarah. I hear you."

"You lawyers are all so suspicious."

"So, it's a lawyer you're playing with?"

"No, it is not a lawyer. I don't play with lawyers."

"What do you do with them?"

"As little as possible. Like everybody else."

"I'm sorry to hear that."

"Except you, of course," she said, giving him a dazzling smile.

She accelerated hard, making the engine scream.

Peter Evans lived in one of the older apartment buildings on Roxbury Drive in the flats of Beverly Hills. There were four units in his building, across the street from Roxbury Park. It was a nice park, a big green expanse, always busy. He saw Hispanic nannies chatting in groups while they minded the children of rich people, and several oldsters sitting in the sun. Off in a corner, a working mother in a business suit had taken off lunch to be with the kids.

The car screeched to a stop. "Here you are."

"Thanks," he said, getting out.

"Isn't it time to move? You've been here five years."

"I'm too busy to move," he said.

"Got your keys?"

"Yeah. But there's always one under the doormat." He reached in his pocket, jingled metal. "All set."

"See you." And she raced off, squealed around the corner, and was gone.

* * *

Evans walked through the little sunlit courtyard, and went up to his apartment, on the second floor. As always, he had found Sarah slightly distressing. She was so beautiful, and so flirtatious. He always had the feeling that she kept men at a distance by keeping them off balance. At least, she kept *him* off balance. He could never tell if she wanted him to ask her out or not. But considering his relationship with Morton, it was a bad idea. He would never do it.

As soon as he walked in the door, the phone began to ring. It was his assistant, Heather. She was going home early because she felt sick. Heather frequently felt sick toward the afternoon, in time to beat rush hour traffic. She tended to call in sick on Fridays or Mondays. Yet the firm showed a surprising reluctance to fire her; she had been there for years.

Some said she had had a relationship with Bruce Black, the founding partner, and that, ever since, Bruce lived in constant dread that his wife would find out, since she had all the money. Others claimed Heather was seeing another of the firm's partners, always unspecified. A third story was that she had been on the scene when the firm moved offices from one Century City skyscraper to another, in the course of which she stumbled on some incriminating documents, and copied them.

Evans suspected the truth was more mundane: that she was a clever woman who had worked in the firm long enough to know everything about wrongful termination suits, and now carefully gauged her repeated infractions against the cost and aggravation of their firing her. And in this way worked about thirty weeks a year.

Heather was invariably assigned to the best junior associate in the firm, on the assumption that a really good attorney wouldn't be hampered by her inconstancy. Evans had tried for years to get rid of her. He was promised a new assistant next year. He saw it as a promotion.

"I'm sorry you don't feel well," he told Heather dutifully. One had to go along with her pretense.

"It's just my stomach," she said. "I have to see the doctor."

"Are you going today?"

"Well, I'm trying to get an appointment . . ."

"All right, then."

"But I wanted to tell you they just set a big meeting for the day after tomorrow. Nine o'clock in the big conference room."

"Oh?"

"Mr. Morton just called it. Apparently ten or twelve people are called."

"You know who?"

"No. They didn't say."

Evans thought: Useless. "Okay," he said.

"And don't forget you have the arraignment for Morton's daughter next week. This time it's Pasadena, not downtown. And Margo Lane's calling about her Mercedes lawsuit. And that BMW dealer still wants to go forward."

"He still wants to sue the church?"

"He calls every other day."

"Okay. Is that it?"

"No, there's about ten others. I'll try to leave the list on your desk if I feel well enough . . ."

That meant she wouldn't. "Okay," he said.

"Are you coming in?"

"No, it's too late. I need to get some sleep."

"Then I'll see you tomorrow."

He realized he was very hungry. There was nothing to eat in the refrigerator except a container of yogurt of indeterminate age, some wilted celery, and a half-finished bottle of wine left over from his last date, about two weeks earlier. He had been seeing a girl named Carol who did product liability at another firm. They'd picked each other up in the gym and had begun a desultory, intermittent affair. They were both busy, and not especially interested in each other, to tell the truth. They met once or twice a week, had passionate sex, and then one of them would plead a breakfast appointment the next day and go home early. Sometimes they went to dinner as well, but not usually. Neither of them wanted to take the time.

He went into the living room to check his answering machine. There was no message from Carol, but there was a message from Janis, another girl he sometimes saw.

Janis was a trainer in the gym, the possessor of one of those LA bodies, perfectly proportioned and rock hard. Sex for Janis was an athletic event, involving multiple rooms, couches, and chairs, and it always left Evans feeling vaguely inadequate, as if his body fat weren't low enough for her. But he continued to see her, feeling vaguely proud that he could have a girl who looked so astonishing, even if the sex wasn't that good. And she was often available on short notice. Janis had a boyfriend who was older, a producer for a cable news station. He was out of town a lot, and she was restless.

Janis had left a message the night before. Evans didn't bother to call her back. With Janis it was always that night, or forget it.

Before Janis and Carol, there had been other women, more or less the same. Evans told himself he should find a more satisfying relationship. Something more serious, more adult. More suited to his age and station in life. But he was busy, and just took things as they came.

Meanwhile he was hungry.

He went back down to his car and drove to the nearest drive-in, a hamburger joint on Pico. They knew him there. He had a double cheeseburger and a strawberry shake.

He went home, intending to go to bed. Then he remembered that he owed Morton a call.

"I'm glad you called," Morton said. "I've just been going over some things with—going over some things. Where are we now on my donations to NERF? The Vanutu lawsuit, all that?"

"I don't know," Evans said. "The papers are drawn and signed, but I don't think anything's been paid yet."

"Good. I want you to hold off payments."

"Sure, no problem."

"Just for a while."

"Okay."

"There's no need to say anything to NERF."

"No, no. Of course not."

"Good."

Evans hung up. He went into the bedroom to get undressed. The phone rang again.

It was Janis. The exercise instructor.

"Hey," she said. "I was thinking about you, and I wondered what you were doing."

"As a matter of fact, I was going to go to bed."

"Oh. Pretty early for that."

"I just got in from Iceland."

"So you must be tired."

"Well," he said. "Not that tired."

"Want company?"

"Sure."

She giggled and hung up.

Evans awoke to the sound of rhythmic gasping. He flung his hand across the bed, but Janis wasn't there. Her side of the bed was still warm. He raised his head slightly, yawning. In the warm morning light he saw one slender, perfectly formed leg rise above the foot of the bed, to be joined by the other legs. Then both legs slowly descended. Gasping. Then legs up again.

"Janis," he said, "what are you doing?"

"I have to warm up." She stood, smiling, naked and at ease, confident of her appearance, every muscle outlined. "I have a class at seven."

"What time is it?"

"Six."

He groaned, and buried his head in the pillow.

"You really should get up now," she said. "It shortens your lifespan to sleep in."

He groaned again. Janis was full of health information; it was her job. "How can it possibly shorten my life to sleep?"

"They did studies on rats. They didn't let them sleep, and you know what? They lived longer."

"Uh-huh. Would you mind turning on the coffee?"

"Okay," she said, "but you really should give up coffee . . ." She drifted out of the room.

He swung his feet onto the floor and said, "Haven't you heard? Coffee prevents strokes."

"It does not," she said, from the kitchen. "Coffee has nine hundred twenty-three different chemicals in it, and it is *not* good for you."

"New study," he said. It was true, too.

"Besides, it causes cancer."

"That's never been shown."

"And miscarriages."

"Not a concern for me."

"And nervous tension."

"Janis, please."

She came back, crossing her arms across her perfect breasts as she leaned against the doorjamb. He could see the veins in her lower abdomen, running down to her groin. "Well, you *are* nervous, Peter. You have to admit it."

"Only when I look at your body."

She pouted. "You don't take me seriously." She turned back into the kitchen, showing him her perfect, high glutes. He heard her open the refrigerator. "There's no milk."

"Black is fine."

He stood, and headed for the shower.

"Did you have any damage?" she said.

"From what?"

"From the earthquake. We had a little one, while you were gone. About 4.3."

"Not that I know."

"Well, it sure moved your TV."

He stopped in mid-stride. "What?"

"It moved your TV. Look for yourself."

The morning sunlight that slanted through the window clearly showed the faint outline where the base of the television had compressed the carpet. The TV had been moved about three inches from its former position. It was an old thirty-two-inch monitor, and damned heavy. It didn't move easily. Looking at it now gave Evans a chill.

"You're lucky," she said. "You have all those glass things on your mantel. They break all the time, even in a small quake. Do you have an insurance policy?"

He didn't answer. He was bent over, looking behind the television at the connections. Everything looked normal. But he hadn't looked behind his TV for about a year. He wouldn't really know.

"By the way," she said, "this is not organic coffee. You should at least drink organic. Are you listening to me?"

"Just a minute." He had crouched down in front of the television, looking for anything unusual beneath the set. He could see nothing out of the ordinary.

"And what is *this?*" she said.

He looked over. She was holding a donut in her hand. "Peter," Janis said severely, "do you know how much fat's in these things? You might as well just eat a stick of butter."

"I know . . . I should give them up."

"Well, you should. Unless you want to develop diabetes later in life. Why are you on the floor?"

"I was checking the TV."

"Why? Is it broken?"

"I don't think so." He got to his feet.

"The water is running in your shower," she said. "That's not environmentally conscious." She poured coffee, handed it to him. "Go and take your shower. I've got to get to my class."

When he came out of the shower, she was gone. He pulled the covers up over the bed (as close as he ever came to making it) and went into the closet to dress for the day.

The law firm of Hassle and Black occupied five floors of an office building in Century City. They were a forward-looking, socially aware firm. They represented many Hollywood celebrities and wealthy activists who were committed to environmental concerns. The fact that they also represented three of the biggest land developers in Orange County was less often publicized. But as the partners said, it kept the firm balanced.

Evans had joined the firm because of its many environmentally active clients, particularly George Morton. He was one of four attorneys who worked almost full-time for Morton, and for Morton's pet charity, the National Environmental Resource Fund, NERF.

Nevertheless, he was still a junior associate, and his office was small, with a window that looked directly at the flat glass wall of the sky-scraper across the street.

Evans looked over the papers on his desk. It was the usual stuff that came to junior attorneys. There was a residential sublet, an employment agreement, written interrogatories for a bankruptcy, a form for the Franchise Tax Board, and two drafted letters threatening lawsuits on behalf of his clients—one for an artist against a gallery refusing to return his unsold paintings, and one for George Morton's girlfriend, who claimed that the parking attendant at Sushi Roku had scratched her Mercedes convertible while parking it.

The mistress, Margaret Lane, was an ex-actress with a bad temper and a propensity for litigation. Whenever George neglected her—which, in recent months, was increasingly often—she would find a reason to sue somebody. And the suit would inevitably land on Evans's desk. He made a note to call Margo; he didn't think she should proceed with this suit, but she would take convincing.

The next item was a spreadsheet from a Beverly Hills BMW dealer who claimed that the "What Would Jesus Drive?" campaign had hurt his business because it denigrated luxury cars. Apparently his dealership was a block from a church, and some parishioners had come around after services and harangued his sales staff. The dealer didn't like that, but it looked to Evans as if his sales figures were higher this year than last. Evans made a note to call him, too.

Then he checked his e-mails, sorting through twenty offers to enlarge his penis, ten offers for tranquilizers, and another ten to get a new mortgage now before rates started to rise. There were only a half-dozen e-mails of importance, the first from Herb Lowenstein, asking to see him. Lowenstein was the senior partner on Morton's account; he did mostly estate management, but handled other aspects of investments as well. For Morton, estate management was a full-time job.

Evans wandered down the hall to Herb's office.

Lisa, Herb Lowenstein's assistant, was listening on the phone. She hung up and looked guilty when Evans entered. "He's talking to Jack Nicholson."

"How is Jack?"

"He's good. Finishing a picture with Meryl. There were some problems."

Lisa Ray was a bright-eyed twenty-seven-year-old, and a dedicated gossip. Evans had long ago come to rely on her for office information of all sorts.

"What's Herb want me for?"

"Something about Nick Drake."

"What's this meeting about tomorrow at nine?"

"I don't *know*," she said, sounding amazed. "I can't find out a *thing*."

"Who called it?"

"Morton's accountants." She looked at the phone on her desk. "Oh, he's hung up. You can go right in."

Herb Lowenstein stood and shook Evans's hand perfunctorily. He was a pleasant-faced balding man, mild-mannered and slightly nerdy. His office was decorated with dozens of pictures of his family, stacked three and four deep on his desk. He got on well with Evans, if only because these days, whenever Morton's thirty-year-old daughter got arrested for cocaine possession, it was Evans who went downtown at midnight to post her bail. Lowenstein had done it for many years, and now was glad to sleep through the night.

"So," he said, "how was Iceland?"

"Good. Cold."

"Is everything okay?"

"Sure."

"I mean, between George and Nick. Everything okay there?"

"I think so. Why?"

"Nick is worried. He called me twice in the last hour."

"About what?"

"Where are we on George's NERF donation?"

"Nick's asking that?"

"Is there a problem about it?"

"George wants to hold off for a while."

"Why?"

"He didn't say."

"Is it this Kenner guy?"

"George didn't say. He just said, hold off." Evans wondered how Lowenstein knew about Kenner.

"What do I tell Nick?"

"Tell him it's in the works and we don't have a date for him yet."

"But there's not a problem with it, is there?"

"Not that I've been told," Evans said.

"Okay," Lowenstein said. "In this room. Tell me: Is there a problem?"

"There might be." Evans was thinking that George rarely held up charitable donations. And there had been a certain tension in the brief talk he had with him the night before.

"What's this meeting about tomorrow morning?" Lowenstein said. "The big conference room."

"Beats me."

"George didn't tell you?"

"No."

"Nick is very upset."

"Well, that's not unusual for Nick."

"Nick has heard of this Kenner guy. He thinks he's a troublemaker. Some kind of anti-environmental guy."

"I doubt that. He's a professor at MIT. In some environmental science."

"Nick thinks he's a troublemaker."

"I couldn't say."

"He overheard you and Morton talking about Kenner on the airplane."

"Nick should stop listening at keyholes."

"He's worried about his standing with George."

"Not surprising," Evans said. "Nick screwed up on a big check. Got deposited in the wrong account."

"I heard about that. It was an error by a volunteer. You can't blame Nick for that."

"It doesn't build confidence."

"It was deposited to the International Wilderness Preservation Society. A great organization. And the money is being transferred back, even as we speak."

"That's fine."

"Where are you in this?"

"Nowhere. I just do what the client says."

"But you advise him."

"If he asks me. He hasn't asked."

"It sounds like you've lost confidence yourself."

Evans shook his head. "Herb," he said. "I'm not aware of any problem. I'm aware of a delay. That's all."

"Okay," Lowenstein said, reaching for the phone. "I'll calm Nick down."

Evans went back to his office. His phone was ringing. He answered it. "What are you doing today?" Morton said.

"Not much. Paperwork."

"That can wait. I want you to go over and see how that Vanutu lawsuit is coming."

"Jeez, George, it's still pretty preliminary. I think the filing is several months away."

"Pay them a visit," Morton said.

"Okay, they're in Culver City, I'll call over there and—"

"No. Don't call. Just go."

"But if they're not expecting—"

"That's right. That's what I want. Let me know what you find out, Peter."

And he hung up.

The Vanutu litigation team had taken over an old warehouse south of Culver City. It was an industrial area, with potholes in the streets. There was nothing to see from the curb: just a plain brick wall, and a door with the street number in battered metal numerals. Evans pushed the buzzer and was admitted to a small walled-off reception area. He could hear the low murmur of voices from the other side of the wall, but he could see nothing at all.

Two armed guards stood on either side of the far door, leading into the warehouse itself. A receptionist sat at a small desk. She gave him an unfriendly look.

"And you are?"

"Peter Evans, Hassle and Black."

"To see?"

"Mr. Balder."

"You have an appointment?"

"No."

The receptionist looked disbelieving. "I will buzz his assistant."

"Thank you."

The receptionist talked on the phone in a low

voice. He heard her mention the name of the law firm. Evans looked at the two guards. They were from a private security firm. They stared back at him, their faces blank, unsmiling.

The receptionist hung up and said, "Ms. Haynes will be out in a moment." She nodded to the guards.

One of them came over and said to Evans, "Just a formality, sir. May I see some identification?"

Evans gave him his driver's license.

"Do you have any cameras or recording equipment on your person?"

"No," Evans said.

"Any disks, drives, flash cards, or other computer equipment?"

"No."

"Are you armed, sir?"

"No."

"Would you mind raising your arms for a moment?" When Evans gave him a strange look, the guard said, "Just think of it like airport security," and he patted him down. But he was also clearly feeling for wires. He ran his fingers over the collar of Evans's shirt, felt the stitching in his jacket, ran his finger around his waistband, and then asked him to take off his shoes. Finally he passed an electronic wand over him.

"You guys are serious," Evans said.

"Yes we are. Thank you, sir."

The guard stepped away, resuming his place at the wall. There was no place to sit, so Evans just stood there and waited. It was probably two minutes before the door opened. An attractive but tough-looking woman in her late twenties, with short dark hair and blue eyes, wearing jeans and a white shirt, said, "Mr. Evans? I'm Jennifer Haynes." Her handshake was firm. "I work with John Balder. Come this way."

They went inside.

They were in a narrow corridor, with a locked door at the far end. Evans realized it was a security lock—two doors to get inside.

"What was that all about?" he said, indicating the guards.

"We've had a little trouble."

"What kind of trouble?"

"People want to know what's going on here."

"Uh-huh . . ."

"We've learned to be careful."

She held her card against the door, and it buzzed open.

They entered an old warehouse—a vast, high-ceilinged space, separated into large rooms by glass partitions. Immediately to his left, behind glass, Evans saw a room filled with computer terminals, each manned by a young person with a stack of documents beside their keyboard. In big lettering on the glass it said, "DATA-RAW."

To his right, there was a matching conference room labeled "SATELLITES/RADIOSONDE." Evans saw four people inside that room, busily discussing huge blowups of a graph on the wall, jagged lines on a grid.

Farther along there was another room marked "GENERAL CIRCULATION MODELS (GCMS)." Here the walls were plastered with large maps of the world, graphical representations in many colors.

"Wow," Evans said. "Big operation."

"Big lawsuit," Jennifer Haynes replied. "These are all our issue teams. They're mostly graduate students in climate science, not attorneys. Each team is researching a different issue for us." She pointed around the warehouse. "The first group does raw data, meaning processed data from the Goddard Institute for Space Studies at Columbia University, in New York, from the USHCN at Oak Ridge, Tennessee, and from Hadley Center in East Anglia, England. Those are the major sources of temperature data from around the world."

"I see," Evans said.

"Then the group over there works on satellite data. Orbiting satellites have recorded temperatures of the upper atmosphere since 1979, so there is more than a twenty-year record. We're trying to figure out what to do about it."

"What to do about it?"

"The satellite data's a problem," she said.

"Why?"

As though she hadn't heard him, she pointed to the next room. "The team there is doing comparative analyses of GCMs—meaning the computer-generated climate models—from the 1970s to the present. As you know, these models are immensely complex, manipulating a million variables or more at once. They are by far the most complex computer models ever created by man. We're dealing with American, British, and German models, primarily."

"I see . . ." Evans was starting to feel overwhelmed.

"And the team down there is doing sea-level

issues. Around the corner is paleoclimate. Those're proxy studies, of course. And the final team is dealing with solar irradiance and aerosols. Then we have an off-site team at UCLA that is doing atmospheric feedback mechanisms, primarily focusing on cloud cover as it varies with temperature change. And that's about all of it." She paused, seeing the confusion on Evans's face. "I'm sorry. Since you work with George Morton, I assumed you were familiar with all this stuff."

"Who said I work with George Morton?"

She smiled. "We know our job, Mr. Evans."

They passed a final glass-walled room that had no label. It was filled with charts and huge photographs, and three-dimensional models of the earth set inside plastic cubes. "What's this?" he said.

"Our AV team. They prepare visuals for the jury. Some of the data is extremely complex, and we're trying to find the simplest and most forceful way to present it."

They walked on. Evans said, "Is it really that complicated?"

"That's correct," she said. "The island nation of Vanutu is actually four coral atolls in the southern Pacific, which have a maximum elevation of twenty feet above sea level. The eight thousand inhabitants of those islands are at risk of being flooded out by rising sea levels caused by global warming."

"Yes," Evans said. "I understand that. But why do you have so many people working on the science?"

She looked at him oddly. "Because we're trying to win the case."

"Yes . . ."

"And it's not an easy case to win."

"What do you mean?" Evans said. "This is global warming. Everybody knows that global warming is—"

A voice boomed from the other end of the warehouse. "Is *what?*"

A bald, bespectacled man came toward them. He had an ungainly gait, and looked like his nickname: the Bald Eagle. As always, John Balder was dressed all in blue: a blue suit, a blue shirt, and a blue tie. His manner was intense, his eyes narrowed as he looked at Evans. In spite of himself, Evans was intimidated to meet the famous litigator.

Evans extended his hand. "Peter Evans, Hassle and Black."

"And you work with George Morton?"

"Yes sir, I do."

"We are indebted to Mr. Morton's generosity. We strive to be worthy of his support."

"I'll tell him that, sir."

"I'm sure you will. You were speaking of global warming, Mr. Evans. Is it a subject that interests you?"

"Yes, sir, it does. And every concerned citizen of the planet."

"I certainly agree. But tell me. What *is* global warming, as you understand it?"

Evans tried to conceal his surprise. He hadn't expected to be quizzed. "Why do you ask?"

"We ask everybody who comes here. We're trying to get a feel for the general state of knowledge. What's global warming?"

"Global warming is the heating up of the earth from burning fossil fuels."

"Actually, that is not correct."

"It's not?"

"Not even close. Perhaps you'd try again."

Evans paused. It was obvious he was being interrogated by a fussy and precise legal mind. He knew the type only too well, from law school. He thought for a moment, choosing his words carefully. "Global warming is, uh, the heating up of the surface of the earth from the excess of carbon dioxide in the atmosphere that is produced by burning fossil fuels."

"Again, not correct."

"Why not?"

"Several reasons. At a minimum, I count four errors in the statement you just made."

"I don't understand," Evans said. "My statement—that's what global warming is."

"In fact, it is not." Balder's tone was crisp, authoritative. "Global warming is the *theory*—"

"—hardly a theory, anymore—"

"No, it is a *theory*," Balder said. "Believe me, I wish it were otherwise. But in fact, global warming is the *theory* that increased levels of carbon dioxide and certain other gases *are causing* an increase in the *average temperature* of the earth's *atmosphere* because of the so-called 'greenhouse effect.'"

"Well, okay," Evans said. "That's a more exact definition, but . . ."

"Mr. Evans, you yourself believe in global warming, I take it?"

"Of course."

"Believe in it strongly?"

"Sure. Everybody does."

"When you have a strongly held belief, don't you think it's important to express that belief accurately?"

Evans was starting to sweat. He really felt like he was back in law school. "Well, sir, I guess . . . not really, in this case. Because when you refer to global warming, everybody knows what you are talking about."

"Do they? I suspect that even you don't know what you are talking about."

Evans felt a burst of hot anger. Before he could check himself, he had blurted, "Look, just because I may not be expressing the fine details of the science—"

"I'm not concerned about *details*, Mr. Evans. I'm concerned about the *core* of your strongly held beliefs. I suspect you have no basis for those beliefs."

"With all due respect, that's ridiculous." He caught his breath. "Sir."

"You mean you do have such a basis?"

"Of course I do."

Balder looked at him thoughtfully. He seemed pleased with himself. "In that case, you can be a great help to this lawsuit. Would you mind giving us an hour of your time?"

"Uh . . . I guess so."

"Would you mind if we videotaped you?"

"No, but . . . why?"

Balder turned to Jennifer Haynes, who said, "We're trying to establish a baseline for what a well-informed person such as yourself knows about global warming. To help us refine our jury presentation."

"Sort of a mock jury of one?"

"Exactly. We've interviewed several people already."

"Okay," Evans said. "I guess I could schedule that at some point."

"*Now* is a good time," Balder said. He turned to Jennifer. "Get your team together in room four."

"Of course I'd like to help," Evans said, "but I came here to get an overview—"

"Because you've heard there are problems with the lawsuit? There aren't. But there are significant challenges," Balder said. He glanced at his watch. "I'm about to go into a meeting," he said. "You spend some time with Ms. Haynes, and when you're done, we'll talk about the litigation as I see it. Is that all right with you?"

There was nothing Evans could do but agree.

They put him in a conference room at the end of a long table, and aimed the video camera at him from the far end. Just like a deposition, he thought.

Five young people drifted into the room and took seats at the table. All were casually dressed, in jeans and T-shirts. Jennifer Haynes introduced them so quickly that Evans didn't catch their names. She explained that they were all graduate students in different scientific disciplines.

While they were setting up, Jennifer slipped into a chair beside his and said, "I'm sorry John was so rough on you. He's frustrated and under a lot of pressure."

"From the case?"

"Yes."

"What kind of pressure?"

"This session may give you some idea what we're dealing with." She turned to the others. "Are we ready?"

Heads nodded, notebooks flipped open. The camera light came on. Jennifer said, "Interview with Peter Evans, of Hassle and Black, on Tuesday, August twenty-fourth. Mr. Evans, we'd like to go over your views about the evidence that supports global warming. This isn't a test; we'd just like to clarify how you think about the issue."

"Okay," Evans said.

"Let's begin informally. Tell us what you know about the evidence for global warming."

"Well," Evans said, "I know that temperatures around the globe have risen dramatically in the last twenty or thirty years as a result of increases in carbon dioxide that is released by industry when fossil fuels are burned."

"Okay. And by a dramatic rise in temperature, you mean how much?"

"I think about a degree."

"Fahrenheit or Celsius?"

"Fahrenheit."

"And this rise has occurred over twenty years?"

"Twenty or thirty, yes."

"And earlier in the twentieth century?"

"Temperatures went up then, too, but not as fast."

"Okay," she said. "Now I am going to show you a graph . . ." She pulled out a graph* on foam core backing.

"Does this look familiar to you?" she asked.

"I've seen it before," Evans said.

"It's taken from the NASA–Goddard data set used by the UN and other organizations. Do you consider the UN a trustworthy source?"

---

* All graphs are generated using tabular data from the following standard data sets: GISS (Columbia); CRU (East Anglia); GHCN and USHCN (Oak Ridge). See Appendix II for a full discussion.

"Yes."

"So we can regard this graph as accurate? Unbiased? No monkey business?"

"Yes."

"Good. Do you know what this graph represents?"

Evans could read that much. He said, "It's the mean global temperature from all the weather stations around the world for the last hundred years or so."

"That's right," she said. "And how do you interpret this graph?"

"Well," he said, "it shows what I was describing." He pointed to the red line. "World temperatures have been rising since about 1890, but they start to go up steeply around 1970, when industrialization is most intense, which is the real proof of global warming."

"Okay," she said. "So the rapid increase in temperature since 1970 was caused by what?"

"Rising carbon dioxide levels from industrialization."

"Good. In other words, as the carbon dioxide goes up, the temperature goes up."

"Yes."

"All right. Now you mentioned the temperature started to rise from 1890, up to about 1940. And we see here that it did. What caused that rise? Carbon dioxide?"

"Um . . . I'm not sure."

"Because there was much less industrialization back in 1890, and yet look how temperatures go up. Was carbon dioxide rising in 1890?"

"I'm not sure."

"Actually, it was. Here is a graph showing carbon dioxide levels and temperature."

"Okay," Evans said. "Just what you would expect. Carbon dioxide goes up, and makes temperatures go up."

"Good," she said. "Now I want to direct your attention to the period from 1940 to 1970. As you see, during that period the global temperature actually went down. You see that?"

"Yes . . ."

"Let me show you a closeup of that period." She took out another chart.

"This is a thirty-year period. One third of a century during which temperatures declined. Crops were damaged by frost in summer, glaciers in Europe advanced. What caused the decline?"

"I don't know."

"Was carbon dioxide rising during that period?"

"Yes."

"So, if rising carbon dioxide is the cause of

Global Temperature vs CO₂ 1940–1970

Source: giss.nasa.gov

rising temperatures, why didn't it cause temperatures to rise from 1940 to 1970?"

"I don't know," Evans said. "There must have been another factor. Or it could be an anomaly. There are anomalies within broad secular trends. Just look at the stock market."

"Does the stock market have anomalies that last thirty years?"

He shrugged. "Or it could have been soot. Or particulate matter in the air. There were a lot of particulates back then, before environmental laws took effect. Or maybe some other factor."

"These graphs show that carbon dioxide rose continuously, but temperature did not. It rose, then fell, then rose again. Even so, I take it you remain convinced that carbon dioxide has caused the most recent temperature rise?"

"Yes. Everybody knows that's the cause."

"Does this graph trouble you at all?"

"No," Evans said. "I admit it raises some questions, but then not everything is known about the climate. So, no. The graph doesn't trouble me."

"Okay, good. I'm glad to hear it. Let's move on. You said this graph was the average of weather stations around the world. How reliable is that weather data, do you think?"

"I have no idea."

"Well, for example, in the late nineteenth century, the data were generated by people going out to a little box and writing down the temperature twice a day. Maybe they forgot for a few days. Maybe somebody in their family was sick. They had to fill it in later."

"That was back then."

"Right. But how accurate do you think weather records are from Poland in the 1930s? Or Russian provinces since 1990?"

"Not very good, I would guess."

"And I would agree. So over the last hundred years, a fair number of reporting stations around the world may not have provided high-quality, reliable data."

"That could be," Evans said.

"Over the years, which country do you imagine has the best-maintained network of weather stations over a large area?"

"The US?"

"Right. I think there is no dispute about that. Here is another graph. Does this graph look like the first one we saw of world temperatures?"

"Not exactly."

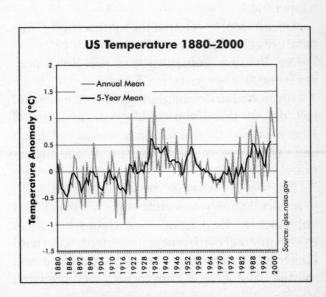

"What is the change in temperature since 1880?"

"Looks like, uh, a third of a degree."

"A third of a degree Celsius in a hundred and twenty years. Not very dramatic." She pointed to the graph. "And what was the warmest year of the last century?"

"Looks like 1934."

"Does this graph indicate to you that global warming is occurring?"

"Well. The temperature *is* going up."

"For the last thirty years, yes. But it went *down* for the previous thirty years. And current temperatures in the US are roughly the same as they were in the 1930s. So: Does this graph argue for global warming?"

"Yes," Evans said. "It's just not as dramatic in the US as it is in the rest of the world, but it's still happening."

"Does it trouble you that the most accurate temperature record shows the least warming?"

"No. Because global warming is a global phenomenon. It's not just the US."

"If you had to defend these graphs in a court of law, do you think you could persuade a jury of your position? Or would a jury look at the graph and say, this global warming stuff is nothing serious?"

"Leading the witness," he said, laughing.

In fact, Evans was feeling slightly uneasy. But only slightly. He'd heard such claims before, at environmental conferences. Industry hacks could slap together data that they had massaged and twisted, and give a convincing, well-prepared speech, and before Evans knew it, he'd start to doubt what he knew.

As if she were reading his mind, Jennifer said, "These graphs show solid data, Peter. Temperature records from Goddard Institute for Space Studies at Columbia University. Carbon dioxide levels from Mauna Loa and the Law Dome ice cores in Antarctica.* All generated by researchers who believe firmly in global warming."

"Yes," he said. "Because the overwhelming consensus of scientists around the world is that global warming *is* happening and it *is* a major worldwide threat."

"Okay, good," she said smoothly. "I'm glad that none of this changes your views. Let's turn to some other questions of interest. David?"

One of the graduate students leaned forward. "Mr. Evans, I'd like to talk to you about land use, the urban heat island effect, and satellite data on the temperature of the troposphere."

Evans thought, *Oh Jesus*. But he just nodded. "Okay . . ."

"One of the issues we're trying to address concerns how surface temperatures change with land use. Are you familiar with that issue?"

"Not really, no." He looked at his watch. "Frankly, you people are working at a level of detail that is beyond me. I just listen to what the scientists say—"

"And we're preparing a lawsuit," Jennifer said,

---

* D. M. Etheridge, et al., 1996, "Natural and anthropogenic changes in atmospheric CO_2 over the last 1,000 years from air in Antarctic ice and firn," *Journal of Geophysical Research* 101 (1996): 4115–28.

"based on what scientists say. This level of detail is where the suit will be fought."

"Fought?" Evans shrugged. "Who's going to fight it? Nobody with any stature. There isn't a reputable scientist in the world who doesn't believe in global warming."

"On that point, you are wrong," she said. "The defense will call full professors from MIT, Harvard, Columbia, Duke, Virginia, Colorado, UC Berkeley, and other prestigious schools. They will call the former president of the National Academy of Sciences. They may also call some Nobel Prize winners. They will bring in professors from England, from the Max Planck Institute in Germany, from Stockholm University in Sweden. These professors will argue that global warming is at best unproven, and at worst pure fantasy."

"Their research paid for by industry, no doubt."

"A few. Not all."

"Arch-conservatives. *Neocons.*"

"The focus in litigation," she said, "will be on the data."

Evans looked at them and saw the concern on their faces. And he thought, *They really believe they might lose this thing.*

"But this is ridiculous," Evans said. "All you have to do is read the newspapers, or watch television—"

"Newspapers and television are susceptible to carefully orchestrated media campaigns. Lawsuits are not."

"Then forget mass media," Evans said, "and just read the scientific journals—"

"We do. They're not necessarily helpful to our side. Mr. Evans, we have a lot to go over. If you'd hold your protestations, we can get on with the issues."

It was at that moment that the phone buzzed, and Balder delivered him from his torment. "Send the guy from Hassle and Black into my office," he said. "I have ten minutes for him."

Balder was ensconced in a glass-walled office, with his feet up on a glass desk, working his way through a stack of briefs and research papers. He didn't take his feet down as Evans came in.

"You find it interesting?" he said. He meant the interrogation.

"In a way," Evans said. "But if you'll pardon my saying so, I get the sense they're worried they might lose."

"I have no doubt that we will win this case," Balder said. "No doubt whatsoever. But I don't want my people thinking that way! I want them worried as hell. I want my team running scared before any trial. And especially this one. We are bringing this suit against the EPA, and in anticipation of that, the agency has retained outside counsel in the person of Barry Beckman."

"Whew," Evans said. "Big guns."

Barry Beckman was the most famous litigator of his generation. A professor at Stanford Law School at twenty-eight, he left the university in his early thirties to go into private practice. He had already represented Microsoft, Toyota, Phillips, and a host of other multinationals. Beckman had an incredibly agile mind, a charming manner, a quick sense of humor, and a photographic memory. Everyone knew that when he argued before the Supreme Court (as he had done three times already) he cited document page numbers as he answered the Justices' questions. "Your honor, I believe you will find that in footnote 17 on the bottom of page 237." Like that.

"Barry has his faults," Balder said. "He has so much information at his fingertips that he can easily slip into irrelevance. He likes to hear himself talk. His arguments drift. I have beaten him once. And lost to him, once. But one thing is sure: We can expect an *extremely* well-prepared opposition."

"Isn't it a little unusual to hire an attorney before you've even filed?"

"It's a tactic," Balder said. "The current administration doesn't want to defend this lawsuit. They believe they will win, but they don't want the negative publicity that will accompany their brief against global warming. So they hope to intimidate us into dropping the case. And of course we never would. Especially now that we are fully funded, thanks to Mr. Morton."

"That's good," Evans said.

"At the same time, the challenges are significant. Barry will argue that there is insufficient evidence for global warming. He will argue that the supporting science is weak. He will argue that the predictions from ten and fifteen years ago have already been shown to be wrong. And he will argue that even leading proponents of global warming have publicly expressed doubts about whether it can be predicted, whether it is a serious problem—and indeed, whether it's occurring at all."

"Leading proponents have said that?"

Balder sighed. "They have. In journals."

"I've never read anything of that sort."

"The statements exist. Barry will dig them out." He shook his head. "Some experts have expressed different views at different times. Some have said rising carbon dioxide isn't a big problem; now they say it is. So far, we don't have a single expert witness that can't be turned. Or made to look very foolish on cross."

Evans nodded sympathetically. He was familiar with this circumstance. One of the first things you learned in law school was that the law was not about truth. It was about dispute resolution. In the course of resolving a dispute, the truth might or might not emerge. Often it did not. Prosecutors might know a criminal was guilty, and still be unable to convict him. It happened all the time.

"That's why," Balder said, "this case is going to hinge on the sea-level records in the Pacific. We are collecting all available data records now."

"Why does the case hinge on that?"

"Because I believe," Balder said, "that this is a case we should bait and switch. The case is about global warming, but that's not where the emotional impact is for a jury. Juries aren't comfortable reading graphs. And all this talk about tenths of a degree Celsius goes right over their heads. It's technical detail; it's the quibbles of experts; and it's incredibly boring for normal people.

"No, the jury will see this as a case about help-less, victimized, impoverished people being flooded out of their ancestral homelands. A case about the terror of sea levels rising precipitously—and inexplicably—with no conceivable cause *unless you accept that something extraordinary and unprecedented has affected the entire world* in recent years. Something that is causing the sea levels to rise and to threaten the lives of innocent men, women, and children."

"And that something is global warming."

Balder nodded. "The jury will have to draw their own conclusions. If we can show them a convincing record of rising sea levels, we will be on very strong ground. When juries see that damage has been done, they are inclined to blame *somebody*."

"Okay." Evans saw where Balder was going. "So the sea-level data is important."

"Yes, but it needs to be solid, irrefutable."

"Is that so hard to obtain?"

Balder cocked an eyebrow. "Mr. Evans, do you know anything about the study of sea levels?"

"No. I just know that sea levels are rising around the world."

"Unfortunately, that claim is in considerable dispute."

"You're joking."

"It is well known," Balder said, "that I have no sense of humor."

"But sea level can't be disputed," Evans said. "It's too simple. You put a mark on a dock at high tide, measure it year after year, watch it go up . . . I mean, how difficult can it be?"

Balder sighed. "You think sea level is simple? Trust me, it's not. Have you ever heard of the geoid? No? The geoid is the equipotential surface of the earth's gravitational field that approximates the mean sea surface. That help you?"

Evans shook his head.

"Well, it is a core concept in the measurement of sea levels." Balder flipped through the stack of papers in front of him. "How about glacio-hydro-isostatic modeling? Eustatic and tectonic effects on shoreline dynamics? Holocene sedimentary sequences? Intertidal foraminifera distributions? Carbon analysis of coastal paleoenvironments? Aminostratigraphy? No? Not ringing a bell? Let me assure you, sea level is a fiercely debated specialty." He tossed the last of the papers aside. "That's what I'm working through now. But the disputes within the field give added importance to finding an unimpeachable set of data."

"And you are obtaining this data?"

"Waiting for them to arrive, yes. The Australians have several sets. The French have at least one in Moorea and perhaps another in Papeete. There is a set that was funded by the V. Allen Willy Foundation, but it may be of too short a duration. And other sets as well. We will have to see."

The intercom buzzed. The assistant said, "Mr. Balder, it's Mr. Drake on the line, from NERF."

"All right." Balder turned to Evans, extended a hand. "Nice talking with you, Mr. Evans. Again, our thanks to George. Tell him any time he wants to have a look around, he can drop by. We are always hard at work here. Good luck to you. Close the door on your way out."

Balder turned away, picking up the phone. Evans heard him say, "Well, Nick, what the fuck is going on at NERF? Are you going to fix this for me, or not?"

Evans closed the door.

He walked out of Balder's office with a sense of nagging unease. Balder was one of the most persuasive men on the planet. He had known Evans was there on behalf of George Morton. He knew Morton was on the verge of making a huge contribution to the lawsuit. Balder should have been totally upbeat, radiating confidence. And he had, indeed, begun that way.

I have no doubt we will win this lawsuit.

But then, Evans had heard:

The challenges are significant.

I do not have a single expert witness who can't be turned.

This is a case we should bait and switch.

This case will hinge on sea-level records.

Sea level is a fiercely debated specialty.

We will have to see.

It certainly wasn't a conversation calculated to raise Evans's level of confidence. Neither, for that matter, was the video session he'd had with Jennifer Haynes, discussing the scientific problems the lawsuit would face.

But then, as he considered it, he decided that these expressions of doubt were actually a sign of confidence on the part of the legal team. Evans was an attorney himself; he had come to learn the issues surrounding the trial, and they had been forthright with him. It was a case they would win, even though it would not be easy, because of the complexity of the data and the short attention span of the jury.

So: would he recommend that Morton continue?

Of course he would.

Jennifer was waiting for him outside Balder's office. She said, "They're ready for you back in the conference room."

Evans said, "I'm really sorry, I can't. My schedule . . ."

"I understand," she said, "we'll do it another time. I was wondering if your schedule was really tight, or whether there was time for you and me to have lunch."

"Oh," Evans said, without missing a beat, "my schedule isn't that tight."

"Good," she said.

They had lunch in a Mexican restaurant in Culver City. It was quiet. There were a handful of film editors in the corner, from nearby Sony Studios. A couple of high school kids necking. A group of older women in sunhats.

They sat in a corner booth and both ordered the special. Evans said, "Balder seems to think the sea-level data is key."

"That's what Balder thinks. Frankly, I'm not so sure."

"Why is that?"

"Nobody's seen all the data. But even if it's high quality, it needs to show a substantial sea-level rise to impress a jury. It may not."

"How could it not?" Evans said. "With glaciers melting, and breaking off Antarctica—"

"Even so, it may not," she said. "You know the Maldive Islands in the Indian Ocean? They were concerned about flooding, so a team of Scandinavian researchers came in to study sea levels. The scientists found no rise in several centuries—and a fall in the last twenty years."

"A fall? Was that published?"

"Last year," she said. The food came; Jennifer

gave a dismissive wave of her hand: enough shop talk for now. She ate her burrito with gusto, wiping her chin with the back of her hand. He saw a jagged white scar running from her palm down the underside of her forearm. She said, "God, I love this food. You can't get decent Mexican food in DC."

"Is that where you're from?"

She nodded. "I came out to help John."

"He asked you?"

"I couldn't turn him down." She shrugged. "So I see my boyfriend on alternate weekends. He comes out here, or I go back there. But if this trial goes forward, it will be a year, maybe two years. I don't think our relationship will make it."

"What does he do? Your boyfriend."

"Attorney."

Evans smiled. "Sometimes I think everyone's an attorney."

"Everyone is. He does securities law. Not my thing."

"What's your thing?"

"Witness prep and jury selection. Psychological analysis of the pool. That's why I'm in charge of the focus groups."

"I see."

"We know that most people we might put on the jury will have heard of global warming, and most will probably be inclined to think it is real."

"Jesus, I'd *hope* so," Evans said. "I mean, it's been an established fact for the last fifteen years."

"But we need to determine what people will believe in the face of contrary evidence."

"Such as?"

"Such as the graphs I showed you today. Or the satellite data. You know about the satellite data?"

Evans shook his head.

"The theory of global warming predicts that the upper atmosphere will warm from trapped heat, just like a greenhouse. The surface of the Earth warms later. But since 1979 we've had orbiting satellites that can continuously measure the atmosphere five miles up. They show that the upper atmosphere is warming much less than the ground is."

"Maybe there's a problem with the data—"

"Trust me, the satellite data have been reanalyzed dozens of times," she said. "They're probably the most intensely scrutinized data in the world. But the data from weather balloons agree with the satellites. They show much less warming than expected by the theory." She shrugged. "Another problem for us. We're working on it."

"How?"

"We think it'll prove too complex for a jury. The details of MSUs—microwave-sounding units, cross-track scanners with four-channel radiance analysis—and the questions about whether channel 2 has been corrected for diurnal drifts and inter-satellite offsets, time-varying nonlinear instrumental responses . . . We hope it will make them throw up their hands. Anyway. Enough of all that." She wiped her face with her napkin and again he saw the white scar that ran down the underside of her arm.

"How'd you get that?" he said.

She shrugged. "In law school."

"And I thought my school was tough."

"I taught an inner-city karate class," she said. "Sometimes it went late. You want any more of these chips?"

"No," he said.

"Shall we get the check?"

"Tell me," he said.

"There's not a lot to tell. One night, I got in my car to drive home, and a kid jumped in the passenger seat and pulled a gun. Told me to start driving."

"Kid from your class?"

"No. An older kid. Late twenties."

"What'd you do?"

"I told him to get out. He told me to drive. So I started the car, and as I put it in gear I asked him where he wanted me to go. And he was stupid enough to point, so I hit him in the windpipe. I didn't hit him hard enough, and he got off a round, blew out the windshield. Then I hit him again with my elbow. Couple, three times."

"What happened to him?" he said.

"He died."

"Jesus," Evans said.

"Some people make bad decisions," she said. "What're you staring at me like that for? He was six-two and two-ten and had a record from here to Nebraska. Armed robbery, assault with a deadly weapon, attempted rape—you name it. You think I should feel sorry for him?"

"No," Evans said quickly.

"You do, I can see it in your eyes. A lot of people do. They go, He was just a kid, how could you do that? Let me tell you, people don't know what the hell they're talking about. One of us was going to get killed that night. I'm glad it wasn't me. But of course, it still bothers me."

"I'll bet."

"Sometimes I wake up in a cold sweat. Seeing the gunshot blow the windshield in front of my face. Realizing how close I came to dying. I was stupid. I should have killed him the first time."

Evans paused. He didn't know what to say.

"You ever had a gun at your head?" she said.

"No . . ."

"Then you have no idea how it feels, do you?"

"Was there trouble about it?" he said.

"You bet your ass there was trouble. For a while I thought I wasn't going to be able to practice law. They claimed I led him on. Do you believe that shit? I never saw the guy in my life. But then a very good attorney came to my rescue."

"Balder?"

She nodded. "That's why I'm here."

"And what about your arm?"

"Ah hell," she said, "the car crashed and I cut it on the broken glass." She signaled to the waitress. "What do you say we get the check?"

"I'll do that."

Minutes later they were back outside. Evans blinked in the milky midday light. They walked down the street. "So," Evans said. "I guess you're pretty good at karate."

"Good enough."

They came to the warehouse. He shook her hand.

"I'd really like to have lunch again some time," she said. She was so direct about it, he wondered whether it was personal, or whether she wanted him to know how the lawsuit was going. Because like Balder, much of what she had said was not encouraging.

"Lunch sounds great," he said.

"Not too long?"

"Deal."

"Will you call me?"

"Count on it," he said.

It was almost dark when he went home to his apartment and parked in the garage facing the alley. He was going up the back stairs when the landlady poked her head out the window. "You just missed them," she said.

"Who?"

"The cable repair people. They just left."

"I didn't call any cable repair people," he said. "Did you let them in?"

"Of course not. They said they would wait for you. They just left."

Evans had never heard of cable repair people waiting for anyone. "How long did they wait?"

"Not long. Maybe ten minutes."

"Okay."

He got up to the second-floor landing. A tag was hooked on his doorknob. "Sorry We Missed You." There was a check box to "Call again to re-schedule service."

Then he saw the problem. The address was listed as 2119 Roxbury. His address was 2129 Roxbury. But the address was on the front door, not the back door. They'd just made a mistake. He lifted his doormat to check on the key he kept there. It was right where he'd left it. It hadn't been moved. There was even a ring of dust around it.

He unlocked the door and went inside. He went to the refrigerator, and saw the old container of yogurt. He needed to go to the supermarket but he was too tired. He checked the messages to see if Janis or Carol had called. They hadn't. Now of course there was the prospect of Jennifer Haynes, but she had a boyfriend, she lived in DC, and . . . he knew it would never work.

He thought of calling Janis, but decided not to. He took a shower, and was considering calling for pizza delivery. He lay down on the bed to relax for a minute before he called. And he fell immediately asleep.

The meeting was held in the big conference room on the fourteenth floor. Morton's four accountants were there; his assistant Sarah Jones; Herb Lowenstein, who did estate planning; a guy named Marty Bren, who did tax work for NERF, and Evans. Morton, who hated all financial meetings, paced restlessly.

"Let's get to it," he said. "I am supposedly giving ten million dollars to NERF, and we have signed papers, is that right?"

"Right," Lowenstein said.

"But now they want to attach a rider to the agreement?"

"Right," Marty Bren said. "It's pretty standard boilerplate for them." He shuffled through his papers. "Any charity wants to have full use of the money they receive, even when it is earmarked for a particular purpose. Maybe that purpose costs more or less than predicted, or it is delayed, or mired in litigation, or set aside for some other reason. In this case, the money has been earmarked for the Vanutu lawsuit, and the relevant phrase NERF wants to add is 'said moneys to be used to defray the cost of the Vanutu litigation, including fees, filing, and copying costs . . . blah blah . . . or for other legal purposes, or for such other purposes as NERF shall see fit in its capacity as an environmental organization.'"

Morton said, "That's the phrase they want?"

"Boilerplate, as I said," Bren said.

"It's been in my previous donation agreements?"

"I don't recall offhand."

"Because," Morton said, "it sounds to me like they want to be able to pull the plug on this lawsuit, and spend the money elsewhere."

"Oh, I doubt that," Herb said.

"Why?" Morton said. "Why else would they want this boilerplate? Look, we had a signed deal. Now they want a change. Why?"

"It's not really a change," Bren said.

"It sure as hell is, Marty."

"If you look at the original agreement," Bren said calmly, "it says that any money not spent on the lawsuit goes to NERF for other purposes."

"But that's only if there's money left after the lawsuit ends," Morton said. "They can't spend it on anything else until the suit is decided."

"I think they imagine there may be long delays here."

"Why should there be delays?" Morton turned to Evans. "Peter? What is going on over there in Culver City?"

"It looks like the suit is going forward," Evans said. "They have a large operation. There must be forty people working on that one case. I don't think they plan to give it up."

"And are there problems with the suit?"

"There are certainly challenges," Evans said. "It's complicated litigation. They face strong opposing counsel. They're working hard."

"Why am I not convinced here?" Morton said. "Six months ago Nick Drake told me this damn lawsuit was a slam dunk and a great publicity opportunity, and now they want a bail-out clause."

"Maybe we should ask Nick."

"I got a better idea. Let's audit NERF."

Murmurs in the room. "I don't think you have that right, George."

"Make it part of the agreement."

"I'm not sure you can do that."

"They want a rider. I want a rider. What's the difference?"

"I'm not sure you can audit their entire operation—"

"George," Herb Lowenstein said. "You and Nick are friends of long standing. You're their Concerned Citizen of the Year. Auditing them seems a little out of character for your relationship."

"You mean it looks like I don't trust them?"

"Put bluntly, yes."

"I don't." Morton leaned on the table and looked at everyone sitting there. "You know what I think? They want to blow off the litigation and spend all the money on this conference on abrupt climate change that Nick is so excited about."

"They don't need ten million for a conference."

"I don't know what they need. He already misplaced two hundred and fifty thousand of my money. It ended up in fucking Vancouver. I don't know what he is doing anymore."

"Well, then you should withdraw your contribution."

"Ah ah," Marty Bren said. "Not so fast. I think they've already made financial commitments based on the reasonable expectation that the money was coming."

"Then give them some amount, and forget the rest."

"No," Morton said. "I'm not going to withdraw the grant. Peter Evans here says the litigation is going forward, and I believe him. Nick says that the two hundred and fifty grand was a mistake, and I believe him. I want you to ask for an audit and I want to know what happens. I will be out of town for the next three weeks."

"You will? Where?"

"I'm taking a trip."

"But we'll have to be able to reach you, George."

"I may be unreachable. Call Sarah. Or have Peter here get in touch with me."

"But George—"

"That's it, guys. Talk to Nick, see what he says. We'll be in contact soon."

And he walked out of the room, with Sarah hurrying after him.

Lowenstein turned to the others. "What the hell was that all about?"

VANCOUVER
THURSDAY, AUGUST 26
12:44 P.M.

Thunder rumbled ominously. Looking out the front windows of his office, Nat Damon sighed. He had always known that that submarine lease would mean trouble. After the check bounced, he had canceled the order, hoping that that would be the end of it. But it wasn't.

For weeks and weeks he had heard nothing, but then one of the men, the lawyer in the shiny suit, had come back unexpectedly to poke a finger in his face and tell him that he had signed a nondisclosure agreement and could not discuss any aspect of the submarine lease with anybody, or risk a lawsuit. "Maybe we'll win, and maybe we'll lose," the lawyer said. "But either way, you're out of business, friend. Your house is mortgaged. You're in debt for the rest of your life. So, think it over. And keep your mouth shut."

All during this, Damon's heart was pounding. Because the fact was, Damon had already been contacted by some sort of revenue service guy. A man named Kenner, who was coming to Damon's office that very afternoon. To ask a few questions, he had said.

Damon had been afraid that this Kenner would

show up while the lawyer was still in his office, but now the lawyer was driving away. His car, a nondescript Buick sedan with Ontario plates, drove through the boatyard, and was gone.

Damon started to clean up the office, getting ready to go home. He was toying with the idea of leaving before Kenner arrived. Kenner was some revenue agent. Damon had done nothing wrong. He didn't have to meet any revenue agent. And if he did, what would he do, say he couldn't answer questions?

The next thing, he'd be subpoenaed or something. Dragged into court.

Damon decided to leave. There was more thunder, and the crack of distant lightning. A big storm was moving in.

As he was closing up, he saw that the lawyer had left his cell phone on the counter. He looked out to see if the lawyer was coming back for it. Not yet, but surely he would realize he had left it, and come back. Damon decided to leave before he showed up.

Hastily, he slipped the cell phone in his pocket, turned out the lights, and locked the office. The first drops of rain were spattering the pavement as he went to his car, parked right in front. He opened the door and was climbing into the car when the cell phone rang. He hesitated, not sure what to do. The phone rang insistently.

A jagged bolt of lightning crashed down, striking the mast of one of the ships in the boatyard. In the next instant there was a burst of light by the car, a blast of furious heat that knocked him to the ground. Dazed, he tried to get up.

He was thinking that his car had exploded, but it hadn't; the car was intact, the door blackened. Then he saw that his trousers were on fire. He stared stupidly at his own legs, not moving. He heard the rumble of thunder and realized that *he had been struck by lightning.*

My God, he thought. I was hit by lightning. He sat up and slapped at his trousers, trying to put out the fire. It wasn't working, and his legs were beginning to feel pain. He had a fire extinguisher inside the office.

Staggering to his feet, he moved unsteadily to his office. He was unlocking the door, his fingers fumbling, when there was another explosion. He felt a sharp pain in his ears, reached up, touched blood. He looked at his bloody fingertips, fell over, and died.

Under normal circumstances, Peter Evans spoke to George Morton every day. Sometimes twice a day. So after a week went by without hearing from him, Evans called his house. He spoke to Sarah.

"I have no idea what is going on," she said. "Two days ago he was in North Dakota. North Dakota! The day before that he was in Chicago. I think he might be in Wyoming today. He's made noises about going to Boulder, Colorado, but I don't know."

"What's in Boulder?" Evans said.

"I haven't a clue. Too early for snow."

"Has he got a new girlfriend?" Sometimes Morton disappeared when he was involved with a new woman.

"Not that I know," Sarah said.

"What's he doing?"

"I have no idea. It sounds like he has a shopping list."

"A shopping list?"

"Well," she said, "sort of. He wanted me to buy some kind of special GPS unit. You know, for locating position? Then he wanted some special video camera using CCD or CCF or something. Had to be rush-ordered from Hong Kong. And yesterday he told me to buy a new Ferrari from a guy in Monterey, and have it shipped to San Francisco."

"Another Ferrari?"

"I know," she said. "How many Ferraris can one man use? And this one doesn't seem up to his usual standards. From the e-mail pictures it looks kind of beat up."

"Maybe he's going to have it restored."

"If he was, he'd send it to Reno. That's where his car restorer is."

He detected a note of concern in her voice. "Is everything okay, Sarah?"

"Between you and me, I don't know," she said. "The Ferrari he bought is a 1972 365 GTS Daytona Spyder."

"So?"

"He already has one, Peter. It's like he doesn't know. And he sounds weird when you talk to him."

"Weird in what way?"

"Just . . . weird. Not his usual self at all."

"Who's traveling with him?"

"As far as I know, nobody."

Evans frowned. That was very odd. Morton hated being alone. Evans's immediate inclination was to disbelieve it.

"What about that guy Kenner and his Nepali friend?"

"Last I heard, they were going to Vancouver, and on to Japan. So they're not with him."

"Uh huh."

"When I hear from him, I'll let him know you called."

Evans hung up, feeling dissatisfied. On an impulse, he dialed Morton's cell phone. But he got the voice mail. "This is George. At the beep." And the quick beep.

"George, this is Peter Evans. Just checking in, to see if there's anything you need. Call me at the office if I can help."

He hung up, and stared out the window. Then he dialed again.

"Center for Risk Analysis."

"Professor Kenner's office, please."

In a moment he got the secretary. "This is Peter Evans, I'm looking for Professor Kenner."

"Oh yes, Mr. Evans. Dr. Kenner said you might call."

"He did?"

"Yes. Are you trying to reach Dr. Kenner?"

"Yes, I am."

"He's in Tokyo at the moment. Would you like his cell phone?"

"Please."

She gave him the number, and he wrote it down on his yellow pad. He was about to call when his assistant, Heather, came in to say that something at lunch had disagreed with her, and she was going home for the afternoon.

"Feel better," he said, sighing.

With her gone, he was obliged to answer his own phone, and the next call was from Margo Lane, George's mistress, asking where the hell

George was. Evans was on the phone with her for the better part of half an hour.

And then Nicholas Drake walked into his office.

"I am very concerned," Drake said. He stood at the window, hands clasped behind his back, staring at the office building opposite.

"About what?"

"This Kenner person that George is spending so much time with."

"I don't know that they're spending time together."

"Of course they are. You don't seriously believe George is *alone*, do you?"

Evans said nothing.

"George is never alone. We both know that. Peter, I don't like this situation at all. Not at all. George is a good man—I don't have to tell you that—but he is susceptible to influence. Including the wrong influence."

"You think a professor at MIT is the wrong influence?"

"I've looked into Professor Kenner," Drake said, "and there are a few mysteries about him."

"Oh?"

"His résumé says he spent a number of years in government. Department of the Interior, Intergovernmental Negotiating Committee, and so on."

"Yes?"

"The Department of the Interior has no record of his working there."

Evans shrugged. "It was more than ten years ago. Government records being what they are . . ."

"Possibly," Drake said. "But there is more. Professor Kenner comes back to MIT, works there for eight years, very successfully. Consultant to the EPA, consultant to Department of Defense, God knows what else—and then he suddenly goes on extended leave, and no one seems to know what happened to him since. He just fell off the radar."

"I don't know," Evans said. "His card says he is Director of Risk Analysis."

"But he's on leave. I don't know what the hell he is doing these days. I don't know who supports him. I take it you've met him?"

"Briefly."

"And now he and George are great pals?"

"I don't know, Nick. I haven't seen or spoken to George in more than a week."

"He's off with Kenner."

"I don't know that."

"But you know that he and Kenner went to Vancouver."

"Actually, I didn't know."

"Let me lay it out for you plainly," Drake said. "I have it on good authority that John Kenner has unsavory connections. The Center for Risk Analysis is wholly funded by industry groups. I needn't say more. In addition, Mr. Kenner spent a number of years advising the Pentagon and in fact was so involved with them that he even underwent some sort of training for a period of time."

"You mean military training?"

"Yes. Fort Bragg and Harvey Point, in North Carolina," Drake said. "There is no question the man has military connections as well as industry connections. And I am told he is hostile toward mainstream environmental organizations. I hate to think of a man like that working on poor George."

"I wouldn't worry about George. He can see through propaganda."

"I hope so. But frankly I do not share your confidence. This military man shows up, and the next thing we know, George is trying to audit us. I mean, my God, why would he want to do that? Doesn't George realize what a waste of resources that involves? Time, money, everything? It would be a *tremendous* drag on my time."

"I wasn't aware an audit was going forward."

"It's being discussed. Of course, we have nothing to hide, and we can be audited at any time. I have always said so. But this is an especially busy time, with the Vanutu lawsuit starting up, and the conference on Abrupt Climate Change to be planned for. All that's in the next few weeks. I wish I could speak to George."

Evans shrugged. "Call his cell."

"I have. Have you?"

"Yes."

"He call you back?"

"No," Evans said.

Drake shook his head. "That man," he said, "is my Concerned Citizen of the Year, and I can't even get him on the phone."

Morton sat at a sidewalk table outside a café on Beverly Drive at eight in the morning, waiting for Sarah to show up. His assistant was ordinarily punctual, and her apartment was not far away. Unless she had taken up with that actor again. Young people had so much time to waste on bad relationships.

He sipped his coffee, glancing at the *Wall Street Journal* without much interest. He had even less interest after an unusual couple sat down at the next table.

The woman was petite and strikingly beautiful, with dark hair and an exotic look. She might have been Moroccan; it was hard to judge from her accent. Her clothing was chic and out of place in casual Los Angeles—tight-fitting skirt, spike heels, Chanel jacket.

The man who accompanied her could not have been more different. He was a red-faced, beefy American, with slightly piggish features, wearing a sweater, baggy khakis, and running shoes. He was as big as a football player. He slumped at the table and said, "I'll have a latte, sweetheart. Non-fat. Grande."

She said, "I thought you would get one for me, like a gentleman."

"I'm not a gentleman," he said. "And you're no fucking lady. Not after you didn't come home last night. So we can forget about ladies and gentlemen, okay?"

She pouted. "*Chéri,* do not make a scene."

"Hey. I asked you to get a fucking latte. Who's making a scene?"

"But *chéri*—"

"You going to get it, or not?" He glared at her. "I've really had it with you, Marisa, you know that?"

"You don't own me," she said. "I do as I please."

"You've made that obvious."

During this conversation, Morton's paper had been slowly drifting downward. Now he folded it flat, set it on his knee, and pretended to read. But in fact he could not take his eyes off this woman. She was extremely beautiful, he decided, although not very young. She was probably thirty-five. Her maturity somehow made her more overtly sexual. He was captivated.

She said to the football player, "William, you are tiresome."

"You want me to leave?"

"Perhaps it is best."

"Oh, fuck you," he said, and slapped her.

Morton could not restrain himself. "Hey," he said, "take it easy there."

The woman gave him a smile. The beefy man stood up, fists bunched. "Mind your own fucking business!"

"You don't hit the lady, pal."

"How about just you and me?" he said, shaking his fist.

At that moment, a Beverly Hills cruiser drove by. Morton looked at it, and waved. The cruiser came over to the curb. "Everything all right?" one of the cops said.

"Just fine, officer," Morton said.

"Fuck this noise," the football player said, and turned away. He stalked off up the street.

The dark woman smiled at Morton. "Thank you for that."

"No problem. Did I hear you say you wanted a latte?"

She smiled again. She crossed her legs, exposing brown knees. "If you would be so kind."

Morton was standing to get it when Sarah called to him, "Hey, George! Sorry to be late." She came jogging up in a tracksuit. As always, she looked very beautiful.

Anger flashed across the dark woman's features. It was fleeting, but Morton caught it and he thought, *Something is wrong here.* He didn't know this woman. She had no reason to be angry. Probably, he decided, she had wanted to teach the boyfriend a lesson. Even now the guy was hanging around at the end of the block, pretending to look in a shop window. But at this early hour, all the shops were closed.

"Ready to go?" Sarah said.

Morton made brief apologies to the woman, who made little gestures of indifference. He had the feeling now that she was French.

"Perhaps we will meet again," he said.

"Yes," she said, "but I doubt it. I am sorry. *Ça va.*"

"Have a nice day."

As they walked off, Sarah said, "Who was that?"

"I don't know. She sat down at the next table."

"Spicy little number."

He shrugged.

"Did I interrupt something? No? That's good." She handed Morton three manila folders. "This one's your contributions to NERF to date. This one is the agreement for the last contribution, so you have the language. And this one is the cashier's check you wanted. Be careful with that. It's a big number."

"Okay. It's not a problem. I'm leaving in an hour."

"You want to tell me where?"

Morton shook his head. "It's better you don't know."

Evans had heard nothing from Morton for almost two weeks. He could not remember ever having gone so long without contact with his client. He had lunch with Sarah, who was visibly anxious. "Do you hear from him at all?" he said.

"Not a word."

"What do the pilots say?"

"They're in Van Nuys. He's rented a different plane. I don't know where he is."

"And he's coming back . . ."

She shrugged. "Who knows?"

And so it was with considerable surprise that he received Sarah's call that day. "You better get going," she said. "George wants to see you right away."

"Where?"

"At NERF. In Beverly Hills."

"He's back?"

"I'll say."

It was a ten-minute drive from his offices in Century City to the NERF building. Of course the National Environmental Resource Fund was head-quartered in Washington, DC, but they had recently opened a west coast office, in Beverly Hills. Cynics claimed that NERF had done it to be closer to the Hollywood celebrities who were so essential to their fund-raising. But that was just gossip.

Evans half expected to find Morton pacing outside, but he was nowhere in sight. Evans went into the reception area and was told that Morton was in the third-floor conference room. He walked up to the third floor.

The conference room was glass-walled on two sides. The interior was furnished with a large, boardroom-style table and eighteen chairs. There was an audiovisual unit in the corner for presentations.

Evans saw three people in the conference room, and an argument in progress. Morton stood at the front of the room, red-faced, gesticulating. Drake was also standing, pacing back and forth, pointing an angry finger at Morton, and shouting back at him. Evans also saw John Henley, the saturnine head of PR for NERF. He was bent over, making notes on a yellow legal pad. It was clearly an argument between Morton and Drake.

Evans was not sure what to do, so he stood there. After a moment, Morton saw him and made a quick jabbing motion, indicating that Evans should sit down outside. He did. And watched the argument through the glass.

It turned out there was a fourth person in the room as well. Evans hadn't seen him at first because he was hunched down behind the podium, but when that person stood, Evans saw a workman in clean, neatly pressed overalls carrying a briefcase-style toolbox and with a couple of electronic meters clipped to his belt. On his chest pocket a logo read AV NETWORK SYSTEMS.

The workman looked confused. Apparently Drake didn't want the workman in the room during the argument, whereas Morton seemed to like an audience. Drake wanted the guy to go; Morton insisted he stay. Caught in the middle, the workman looked uncomfortable, and ducked down out of sight again. But soon after, Drake prevailed, and the workman left.

As the workman walked past him, Evans said, "Rough day?"

The workman shrugged. "They got a lot of network problems in this building," he said. "Myself, I think it's bad Ethernet cable, or the routers are overheating. . . ." And he walked on.

Back inside, the argument raged, fiercer than ever. It continued for another five minutes. The glass was almost entirely soundproof, but from time to time, when they shouted, Evans could hear a phrase. He heard Morton yell, "God damn it, I want to win!" and he heard Drake reply, "It's just too risky." Which made Morton even angrier.

And later Morton said, "Don't we have to fight for the most important issue facing our planet?" And Drake answered something about being practical, or facing reality. And Morton said, "Fuck reality!"

At which point the PR guy, Henley, glanced up and said, "My sentiments exactly." Or something like that.

Evans had the distinct impression that this

argument concerned the Vanutu lawsuit, but it seemed to range over a number of other subjects as well.

And then, quite abruptly, Morton came out, slamming the door so hard that the glass walls shook. "Fuck those guys!"

Evans fell into step with his client. Through the glass, he saw the other two men huddle, whispering together.

"Fuck 'em!" George said loudly. He paused and looked back. "If we have right on our side, shouldn't we be telling the truth?"

Inside, Drake just shook his head sorrowfully.

"Fuck 'em," Morton said again, walking off.

Evans said, "You wanted me here?"

"Yes." Morton pointed. "You know who that other guy was?"

"Yes," he said. "John Henley."

"Correct. Those two guys *are* NERF," George said. "I don't care how many celebrity trustees they have on their letterhead. Or how many lawyers they keep on staff. Those two run the show, and everyone else rubberstamps. None of the trustees really knows anything about what is going on. Otherwise they wouldn't be a part of this. And let me tell you, I'm not going to be a part of this. Not anymore."

They started walking down the stairs.

"Meaning what?" Evans said to him.

"Meaning," Morton said, "I'm not giving them that ten-million-dollar grant for the lawsuit."

"You told them that?"

"No," he said, "I did not tell them that. And you will not tell them that either. I think I'll let it be a surprise, for later." He smiled grimly. "But draw up the papers now."

"Are you sure about this, George?"

"Don't piss me off, kid."

"I'm just asking—"

"And I said draw up the papers. So do it."

Evans said he would.

"*Today.*"

Evans said he would do it at once.

Evans waited until they got to the parking garage before he spoke again. He walked Morton to his waiting town car. His driver, Harry, opened the door for him. Evans said, "George, you have that NERF banquet honoring you next week. Is that still going ahead?"

"Absolutely," Morton said. "I wouldn't miss it for the world."

He got in the car, and Harry closed the door.

"Good day, sir," Harry said to Evans.

And the car drove off into the morning sunlight.

He called from his car: "Sarah."

"I know, I know."

"What is going on?"

"He won't tell me. But he's really angry, Peter. *Really* angry."

"I got that impression."

"And he just left again."

"What?"

"He left. Said he would be back in a week. In

time to fly everybody up to San Francisco for the banquet."

Drake called Evans's cell phone. "What is going on, Peter?"

"I have no idea, Nick."

"The man's demented. The things he was saying . . . could you hear him?"

"No, actually."

"He's demented. I really am worried about him. I mean as a friend. To say nothing of our banquet next week. I mean, is he going to be all right?"

"I think so. He's taking a planeload of friends up there."

"Are you sure?"

"That's what Sarah says."

"Can I talk to George? Can you set something up?"

"My understanding," Evans said, "is that he just went out of town again."

"It's that damn Kenner. He's behind all this."

"I don't know what's going on with George, Nick. All I know is, he's coming to the banquet."

"I want you to promise me you'll deliver him."

"Nick," Evans said. "George does what he wants."

"That's what I'm afraid of."

Flying up on his Gulfstream, Morton brought several of the most prominent celebrity supporters of NERF. These included two rock stars, the wife of a comedian, an actor who played the president on a television series, a writer who had recently run for governor, and two environmental lawyers from other firms. Over white wine and smoked salmon canapés, the discussion became quite lively, focusing on what the United States, as the world's leading economy, should be doing to promote environmental sanity.

Uncharacteristically, Morton did not join in. Instead, he slumped in the back of the plane, looking irritable and gloomy. Evans sat beside him, keeping him company. Morton was drinking straight vodka. He was already on his second.

"I brought the papers cancelling your grant," Evans said, taking them out of his briefcase. "If you still want to do this."

"I do." Morton scribbled his signature, hardly looking at the documents. He said, "Keep those safe until tomorrow." He looked back at his guests, who were now trading statistics on species loss as the rain forests of the world were cut down. Off to one side, Ted Bradley, the actor who played the president, was talking about how he preferred his electric car—which, he pointed out, he had owned for many years now—to the new hybrids that were so popular. "There's no comparison," he was saying. "The hybrids are nice, but they're not the real thing."

At the center table, Ann Garner, who sat on the boards of environmental organizations, was arguing that Los Angeles needed to build more public transportation so that people could get out of their cars. Americans, she said, belched out more carbon dioxide than any other people on the planet, and it was disgraceful. Ann was the beautiful wife of a famous attorney, and always intense, especially on environmental issues.

Morton sighed. He turned to Evans. "Do you know how much pollution we're creating right this minute? We'll burn four hundred fifty gallons of aviation fuel to take twelve people to San Francisco. Just by making this trip, they're generating more pollution per capita than most people on the planet will generate in a year."

He finished his vodka, and rattled the ice in the glass irritably. He handed the glass to Evans, who dutifully signaled for more.

"If there's anything worse than a limousine liberal," Morton said, "it's a Gulfstream environmentalist."

"But George," Evans said. "You're a Gulfstream environmentalist."

"I know it," Morton said. "And I wish it bothered me more. But you know what? It doesn't. I *like* flying around in my own airplane."

Evans said, "I heard you were in North Dakota and Chicago."

"I was. Yes."

"What'd you do there?"

"I spent money. A lot of money. A *lot*."

Evans said, "You bought some art?"

"No. I bought something far more expensive than art. I bought integrity."

"You've always had integrity," Evans said.

"Oh, not my integrity," Morton said. "I bought somebody else's."

Evans didn't know what to say to that. For a minute he thought Morton was joking.

"I was going to tell you about it," Morton continued. "I got a list of numbers, kid, and I want you to get it to Kenner. It is very much—for later. Hello, Ann!"

Ann Garner was coming toward them. "So, George, are you back for a while? Because we need you here now. The Vanutu lawsuit, which thank God you are backing, and the climate change conference that Nick has scheduled, and it's so important—my God, George. This is crunch time."

Evans started to stand to let Ann take his seat, but Morton pushed him back down again.

"Ann," he said, "I must say you look more lovely than ever, but Peter and I are having a small business discussion."

She glanced at the papers, and Evans's open briefcase. "Oh. I didn't know I was interrupting."

"No, no, if you'd just give us a minute."

"Of course. I'm sorry." But she lingered. "This

is so unlike you, George, doing business on the plane."

"I know," Morton said, "but, if you must know, I am feeling quite unlike myself these days."

That made her blink. She didn't know how to take it, so she smiled, nodded, and moved away. Morton said, "She looks wonderful. I wonder who did her work."

"Her work?"

"She's had more, in the last few months. I think eyes. Maybe chin. Anyway," he said, waving his hand, "about the list of numbers. You are to tell this to no one, Peter. *No one.* Not anyone in the law firm. And especially not anyone at—"

"George, damn it, why are you hiding back there?" Evans looked over his shoulder and saw Ted Bradley coming toward them. Ted was already drinking heavily, though it was only noon. "It hasn't been the same without you, George. My God, the world without Bradley is a boring world. Oops! I mean, without George Morton, is a boring world. Come on, George. Get up out of there. That man is a lawyer. Come and have a drink."

Morton allowed himself to be led away. He glanced over his shoulder at Evans. "Later," he said.

The Grand Ballroom of the Mark Hopkins Hotel was darkened for the after-dinner speeches. The audience was elegant, the men in tuxedos, the women in ball gowns. Beneath the ornate chandeliers, the voice of Nicholas Drake boomed from the podium.

"Ladies and gentlemen, it is no exaggeration to say that we face an environmental crisis of unprecedented proportions. Our forests are disappearing. Our lakes and rivers are polluted. The plants and animals that make up our biosphere are vanishing at unprecedented rates. Forty thousand species become extinct every year. That's fifty species every single day. At present rates, we will lose half of all species on our planet in the next few decades. It is the greatest extinction in the history of earth.

"And what is the texture of our own lives? Our food is contaminated with lethal pesticides. Our crops are failing from global warming. Our weather is growing worse, and more severe. Flooding, droughts, hurricanes, tornadoes. All around the globe. Our sea levels are rising—twenty-five feet in the next century, and possibly more. And most fearsome of all, new scientific evidence points to the specter of abrupt climate change, as a result of our destructive behavior. In short, ladies and gentlemen, we are confronted by a genuine global catastrophe for our planet."

Sitting at the center table, Peter Evans looked around at the audience. They were staring down at their plates, yawning, leaning over and talking to one another. Drake wasn't getting a lot of attention.

"They've heard it before," Morton growled. He shifted his heavy frame and gave a soft belch. He had been drinking steadily through the evening, and was now quite drunk.

". . . Loss of biodiversity, shrinking of habitat, destruction of the ozone layer . . ."

Nicholas Drake appeared tall and ungainly, his tuxedo ill-fitting. The collar of his shirt was bunched up around his scrawny neck. As always, he gave the impression of an impoverished but dedicated academic, a latter-day Ichabod Crane. Evans thought no one would ever guess that Drake was paid a third of a million dollars a year to head the Fund, plus another hundred thousand in expenses. Or that he had no science background at all. Nick Drake was a trial attorney, one of five who had started NERF many years before. And like all trial attorneys, he knew the importance of not dressing too well.

". . . the erosion of bio-reservoirs, the rise of ever more exotic and lethal diseases . . ."

"I wish he'd hurry up," Morton said. He drummed his fingers on the table. Evans said nothing. He had attended enough of these functions

to know that Morton was always tense if he had
to speak.

At the podium, Drake was saying ". . . glimmers
of hope, faint rays of positive energy, and none
more positive and hopeful than the man whose
lifelong dedication we are here to honor
tonight . . ."

"Can I get another drink?" Morton said, finishing the last of his martini. It was his sixth. He
set the glass on the table with a thud. Evans turned
to look for the waiter, raising his hand. He was
hoping the waiter wouldn't come over in time.
George had had enough.

". . . for three decades has dedicated his considerable resources and energy to making our
world a better, healthier, saner place. Ladies and
gentlemen, the National Environmental Resource
Fund is proud . . ."

"Ah screw, never mind," Morton said. He tensed
his body, ready to push back from the table. "I
hate making a fool of myself, even for a good
cause."

"Why should you make a fool of—" Evans
began.

". . . my good friend and colleague and this
year's concerned citizen . . . Mr. *George Morton!*"

The room filled with applause, and a spotlight
hit Morton as he stood and headed toward the
podium, a hunched bear of a man, physically
powerful, solemn, head down. Evans was alarmed
when Morton stumbled on the first step, and for
a moment he feared his boss would fall backward, but Morton regained his balance, and as
he stepped to the stage he seemed all right. He

shook hands with Drake and moved to the podium, gripping it on both sides with his large hands. Morton looked out at the room, turning his head from side to side, surveying the audience. He did not speak.

He just stood there, and said nothing.

Ann Garner, sitting beside Evans, gave him a nudge. "Is he all right?"

"Oh yes. Absolutely," Evans said, nodding. But in truth, he wasn't sure.

Finally George Morton began to speak. "I'd like to thank Nicholas Drake and the National Environmental Resource Fund for this award, but I don't feel I deserve it. Not with all the work that remains to be done. Do you know, my friends, that we know more about the moon than we do about the Earth's oceans? That's a real environmental problem. We don't know enough about the planet we depend on for our very lives. But as Montaigne said three hundred years ago, 'Nothing is so firmly believed as that which is least known.'"

Evans thought: Montaigne? George Morton quoting Montaigne?

In the glare of the spotlight, Morton was distinctly weaving back and forth. He was gripping the podium for balance. The room was absolutely silent. People were not moving at all. Even the waiters had stopped moving between the tables. Evans held his breath.

"All of us in the environmental movement," Morton said, "have seen many wonderful victories over the years. We have witnessed the creation of the EPA. We have seen the air and water made cleaner, sewage treatment improved, toxic dumps cleaned up, and we have regulated common poisons like lead for the safety of all. These are real victories, my friends. We take justifiable pride in them. And we know more needs to be done."

The audience was relaxing. Morton was moving onto familiar ground.

"But will the work get done? I am not sure. I know my mood has been dark, since the death of my beloved wife, Dorothy."

Evans sat bolt upright in his chair. At the next table, Herb Lowenstein looked shocked, his mouth open. George Morton had no wife. Or rather, he had six ex-wives—none named Dorothy.

"Dorothy urged me to spend my money wisely. I always thought I did. Now I am less sure. I said before that we don't know enough. But I fear that today, the watchword of NERF has become, We don't sue enough."

You could hear breath sucked in sharply all around the room.

"NERF is a law firm. I don't know if you realize that. It was started by lawyers and it is run by lawyers. But I now believe money is better spent on research than litigation. And that is why I am withdrawing my funding for NERF, and why I am—"

For the next few moments Morton could not be heard above the excited jabber of the crowd. Everyone was talking loudly. There were scattered boos; some guests got up to leave. Morton continued to talk, seemingly oblivious to the effect he was having. Evans caught a few phrases: ". . . one environmental charity is under FBI investigation . . . complete lack of oversight . . ."

Ann Garner leaned over and hissed, *"Get him off there."*

"What do you want me to do?" Evans whispered.

"Go and get him. He's obviously drunk."

"That may be, but I can't—"

"You have to stop this."

But on the stage, Drake was already moving forward, saying "All right, thank you, George—"

"Because to tell the truth right now—"

"Thank you, George," Drake said again, moving closer. He was actually pushing against Morton's bulk, trying to shove him away from the podium.

"Okay, okay," Morton said, clinging to the podium. "I said what I did for Dorothy. My dear dead wife—"

"Thank you, George." Drake was applauding now, holding his hands up at head height, nodding to the audience to join with him. "Thank you."

". . . who I miss desperately . . ."

"Ladies and gentlemen, please join me in thanking—"

"Yeah, okay, I'm leaving."

To muted applause, Morton shambled off the stage. Drake immediately stepped up to the podium and signaled the band. They started into a rousing rendition of Billy Joel's "You May Be Right," which someone had told them was Morton's favorite song. It was, but it seemed a poor choice under the circumstances.

Herb Lowenstein leaned over from the next

table and grabbed Evans by the shoulder, pulling him close. "Listen," he whispered fiercely. *"Get him out of here."*

"I will," Evans said. "Don't worry."

"Did you know this was going to happen?"

"No, I swear to God."

Lowenstein released Evans just as George Morton returned to the table. The assembled group was stunned. But Morton was singing cheerfully with the music, "You may be right, I may be crazy . . ."

"Come on, George," Evans said, standing up. "Let's get out of here."

Morton ignored him. ". . . But it just may be a loo-natic you're looking for . . ."

"George? What do you say?" Evans took him by the arm. "Let's go."

". . . Turn out the light, don't try to save me . . ."

"I'm not trying to save you," Evans said.

"Then how about another damn martini?" Morton said, no longer singing. His eyes were cold, a little resentful. "I think I fucking earned it."

"Harry will have one for you in the car," Evans said, steering Morton away from the table. "If you stay here, you'll have to wait for it. And you don't want to wait for a drink right now . . ." Evans continued talking, and Morton allowed himself to be led out of the room.

". . . too late to fight," he sang, "too late to change me . . ."

Before they could get out of the room, there was a TV camera with lights shining in their faces, and two reporters shoving small tape recorders in front of Morton. Everybody was yelling questions. Evans put his head down and said, "Excuse us, sorry, coming through, excuse us . . ."

Morton never stopped singing. They made their way through the hotel lobby. The reporters were running in front of them, trying to get some distance ahead, so they could film them walking forward. Evans gripped Morton firmly by the elbow as Morton sang:

"I was only having fun, wasn't hurting anyone, and we all enjoyed the weekend for a change . . ."

"This way," Evans said, heading for the door.

"I was stranded in the combat zone . . ."

And then at last they were through the swinging doors, and outside in the night. Morton stopped singing abruptly when the cold air hit him. They waited for his limousine to pull around. Sarah came out, and stood beside Morton. She didn't say anything, she just put her hand on his arm.

Then the reporters came out, and the lights came on again. And then Drake burst through the doors, saying "God damn it, George—"

He broke off when he saw the cameras. He glared at Morton, turned, and went back inside. The cameras remained on, but the three of them just stood there. It was awkward, just waiting. After what seemed like an eternity, the limousine pulled up. Harry came around, and opened the door for George.

"Okay, George," Evans said.

"No, not tonight."

"Harry's waiting, George."

"I said, *not tonight.*"

There was a deep-throated growl in the darkness, and a silver Ferrari convertible pulled up alongside the limousine.

"My car," Morton said. He started down the stairs, lurching a bit.

Sarah said, "George, I don't think—"

But he was singing again: "And you told me not to drive, but I made it home alive, so you said that only proves that I'm in-sayyy-nnne."

One of the reporters muttered, "He's insane, all right."

Evans followed Morton, very concerned. Morton gave the parking attendant a hundred dollar bill, saying "A twenty for you, my good man." He fumbled with the Ferrari door. "These crummy Italian imports." Then he got behind the wheel of the convertible, gunned the engine, and smiled. "Ah, a manly sound."

Evans leaned over the car. "George, let Harry drive you. Besides," he added, "don't we need to talk about something?"

"We do not."

"But I thought—"

"Kid, get out of my way." The camera lights were still on them. But Morton moved so that he was in the shadow cast by Evans's body. "You know, the Buddhists have a saying."

"What saying?"

"Remember it, kid. Goes like this: 'All that matters is not remote from where the Buddha sits.' "

"George, I really think you should not be driving."

"Will you remember what I just said to you?"

"Yes."

"Wisdom of the ages. Good-bye, kid."

And he accelerated, roaring out of the parking lot as Evans jumped back. The Ferrari squealed around the corner, ignoring a stop sign, and was gone.

"Peter, come on."

Evans turned, and saw Sarah standing by the limousine. Harry was getting in behind the wheel. Evans got in the back seat with Sarah, and they drove off after Morton.

The Ferrari turned left at the bottom of the hill, disappearing around the corner. Harry accelerated, handling the huge limousine with skill.

Evans said, "Do you know where he's going?"

"No idea," she said.

"Who wrote his speech?"

"He did."

"Really?"

"He was working in the house all day yesterday, and he wouldn't let me see what he was doing . . ."

"Jesus," Evans said. "Montaigne?"

"He had a book of quotations out."

"Where'd he come up with Dorothy?"

She shook her head. "I have no idea."

They passed Golden Gate Park. Traffic was light; the Ferrari was moving fast, weaving among the cars. Ahead was the Golden Gate Bridge, brightly lit in the night. Morton accelerated. The Ferrari was going almost ninety miles an hour.

"He's going to Marin," Sarah said.

Evans's cell phone rang. It was Drake. "Will you tell me what the hell that was all about?"

"I'm sorry, Nick. I don't know."

"Was he serious? About withdrawing his support?"

"I think he was."

"That's unbelievable. He's obviously suffered a nervous breakdown."

"I couldn't say."

"I was afraid of this," Drake said. "I was afraid something like this might happen. You remember, on the plane coming back from Iceland? I said it to you, and you told me I shouldn't worry. Is that your opinion now? That I shouldn't worry?"

"I don't know what you're asking, Nick."

"Ann Garner said he signed some papers on the plane."

"That's right. He did."

"Are they related to this sudden and inexplicable withdrawal of support for the organization that he loved and cherished?"

"He seems to have changed his mind about that," Evans said.

"And why didn't you tell me?"

"He instructed me not to."

"Fuck you, Evans."

"I'm sorry," Evans said.

"Not as sorry as you will be."

The phone went dead. Drake had hung up. Evans flipped the phone shut.

Sarah said, "Drake is mad?"

"Furious."

Off the bridge, Morton headed west, away from the lights of the freeway, onto a dark road skirting the cliffs. He was driving faster than ever.

Evans said to Harry, "Do you know where we are?"

"I believe we're in a state park."

Harry was trying to keep up, but on this narrow, twisting road, the limousine was no match for the Ferrari. It moved farther and farther ahead. Soon they could see only the taillights, disappearing around curves a quarter mile ahead.

"We're going to lose him," Evans said.

"I doubt it, sir."

But the limousine fell steadily behind. After Harry took one turn too fast—the big rear end lost traction and swung wide toward a cliff's edge—they were obliged to slow down even more. They were in a desolate area now. The night was dark and the cliffs deserted. A rising moon put a streak of silver on the black water far below.

Up ahead, they no longer saw any taillights. It seemed they were alone on the dark road.

They came around a curve, and saw the next curve a hundred yards ahead—obscured by billowing gray smoke.

"Oh no," Sarah said, putting her hand to her mouth.

The Ferrari had spun out, struck a tree, and flipped over. It now lay upside down, a crumpled and smoking mass. It had very nearly gone off the cliff itself. The nose of the car was hanging over the edge.

Evans and Sarah ran forward. Evans got down on his hands and knees and crawled along the cliff's edge, trying to see into the driver's compartment. It was hard to see much of anything—the front windshield was flattened, and the Ferrari lay almost flush to the pavement. Harry came over with a flashlight, and Evans used it to peer inside.

The compartment was empty. Morton's black bow tie was dangling from the doorknob, but otherwise he was gone.

"He must have been thrown."

Evans shone the light down the cliff. It was crumbling yellow rock, descending steeply for eighty feet to the ocean below. He saw no sign of Morton.

Sarah was crying softly. Harry had gone back to get a fire extinguisher from the limousine. Evans swung his light back and forth over the rock face. He did not see George's body. In fact, he did not see any sign of George at all. No disturbance, no path, no bits of clothing. Nothing.

Behind him he heard the whoosh of the fire extinguisher. He crawled away from the cliff's edge.

"Did you see him, sir?" Harry said, his face full of pain.

"No. I didn't see anything."

"Perhaps . . . over there." Harry pointed toward the tree. And he was right; if Morton had been thrown from the car by the initial impact, he might be twenty yards back, on the road.

Evans walked back, and shone his flashlight down the cliff again. The battery was running down, the beam was weakening. But almost immediately, he saw a glint of light off a man's patent leather slipper, wedged among the rocks at the edge of the water.

He sat down in the road and put his head in his hands. And cried.

By the time the police were finished talking with them, and a rescue team had rappelled down the cliff to recover the shoe, it was three o'clock in the morning. They found no other sign of the body, and the cops, talking among themselves, agreed that the prevailing currents would probably carry the body up the coast to Pismo Beach. "We'll find him," one said, "in about a week or so. Or at least, what's left by the great whites."

Now the wreck was being cleared away, and loaded onto a flatbed truck. Evans wanted to leave, but the highway patrolman who had taken Evans's statement kept coming back to ask for more details. He was a kid, in his early twenties. It seemed he had not filled out many of these forms before.

The first time he came back to Evans, he said, "How soon after the accident would you say you arrived on the scene?"

Evans said, "I'm not sure. The Ferrari was about half a mile ahead of us, maybe more. We were probably going forty miles an hour, so . . . maybe a minute later?"

The kid looked alarmed. "You were going forty in that limo? On this road?"

"Well. Don't hold me to it."

Then he came back and said, "You said you were the first on the scene. You told me you crawled around at the edge of the road?"

"That's right."

"So you would have stepped on broken glass, on the road?"

"Yes. The windshield was shattered. I had it on my hands, too, when I crouched down."

"So that explains why the glass was disturbed."

"Yes."

"Lucky you didn't cut your hands."

"Yes."

The third time he came back, he said, "In your estimation, what time did the accident occur?"

"What time?" Evans looked at his watch. "I have no idea. But let me see . . ." He tried to work backward. The speech must have started about eight-thirty. Morton would have left the hotel at nine. Through San Francisco, then over the bridge . . . "Maybe nine-forty-five, or ten at night."

"So, five hours ago? Roughly?"

"Yes."

The kid said, "Huh." As if he were surprised.

Evans looked over at the flatbed truck, which now held the crumpled remains of the Ferrari. One cop was standing on the flatbed, beside the car. Three other cops were on the street, talking with some animation. There was another man there, wearing a tuxedo. He was talking to the cops. When the man turned, Evans was surprised to see that it was John Kenner.

"What's going on?" Evans asked the kid.

"I don't know. They just asked me to check on the time of the accident."

Then the driver got into the flatbed truck, and started the engine. One of the cops yelled to the kid, "Forget it, Eddie!"

"Never mind, then," the kid said to Evans. "I guess everything's okay."

Evans looked over at Sarah, to see if she had noticed Kenner. She was leaning on the limousine, talking on the phone. Evans looked back in time to see Kenner get into a dark sedan driven by the Nepali guy, and drive off.

The cops were leaving. The flatbed turned around and headed up the road, toward the bridge.

Harry said, "Looks like it's time to go."

Evans got into the limousine. They drove back toward the lights of San Francisco.

Morton's jet flew back to Los Angeles at noon. The mood was somber. All the same people were on board, and a few more, but they sat quietly, saying little. The late-edition papers had printed the story that millionaire philanthropist George Morton, depressed by the death of his beloved wife, Dorothy, had given a disjointed speech (termed "rambling and illogical" by the *San Francisco Chronicle*) and a few hours later had died in a tragic automobile crash while test-driving his new Ferrari.

In the third paragraph, the reporter mentioned that single-car fatalities were frequently caused by undiagnosed depression and were often disguised suicides. And this, according to a quoted psychiatrist, was the likely explanation for Morton's death.

About ten minutes into the flight, the actor Ted Bradley said, "I think we should drink a toast in memory of George, and observe a minute of silence." And to a chorus of "Hear, hear," glasses of champagne were passed all around.

"To George Morton," Ted said. "A great American, a great friend, and a great supporter of the environment. We, and the planet, will miss him."

For the next ten minutes, the celebrities on board remained relatively subdued, but slowly the conversation picked up, and finally they began to talk and argue as usual. Evans was sitting in the back, in the same seat he had occupied when they flew up. He watched the action at the table in the center, where Bradley was now explaining that the US got only 2 percent of its energy from sustainable sources and that we needed a crash program to build thousands of offshore wind farms, like England and Denmark were doing. The talk moved on to fuel cells, hydrogen cars, and photovoltaic households running off the grid. Some talked about how much they loved their hybrid cars, which they had bought for their staff to drive.

Evans felt his spirits improve as he listened to them. Despite the loss of George Morton, there were still lots of people like these—famous, high-profile people committed to change—who would lead the next generation to a more enlightened future.

He was starting to drift off to sleep when Nicholas Drake dropped into the seat beside his. Drake leaned across the aisle. "Listen," he said. "I owe you an apology for last night."

"That's all right," Evans said.

"I was way out of line. And I want you to know I'm sorry for how I behaved. I was upset, and very worried. You know George has been acting weird as hell the last couple of weeks. Talking strangely, picking fights. I guess in retrospect he was beginning to have a nervous breakdown. But I didn't know. Did you?"

"I am not sure it was a nervous breakdown."

"It must have been," Drake said. "What else could it have been? My God, the man disowns his life's work, and then goes out and kills himself. By the way, you can forget about any documents that he signed yesterday. Under the circumstances, he obviously was not in his right mind. And I know," he added, "that you wouldn't argue the point differently. You're already conflicted enough, doing work both for him and for us. You really should have recused yourself and seen to it that any papers were drawn up by a neutral attorney. I'm not going to accuse you of malpractice, but you've shown highly questionable judgment."

Evans said nothing. The threat was plain enough.

"Well, anyway," Drake said, resting his hand on Evans's knee, "I just wanted to apologize. I know you did your best with a difficult situation, Peter. And . . . I think we're going to come out of this all right."

The plane landed in Van Nuys. A dozen black SUV limos, the latest fashion, were lined up on the runway, waiting for the passengers. All the celebrities hugged, kissed air, and departed.

Evans was the last to leave. He didn't rate a car and driver. He climbed into his little Prius hybrid, which he'd parked there the day before, and drove through the gates and onto the freeway. He thought he should go to the office, but unexpected tears came to his eyes as he negotiated the midday traffic. He wiped them away and decided he was too damned tired to go to the office. Instead, he would go back to his apartment to get some sleep.

He was almost home when his cell phone rang. It was Jennifer Haynes, at the Vanutu litigation team. "I'm sorry about George," she said. "It's just terrible. Everybody here is very upset, as you can imagine. He pulled the funding, didn't he?"

"Yes, but Nick will fight it. You'll get your funding."

"We need to have lunch," she said.

"Well, I think—"

"Today?"

Something in her voice made him say, "I'll try."

"Phone me when you're here."

He hung up. The phone rang again almost immediately. It was Margo Lane, Morton's mistress. She was angry. "What the fuck is going on?"

"How do you mean?" Evans said.

"Was anybody going to fucking call me?"

"I'm sorry, Margo—"

"I just saw it on TV. Missing in San Francisco and presumed dead. They had pictures of the car."

"I was going to call you," Evans said, "when I got to my office." The truth was, she had completely slipped his mind.

"And when would that have been, next week? You're as bad as that sick assistant of yours. You're his lawyer, Peter. Do your fucking job. Because, you know, let's face it, this is not a surprise. I knew this was going to happen. We all did. I want you to come over here."

"I have a busy day."

"Just for a minute."

"All right," he said. "Just for a minute."

Margo Lane lived on the fifteenth floor of a high-rise apartment building in the Wilshire Corridor. The doorman had to call up before Evans was allowed in the elevator. Margo knew he was coming up, but she still answered the door wrapped in a towel. "Oh! I didn't realize you'd be here so soon. Come in, I just got out of the shower." She frequently did something like this, flaunting her body. Evans came into the apartment and sat on the couch. She sat opposite him. The towel barely covered her torso.

"So," she said, "what's all this about George?"

"I'm sorry," Evans said, "but George crashed his Ferrari at very high speed and was thrown from the car. He fell down a cliff—they found a shoe at the bottom—and into the water. His body hasn't been recovered but they expect it to turn up in a week or so."

With her love of drama, he was sure Margo would start to cry, but she didn't. She just stared at him. "That's bullshit," she said.

"Why do you say that, Margo?"

"Because. He's hiding or something. You know it."

"Hiding? From what?"

"Probably nothing. He'd become completely paranoid. You know that."

As she said it, she crossed her legs. Evans was careful to keep his eyes on her face.

"Paranoid?" he asked.

"Don't act like you didn't know, Peter. It was obvious."

Evans shook his head. "Not to me."

"The last time he came here was a couple of days ago," she said. "He went right to the window and stood back behind the curtain, looking down onto the street. He was convinced he was being followed."

"Had he done that before?"

"I don't know. I hadn't seen him much lately; he was traveling. But whenever I called him and asked when he was coming over, he said it wasn't safe to come here."

Evans got up and walked to the window. He stood to one side and looked down at the street below.

"Are you being followed, too?" she said.

"I don't think so."

Traffic on Wilshire Boulevard was heavy, the start of afternoon rush hour. Three lanes of cars moving fast in each direction. He could hear the roar of the traffic, even up there. But there was no place to park, to pull out from the traffic. A blue Prius hybrid had pulled to the curb across the street, and traffic was backing up behind it, honking. After a moment, the Prius started up again.

No place to stop.

"Do you see anything suspicious?" she asked.

"No."

"I never did either. But George did—or thought he did."

"Did he say who was following him?"

"No." She shifted again. "I thought he should have medication. I told him."

"And what did he say to that?"

"He said I was in danger, too. He told me I should leave town for a while. Go visit my sister in Oregon. But I won't."

Her towel was coming loose. Margo tightened it, lowering it across her firm, enhanced breasts. "So I'm telling you, George went into hiding," she said. "And I think you better find him fast, because the man needs help."

"I see," Evans said. "But I suppose it's possible he isn't in hiding, that he really crashed his car. . . . In which case, there are things you need to do now, Margo."

He explained to her that if George remained missing, his assets could be ordered frozen. Which meant that she ought to withdraw everything from the bank account into which he put money for her every month. So she would be sure to have money to live on.

"But that's silly," she protested. "I know he'll be back in a few days."

"Just in case," Evans said.

She frowned. "Do you know something you're not telling me?"

"No," Evans said. "I'm just saying, it could be a while before this thing gets cleared up."

"Look," she said. "He's sick. You're supposed to be his friend. Find him."

Evans said that he would try. When he left, Margo was flouncing off to the bedroom to get dressed before going to the bank.

Outside, in the milky afternoon sunlight, fatigue overwhelmed him. All he wanted to do was go home and go to sleep. He got in his car and started driving. He was within sight of his apartment when his phone rang again.

It was Jennifer, asking where he was.

"I'm sorry," he said. "I can't come today."

"It's important, Peter. Really."

He said he was sorry, and would call her later.

Then Lisa, Herb Lowenstein's secretary, called to say that Nicholas Drake had been trying to reach him all afternoon. "He really wants to talk to you."

"Okay," Evans said, "I'll call."

"He sounds pissed."

"Okay."

"But you better call Sarah first."

"Why?"

His phone went dead. It always did in the back alley of his apartment; it was a dead spot in the cellular net. He slipped the phone into his shirt pocket; he'd call in a few minutes. He drove down the alley, and pulled into his garage space.

He walked up the back stairs to his apartment and unlocked the door.

And stared.

* * *

The apartment was a mess. Furniture torn apart, cushions slashed open, papers all over the place, books tumbled out of the bookshelves and lying scattered on the floor.

He stood in the entrance, stunned. After a moment he walked into the room, straightened one of the toppled chairs and sat down in it. It occurred to him that he had to call the police. He got up, found the phone on the floor, and dialed them. But almost immediately the cell phone in his pocket began to ring. He hung up on the police and answered the cell phone. "Yes."

It was Lisa. "We got cut off," she said. "You better call Sarah right away."

"Why?"

"She's over at Morton's house. There was a robbery there."

"*What?*"

"I know. You better call her," she said. "She sounded upset."

Evans flipped the phone shut. He stood and walked into the kitchen. Everything was a mess there, too. He glanced into the bedroom. Everything was a mess. All he could think was the maid wasn't coming until next Tuesday. How could he ever clean this up?

He dialed his phone.

"Sarah?"

"Is that you, Peter?"

"Yes. What happened?"

"Not on the phone. Have you gone home yet?"

"Just got here."

"So . . . did it happen to you too?"

"Yes. Me too."

"Can you come here?"

"Yes."

"How soon?" She sounded frightened.

"Ten minutes."

"Okay. See you." She hung up.

Evans turned the ignition of his Prius and it hummed to life. He was pleased to have the hybrid; the waiting list in Los Angeles to get one was now more than six months. He'd had to take a light gray one, which wasn't his preferred color, but he loved the car. And he took a quiet satisfaction in noticing how many of them there were on the streets these days.

He drove down the alley to Olympic. Across the street he saw a blue Prius, just like the one he had seen below Margo's apartment. It was electric blue, a garish color. He thought he liked his gray better. He turned right, and then left again, heading north through Beverly Hills. He knew there would be rush hour traffic starting at this time of day and he should get up to Sunset, where traffic moved a little better.

When he got to the traffic light at Wilshire, he saw another blue Prius behind him. That same ugly color. Two guys in the car, not young. When he made his way to the light at Sunset, the same car was still behind him. Two cars back.

He turned left, toward Holmby Hills.

The Prius turned left, too. Following him.

Evans pulled up to Morton's gate and pressed the buzzer. The security camera above the box blinked on. "Can I help you?"

"It's Peter Evans for Sarah Jones."

A momentary pause, and then a buzz. The gates swung open slowly, revealing a curving roadway. The house was still hidden from view.

While he waited, Evans glanced down the road to his left. A block away, he saw the blue Prius coming up the road toward him. It passed him without slowing down, and disappeared around a curve.

So. Perhaps he was not being followed after all.

He took a deep breath, and let it out slowly.

The gates swung wide, and he drove inside.

It was almost four o'clock as Evans drove up the driveway to Morton's house. The property was crawling with security men. There were several searching among the trees near the front gate, and more in the driveway, clustered around several vans marked ANDERSON SECURITY SERVICE.

Evans parked next to Sarah's Porsche. He went to the front door. A security man opened it. "Ms. Jones is in the living room."

He walked through the large entryway and past the staircase that curved up to the second floor. He looked into the living room, prepared to see the same disarray that he'd witnessed at his own apartment, but here everything seemed to be in its place. The room appeared exactly as Evans remembered it.

Morton's living room was arranged to display his extensive collection of Asian antiquities. Above the fireplace was a large Chinese screen with shimmering gilded clouds; a large stone head from the Angkor region of Cambodia, with thick lips and a half-smile, was mounted on a pedestal near the couch; against one wall stood a seventeenth-century Japanese *tansu*, its rich wood glowing. Extremely rare, two hundred-year-old woodcuts by Hiroshige hung on the back wall. A standing Burmese Buddha, carved in faded wood, stood at the entrance to the media room, next door.

In the middle of the room, surrounded by these antiquities, Sarah sat slumped on the couch, staring blankly out the window. She looked over as Evans came in. "They got your apartment?"

"Yes. It's a mess."

"This house was broken into, too. It must have happened last night. All the security people here are trying to figure out how it could have happened. Look here."

She got up and pushed the pedestal that held the Cambodian head. Considering the weight of the head, the pedestal moved surprisingly easily, revealing a safe sunk in the floor. The safe door stood open. Evans saw neatly stacked manila folders inside.

"What was taken?" he said.

"As far as I can tell, nothing," she said. "Seems like everything is still in its place. But I don't know exactly what George had in these safes. They were his safes. I rarely went into them."

She moved to the *tansu*, sliding open a center panel, and then a false back panel, to expose a safe in the wall behind. It, too, was open. "There are six safes in the house," she said. "Three down here, one in the second-floor study, one in the basement, and one up in his bedroom closet. They opened every one."

"Cracked?"

"No. Someone knew the combinations."

Evans said, "Did you report this to the police?"

"No."

"Why not?"

"I wanted to talk to you first."

Her head was close to his. Evans could smell a faint perfume. He said, "Why?"

"Because," she said. "Someone knew the combinations, Peter."

"You mean it was an inside job."

"It had to be."

"Who stays in the house at night?"

"Two housekeepers sleep in the far wing. But last night was their night off, so they weren't here."

"So nobody was in the house?"

"That's right."

"What about the alarm?"

"I armed it myself, before I went to San Francisco yesterday."

"The alarm didn't go off?"

She shook her head.

"So somebody knew the code," Evans said. "Or knew how to bypass it. What about the security cameras?"

"They're all over the property," she said, "inside the house and out. They record onto a hard drive in the basement."

"You've played it back?"

She nodded. "Nothing but static. It was scrubbed. The security people are trying to recover something, but . . ." She shrugged. "I don't think they'll get anywhere."

It would take pretty sophisticated burglars to

know how to wipe a hard drive. "Who has the alarm codes and safe combinations?"

"As far as I know, just George and me. But obviously somebody else does, too."

"I think you should call the police," he said.

"They're looking for something," she said. "Something that George had. Something they think one of us has now. They think George gave it to one of us."

Evans frowned. "But if that's true," he said, "why are they being so obvious? They smashed my place so I couldn't help notice. And even here, they left the safes wide open, to be sure you'd know you'd been robbed . . ."

"Exactly," she said. "They want us to know what they're doing." She bit her lip. "They want us to panic, and rush off to retrieve this thing, whatever it is. Then they'll follow us, and take it."

Evans thought it over. "Do you have any idea what it could be?"

"No," she said. "Do you?"

Evans was thinking of the list George had mentioned to him, on the airplane. The list he never got around to explaining, before he died. But certainly the implication was that Morton had paid a lot of money for some sort of list. But something made Evans hesitate to mention it now.

"No," he said.

"Did George give you anything?"

"No," he said.

"Me neither." She bit her lip again. "I think we should leave."

"Leave?"

"Get out of town for a while."

"It's natural to feel that way after a robbery," he said. "But I think the proper thing to do right now is to call the police."

"George wouldn't like it."

"George is no longer with us, Sarah."

"George hated the Beverly Hills police."

"Sarah . . ."

"He never called them. He always used private security."

"That may be, but . . ."

"They won't do anything but file a report."

"Perhaps, but . . ."

"Did you call the police, about your place?"

"Not yet. But I will."

"Okay, well you call them. See how it goes. It's a waste of time."

His phone beeped. There was a text message. He looked at the screen. It said: N. DRAKE COME TO OFFICE IMMED. URGENT.

"Listen," he said. "I have to go see Nick for a bit."

"I'll be fine."

"I'll come back," he said, "as soon as I can."

"I'll be fine," she repeated.

He stood, and she stood, too. On a sudden impulse he gave her a hug. She was so tall they were almost shoulder to shoulder. "It's going to be okay," he said. "Don't worry. It'll be okay."

She returned the hug, but when he released her, she said, "Don't ever do that again, Peter. I'm not hysterical. I'll see you when you get back."

He left hastily, feeling foolish. At the door, she said, "By the way, Peter: Do you have a gun?"

"No," he said. "Do you?"

"Just a 9-millimeter Beretta, but it's better than nothing."

"Oh, okay." As he went out the front door, he thought, so much for manly reassurances for the modern woman.

He got in the car, and drove to Drake's office.

It was not until he had parked his car and was walking in the front door to the office that he noticed the blue Prius parked at the end of the block, with two men sitting inside it.

Watching him.

"No, no, *no!*" Nicholas Drake stood in the NERF media room, surrounded by a half-dozen stunned-looking graphic designers. On the walls and tables were posters, banners, flyers, coffee mugs, and stacks of press releases, and media kits. All were emblazoned with a banner that went from green to red, with the superimposed words: "Abrupt Climate Change: The Dangers Ahead."

"I hate it," Drake said. "I just fucking *hate* it."

"Why?"

"Because it's *boring.* It sounds like a damn PBS special. We need some punch here, some pizzazz."

"Well, sir," one of the designers said, "if you remember, you originally wanted to avoid anything that looked like overstatement."

"I did? No, I didn't. Henley wanted to avoid overstatement. Henley thought it should be made to look exactly like a normal academic conference. But if we do that, the media will tune us out. I mean, shit, do you know how many climate change conferences there are every year? All around the world?"

"No sir, how many?"

"Well, um, forty-seven. Anyway, that's not the point." Drake rapped the banner with his knuckles. "I mean look at this, 'Dangers.' It's so vague; it could refer to anything."

"I thought that's what you wanted—that it could refer to anything."

"No, I want 'Crisis' or 'Catastrophe.' 'The Crisis Ahead.' 'The Catastrophe Ahead.' That's better. 'Catastrophe' is much better."

"You used 'Catastrophe' for the last conference, the one on species extinction."

"I don't care. We use it because it works. This conference must point to a catastrophe."

"Uh, sir,". one said, "with all due respect, is it really accurate that abrupt climate change will lead to catastrophe? Because the background materials we were given—"

"Yes, God damn it," Drake snapped, "it'll lead to a catastrophe. Believe me, it will! Now make the damn changes!"

The graphic artists surveyed the assembled materials on the table. "Mr. Drake, the conference starts in four days."

"You think I don't know it?" Drake said. "You think I fucking don't know it?"

"I'm not sure how much we can accomplish—"

"Catastrophe! Lose 'Danger,' add 'Catastrophe'! That's all I'm asking for. How difficult can it be?"

"Mr. Drake, we can redo the visual materials and the banners for the media kits, but the coffee mugs are a problem."

"Why are they a problem?"

"They're made for us in China, and—"

"*Made in China?* Land of pollution? Whose idea was that?"

"We always have the coffee mugs made in China for—"

"Well, we definitely can't use them. This is NERF, for Christ's sake. How many cups do we have?"

"Three hundred. They're given to the media in attendance, along with the press kit."

"Well get some damn eco-acceptable mugs," Drake said. "Doesn't Canada make mugs? Nobody ever complains about anything Canada does. Get some Canadian mugs and print 'Catastrophe' on them. That's all."

The artists were looking at one another. One said, "There's that supply house in Vancouver . . ."

"But their mugs are cream-colored . . ."

"I don't care if they're chartreuse," Drake said, his voice rising. "Just do it! Now what about the press releases?"

Another designer held up a sheet. "They're four-color banners printed in biodegradable inks on recycled bond paper."

Drake picked up a sheet. "This is recycled? It looks damn good."

"Actually, it's fresh paper." The designer looked nervous. "But no one will know."

"You didn't tell me that," Drake said. "It's essential that recycled materials look good."

"And they do, sir. Don't worry."

"Then let's move on." He turned to the PR people. "What's the timeline of the campaign?"

"It's a standard starburst launch to bring public awareness to abrupt climate change," the first rep said, standing up. "We have our initial press break on Sunday-morning talk shows and in the Sunday newspaper supplements. They'll be talking about the start of the conference Wednesday and interviewing major photogenic principals. Stanford, Levine, the other people who show well on TV. We've given enough lead time to get into all the major weekly newsbooks around the world, *Time, Newsweek, Der Spiegel, Paris Match, Oggi, The Economist.* All together, fifty news magazines to inform lead opinion makers. We've asked for cover stories, accepting banner folds with a graphic. Anything less and they didn't get us. We expect covers on at least twenty."

"Okay," Drake said, nodding.

"We start the conference on Wednesday. Well-known, charismatic environmentalists and major politicians from industrialized nations are scheduled to appear. We have delegates from around the world, so B-roll reaction shots of the audience will be satisfactorily color-mixed. Industrialized countries now include India and Korea and Japan, of course. The Chinese delegation will participate but there will be no speakers.

"Our two hundred invited television journalists will stay at the Hilton, and we will have interview facilities there as well as in the conference halls, so our speakers can spread the message to video audiences around the world. We will also have a number of print media people to carry the word to elite opinion makers, the ones that read but do not watch TV."

"Good," Drake said. He appeared pleased.

"Each day's theme will be identified by a distinctive graphic icon, emphasizing flood, fire, rising sea levels, drought, icebergs, typhoons, and hurricanes, and so on. Each day we have a fresh contingent of politicians from around the world coming to attend and give interviews explaining the high level of their dedication and concern about this newly emerging problem."

"Good, good." Drake nodded.

"The politicians will stay for only a day—some only a few hours—and they will not have time to attend the conferences beyond a brief photo-op showing them in the audience, but they are briefed and will be effective. Then we have local schoolchildren, grades four to seven, coming each day to learn about the dangers—sorry, the catastrophe—in their futures, and we have educational kits for grade-school teachers, so they can teach their kids about the crisis of abrupt climate change."

"When do those kits go out?"

"They were going out today, but now we'll hold them for re-bannering."

"Okay," Drake said. "And for high schools?"

"We have some trouble there," the PR guy said. "We showed the kits to a sample of high school science teachers and, uh . . ."

"And what?" Drake said.

"The feedback we got was they might not go over so well."

Drake's expression turned dark. "And why not?"

"Well, the high school curriculum is very

college oriented, and there isn't a lot of room for electives . . ."

"This is hardly an *elective* . . ."

"And, uh, they felt it was all speculative and unsubstantiated. They kept saying things like, 'Where's the hard science here?' Just reporting, sir."

"God damn it," Drake said, "it is *not* speculative. It is *happening!*"

"Uh, perhaps we didn't get the right materials that show what you are saying . . ."

"Ah fuck. Never mind now," Drake said. "Just trust me, it's happening. Count on it." He turned, and said in a surprised voice, "Evans, how long have you been here?"

Peter Evans had been standing in the doorway for at least two minutes and had overheard a good deal of the conversation. "Just got here, Mr. Drake."

"All right." Drake turned to the others. "I think we've gone through this. Evans, you come with me."

Drake shut the door to his office. "I need your counsel, Peter," he said quietly. He walked around to his desk, picked up some papers, and slid them toward Evans. "What the fuck is this?"

Evans looked. "That is George's withdrawal of support."

"Did you draw it up?"

"I did."

"Whose idea was paragraph 3a?"

"Paragraph 3a?"

"Yes. Did you add that little bit of wisdom?"

"I don't really remember—"

"Then let me refresh your memory," Drake said. He picked up the document and started to read. " 'In the event of any claim that I am not of sound mind, there may be an attempt to obtain injunctive relief from the terms of this document. Therefore this document authorizes the payment of fifty thousand dollars per week to NERF while awaiting the judgment of a full trial. Said monies shall be deemed sufficient to pay ongoing costs incurred by NERF and shall by said payment deny injunctive relief.' Did you write this, Evans?"

"I did."

"Whose idea was it?"

"George's."

"George is not a lawyer. He had help."

"Not from me," Evans said. "He more or less dictated that clause. I wouldn't have thought of it."

Drake snorted in disgust. "Fifty thousand a week," he said. "At that rate, it will take us four years to receive the ten-million-dollar grant."

"That's what George wanted the document to say," Evans said.

"But whose idea was it?" Drake said. "If it wasn't you, who was it?"

"I don't know."

"Find out."

"I don't know if I can," Evans said. "I mean, George is dead now, and I don't know who he might have consulted—"

Drake glared at Evans. "Are you with us here, Peter, or not?" He started pacing back and forth. "Because this Vanutu litigation is undoubtedly the most significant lawsuit we have ever filed." He lapsed into his speech-making mode. "The stakes are enormous, Peter. Global warming is the greatest crisis facing mankind. You know that. I know that. Most of the civilized world knows that. We *must* act to save the planet, before it is too late."

"Yes," Evans said. "I know that."

"Do you?" Drake said. "We have a lawsuit, a very important lawsuit, that needs our help. And fifty thousand dollars a week will strangle it."

Evans was sure that was not true. "Fifty thousand is a lot of money," he said, "I don't see why it should strangle—"

"Because it will!" Drake snapped. *"Because I am telling you it will!"* He seemed surprised by his own outburst. He gripped the desk, got control of himself. "Look," he said. "We can never forget about our opponents here. The forces of industry are strong, phenomenally strong. And industry wants to be left alone to pollute. It wants to pollute here, and in Mexico, and in China, and wherever else it does its business. The stakes are huge."

"I understand," Evans said.

"Many powerful forces are taking an interest in this case, Peter."

"Yes, I'm sure."

"Forces that will stop at nothing to be sure that we lose it."

Evans frowned. What was Drake telling him?

"Their influence is everywhere, Peter. They may have influence with members of your law firm. Or other people you know. People whom you believe you can trust—but you can't. Because they are on the other side, and they don't even know it."

Evans said nothing. He was just looking at Drake.

"Be prudent, Peter. Watch your back. Don't discuss what you are doing with anyone—with *anyone*—except me. Try not to use your cell phone. Avoid e-mail. And keep an eye out in case you are followed."

"Okay. . . . But actually I've already been followed," Evans said. "There's a blue Prius—"

"Those were our guys. I don't know what they are doing. I called them off days ago."

"Your guys?"

"Yes. It's a new security firm we've been trying out. They're obviously not very competent."

"I'm confused," Evans said. "NERF has a security firm?"

"Absolutely. For years, now. Because of the danger we face. Please understand me: *We are all in danger,* Peter. Don't you understand what this lawsuit means if we win? Trillions of dollars that industry must pay in the coming years, to halt their emissions that are causing global warming. *Trillions.* With those stakes, a few lives don't matter. So: Be very damn careful."

Evans said that he would. Drake shook his hand.

"I want to know who told George about the paragraph," Drake said. "And I want that money freed up for us to use it as we see fit. This is all riding on you now," he said. "Good luck, Peter."

On his way out of the building, Evans ran into a young man who was sprinting up the stairs. They collided so hard that Evans was almost knocked down. The young man apologized hastily, and continued on his way. He looked like one of the kids working on the conference. Evans wondered what the crisis could be, now.

When he got back outside, he looked down the street. The blue Prius was gone.

He got into the car and drove back to Morton's, to see Sarah.

Traffic was heavy. He crept slowly along Sunset; he had plenty of time to think. The conversation with Drake left him feeling odd. There had been a funny quality to the actual meeting. As if it didn't really need to happen, as if Drake just wanted to make sure he was able to call Evans in, and Evans would come. As if he were asserting his authority. Or something like that.

Anyway, Evans felt, something was off.

And Evans also felt a little strange about the security firm. That just didn't seem right. After all, NERF was one of the good guys. They shouldn't be sneaking around and following people. And Drake's paranoid warnings were somehow not persuasive. Drake was overreacting, as he so often did.

Drake was dramatic by nature. He couldn't help it. Everything was a crisis, everything was desperate, everything was vitally important. He lived in a world of extreme urgency, but it wasn't necessarily the real world.

Evans called his office, but Heather had gone for the day. He called Lowenstein's office and spoke to Lisa. "Listen," he said, "I need your help."

Her voice was lower, conspiratorial. "Of course, Peter."

"My apartment was robbed."

"No—you, too?"

"Yes, me, too. And I really need to talk to the police—"

"Well, yes, you certainly do—my goodness— did they take anything?"

"I don't think so," he said, "but just to file a report, all that—I'm kind of busy right now, dealing with Sarah . . . it may go later into the night . . ."

"Well, of course, do you need me to deal with the police about your robbery?"

"Could you?" he said. "It would help so much."

"Why of course, Peter," she said. "Leave it to me." She paused. When she spoke again, it was almost a whisper. "Is there, ah, anything you don't want the police to find?"

"No," he said.

"I mean, it's all right with me, everybody in LA has a few bad habits, otherwise we wouldn't be here—"

"No, Lisa," he said. "Actually, I don't have any drugs, if that's what you mean."

"Oh, no," she said quickly. "I wasn't assuming anything. No pictures or anything like that?"

"No, Lisa."

"Nothing, you know, underage?"

"Afraid not."

"Okay, I just wanted to be sure."

"Well, thanks for doing this. Now to get in through the door—"

"I know," she said, "the key is under the back mat."

"Yes." He paused. "How'd you know that?"

"Peter," she said, sounding a little offended. "You can count on me to know things."

"All right. Well, thanks."

"Don't mention it. Now, what about Margo? How's she doing?" Lisa said.

"She's fine."

"You went to see her?"

"This morning, yes, and—"

"No, I mean at the hospital. Didn't you hear? Margo was coming back from the bank today and walked in while her apartment was being robbed. Three robberies in one day! You, Margo, Sarah! What is going on? Do you know?"

"No," Evans said. "It's very mysterious."

"It *is*."

"But about Margo . . . ?"

"Oh yes. So I guess she decided to fight these guys, which was the wrong thing to do, and they beat her up, maybe knocked her unconscious. She had a black eye, I heard, and while the cops were there interviewing her, she passed out. Got completely paralyzed and couldn't move. And she even stopped breathing."

"You're kidding."

"No. I had a long conversation with the detective who was there. He told me it just came over her, and she was unable to move and was dark blue before the paramedics showed up and took her to UCLA. She's been in intensive care all afternoon. The doctors are waiting to ask her about the blue ring."

"What blue ring?"

"Just before she became paralyzed, she was

slurring her words but she said something about the blue ring, or the blue ring of death."

"The blue ring of death," Evans said. "What does that mean?"

"They don't know. She isn't able to talk yet. Does she take drugs?"

"No, she's a health nut," Evans said.

"Well, I hear the doctors say she'll be okay. It was some temporary paralysis."

"I'll go see her later," he said.

"When you do, will you call me afterward? And I'll handle your apartment, don't worry."

It was dark when he got to Morton's house. The security people were gone; the only car parked in front was Sarah's Porsche. She opened the front door when he rang. She had changed into a tracksuit. "Everything all right?" he said.

"Yes," she said. They came into the hallway, and they crossed to the living room. The lights were on, and the room was warm and inviting.

"Where are the security people?"

"They left for dinner. They'll be back."

"They *all* left?"

"They'll be back. I want to show you something," she said. She pulled out a wand with an electronic meter attached to it. She ran it over his body, like an airport security check. She tapped his left pocket. "Empty it."

The only thing in his pocket were his car keys. He dropped them on the coffee table. Sarah was running the wand over his chest, his jacket. She touched his right jacket pocket, gestured for him to empty it out.

"What's this about?" he said.

She shook her head, and didn't speak.

He pulled out a penny. Set it on the counter.

She waved her hand: more?

He felt again. Nothing.

She ran the wand over his car keys. There was a plastic rectangle on the chain, which unlocked his car door. She pried it open with a pocketknife.

"Hey, listen . . ."

The rectangle popped open. Evans saw electronic circuits inside, a watch battery. Sarah pulled out a tiny bit of electronics hardly bigger than the tip of a lead pencil. "Bingo."

"Is that what I think it is?"

She took the electronic unit and dropped it into a glass of water. Then she turned to the penny. She examined it minutely, then twisted it in her fingers. To Evans's surprise, it broke in half, revealing a small electronic center.

She dropped that in the glass of water, too. "Where's your car?" she said.

"Out in front."

"We can check it later."

He said, "What's this about?"

"The security guys found bugs on me," she said. "And all over the house. The best guess is that was the reason for the robbery—to plant bugs. And guess what? You have bugs, too."

He looked around. "Is the house okay?"

"The house has been electronically swept and cleared. The guys found about a dozen bugs. Supposedly it's clean now."

They sat together on the couch. "Whoever is doing all this, they think we know something," she said. "And I'm beginning to believe they're right."

Evans told her about Morton's comments about the list.

"He bought a list?" she said.

Evans nodded. "That's what he said."

"Did he say what kind of a list?"

"No. He was going to tell me more, but he never got around to it."

"He didn't say anything more to you, when you were alone with him?"

"Not that I remember."

"Going up on the plane?"

"No . . ."

"At the table, at dinner?"

"I don't think so, no."

"When you walked him to his car?"

"No, he was singing all that time. It was sort of embarrassing, to tell you the truth. And then he got in his car . . . Wait a minute." Evans sat up. "He did say one funny thing."

"What was that?"

"It was some Buddhist philosophical saying. He told me to remember it."

"What was it?"

"I don't remember," Evans said. "At least not exactly. It was something like 'Everything that matters is near where the Buddha sits.'"

"George wasn't interested in Buddhism," Sarah said. "Why would he say that to you?"

"Everything that matters is near where the Buddha sits," Evans said, repeating it again.

He was staring forward, into the media room adjacent to the living room.

"Sarah . . ."

Directly facing them, under dramatic overhead lighting, was a large wooden sculpture of a seated Buddha. Burmese, fourteenth century.

Evans got up and walked into the media room. Sarah followed him. The sculpture was four feet high, and mounted on a high pedestal. Evans walked around behind the statue.

"You think?" Sarah said.

"Maybe."

He ran his fingers around the base of the statue. There was a narrow space there, beneath the crossed legs, but he could feel nothing. He crouched, looked: nothing. There were some wide cracks in the wood of the statue, but nothing was there.

"Maybe move the base?" Evans said.

"It's on rollers," Sarah said.

They slid it to one side, exposing nothing but white carpet.

Evans sighed.

"Any other Buddhas around here?" he said, looking around the room.

Sarah was down on her hands and knees. "Peter," she said.

"What?"

"Look."

He crouched down. There was a roughly one-inch gap between the base of the pedestal and the floor. Barely visible in that gap was the corner of an envelope, attached to the inside of the pedestal.

"I'll be damned."

"It's an envelope."

She slid her fingers in.

"Can you reach it?"

"I . . . think so . . . got it!"

She pulled it out. It was a business-size envelope, sealed and unmarked.

"This could be it," she said, excited. "Peter, I think we may have found it!"

The lights went out, and the house was plunged into darkness.

They scrambled to their feet.

"What happened?" Evans said.

"It's okay," she said. "The emergency generator will cut in at any second."

"Actually, it won't," a voice in the darkness said.

Two powerful flashlights shone directly in their faces. Evans squinted in the harsh light; Sarah raised her hand to cover her eyes.

"May I have the envelope, please," the voice said.

Sarah said, "No."

There was a mechanical click, like the cocking of a gun.

"We'll take the envelope," the voice said. "One way or another."

"No you won't," Sarah said.

Standing beside her, Evans whispered, *"Sar-ah . . ."*

"Shut up, Peter. They can't have it."

"We'll shoot if we have to," the voice said.

"Sarah, give them the fucking envelope," Evans said.

"Let them take it," Sarah said defiantly.

"Sar-ah . . ."

"Bitch!" the voice screamed, and a gunshot sounded. Evans was embroiled in chaos and blackness. There was another scream. One of the flashlights bounced on the floor and rolled, pointing in a corner. In the shadows Evans saw a large dark figure attack Sarah, who screamed and kicked. Without thinking, Evans threw himself against the attacker, grabbing an arm in a leather jacket. He could smell the man's beery breath, hear him grunting. Then someone else pulled him off, slamming him to the ground, and he was kicked in the ribs.

He rolled away, banging against the furniture, and then a new, deep voice held up a flashlight and said, "Move away *now*." Immediately the attacker stopped fighting with them, and turned to this new voice. Evans looked back to see Sarah, who was on the floor. Another man got up and turned toward the flashlight.

There was a crackling sound and the man screamed and fell backward. The flashlight swung to the man who had been kicking Peter.

"You. Down."

The man immediately lay on the carpet.

"Face down."

The man rolled over.

"That's better," the new voice said. "Are you two all right?"

"I'm fine," Sarah said, panting, staring into the light. "Who the hell are you?"

"Sarah," the voice said. "I'm disappointed you don't recognize me."

Just then, the lights came back up in the room.

Sarah said, "John!"

And to Evans's astonishment, she stepped across the body of the fallen attacker to give a grateful hug to John Kenner, professor of Geo-environmental Engineering at MIT.

"I think I deserve an explanation," Evans said. Kenner had crouched down and was handcuffing the two men lying on the floor. The first man was still unconscious.

"It's a modulated taser," Kenner said. "Shoots a five-hundred-megahertz dart that delivers a four-millisecond jolt that inactivates cerebellar functioning. Down you go. Unconsciousness is immediate. But it only lasts a few minutes."

"No," Evans said. "I meant—"

"Why am I here?" Kenner said, looking up with a faint smile.

"Yes," Evans said.

"He's a good friend of George's," Sarah said.

"He is?" Evans said. "Since when?"

"Since we all met, a while back," Kenner said. "And I believe you remember my associate, Sanjong Thapa, as well."

A compact, muscular young man with dark skin and a crew cut came into the room. As before, Evans was struck by his vaguely military bearing, and British accent. "Lights are all back on, Professor," Sanjong Thapa said. "Should I call the police?"

"Not just yet," Kenner said. "Give me a hand here, Sanjong." Together, Kenner and his friend went through the pockets of the handcuffed men. "As I thought," Kenner said, straightening at last. "No identification on them."

"Who are they?"

"That'll be a question for the police," he said. The men were beginning to cough, and wake up. "Sanjong, let's get them to the front door." They hauled the intruders to their feet, and half-led, half-dragged them out of the room.

Evans was alone with Sarah. "How did Kenner get in the house?"

"He was in the basement. He's been searching the house most of the afternoon."

"And why didn't you tell me?"

"I asked her not to," Kenner said, walking back into the room. "I wasn't sure about you. This is a complicated business." He rubbed his hands together. "Now then, shall we have a look at that envelope?"

"Yes." Sarah sat down on the couch, and tore it open. A single sheet of paper, neatly folded, was inside. She stared at it in disbelief. Her face fell.

"What is it?" Evans said.

Without a word, she handed it to him.

It was a bill from the Edwards Fine Art Display Company of Torrance, California, for construction of a wooden pedestal to support a statue of a Buddha. Dated three years ago.

Feeling dejected, Evans sat down on the couch next to Sarah.

"What?" Kenner said. "Giving up already?"

"I don't know what else to do."

"You can begin by telling me exactly what George Morton said to you."

"I don't remember exactly."

"Tell me what you do remember."

"He said it was a philosophical saying. And it was something like, 'Everything that matters is near where the Buddha sits.'"

"No. That's impossible," Kenner said, in a definite tone.

"Why?"

"He wouldn't have said that."

"Why?"

Kenner sighed. "I should think it's self-evident. If he was giving instructions—which we presume he was—he wouldn't be so inexact. So he must have said something else."

"That's all I remember," Evans said, defensively. Evans found Kenner's quick manner to be brusque, almost insulting. He was beginning not to like this man.

"That's all you remember?" Kenner said. "Let's try again. *Where* did George make this statement to you? It must have been after you left the lobby."

At first Evans was puzzled. Then he remembered: "Were you there?"

"Yes, I was. I was in the parking lot, off to one side."

"Why?" Evans said.

"We'll discuss that later," Kenner said. "You were telling me, you and George went outside . . ."

"Yes," Evans said. "We went outside. It was cold, and George stopped singing when he felt the cold. We were standing on the steps of the hotel, waiting for the car."

"Uh-huh . . ."

"And when it came, he got into the Ferrari, and I was worried he shouldn't be driving, and I asked him about that, and George said, 'This reminds me of a philosophical saying.' And I said, 'What is it?' And he said. 'Everything that matters is not far from where the Buddha sits.'"

"Not far?" Kenner said.

"That's what he said."

"All right," Kenner said. "And at this moment, you were . . ."

"Leaning over the car."

"The Ferrari."

"Yes."

"Leaning over. And when George told you this philosophical saying, what did you answer back?"

"I just asked him not to drive."

"Did you repeat the phrase?"

"No," Evans said.

"Why not?"

"Because I was worried about him. He shouldn't be driving. Anyway, I remember thinking it was sort of awkwardly phrased. 'Not remote from where the Buddha sits.'"

"Not remote?" Kenner said.

"Yes," Evans said.

"He said to you, 'not remote'?"

"Yes."

"*Much* better," Kenner said. He was moving restlessly around the room, his eyes flicking from object to object. Touching things, dropping them, moving on.

"Why is it much better?" Evans said irritably.

Kenner gestured around the room. "Look around you, Peter. What do you see?"

"I see a media room."

"Exactly."

"Well, I don't understand—"

"Sit down on the couch, Peter."

Evans sat down, still furious. He crossed his arms over his chest and glowered at Kenner.

The doorbell rang. They were interrupted by the arrival of the police. Kenner said, "Let me handle this. It's easier if they don't see you," and he again walked out of the room. From the hallway, they heard several low voices discussing the two captured intruders. It sounded all very chummy.

Evans said, "Does Kenner have something to do with law enforcement?"

"Not exactly."

"What does that mean?"

"He just seems to know people."

Evans stared at her. "He knows people," he repeated.

"Different sorts of people. Yes. He sent George off to see a lot of them. Kenner has a tremendously wide range of contacts. Particularly in the environmental area."

"Is that what the Center for Risk Analysis does? Environmental risks?"

"I'm not sure."

"Why is he on sabbatical?"

"You should ask him these things."

"Okay."

"You don't like him, do you?" she said.

"I like him fine. I just think he's a conceited asshole."

"He's very sure of himself," she said.

"Assholes usually are."

Evans got up, and walked to where he could see into the hallway. Kenner was talking to the policemen, signing some documents, and turning over the intruders. The police were joking with him. Standing to one side was the dark man, Sanjong.

"And what about the little guy with him?"

"Sanjong Thapa," she said. "Kenner met him in Nepal when he was climbing a mountain there. Sanjong was a Nepali military officer assigned to help a team of scientists studying soil erosion in the Himalaya. Kenner invited him back to the States to work with him."

"I remember now. Kenner's a mountain climber, too. And he was almost on the Olympic ski team." Evans couldn't conceal his annoyance.

Sarah said, "He's a remarkable man, Peter. Even if you don't like him."

Evans returned to the couch, sat down again, folded his arms. "Well, you're right about that," he said. "I don't."

"I have the feeling you're not alone there," she said. "The list of people who dislike John Kenner is a long one."

Evans snorted, and said nothing.

They were still sitting on the couch when Kenner came bounding back into the room. He was again rubbing his hands. "All right," he said. "All the two boys have to say is that they want to talk to a lawyer, and they seem to know one. Imagine that. But we'll know more in a few hours." He turned to Peter. "So: mystery solved? Concerning the Buddha?"

Evans glared at him. "No."

"Really? It's quite straightforward."

"Why don't you just tell us," Evans said.

"Reach your right hand out to the end table," Kenner said.

Evans put his hand out. There were five remote controls on the table.

"Yes?" he said. "And?"

"What are they for?"

"It's a media room," Evans said. "I think we've established that."

"Yes," Kenner said. "But *what are they for?*"

"Obviously," Evans said, "to control the television, the satellite, the DVD, the VHS, all that."

"Which one does which?" Kenner said.

Evans stared at the table. And suddenly he got it. "Oh my God," he said. "You're absolutely right."

He was flipping them over, one after another.

"This one's the flat panel . . . DVD . . . satellite . . . high def . . ." He stopped. There was one more. "Looks like there are two DVD controllers." The second one was stubby and black and had all the usual buttons, but it was slightly lighter than the other.

Evans pulled open the battery compartment. Only one battery was there. In place of the other was a tightly rolled piece of paper.

"Bingo," he said.

He took the paper out.

All that matters is not remote from where the Buddha sits. That's what George had said. Which meant that this paper was all that matters.

Carefully, Evans unrolled the tiny sheet and pressed it flat on the coffee table with the heel of his hand, smoothing out the wrinkles.

And then he stared.

The paper contained nothing but columns of numbers and words:

662262	3982293	24FXE 62262 82293	**TERROR**
882320	4898432	12FXE 82232 54393	**SNAKE**
774548	9080799	02FXE 67533 43433	**LAUGHER**
482320	5898432	22FXE 72232 04393	**SCORPION**
ALT			
662262	3982293	24FXE 62262 82293	**TERROR**
382320	4898432	12FXE 82232 54393	**SEVER**
244548	9080799	02FXE 67533 43433	**CONCH**
482320	5898432	22FXE 72232 04393	**SCORPION**
ALT			
662262	3982293	24FXE 62262 82293	**TERROR**
382320	4898432	12FXE 82232 54393	**BUZZARD**
444548	7080799	02FXE 67533 43433	**OLD MAN**
482320	5898432	22FXE 72232 04393	**SCORPION**
ALT			
662262	3982293	24FXE 62262 82293	**TERROR**
382320	4898432	12FXE 82232 54393	**BLACK MESA**
344548	9080799	02FXE 67533 43433	**SNARL**
482320	5898432	22FXE 72232 04393	**SCORPION**

Evans said, "Is *this* what everybody's after?"

Sarah was looking at the paper over his shoulder. "I don't get it. What does it mean?"

Evans passed the paper to Kenner. He hardly glanced at it before he said, "No wonder they were so desperate to get this back."

"You know what it is?"

"There's no doubt about what it is," Kenner said, handing the paper to Sanjong. "It's a list of geographic locations."

"Locations? Where?"

"We'll have to calculate that," Sanjong said. "They're recorded in UTM, which may mean the listing was intended for pilots." Kenner saw the blank looks on the others' faces. "The world is a globe," he said, "and maps are flat. Therefore all maps are projections of a sphere onto a flat surface. One projection is the Universal Transverse Mercator grid, which divides the globe into six-degree grids. It was originally a military projection, but some pilot charts use it."

Evans said, "So these numbers are latitude and longitude in a different form?"

"Correct. A military form." Kenner ran his finger down the page. "It appears to be several alternate sets of four locations. But in every instance the first and last locations are the same. For whatever reason . . ." He frowned, and stared off into space.

"Is that bad?" Sarah said.

"I'm not sure," Kenner said. "But it might be, yes." He looked at Sanjong.

Sanjong nodded gravely. "What is today?" he said.

"Tuesday."

"Then . . . time is very short."

Kenner said, "Sarah, we're going to need George's plane. How many pilots does he have?"

"Two, usually."

"We'll need at least four. How soon can you get them?"

"I don't know. Where do you want to go?" she said.

"Chile."

"Chile! And leave when?"

"As soon as possible. Not later than midnight."

"It'll take me some time to arrange—"

"Then get started now," Kenner said. "Time is short, Sarah. Very short."

Evans watched Sarah go out of the room. He turned back to Kenner. "Okay," he said. "I give up. What's in Chile?"

"A suitable airfield, I presume. With adequate jet fuel." Kenner snapped his fingers. "Good point, Peter. Sarah," he called into the next room, "what kind of a plane is it?"

"G-five!" she called back.

Kenner turned to Sanjong Thapa, who had taken out a small handheld computer and was tapping away at it. "Are you connected to Akamai?"

"Yes."

"Was I right?"

"I've only checked the first location so far," Sanjong said. "But yes. We need to go to Chile."

"Then Terror is Terror?" Kenner said.

"I think so, yes."

Evans looked from one man to the other. "Terror is Terror?" he said, puzzled.

"That's right," Kenner said.

Sanjong said, "You know, Peter's got a point."

Evans said, "Are you guys ever going to tell me what's going on?"

"Yes," Kenner said. "But first, you have your passport?"

"I always carry it."

"Good man." Kenner turned back to Sanjong. "What point?"

"It's UTM, Professor. It's a six-degree grid."

"Of course!" Kenner said, snapping his fingers again. "What's the matter with me?"

"I give up," Evans said. "What's the matter with you?"

But Kenner didn't answer; he now seemed almost hyperactive, his fingers twitching nervously as he picked up the remote control from the table beside Peter and peered at it closely, turning it in the light. Finally, he spoke.

"A six-degree grid," Kenner said, "means that these locations are only accurate to a thousand meters. Roughly half a mile. That's simply not good enough."

"Why? How accurate should it be?"

"Three meters," Sanjong said. "About ten feet."

"Assuming they are using PPS," Kenner said, still squinting at the remote control. "In which case . . . Ah. I thought so. It's the oldest trick in the book."

He pulled the entire back of the remote off, exposing the circuit board. He lifted that away to reveal a second folded sheet of paper. It was thin, hardly more than tissue paper. It contained rows of numbers and symbols.

-2147483640,8,0*x°%ÁgKÀ__^O#_QÀ__cÁ«ªªªªÚ?___ÿÿÿ__å
-2147483640,8,0%h° â#KÀ_O__@BÀ__cÁ«ªªªªÚ?ÿÿÿÿ__ÿÿÿ__
-2147483640,8,0ã'»^$PNÀ_N__éxFÀ__cÁ¬ªªªªÚ¿__ÿÿÿ__Â
-2147483640,8,06W»1/4_OÀ   ò°q_IMÀ__cÁ«ªªªªÚ?ÿÿÿÿ__ÿÿÿ__¥
-2147483640,8,0‰œ°'/Ñ_LÀøø_8_ÔPÀ__cÁ«ªªªªÚ?___ÿÿÿ__

```
-2147483640,8,0*x°%ÁgKÀ__^O#_QÀ__cÁ«ªªªªÚ?_ ___ÿÿÿ__å
-2147483640,8,0%h° â#KÀ_O,__@BÀ__cÁ«ªªªªÚ?ÿÿÿÿ__ÿÿÿ__
-2147483640,8,0óW»1/4_OÀ   ò°q_IMÀ__cÁ«ªªªªÚ?ÿÿÿÿ__ÿÿÿ__¥
-2147483640,8,0ë(»I_'OÀã°°"d,LÀ__cÁ¬ªªªªÚ¿__ÿÿÿ
-2147483640,8,0%∞œ°/Ñ_LÀøø_8_ÔPÀ__cÁ«ªªªªÚ?___ÿÿÿ__

-2147483640,8,0*x°%ÁgKÀ__^O#_QÀ__cÁ«ªªªªÚ?_ ___ÿÿÿ__å
-2147483640,8,0%h° â#KÀ_O,__@BÀ__cÁ«ªªªªÚ?ÿÿÿÿ__ÿÿÿ__
-2147483640,8,0óW»1/4_OÀ   ò°q_IMÀ__cÁ«ªªªªÚ?ÿÿÿÿ__ÿÿÿ__¥
-2147483640,8,0ë(»I_'OÀã°°"d,LÀ__cÁ¬ªªªªÚ¿__ÿÿÿ
-2147483640,8,0%∞œ°/Ñ_LÀøø_8_ÔPÀ__cÁ«ªªªªÚ?___ÿÿÿ__
```

"All right," Kenner said. "This is more like it."

"And these are?" Evans said.

"True coordinates. Presumably for the same locations."

"Terror is Terror?" Evans said. He was starting to feel foolish.

Kenner said, "Yes. We're talking about Mount Terror, Peter. An inactive volcano. You have heard of it?"

"No."

"Well, we're going there."

"Where is it?"

"I thought you'd have guessed that by now," Kenner said. "It's in Antarctica, Peter."

II

TERROR

Van Nuys Airport sank beneath them. The jet turned south, crossing the flat, glowing expanse of the Los Angeles Basin. The flight attendant brought Evans coffee. On the little screen, it said 6,204 miles to destination. Flying time was nearly twelve hours.

The flight attendant asked them if they wanted dinner, and went off to prepare it.

"All right," Evans said. "Three hours ago, I'm coming to help Sarah deal with a robbery. Now I'm flying to Antarctica. Isn't it time somebody told me what this is about?"

Kenner nodded. "Have you heard of the Environmental Liberation Front? ELF?"

"No," Evans said, shaking his head.

"Not me," Sarah said.

"It's an underground extremist group. Supposedly made up of ex-Greenpeace and Earth First! types who thought those organizations had gone soft. ELF engages in violence on behalf of environmental causes. They've burned hotels in Colorado, houses on Long Island, spiked trees in Michigan, torched cars in California."

Evans nodded. "I read about them. . . . The

FBI and other law enforcement agencies can't infiltrate them because the organization consists of separate cells that never communicate with one another."

"Yes," Kenner said. "Supposedly. But cell phone conversations have been recorded. We've known for some time that the group was going global, planning a series of major events around the world, starting a few days from now."

"What kind of events?"

Kenner shook his head. "That, we don't know. But we have reason to think they'll be big—and destructive."

Sarah said, "What does this have to do with George Morton?"

"Funding," Kenner said. "If ELF is preparing actions around the world, they need a lot of money. The question is, where are they getting it?"

"Are you saying George has funded an extremist group?"

"Not intentionally. ELF is a criminal organization, but even so, radical groups like PETA fund them. Frankly, it's a disgrace. But the question became whether better-known environmental groups were funding them, too."

"Better-known groups? Like who?"

"Any of them," Kenner said.

"Wait a minute," Sarah said. "Are you suggesting that the Audubon Society and the Sierra Club fund terrorist groups?"

"No," Kenner said. "But I'm telling you that nobody knows exactly what any of these groups do with their money. Because government oversight of foundations and charities is extraordinarily lax. They don't get audited. The books don't get inspected. Environmental groups in the US generate half a billion dollars a year. What they do with it is unsupervised."

Evans frowned. "And George knew this?"

"When I met him," Kenner said, "he was already worrying about NERF. What it was doing with its money. It dispenses forty-four million dollars a year."

Evans said, "You're not going to tell me that NERF—"

"Not directly," Kenner said. "But NERF spends nearly sixty percent of its money on fund-raising. It can't admit that, of course. It'd look bad. It gets around the numbers by contracting nearly all of its work to outside direct-mail advertisers and telephone solicitation groups. These groups have misleading names, like the International Wildlife Preservation Fund—that's an Omaha-based direct-mail organization, that in turn outsources the work to Costa Rica."

"You're kidding," Evans said.

"No. I am not. And last year the IWPF spent six hundred fifty thousand dollars to gather information on environmental issues, including three hundred thousand dollars to something called the Rainforest Action and Support Coalition, RASC. Which turns out to be a drop box in Elmira, New York. And an equal sum to Seismic Services in Calgary, another drop box."

"You mean . . ."

"A drop box. A dead end. That was the true basis of the disagreement between Morton and Drake. Morton felt that Drake wasn't minding the store. That's why he wanted an external audit of the organization, and when Drake refused, Morton got really worried. Morton is on the NERF board; he has liability. So he hired a team of private investigators to investigate NERF."

"He did?" Evans said.

Kenner nodded. "Two weeks ago."

Evans turned to Sarah. "Did you know this?"

She looked away, then back. "He told me I couldn't tell anyone."

"George did?"

"I did," Kenner said.

"So you were behind this?"

"No, I merely consulted with George. It was his ball game. But the point is, once you outsource the money, you no longer control how it is spent. Or, you have deniability about how it is spent."

"Jesus," Evans said. "All this time, I just thought George was worried about the Vanutu lawsuit."

"No," Kenner said. "The lawsuit is probably hopeless. It is very unlikely it will ever go to trial."

"But Balder said when he gets good sea-level data—"

"Balder already has the good data. He has had it for months."

"What?"

"The data show no rise in South Pacific sea levels for the last thirty years."

"*What?*"

Kenner turned to Sarah. "Is he always like this?"

The flight attendant set out placemats, napkins, and silverware. "I've got fusilli pasta with chicken, asparagus, and sun-dried tomatoes," she said, "and a mixed green salad to follow. Would anyone like wine?"

"White wine," Evans said.

"I have Puligny-Montrachet. I'm not sure of the year, I think it's '98. Mr. Morton usually kept '98 on board."

"Just give me the whole bottle," Evans said, trying to make a joke. Kenner had unnerved him. Earlier in the evening, Kenner had been excited, almost twitchy-nervous. But now, sitting on the airplane, he was very still. Implacable. He had the manner of a man who was telling obvious truths, even though none of it was obvious to Peter. "I had it all wrong," Evans said finally. "If what you're saying is true . . ."

Kenner just nodded slowly.

Evans thought: He's letting me put it together. He turned to Sarah. "Did you know this, too?"

"No," she said. "But I knew something was wrong. George was very upset for the last two weeks."

"You think that's why he gave that speech, and then killed himself?"

"He wanted to embarrass NERF," Kenner said. "He wanted intense media scrutiny of that organization. Because he wanted to stop what is about to happen."

The wine came in cut glass crystal. Evans gulped it, held out his glass for more. "And what is about to happen?" he said.

"According to that list, there will be four events," Kenner said. "In four locations in the world. Roughly one day apart."

"What kind of events?"

Kenner shook his head. "We now have three good clues."

Sanjong fingered his napkin. "This is real linen," he said, in an awestruck tone. "And real crystal."

"Nice, huh?" Evans said, draining his glass again.

Sarah said, "What are the clues?"

"The first is the fact that the timing is not exact. You might think a terrorist event would be precisely planned, down to the minute. These events are not."

"Maybe the group isn't that well organized."

"I doubt that's the explanation. The second clue we got tonight, and it's very important," Kenner said. "As you saw from the list, there are several alternate locations for these events. Again, you'd think a terrorist organization would pick one location and stick to it. But this group hasn't done that."

"Why not?"

"I assume it reflects the kind of events that are planned. There must be some uncertainty inherent in the event itself, or in the conditions needed for it to take place."

"Pretty vague."

"It's more than we knew twelve hours ago."

"And the third clue?" Evans said, gesturing to the flight attendant to refill his glass.

"The third clue we have had for some time. Certain government agencies track the sale of restricted high technologies that might be useful to terrorists. For example, they track everything

that can be used in nuclear weapons production—
centrifuges, certain metals, and so on. They
track the sale of all conventional high explosives. They track certain critical biotechnologies.
And they track equipment that might be used to
disrupt communications networks—that generate electromagnetic impulses, for example, or
high-intensity radio frequencies."

"Yes . . ."

"They do this work with neural network
pattern-recognition computers that search for regularities in great masses of data—in this case,
basically thousands of sales invoices. About eight
months ago, the computers detected a very faint
pattern that seemed to indicate a common origin
for the widely scattered sale of certain field and
electronic equipment."

"How did the computer decide that?"

"The computer doesn't tell you that. It just
reports the pattern, which is then investigated by
agents on the ground."

"And?"

"The pattern was confirmed. ELF was buying
very sophisticated high technology from companies in Vancouver, London, Osaka, Helsinki, and
Seoul."

"What kind of equipment?" Evans said.

Kenner ticked them off on his fingers. "Fer-
mentation tanks for AOB primers—that's
ammonia-oxidizing bacteria. Mid-level particle-
dispersal units, military grade. Tectonic impulse
generators. Transportable MHD units. Hypersonic
cavitation generators. Resonant impact processor
assemblies."

"I don't know what any of that is," Evans said.

"Few people do," Kenner said. "Some of it's fairly standard environmental technology, like the AOB primer tanks. They're used in industrial wastewater treatment. Some of it's military but sold on the open market. And some of it's highly experimental. But it's all expensive."

Sarah said, "But how is it going to be used?"

Kenner shook his head. "Nobody knows. That's what we're going to find out."

"How do you *think* it's going to be used?"

"I hate to speculate," Kenner said. He picked up a basket of rolls. "Bread, anyone?"

The jet flew through the night.

The front of the cabin was darkened; Sarah and Sanjong were sleeping on makeshift beds, but Evans couldn't sleep. He sat in the back, staring out the window at the carpet of clouds glowing silver in the moonlight.

Kenner sat opposite him. "It's a beautiful world, isn't it?" he said. "Water vapor is one of the distinctive features of our planet. Makes such beauty. It's surprising there is so little scientific understanding of how water vapor behaves."

"Really?"

"The atmosphere is a bigger mystery than anyone will admit. Simple example: No one can say for sure if global warming will result in more clouds, or fewer clouds."

"Wait a minute," Evans said. "Global warming is going to raise the temperature, so more moisture will evaporate from the ocean, and more moisture means more clouds."

"That's one idea. But higher temperature also means more water vapor in the air and therefore fewer clouds."

"So which is it?"

"Nobody knows."

"Then how do they make computer models of climate?" Evans said.

Kenner smiled. "As far as cloud cover is concerned, they guess."

"They *guess?*"

"Well, they don't call it a guess. They call it an estimate, or parameterization, or an approximation. But if you don't understand something, you can't approximate it. You're really just guessing."

Evans felt the beginnings of a headache. He said, "I think it's time for me to get some sleep."

"Good idea," Kenner said, glancing at his watch. "We still have another eight hours before we land."

The flight attendant gave Evans some pajamas. He went into the bathroom to change. When he came out, Kenner was still sitting there, staring out the window at the moonlit clouds. Against his better judgment, Evans said, "By the way. You said earlier that the Vanutu lawsuit won't go to trial."

"That's right."

"Why not? Because of the sea-level data?"

"In part, yes. It's hard to claim global warming is flooding your country if sea levels aren't rising."

"It's hard to believe sea levels aren't rising," Evans said. "Everything you read says that they are. All the television reports . . ."

Kenner said, "Remember African killer bees? There was talk of them for years. They're here now, and apparently there's no problem. Remember Y2K? Everything you read back then said disaster was imminent. Went on for months. But in the end, it just wasn't true."

Evans thought that Y2K didn't prove anything about sea levels. He felt an urge to argue that point, but found himself suppressing a yawn.

"It's late," Kenner said. "We can talk about all this in the morning."

"You're not going to sleep?"

"Not yet. I have work to do."

Evans went forward to where the others were sleeping. He lay down across the aisle from Sarah, and pulled the covers up to his chin. Now his feet were exposed. He sat up, wrapped the blanket around his toes, and then lay down again. The blanket only came to mid-shoulder. He thought about getting up and asking the flight attendant for another.

And then he slept.

He awoke to harsh, glaring sunlight. He heard the clink of silverware, and smelled coffee. Evans rubbed his eyes, and sat up. In the back of the plane, the others were eating breakfast.

He looked at his watch. He'd slept for more than six hours.

He walked to the back of the plane.

"Better eat," Sarah said, "we land in an hour."

They stepped out onto the runway of Marso del Mar, shivering in the chill wind that whipped in off the ocean. The land around them was low, green, marshy, and cold. In the distance Evans saw the jagged, snow-covered spires of the El Fogara range of southern Chile.

"I thought this was summer," he said.

"It is," Kenner said. "Late spring, anyway."

The airfield consisted of a small wooden terminal, and a row of corrugated steel hangars, like oversize Quonset huts. There were seven or eight other aircraft on the field, all four-engine prop planes. Some had skis that were retracted above the landing wheels.

"Right on time," Kenner said, pointing to the hills beyond the airport. A Land Rover was bouncing toward them. "Let's go."

Inside the little terminal, which was little more than a single large room, its walls covered with faded, stained air charts, the group tried on parkas, boots, and other gear brought by the Land Rover. The parkas were all bright red or orange. "I tried to get everybody's size right," Kenner said. "Make sure you take long johns and microfleece, too."

Evans glanced at Sarah. She was sitting on the floor, pulling on heavy socks and boots. Then she unselfconsciously stripped down to her bra, and pulled a fleece top over her head. Her movements were quick, businesslike. She didn't look at any of the men.

Sanjong was staring at the charts on the wall, and seemed particularly interested in one. Evans went over. "What is it?"

"It's the record from the weather station at Punta Arenas, near here. It's the closest city to Antarctica in the world." He tapped the chart and laughed. "There's your global warming."

Evans frowned at the chart.

Punta Arenas 1888–2004

Source: giss.nasa.gov

"Finish up, everybody," Kenner said, glancing at his watch. "Our plane leaves in ten minutes."

Evans said, "Where exactly are we going?"

"To the base nearest Mount Terror. It's called Weddell Station. Run by New Zealanders."

"What's there?"

"Not much, mate," the Land Rover driver said, and he laughed. "But the way the weather's been lately, you'll be lucky if you can get there at all."

Evans stared out the narrow window of the Hercules. The vibration of the props made him sleepy, but he was fascinated by what he saw beneath him—mile after mile of gray ice, a vista broken by intermittent fog, and the occasional outcrop of black rock. It was a monochromatic, sunless world. And it was huge.

"Enormous," Kenner said. "People have no perspective on Antarctica, because it appears as a fringe at the bottom of most maps. But in fact, Antarctica is a major feature on the Earth's surface, and a major factor in our climate. It's a big continent, one and a half times the size of either Europe or the United States, and it holds ninety percent of all the ice on the planet."

"Ninety percent?" Sarah said. "You mean there's only ten percent in the rest of the world?"

"Actually, since Greenland has four percent, all the other glaciers in the world—Kilimanjaro, the Alps, the Himalaya, Sweden, Norway, Canada, Siberia—they all account for six percent of the planet's ice. The overwhelming majority of the frozen water of our planet is in the continent of

Antarctica. In many places the ice is five or six miles thick."

"No wonder they're concerned that the ice here is melting," Evans said.

Kenner said nothing.

Sanjong was shaking his head.

Evans said, "Come on, guys. Antarctica *is* melting."

"Actually, it's not," Sanjong said. "I can give you the references, if you like."

Kenner said, "While you were asleep, Sanjong and I were talking about how to clarify things for you, since you seem to be so ill-informed."

"Ill-informed?" Evans said, stiffening.

"I don't know what else one would call it," Kenner said. "Your heart may be in the right place, Peter, but you simply don't know what you're talking about."

"Hey," he said, controlling his anger. "Antarctica *is* melting."

"You think repetition makes something true? The data show that one relatively small area called the Antarctic Peninsula is melting and calving huge icebergs. That's what gets reported year after year. But the continent as a whole is getting colder, and the ice is getting thicker."

"Antarctica is getting *colder?*"

Sanjong had taken out a laptop and was hooking it up to a small portable bubble jet printer. He flipped open his laptop screen.

"What we decided," Kenner said, "is that we're going to give you references from now on. Be-

cause it's too boring to try and explain everything to you."

A sheet of paper began to buzz out of the
printer. Sanjong passed it to Evans.

Doran, P. T., Priscu, J. C., Lyons, W. B., Walsh, J. E., Fountain, A. G.,
McKnight, D. M., Moorhead, D. L., Virginia, R. A., Wall, D. H., Clow,
G. D., Fritsen, C. H., McKay, C. P., and Parsons, A. N., 2002,
"Antarctic climate cooling and terrestrial ecosystem response,"
Nature **415**: 517–20.

**From 1986 to 2000 central Antarctic valleys cooled
.7°C per decade with serious ecosystem damage from
cold.**

Comiso, J. C., 2000, "Variability and trends in Antarctic surface
temperatures from *in situ* and satellite infrared measurements,"
Journal of Climate **13**: 1674–96.

**Both satellite data and ground stations show slight
cooling over the last 20 years.**

Joughin, I., and Tulaczyk, S., 2002, "Positive mass balance of the
Ross Ice Streams, West Antarctica," *Science* **295**: 476–80.

**Side-looking radar measurements show West Antarctic
ice is increasing at 26.8 gigatons/yr. Reversing the melting
trend of the last 6,000 years.**

Thompson, D. W. J., and Solomon, S., 2002, "Interpretation of
recent Southern Hemisphere climate change," *Science* **296**:
895–99.

**Antarctic peninsula has warmed several degrees while
interior has cooled somewhat. Ice shelves have retreated
but sea ice has increased.**

Petit, J. R., Jouzel, J., Raynaud, D., Barkov, N. I., Barnola, J.-M.,
Basile, I., Bender, M., Chappellaz, J., Davis, M., Delaygue, G.,
Delmotte, M., Kotlyakov, V. M., Legrand, M., Lipenkov, V. Y., Lorius,
C., Pepin, L., Ritz, C., Saltzman, E., and Stievenard, M., 1999,
"Climate and atmospheric history of the past 420,000 years from
the Vostok ice core, Antarctica," *Nature* **399**: 429–36.

**During the last four interglacials, going back 420,000
years, the Earth was warmer than it is today.**

Anderson, J. B., and Andrews, J. T., 1999, "Radiocarbon constraints
on ice sheet advance and retreat in the Weddell Sea, Antarctica,"
Geology **27**: 179–82.

Less Antarctic ice has melted today than occurred during the last interglacial.

Liu, J., Curry, J. A., and Martinson, D. G., 2004, "Interpretation of recent Antarctic sea ice variability," *Geophysical Research Letters* **31**: 10.1029/2003 GL018732.
Antarctic sea ice has increased since 1979.

Vyas, N. K., Dash, M. K., Bhandari, S. M., Khare, N., Mitra, A., and Pandey, P. C., 2003, "On the secular trends in sea ice extent over the antarctic region based on OCEANSAT-1 MSMR observations," *International Journal of Remote Sensing* **24**: 2277–87.
Trend toward more sea ice may be accelerating.

Parkinson, C. L., 2002, "Trends in the length of the southern Ocean sea-ice season, 1979–99," *Annals of Glaciology* **34**: 435–40.
The greater part of Antarctica experiences a longer sea-ice season, lasting 21 days longer than it did in 1979.

"Okay, well, I see *slight* cooling referred to here," Evans said. "I also see warming of the peninsula of *several degrees*. That certainly seems more significant. And that peninsula's a pretty big part of the continent, isn't it?" He tossed the paper aside. "Frankly, I'm not impressed."

Sanjong said, "The peninsula is two percent of the continent. And frankly, I am surprised that you did not comment on the most significant fact in the data you were given."

"Which is?"

"When you said earlier that the Antarctic is melting," Sanjong said, "were you aware that it has been melting for the last *six thousand years?*"

"Not specifically, no."

"But generally, you knew that?"

"No," Evans said. "I wasn't aware of that."

"You thought that the Antarctic melting was something new?"

"I thought it was melting faster than previously," Evans said.

"Maybe we won't bother anymore," Kenner said.

Sanjong nodded, and started to put the computer away.

"No, no," Evans said. "I'm interested in what you have to say. I'm not closed-minded about this. I'm ready to hear new information."

"You just did," Kenner said.

Evans picked up the sheet of paper again, and folded it carefully. He slipped it into his pocket. "These studies are probably financed by the coal industry," he said.

"Probably," Kenner said. "I'm sure that explains it. But then, everybody's paid by somebody. Who pays your salary?"

"My law firm."

"And who pays them?"

"The clients. We have several hundred clients."

"You do work for all of them?"

"Me, personally? No."

"In fact, you do most of your work for environmental clients," Kenner said. "Isn't that true?"

"Mostly. Yes."

"Would it be fair to say that the environmental clients pay your salary?" Kenner said.

"You could make that argument."

"I'm just asking, Peter. Would it be fair to say environmentalists pay your salary?"

"Yes."

"Okay. Then would it be fair to say the opinions you hold are because you work for environmentalists?"

"Of course not—"

"You mean you're not a paid flunky for the environmental movement?"

"No. The fact is—"

"You're not an environmental stooge? A mouthpiece for a great fund-raising and media machine—a multi-billion-dollar industry in its own right—with its own private agenda that's not necessarily in the public interest?"

"God damn it—"

"Is this pissing you off?" Kenner said.

"You're damn right it is!"

"Good," Kenner said. "Now you know how legitimate scientists feel when their integrity is impugned by slimy characterizations such as the one you just made. Sanjong and I gave you a careful, peer-reviewed interpretation of data. Made by several groups of scientists from several different countries. And your response was first to ignore it, and then to make an ad hominem attack. You didn't answer the data. You didn't provide counter evidence. You just smeared with innuendo."

"Oh, fuck you," Evans said. "You think you have an answer for everything. But there's only one problem: Nobody agrees with you. Nobody in the world thinks that Antarctica is getting colder."

"These scientists do," Kenner said. "They published the data."

Evans threw up his hands. "The hell with it," he said. "I don't want to talk about this anymore."

He walked to the front of the plane and sat down, crossed his arms, and stared out the window.

Kenner looked at Sanjong and Sarah. "Anyone feel like coffee?"

Sarah had watched Kenner and Evans with a certain amount of uneasiness. Even though she had worked for the past two years for Morton, she had never shared her employer's passion for environmental issues. All during that time, Sarah had been in a tempestuous, exciting relationship with a handsome young actor. Their time together consisted of an unending series of passionate evenings, angry confrontations, slammed doors, tearful reconciliations, jealousies, and infidelities—and it had consumed her more than she cared to admit. The truth was that she had paid no more attention to NERF or Morton's other environmental interests than the job required. At least, until the son-of-a-bitch actor appeared in the pages of *People* magazine with a young actress from his TV show, and Sarah finally decided she had had enough, erased the guy from her cell phone, and threw herself into her work.

But she certainly held the same general view about the state of the world as Evans did. Perhaps Evans was more aggressive in stating his views, and more trusting of his assumptions, but she basically agreed with him. And here was Kenner, casting doubt after doubt.

It left her wondering whether Kenner was really correct about everything he was saying. And it also made her wonder just how he and Morton had become friends.

She asked Kenner, "Did you have these same discussions with George?"

"In the last weeks of his life, yes."

"And did he argue with you the way Evans is?"

"No." Kenner shook his head. "Because by then, he knew."

"Knew what?"

They were interrupted by the pilot's voice on the intercom. "Good news," he said. "The weather's broken over Weddell, and we will land in ten minutes. For those of you who have never made a landing on ice, seat belts should be low and tight, and all your gear safely stowed. And we really mean it."

The plane began a slow, curving descent. Sarah looked out the window at a crusty expanse of white, snow-covered ice. In the distance she saw a series of brightly colored buildings—red, blue, green—built on a cliff, overlooking the gray and choppy ocean.

"That's Weddell Station," Kenner said.

Trudging toward structures that looked like over-size children's building blocks, Evans kicked a clump of ice out of his path. He was in a grumpy mood. He felt relentlessly bullied by Kenner, whom he now recognized as one of those perpetual contrarians who argued against all conventional wisdom, simply because it was conventional.

But since Evans was stuck with this lunatic—at least for the next few days—he decided to avoid Kenner as much as possible. And certainly not engage him in any more conversations. There was no point in arguing with extremists.

He looked at Sarah, walking across the ice airfield beside him. Her cheeks were flushed in the cold air. She looked very beautiful. "I think the guy is a nut," Evans said.

"Kenner?"

"Yeah. What do you think?"

She shrugged. "Maybe."

"I bet those references he gave me are fake," he said.

"They'll be easy enough to check," she said. They stamped their feet and entered the first building.

* * *

Weddell Research Station turned out to be home to thirty-odd scientists, graduate students, technicians, and support staff. Evans was pleasantly surprised to find it was quite comfortable inside, with a cheerful cafeteria, a game room, and a large gym with a row of treadmills. There were big picture windows with views of the choppy, restless ocean. Other windows looked out over the vast, white expanse of the Ross Ice Shelf, stretching away to the west.

The head of the station greeted them warmly. He was a heavyset, bearded scientist named MacGregor who looked like Santa Claus in a Patagonia vest. Evans was annoyed that MacGregor seemed to know Kenner, at least by reputation. The two men immediately struck up a friendly conversation.

Evans excused himself, saying he wanted to check his e-mail. He was shown to a room with several computer terminals. He signed on to one, and went directly to the site for *Science* magazine.

It took him only a few moments to determine that the references Sanjong had given him were genuine. Evans read the online abstracts, and then the full text. He began to feel a little better. Kenner had summarized the raw data correctly, but he had drawn a different interpretation from that of the authors. The authors of those papers were firmly committed to the idea of global warming—and said so in the text.

Or at least, most of them did.

It was a bit complicated. In one paper, it was clear that even though the authors gave lip service to the threat of global warming, their data seemed to suggest the opposite of what they were saying in the text. But that apparent confusion, Evans suspected, was probably just the result of drawing up a paper with half a dozen authors. What they *said* was they supported the idea of global warming. And that was what counted.

More disturbing was the paper on the increase in ice thickness in the Ross Ice Shelf. Here Evans found some troubling points. First, the author did say that the shelf had been melting for the last six thousand years, ever since the Holocene era. (Though Evans could not remember reading, in any article about melting Antarctic ice, that it had been going on for the last six thousand years.) If that were true, it wasn't exactly news. On the contrary, the author suggested that the real news was the end of this long-term melting trend, and the first evidence of ice thickening. The author was hinting that this might be the first sign of the start of the next Ice Age.

Jesus!

The next *Ice Age?*

There was a knock on the door behind him. Sarah stuck her head in. "Kenner wants us," she said. "He's discovered something. Looks like we're going out on the ice."

The map covered the entire wall, showing the enormous, star-shaped continent. In the lower right-hand corner was Weddell Station, and the curving arc of the Ross Ice Shelf.

"We've learned," Kenner said, "that a supply

ship docked five days ago bringing boxes of field material for an American scientist named James Brewster, from the University of Michigan. Brewster is a very recent arrival who was permitted to come at the last minute because the terms of his research grant were unusually generous in their allowance for overhead—meaning the station would get some much-needed money for operations."

"So he bought his way in?" Evans said.

"In effect."

"When did he get here?"

"Last week."

"Where is he now?"

"Out in the field." Kenner pointed to the map. "Somewhere south of the slopes of Mount Terror. And that's where we're going."

"You say this guy's a scientist from Michigan?" Sarah said.

"No," Kenner said. "We just checked with the university. They have a Professor James Brewster, all right. He's a geophysicist at the University of Michigan, and right now he's in Ann Arbor waiting for his wife to deliver a baby."

"So who is this guy?"

"Nobody knows."

"And what was his offloaded equipment?" Evans said.

"Nobody knows that, either. It was helicoptered out to the field, still in the original crates. The guy's been out there a week with two so-called graduate students. Whatever he's doing, he's apparently working across a large area, so he moves his base camp frequently. Nobody here knows precisely where he is." Kenner lowered his voice. "One of the graduate students came back yesterday to do some computer work. But we won't use him to lead us out there, for obvious reasons. We'll use one of the staff people at Weddell, Jimmy Bolden. He's very knowledgeable.

"The weather's too dicey for helicopters, so we have to take snowtracks. It's seventeen miles to the camp. The snowtracks should get us there in two hours. The outside temperature's perfect for springtime in Antarctica—minus twenty-five degrees Fahrenheit. So, bundle up. Any questions?"

Evans glanced at his watch. "Won't it get dark soon?"

"We have much less nighttime now that spring is here. We'll have daylight all the time we're out there. The only problem we face is right here," Kenner said, pointing to the map. "We have to cross the shear zone."

"The shear zone?" Jimmy Bolden said, as they trudged toward the vehicle shed. "There's nothing to it. You just have to be careful, that's all."

"But what is it?" Sarah said.

"It's a zone where the ice is subjected to lateral forces, shear forces, a bit like the land in California. But instead of having earthquakes, you get crevasses. Lots of 'em. Deep ones."

"We have to cross that?"

"It's not a problem," Bolden said. "Two years ago they built a road that crosses the zone safely. They filled in all the crevasses along the road."

They went into the corrugated steel shed. Evans saw a row of boxy vehicles with red cabs and tractor treads. "These are the snowtracks," Bolden said. "You and Sarah'll go in one, Dr. Kenner in one, and I'll be in the third, leading you."

"Why can't we all go in one?"

"Standard precaution. Keep the weight down. You don't want your vehicle to fall through into a crevasse."

"I thought you said there was a road where the crevasses were filled in?"

"There is. But the road is on an ice field, and

the ice moves a couple of inches a day. Which means the road moves. Don't worry, it's clearly marked with flags." Bolden climbed up onto the tread. "Here, let me show you the features of the snowtrack. You drive it like a regular car: clutch there, handbrake, accelerator, steering wheel. You run your heater on this switch here—" he pointed to a switch "—and keep it on at all times. It will maintain the cab at around ten above zero. This bulgey orange beacon on the dashboard is your transponder. It turns on when you push this button here. It also turns on automatically if the vehicle shifts more than thirty degrees from horizontal."

"You mean if we fall into a crevasse," Sarah said.

"Trust me; that isn't going to happen," Bolden said. "I'm just showing you the features. Transponder broadcasts a unique vehicle code, so we can come and find you. If for any reason you need to be rescued, you should know the average time to rescue is two hours. Your food is here; water here; you have enough for ten days. Medical kit here, including morphine and antibiotics. Fire extinguisher here. Expedition equipment in this box—crampons, ropes, carabiners, all that. Space blankets here, equipped with mini heaters; they'll keep you above freezing for a week, if you crawl inside 'em. That's about it. We communicate by radio. Speaker in the cab. Microphone above the windshield. Voice-activated—just talk. Got it?"

"Got it," Sarah said, climbing up.

"Then let's get started. Professor, you clear on everything?"

"I am," Kenner said, climbing up into the adjacent cab.

"Okay," Bolden said. "Just remember that whenever you are outside your vehicle, it is going to be thirty below zero. Keep your hands and face covered. Any exposed skin will get frostbite in less than a minute. Five minutes, and you're in danger of losing anatomy. We don't want you folks going home without all your fingers and toes. Or noses."

Bolden went to the third cab. "We proceed single file," he said. "Three cab-lengths apart. No closer under any circumstances, and no farther. If a storm comes up and visibility drops, we maintain the same distance but reduce our speed. Got it?"

They all nodded.

"Then let's go."

At the far end of the shed, a corrugated door rolled up, the icy metal screeching. Bright sunlight outside.

"Looks like a beautiful day in the neighborhood," Bolden said. And with a sputter of diesel exhaust, he drove the first snowtrack out through the door.

It was a bouncing, bone-jolting ride. The ice field that had looked so flat and featureless from a distance was surprisingly rugged when experienced up close, with long troughs and steep hillocks. Evans felt like he was in a boat, crashing through choppy seas, except of course this sea was frozen, and they were moving slowly through it.

Sarah drove, her hands confident on the wheel.

Evans sat in the passenger seat beside her, clutching the dashboard to keep his balance.

"How fast are we going?"

"Looks like fourteen miles an hour."

Evans grunted as they nosed down a short trench, then up again. "We've got two hours of this?"

"That's what he said. By the way, did you check Kenner's references?"

"Yes," Evans said, in a sulky voice.

"Were they made up?"

"No."

Their vehicle was third in the row. Ahead was Kenner's snowtrack, following behind Bolden's in the lead.

The radio hissed. "Okay," they heard Bolden say, over the speaker. "Now we're coming into the shear zone. Maintain your distance and stay within the flags."

Evans could see nothing different—it just looked like more ice field, glistening in the sun—but here there were red flags on both sides of the route. The flags were mounted on six-foot-high posts.

As they moved deeper into the field, he looked beyond the road to the openings of crevasses in the ice. They had a deep blue color, and seemed to glow.

"How deep are they?" Evans said.

"The deepest we've found is a kilometer," Bolden said, over the radio. "Some of them are a thousand feet. Most are a few hundred feet or less."

"They all have that color?"

"They do, yes. But you don't want a closer look."

Despite the dire warnings, they crossed the field in safety, leaving the flags behind. Now they saw to the left a sloping mountain, with white clouds.

"That's Erebus," Bolden said. "It's an active volcano. That's steam coming from the summit. Sometimes it lobs chunks of lava, but never this far out. Mount Terror is inactive. You see it ahead. That little slope."

Evans was disappointed. The name, Mount Terror, had suggested something fearsome to him—not this gentle hill with a rocky outcrop at the top. If the mountain hadn't been pointed out to him, he might not have noticed it at all.

"Why is it called Mount Terror?" he said. "It's not terrifying."

"Has nothing to do with that. The first Antarctic landmarks were named after the ships that discovered them," Bolden said. "Terror was apparently the name of a ship in the nineteenth century."

"Where's the Brewster camp?" Sarah said.

"Should be visible any minute now," Bolden said. "So, you people are some kind of inspectors?"

"We're from the IADG," Kenner said. "The international inspection agency. We're required to make sure that no US research project violates the international agreements on Antarctica."

"Uh-huh . . ."

"Dr. Brewster showed up so quickly," Kenner went on, "he never submitted his research grant proposal for IADG approval. So we'll check in the field. It's just routine."

They bounced and crunched onward for several minutes in silence. They still did not see a camp.

"Huh," Bolden said. "Maybe he moved it."

"What type of research is he doing?" Kenner said.

"I'm not sure," Bolden said, "but I heard he's studying the mechanics of ice calving. You know, how the ice flows to the edge, and then breaks off the shelf. Brewster's been planting GPS units in the ice to record how it moves toward the sea."

"Are we close to the sea?" Evans said.

"About ten or eleven miles away," Bolden said. "To the north."

Sarah said, "If he's studying iceberg formation, why is he working so far from the coast?"

"Actually, this isn't so far," Kenner said. "Two years ago an iceberg broke off the Ross Shelf that was four miles wide and forty miles long. It was as big as Rhode Island. One of the biggest ever seen."

"Not because of global warming, though," Evans said to Sarah, with a disgusted snort. "Global warming couldn't be responsible for that. Oh no."

"Actually, it wasn't responsible," Kenner said. "It was caused by local conditions."

Evans sighed. "Why am I not surprised?"

Kenner said, "There's nothing wrong with the idea of local conditions, Peter. This is a *continent*. It would be surprising if it didn't have its own distinctive weather patterns, irrespective of global trends that may or may not exist."

"And that's very true," Bolden said. "There are definitely local patterns here. Like the katabatic winds."

"The what?"

"Katabatic winds. They're gravitational winds. You've probably noticed that it's a lot windier here than in the interior. The interior of the continent is relatively calm."

"What's a gravitational wind?" Evans said.

"Antarctica's basically one big ice dome," Bolden said. "The interior is higher than the coast. And colder. Cold air flows downhill, and gathers speed as it goes. It can be blowing fifty, eighty miles an hour when it reaches the coast. Today is not a bad day, though."

"That's a relief," Evans said.

And then Bolden said, "See there, dead ahead. That's Professor Brewster's research camp."

It wasn't much to look at: a pair of orange domed tents, one small, one large, flapping in the wind. It looked like the large one was for equipment; they could see the edges of boxes pressing against the tent fabric. From the camp, Evans could see orange-flagged units stuck into the ice every few hundred yards, in a line stretching away into the distance.

"We'll stop now," Bolden said. "I'm afraid Dr. Brewster's not here at the moment; his snowtrack is gone."

"I'll just have a look," Kenner said.

They shut the engines and climbed out. Evans had thought it was chilly in the cab, but it was a shock to feel the cold air hit him as he stepped out onto the ice. He gasped and coughed. Kenner appeared to have no reaction; he went straight for the supply tent and disappeared inside.

Bolden pointed down the line of flags. "You see his vehicle tracks there, parallel to the sensor units? Dr. Brewster must have gone out to check his line. It runs almost a hundred miles to the west."

Sarah said, "A hundred miles?"

"That's right. He has installed GPS radio units all along that distance. They transmit back to him, and he records how they move with the ice."

"But there wouldn't be much movement . . ."

"Not in the course of a few days, no. But these sensors will remain in place for a year or more. Sending back the data by radio to Weddell."

"Dr. Brewster is staying that long?"

"Oh no, he'll go back, I'm sure. It's too expensive to keep him here. His grant allows an initial twenty-one-day stay only, and then monitoring visits of a week every few months. But we'll be forwarding his data to him. Actually, we just put it up on the Internet; he takes it wherever he happens to be."

"So you assign him a secure web page?"

"Exactly."

Evans stamped his feet in the cold. "So, is Brewster coming back, or what?"

"Should be coming back. But I couldn't tell you when."

From within the tent, Kenner shouted, "Evans!"

"I guess he wants me."

Evans went to the tent. Bolden said to Sarah, "Go ahead with him, if you want to." He pointed off to the south, where clouds were darkening. "We don't want to be staying here too long. Looks like weather coming up. We have two hours ahead of us, and it won't be any fun if it socks in. Visibility drops to ten feet or less. We'd have to stay put until it cleared. And that might be two or three days."

"I'll tell them," she said.

* * *

Evans pushed the tent flap aside. The interior glowed orange from the fabric. There were the remains of wooden crates, broken down and stacked on the ground. On top of them were dozens of cardboard boxes, all stenciled identically. They each had the University of Michigan logo, and then green lettering:

University of Michigan
Dept. of Environmental Science
Contents: Research Materials
Extremely Sensitive
HANDLE WITH CARE
This Side Up

"Looks official," Evans was saying. "You sure this guy isn't an actual research scientist?"

"See, for yourself," Kenner said, opening one cardboard carton. Within it, Evans saw a stack of plastic cones, roughly the size of highway cones. Except they were black, not orange. "You know what these are?"

"No." Evans shook his head.

Sarah came into the tent. "Bolden says bad weather coming, and we shouldn't stay here."

"Don't worry, we won't," Kenner said. "Sarah, I need you to go into the other tent. See if you can find a computer there. Any kind of computer—laptop, lab controller, PDA—anything with a microprocessor in it. And see if you can find any radio equipment."

"You mean transmitters, or radios for listening?"

"Anything with an antenna."

"Okay." She turned and went outside again.

Evans was still going through the cartons. He opened three, then a fourth. They all contained the same black cones. "I don't get it."

Kenner took one cone, turned it to the light. In raised lettering it said: "Unit PTBC-XX-904/8776-AW203 US DOD."

Evans said, "These are military?"

"Correct," Kenner said.

"But what are they?"

"They're the protective containers for coned PTBs."

"PTBs?"

"Precision-timed blasts. They're explosives detonated with millisecond timing by computer in order to induce resonant effects. The individual blasts are not particularly destructive, but the timing sets up standing waves in the surrounding material. That's where the destructive power comes from—the standing wave."

"What's a standing wave?" Evans said.

"You ever watch girls play jump rope? Yes? Well, if instead of spinning the rope, they shake it up and down, they generate loopy waves that travel along the length of the rope, back and forth."

"Okay . . ."

"But if the girls shake it just right, the waves appear to stop moving back and forth. The rope takes on a single curved shape and holds it. You've seen that? Well, that's a standing wave. It reflects back and forth in perfect synchronization so it doesn't seem to move."

"And these explosives do that?"

"Yes. In nature, standing waves are incredibly powerful. They can shake a suspension bridge to pieces. They can shatter a skyscraper. The most destructive effects of earthquakes are caused by standing waves generated in the crust."

"So Brewster's got these explosives . . . set in a row . . . for a hundred miles? Isn't that what Bolden said? A hundred miles?"

"Right. And I think there's no question what he intends. Our friend Brewster is hoping to fracture the ice for a hundred miles, and break off the biggest iceberg in the history of the planet."

Sarah stuck her head in.

Kenner said, "Did you find a computer?"

"No," she said. "There's nothing there. Nothing at all. No sleeping bag, no food, no personal effects. Nothing but a bare tent. The guy's gone."

Kenner swore. "All right," he said. "Now, listen carefully. Here's what we are going to do."

"Oh no," Jimmy Bolden said, shaking his head. "I'm sorry, but I can't allow that, Dr. Kenner. It's too dangerous."

"Why is it dangerous?" Kenner said. "You take these two back to the station, and I'll follow Brewster's snowtracks until I meet up with him."

"No, sir, we all stay together, sir."

"Jimmy," Kenner said firmly, "we're not going to do that."

"With all due respect, sir, you don't know your way around this part of the world . . ."

"You forget, I am an IADG inspector," Kenner said. "I was resident in Vostok Station for six months in the winter of '99. And I was resident in Morval for three months in '91. I know exactly what I'm doing."

"Gee, I don't know . . ."

"Call back to Weddell. The station chief will confirm it."

"Well, sir, if you put it that way . . ."

"I do," Kenner said firmly. "Now get these two people back to base. Time is wasting."

"Okay, if you'll be all right . . ." Bolden turned

to Evans and Sarah. "Then I guess we go. Mount up, folks, and we'll head out."

Within minutes, Evans and Sarah were jouncing along on the ice, following behind Bolden's snowtrack. Behind them, Kenner was driving parallel to the line of flags, heading east. Evans looked back just in time to see Kenner stop, get out, check one of the flags briefly, then get back in again and drive on.

Bolden saw it, too. "What is he doing?" he said in an anxious tone.

"Just looking at the unit, I guess."

"He shouldn't be getting out of his vehicle," Bolden said. "And he shouldn't be alone on the shelf. It's against regulations."

Sarah had the feeling Bolden was about to turn back. She said, "I can tell you something about Dr. Kenner, Jimmy."

"What's that?"

"You don't want to make him mad."

"Really?"

"No, Jimmy. You don't."

"Well . . . okay then."

They drove on, climbing a long rise, descending on the other side. Brewster's camp was gone, and so was Kenner's snowtrack. Ahead lay the vast white field of the Ross Ice Shelf, stretching away to the gray horizon.

"Two hours, folks," Bolden said. "And then a hot shower."

The first hour passed uneventfully. Evans started to fall asleep, only to be jolted awake by the sharp movements of the vehicle. Then he would drift off again, his head nodding until the next shock.

Sarah was driving. He said to her, "Aren't you tired?"

"No, not at all," she said.

The sun was now low on the horizon, and obscured by fog. The landscape was shades of pale gray, with almost no separation between land and sky. Evans yawned. "Want me to take over?"

"I've got it, thanks."

"I'm a good driver."

"I know you are."

He was thinking she had a definite bossy side, despite her charm and her beauty. She was the kind of woman who would want to control the remote.

"I bet you want the remote," he said.

"You think so?" She smiled.

It was irritating in a certain way, he thought, that she did not take him seriously as a man. At least, not as a man she could be interested in. In truth, she was a little too cool for his taste. A little too ice blond. A little too controlled, beneath that beautiful exterior.

The radio clicked. Bolden said, "I don't like this weather coming in. We better take a shortcut."

"What shortcut?"

"It's only half a mile, but it'll save twenty minutes on our time. Follow me." He turned his snowtrack left, leaving the packed snow road, and heading off onto the ice fields.

"Okay," Sarah said. "Right behind you."

"Good work," Bolden said. "We're still an hour from Weddell. I know this route, it's a piece of-

cake. Just stay directly behind me. Not to the left
or right, but directly behind, you understand?"

"Got it," Sarah said.

"Good."

In a matter of minutes, they had moved several hundred yards from the road. The ice there
was bare and hard, the treads of the snowtracks
scratching and squeaking as they crossed it.

"You're on ice now," Bolden said.

"I noticed."

"Won't be long now."

Evans was looking out the window. He could
no longer see the road. In fact, he wasn't sure
anymore in which direction it lay. Everything
now looked the same. He felt anxious suddenly.
"We're really in the middle of nowhere."

The snowtrack slid laterally a little, across the
ice. He grabbed for the dashboard. Sarah immediately brought the vehicle back under control.

"Jeez," Evans said, clinging to the dashboard.

"Are you a nervous passenger?" she said.

"Maybe a little."

"Too bad we can't get some music. Is there any
way to get music?" she asked Bolden.

"You should," Bolden said. "Weddell broadcasts
twenty-four hours. Just a minute." He stopped his
snowtrack, and walked back to their stopped
vehicle. He climbed up on the tread and opened
the door, in a blast of freezing air. "Sometimes
you get interference from this," he said, and unclipped the transponder from the dash. "Okay.
Try your radio now."

Sarah fiddled with the receiver, twisting the
knob. Bolden walked back to his red cab, carry-

ing the transponder. His diesel engine spit a cloud of black exhaust as he put the snowtrack in gear.

"You think they'd be a little more ecologically minded," Evans said, looking at the exhaust as Bolden's snowtrack chugged forward.

"I'm not getting any music," Sarah said.

"Never mind," Evans said. "I don't care that much."

They drove another hundred yards. Then Bolden stopped again.

"Now what?" Evans said.

Bolden climbed out of his vehicle, walked to the back of it, and looked at his own treads.

Sarah was still fiddling with the radio. Punching the buttons for the different transmission frequencies, she got bursts of static for each.

"I'm not sure this is an improvement," Evans said. "Just let it go. Why have we stopped, anyway?"

"I don't know," Sarah said. "He seems to be checking something."

Now Bolden turned and looked back at them. He didn't move. He just stood there and stared.

"Should we get out?" Evans said.

The radio crackled and they heard "—is Weddell CM to—401. Are you there, Dr. Kenner? Weddell CM to—Kenner. Can you hear—?"

"Hey," Sarah said, smiling. "I think we finally got something."

The radio hissed and sputtered.

"—just found Jimmy Bolden unconscious in— maintenance room. We don't know who is—out there with—but it's not—"

"Oh shit," Evans said, staring at the man in front of them. "That guy's not Bolden? Who is he?"

"I don't know, but he's blocking the way," Sarah said. "And he's waiting."

"Waiting for what?"

There was a loud *crack!* from beneath them. Inside the cab, the sound echoed like a gunshot. Their vehicle shifted slightly.

"Screw this," Sarah said. "We're getting out of here, even if I have to ram the bastard." She put the snowtrack in gear, and started to back away from the vehicle in front of them. She shifted, starting the snowtrack forward again.

Another *crack!*

"Let's go!" Evans said. "Let's *go!*"

Crack! Crack! Their vehicle lurched beneath them, tilted sideways at an angle. Evans looked out at the guy pretending to be Bolden.

"It's the ice," Sarah said. "He's waiting for our weight to break through."

"Ram him!" Evans said, pointing ahead. The bastard was making some hand gesture to them. It took him a moment for Evans to understand what it meant. Then he got it.

The man was waving goodbye.

Sarah stomped on the accelerator and the engine rumbled forward, but in the next moment the ground gave way completely beneath them, and their vehicle nosed down. Evans saw the blue-ice wall of a crevasse. Then the vehicle began to tumble forward, and they were encased for an instant in a world of eerie blue before they plunged onward into the blackness below.

SHEAR ZONE
WEDNESDAY, OCTOBER 6
3:51 P.M.

Sarah opened her eyes and saw a huge blue star-burst, streaks radiating outward in all directions. Her forehead was icy cold, and she had terrible pain in her neck. Tentatively, she shifted her body, checking each of her limbs. They hurt, but she could move all of them except her right leg, which was pinned under something. She coughed and paused, taking stock. She was lying on her side, her face shoved up against the windshield, which she had shattered with her forehead. Her eyes were just inches from the fractured glass. She eased away, and slowly looked around.

It was dark, a kind of twilight. Faint light coming from somewhere to her left. But she could see that the whole cab of the snowtrack was lying on its side, the treads up against the ice wall. They must have landed on a ledge of some kind. She looked upward—the mouth of the crevasse was surprisingly close, maybe thirty or forty yards above her. It was near enough to give her a burst of encouragement.

Next she looked down, trying to see Evans. But it was dark everywhere beneath her. She couldn't see him at all. Her eyes slowly adjusted. She gasped. She saw her true situation.

There was no ledge.

The snowtrack had tumbled into the narrowing crevasse, and wedged itself sideways within the crevasse walls. The treads were against one wall, the roof of the cab against the other, and the cab itself was suspended over the inky downward gash. The door on Evans's side hung open.

Evans was not in the cab.

He had fallen out.

Into the blackness.

"Peter?"

No answer.

"Peter, can you hear me?"

She listened. There was nothing. No sound or movement.

Nothing at all.

And then the realization hit her: *She was alone down there.* A hundred feet down in a freezing crevasse, in the middle of a trackless ice field, far off the road, miles from anywhere.

And she realized, with a chill, that this was going to be her tomb.

Bolden—or whoever he was—had planned it very well, Sarah thought. He had taken their transponder. He could drive a few miles, drop it down the deepest crevasse he could find, and then go back to the base. When the rescue parties set out, they would head for the transponder. It would be nowhere near where she was. The party might search for days in a deep crevasse before giving up.

And if they widened the search? They still wouldn't find the snowtrack. Even though it was only about forty yards below the surface, it might as well be four hundred yards below. It was too deep to be seen by a passing helicopter, or even a vehicle as it drove by. Not that any vehicle would. They would think the snowtrack had gone off the marked road, and they would search along the edge of the road. Not way out here, in the middle of the ice field. The road was seventeen miles long. They would spend days searching.

No, Sarah thought. They would never find her.

And even if she could get herself to the surface, what then? She had no compass, no map, no GPS. No radio—it lay smashed beneath her knee. She didn't even know in what direction Weddell Station might be from her present location.

Of course, she thought, she had a bright red parka that would be visible from a distance, and she had supplies, food, equipment—all the equipment that guy had talked about, before they set out. What was it, exactly? She vaguely remembered something about climbing supplies. Crampons and ropes.

Sarah bent down, managed to free herself from a toolbox that had pinned her foot to the floor, and then crawled to the rear of the cab, balancing carefully to avoid the gaping, wide-open door beneath her. In the perpetual twilight of the crevasse, she saw the supply locker. It was crumpled slightly from the impact, and she couldn't get it open.

She went back to the toolbox, opened it, took out a hammer and a screwdriver, and spent the better part of the next half hour trying to pry the locker open. At last, with a metallic screech, the door swung wide. She peered inside.

The locker was empty.

No food, no water, no climbing supplies. No space blankets, no heaters.

Nothing at all.

Sarah took a deep breath, let it out slowly. She remained calm, refusing to panic. She considered her options. Without ropes and crampons, she could not get to the surface. What could she use instead? She had a toolbox. Could she use the screwdriver as an ice axe? Probably too small. Perhaps she could disassemble the gearshift and make an ice axe out of the parts. Or perhaps she could take apart some of the tread and find parts to use.

She had no crampons, but if she could find sharp pointed things, screws or something like that, she could push them through the soles of her boots and then climb. And for a rope? Some sort of cloth perhaps . . . She looked around the interior. Maybe she could tear the fabric off the seats? Or cut it off in strips? That might work.

In this way, she kept her spirits up. She kept herself moving forward. Even if her chance of success was small, there was still a chance. A *chance*.

She focused on that.

Where was Kenner? What would he do when he heard the radio message? He probably had, already. Would he come back to Weddell? Almost certainly. And he would look for that guy, the one they thought of as Bolden. But Sarah was pretty sure that guy had disappeared.

And with his disappearance, her hopes for rescue.

The crystal of her watch was smashed. She didn't know how long she had been down there, but she noticed that it was darker than before. The gap above her was not as bright. Either the weather on the surface was changing, or the sun was low on the horizon. That would mean she had been down there for two or three hours already.

She was aware of a stiffening in her body—not just from the fall, but also, she realized, because she was cold. The cab had lost its heat.

It occurred to her that perhaps she could start the motor, and get heat going. It was worth a try. She flicked on the headlights, and one of them worked, glaring off the ice wall. So there was still electricity from the battery.

She turned the key. The generator made a grinding sound. The engine did not kick on.

And she heard a voice yell, "Hey!"

Sarah looked up, toward the surface. She saw nothing but the gap and the strip of gray sky beyond.

"Hey!"

She squinted. Was somebody really up there? She yelled back: "Hey! I'm down here!"

"I know where you are," the voice said.

And then she realized the voice was coming from *below* her.

She looked down, into the depths of the crevasse.

"Peter?" she said.

"I'm fucking freezing," he said. His voice floated up from the darkness.

"Are you hurt?"

"No, I don't think so. I don't know. I can't move. I'm wedged in some kind of cleft or something."

"How far down are you?"

"I don't know. I can't turn my head to look up. I'm stuck, Sarah." His voice trembled. He sounded frightened.

"Can you move at all?" she said.

"Just one arm."

"Can you see anything?"

"Ice. I see a blue wall. It's about two feet away."

Sarah was straddling the open door, peering down into the crevasse, straining to see. It was very dark down there. But it seemed as if the crevasse narrowed quickly, farther down. If so, he might not be that far beneath her.

"Peter. Move your arm. Can you move your arm?"

"Yes."

"Wave it."

"I am."

She didn't see anything. Just darkness.

"Okay," she said. "Stop."

"Did you see me?"

"No."

"Shit." He coughed. "It's really cold, Sarah."

"I know. Hang on."

She had to find a way to see down into the cleft. She looked under the dashboard, near where the fire extinguisher was clipped to the car wall. If there was a fire extinguisher, there was probably a flashlight there, too. They would be sure to have a flashlight . . . someplace.

Not under the dashboard.

Maybe the glove compartment. She opened it, shoved her hand in, feeling in the darkness. Crunching paper. Her fingers closed around a thick cylinder. She brought it out.

It was a flashlight.

She flicked it on. It worked. She shone it down into the depths of the crevasse.

"I see that," Peter said. "I see the light."

"Good," she said. "Now swing your arm again."

"I am."

"Now?"

"I'm doing it now."

She stared. "Peter, I don't see—wait a minute." She *did* see him—just the tips of his fingers in their red gloves, protruding briefly beyond the tractor treads, and the ice below.

"Peter."

"What."

"You're very near me," she said. "Just five or six feet below me."

"Great. Can you get me out?"

"I could, if I had a rope."

"There's no rope?" he said.

"No. I opened the supply chest. There's nothing at all."

"But it's not in the supply chest," he said. "It's under the seat."

"What?"

"Yeah, I saw it. The ropes and stuff are under the passenger seat."

She looked. The seat was on a steel base anchored firmly to the floor of the snowtrack. There were no doors or compartments in the base. It was difficult to maneuver around the seat to see, but she was sure: no doors. On a sudden impulse, she lifted up the seat cushion, and saw a compartment beneath it. The light of her flashlight revealed ropes, hooks, snow axes, crampons . . .

"Got it," she said. "You were right. It's all here."

"Whew," he said.

She brought the equipment out carefully, making sure none of it fell through the open door. Already her fingers were growing numb, and she felt clumsy as she held a fifty-foot length of nylon rope with a three-pronged ice hook at one end.

"Peter," she said. "If I lower a rope, can you grab it?"

"Maybe. I think so."

"Can you hold the rope tight, so I can pull you out?"

"I don't know. I just have the one arm free. The other one's pinned under me."

"Are you strong enough to hold the rope with one arm?"

"I don't know. I don't think so. I mean, if I got my body partway out, and lost my grip . . ." His voice broke off. He sounded on the verge of tears.

"Okay," she said. "Don't worry."

"I'm *trapped*, Sarah!"

"No, you're not."

"I am, I'm trapped, I'm fucking trapped!" Now there was panic. "I'm going to die here!"

"Peter. Stop." She was coiling the rope around her waist as she spoke. "It's going to be all right. I have a plan."

"What plan?"

"I'm going to lower an ice hook on the rope," she said. "Can you hook it onto something? Like your belt?"

"Not my belt . . . No. I'm wedged in here, Sarah. I can't move. I can't reach my belt."

She was trying to visualize his situation. He must be wedged in some sort of cleft in the ice. It was frightening just to imagine it. No wonder he was scared. "Peter," she said, "can you hook it onto anything?"

"I'll try."

"Okay, here it comes," she said, lowering the rope. The hook disappeared into the darkness. "Do you see it?"

"I see it."

"Can you reach it?"

"No."

"Okay, I'll swing it toward you." She turned her wrist gently, starting the rope in a lateral swing. The hook vanished out of sight, then swung back, then out of sight again.

"I can't . . . keep doing it, Sarah."

"I am."

"I can't get it, Sarah."

"Keep trying."

"It has to be lower."

"Okay. How much lower?"

"About a foot."

"Okay." She lowered it a foot. "How's that?"

"Good, now swing it."

She did. She heard him grunting, but each time the hook swung back into view.

"I can't do it, Sarah."

"Yes you can. Keep trying."

"I can't. My fingers are too cold."

"Keep trying," she said. "Here it is again."

"I can't, Sarah, I can't . . . Hey!"

"What?"

"I almost got it."

Looking down, she saw the hook spinning when it came back into view. He'd touched it.

"Once more," she said. "You'll do it, Peter."

"I'm trying, it's just I have so little—I got it, Sarah. *I got it!*"

She gave a long sigh of relief.

He was coughing in the darkness. She waited.

"Okay," he said. "I got it hooked on my jacket."

"Where?"

"Right on the front. Just on my chest."

She was visualizing that if the hook ripped free, it would tear right into his chin. "No, Peter. Hook it on the armpit."

"I can't, unless you pull me out a couple of feet."

"Okay. Say when."

He coughed. "Listen, Sarah. Are you strong enough to pull me out?"

She had avoided thinking about that. She just

assumed that somehow she could. Of course she didn't know how hard he was wedged in, but . . . "Yes," she said. "I can do it."

"Are you sure? I weigh a hundred and sixty." He coughed again. "Maybe a little more. Maybe ten more."

"I've got you tied off on the steering wheel."

"Okay, but . . . don't drop me."

"I won't drop you, Peter."

There was a pause. "How much do you weigh?"

"Peter, you never ask a lady that question. Especially in LA."

"We're not in LA."

"I don't know how much I weigh," she said. Of course she knew exactly. She weighed a hundred and thirty-seven pounds. He weighed over thirty pounds more than that. "But I know I can pull you up," she said. "Are you ready?"

"Shit."

"Peter, are you ready or not?"

"Yeah. Go."

She drew the rope tight, then crouched down, planting her feet firmly on either side of the open door. She felt like a sumo wrestler at the start of a match. But she knew her legs were much stronger than her arms. This was the only way she could do it. She took a deep breath.

"Ready?" she said.

"I guess."

Sarah began to stand upright, her legs burning with effort. The rope stretched taut, then moved upward—slowly at first, just a few inches. But it was moving.

It was moving.

* * *

"Okay, stop. Stop!"

"What?"

"*Stop!*"

"Okay." She was in mid-crouch. "But I can't hold this for long."

"Don't hold it at all. Let it out. Slowly. About three feet."

She realized that she must have already pulled him part of the way out of the cleft. His voice sounded better, much less frightened, though he was coughing almost continuously.

"Peter?"

"Minute. I'm hooking it on my belt."

"Okay . . ."

"I can see up now," he said. "I can see the tread. The tread is about six feet above my head."

"Okay."

"But when you pull me up, the rope's going to rub on the edge of the tread."

"It'll be okay," she said.

"And I'll be hanging right over the, uh . . ."

"I won't let you go, Peter."

He coughed for a while. She waited. He said, "Tell me when you're ready."

"I'm ready."

"Then let's get this over with," he said, "before I get scared."

There was only one bad moment. She had pulled him up about four feet, and he came free of the cleft, and she suddenly took the full weight of his body. It shocked her; the rope slid three feet down. He howled.

"Sar-ah!"

She gripped the rope, stopped it. "Sorry."

"Fuck!"

"Sorry." She adjusted to the added weight, started pulling again. She was groaning with the effort but it was not long before she saw his hand appear above the tread, and he gripped it, and began to haul himself over. Then two hands, and his head appeared.

That shocked her, too. His face was covered in thick blood, his hair matted red. But he was smiling.

"Keep pulling, sister."

"I am, Peter. I am."

Only after he finally had scrambled into the cab did Sarah sink to the floor. Her legs began to shake violently. Her body trembled all over. Evans, lying on his side, coughing and wheezing beside her, hardly noticed. Eventually the trembling passed. She found the first-aid kit and began to clean his face up.

"It's only a superficial cut," she said, "but you'll need stitches."

"If we ever get out of here . . ."

"We'll get out, all right."

"I'm glad you're confident." He looked out the window at the ice above. "You done much ice climbing?"

She shook her head. "But I've done plenty of rock climbing. How different can it be?"

"More slippery? And what happens when we get up there?" he said.

"I don't know."

"We have no idea where to go."

"We'll follow the guy's snowtracks."

"If they're still there. If they haven't blown away. And you know it's at least seven or eight miles to Weddell."

"Peter," she said.

"If a storm comes up, maybe we're better off down here."

"I'm not staying here," she said. "If I'm going to die, I'll die in daylight."

The actual climb up the crevasse wall was not so bad, once Sarah got used to the way she had to kick her boots with the crampons, and how hard she had to swing the axe to make it bite into the ice. It took her only seven or eight minutes to cover the distance, and clamber onto the surface.

The surface looked exactly the same as before. The same dim sunlight, the same gray horizon that blended with the ground. The same gray, featureless world.

She helped Evans up. His cut was bleeding again, and his mask was red, frozen stiff against his face.

"Shit it's cold," he said. "Which way, do you think?"

Sarah was looking at the sun. It was low on the horizon, but was it sinking, or rising? And which direction did the sun indicate, anyway, when you were at the South pole? She frowned: She couldn't work it out, and she didn't dare make a mistake.

"We'll follow the tracks," she said at last. She took off her crampons and started walking.

She had to admit, Peter was right about one thing: It was much colder here on the surface. After half an hour, the wind came up, blowing strongly; they had to lean into it as they trudged forward. Worse, the snow began to blow across the ground beneath their feet. Which meant—

"We're losing the tracks," Evans said.

"I know."

"They're getting blown away."

"I *know*." Sometimes he was such a baby. What did he expect her to do about the wind?

"What do we do?" he said.

"I don't *know*, Peter. I've never been lost in Antarctica before."

"Well, me neither."

They trudged onward.

"But it was your idea to come up here."

"Peter. Pull yourself together."

"Pull myself together? It's fucking freezing, Sarah. I can't feel my nose or my ears or my fingers or my toes or—"

"Peter." She grabbed him by the shoulders and shook him. *"Shut up!"*

He was silent. Through slots in his facemask, he stared out at her. His eyelashes were white with ice.

"I can't feel my nose either," Sarah said. "We have to keep a grip."

She looked around, turning a full circle, trying to conceal her own growing desperation. The wind was blowing more snow now. It was becoming harder to see. The world was flatter and grayer, with almost no sense of depth. If this weather continued, they would soon not be able to see the ground well enough to avoid the crevasses.

Then they would have to stop where they were.

In the middle of nowhere.

He said, "You're beautiful when you're angry, you know that?"

"Peter, for Christ's sake."

"Well, you are."

She started walking, looking down at the ground, trying to see the tread marks. "Come on, Peter." Perhaps the tracks would return soon to the road. If they did, the road would be easier to follow in a storm. And safer for walking.

"I think I'm falling in love, Sarah."

"Peter . . ."

"I had to tell you. This may be my last chance." He started coughing again.

"Save your breath, Peter."

"Fucking freezing."

They stumbled on, no longer speaking. The wind howled. Sarah's parka was pressed flat against her body. It became harder and harder to move forward. But she pressed on. She did not know how much longer she continued in that way before she raised a hand, and stopped. Evans must not have been able to see her, because he walked into her back, grunted, and stopped.

They had to put their heads together and shout to hear each other above the wind.

"We have to stop!" she yelled.

"I know!"

And then, because she didn't know what else to do, she sat down on the ground and pulled her legs up and lowered her head to her knees, and tried not to cry. The wind grew louder and louder. Now it was shrieking. The air was thick with flying snow.

Evans sat down beside her. "We're going to fucking die," he said.

She started shivering, little tremulous bursts at first, and then almost continuously. She felt as if she were having a seizure. From skiing, she knew what that meant. Her core temperature had dropped dangerously, and the shivering was an automatic physiological attempt to warm her body up.

Her teeth chattered. It was hard to speak. But her mind was still working, still looking for a way out. "Isn't there a way to build a snow house?"

Evans said something. The wind whipped his words away.

"Do you know how?" she said.

He didn't answer her.

But it was too late, anyway, she thought. She was losing control of her body. She could hardly even keep her arms wrapped around her knees, the shaking was so bad.

And she was starting to feel sleepy.

She looked over at Evans. He was lying on his side on the ice.

She nudged him to get up. She kicked him. He didn't move. She wanted to yell at him but she couldn't, because her teeth were chattering so badly.

Sarah fought to retain consciousness, but the desire to sleep was becoming overpowering. She struggled to keep her eyes open and, to her astonishment, began to see swift scenes from her life—her childhood, her mother, her kindergarten class, ballet lessons, the high school prom . . .

Her whole life was passing before her. Just like the books said happened, right before you died. And when she looked up, she saw a light in the distance, just like they said happened. A light at the end of a long, dark tunnel . . .

She couldn't fight it any longer. She lay down. She couldn't feel the ground anyway. She was lost in her own, private world of pain and exhaustion. And the light before her was growing brighter and brighter, and now there were two other lights, blinking yellow and green . . .

Yellow and green?

She fought the sleepiness. She tried to push herself upright again, but she couldn't. Her muscles were too weak, her arms blocks of frozen ice. She couldn't move.

Yellow and green lights, growing larger. And a white light in the center. Very white, like halogen. She was starting to see details through the swirling snow. There was a silver dome, and wheels, and large glowing letters. The letters said—

NASA.

She coughed. The thing emerged from the snow. It was some kind of small vehicle—about three feet high, no larger than those Sunday lawn-mowers that people drove around on. It had big wheels and a flattened dome, and it was beeping as it came directly toward her.

In fact, it was going to drive right over her. She realized it without concern. She could do nothing to prevent it. She lay on the ground, dazed, indifferent. The wheels grew larger and larger. The last thing she remembered was a mechanical voice saying, "Hello. Hello. Please move out of the way. Thank you very much for your cooperation. Hello. Hello. Please move out of the way . . ."

And then nothing.

Darkness. Pain. Harsh voices.

Pain.

Rubbing. All over her body, arms and legs. Like fire rubbed on her body.

She groaned.

A voice spoke, rasping and distant. It sounded like "Coffee grounds."

The rubbing continued, brisk and harsh and excruciating. And a sound like sandpaper—scratching, rough, terrible.

Something struck her in the face, on the mouth. She licked her lips. It was snow. Freezing snow.

"Cousins set?" a voice said.

"Nod eely."

It was a foreign language, Chinese or something. Sarah heard several voices now. She tried to open her eyes but could not. Her eyes were held shut by something heavy over her face, like a mask, or—

She tried to reach up, but couldn't. All her limbs were held down. And the rubbing continued, rubbing, rubbing . . .

She groaned. She tried to speak.

"Thin song now whore nod?"

"Don thin song."

"Kee pub yar wok."

Pain.

They rubbed her, whoever they were, while she lay immobilized in darkness, and gradually more sensation returned to her limbs and to her face. She was not glad for it. The pain grew worse and worse. She felt as if she were burned everywhere on her body.

The voices seemed to float around her, disembodied. There were more of them now. Four, five—she was not sure anymore. All women, it sounded like.

And now they were doing something else, she realized. Violating her. Sticking something in her body. Dull and cold. Not painful. Cold.

The voices floated, slithered all around her. At her head, at her feet. Touching her roughly.

It was a dream. Or death. Maybe she was dead, she thought. She felt oddly detached about it. The pain made her detached. And then she heard a woman's voice in her ear, very close to her ear, and very distinct. The voice said:

"Sarah."

She moved her mouth.

"Sarah, are you awake?"

She nodded slightly.

"I am going to take the icepack off your face, all right?"

She nodded. The weight, the mask was lifted.

"Open your eyes. Slowly."

She did. She was in a dimly lit room with white walls. A monitor to one side, a tangle of green lines. It was like a hospital room. A woman looked down at her with concern. The woman wore a white nurse's uniform and a down vest. The room was cold. Sarah could see her breath.

She said, "Don't try to speak."

Sarah didn't.

"You're dehydrated. It'll be a few hours yet. We're bringing your temperature up slowly. You're very lucky, Sarah. You're not going to lose anything."

Not lose anything.

She felt alarmed. Her mouth moved. Her tongue was dry, thick feeling. A sort of hissing sound came from her throat.

"Don't speak," the woman said. "It's too soon. Is your pain bad? Yes? I'll give you something for it." She raised a syringe. "Your friend saved your life, you know. He managed to get to his feet, and open the radiophone on the NASA robot. That's how we knew where to find you."

Her lips moved.

"He's in the next room. We think he'll be all right, too. Now just rest."

She felt something cold in her veins.

Her eyes closed.

The nurses left Peter Evans alone to get dressed. He put on his clothes slowly, taking stock of himself. He was all right, he decided, though his ribs hurt when he breathed. He had a big bruise on the left side of his chest, another big bruise on his thigh, and an ugly purple welt on his shoulder. A line of stitches on his scalp. His whole body was stiff and aching. It was excruciating to put on his socks and shoes.

But he was all right. In fact, better than that— he felt new somehow, almost reborn. Out there on the ice, he had been certain he was going to die. How he found the strength to get to his feet, he did not know. He had felt Sarah kicking him, but he did not respond to her. Then he'd heard the beeping sound. And when he looked up, he saw the letters "NASA."

He'd realized vaguely that it was some kind of vehicle. So there must be a driver. The front tires had stopped just inches from his body. He managed to get to his knees, and haul himself up over the tires, grabbing onto the struts. He hadn't understood why the driver hadn't climbed out and helped him. Finally, he managed to get to his knees in the howling wind. He realized that the vehicle was low and bulbous, barely four feet off the ground. It was too small for any human operator—it was some kind of robot. He scraped snow away from the dome-like shell. The lettering read, "NASA Remote Vehicle Meteorite Survey."

The vehicle was talking, repeating a taped voice over and over. Evans couldn't understand what it was saying because of the wind. He brushed away the snow, thinking there must be some method of communication, some antenna, some—

Then his fingers had touched a panel with a finger hole. He pulled it open. Inside he saw a telephone—a regular telephone handset, bright red. He held it to his frozen mask. He could not hear anything from it, but he said, "Hello? Hello?"

Nothing more.

He collapsed again.

But the nurses told him what he had done was enough to send a signal to the NASA station at Patriot Hills. NASA had notified Weddell, who sent out a search party, and found them in ten minutes. They were both still alive, barely.

That had been more than twenty-four hours ago.

It had taken the medical team twelve hours to bring their body temperatures back to normal, because, the nurse said, it had to be done slowly. They told Evans he was going to be fine, but he might lose a couple of his toes. They would have to wait and see. It would be a few days.

His feet were bandaged with some kind of protective splints around the toes. He couldn't fit into his regular shoes, but they had found him an oversized pair of sneakers. They looked like they belonged to a basketball player. On Evans, they made huge clown feet. But he could wear them, and there wasn't much pain.

Tentatively, he stood. He was tremulous, but he was all right.

The nurse came back. "Hungry?"

He shook his head. "Not yet."

"Pain?"

He shook his head. "Just, you know, everywhere."

"That'll get worse," she said. She gave him a small bottle of pills. "Take one of these every four hours if you need it. And you'll probably need it to sleep, for the next few days."

"And Sarah?"

"Sarah will be another half hour or so."

"Where's Kenner?"

"I think he's in the computer room."

"Which way is that?"

She said, "Maybe you better lean on my shoulder . . ."

"I'm fine," he said. "Just tell me the way."

She pointed, and he started walking. But he was more unsteady than he realized. His muscles weren't working right; he felt shaky all over. He started to fall. The nurse quickly ducked, sliding her shoulder under his arm.

"Tell you what," she said. "I'll just show you the way."

This time he did not object.

* * *

Kenner sat in the computer room with the bearded station chief, MacGregor, and Sanjong Thapa. Everybody was looking grim.

"We found him," Kenner said, pointing to a computer monitor. "Recognize your friend?"

Evans looked at the screen. "Yeah," he said. "That's the bastard."

On the screen was a photo of the man Evans knew as Bolden. But the ID form onscreen gave his name as David R. Kane. Twenty-six years old. Born Minneapolis. BA, Notre Dame; MA, University of Michigan. Current Status: PhD candidate in oceanography, University of Michigan, Ann Arbor. Research Project: Dynamics of Ross Shelf Flow as measured by GPS sensors. Thesis Advisor/ Project Supervisor: James Brewster, University of Michigan.

"His name's Kane," the Weddell chief said. "He's been here for a week, along with Brewster."

"Where is he now?" Evans said darkly.

"No idea. He didn't come back to the Station today. Neither did Brewster. We think they may have gone to McMurdo and hopped the morning transport out. We have a call in to McMurdo to do a vehicle count, but they haven't gotten back to us yet."

"You're sure he's not still here?" Evans said.

"Quite sure. You need an ID tag to open the exterior doors here, so we always know who's where. Neither Kane nor Brewster opened any doors in the last twelve hours. They aren't here."

"So you think they may be on the plane?"

"McMurdo Tower wasn't sure. They're pretty

casual about the daily transport—if somebody wants to go, they just hop on and leave. It's a C-130, so there's always plenty of room. You see, a lot of the research grants don't permit you to leave during the period of your research, but people have birthdays and family events back on the mainland. So they just go, and come back. It's unrecorded."

"If I recall," Kenner said, "Brewster came here with two graduate students. Where's the other one?"

"Interesting. He left from McMurdo yesterday, the day you arrived."

"So they all got out," Kenner said. "Got to give them credit: They're smart." He looked at his watch. "Now let's see what, if anything, they left behind."

The name on the door said "Dave Kane, U. Mich." Evans pushed it open, and saw a small room, an unmade bed, a small desk with a messy stack of papers, and four cans of Diet Coke. There was a suitcase lying open in the corner.

"Let's get started," Kenner said. "I'll take the bed and the suitcase. You check the desk."

Evans began to go through the papers on the desk. They all seemed to be reprints of research articles. Some were stamped U MICH GEO LIB followed by a number.

"Window dressing," Kenner said, when he was shown the papers. "He brought those papers with him. Anything else? Anything personal?"

Evans didn't see anything of interest. Some of the papers were highlighted in yellow marker.

There was a stack of 3-by-5 notecards, with some notes written on them, but they seemed to be genuine, and related to the stack of papers.

"You don't suppose this guy is really a graduate student?"

"Could be, though I doubt it. Eco-terrorists aren't usually well educated."

There were pictures of glacier flows, and satellite images of various sorts. Evans shuffled through them quickly. Then he paused at one:

ISS006.ESC1.03003375 SCORPION B

What caught his eye was the caption. "Listen," he said, "on that list of four locations, wasn't one of them called 'Scorpion'?"

"Yes . . ."

"It's right here, in Antarctica," Evans said. "Look at this."

Kenner started to say, "But it can't be—" and abruptly broke off. "This is extremely interesting, Peter. Well done. It was in that stack? Good. Anything else?"

Despite himself, Evans felt pleased by Kenner's approval. He searched quickly. A moment later he said, "Yes. There's another one."

ISS006.ESC1.03003375 SCORPION B

"It's the same basic pattern of rock outcrops in the snow," Evans said, excitedly. "And, I don't know about these faint lines . . . roads? Rocks covered in snow?"

"Yes," Kenner said. "I think that's almost certainly correct."

"And if they're aerial photographs, there must be a way to trace them. Do you think these numbers are references of some kind?"

"There's no question." Kenner pulled out a small pocket magnifying glass, and scanned the image, peering closely. "Yes, Peter. Very well done."

Evans beamed.

From the doorway, MacGregor said, "You found something? Can I help?"

"I don't think so," Kenner said. "We'll deal with this ourselves."

Evans said, "But maybe he will recognize—"

"No," Kenner said. "We'll get the ID off the NASA image files. Let's continue."

They searched in silence for several minutes

more. Kenner took out a pocketknife and began cutting the lining of the suitcase lying open in the corner of the room. "Ah." He straightened. In his fingers, he held two curved arcs of pale rubber.

"What are those?" Evans said. "Silicon?"

"Or something very similar. A kind of soft plastic, at any rate." Kenner seemed very pleased.

"What're they for?" Evans said.

"I have no idea," Kenner said. He resumed his search of the suitcase. Privately, Evans wondered why Kenner was so pleased. Probably he was not saying what he knew in front of MacGregor. But what could two bits of rubber mean, anyway? What could they be used for?

Evans went through the documents on the desk a second time, but found nothing more. He lifted the desk lamp and looked under the base. He crouched down and looked under the desk, in case something was taped there. He found nothing.

Kenner closed the suitcase. "As I thought, nothing more. We were very lucky to find what we did." He turned to MacGregor. "Where's Sanjong?"

"In the server room, doing what you requested—cutting Brewster and his team out of the system."

The "server room" was hardly larger than a closet. There were twin racks of processors running floor to ceiling, and the usual mesh ceiling for cabling. There was a master terminal in the room, on a small steel table. Sanjong was crowded in there with a Weddell technician at his side, looking frustrated.

Kenner and Evans stood outside, in the hallway. Evans was pleased that he felt steady enough to stand. His strength was coming back quickly.

"It hasn't been easy," Sanjong said to Kenner. "The procedure here is to give each Weddell researcher private storage space and also direct radio and Internet connections. And these three guys knew how to take advantage of it. Apparently the third man with Brewster was the computer guy. Within a day of his arrival, he got into the system as root, and installed back doors and trojans all over the place. We're not sure how many. We're trying to get them out."

"He also added a few dummy user accounts," the technician said.

"Like about twenty," Sanjong said. "But I'm not worried about those. They're probably just that—dummies. If this guy was smart—and he was—he'd have given himself access to the system through an existing user, so he'd go undetected. We're looking now for any users who have added a new secondary password in the last week. But this system doesn't have a lot of maintenance utilities. It's slow going."

"What about the trojans?" Kenner said. "How are they timed?" In computer slang, a trojan was an innocent-looking program installed in the system. It was designed to wake up at a later time and carry out some action. It derived its name from the way the Greeks won the Trojan war—by making a huge horse and presenting it to the Trojans as a gift. Once the horse was within the walls of Troy, the Greek soliders who had been hiding inside it came out and attacked the city.

The classic trojan was one installed by a disgruntled employee. It erased all the hard drives in a business three months after the employee was fired. But there were many variations.

"Timing on all of the ones I found here is short," Sanjong said. "One day, two days from now. We found one that is three days from now. Nothing after that."

"So. Just as we suspected," Kenner said.

"Exactly," Sanjong said, nodding. "They intended it to happen soon."

"Intended what?" Evans said.

"The calving of the big iceberg," Kenner said.

"Why soon? They would still have been here."

"I'm not sure they would have. But in any case the timing was determined by something else."

"Yes? What?" Evans said.

Kenner gave him a look. "We can go into it later." He turned back to Sanjong. "And what about the radio connects?"

"We disabled all the direct connects right away," he said. "And I assume you did work on the ground at the location itself."

"I did," Kenner said.

"What did you do on the ground?" Evans said.

"Random disconnects."

"Of what?"

"Tell you later."

"So we're redundant," Sanjong said.

"No. Because we can't be sure there's not someone else embedded in this place who will undo our work."

"I wish," Evans said, "I knew what the hell you guys were talking about . . ."

"*Later,*" Kenner said. This time the look was sharp.

Evans was silent. He felt a little wounded.

MacGregor said, "Ms. Jones is awake, and getting dressed."

"All right," Kenner said. "I believe our work here is done. Wheels up in an hour."

"To go where?" Evans said.

"I thought that was obvious," Kenner said. "Helsinki, Finland."

The plane flew back through the dazzling morning light. Sarah was sleeping. Sanjong was working on his laptop. Kenner stared out the window.

Evans said, "All right, what did you disconnect randomly?"

"The cone charges," Kenner said. "They were laid out in a precise pattern, four hundred meters apart. I disconnected fifty at random, mostly along the eastern end of the line. That will suffice to prevent the standing wave from being generated."

"So, no iceberg?"

"That's the idea."

"And why are we going to Helsinki?"

"We're not. I only said that for the benefit of the technician. We're going to Los Angeles."

"Okay. And why are we going to Los Angeles?"

"Because that's where the NERF Conference on Abrupt Climate Change is being held."

"This is all related to the conference?"

Kenner nodded.

"These guys are trying to break off an iceberg to coincide with the conference?"

"Exactly. All part of any good starburst media

plan. You arrange an event with good visuals that reinforces the point of the conference."

"You seem awfully calm about it," Evans said.

"It's the way things are done, Peter." Kenner shrugged. "Environmental concerns don't come to the public's attention by accident, you know."

"What do you mean?"

"Well, take your favorite fear, global warming. The arrival of global warming was announced dramatically by a prominent climatologist, James Hansen, in 1988. He gave testimony before a joint House and Senate committee headed by Senator Wirth of Colorado. Hearings were scheduled for June, so Hansen could deliver his testimony during a blistering heat wave. It was a setup from the beginning."

"That doesn't bother me," Evans said. "It's legitimate to use a government hearing as a way to make the public aware—"

"Really? So you're saying that in your mind, there's no difference between a government hearing and a press conference?"

"I'm saying hearings have been used that way many times before."

"True. But it is unquestionably manipulative. And Hansen's testimony wasn't the only instance of media manipulation that's occurred in the course of the global warming sales campaign. Don't forget the last-minute changes in the 1995 IPCC report."

"IPCC? What last-minute changes?"

"The UN formed the Intergovernmental Panel on Climate Change in the late 1980s. That's the

IPCC, as you know—a huge group of bureaucrats, and scientists under the thumb of bureaucrats. The idea was that since this was a global problem, the UN would track climate research and issue reports every few years. The first assessment report in 1990 said it would be very difficult to detect a human influence on climate, although everybody was concerned that one might exist. But the 1995 report announced with conviction that there was now 'a discernable human influence' on climate. You remember that?"

"Vaguely."

"Well, the claim of 'a discernable human influence' was written into the 1995 summary report after the scientists themselves had gone home. Originally, the document said scientists couldn't detect a human influence on climate for sure, and they didn't know when they would. They said explicitly, 'we don't know.' That statement was deleted, and replaced with a new statement that a discernable human influence did indeed exist. It was a major change."

"Is that true?" Evans said.

"Yes. Changing the document caused a stir among scientists at the time, with opponents and defendants of the change coming forward. If you read their claims and counter-claims, you can't be sure who's telling the truth. But this is the Internet age. You can find the original documents and the list of changes online and decide for yourself. A review of the actual text changes makes it crystal clear that the IPCC is a political organization, not a scientific one."

Evans frowned. He wasn't sure how to answer. He'd heard of the IPCC, of course, although he didn't know much about it. . . .

"But my question is simpler, Peter. If something is real, if it is a genuine problem that requires action, why does anybody have to exaggerate their claims? Why do there have to be carefully executed media campaigns?"

"I can give you a simple answer," Evans said. "The media is a crowded marketplace. People are bombarded by thousands of messages every minute. You have to speak loudly—and yes, maybe exaggerate a little—if you want to get their attention. And try to mobilize the entire world to sign the Kyoto treaty."

"Well, let's consider that. When Hansen announced in the summer of 1988 that global warming was here, he predicted temperatures would increase .35 degrees Celsius over the next ten years. Do you know what the actual increase was?"

"I'm sure you'll tell me it was less than that."

"*Much* less, Peter. Dr. Hansen overestimated by three hundred percent. The actual increase was .11 degrees."

"Okay. But it *did* increase."

"And ten years after his testimony, he said that the forces that govern climate change are so poorly understood that long-term prediction is impossible."

"He did not say that."

Kenner sighed. "Sanjong?"

Sanjong pecked at his laptop. "Proceedings of

the National Academy of Sciences, October 1998."*

"Hansen didn't say that prediction was *impossible*."

"He said, quote, 'The forcings that drive long-term climate change are not known with an accuracy sufficient to define future climate change,' endquote. And he argued that, in the future, scientists should use multiple scenarios to define a range of possible climate outcomes."

"Well that isn't exactly—"

"Stop quibbling," Kenner said. "He said it. Why do you think Balder is worried about his witnesses in the Vanutu case? It's because of statements like these. However you attempt to reframe it, it's a clear statement of limited knowledge. And it's hardly the only one. The IPCC itself made many limiting statements."†

"But Hansen still believes in global warming."

"Yes, he does. And his 1988 prediction," Kenner said, "was wrong by three hundred percent."

"So what?"

"You are ignoring the implication of an error that large," Kenner said. "Compare it to other fields.

---

* James E. Hansen, Makiko Sato, Andrew Lacis, Reto Ruedy, Ina Tegen, and Elaine Matthews, "Climate Forcings in the Industrial Era," *Proceedings of the National Academy of Sciences* 95 (October 1998): 12753–58.

† IPCC. *Climate Change 2001: The Scientific Basis.* Cambridge, UK: Cambridge University Press, 2001, p. 774: "In climate research and modelling [*sic*], we should recognize that we are dealing with a coupled non-linear chaotic system, and therefore that the long-term prediction of future climate states is not possible." See also: IPCC. *Climate Change 1995: The Science of Climate Change*, p. 330. "Natural climate variability on long time-scales will continue to be problematic for CO_2 climate change analysis and detection."

For example, when NASA launched the rocket carrying the Mars Rover, they announced that in two hundred and fifty-three days, the Rover would land on the surface of Mars at 8:11 P.M., California time. In fact, it landed at 8:35 P.M. That is an error of a few *thousandths* of a percent. The NASA people knew what they were talking about."

"Okay, fine. But there are some things you have to estimate."

"You're absolutely right," Kenner said. "People estimate all the time. They estimate sales, they estimate profits, they estimate delivery dates, they estimate—by the way, do you estimate your taxes for the government?"

"Yes. Quarterly."

"How accurate does that estimate have to be?"

"Well, there's no fixed rule—"

"Peter. How accurate, without penalty?"

"Maybe fifteen percent."

"So if you were off by three hundred percent, you'd pay a penalty?"

"Yes."

"Hansen was off by three hundred percent."

"Climate is not a tax return."

"In the real world of human knowledge," Kenner said, "to be wrong by three hundred percent is taken as an indication you don't have a good grasp on what you are estimating. If you got on an airplane and the pilot said it was a three-hour flight, but you arrived in one hour, would you think that pilot was knowledgeable or not?"

Evans sighed. "Climate is more complicated than that."

"Yes, Peter. Climate *is* more complicated. It is

so complicated that no one has been able to predict future climate with accuracy. Even though billions of dollars are being spent, and hundreds of people are trying all around the world. Why do you resist that uncomfortable truth?"

"Weather prediction is much better," Evans said. "And that's because of computers."

"Yes, weather prediction has improved. But nobody tries to predict weather more than ten days in advance. Whereas computer modelers are predicting what the temperature will be one hundred years in advance. Sometimes a thousand years, three thousand years."

"And they are doing better."

"Arguably they aren't. Look," Kenner said. "The biggest events in global climate are the El Niños. They happen roughly every four years. But climate models can't predict them—not their timing, their duration, or their intensity. And if you can't predict El Niños, the predictive value of your model in other areas is suspect."

"I heard they can predict El Niños."

"That was claimed in 1998. But it is not true."* Kenner shook his head. "Climate science simply isn't there yet, Peter. One day it will be. But not now."

---

* C. Landsea, et al., 2000, "How Much Skill Was There in Forecasting the Very Strong 1997–98 El Niño?" *Bulletin of the American Meteorological Society* 81: 2107-19. ". . . one could have even less confidence in anthropogenic global warming studies because of the lack of skill in predicting El Niño . . . the successes in ENSO forecasting have been overstated (sometimes drastically) and misapplied in other arenas."

Another hour passed. Sanjong was working continuously on the laptop. Kenner sat motionless, staring out the window. Sanjong was accustomed to this. He knew that Kenner could stay silent and immobile for several hours. He only turned away from the window when Sanjong swore.

"What's the matter?" Kenner said.

"I lost our satellite connection to the Internet. It's been in and out for a while."

"Were you able to trace the images?"

"Yes, that was no problem. I have the location fixed. Did Evans really think these were images from Antarctica?"

"Yes. He thought they showed black outcrops against snow. I didn't disagree with him."

"The actual location," Sanjong said, "is a place called Resolution Bay. It's in northeast Gareda."

"How far from Los Angeles?"

"Roughly six thousand nautical miles."

"So the propagation time is twelve or thirteen hours."

"Yes."

"We'll worry about it later," Kenner said. "We have other problems first."

Peter Evans slept fitfully. His bed consisted of a padded airplane seat laid flat, with a seam in the middle, right where his hip rested. He tossed and turned, waking briefly, hearing snatches of conversation between Kenner and Sanjong at the back of the plane. He couldn't hear the whole conversation over the drone of the engines. But he heard enough.

Because of what I need him to do.

He'll refuse, John.

... he likes it or not ... Evans is at the center of everything.

Peter Evans was suddenly awake. He strained to hear now. He raised his head off the pillow so he could hear better.

Didn't disagree with him.

Actual location ... Resolution Bay ... Gareda.

How far ... ?

... thousand miles ...

... the propagation time ... thirteen hours ...

He thought: *Propagation time? What the hell were they talking about?* On impulse he jumped up, strode back there, and confronted them.

Kenner didn't blink. "Sleep well?"

"No," Evans said, "I did not sleep well. I think you owe me some explanations."

"About what?"

"The satellite pictures, for one."

"I couldn't very well tell you right there in the

room, in front of the others," Kenner said. "And I hated to interrupt your enthusiasm."

Evans went and poured himself a cup of coffee. "Okay. What do the pictures really show?"

Sanjong flipped his laptop around to show Evans the screen. "Don't feel bad. You would never have had any reason to suspect. The images were negatives. They're often used that way, to increase contrast."

"Negatives . . ."

"The black rocks are actually white. They're clouds."

Evans sighed.

"And what is the land mass?"

"It's an island called Gareda, in the southern part of the Solomon chain."

"Which is . . ."

"Off the coast of New Guinea. North of Australia."

"So this is an island in the South Pacific," Evans said. "This guy in Antarctica had a picture of a Pacific island."

"Correct."

"And the SCORPION reference is . . ."

"We don't know," Sanjong said. "The actual location is called Resolution Bay on the charts. But it may be known locally as Scorpion Bay."

"And what are they planning down there?"

Kenner said, "We don't know that, either."

"I heard you talking about propagation times. Propagation times for what?"

"Actually, you misheard me," Kenner said smoothly. "I was talking about interrogation times."

"Interrogation times?" Evans said.

"Yes. We were hoping we'd be able to identify at least one of the three men in Antarctica, since we have good photographs of all three. And we know the photographs are accurate because people on the base saw them. But, I'm afraid we're out of luck."

Sanjong explained that they had transmitted photos of Brewster and the two graduate students to several databases in Washington, where pattern-recognition computers checked them against individuals with known criminal records. Sometimes you got lucky, and the computer found a match. But this time, no match had come back.

"It's been several hours, so I think we're out of luck."

"As we expected," Kenner said.

"Yes," Sanjong said. "As we expected."

"Because these guys don't have criminal records?" Evans said.

"No. They very well may."

"Then why didn't you get a match?"

"Because this is a netwar," Kenner said. "And at the moment, we are losing it."

In media accounts, Kenner explained, the Environmental Liberation Front was usually characterized as a loose association of eco-terrorists, operating in small groups on their own initiative, and employing relatively unsophisticated means to create havoc—starting fires, trashing SUVs in car lots, and so on.

The truth was quite different. Only one member of ELF had ever been apprehended—a twenty-nine-year-old graduate student at the University of California at Santa Cruz. He was caught sabotaging an oil rig in El Segundo, California. He denied any association with the group, and insisted he was acting alone.

But what troubled authorities was the fact that he was wearing an appliance on his forehead that changed the shape of his skull and made his eyebrows jut out prominently. He was also wearing false ears. It wasn't much of a disguise. But it was troubling, because it suggested that he knew quite a lot about the pattern-matching programs used by the government.

Those programs were tuned to look past changes in facial hair—wigs, beards, and mustaches—since that was the most common method of disguise. They were also designed to compensate for changes in age, such as increased heaviness in the face, drooping features, receding hairlines.

But ears didn't change. The shape of the forehead didn't change. So the programs were therefore weighted to rely on the configuration of ears, and the shape of the forehead. Changing these parts of the face would result in a "no-match" outcome on a computer.

The guy from Santa Cruz knew that. He knew security cameras would photograph him when he got near the rig. So he changed his appearance in a way that would prevent identification by computer.

Similarly, the three extremists at Weddell clearly had formidable backing to carry out their high-tech terrorist act. It took months of planning. Costs were high. And they obviously had in-depth support to obtain academic credentials, university stencils on their shipping boxes, shell companies for their Antarctic shipments, false websites, and dozens of other details necessary for the undertaking. There was nothing unsophisticated about their plan or the way they had executed it.

"And they would have succeeded," Kenner said, "except for that list George Morton obtained shortly before his death."

All of which suggested that if ELF was once a loose association of amateurs, it was no longer. Now it was a highly organized network—one that employed so many channels of communication among its members (e-mail, cell phones, radio, text messaging) that the network as a whole eluded detection. The governments of the world had long worried about how to deal with such networks, and the "netwars" that would result from trying to fight them.

"For a long time, the concept of a netwar was theoretical," Kenner said. "There were studies coming out of RAND, but nobody in the military was really focusing on it. The notion of a networked enemy, or terrorists, or even criminals was too amorphous to bother with."

But it was the amorphous quality of the network—fluid, rapidly evolving—that made it so difficult to combat. You couldn't infiltrate it. You couldn't listen in on it, except by accident. You couldn't locate it geographically because it wasn't in any one place. In truth, the network represented a radically new kind of opponent, and one that required radically new techniques to combat it.

"The military just didn't get it," Kenner said. "But like it or not, we're in a netwar right now."

"And how do you fight a netwar?" Evans said.

"The only way to oppose a network is with another network. You expand your listening posts. You decrypt around the clock. You employ techniques of networked deception and entrapment."

"Such as what?"

"It's technical," Kenner said vaguely. "We rely on the Japanese to spearhead that effort. They are the best at it in the world. And of course we extend our feelers in multiple directions at the same time. Based on what we've just learned at Weddell, we have lots of irons in the fire." Kenner had databases being searched. He had state organizations mobilized. He had inquiries into where the terrorists had obtained their academic credentials, their encrypted radio transmitters, their explosive charges, their computerized detonation timers. None of this was commonplace stuff and it could be traced, given enough time.

"Is there enough time?" Evans said.

"I'm not sure."

Evans could see that Kenner was worried. "So: What is it you want me to do?"

"Just one very simple thing," Kenner said.

"What's that?"

Kenner smiled.

III

ANGEL

"Is this really necessary?" Peter Evans said, with a worried look.

"It is," Kenner said.

"But it's illegal," Evans said.

"It's not," Kenner said firmly.

"Because you are a law-enforcement officer?" Evans said.

"Of course. Don't worry about it."

They were flying in over Los Angeles, approaching the runway at Van Nuys. The California sun shone through the windows. Sanjong was hunched over the dining table in the middle of the plane. In front of him lay Evans's cell phone, the back removed. Sanjong was attaching a thin gray plate the size of his thumbnail right on top of the battery.

"But what exactly is it?" Evans said.

"Flash memory," Sanjong said. "It'll record four hours of conversation in a compressed format."

"I see," Evans said. "And what am I supposed to do?"

"Just carry the phone in your hand, and go about your business."

"And if I get caught?" he said.

"You won't get caught," Kenner said. "You can take it anywhere. You'll go right through any security, no problem."

"But if they have bug sweepers . . ."

"They won't detect you, because you're not transmitting anything. It's got a burst transmitter. For two seconds every hour, it transmits. The rest of the time, nothing." Kenner sighed. "Look, Peter. It's just a cell phone. Everyone has them."

"I don't know," Evans said. "I feel bad about this. I mean, I'm not a stool pigeon."

Sarah came to the back, yawning, clearing her ears. "Who's a stool pigeon?"

"It's how I feel," Evans said.

"That's not the issue," Kenner said. "Sanjong?"

Sanjong took out a printed list, passed it to Evans. It was Morton's original sheet, now with additions to it:

662262	3982293	24FXE 62262 82293	TERROR	Mt. Terror, Antarctica
882320	4898432	12FXE 82232 54393	SNAKE	Snake Butte, Arizona
774548	9080799	02FXE 67533 43433	LAUGHER	Laugher Cay, Bahamas
482320	5898432	22FXE 72232 04393	SCORPION	Resolution, Solomon Is.

ALT

662262	3982293	24FXE 62262 82293	TERROR	Mt. Terror, Antarctica
382320	4898432	12FXE 82232 54393	SEVER	Sever City, Arizona
244548	9080799	02FXE 67533 43433	CONCH	Conch Cay, Bahamas
482320	5898432	22FXE 72232 04393	SCORPION	Resolution, Solomon Is.

ALT				
662262	3982293	24FXE 62262 82293	TERROR	Mt. Terror, Antarctica
382320	4898432	12FXE 82232 54393	BUZZARD	Buzzard Gulch, Utah
444548	7080799	02FXE 67533 43433	OLD MAN	Old Man Is., Turks & Caicos
482320	5898432	22FXE 72232 04393	SCORPION	Resolution, Solomon Is.
ALT				
662262	3982293	24FXE 62262 82293	TERROR	Mt. Terror, Antarctica
382320	4898432	12FXE 82232 54393	BLACK MESA	Black Mesa, New Mexico
344548	9080799	02FXE 67533 43433	SNARL	Snarl Cay, BWI
482320	5898432	22FXE 72232 04393	SCORPION	Resolution, Solomon Is.

"As you see, Sanjong has identified the precise GPS locations," Kenner said. "You've undoubtedly noticed a pattern in the list. The first incident we know about. The second incident will take place somewhere in the American desert—either Utah, Arizona, or New Mexico. The third incident will be somewhere in the Caribbean, east of Cuba. And the fourth incident will be in the Solomon Islands."

"Yes? So?"

"Our concern right now is for the second incident," Kenner said. "And the problem is that from Utah to Arizona to New Mexico there are fifty thousand square miles of desert. Unless we can get additional information, we'll never find these guys."

"But you have exact GPS locations . . ."

"Which they will undoubtedly change, now that they know of the trouble in Antarctica."

"You think they have already changed plans?"

"Of course. Their network knew something was wrong as soon as we arrived at Weddell yesterday. I think that's why the first guy left. I think he's actually the leader of the three. The other two were just foot soldiers."

"So you want me to go see Drake," Evans said.

"Right. And find out whatever you can."

"I hate this," Evans said.

"I understand," Kenner said. "But we need you to do it."

Evans looked at Sarah, who was rubbing her eyes, still sleepy. He was annoyed to see that she had arisen from her bed perfectly composed, her face uncreased, beautiful as ever. "How are you?" he said to her.

"I need to brush my teeth," she said. "How long until we land?"

"Ten minutes."

She got up, and walked to the back of the plane.

Evans looked out the window. The sunlight was glaring, harsh. He hadn't had enough sleep. The line of stitches in his scalp pinched. His body ached from being wedged in the damned crevasse for so long. Just to rest his elbow on the armrest of the seat was painful.

He sighed.

"Peter," Kenner said, "those guys tried to kill you. I wouldn't be too careful about the niceties when you fight back."

"Maybe so, but I'm a lawyer."

"And you could be a dead lawyer," Kenner said. "I don't advise it."

* * *

It was with a sense of unreality that Peter Evans merged his hybrid car onto the San Diego freeway, twelve lanes of roaring traffic on an expanse of concrete as wide as half a football field. Sixty-five percent of the surface area of Los Angeles was devoted to cars. People had to wedge themselves in what little was left. It was an inhuman design and it was environmentally absurd. Everything was so far apart, you couldn't walk anywhere, the pollution was incredible.

And people like Kenner did nothing but criticize the good work of environmental organizations, without whose efforts the environment of a place like Los Angeles would be much, much worse.

Face it, he thought. The world needed help. It desperately needed an environmental perspective. And nothing in Kenner's smooth manipulation of facts would change that truth.

His thoughts rambled on in this way for another ten minutes, until he crossed Mulholland Pass and came down toward Beverly Hills.

He looked at the passenger seat beside him. The doctored cell phone glinted in the sunlight. He decided to take it to Drake's office right away. Get this whole thing over with.

He telephoned Drake's office and asked to talk to him; he was told Drake was at the dentist and would return later in the day. The secretary wasn't sure exactly when.

Evans decided to go to his apartment and take a shower.

* * *

He parked in the garage and walked through the little garden to his apartment. The sun was shining down between the buildings; the roses were in bloom, beautiful. The only thing that marred it, he thought, was the lingering odor of cigar smoke in the air. It was offensive to think that somebody had smoked a cigar and that what remained was—

"Sssst! Evans!"

He paused. He looked around. He could see nothing.

Evans heard an intense whisper, like a hiss: "Turn right. Pick a damn rose."

"What?"

"Don't talk, you idiot. And stop looking around. Come over here and pick a rose."

Evans moved toward the voice. The cigar smell was stronger. Behind the tangle of the bushes, he saw an old stone bench that he had never noticed before. It was crusted with algae. Hunched down on the bench was a man in a sport coat. Smoking a cigar.

"Who are—"

"Don't talk," the man whispered. "How many times do I have to tell you. Take the rose, and smell it. That'll give you a reason to stay a minute. Now listen to me. I'm a private investigator. I was hired by George Morton."

Evans smelled the rose. Inhaling cigar smoke.

"I have something important for you," the guy said. "I'll bring it to your apartment in two hours. But I want you to leave again, so they'll follow you. Leave your door unlocked."

Evans turned the rose in his fingers, pretending to examine it. In fact, he was looking past the rose at the man on the bench. The man's face was familiar, somehow. Evans was sure he had seen him before . . .

"Yeah, yeah," the man said, as if reading his thoughts. He turned his lapel, to show a badge. "AV Network Systems. I was working in the NERF building. Now you remember, right? Don't *nod*. For Christ's sake. Just go upstairs, change your clothes, and leave for a while. Go to the gym or whatever. Just go. These assholes"—he jerked his head toward the street—"have been waitin' for you. So don't disappoint them. Now *go*."

His apartment had been put back together very well. Lisa had done a good job—the slashed cushions had been flipped over; the books were back in the bookcase. They were out of order, but he would deal with that later.

From the large windows in his living room, Evans looked out toward the street. He could see nothing except the green expanse of Roxbury Park. The kids playing at midday. The clusters of gossiping nannies. There was no sign of surveillance.

It looked perfectly normal.

Self-consciously, he started unbuttoning his shirt, and turned away. He went to the shower, letting the hot spray sting his body. He looked at his toes, which were dark purple, a worrisome, unnatural color. He wiggled them. He didn't have much sensation, but other than that, they seemed to be all right.

He toweled off, and checked his messages. There was a call from Janis, asking if he was free tonight. Then another, nervous one from her, saying her boyfriend had just come back into town and she was busy (which meant, don't call her back). There was a call from Lisa, Herb Lowenstein's assistant, asking where he was. Lowenstein wanted to go over some documents with him; it was important. A call from Heather, saying that Lowenstein was looking for him. A call from Margo Lane, saying she was still in the hospital and why hadn't he called her back? A call from his client the BMW dealer, asking when he was coming to the showroom.

And about ten hang-ups. Far more than he usually had.

The hang-ups gave him a creepy feeling.

Evans dressed quickly, putting on a suit and tie. He came back into the living room and, feeling uneasy, clicked on the television set, just in time for the local noon news. He was heading for the door when he heard: "Two new developments emphasize once again the dangers of global warming. The first study, out of England, says global warming is literally changing the rotation of the Earth, shortening the length of our day."

Evans turned back to look. He saw two co-anchors, a man and a woman. The man was explaining that even more dramatic was a study that showed that the Greenland ice cap was going to melt entirely away. That would cause sea levels to rise twenty feet.

"So, I guess it's good-bye Malibu!" the anchor said cheerfully. Of course, that wouldn't happen for a few years yet. "But it's coming . . . unless we all change our ways."

Evans turned away from the television and headed for the door. He wondered what Kenner would have to say about this latest news. Changing the rotation speed of the Earth? He shook his head at the sheer enormity of it. And melting all the ice in Greenland? Evans could imagine Kenner's discomfiture.

But then, he'd probably just deny it all, the way he usually did.

Evans opened the door, carefully ensured that it would remain unlocked, closed it behind him, and headed for his office.

He ran into Herb Lowenstein in the hall, walking toward a conference room. "Jesus," Lowenstein said, "where the hell have you been, Peter? Nobody could find you."

"I've been doing a confidential job for a client."

"Well next time tell your damn secretary how to reach you. You look like shit. What happened, you get in a fight or something? And what's that above your ear? Jesus, are those stitches?"

"I fell."

"Uh-huh. What client were you doing this confidential job for?"

"Nick Drake, actually."

"Funny. He didn't mention it."

"No?"

"No, and he just left. I spent the whole morning with him. He's very unhappy about the document rescinding the ten-million-dollar grant from the Morton Foundation. Especially that clause."

"I know," Evans said.

"He wants to know where the clause came from."

"I know."

"Where did it come from?"

"George asked me not to divulge that."

"George is dead."

"Not officially."

"This is bullshit, Peter. Where did the clause come from?"

Evans shook his head. "I'm sorry, Herb. I have specific instructions from the client."

"We're in the same firm. And he's my client, too."

"He instructed me in writing, Herb."

"In *writing?* Horseshit. George didn't write anything."

"Handwritten note," Evans said.

"Nick wants the terms of the document broken."

"I'm sure he does."

"And I told him we'd do that for him," Lowenstein said.

"I don't see how."

"Morton was not in his right mind."

"But he was, Herb," Evans said. "You'll be taking ten million out of his estate and if anybody whispers in the ear of his daughter—"

"She's a total cokehead—"

"—who goes through cash like a monkey through bananas. And if anybody whispers in her ear, this firm will be liable for the ten million, and for punitive damages for conspiracy to defraud. Have you talked to the other senior partners about this course of action?"

"You're being obstructive."

"I'm being cautious. Maybe I should express my concerns in an e-mail to you."

"This is not how you advance in this firm, Peter."

Evans said, "I think I am acting in the firm's best interest. I certainly don't see how you can abrogate this document without, at the very least, first obtaining written opinions from attorneys outside the firm."

"But no outside attorney would countenance—" He broke off. He glared at Evans. "Drake is going to want to talk to you about this."

"I'll be happy to do that."

"I'll tell him you'll call."

"Fine."

Lowenstein stalked off. Then he turned back. "And what was all that business about the police and your apartment?"

"My apartment was robbed."

"For what? Drugs?"

"No, Herb."

"My assistant had to leave the office to help you with a police matter."

"That's true. As a personal favor. And it was after hours, if I recall."

Lowenstein snorted, and stomped off down the hall.

Evans made a mental note to call Drake. And get this entire business behind him.

In the hot midday sun, Kenner parked his car in the downtown lot and walked with Sarah out onto the street. Heat shimmered off the pavement. The signs there were all in Spanish, except for a few English phrases—"Checks Cashed" and "Money Loaned." From scratchy loudspeakers, mariachi music blared out.

Kenner said, "All set?"

Sarah checked the small sports bag on her shoulder. It had nylon mesh at either end. The mesh concealed the video lens. "Yes," she said. "I'm ready."

Together, they walked toward the large store on the corner, "Brader's Army/Navy Surplus."

Sarah said, "What're we doing here?"

"ELF purchased a large quantity of rockets," Kenner said.

She frowned. "Rockets?"

"Small ones. Lightweight. About two feet long. They're outdated versions of an '80s Warsaw Pact device called Hotfire. Handheld, wire-guided, solid propellant, range of about a thousand yards."

Sarah wasn't sure what all that meant. "So, these are weapons?"

"I doubt that's why they bought them."

"How many did they buy?"

"Five hundred. With launchers."

"Wow."

"Let's just say they're probably not hobbyists."

Above the doors, a banner in flaking yellow and green paint read, Camping Gear Paintball Paratrooper Jackets Compass Sleeping Bags Much, Much More!

The front door chimed as they went in.

The store was large and disorderly, filled with military stuff on racks and piled in untidy heaps on the floor. The air smelled musty, like old canvas. There were few people inside at this hour. Kenner walked directly to the kid at the cash register, flashed his wallet, and asked for Mr. Brader.

"In the back."

The kid smiled at Sarah. Kenner went to the back of the store. Sarah stayed at the front.

"So," she said. "I need a little help."

"Do my best." He grinned. He was a crew-cut kid, maybe nineteen or twenty. He had a black T-shirt that said "The Crow." His arms looked like he worked out.

"I'm trying to find a guy," Sarah said, and slid a sheet of paper toward him.

"You think any guy would be trying to find you," the kid said. He picked up the paper. It showed a photograph of the man they knew as Brewster, who had set up camp in Antarctica.

"Oh yeah," the kid said immediately. "Sure, I know him. He comes in sometimes."

"What's his name?"

"I don't know, but he's in the store now."

"Now?" She glanced around for Kenner, but he was in the back, huddled with the owner. She didn't want to call to him or do anything to cause attention.

The kid was standing on tiptoes, looking around. "Yeah, he's here. I mean, he was in here a few minutes ago. Came in to buy some timers."

"Where are your timers?"

"I'll show you." He came around the counter, and led her through the stacks of green clothing and the boxes piled seven feet high. She couldn't see over them. She could no longer see Kenner.

The kid glanced over his shoulder at her. "What are you, like a detective?"

"Sort of."

"You want to go out?"

They were moving deeper into the store when they heard the chime of the front door. She turned to look. Over stacks of flak jackets, she had a glimpse of a brown head, a white shirt with a red collar, and the door closing.

"He's leaving . . ."

She didn't think. She just turned and sprinted for the door. The bag banged against her hip. She jumped over stacked canteens, running hard.

"Hey," the kid yelled behind her. "You coming back?"

She banged through the door.

She was out on the street. Glaring hot sun and shoving crowds. She looked left and right. She didn't see the white shirt and red collar anywhere.

There hadn't been time for him to cross the street. She looked around the corner, and saw him strolling casually away from her, toward Fifth Street. She followed him.

He was a man of about thirty-five, dressed in cheap golf-type clothes. His pants were rumpled. He wore dirty hiking boots. He had tinted glasses and a small, trim moustache. He looked like a guy who spent a lot of time outdoors, but not a construction guy—more of a supervisor. Maybe a building contractor. Building inspector. Something like that.

She tried to notice the details, to remember them. She gained on him, then decided that was a bad idea, and dropped back. "Brewster" stopped in front of one window and looked at it intently for a few moments, then went on.

She came to the window. It was a crockery store, displaying cheap plates. She wondered, then, if he already knew he was being followed.

To trail a terrorist on a downtown street felt like something out of a movie, but it was more frightening than she anticipated. The surplus store seemed very far behind her. She didn't know where Kenner was. She wished he were here. Also, she was hardly inconspicuous; the crowd on the sidewalk was largely Hispanic, and Sarah's blond head stuck up above most people's.

She stepped off the curb, and walked along the street gutter, hanging at the edge of the crowd. That way she lost six inches of height. But still, she was uncomfortably aware that her hair was distinctively blonde. But there was nothing she could do about that.

She let Brewster get twenty yards ahead of her. She didn't want to allow more distance than that because she was afraid she'd lose him.

Brewster crossed Fifth Street, and continued on. He went another half a block, and then turned left, down an alley. Sarah got to the alley entrance, and paused. There were garbage bags stacked at intervals. She could smell the rotten odor from where she was. A big delivery truck blocked the far end of the alley.

And no Brewster.

He had vanished.

It wasn't possible, unless he had walked through one of the back doors that opened onto the alley. There were doors every twenty feet or so, many of them recessed into the brick wall.

She bit her lip. She didn't like the idea that she couldn't see him. But there were delivery men down at the truck. . . .

She started down the alley.

She looked at each door as she passed it. Some were boarded shut, some were locked. A few had grimy signs giving the name of the firm, and saying USE FRONT ENTRANCE or PRESS BELL FOR SERVICE.

No Brewster.

She had gotten halfway down the alley when something made her look back. She was just in time to see Brewster step out of a doorway and head back to the street, moving quickly away from her.

She ran.

As she passed the doorway, she saw an elderly woman standing in the door. The sign on the door said, Munro Silk and Fabrics.

"Who is he?" she shouted.

The old woman shrugged, shaking her head. "Wrong door. They all do—" She said something more, but by then Sarah couldn't hear.

She was back on the sidewalk, still running. Heading toward Fourth. She could see Brewster half a block ahead. He was walking quickly, almost a jog.

He crossed Fourth. A pickup truck pulled over to the side, a few yards ahead. It was battered blue, with Arizona license plates. Brewster jumped in the passenger side, and the truck roared off.

Sarah was scribbling down the license plate when Kenner's car screeched to a stop alongside her. "Get in."

She did, and he accelerated forward.

"Where were you?" she said.

"Getting the car. I saw you leave. Did you film him?"

She had forgotten all about the bag on her shoulder. "Yes, I think so."

"Good. I got a name for this guy, from the store owner."

"Yes?"

"But it's probably an alias. David Poulson. And a shipping address."

"For the rockets?"

"No, for the launch stands."

"Where?"

Kenner said, "Flagstaff, Arizona."

Ahead, they saw the blue pickup.

They followed the pickup down Second, past the *Los Angeles Times* building, past the criminal courts, and then onto the freeway. Kenner was skilled; he managed to stay well back, but always kept the truck in sight.

"You've done this before," Sarah said.

"Not really."

"What is that little card you show everybody?"

Kenner pulled out his wallet, and handed it to her. There was a silver badge, looking roughly like a police badge, except it said "NSIA" on it. And there was an official license for "National Security Intelligence Agency," with his photograph.

"I've never heard of the National Security Intelligence Agency."

Kenner nodded, took the wallet back.

"What does it do?"

"Stays below the radar," Kenner said. "Have you heard from Evans?"

"You don't want to tell me?"

"Nothing to tell," Kenner said. "Domestic terrorism makes domestic agencies uncomfortable. They're either too harsh or too lenient. Everyone in NSIA is specially trained. Now, call Sanjong and read him the license plate on that pickup, see if he can trace it."

"So you do domestic terrorism?"

"Sometimes."

Ahead, the pickup truck moved onto the Interstate 5 freeway, heading east, past the clustered yellowing buildings of County General Hospital.

"Where are they going?" she said.

"I don't know," he said. "But this is the road to Arizona."

She picked up the phone and called Sanjong.

Sanjong wrote down the license, and called back in less than five minutes. "It's registered to the Lazy-Bar Ranch, outside Sedona," he told Kenner. "It's apparently a guest ranch and spa. The truck hasn't been reported stolen."

"Okay. Who owns the ranch?"

"It's a holding company: Great Western Environmental Associates. They own a string of guest ranches in Arizona and New Mexico."

"Who owns the holding company?"

"I'm checking on that, but it'll take some time."

Sanjong hung up.

Ahead, the pickup truck moved into the right lane, and turned on its blinker.

"It's pulling off the road," Kenner said.

They followed the truck through an area of seedy industrial parks. Sometimes the signs said SHEET WORKS or MACHINE TOOLING, but most of the buildings were blocky and unrevealing. The air was hazy, almost a light fog.

After two miles, the truck turned right again, just past a sign that said LTSI CORP. And beneath that, a small picture of an airport, with an arrow.

"It must be a private airfield," Kenner said.

"What's LTSI?" she said.

He shook his head. "I don't know."

Farther down the road, they could see the little airfield, with several small prop planes, Cessnas and Pipers, parked to one side. The truck drove up and parked alongside a twin-engine plane.

"Twin Otter," Kenner said.

"Is that significant?"

"Short takeoff, large payload. It's a workhorse aircraft. Used for firefighting, all sorts of things."

Brewster got out of the truck, and walked to the cockpit of the plane. He spoke briefly to the pilot. Then he got back in the truck, and drove a hundred yards down the road, pulling up in front of a huge rectangular shed of corrugated steel. There were two other trucks parked alongside it. The sign on the shed said LTSI, in big blue letters.

Brewster got out of the truck, and came around the back as the driver of the truck got out.

"Son of a bitch," Sarah said.

The driver was the man they knew as Bolden. He was now wearing jeans, a baseball cap, and sunglasses, but there was no doubt about his identity.

"Easy," Kenner said.

They watched as Brewster and Bolden walked into the shed through a narrow door. The door closed behind them with a metallic clang.

Kenner turned to Sarah. "You stay here."

He got out of the car, walked quickly to the shed, and went inside.

She sat in the passenger seat, shading her eyes against the sun, and waited. The minutes dragged. She squinted at the sign on the side of the shed, because she could detect small white lettering beneath the large LTSI initials. But she was too far away to make out what it said.

She thought of calling Sanjong, but didn't. She worried about what would happen if Brewster and Bolden came out, but Kenner remained inside. She would have to follow them alone. She couldn't let them get away. . . .

That thought led her to slide over into the driver's seat. She rested her hands on the wheel. She looked at her watch. Surely nine or ten minutes had already passed. She scanned the shed for any sign of activity, but the building was clearly made to be as unobtrusive and as unrevealing as possible.

She looked at her watch again.

She began to feel like a coward, just sitting there. All her life, she had confronted the things that frightened her. That was why she had learned to ski black diamond ice, to rock climb (even though she was too tall), to scuba dive wrecks.

Now, she was just sitting in a hot car, waiting as the minutes ticked by.

The hell with it, she thought. And she got out of the car.

At the door to the shed, there were two small signs. One said LTSI LIGHTNING TEST SYSTEMS INTERNATIONAL. The second said WARNING: DO NOT ENTER TEST BED DURING DISCHARGE INTERVALS.

Whatever that meant.

Sarah opened the door cautiously. There was a reception area, but it was deserted. On a plain wooden desk was a handwritten sign and a buzzer. PRESS BUZZER FOR ASSISTANCE.

She ignored the buzzer, and opened the inner door, which was ominously marked:

NO TRESPASSING
HIGH VOLTAGE DISCHARGE
AUTHORIZED PERSONNEL ONLY

She went through the door and came into an open, dimly lit industrial space—pipes on the ceiling, a catwalk, rubber-tile floor underfoot. It was all quite dark except for a two-story glass-walled chamber in the center, which was brightly lit. It was a fairly large space, roughly the size of her living room. Inside the chamber she saw what looked like an airplane jet engine, mounted on a small section of wing. At the side of the room was a large metal plate, set against the wall. And outside the room was a control panel. A man was sitting in front of the panel. Brewster and Bolden were nowhere to be seen.

Inside the room, a recessed monitor screen flashed CLEAR AREA NOW. A computer voice said, "Please clear the test area. Testing begins in . . . thirty seconds." Sarah heard a slowly building whine, and the chugging of a pump. But nothing was happening that she could see.

Curious, she moved forward.

"Ssst!"

She looked around, but could not see where the sound was coming from.

"Ssst!"

She looked up. Kenner was above her, on the catwalk. He gestured for her to join him, pointing to a set of stairs at the corner of the room.

The computer voice said, "Testing begins in . . . twenty seconds."

She climbed the stairs and crouched beside Kenner. The whine had now built to a shriek, and the chugging was rapid, almost a continuous sound. Kenner pointed to the jet engine, and whispered, "They're testing airplane parts." He explained quickly that airplanes were frequently struck by lightning, and all their components had to be lightning proof. He said something else, too, but she couldn't really hear him over the increasing noise.

Inside the center room, the lights went off, leaving just a faint blue glow over the jet engine and its smoothly curved cowling. The computer voice was counting backward from ten.

"Testing begins . . . now."

There was a *snap!* so loud it sounded like a gunshot, and a bolt of lightning snaked out from the wall and struck the engine. It was immediately followed by more bolts from the other walls, striking the engine from all sides. The lightning crackled over the cowling in jagged white-hot fingers, then abruptly shot down to the floor, where Sarah saw a dome-shaped piece of metal about a foot in diameter.

She noticed a few of the lightning bolts seemed to shoot directly to this dome, missing the engine entirely.

As the test continued, the lightning bolts grew thicker, brighter. They made a long *crack!* as they shot through the air, and etched black streaks over the metal cowl. The fan blades were struck by one bolt, causing the fan to spin silently.

As Sarah watched, it seemed as if more and more of the bolts did not strike the engine, but instead struck the small dome on the floor until finally there was a white spider web of lightning strikes, coming from all sides, going directly to the dome.

And then, abruptly, the test ended. The whining sound stopped, and the room lights came on. Faint, hazy smoke rose from the engine cowling. Sarah looked over at the console, and saw Brewster and Bolden standing behind the seated technician. All three men walked into the central room, where they crouched beneath the engine and inspected the metal dome.

"What is it?" Sarah whispered.

Kenner put a finger to his lips, and shook his head. He looked unhappy.

Inside the room, the men upended the dome, and Sarah had a glimpse of its complexity—green circuit boards and shiny metal attachments. But the men were clustered around it, talking excitedly, and it was hard for her to see. Then they put the dome back down on the floor again, and walked out of the room.

They were laughing and slapping each other on the back, apparently very pleased with the test. She heard one of them say something about buying a round of beer, and there was more laughter, and they walked out through the front door. The test area was silent.

They heard the outer door slam shut.

She and Kenner waited.

She looked at Kenner. He waited, motionless for a full minute, just listening. Then, when they still heard nothing, he said, "Let's have a look at that thing."

They climbed down from the catwalk.

On the ground level, they saw and heard nothing. The facility was apparently deserted. Kenner pointed to the inner chamber. They opened the door, and went inside.

The interior of the chamber was bright. There was a sharp smell in the air.

"Ozone," Kenner said. "From the strikes."

He walked directly to the dome on the floor.

"What do you think it is?" Sarah said.

"I don't know, but it must be a portable charge generator." He crouched, turned the dome over. "You see, if you can generate a strong enough negative charge—"

He broke off. The dome was empty. Its electronic innards had been removed.

With a *clang*, the door behind them slammed shut.

Sarah whirled. Bolden was on the other side of the door, calmly locking it with a padlock.

"Oh shit," she said. Over at the console she saw Brewster, turning knobs, flipping switches. He flicked an intercom.

"There's no trespassing in this facility, folks. It's clearly marked. Guess you didn't read the signs . . ."

Brewster stepped away from the console. The room lights went dark blue. Sarah heard the start of the whine, beginning to build. The screen flashed CLEAR AREA NOW. And she heard a computer voice say, "Please clear the test area. Testing begins in . . . thirty seconds."

Brewster and Bolden walked out, without looking back.

Sarah heard Bolden say, "I hate the smell of burning flesh."

And they were gone, slamming the door.

The computer voice said, "Testing begins in . . . fifteen seconds."

Sarah turned to Kenner. "What do we do?"

Outside the facility, Bolden and Brewster got into their car. Bolden started the engine. Brewster put a hand on the other man's shoulder.

"Let's just wait a minute."

They watched the door. A red light began to flash, slowly at first, then faster and faster.

"Test has started," Brewster said.

"Damn shame," Bolden said. "How long you figure they can survive?"

"One bolt, maybe two. But by the third one, they're definitely dead. And probably on fire."

"Damn shame," Bolden said again. He put the car in gear, and drove toward the waiting airplane.

IV

FLASH

Inside the test chamber, the air took on a sizzly, electric quality, like the atmosphere before a storm. Sarah saw the hairs on her arm standing up. Her clothing was sticking to her body, flattened by the electric charge.

"Got a belt?" Kenner said.

"No . . ."

"Hairclip?"

"No."

"Anything metal?"

"No! Damn it, no!"

Kenner flung himself against the glass wall, but just bounced off. He kicked it with his heel; nothing happened. He slammed his weight against the door, but the lock was strong.

"Ten seconds to test," the computer voice said.

"What are we going to do?" Sarah said, panicked.

"Take your clothes off."

"What?"

"Now. Do it." He was stripping off his shirt, ripping it off, buttons flying. "Come on, Sarah. Especially the sweater."

She had a fluffy angora sweater, and bizarrely,

she recalled it had been a present from her boy-friend, one of the first things he ever bought her. She tore it off, and the T-shirt beneath.

"Skirt," Kenner said. He was down to his shorts, pulling off his shoes.

"What is this—"

"It's got a zipper!"

She fumbled, getting the skirt off. She was down to her sports bra and panties. She shivered. The computer voice was counting backward. "Ten . . . nine . . . eight . . ."

Kenner was draping the clothes over the engine. He took her skirt, draped it over, too. He arranged the angora sweater to lie on the top.

"What are you doing?"

"Lie down," he said. "Lie flat on the floor—make yourself as flat as you can—and *don't move.*"

She pressed her body against the cold concrete. Her heart was pounding. The air was bristling. She felt a shiver down the back of her neck.

"Three . . . two . . . one . . ."

Kenner threw himself on the ground next to her and the first lightning bolt crashed through the room. She was shocked by the violence of it, the blast of air rushing over her body. Her hair was rising into the air, she could feel the weight of it lift off her neck. There were more bolts—the crashing sound was terrifying—blasting blue light, so bright she saw it even though she squeezed her eyes shut. She pressed herself against the ground, willing herself to be even flatter, exhaling, thinking *Now is a time for prayer.*

But suddenly there was another kind of light

in the room, yellower, flickering, and a sharp acrid smell.

Fire.

A piece of her flaming sweater fell on her bare shoulder. She felt searing pain.

"It's a fire—"

"Don't move!" Kenner snarled.

The bolts were still blasting, coming faster and faster, crackling over the room, but she could see out of the corner of her eye that the clothes heaped on the engine were aflame, the room was filling with smoke.

She thought, *My hair is burning.* And she could feel it suddenly hot at the base of her neck, along her scalp . . .

And suddenly the room was filled with blasting water, and the lightning had stopped, and the sprinkler nozzles hissed overhead. She felt cold; the fires went out; the concrete was wet.

"Can I get up now?"

"Yes," Kenner said. "You can get up now."

He spent several more minutes trying to break the glass without success. Finally he stopped and stared, his hair matted by the sizzling water. "I don't get it," he said. "You can't have a room like this without a safety mechanism to enable someone to get out."

"They locked the door, you saw it yourself."

"Right. Locking it from the outside with a padlock. That padlock must be there to make sure nobody can enter the room from the outside while the facility is closed. But there still has to be some way to get out *from the inside.*"

"If there is, I don't see it." She was shivering. Her shoulder hurt where she was burned. Her underwear was soaked through. She wasn't modest, but she was cold, and he was nattering on . . .

"There just has to be a way," he said, turning slowly, looking.

"You can't break the glass . . ."

"No," he said. "You can't." But that seemed to suggest something to him. He bent and carefully examined the glass frame, looking at the seam where the glass met the wall. Running his finger along it.

She shivered while she watched him. The sprinklers were still on, still spraying. She was standing in three inches of water. She could not understand how he could be so focused, so intent on—

"I'll be damned," he said. His fingers had closed on a small latch, flush with the mounting. He found another on the opposite side of the window, flicked it open. And then he pushed the window, which was hinged in the center, and rotated it open.

He stepped through into the outer room.

"Nothing to it," he said. He extended his hand. "Can I offer you some dry clothes?"

"Thank you," she said, and took his hand.

The LTSI washrooms weren't anything to write home about, but Sarah and Kenner dried off with paper towels and found some warm coveralls, and Sarah began to feel better. Staring in the mirror, she saw that she'd lost two inches of hair around her left side. The ends were ragged, black, twisted.

"Could have been worse," she said, thinking *Ponytails for a while.*

Kenner tended to her shoulder, which he said was just a first-degree burn with a few blisters. He put ice on it, telling her that burns were not a thermal injury but were actually a nerve response within the body, and that ice in the first ten minutes reduced the severity of the burn by numbing the nerve, and preventing the response. So, if you were going to blister, ice prevented it from happening.

She tuned out his voice. She couldn't actually see the burned area, so she had to take his word for it. It was starting to hurt. He found a first-aid kit, brought back aspirin.

"Aspirin?" Sarah said.

"Better than nothing." He dropped two tablets in her hand. "Actually, most people don't know it, but aspirin's a true wonder drug, it has more pain-killing power than morphine, and it is anti-inflammatory, anti-fever—"

"Not right now," she said. "Please." She just couldn't take another of his lectures.

He said nothing. He just put on the bandage. He seemed to be good at that, too.

"Is there anything you're not good at?" she said.

"Oh sure."

"Like what? Dancing?"

"No, I can dance. But I'm terrible at languages."

"That's a relief." She herself was good at languages. She'd spent her junior year in Italy, and was reasonably fluent in Italian and French. And she'd studied Chinese.

"And what about you?" he said. "What are you bad at?"

"Relationships," she said. Staring in the mirror and pulling at the blackened strands of her hair.

As Evans climbed the steps to his apartment, he could hear the television blaring. It seemed louder than before. He heard cheers and laughter. Some sort of show with a live studio audience.

He opened the door, and went into the living room. The private investigator from the courtyard was sitting on the couch, his back to Evans while he watched television. His jacket was off and flung over a nearby chair. He had his arm draped across the back of the sofa. His fingers drummed impatiently.

"I see you've made yourself at home," Evans said. "Pretty loud, don't you think? Would you mind turning it down?"

The man didn't answer, he just continued to stare at the TV.

"Did you hear me?" Evans said. "Turn it down, would you?"

The man did not move. Just his fingers, moving restlessly on the back of the couch.

Evans walked around to face the man. "I'm sorry, I don't know your name but—"

He broke off. The investigator hadn't turned to look at him but continued to stare fixedly at the

TV. In fact, no part of his body moved. He was immobile, rigid. His eyes didn't move. They didn't even blink. The only part of his body that moved was his fingers, on the top of the couch. They almost seemed to be twitching. In spasm.

Evans stepped directly in front of the man. "Are you all right?"

The man's face was expressionless. His eyes stared forward, seeming to look straight through Evans.

"Sir?"

The investigator was breathing shallowly, his chest hardly moving. His skin was tinged with gray.

"Can you move at all? What happened to you?"

Nothing. The man was rigid.

Just like the way they described Margo, Evans thought. The same rigidity, the same blankness. Evans picked up the phone and dialed 911, called for an ambulance to his address.

"Okay, help is coming," he said to the man. The private detective gave no visible response, but even so, Evans had the impression that the man could hear, that he was fully aware inside his frozen body. But there was no way to be sure.

Evans looked around the room, hoping to find clues as to what had happened to this man. But the apartment seemed undisturbed. One chair in the corner seemed to have been moved. The guy's smelly cigar was on the floor in the corner, as if it had rolled there. It had burned the edge of the rug slightly.

Evans picked up the cigar.

He brought it back to the kitchen, ran it under

the faucet, and tossed it in the wastebasket. Then he had an idea. He went back to the man. "You were going to bring me something . . ."

There was no movement. Just the fingers on the couch.

"Is it here?"

The fingers stopped. Or almost stopped. They still moved slightly. But there was clearly an effort being made.

"Can you control your fingers?" Evans said.

They started, then stopped again.

"So you can. Okay. Now: is the thing you wanted me to see here?"

Fingers moved.

Then stopped.

"I take that as a yes. Okay." Evans stepped back. In the distance, he heard an approaching siren. The ambulance would be here in a few minutes. He said, "I am going to move in one direction, and if it is the right direction, move your fingers."

The fingers started, then stopped, as if to signal "yes."

"Okay," Evans said. He turned and took several steps to his right, heading toward the kitchen. He looked back.

The fingers did not move.

"So it's not that way." He now moved toward the television, directly in front of the man.

The fingers did not move.

"All right, then." Evans turned left, walking toward the picture windows. Still the fingers did not move. There was only one direction remaining: he moved behind the investigator, heading toward the door. Since the man could not see him, Evans said, "Now I am walking away from you, toward the front door . . ."

The fingers did not move.

"Maybe you didn't understand," Evans said. "I wanted you to move your fingers if I was heading in the right direction . . ."

Fingers moved. Scratching the couch.

"Yeah, okay, but which direction? I went in all four directions and—"

The doorbell rang. Evans opened it, and two paramedics rushed in, bringing a stretcher. And now there was pandemonium, they were asking him rapid-fire questions, and loading the guy onto the stretcher. The police arrived a few moments later, with still more questions. They were the Beverly Hills police, so they were polite, but they were insistent. This man was paralyzed in Evans's apartment, and Evans did not seem to know anything about it.

Finally, a detective came through the door. He wore a brown suit and introduced himself as Ron Perry. He gave Evans his card. Evans gave him his own card. Perry looked at it, then looked at Evans and said, "Haven't I seen this card before? It looks familiar. Oh yeah, I remember. It was at that apartment on Wilshire where the lady was paralyzed."

"She was my client."

"And now it's happened again, the same paralysis," Perry said. "Is that a coincidence or what?"

"I don't know," Evans said, "because I wasn't here. I don't know what happened."

"Somehow people just become paralyzed wherever you go?"

"No," Evans said. "I told you, I don't know what happened."

"Is this guy a client, too?"

"No."

"Then who is he?"

"I have no idea who he is."

"No? How'd he get in here?"

Evans was about to say he had left the door open for him, but he realized that was going to be a long explanation, and a difficult one.

"I don't know. I, uh . . . Sometimes I don't lock my door."

"You should always lock your door, Mr. Evans. That's just common sense."

"Of course, you're right."

"Doesn't your door lock automatically, when you leave?"

"I told you, I don't know how he got in my apartment," Evans said, looking directly into the detective's eyes.

The detective returned the stare. "How'd you get those stitches in your head?"

"I fell."

"Looks like quite a fall."

"It was."

The detective nodded slowly. "You could save us a lot of trouble if you'd just tell me who this guy is, Mr. Evans. You've got a man in your apartment, you don't know who he is, you don't know how he got here. Forgive me if I feel you're maybe leaving something out."

"I am."

"Okay." Perry took out his notebook. "Go ahead."

"The guy's a private detective."

"I know that."

"You do?" Evans said.

"The paramedics checked his pockets, found a license in his wallet. Go on."

"He told me he had been hired by a client of mine."

"Uh-huh. Which client is that?" Perry was writing.

"I can't tell you that," Evans said.

He looked up from his pad. "Mr. Evans—"

"I'm sorry. That's privileged."

The detective gave a long sigh. "Okay, so this guy is a private investigator hired by a client of yours."

"Right," Evans said. "The investigator contacted me and said he wanted to see me, to give me something."

"To give you something?"

"Right."

"He didn't want to give it to the client?"

"He couldn't."

"Because?"

"The client is, uh, unavailable."

"I see. So he came to you instead?"

"Yes. And he was a bit paranoid, and wanted to meet me in my apartment."

"So you left the door to your apartment open for him."

"Yes."

"Some guy you'd never seen before?"

"Yes, well, I knew he was working for my client."

"How did you know that?"

Evans shook his head. "Privileged."

"Okay. So this guy comes into your apartment. Where are you?"

"I was at my office."

Evans quickly recounted his movements during the intervening two hours.

"People saw you at the office?"

"Yes."

"Conversations?"

"Yes."

"More than one person?"

"Yes."

"You see anybody else besides people in the law firm?"

"I stopped to get gas."

"Attendant will recognize you?"

"Yes. I had to go in to use my credit card."

"Which station?"

"Shell on Pico."

"Okay. So you were gone two hours, you come back here, and the guy is . . ."

"As you saw him. Paralyzed."

"And what was he going to give you?"

"I have no idea."

"You didn't find anything in the apartment?"

"No."

"Anything else you want to tell me?"

"No."

Another long sigh. "Look, Mr. Evans. If two people I knew were mysteriously paralyzed, I'd be a little worried. But you don't seem worried."

"Believe me, I'm worried," Evans said.

The detective frowned at him. "Okay," he said finally. "You have a client privilege you're invoking. I have to tell you that I've gotten calls from UCLA and from the CDC on this paralysis thing. Now that there's a second case, there are going to be more calls." He flipped his notebook shut. "I'm going to need you to come by the station and give us a signed statement. Can you do that later today?"

"I think so."

"Four o'clock?"

"Yes. Fine."

"The address is on the card. Just ask for me at the desk. Parking is under the building."

"Okay," Evans said.

"See you then," the detective said, and turned to leave.

Evans shut the door behind him and leaned against it. He was glad to finally be alone. He walked around the apartment slowly, trying to focus his thoughts. The television was still on, but the sound was turned off. He looked at the couch where the private investigator had been sitting. The indentation of his body was still visible.

He still had half an hour before he was supposed to meet with Drake. But he wanted to know what the PI had brought to him. Where was it? Evans had moved in every direction of the compass, and each time the man had indicated with his fingertips that it was the wrong direction.

Which meant what? He hadn't brought the thing? It was somewhere else? Or that whoever paralyzed him had taken it, so it was no longer there?

Evans sighed. The critical question—is it

here?—was one he hadn't asked the detective. Evans just assumed it was there.

And suppose it was? Where would it be?

North, south, east, west. All wrong.

Which meant . . .

What?

He shook his head. He was having trouble concentrating. The truth was, the private investigator's paralysis had unnerved him more than he wanted to admit. He looked at the couch, and the indentation. The guy couldn't move. It must have been terrifying. And the paramedics had lifted him up bodily, like a sack of potatoes, and put him on the stretcher. The cushions on the couch were in disarray, a reminder of their efforts.

Idly, Evans straightened up the couch, putting the cushions in place, fluffing them . . .

He felt something. Inside a slit in one cushion. He stuck his hand deeper into the padding.

"Damn," he said.

Of course it was obvious in retrospect. Moving away in every direction was wrong, because the investigator wanted Evans to move *toward* him. The guy was sitting on the thing, which he had slipped inside the couch cushion.

It turned out to be a shiny DVD.

Evans dropped it in the DVD player, and watched as a menu came up, a list of dates. They were all in the last few weeks.

Evans clicked on the first date.

He saw a view of the NERF conference room. It was a side angle, from the corner of the room, waist high. It must have been from a camera hidden in the speaker's podium or something, Evans thought. Undoubtedly the investigator had installed the camera the day Evans had seen him in the NERF conference room.

At the bottom of the screen was a running time code, numbers flickering. But Evans stared at the image itself, which showed Nicholas Drake talking to John Henley, the PR guy. Drake was upset, throwing up his hands.

"I *hate* global warming," Drake said, almost shouting. "I fucking *hate* it. It's a goddamn disaster."

"It's been established," Henley said calmly. "Over many years. It's what we have to work with."

"To work with? But *it doesn't work*," Drake said. "That's my point. You can't raise a dime with it, especially in winter. Every time it snows people forget all about global warming. Or else they decide some warming might be a good thing after all. They're trudging through the snow, *hoping* for a little global warming. It's not like pollution, John. Pollution *worked*. It still works. Pollution scares the shit out of people. You tell 'em they'll get cancer, and the money rolls in. But nobody is scared of a little warming. Especially if it won't happen for a hundred years."

"You have ways to play it," Henley said.

"Not anymore," Drake said. "We've tried them all. Species extinction from global warming—nobody gives a shit. They've heard that most of the species that will become extinct are insects. You can't raise money on insect extinctions,

John. Exotic diseases from global warming—nobody cares. Hasn't happened. We ran that huge campaign last year connecting global warming to the Ebola and Hanta viruses. Nobody went for it. Sea-level rise from global warming—we all know where that'll end up. The Vanutu lawsuit is a fucking disaster. Everybody'll assume the sea level isn't rising anywhere. And that Scandinavian guy, that sea level expert. He's becoming a pest. He's even attacking the IPCC for incompetence."

"Yes," Henley said patiently. "That's all true . . ."

"So you tell me," Drake said, "how the hell I'm supposed to *play* global warming. Because you know what I have to raise to keep this organization going, John. I need forty-four million dollars a year. The foundations will only give me a quarter of that this year. The celebrities show up at the fund-raisers, but they don't give us shit. They're so egotistical they think showing up should be payment enough. Of course we sue the EPA every year, and they may cough up three, four million. With EPA grants, maybe five total. That still leaves a big gap, John. Global warming isn't going to cut it. I need a fucking *cause*. A cause that *works!*"

"I understand," Henley said, still very calm. "But you are forgetting the conference."

"Oh, Christ, the conference," Drake said. "These assholes can't even get the posters right. Bendix is our best speaker; he's got a family problem. Wife is having chemo. Gordon was scheduled, but he's got some lawsuit about his research . . . Seems his notebooks were faked . . ."

"Those are details, Nicholas," Henley said. "I'm asking you to stay with the big picture—"

At that moment, the phone rang. Drake answered it, listened briefly. Then he put his hand over the phone and turned to Henley.

"We have to continue this later, John. I've got an emergency here."

Henley got up, and left the room.

The clip ended.

The screen went black.

Evans stared at the blank screen. He felt as if he were going to be ill. A wave of dizziness passed over him. His stomach churned. He held the remote in his hand, but he did not press the buttons.

The moment passed. He took a breath. On reflection, he realized that what he had seen wasn't really surprising. Perhaps Drake was more explicit in private—everyone was—and obviously he felt under pressure to raise money. But the frustration he expressed was perfectly understandable. From the beginning, the movement had had to fight apathy in the broader society. Human beings didn't think in the long term. They didn't see the slow degradation of the environment. It had always been an uphill battle to rouse the public to do what was really in its own best interest.

That fight was far from over. In fact, it was just beginning.

And it was probably true that it wasn't easy to raise money for global warming. So Nicholas Drake had his work cut out for him.

And environmental organizations were really

working with very small funds. Forty-four million for NERF, the same for the NRDC, maybe fifty for the Sierra Club. The big one was the Nature Conservancy, they had three quarters of a billion. But what was that compared with the zillions of dollars that could be mobilized by corporations? It was David and Goliath. And Drake was David. As he had said himself, on every occasion.

Evans glanced at his watch. In any case, it was time to go see Drake.

He took the DVD out of the player, slipped it into his pocket, and left the apartment. On his way, he reviewed what he was going to say. He went over it, again and again, trying to make it perfect. He had to do it carefully, because everything Kenner had told him to say was a lie.

"Peter, Peter," Nicholas Drake said, shaking his hand warmly. "I am very pleased to see you. You've been away."

"Yes."

"But you haven't forgotten my request."

"No, Nick."

"Have a seat."

Evans sat down and Drake sat behind the desk. "Go ahead."

"I traced the origin of that clause."

"Yes?"

"Yes. You were right. George did get the idea from a lawyer."

"I knew it! Who?"

"An outside attorney, not in our firm." Evans spoke carefully, saying just what Kenner had instructed him to say.

"Who?"

"Unfortunately, Nick, there's documentation. Red-lined drafts with George's handwritten comments."

"Ah, shit. From when?"

"Six months ago."

"Six months!"

"Apparently George has been concerned for some time about . . . things. The groups he supports."

"He never told me."

"Nor me," Evans said. "He chose an outside attorney."

"I want to see this correspondence," Drake said.

Evans shook his head. "The attorney will never permit it."

"George is dead."

"Privilege continues after death. *Swidler and Berlin v. United States.*"

"This is bullshit, Peter, and you know it."

Evans shrugged. "But this attorney plays by the book. And I have arguably overstepped proper bounds by saying as much as I have."

Drake drummed his fingers on the desk top. "Peter, the Vanutu lawsuit is desperately in need of that money."

"I keep hearing," Evans said, "that that lawsuit may be dropped."

"Nonsense."

"Because the data sets don't show any rise in Pacific sea level."

"I'd be careful about saying things like that," Drake said. "Where did you hear that? Because that has to be disinformation from industry, Peter. There is *no question* sea levels are rising around the world. It's been scientifically demonstrated time and again. Why, just the other day I was looking at the satellite measurements of sea level, which are a relatively new way to make those measurements. The satellites show a rise of several millimeters, just in the last year."

"Was that published data?" Evans said.

"I don't remember offhand," Drake said, giving him an odd look. "It was in one of the briefing summaries I get."

Evans hadn't planned to ask questions like these. They had just somehow come out of his mouth, unbidden. And he was uncomfortably aware that his tone was skeptical. No wonder Drake was giving him an odd look.

"I don't mean anything," Evans said quickly. "It's just that I heard these rumors . . ."

"And you wanted to get to the bottom of it," Drake said, nodding. "As is only natural. I'm glad you brought this to my attention, Peter. I'll get on the horn with Henley and find out what's being disseminated. Of course it's an endless battle. You know we have those Neanderthals at the Competitive Enterprise Institute, and the Hoover Foundation, and the Marshall Institute to deal with. Groups financed by right-wing radicals and brain-dead fundamentalists. But, unfortunately, they have a tremendous amount of money at their disposal."

"Yes, I understand," Evans said. He turned to go. "Do you need me for anything else?"

"I'll be frank," Drake said, "I'm not happy. Are we back to fifty thousand a week?"

"Under the circumstances, I think we have no option."

"Then we will have to manage," Drake said. "The lawsuit's going fine, by the way. But I have to focus my energies on the conference."

"Oh, right. When does that start?"

"Wednesday," Drake said. "Four days from now. Now, if you'll excuse me . . ."

"Of course," Evans said. He walked out of the office, leaving his cell phone on the side table across from the desk.

Evans had gone all the way down the stairs to the ground floor before he realized Drake hadn't asked him about his stitches. Everyone else he had seen that day had made some comment about them, but not Drake.

Of course, Drake had a lot on his mind, with the preparations for the conference. Directly ahead, Evans saw the ground-floor conference room bustling with activity. The banner on the wall read, ABRUPT CLIMATE CHANGE—THE CATASTROPHE AHEAD. Twenty young people clustered around a large table, on which stood a scale model of the interior of an auditorium, and the surrounding parking lot. Evans paused to watch for a moment.

One of the young people was putting wooden blocks in the parking lot, to simulate cars.

"He won't like that," another one said. "He wants the slots nearest the building reserved for news vans, not buses."

"I left three spaces over here for news," the first kid said. "Isn't that enough?"

"He wants ten."

"Ten spaces? How many news crews does he think are going to show up for this thing?"

"I don't know, but he wants ten spaces and he's told us to arrange extra power and phone lines."

"For an academic conference on abrupt climate change? I don't get it. How much can you say about hurricanes and droughts? He'll be lucky to have three crews."

"Hey, he's the boss. Mark off the ten slots and be done with it."

"That means the buses have to go way in the back."

"Ten slots, Jake."

"Okay, okay."

"Next to the building, because the line feeds are very expensive. The auditorium's charging us an arm and a leg for the extra utilities."

At the other end of the table, a girl was saying, "How dark will it be in the exhibition spaces? Will it be dark enough to project video?"

"No, they're limited to flat panels."

"Some of the exhibitors have all-in-one projectors."

"Oh, that should be all right."

A young woman came up to Evans as he was standing looking into the room. "Can I help you, sir?" She looked like a receptionist. She had that bland prettiness.

"Yes," he said, nodding toward the conference room. "I was wondering how I arrange to attend this conference."

"It's by invitation only, I'm afraid," she said. "It's an academic conference, not really open to the public."

"I've just left Nick Drake's office," Evans said, "and I forgot to ask him—"

"Oh. Well, actually, I have some comp tickets

at the reception desk. Do you know which day you'll be attending?"

"All of them," Evans said.

"That's quite a commitment," she said, smiling. "If you'll come this way, sir . . ."

It was only a short drive from NERF to the conference headquarters, in downtown Santa Monica. Workmen on a cherry picker were placing letters on the large sign: so far it said, ABRUPT CLIMATE CHA, and beneath, THE CATASTR.

His car was hot in the midday sun. Evans called Sarah on the car phone. "It's done. I left my phone in his office."

"Okay. I was hoping you'd call earlier. I don't think that matters anymore."

"No? Why?"

"I think Kenner already found out what he needed."

"He did?"

"Here, talk to him."

Evans thought, she's with him?

"Kenner speaking."

"It's Peter," he said.

"Where are you?"

"In Santa Monica."

"Go back to your apartment and pack some hiking clothes. Then wait there."

"For what?"

"Change all the clothes you are wearing now. Take nothing with you that you are wearing right now."

"Why?"

"Later."

Click. The phone was dead.

Back in his apartment, he hastily packed a bag. Then he went back to the living room. While he waited, he put the DVD back into the player and waited for the menu of dates.

He chose the second date on the list.

On the screen, he once again saw Drake and Henley. It must have been the same day, because they were dressed in the same clothes. But now it was later. Drake had his jacket off, hung over a chair.

"I've listened to you before," Drake was saying. He sounded resentful. "And your advice didn't work."

"Think structurally," Henley said, leaning back in his chair, staring up at the ceiling, fingertips tented.

"What the hell does that mean?" Drake said.

"Think structurally, Nicholas. In terms of how information functions. What it holds up, what holds it up."

"This is just PR bullshit."

"Nicholas," Henley said, sharply. "I am trying to help you."

"Sorry." Drake looked chastened. He hung his head a little.

Watching the video, Evans thought: *Is Henley in charge here?* For a moment, it certainly appeared that way.

"Now then," Henley said. "Let me explain how you are going to solve your problem, Nicholas. The solution is simple. You have already told me—"

There was a loud pounding on Evans's door. Evans stopped the DVD, and just to be safe, removed it from the player and slipped it into his pocket. The pounding continued, impatient, as he went to the door.

It was Sanjong Thapa. He looked grim.

"We have to leave," he said. "Right now."

V

SNAKE

The helicopter thumped over the Arizona desert, twenty miles east of Flagstaff, not far from Canyon Diablo. In the back seat, Sanjong handed Evans pictures and computer printouts. Speaking of the Environmental Liberation Front, he said, "We assume their networks are up, but so are ours. All our networks are running," he said, "and we picked up an unexpected clue from one of them. Of all things, the Southwestern Parks Management Association."

"Which is?"

"It's an organization of state park managers from all the western states. And they discovered that something very odd had happened." A large percentage of the state parks in Utah, Arizona, and New Mexico were booked in advance, and paid for, to reserve them for company picnics, school celebrations, institutional birthday parties, and so on, for this weekend. In each case they were family affairs, involving parents and kids, sometimes grandparents, too.

True, this was a long three-day weekend. But nearly all the advance bookings were for Monday. Only a handful had been for Saturday or

Sunday. None of the park superintendents could remember such a thing happening before.

"I don't get it," Evans said.

"They didn't either," Sanjong said. "They thought it might be some cult thing, and because the parks can't be used for religious purposes, they got on the phone and called some of the organizations. And they found in every case that the organization had received a special donation to fund the function on this particular weekend."

"Donation from whom?"

"Charitable organizations. In every case the situation was the same. They'd receive a letter saying 'Thank you for your recent request for funding. We are pleased to say we can support your get-together at such-and-such park on Monday, October eleventh. The check has already been sent in your name. Enjoy your gathering.' "

"But the groups never requested the booking?"

"No. So they'd call the charity, and someone would tell them it must have been a mixup, but since the checks were already sent out, they might as well go ahead and use the park that day. And a lot of the groups decided they would."

"And these charitable organizations were?"

"None you ever heard of. The Amy Rossiter Fund. The Fund for a New America. The Roger V. and Eleanor T. Malkin Foundation. The Joiner Memorial Foundation. All together, about a dozen charities."

"Real charities?"

Sanjong shrugged. "We assume not. But we're checking that now."

Evans said, "I still don't get it."

"Somebody wants those parks used this weekend."

"Yes, but why?"

Sanjong handed him a photograph. It was an aerial shot in false colors, and it showed a forest, the trees bright red against a dark blue ground. Sanjong tapped the center of the picture. There, in a clearing in the forest, Evans saw what looked like a spiderweb on the ground—a series of concentric lines connecting fixed points. Like a spiderweb.

"And that is?"

"It's a rocket array. The launchers are the fixed points. The lines are the power cables to control the launch." His finger moved across the picture. "And you see, there's another array here. And a third one here. The three arrays form a triangle, approximately five miles on each side."

Evans could see it. Three separate spiderwebs, set in clearings in the forest.

"Three rocket arrays . . ."

"Yes. We know they have purchased five hundred solid-state rockets. The rockets themselves are quite small. Close analysis of the picture elements indicates that the launchers are four to six inches in diameter, which means the rockets are capable of going up about a thousand feet or so. Not more than that. Each array has about fifty rockets, wired together. Probably not set to fire at the same time. And you notice the launchers are placed quite far apart . . ."

"But for what purpose?" Evans said. "These

things are out in the middle of nowhere. They shoot up a thousand feet, and then fall back down? Is that it? What's the point of that?"

"We don't know," Sanjong said. "But we have another clue. The picture you're holding in your hands was taken yesterday. But here is a picture from a flyby this morning." He handed Evans a second picture, showing the same terrain.

The spiderwebs were gone.

"What happened?" Evans said.

"They packed up and left. You see in the first picture, there are vans parked at the edge of the clearings. Apparently, they just put everything in the vans and moved."

"Because they were spotted?"

"It's unlikely they know they were spotted."

"Then what?"

"We think they had to move to a more favorable setting."

"More favorable for what?" Evans said. "What's going on?"

"It may be significant," Sanjong said, "that at the time they purchased the rockets, they also purchased a hundred and fifty kilometers of microfilament wire."

He was nodding to Evans, as if that was supposed to explain everything.

"A hundred and fifty kilometers . . ."

Sanjong flicked his eyes toward the helicopter pilot, and shook his head. "We can go into it in greater detail later on, Peter."

And then he looked out the window.

* * *

Evans stared out the opposite window. He saw mile after mile of eroded desert landscape, cliffs brown with streaks of orange and red. The helicopter rumbled northward. He could see the helicopter's shadow racing over the sand. Distorted, twisted, then recognizable again.

Rockets, he thought. Sanjong had given him this information as if he were supposed to figure it out on his own. Five hundred rockets. Groups of fifty launchers, set widely apart. One hundred and fifty kilometers of microfilament wire.

Perhaps that was supposed to mean something, but Peter Evans didn't have the faintest idea what it could possibly be. Groups of small rockets, for what?

Microfilament, for what?

In his head, it was easy enough to calculate that if this microfilament was attached to the rockets, each rocket would have about a third of a kilometer of wire. And a third of a kilometer was . . . roughly a thousand feet.

Which was how high Sanjong said the rockets could go, anyway.

So these rockets were flying a thousand feet into the air, dragging a microfilament wire behind them? What was the point of that? Or was the wire intended to be used to retrieve them, later on? But no, he thought, that couldn't be. The rockets would fall back into the forest, and any microfilament would snap.

And why were the rockets spaced widely apart? If they were only a few inches in diameter, couldn't they be packed closer together?

He seemed to recall that the military had rocket launchers where the rockets were so close together the fins almost touched. So why should these rockets be far apart?

A rocket flies up . . . dragging a thin wire . . . and it gets to a thousand feet . . . and . . .

And what?

Perhaps, he thought, there was some instrumentation in the nose of each rocket. The wire was a way to transmit information back to the ground. But what instrumentation?

What was the point of all this?

He glanced back at Sanjong, who was now hunched over another photograph.

"What're you doing?"

"Trying to figure out where they've gone."

Evans frowned as he saw the picture in Sanjong's hand. It was a satellite weather map.

Sanjong was holding a weather map.

Did all this have to do with weather?

"Yes," Kenner said, leaning forward in the booth of the restaurant. They were in the back of a steakhouse in Flagstaff. The jukebox at the bar was playing old Elvis Presley: "Don't Be Cruel." Kenner and Sarah had showed up just a few minutes before. Sarah, Evans thought, looked drawn and worried. Not her usual cheerful self.

"We think this is all about the weather," Kenner was saying. "In fact, we're sure it is." He paused while a waitress brought salads, then continued. "There are two reasons to think so. First, ELF has bought a considerable amount of expensive technology that seems to have no use in common, except perhaps attempts to influence the weather. And second, the—"

"Hold on, hold on," Evans said. "You said attempts to influence the weather?"

"Exactly."

"Influence how?"

"Control it," Sanjong said.

Evans leaned back in the booth. "This is crazy," he said. "I mean, you're telling me these guys think they can control the weather?"

"They can," Sarah said.

"But how?" Evans said. "How could they do it?"

"Most of the research is classified."

"Then how do they get it?"

"Good question," Kenner said. "And we'd like to know that answer. But the point is, we assume that these rocket arrays are designed to produce major storms, or to amplify the power of existing storms."

"By doing what?"

"They cause a change in the electric potentials of the infra-cumulus strata."

"I'm glad I asked," Evans said. "That's very clear."

"We don't really know the details," Kenner said, "although I'm sure we'll find out soon enough."

"The strongest evidence," Sanjong said, "comes from the pattern of park rentals. These guys have arranged for lots of picnics over a large area— three states, in point of fact. Which means they are probably going to decide at the last minute where to act, based on existing weather conditions."

"Decide what?" Evans said. "What are they going to do?"

Nobody spoke.

Evans looked from one to another.

"Well?"

"We know one thing," Kenner said. "They want it documented. Because if there's one thing you can count on at a school picnic or a company outing with families and kids, it's lots of cameras. Lots of video, lots of stills."

"And then of course the news crews will come," Sanjong said.

"They will? Why?"

"Blood draws cameras," Kenner said.

"You mean they're going to hurt people?"

"I think it's clear," Kenner said, "that they're going to try."

An hour later they all sat on lumpy motel beds while Sanjong hooked a portable DVD player to the television set in the room. They were in a crappy motel room in Shoshone, Arizona, twenty miles north of Flagstaff.

On the screen, Evans once again saw Henley talking to Drake.

"I've listened to you before," Drake said resentfully. "And your advice didn't work."

"Think structurally," Henley answered. He was leaning back in his chair, staring up at the ceiling, fingertips tented.

"What the hell does that mean?" Drake said.

"Think structurally, Nicholas. In terms of how information functions. What it holds up, what holds it up."

"This is just PR bullshit."

"Nicholas," Henley said, sharply. "I am trying to help you."

"Sorry." Drake looked chastened. He hung his head a little.

Watching the screen, Evans said, "Does it look like Henley is in charge here?"

"He's always been in charge," Kenner said. "Didn't you know that?"

On the screen, Henley was saying, "Let me explain how you are going to solve your problem, Nicholas. The solution is simple. You have already told me that global warming is unsatisfactory because whenever there is a cold snap, people forget about it."

"Yes, I told you—"

"So what you need," Henley said, "is to structure the information so that whatever kind of weather occurs, it always confirms your message. That's the virtue of shifting the focus to abrupt climate change. It enables you to use everything that happens. There will always be floods, and freezing storms, and cyclones, and hurricanes. These events will always get headlines and airtime. And in every instance, you can claim it is an example of abrupt climate change caused by global warming. So the message gets reinforced. The urgency is increased."

"I don't know," Drake said doubtfully. "That's been tried, the last couple of years."

"Yes, on a scattered, individual basis. Isolated politicians, making claims about isolated storms or floods. Clinton did it, Gore did it, that blithering science minister in England did it. But we're not talking about isolated politicians, Nicholas. We are talking about an organized campaign throughout the world to make people understand that global warming is responsible for abrupt and extreme weather events."

Drake was shaking his head. "You know," he said, "how many studies show no increase in extreme weather events."

"Please." Henley snorted. "Disinformation from skeptics."

"That's hard to sell. There are too many studies . . ."

"What are you talking about, Nicholas? It's a snap to sell. The public already believes that industry is behind any contrary view." He sighed. "In any case, I promise you there will soon be more computer models showing that extreme weather *is* increasing. The scientists will get behind this and deliver what is needed. You know that."

Drake paced. He looked unhappy. "But it just doesn't make sense," he said. "It's not logical to say that freezing weather is caused by global warming."

"What's logic got to do with it?" Henley said. "All we need is for the media to report it. After all, most Americans believe that crime in their country is increasing, when it has actually been declining *for twelve years*. The US murder rate is as low as it was in the early 1970s, but Americans are more frightened than ever, because so much more airtime is devoted to crime, they naturally assume there is more in real life, too." Henley sat up in his chair. "Think about what I am saying to you, Nicholas. A twelve-year trend, and they still don't believe it. There is no greater proof that all reality is media reality."

"The Europeans are more sophisticated—"

"Trust me—it'll be even easier to sell abrupt climate change in Europe than in the US. You just do it out of Brussels. Because bureaucrats *get it,* Nicholas. They'll see the advantages of this shift in emphasis."

Drake did not reply. He walked back and forth, hands in his pockets, staring at the floor.

"Just think how far we have come!" Henley said. "Back in the 1970s, all the climate scientists believed an ice age was coming. They thought the world was getting colder. But once the notion of global *warming* was raised, they immediately recognized the advantages. Global warming creates a crisis, a call to action. A crisis needs to be studied, it needs to be funded, it needs political and bureaucratic structures around the world. And in no time at all, a huge number of meteorologists, geologists, oceanographers suddenly became 'climate scientists' engaged in the management of this crisis. This will be the same, Nicholas."

"Abrupt climate change has been discussed before, and it hasn't caught on."

"That's why you are holding a conference," Henley said patiently. "You hold a well-publicized conference and it happens to coincide with some dramatic evidence for the dangers of abrupt climate. And by the end of the conference, you will have established abrupt climate change as a genuine problem."

"I don't know . . ."

"Stop whining. Don't you remember how long it took to establish the global threat of nuclear winter, Nicholas? It took *five days.* On one Saturday in 1983, nobody in the world had ever heard of nuclear winter. Then a big media conference was held and by the following Wednesday the entire world was worried about nuclear winter. It was established as a bona fide threat to the planet. Without a single published scientific paper."

Drake gave a long sigh.

"Five days, Nicholas," Henley said. "They did it. You'll do it. Your conference is going to change the ground rules for climate."

The screen went black.

"My God," Sarah said.

Evans said nothing. He just stared at the screen.

Sanjong had stopped listening some minutes before. He was working with his laptop.

Kenner turned to Evans. "When was that segment recorded?"

"I don't know." Evans slowly came out of his fog. He looked around the room in a daze. "I have no idea when it was recorded. Why?"

"You've got the remote in your hand," Kenner said.

"Oh, sorry." Evans pressed the buttons, brought the menu up, saw the date. "It was two weeks ago."

"So Morton's been bugging Drake's offices for two weeks," Kenner said.

"Looks like it."

Evans watched as the recording ran again, this time with the sound off. He stared at the two men, Drake pacing and worried, Henley just sitting there, sure of himself. Evans was struggling to assimilate what he had heard. The first recording had seemed reasonable enough to him. There, Drake was complaining about the problems of publicizing a genuine environmental threat, global warming, when everybody naturally ceased to care about the topic in the middle of a snowstorm. All that made sense to Evans.

But this conversation . . . He shook his head. This one worried him.

Sanjong clapped his hands together and said, "I got it! I have the location!" He turned his laptop so everyone could see the screen. "This is NEXRAD radar from Flagstaff-Pulliam. You can see the precipitation center forming northeast of Payson. There should be a storm there by midday tomorrow."

"How far is that from us?" Sarah said.

"About ninety miles."

Kenner said, "I think we better get in the helicopter."

"And do what?" Evans said. "It's ten o'clock at night, for God's sake."

"Dress warmly," Kenner said.

The world was green and black, the trees slightly fuzzy through the lenses. The night-vision goggles pressed heavily against his forehead. There was something wrong with the straps: they cut into his ears and were painful. But everybody was wearing them, looking out the windows of the helicopter at the miles of forest below.

They were looking for clearings, and had already passed a dozen or more. Some were inhabited, the houses dark rectangles with glowing windows. In a couple of clearings, the buildings were completely black—ghost towns, abandoned mining communities.

But they hadn't yet found what they were looking for.

"There's one," Sanjong said, pointing.

Evans looked off to his left, and saw a large clearing. The familiar spiderweb pattern of launchers and cables was partially obscured in tall grass. To one side stood a large trailer truck of the size used to deliver groceries to supermarkets. And indeed, in black lettering, he saw "A&P" printed on the side panels.

"Food terrorists," Sarah said. But no one laughed.

And then the clearing had flashed past, the helicopter continuing onward. The pilot had explicit instructions not to slow down or to circle any clearing.

"That was definitely one," Evans said. "Where are we now?"

"Tonto Forest, west of Prescott," the pilot said. "I've marked the coordinates."

Sanjong said, "We should find two more, in a five-mile triangle."

The helicopter thumped onward into the night. It was another hour before they located the remaining spiderwebs, and the helicopter headed home.

The morning was warm and sunny, although dark clouds threatened to the north. At McKinley State Park, the Lincoln Middle School was having its annual outing. There were balloons attached to the picnic tables, the barbecue grills were smoking, and about three hundred kids and their families were playing on the grassy field beside the waterfall, throwing Frisbees and baseballs. More were playing along the banks of the nearby Cavender River, which meandered peacefully through the park. The river was low at the moment, with sandy banks on either side, and small rocky pools where the younger children played.

Kenner and the others were parked to one side, watching.

"When that river overflows," Kenner said, "it'll take out the entire park and everyone in it."

"It's a pretty big park," Evans said. "Will it really overflow that much?"

"Doesn't take much. The water will be muddy and fast moving. Six inches of fast water is enough to knock a person off his feet. Then they slide; it's slippery, they won't be able to get back up again. There're rocks and debris in the water; mud blinds them, they hit things, lose consciousness. Most drownings occur because people try to move across very low water."

"But six inches . . ."

"Muddy water has power," Kenner said. "Six inches of mud will take a car, no problem. Lose traction, sweep it right off the road. Happens all the time."

Evans found this hard to believe, but Kenner was now talking about some famous flood in Colorado, the Big Thompson, where a hundred and forty people died in a matter of minutes. "Cars crushed like beer cans," he said. "People with clothes ripped off their bodies by mud. Don't kid yourself."

"But here," Evans said, pointing to the park. "If the water starts to rise, there will be enough time to get out . . ."

"Not if it's a flash flood. Nobody here will know until it's too late. That's why we're going to make sure they don't have a flash flood."

He checked his watch, looked up at the darkening sky, and then walked back to the cars. They had three SUVs in a row. Kenner would drive one; Sanjong would drive one; Peter and Sarah would drive the third.

Kenner opened the back door to his car. He said to Peter, "Do you have a gun?"

"No."

"You want one?"

"You think I need one?"

"You might. When was the last time you were on a range?"

"Uh, it's been a while." In truth, Evans had never fired a gun in his life. And until this moment, he was proud of it. He shook his head. "I'm not much of a gun guy."

Kenner had a revolver in his hands. He had opened the cylinder and was checking it. Sanjong was over by his own car, checking an evil-looking rifle, matte black stock with a telescopic sight. His manner was quick, practiced. A soldier. Uneasily, Evans thought: *What is this, the O.K. Corral?*

"We'll be all right," Sarah said to Kenner. "I have a gun."

"You know how to use it?"

"I do."

"What is it?"

"A .38 Revolver."

Kenner shook his head. "Can you handle an automatic?"

"Sure."

He gave her a 9-millimeter Beretta and a holster. She clipped the holster to the waistband of her jeans. She seemed to know what she was doing.

Evans said, "Do you really expect us to shoot somebody?"

"Not unless you have to," Kenner said. "But you may need to defend yourself."

"You think they'll have guns?"

"They might. Yes."

"Jesus."

"It's okay," Sarah said. "Personally, I'll be

happy to shoot the bastards." Her voice was hard, angry.

"All right, then," Kenner said. "That about does it. Let's mount up."

Evans thought, *Mount up.* Jesus. This *was* the O.K. Corral.

Kenner drove to the other side of the park and spoke briefly to a state trooper, whose black-and-white patrol car stood at the edge of a clearing. Kenner had arranged radio contact with the trooper. In fact, they were all going to be in radio contact, because the plan required a high degree of coordination. They would have to hit the three spiderweb sites at the same time.

As Kenner explained it, the rockets were intended to do something called "charge amplification" of the storm. It was an idea from the last ten years, when people first began to study lightning in the field, in actual storms. The old idea was that each lightning strike decreased the storm's intensity, because it reduced the difference in electrical charge between the clouds and the ground. But some researchers had concluded that lightning strikes had the opposite effect— they increased the power of storms dramatically. The mechanism for this was not known, but was presumed to be related to the sudden heat of the lightning bolt, or the shockwave it created, adding turbulence to the already turbulent storm center. In any case, there was now a theory that if you could make more lightning, the storm would get worse.

"And the spiderwebs?" Evans said.

"They're little rockets with microfilaments attached. They go up a thousand feet into the cloud layer, where the wire provides a low-resistance conduction pathway and creates a lightning strike."

"So the rockets cause more lightning? That's what they're for?"

"Yes. That's the idea."

Evans remained doubtful. "Who pays for all this research?" he said. "The insurance companies?"

Kenner shook his head. "It's all classified," he said.

"You mean it's military?"

"Correct."

"The military pays for weather research?"

"Think about it," Kenner said.

Evans was not inclined to do so. He was deeply skeptical of all things military. The notion that they were paying for weather research struck him as the same sort of ludicrous excess as the six-hundred-dollar toilet seats and thousand-dollar wrenches that had become so notorious. "If you ask me, it's all a waste of money."

"ELF doesn't think so," Kenner said.

It was then that Sanjong spoke, with considerable intensity. Evans had forgotten that he was a soldier. Sanjong said that whoever could control the weather would control the battlefield. It was an age-old military dream. Of course the military would spend money on it.

"You're saying it actually works."

"Yes," Sanjong said. "Why do you think we are here?"

* * *

The SUV wound up into the wooded hills north of McKinley Park. This was an area of intermittent dense forest and open grassy fields. In the passenger seat, Sarah looked at Peter. He was good-looking, and he had the strong physique of an athlete. But sometimes he behaved like such a wimp.

"You ever do any sports?" she said.

"Sure."

"What?"

"Squash. A little soccer."

"Oh."

"Hey," he said. "Just because I don't shoot guns . . . I'm a lawyer, for Christ's sake."

She was disappointed with him and not even sure why. Probably, she thought, because she was nervous and wanted somebody competent to be with her. She liked being around Kenner. He was so knowledgeable, so skilled. He knew what was going on. He was quick to respond to any situation.

Whereas Peter was a nice guy, but . . .

She watched his hands on the wheel. He drove well. And that was important today.

It was no longer sunny. They were close to the storm clouds. The day was dark, gloomy, threatening. The road ahead was deserted as it wound through the forests. They hadn't seen a car since they left the park.

"How much farther?" Evans said.

Sarah consulted the GPS. "Looks like another five miles."

He nodded. Sarah shifted in her seat, moving

so the holstered gun would not press against her
hip. She glanced at the passenger-side mirror.

"Oh shit."

"What?"

Behind them was a battered blue pickup truck.
With Arizona plates.

"We've got trouble," Sarah said.

"Why?" Evans said. He glanced in the rearview mirror, saw the truck. "What is it?"

Sarah had the radio in her hand. "Kenner. They spotted us."

"Who did?" Evans said. "Who are they?"

The radio clicked. "Where are you?" Kenner said.

"On Highway 95. We're about four miles away."

"Okay," Kenner said. "Stick with the plan. Do your best."

"Who is it?" Evans said, looking in the mirror.

The blue pickup was advancing fast. Very fast. In the next instant, it banged into the back of their car. Evans was startled, swerved, got control again. "What the *fuck?*" he said.

"Just drive, Peter."

Sarah took the revolver from its holster. She held the gun on her lap, looked out the side mirror.

The blue truck had dropped back for a moment, but now raced forward again.

"Here he comes—"

Perhaps because Peter stepped on the gas, the impact was surprisingly gentle. It was hardly more than a nudge. Peter careened around the curves, glancing at the rearview mirror.

Again, the blue truck dropped back. It followed them for the next half mile, but it was never closer than five or six car lengths.

"I don't get it," Evans said. "Are they going to ram us or not?"

"Guess not," she said. "See what happens if you slow down."

He slowed the SUV, dropping their speed to forty.

The blue truck slowed too, falling back farther.

"They're just following us," she said.

Why?

The first scattered drops of rain spattered the windshield. The road ahead was spotted. But they weren't yet in full rain.

The blue truck dropped even farther back now.

They came around a curve, and immediately ahead of them saw a big silver eighteen-wheeler, with a big trailer. It was rumbling slowly along the road, not going more than thirty miles an hour. On its back doors it said, "A&P."

"Oh shit," Evans said. In the back mirror, they saw the blue truck, still following. "They've got us front and back."

He swerved out, trying to pass the big trailer, but as soon as he did, the driver moved toward the center of the road. Evans immediately fell back.

"We're trapped," he said.

"I don't know," she said. "I don't get it."

The trailer blocked them at the front, but behind them the blue truck was farther back than ever, several hundred yards down the road.

She was still puzzling over this situation when a bolt of lightning crashed down at the side of the road as they drove past. It couldn't have been more than ten yards away, a white-hot, dazzling blast of light and sound. They both jumped.

"Jesus, that was close," Evans said.

"Yes . . ."

"I've never seen one that close."

Before she could answer, a second bolt crashed down, directly in front of them. The sound was explosive; Evans swerved involuntarily, even though the bolt was gone.

"Holy shit."

By then Sarah had a suspicion, just as the third bolt hit the car itself, a deafening crash and a sudden pressure that made knife pains in her ears and a blast of white that enveloped the car. Evans screamed in fear and let go of the wheel; Sarah grabbed it and straightened the car in the road.

A fourth bolt smashed down by the driver's side, just inches from the car. The driver's-side window cracked and splintered.

"Holy shit," Evans was saying. "Holy shit! What is this?"

To Sarah, it was only too obvious.

They were attracting lightning.

The next bolt cracked down, and was immediately followed by another, which smashed into the hood and spread burning white, jagged fingers over the car, and then was gone. There was a huge black indentation in the hood.

"I can't do this," Evans was saying. "I can't, I can't do this."

"Drive, Peter," Sarah said, grabbing his arm and squeezing hard. *"Drive."*

Two more bolts hit them, in rapid succession. Sarah smelled the odor of something burning—she wasn't sure what. But now she understood why they had been so gently rammed.

The blue pickup had stuck something onto their car. Some kind of electronic thing. And it was drawing the lightning to them.

"What do we do? What do we do?" Evans was whimpering. He howled as each new bolt struck.

But they were trapped, driving on a narrow road, hemmed in by dense pine forest on both sides of the road . . .

Something she should know.

Forest . . . What about the forest?

A lightning bolt cracked the rear window with explosive force. Another bolt struck them so hard it bounced the car on the macadam, as if it had been hit by a hammer.

"The hell with this," Evans said, and spun the wheel, turning off the highway and onto a dirt track in the forest. Sarah saw a sign flash by, the name of a town on a battered post. They were plunged into near darkness under the huge, green pines. But the lightning immediately stopped.

Of course, she thought. *The trees.*

Even if their car was attracting lightning, it would strike the taller trees first.

A moment later, it did. They heard a sharp crack just behind them, and lightning flashed down the side of a tall pine, splitting the trunk open with what looked like steam and bursting the tree into flames.

"We're going to start a forest fire."

"I don't care," Evans said. He was driving fast. The vehicle was bouncing over the dirt road, but it was an SUV and it rode high so Sarah knew they would be all right.

Looking back, she saw the tree burning, and the fire spreading laterally in fingers along the ground.

Kenner on the radio: "Sarah, what's happening?"

"We had to leave the road. We're being struck by lightning."

"A lot!" Evans yelled. "All the time!"

"Find the attractor," Kenner said.

"I think it's attached to the car," Sarah said. As she spoke, a bolt smashed down on the road just ahead of them. The glare was so bright she saw green streaks before her eyes.

"Then dump the car," Kenner said. "Go out as low as you can."

He clicked off. Evans continued to race forward, the SUV bouncing on the ruts. "I don't want to leave," he said. "I think we're safer inside. They always say don't leave your car because you're safer inside. The rubber tires insulate you."

"But something's on fire," she said, sniffing.

The car jolted and bounced. Sarah tried to keep her balance, just holding onto her seat, not touching the metal of the doors.

"I don't care, I think we should stay," Evans said.

"The gas tank might explode . . ."

"I don't want to leave," he said. "I'm not leaving." His knuckles were white, gripping the wheel. Ahead, Sarah saw a clearing in the forest. It was a large clearing, with high, yellow grass.

A lightning bolt smashed down with a fearsome crack, shattering the side mirror, which blew apart like a bomb. A moment later, they heard a soft *whump*. The car tilted to one side. "Oh shit," Evans said. "It blew a tire."

"So much for the insulation," she said.

The car was now grinding, the underside scraping over a dirt rut, metal squealing.

"Peter," she said.

"All right, all right, just let me get to the clearing."

"I don't think we can wait."

But the rut ended, the road flattened, and Evans drove forward, creaking on the rim, into the clearing. Raindrops spattered the windshield. Above the grass, Sarah saw the roofs of wooden buildings bleached by the sun. It took her a moment to realize that this was a ghost town. Or a mining town.

Directly ahead was a sign, AURORAVILLE, POP. 82. Another lightning bolt crashed down, and Evans hit the sign, knocking it over.

"Peter, I think we're here."

"Okay, yeah, let me get a little closer—"

"Now, Peter!"

He stopped the car, and they flung open their doors in unison. Sarah threw herself bodily onto the ground, and another bolt crashed so close to her that the blast of hot air knocked her sideways and sent her rolling on the ground. The roar of the lightning was deafening.

She got up on hands and knees, and scrambled around to the back of the vehicle. Evans was on the other side of the SUV, yelling something, but she couldn't hear him. She examined the rear bumper. There was no attachment, no device.

There was nothing there.

But she had no time to think, because another bolt struck the back of the SUV, rocking it, and the rear window shattered, sprinkling her with shards of glass. She fought panic and scrambled forward, staying low as she moved around the SUV and through the grass toward the nearest building.

Evans was somewhere ahead, yelling to her. But she couldn't hear him over the rumbling thunder. She just didn't want another bolt, not now, if she could just go a few more seconds . . .

Her hands touched wood. A board.

A step.

She crawled forward quickly, pushing aside the grass, and now she saw a porch, a dilapidated building, and swinging from the roof a sign bleached so gray she couldn't see what it said. Evans was inside, and she scrambled forward, ignoring the splinters in her hands, and he was yelling, yelling.

And she finally heard what he was saying:

"Look out for the scorpions!"

They were all over the wooden porch—tiny, pale yellow, with their stingers in the air. There must have been two dozen. They moved surprisingly fast, scampering sideways, like crabs.

"Stand up!"

She got to her feet, and ran, feeling the arachnids crunch under her feet. Another lightning bolt smashed into the building's roof, knocking down the sign, which fell in a cloud of dust onto the porch.

But then she was inside the building. And Evans was standing there, fists raised, yelling, "Yes! Yes! We did it!"

She was gasping for breath. "At least they weren't snakes," she said, chest heaving.

Evans said, "What?"

"There're always rattlers in these old buildings."

"Oh Jesus."

Outside, thunder rumbled.

And the lightning started again.

Through the shattered, grimy window Sarah was looking at the SUV, and thinking that now that they had left the car, there were no more lightning strikes on the SUV . . . thinking . . . nothing on the bumper . . . then why had the pickup nudged the SUV? What was the point? She turned to ask Evans if he had noticed—

And a lightning bolt blasted straight down through the roof, smashing it open to the dark sky, sending boards flying in all directions, and blasting into the ground right where she had been standing. The lightning left a blackened pattern of jagged streaks, like the shadow of a thorn bush on the floor. The ozone smell was strong. Wisps of smoke drifted up from the dry floorboards.

"This whole building could go," Evans said. He was already flinging a side door open, heading outside.

"Stay low," Sarah said, and followed him out.

The rain was coming down harder, big splattering drops that struck her back and shoulders as she ran to the next building. It had a brick chimney, and looked generally better built. But the windows were the same, broken and thickly coated with dust and grime.

They tried the nearest door, but it was jammed shut, so they ran around to the front, and found that door wide open. Sarah ran inside. A lightning bolt smashed down behind her, sagging the roof over the porch, splintering one of the side posts as it streaked down into the ground. The shockwave blasted the front windows in a shower of dirty glass. Sarah turned away, covering her face, and when she looked out again, she realized she was in a blacksmith's shop. There was a large firepit in the center of the room, and above it all sorts of iron implements hanging from the ceiling.

And on the walls, she saw horseshoes, tongs, metal of all sorts.

This room was full of metal.

The thunder rumbled ominously. "We have to get out of here," Evans shouted. "This is the wrong place to—"

He never finished. The next bolt knocked him

off his feet as it came crashing down through the ceiling, spinning the iron implements, then smashing into the firepit, blasting the bricks outward in all directions. Sarah ducked, covering her head and ears, felt bricks striking her shoulders, back, legs—knocking her over—and then there was a burst of pain in her forehead, and she saw brief stars before blackness settled over her and the rumble of thunder faded to endless silence.

Kenner was fifteen miles away, driving east on Route 47, listening to Sarah's radio. Her transmitter was still on, clipped to her belt. It was hard to be sure what was happening because each lightning strike produced a burst of static that lasted for the next fifteen seconds. Nevertheless he understood the most important point—Evans and Sarah had gotten away from the SUV, but the lightning hadn't stopped. In fact it seemed that the lightning was following them.

Kenner had been yelling into his handset, trying to get Sarah's attention, but apparently she had turned her volume down, or was too busy dealing with what was happening in the ghost town. He kept saying, "It's following you!" over and over.

But she never answered.

Now there was a long burst of static, followed by silence. Kenner switched channels.

"Sanjong?"

"Yes, Professor."

"Have you been listening?"

"Yes."

"Where are you?" Kenner said.

"I am on Route 190, going north. I estimate I am three miles from the web."

"Any lightning yet?"

"No. But the rain has just started here. First drops on the windshield."

"Okay. Hang on."

He went back to Sarah's channel. There was still static, but it was fading.

"Sarah! Are you there? Sarah! Sarah!"

Kenner heard a cough, a distant cough.

"Sarah!"

A click. A bang. Someone fumbling with the radio. A cough. "This is Peter. Evans."

"What's happening there?"

"—dead."

"What?"

"She's dead. Sarah's dead. She got hit with a brick, and she fell and then there was a lightning strike that hit her full on the body and she's dead. I'm right here beside her. She's dead, oh shit, she's dead . . ."

"Try mouth-to-mouth."

"I'm telling you, she's dead."

"Peter. *Mouth-to-mouth*."

"Oh God . . . She's *blue* . . ."

"That means she's alive, Peter."

"—like a corpse, a—corpse—"

"Peter, listen to me."

But Evans wasn't hearing anything. The idiot had his finger on the radio button. Kenner swore in frustration. And then suddenly a new blast of static. Kenner knew what it meant.

There had been another lightning strike. A bad one.

"Sanjong?"

Now, Kenner heard nothing but static on Sanjong's channel, too. It lasted ten seconds, fifteen seconds. So Sanjong had a strike, too. Only then did Kenner realize what must be causing it.

Sanjong came back, coughing.

"Are you all right?"

"I had a lightning strike. Very near the car. I cannot imagine, so close."

"Sanjong," Kenner said. "I think it's the radios."

"You think?"

"Where'd we get them?"

"I had them FedExed from DC."

"Package delivered to you personally?"

"No. To the motel. The owner gave it to me when I checked in . . . But the box was sealed . . ."

"Throw your radio away," Kenner said.

"There's no cellular net, we won't be in communic—"

Nothing more. Just a blast of static.

"Peter."

There was no answer. Only silence on the radio. Not even static now.

"Peter. Answer me. Peter. Are you there?"

Nothing. Dead.

Kenner waited a few moments. There was no answer from Evans.

The first drops of rain splashed on Kenner's

windshield. He rolled down his window, and threw his radio away. It bounced on the pavement, and went into the grass on the other side of the road.

Kenner had gone another hundred yards down the road when a bolt of lightning crashed down behind him on the opposite side of the road.

It was the radios, all right.

Somebody had gotten to the radios. In DC? Or in Arizona? It was hard to know for sure, and at this point it didn't matter. Their carefully coordinated plan was now impossible to carry out. The situation was suddenly very dangerous. They had planned to hit all three rocket arrays at the same time. That would not happen now. Of course Kenner could still hit his array. If Sanjong was still alive, he might get to the second array, but their attack would not be coordinated. If one of them were later than the other, the second rocket team would have been informed by radio, and would be waiting with guns ready. Kenner had no doubt about that.

And Sarah and Evans were either dead or unable to function. Their car was broken down. Certainly they would never make it to the third array.

So. Just one rocket array taken out. Maybe two.

Would that be enough?

Maybe, he thought.

Kenner looked at the road ahead, a pale strip under dark skies. He did not think about whether his friends were alive or not. Perhaps all three were dead. But if Kenner did not stop the storm, there would be hundreds dead. Children, families.

Paper plates in the mud, while the searchers dug out the bodies.

Somehow he had to stop it.

He drove forward, into the storm.

"Mommy! Mommy! Brad hit me! Mommy! Make him stop!"

"All right, kids . . ."

"Bradley? How many times do I have to tell you? Leave your sister alone!"

Standing to one side of McKinley Park, Trooper Miguel Rodriguez of the Arizona Highway Patrol stood by his car and watched the picnic in progress. It was now eleven-thirty in the morning, and the kids were getting hungry. They were starting to fight. All around the park, barbecues were going, the smoke rising into an ever-darkening sky. Some of the parents looked upward with concern, but nobody was leaving the park. And the rain hadn't started here, even though they had heard the crack of lightning and the rumble of thunder a few miles to the north.

Rodriguez glanced at the bullhorn resting on the seat of his car. For the last half hour, he had waited impatiently for the radio call from Agent Kenner, telling him to clear the park.

But the call hadn't yet come.

And Agent Kenner had given him explicit instructions. Do not clear McKinley Park before he was given the word.

Trooper Rodriguez didn't understand why it was necessary to wait, but Kenner had been insistent. He said it was a matter of national security. Rodriguez didn't understand that either. How was a damn picnic in a park a matter of national security?

But he knew an order when he heard one. So Rodriguez waited, impatient and uneasy, and watched the sky. Even when he heard the weather service announce a flash flood advisory for the eastern counties from Kayenta to Two Guns and Camp Payson—an area that included McKinley—Rodriguez still waited.

He could not know that the radio call he was waiting for would never come.

In retrospect, what saved Peter Evans was the slight tingling he had felt, holding the radio in his sweating palm. In the minutes before, Evans had realized that something was causing the lightning to follow them wherever they went. He didn't know any science, but assumed it must be something metallic or electronic. Talking to Kenner, he had felt the faint electric tingle from the handset—and on an impulse he had flung it across the room. It landed against a large iron viselike contraption that looked like a bear trap.

The lightning crashed down a moment later, glaring white and roaring, and Evans threw himself flat, across Sarah's dead body. Lying there, dizzy with fear, his ears ringing from the blast, he thought for a moment that he felt some movement from her body beneath him.

He got up quickly and began to cough. The room was full of smoke. The opposite wall was on fire, the flames still small, but already licking up the wall. He looked back at Sarah, blue and cold. There was no question in his mind that she was dead. He must have imagined her movement, but—

He pinched her nose and began to give her mouth-to-mouth. Her lips were cold. It frightened him. He was sure she was dead. He saw hot embers and ash floating in the smoky air. He would have to leave before the entire building came down around him. He was losing his count, blowing into her lungs.

There was no point anyway. He heard the flames crackling around him. He looked up and saw that the ceiling timbers were starting to burn.

He felt panic. He jumped to his feet, ran to the door, and threw it open and went outside.

He was stunned to feel hard rain coming down—pelting him, soaking him instantly. It shocked him to his senses. He looked back and saw Sarah lying on the floor. He couldn't leave her.

He ran back, grabbed both her arms, and dragged her out of the house. Her inert body was surprisingly heavy. Her head sagged back, eyes closed, her mouth hanging open. She was dead, all right.

Out in the rain once more, he dropped her in the yellow grass, got down on his knees, and gave her more mouth-to-mouth. He was not sure how long he kept up his steady rhythm. One minute, two minutes. Maybe five. It was clearly pointless, but he continued long past any reason, because in a strange way the rhythm relieved his own sense of panic, it gave him something to concentrate on. He was out there in the middle of a pelting downpour with a ghost town in flames around him anyway, and—

Sarah retched. Her body rose up suddenly, and he released her in astonishment. She had a spasm of dry heaves, and then fell into a fit of coughing.

"Sarah . . ."

She groaned. She rolled over. He grabbed her in his arms, and held her. She was breathing. But her eyes fluttered wildly. She didn't seem to be conscious.

"Sarah, come on . . ."

She was coughing, her body shaking. He wondered if she was choking to death.

"Sarah . . ."

She shook her head, as if to clear it. She opened her eyes and stared at him. "Oh man," she said. "Do I have a *headache*."

He thought he was going to cry.

Sanjong glanced at his watch. The rain was coming down harder now, the wipers flicking back and forth. It was very dark, and he had turned on his headlights.

He had thrown his radio away many minutes before, and the lightning had stopped around his car. But it was continuing elsewhere—he heard the rumble of distant thunder. Checking the GPS, he realized he was only a few hundred yards from the spiderweb he was meant to disrupt.

He scanned the road ahead, looking for the turnoff. That was when he saw the first cluster of rockets firing skyward, like black birds streaking straight up into the dark and roiling clouds.

And in a moment, a cluster of lightning bolts came blasting downward, carried on the wires.

* * *

Ten miles to the north, Kenner saw the rocket array fire upward from the third spiderweb. He guessed there were only about fifty rockets in that array, which meant there were another hundred still on the ground.

He came to the side road, turned right, and came instantly into a clearing. There was a large eighteen-wheeler parked to one side. There were two men in yellow rain slickers standing beside the cab. One of them held a box in his hands—the firing device.

Kenner didn't hesitate. He spun the wheel of the SUV and drove right for the cab. The men were stunned for a moment, and at the last moment jumped aside just as Kenner scraped along the side of the cab, screeching metal, and then turned into the rocket field itself.

In his rearview mirror he saw the men scrambling up, but by now he was within the spiderweb array, driving along the line of wires, trying to crush the launch tubes under his wheels. As he hit them he could hear: *Thunk! Thunk! Thunk!* He hoped that would disrupt the firing pattern, but he was wrong.

Directly ahead, he saw another fifty rockets spout flames, and rush upward into the sky.

Sanjong was inside the second clearing. He saw a wooden cabin off to the right, and a large truck parked beside it. There were lights in the cabin, and he saw shapes moving in the windows. There were men in there. Wires came out from the front door of the cabin and disappeared in the grass.

He drove straight for the cabin, and he pushed the cruise control on the steering wheel.

From the front door he saw one man come out, cradling a machine gun. Flame spurted from the barrel and Sanjong's windshield shattered. He threw open his door and jumped out of the SUV, holding his rifle away from his body, then landing and rolling in the grass.

He looked up just in time to see the SUV smash into the cabin. There was a lot of smoke and shouting. Sanjong was only about twenty yards away. He waited. After a moment, the man with the machine gun came running around to the side of the SUV, to look for the driver. He was shouting excitedly.

Sanjong fired once. The man fell backward.

He waited. A second man came out, yelling in the rain. He saw the fallen man, and jumped back, huddling behind the front bumper of the SUV. He leaned forward and called to the fallen man.

Sanjong shot at him. The man disappeared, but Sanjong was not certain he had hit him.

He had to change position now. The rain had matted down the grass, so there was not as much cover as he would have liked. He rolled quickly, moving laterally about ten yards, and then crawled forward cautiously, trying to get a view into the cabin. But the car had smashed in the front door, and the lights inside were now out. He was sure there were more men in the cabin but he did not see anyone now. The shouting had stopped. There was just the rumble of thunder and the patter of rain.

He strained, listening. He heard the crackle of radios. And voices.

There were still men in the cabin.

He waited in the grass.

Rain dripped in Evans's eyes as he spun the wrench, tightening the lug nuts on the front wheel of the SUV. The spare tire was now securely in place. He wiped his eyes, and then briefly tightened each lug nut in turn. Just to be sure. It was a rough road going back to the main highway, and now with this rain it would be muddy. He didn't want the wheel coming loose.

Sarah was waiting for him in the passenger seat. He had half-dragged, half-carried her back to the vehicle. She was still dazed, out of it, so he was surprised to hear her shouting something over the sound of the rain.

Evans looked up.

He saw headlights, in the distance. On the far side of the clearing.

He squinted.

It was the blue pickup truck.

"Peter!"

He dropped the lug wrench and ran for the driver's side. Sarah had already started the engine. He got behind the wheel and put the SUV in gear. The blue truck was gaining on them, coming across the clearing.

"Let's go," Sarah said.

Evans stepped on the gas, turned, and drove into the forest—heading back the way they had come. Behind them, the burning building had been put out by the rain. It was now a smoldering wreck, hissing clouds of steam.

The blue pickup drove past the building without a pause. And came down the road after them.

Kenner turned, and came back toward the eighteen-wheeler. The men were standing there, holding the firing box. One had a pistol out, and began firing at Kenner. Kenner accelerated hard, driving straight at them. He hit the man with the pistol. His body was thrown into the air, over the top of the SUV. The second man had somehow gotten away. Kenner spun the wheel.

As he came back he saw the man he had hit staggering to his feet in the grass. The other man was nowhere to be seen. The staggering man raised his gun just as Kenner hit him again. He went down, and the SUV bounced over his body. Kenner was looking for the other man—the man with the firing box.

He didn't see him anywhere.

He spun the wheel. There was only one place the man could have gone.

Kenner drove straight for the truck.

Sanjong was waiting in the grass when he heard the sound of a truck engine. His view was blocked by his own crashed SUV. The truck was behind the SUV. He heard someone put it into gear, backing up.

Sanjong got to his feet and began to run. A bullet whined past him. He dropped to the ground again.

They had left someone in the house.

He stayed low in the grass, and crawled forward, heading for the truck. Bullets snapped in the grass all around him. Somehow they had his position, even in the grass. That meant . . .

He twisted, turning to face the house. He wiped the rain out of his eyes and looked through the sights of his rifle.

The guy was on the roof of the cabin. Barely visible, except when he rose up to fire.

Sanjong fired just below the roofline. He knew the bullet would pass right through the wood. He didn't see the man again. But the man's rifle slid down the roof as Sanjong watched.

He got to his feet and ran toward the truck, but it was already driving away, heading out from the clearing, a pair of red taillights in the rain, disappearing onto the main road.

Kenner was out of his SUV, and on the ground. He could see the last guy, a silhouette under the big eighteen-wheeler.

"Don't shoot me, don't shoot me!" the guy was yelling.

"Come out slowly, with your hands empty," Kenner shouted. "I want to see your hands."

"Just don't shoot . . ."

"Come out. Real slow and—"

A sudden burst of machine gun fire. The wet grass around him snapped.

Kenner pressed his face into the wet earth, and waited.

* * *

"Go faster!" Sarah said, looking over her shoulder.

Their SUV bounced in the mud, headlights jumping wildly.

"I don't think I can . . ." Evans said.

"They're gaining!" she said. "You have to go faster!"

They were almost out of the forest. Evans could see the highway just a few dozen yards ahead. He remembered that the last section of the dirt track was less eroded, and he accelerated, heading there.

And came out onto the highway, going south.

"What are you doing?" Sarah said. "We have to go to the rocket field."

"It's too late now," he said. "We're going back to the park."

"But we promised Kenner—"

"It's too late," he said. "Look at the storm. It's already full blown. We have to get back to help those families in the park."

He turned the windshield wipers on full force, and raced down the road in the storm.

Behind them, the pickup truck turned and followed them.

Trooper Miguel Rodriguez had been watching the waterfall. An hour ago, it had been a clear mist, coming over the cliff's edge. Now it was tinged with brown, and it had more volume. The river, too, was starting to rise. It was flowing faster, and beginning to turn a muddy brown.

But it was still not raining at the park. The air had turned distinctly humid, and there had been scattered raindrops for a few minutes, but then the rain had stopped. A few families had abandoned their barbecues. A half-dozen more were packing up their cars in anticipation of the coming storm. But most had chosen to ignore it. The school principal was walking among the picnickers, telling people the weather would pass, urging everyone to stay.

Rodriguez was edgy. He tugged at his uniform collar, uncomfortable in the dampness. He paced back and forth beside his open car door. He heard the police radio announce flash flood warnings for Clayton County, which was where McKinley Park was located. He didn't want to wait any longer, but still he hesitated.

He couldn't understand why Kenner hadn't called him. The park was located in a canyon, and there was every sign of a potential flash flood. Rodriguez had lived in northern Arizona his whole life. He knew he should clear the park now.

Why hadn't Kenner called?

He drummed his fingers on the door of the car.

He decided to give it five more minutes.

Five minutes. No more.

What worried him most at the moment was the waterfall. The brown tinge had put people off, and most of the crowd had moved away. But a few teenagers were still playing in the pool at the base of the fall. Rodriguez knew that rocks could come over the cliff any minute now. Even small rocks would have enough force to kill a person at the bottom.

Rodriguez was thinking about clearing the waterfall area when he noticed something strange. Up at the top of the cliff, where the water came over the lip, he saw a van with an antenna. It looked like a TV station van. There was no lettering on the side, but there was a logo of some kind. Still he couldn't make it out from this distance. He saw a cameraman get out of the van and take a position by the waterfall, crouching down with a camera mounted on his shoulder and looking down into the park. A woman in a skirt and blouse stood by his side, pointing in this direction and that. Apparently telling him where to film, because he was turning the camera where she pointed.

It was definitely a news crew.

He thought: *A news crew for a school picnic?*

Rodriguez squinted, trying to identify the van's logo. It was yellow and blue, sort of swirly interlocking circles. He didn't recognize it as one of the local stations. But there was something distinctly creepy about this crew, coming here right as the storm was descending on the park. He decided he'd better walk over and have a talk with them.

Kenner didn't want to kill the guy now huddled beneath the semi. No member of ELF had ever been captured, and this one seemed a likely candidate. Kenner could tell from the sound of the guy's voice that he was scared. And he sounded young, maybe in his twenties. Probably he was shaken by the death of his friend. Certainly he couldn't handle a machine gun very well.

Now this guy was afraid he was going to die, too. Maybe he was having second thoughts about his cause.

"Come out now," Kenner yelled to him. "Come out, and everything will be all right."

"Fuck you," the guy said. "Who the fuck are you, anyway? What is your fucking problem? Don't you get it, man? We're trying to save the planet."

"You're breaking the law," Kenner said.

"The *law*," the guy said contemptuously. "The law's owned by the corporations that pollute the environment and destroy human life."

"The only one killing people is you," Kenner said. Thunder was rumbling and lightning flickered dimly behind the inky clouds. It was absurd to be having this conversation in the middle of a storm.

But it was worth it to get the guy alive.

"Hey, I'm not killing anyone," the guy said. "Not even you."

"You're killing little kids," Kenner said, "in the park. You're killing families on a picnic."

"Casualties are inevitable in accomplishing social change. History tells us that."

Kenner wasn't sure whether the guy believed what he was saying, had been fed it at college, or was just distracted by fear. Then again, maybe it was meant to be a distraction . . .

He looked to his right, beneath his own vehicle. And he saw a pair of feet moving around the SUV and heading toward him.

Ah hell, he thought. It was disappointing. He aimed carefully and shot once, hitting the man behind the SUV in the ankle. The guy screamed in pain and went down on his back. Kenner could see him under the car. He wasn't young, maybe forty or forty-five. Bearded. He carried a machine gun, and he was rolling over to shoot—

Kenner fired twice. The man's head jerked back. He dropped the machine gun and did not move, his body sprawled awkwardly in the grass.

The man under the semi began to fire his own machine gun. The bullets were flying wildly. Kenner heard several *thunk* into his SUV. Kenner lay in the grass, head down.

When the shooting stopped, he yelled, "Last chance!"

"Fuck you!"

Kenner waited. There was a long pause. He listened to the sound of the rain. It was coming down very hard, now.

He waited.

The guy yelled, "Did you hear me, you fucking asshole?"

"I heard you," Kenner said, and shot once.

It was a real desert downpour, Evans thought, gripping the steering wheel. The rain was coming down in dense sheets. Even with the windshield wipers going as fast as they could, he found it almost impossible to see the road ahead. He had dropped his speed to fifty, then forty. Now he was down to thirty. The pickup truck behind them had slowed, too. There was no real choice.

He passed one or two other cars, but they were all pulled over to the side of the road. It was the sensible thing to do.

The pavement was awash in water, and whenever the pavement dipped a little, it formed a lake, or a rushing rivulet. Sometimes he could not tell how deep the water was, and he didn't want to soak his ignition. He gunned the engine to keep it dry.

He didn't see any road signs. It was almost as dark as night out there, and he had his headlights on, but they seemed to make no difference. He could see only a few yards ahead through the rain.

He looked over at Sarah, but she was just staring forward. Not moving, not speaking. He wondered if she was all right.

Looking in the rearview mirror, he could sometimes see the lights of the pickup truck following him, and sometimes not. There was that much rain.

"I think we're almost to the park," he said. "But I can't be sure."

The interior of the windshield was starting to fog up. He rubbed it with the back of his arm and his elbow, making a squeaking sound on the glass. Now he could see a little better. They were at the top of a gentle hill, heading down toward—

"Oh shit."

"What?" Sarah said.

"Look."

At the bottom of the hill was a fifteen-foot culvert, the road passing over a series of large pipes carrying water from a small stream. Earlier, the stream had been little more than a silvery trickle in a rocky bed. But it had broadened and risen so that it now flowed over the surface of the road, the water moving swiftly.

Evans couldn't tell how deep it was. Probably not very deep.

"Peter," Sarah said. "You've stopped the car."

"I know."

"You can't stop."

"I don't know if I can go through this," he said. "I don't know how deep—"

Six inches of water is enough to carry away a car.

"You've got no choice."

In his rearview mirror, he saw the lights of the pickup truck. He headed down the hill, toward the culvert. He kept his eyes on the mirror, waiting to see what the truck did. It had slowed as well, but it was still following as he drove the SUV down the hill.

"Keep your fingers crossed," Evans said.

"I've got everything crossed."

He entered the water. It was whooshing up on the sides of the car, spraying up as high as the windows, and gurgling under the floorboards. He was terrified that he would lose the ignition, but so far, so good.

He gave a sigh. He was approaching the middle now, and it wasn't that deep. No more than two, two and a half feet. He would make it okay.

"Peter . . ." Sarah pointed ahead.

There was a large eighteen-wheeler coming down the road toward them. Its lights were flaring. It wasn't slowing down at all.

"He's an idiot," Evans said.

Moving slowly in the water, he turned right, moving farther toward his side of the road, to make room.

In response, the truck moved directly into his lane.

It did not slow down.

Then he saw the logo above the cab.

It said in red letters, "A&P."

"Peter, *do something!*"

"Like *what?*"

"*Do something!*"

Several tons of roaring steel were coming right at him. He glanced in the rearview mirror. The blue pickup truck was still behind him, closing in.

They had him front and back.

They were going to drive him off the road.

The semi was in deeper water now, roaring forward. The water plumed high on both sides.

"*Peterrrrr!*"

There wasn't any choice.

He spun the wheel and drove off the road, plunging into the water of the rushing stream.

The SUV nosed down, and water came over the hood, up to the windshield, and for a moment he thought they were going to sink right there. Then the bumper crunched against the rocks of the streambed, and the wheels gained purchase, and the car straightened.

For a thrilling moment he thought he was going to be able to drive the car along the streambed— the river wasn't that deep, not really—but almost at once, the engine died, and he felt the rear end pull loose and spin around.

And they were carried helplessly along in the river.

Evans turned the ignition, trying to start the engine again, but it wasn't working. The SUV moved gently, rocking and bumping against rocks. Occasionally it would stop, and he considered getting out, but then it would begin to float downstream again.

He looked over his shoulder. The road was surprisingly far back. Now that the engine was out, the car was fogging up quickly. He had to rub all the windows, to see out.

Sarah was silent. Gripping the arms of her seat.

The car came to a stop again, against a rock. "Should we get out?" she said.

"I don't think so," he said. He could feel the car shuddering in the moving water.

"I think we should," she said.

The car started to move again. He tried the ignition, but it would not start up. The alternator whirred and sputtered. Then he remembered.

"Sarah," he said. "Open your window."

"What?"

"Open your window."

"Oh." She flicked the switch. "It doesn't work."

Evans tried his own window on the driver's side. It didn't work, either. The electrical systems were shot.

On a chance, he tried the rear windows. The left window opened smoothly.

"Hey! Success."

Sarah said nothing. She was looking forward.

The stream was moving faster, the car picking up speed.

He kept rubbing the fogged windows, trying to see, but it was difficult and suddenly the car gave a sharp jolt, and afterward the movement was different. It went swiftly ahead, turning slowly in circles. The wheels no longer touched rock.

"Where are we? What happened?" Together, they rubbed the windshield frantically to get it clean.

"Oh Jesus," Sarah said, when she saw.

They were in the middle of a rushing river. Muddy brown, and moving fast, standing waves of churning water. There were big tree branches and debris moving swiftly along. The car was going faster and faster every second.

And water was coming in through the floor now. Their feet were wet. Evans knew what that meant.

They were sinking.

"I think we should get out, Peter."

"No." He was looking at the standing waves of churning water. There were rapids, big boulders, sinkholes. Maybe if they had helmets and body protection, they might try to go into the current. But without helmets they would die.

The car tilted to the right, then came back up. But he had the feeling that sooner or later it would roll onto its side and sink. And he had the feeling it would sink fast.

He looked out the window and said, "Does this look familiar? What river is this?"

"Who cares?" Sarah yelled.

And then Evans said, "Look!"

Trooper Rodriguez saw the SUV bouncing and spinning down the river and immediately hit his car siren. He grabbed the bullhorn and turned to the picnickers.

"Folks, please clear the area! We have a flash flood *now*. Everybody move to higher ground, and do it now!"

He hit the siren again.

"Now, folks! Leave your things for later. *Go now!*"

He looked back at the SUV, but it was already almost out of sight, headed down the river toward the McKinley overpass. And right beyond the McKinley overpass was the cliff's edge, a ninety-foot drop.

The car and its occupants wouldn't survive it.

And there was nothing they could do about it.

Evans couldn't think, couldn't plan—it was all he could do to hang on. The SUV rolled and turned in the churning water. The vehicle was sinking lower, and the water now sloshing at knee height was freezing cold, and seemed to make the car more unstable, its movements more unpredictable.

At one point he banged heads with Sarah, who grunted, but she was not saying anything either. Then he banged his head on the door post, saw stars briefly.

Ahead, he saw an overpass, a roadway held up with big concrete stanchions. Each stanchion had caught debris floating downriver; the pylons were now wrapped with a tangled mat of tree branches, burned trunks, old boards, and floating junk, so that there was little room to pass by.

"Sarah," he yelled, "unbuckle your seat belt." His own belt was now under the chilly water. He fumbled with it, as the car rolled.

"I can't," she said. "I can't get it."

He bent to help her.

"What are we going to do?"

"We're going to get out," he said.

The car raced forward, then slammed into a mass of branches. It shuddered in the current, but held position. It clanged against an old refrigerator (*a refrigerator?* Evans thought) that bobbed in the water nearby. The pylon loomed above them. The river was so high, the road overpass was only about ten feet above them.

"We have to get out, Sarah," he said.

"My belt is stuck; I can't."

He bent to help her, plunging his hands into the water, fumbling for the belt. He couldn't see it in the mud. He had to do it by feel.

And he felt the car begin to move.

It was going to break free.

Sanjong was driving furiously along the upper road. He saw Peter and Sarah in their SUV, riding the current toward the bridge. He saw them crash against the pylon, and hold precariously there.

The traffic on the bridge was swarming away from the park, passengers panicking, honking horns, confusion. Sanjong drove across the bridge, and jumped out of his car. He began to run across the bridge, toward the car in the water below.

Evans hung on desperately as the SUV rolled and spun in the churning water. The refrigerator clanged against them, again and again. Branches stuck through the shattered windows, the tips quivering like fingers. Sarah's seat belt was jammed, the latch was crumpled or something. Evans's fingers were numb in the cold. He knew that the car wouldn't stay in position very long. He could feel the current pulling at it, dragging it laterally.

"I can't get it open, Sarah," he said.

The water had risen; it was now almost chest high.

"What do we do?" she said. Her eyes were panicky.

For an instant he didn't know, and then he thought *I'm an idiot* and he threw himself bodily across her, plunged his head underwater, and felt for the door post on her side of the car. He dragged a three-foot length of the seat belt away from the post, and brought his head back up, gasping for air.

"Slide out!" he yelled. "Slide out!"

She understood immediately, putting her hands on his shoulder and shoving as she slithered out from the belt. His head went back under the water, but he could feel her getting free. She moved into the backseat, kicking him in the head as she went.

He was back up above the water, gasping.

"Now climb out!" he yelled.

The car was starting to move. The branches creaking. The refrigerator clanging.

Sarah's athleticism stood her in good stead. She slipped through the rear window, and hung onto the car.

"Go for the branches! Climb!" He was afraid the current would take her if she held onto the car. He was scrambling back into the rear seat, then squeezing himself through the window. The car was pulling loose, trembling at first, then distinctly moving, rolling around the debris pile, and he was still half out the window.

"Peter!" Sarah shouted.

He lunged, throwing himself forward into the branches, scratching his face but feeling his hands close around large branches and he pulled his body clear of the car just as the current ripped it away, dragging it under the bridge.

The car was gone.

He saw Sarah climbing up the debris stack, reaching up for the concrete railing of the roadway. He followed her, shivering from cold and fear. In a few moments, he felt a strong hand reach down and pull him up the rest of the way. He looked up and saw Sanjong grinning at him.

"My friend. You are a lucky one."

Evans came over the railing and toppled onto the ground, gasping, exhausted.

Distantly, he heard the sound of a police siren, and a bullhorn barking orders. He became aware of the traffic on the bridge, the honking horns, the panic.

"Come on," Sarah said, helping him up. "Somebody's going to run over you if you stay here."

* * *

Trooper Rodriguez was still getting everybody into their cars, but there was pandemonium in the parking lot and a traffic jam on the bridge. The rain was starting to come down hard. That was making people move faster.

Rodriguez cast a worried eye at the waterfall, noting that it was a darker brown, and flowing more heavily than before. He saw then that the TV crew had gone. The van was no longer atop the cliff. That was odd, he thought. You'd think they'd have stayed to film the emergency exit.

Cars were honking on the bridge, where traffic was stalled. He saw a number of people standing there, looking over the other side. Which could only mean that the SUV had gone over the cliff.

Rodriguez slipped behind the wheel to radio for an ambulance. That was when he heard that an ambulance had already been called to Dos Cabezas, fifteen miles to the north. Apparently a group of hunters had gotten into a drunken argument, and there had been some shooting. Two men were dead and a third was injured. Rodriguez shook his head. Damn guys went out with a rifle and a bottle of bourbon each, and then had to sit around drinking because of the rain, and before you knew it, couple of them were dead. Happened every year. Especially around the holidays.

"I don't see why this is necessary," Sarah said, sitting up in bed. She had electrodes stuck to her chest and legs.

"Please don't move," the nurse said. "We're trying to get a record."

They were in a small, screened-off cubicle in the Flagstaff hospital emergency room. Kenner, Evans, and Sanjong had insisted she come there. They were waiting outside. She could hear them talking softly.

"But I'm twenty-eight years old," Sarah said. "I'm not going to have a heart attack."

"The doctor wants to check your conduction pathways."

"My conduction pathways?" Sarah said. "There's nothing wrong with my conduction pathways."

"Ma'am? Please lie down and don't move."

"But this is—"

"And don't talk."

She lay down. She sighed. She glanced at the monitor, which showed squiggly white lines. "This is ridiculous. There's nothing wrong with my heart."

"No, there doesn't seem to be," the nurse said, nodding to the monitor. "You're very lucky."

Sarah sighed. "So, can I get up now?"

"Yes. And don't you worry yourself about those burn marks," the nurse said. "They'll fade over time."

Sarah said, "What burn marks?"

The nurse pointed to her chest. "They're very superficial."

Sarah sat up and looked down her blouse. She saw the white adhesive tags of the electrodes. But she also saw pale brown streaks, jagged marks that ran across her chest and abdomen. Like zig-zags or something—

"What is this?" she said.

"It's from the lightning."

She said, "What?"

"You were struck by lightning," the nurse said.

"What are you talking about?"

The doctor came in, an absurdly young man, prematurely balding. He seemed very busy and preoccupied. He said, "Don't worry about those burn marks, they'll fade in no time at all."

"It's from lightning?"

"Pretty common, actually. Do you know where you are?"

"In Flagstaff hospital."

"Do you know what day it is?"

"Monday."

"That's right. Very good. Look at my finger, please." He held his finger up in front of her face, moved it left and right, up and down. "Follow it. That's good. Thank you. You have a headache?"

"I did," she said. "Not anymore. Are you telling me I was struck by lightning?"

"You sure as heck were," he said, bending to hit her knees with a rubber hammer. "But you're not showing any signs of hypoxia."

"Hypoxia . . ."

"Lack of oxygen. We see that when there's a cardiac arrest."

She said, "What are you talking about?"

"It's normal not to remember," the doctor said. "But according to your friends out there, you arrested and one of them resuscitated you. Said it took four or five minutes."

"You mean I was dead?"

"Would have been, if you hadn't gotten CPR."

"*Peter* resuscitated me?" It had to be Peter, she thought.

"I don't know which one." Now he was tapping her elbows with the hammer. "But you're a very lucky young woman. Around here, we get three, four deaths a year from strikes. And sometimes very serious burns. You're just fine."

"Was it the young guy?" she said. "Peter Evans? Him?"

The doctor shrugged. He said, "When was your last tetanus?"

"I don't understand," Evans said. "On the news report it said they were hunters. A hunting accident or an argument of some kind."

"That's right," Kenner said.

"But you're telling me you guys shot them?" Evans looked from Kenner to Sanjong.

"They shot first," Kenner said.

"Jesus," Evans said. "Three deaths?" He bit his lip.

But in truth, he was feeling a contradictory reaction. He would have expected his native caution to take over—a series of killings, possibly murders, he was an accomplice or at the very least a material witness, he could be tied up in court, disgraced, disbarred. . . . That was the path his mind usually followed. That was what his legal training had emphasized.

But at this moment he felt no anxiety at all. Extremists had been discovered and they had been killed. He was neither surprised nor disturbed by the news. On the contrary, he felt quite satisfied to hear it.

He realized then that his experience in the crevasse had changed him—and changed him permanently. Someone had tried to kill him. He could never have imagined such a thing growing up in suburban Cleveland, or in college, or law school. He could never have imagined such a thing while living his daily life, going to work at his firm in Los Angeles.

And so he could not have predicted the way that he felt changed by it now. He felt as if he had been physically moved—as if someone had picked him up and shifted him ten feet to one side. He was no longer standing in the same place. But he had also been changed internally. He felt a kind of solid impassivity he had not known before. There were unpleasant realities in the world, and previously he had averted his eyes from them, or changed the subject, or made excuses for what had occurred.

He had imagined that this was an acceptable strategy in life—in fact, that it was a more humane strategy. He no longer believed that.

If someone tried to kill you, you did not have the option of averting your eyes or changing the subject. You were forced to deal with that person's behavior. The experience was, in the end, a loss of certain illusions.

The world was not how you wanted it to be.

The world was how it was.

There were bad people in the world. They had to be stopped.

"That's right," Kenner was saying, nodding slowly. "Three deaths. Isn't that right, Sanjong?"

"That's right," Sanjong said.

"Screw 'em," Evans said.

Sanjong nodded.

Kenner said nothing.

The jet flew back to Los Angeles at six o'clock. Sarah sat in the front, staring out the window. She listened to the men in the back. Kenner was talking about what would happen next. The dead men were being ID'd. Their guns and trucks and clothes were being traced. And the television film crew had already been found: it was a truck from KBBD, a cable station in Sedona. They'd gotten an anonymous call saying that the highway patrol had been derelict and had allowed a picnic to proceed despite flash flood warnings, and disaster was probable. That was why they had gone to the park.

Apparently it never occurred to anyone to question why they'd got an anonymous call half an hour before a flash flood warning had been issued from the NEXRAD center. The call had been traced, however. It had been placed from a pay phone in Calgary, Canada.

"That's organization," Kenner said. "They knew the phone number of the station in Arizona before they ever started this thing."

"Why Calgary?" Evans said. "Why from there?"

"That seems to be one primary location for this group," Kenner said.

Sarah looked at the clouds. The jet was above the weather. The sun was setting, a golden band in the west. The view was serene. The events of the day seemed to have occurred months before, years before.

She looked down at her chest and saw the faint brownish markings from the lightning. She'd taken an aspirin, but it was still beginning to hurt slightly, to burn. She felt marked. A marked woman.

She no longer listened to what the men were saying, only to the sound of their voices. She noticed that Evans's voice had lost its boyish hesitancy. He was no longer protesting everything Kenner said. He sounded older somehow, more mature, more solid.

After a while, he came up to sit with her. "You mind company?"

"No." She gestured to a seat.

He dropped into it, wincing slightly. He said, "You feel okay?"

"I'm okay. You?"

"A little sore. Well. Very sore. I think I got banged around in the car."

She nodded, and looked out the window for a while. Then she turned back. "When were you going to tell me?" she said.

"Tell you what?"

"That you saved my life. For the second time."

He shrugged. "I thought you knew."

"I didn't."

She felt angry when she said it. She didn't know why it should make her angry, but it did. Maybe because now she felt a sense of obligation, or . . . or . . . she didn't know what. She just felt angry.

"Sorry," he said.

"Thanks," she said.

"Glad to be of service." He smiled, got up, and went to the back of the plane again.

It was odd, she thought. There was something about him. Some surprising quality she hadn't noticed before.

When she looked out the window again, the sun had set. The golden band was turning richer, and darker.

In the back of the plane, Evans drank a martini and stared at the monitor mounted on the wall. They had the satellite linkup of the news station in Phoenix. There were three anchors, two men and a woman, at a curved table. The graphic behind their heads read "Killings in Canyon Country" and apparently referred to the deaths of the men in Flagstaff, but Evans had come in too late to hear the news.

"There's other news from McKinley State Park, where a flash flood warning saved the lives of three hundred schoolchildren on a school picnic. Officer Mike Rodriguez told our own Shelly Stone what happened."

There followed a brief interview with the highway patrol officer, who was suitably laconic. Neither Kenner nor his team was mentioned.

Then there was footage of Evans's overturned SUV, smashed at the bottom of the cliff. Rodriguez explained that fortunately no one was in the car when it was carried away by the floodwater.

Evans gulped his martini.

Then the anchors came back onscreen, and

one of the men said, "Flood advisories remain in effect, even though it is unseasonable for this time of year."

"Looks like the weather's changing," the anchorwoman said, tossing her hair.

"Yes, Marla, there is no question the weather is changing. And here, with that story, is our own Johnny Rivera."

They cut to a younger man, apparently the weatherman. "Thanks, Terry. Hi, everybody. If you're a longtime resident of the Grand Canyon State, you've probably noticed that our weather is changing, and scientists have confirmed that what's behind it is our old culprit, global warming. Today's flash flood is just one example of the trouble ahead—more extreme weather conditions, like floods and tornadoes and droughts—all as a result of global warming."

Sanjong nudged Evans, and handed him a sheet of paper. It was a printout of a press release from the NERF website. Sanjong pointed to the text: ". . . scientists agree there will be trouble ahead: more extreme weather events, like floods and tornadoes and drought, all as a result of global warming."

Evans said, "This guy's just reading a press release?"

"That's how they do it, these days," Kenner said. "They don't even bother to change a phrase here and there. They just read the copy outright. And of course, what he's saying is not true."

"Then what's causing the increase in extreme weather around the world?" Evans said.

"There is no increase in extreme weather."

"That's been studied?"

"Repeatedly. The studies show no increase in extreme weather events over the past century. Or in the last fifteen years. And the GCMs don't predict more extreme weather. If anything, global warming theory predicts *less* extreme weather."

"So he's just full of shit?" Evans said.

"Right. And so is the press release."

Onscreen, the weatherman was saying, "—is becoming so bad, that the latest news is—get this—glaciers on Greenland are melting away and will soon vanish entirely. Those glaciers are three miles thick, folks. That's a lotta ice. A new study estimates sea levels will rise twenty feet or more. So, sell that beach property now."

Evans said, "What about that one? It was on the news in LA yesterday."

"I wouldn't call it news," Kenner said. "Scientists at Reading ran computer simulations that suggested that Greenland *might* lose its ice pack in the next thousand years."

"Thousand years?" Evans said.

"Might."

Evans pointed to the television. "He didn't say it could happen a thousand years from now."

"Imagine that," Kenner said. "He left that out."

"But you said it isn't news . . ."

"You tell me," Kenner said. "Do you spend much time worrying about what might happen a thousand years from now?"

"No."

"Think anybody should?"

"No."

"There you are."

When he had finished his drink he suddenly felt sleepy. His body ached; however he shifted in his seat, something hurt—his back, his legs, his hips. He was bruised and exhausted. And a little tipsy.

He closed his eyes, thinking of news reports of events a thousand years in the future.

All reported as if it were up-to-the-minute, important life-and-death news.

A thousand years from now.

His eyes were heavy. His head fell to his chest, then jerked up abruptly as the intercom came on.

"Fasten your seat belts," the captain said. "We are landing in Van Nuys."

All he wanted to do was sleep. But when he landed, he checked his cell phone messages and discovered that he had been missed, to put it mildly:

"Mr. Evans, this is Eleanor in Nicholas Drake's office. You left your cell phone. I have it for you. And Mr. Drake would like to speak to you."

"Peter, it's Jennifer Haynes at John Balder's office. We'd like you to come to the office no later than ten o'clock tomorrow please. It's quite important. Call me if for some reason you can't make it. See you then."

"Peter, call me. It's Margo. I'm out of the hospital."

"Mr. Evans, this is Ron Perry at the Beverly Hills police department. You've missed your four o'clock appointment to dictate a statement. I don't want to issue a warrant for your arrest. Call me. You have the number."

"This is Herb Lowenstein. Where the hell are you? We don't hire junior associates to have them disappear day after day. There is work to be done here. Balder's office has been calling. They want you at the Culver City office tomorrow morning by ten A.M. sharp. My advice is, be there, or start looking for another job."

"Mr. Evans, this is Ron Perry from Beverly Hills police. Please return my call ASAP."

"Peter, call me. Margo."

"Peter, want to get together tonight? It's Janis. Call me."

"Mr. Evans, I have Mr. Drake for you, at the NERF office."

"Peter, it's Lisa in Mr. Lowenstein's office. The police have been calling for you. I thought you would want to know."

"Peter, it's Margo. When I call my lawyer I expect to get a call back. Don't be an asshole. Call me."

"This is Ron Perry from the Beverly Hills police department. If I do not hear from you I will have to ask the judge to issue a warrant for your arrest."

"Evans, it's Herb Lowenstein. You really are a dumb shit. The police are going to issue a warrant for your arrest. Deal with it at once. Members of this firm do not get arrested."

Evans sighed, and hung up.

Sarah said, "Trouble?"

"No. But it doesn't look like I will be getting any sleep for a while."

He called the detective, Ron Perry, and was told that Perry was gone for the day, and would be in court in the morning. His cell phone would be off. Evans left a number for him to call back.

He called Drake, but he was gone for the day.

He called Lowenstein, but he was not in the office.

He called Margo, but she did not answer.

He called Jennifer Haynes and said that he would be there tomorrow, at ten o'clock.

"Dress professionally," she said.

"Why?"

"You're going to be on television."

There were two white camera trucks parked out-side the offices of the Vanutu litigation team. Evans went inside and found workmen setting up lights and changing fluorescent light bulbs in the ceiling. Four different video crews were walking around, inspecting different angles. But nobody was shooting yet.

The offices themselves, he noticed, had been considerably transformed. The graphs and charts on the walls were now much more complicated and technical looking. There were huge, blowup photographs of the Pacific nation of Vanutu, as seen from the air and from the ground. Several featured the erosion of the beaches, and houses leaning at an angle, ready to slide into the water. There was a school picture from the Vanutu school, beautiful brown-skinned kids with smil-ing faces. In the center of the room, there was a three-dimensional model of the main island, specially lit for cameras.

Jennifer was wearing a skirt and blouse and heels. She looked startlingly beautiful in a dark, mysterious way. Evans noticed that everyone was better dressed than at his first visit; all the researchers were now in jackets and ties. The jeans and T-shirts were gone. And there seemed to be a lot more researchers.

"So," Evans said, "what is this about?"

"B-roll," Jennifer said. "We're shooting B-roll for the stations to use as background and cut-aways. And of course we're making a video press kit as well."

"But you haven't announced the lawsuit yet."

"That happens this afternoon, here outside the warehouse. Press conference at one P.M. You'll be there, of course?"

"Well, I didn't—"

"I know John Balder wants you there. Representing George Morton."

Evans felt uneasy. This could create a political problem for him at the firm. "There are several attorneys more senior than I who handled George's—"

"Drake specifically asked for you."

"He did?"

"Something about your involvement in getting the papers signed to finance this suit."

So that was it, Evans thought. They were putting him on television so he would not be able later to say anything about the gift of ten million dollars to NERF. No doubt they would stick him in the background for the announcement ceremony, maybe make a brief acknowledgment of his presence. Then Drake would say that the ten million was coming, and unless Evans stood up and contradicted him, his silence would be taken as acquiescence. Later, if he developed any qualms, they could say, But you were there, Evans. Why didn't you speak up then?

"I see," Evans said.

"You look worried."

"I am . . ."

"Let me tell you something," she said. "Don't worry about it."

"But you don't even know—"

"Just listen to me. Don't worry about it." She was looking directly into his eyes.

"Okay . . ."

Of course she meant well, but despite her words, Evans was experiencing an unpleasant, sinking feeling. The police were threatening to issue a warrant for his arrest. The firm was complaining about his absences. Now this effort to force him into silence—by putting him on television.

He said, "Why did you want me here so early?"

"We need you to sit in the hot seat again, as part of our test for jury selection."

"I'm sorry, I can't—"

"Yes. You have to. Same thing as before. Want some coffee?"

"Sure."

"You look tired. Let's get you to hair and makeup."

Half an hour later he was back in the deposition room, at the end of the long table. There was again a crew of eager young scientific types looking down at him.

"Today," Jennifer said, "we would like to

consider issues of global warming and land use. Are you familiar with this?"

"Only slightly," Evans said.

Jennifer nodded to one of the researchers at the far end. "Raimundo? Will you give him the background?"

The researcher had a heavy accent, but Evans could follow him. "It is well known," he said, "that changes in land use will cause changes in average ground temperature. Cities are hotter than the surrounding countryside—what is called the 'urban heat island' effect. Croplands are warmer than forested lands, and so on."

"Uh-huh," Evans said. Nodding. He hadn't heard about these land use concepts, but it certainly stood to reason.

Raimundo continued, "A high percentage of weather stations that were out in the countryside forty years ago are now surrounded by concrete and skyscrapers and asphalt and so on. Which makes them register warmer."

"I understand," Evans said. He glanced away, through the glass wall. He saw film crews moving around the warehouse, shooting various things. He hoped the crews wouldn't come in. He didn't want to sound stupid in front of them.

"These facts," Raimundo said, "are well known within the field. So researchers take the raw temperature data from stations near cities and reduce them by some amount to compensate for the urban heat island effect."

Evans said, "And how is this reduction calculated?"

"Different ways, depending on who does it.

But most algorithms are based on population size. The larger the population, the greater the reduction."

Evans shrugged. "That sounds like the right way to do it."

"Unfortunately," he said, "it probably isn't. Do you know about Vienna? It was studied by Bohm a few years back. Vienna has had no increase in population since 1950, but it has more than doubled its energy use and increased living space substantially. The urban heat island effect has increased, but the calculated reduction is unchanged, because it only looks at population change."*

"So the heating from cities is being underestimated?" Evans said.

"It's worse than that," Jennifer said. "It used to be assumed that urban heating was unimportant because the urban heat island effect was only a fraction of total warming. The planet warmed about .3 degrees Celsius in the last thirty years. Cities are typically assumed to have heated by around .1 degree Celsius."

"Yes? So?"

"So those assumptions are wrong. The Chinese report that Shanghai warmed 1 degree Celsius in the last twenty years alone.[†] That's more than the

---

* R. Bohm, "Urban bias in temperature time series—a case study for the city of Vienna, Austria," *Climatic Change* 38, (1998): 113–1128. Ian G. McKendry, "Applied Climatology," *Progress in Physical Geography* 27, 4 (2003): 597–606. "Population-based adjustments for the UHI in the USA may be underestimating the urban effect."

[†] L. Chen, et al., 2003, "Characteristics of the heat island effect in Shanghai and its possible mechanism," *Advances in Atmospheric Sciences* 20: 991–1001.

total global warming of the planet in the last hundred years. And Shanghai is not unique. Houston increased .8 degrees Celsius in the last twelve years.* Cities in South Korea are heating rapidly.† Manchester, England, is now 8 degrees warmer than the surrounding countryside.‡ Even small towns are much hotter than the surrounding areas."

Jennifer reached for her charts. "Anyway," she said, "the point is that the graphs you see are not raw data. They have already been adjusted with fudge factors to compensate for urban heating. But probably not enough."

At that moment, the door opened and one of the four video crews came in, their camera light shining. Without hesitation, Jennifer reached for some charts, and brought them up. She whispered, "B-roll is silent, so we need to be active and provide visuals."

She turned toward the camera and said, "Let me show you some examples of weather station data. Here, for instance, is a record of the average temperature for Pasadena since 1930."§

---

* D. R. Streutker, "Satellite-measured growth of the urban heat island of Houston, Texas," *Remote Sensing of Environment* 85 (2003): 282–289. "Between 1987 and 1999, the mean nighttime surface temperature heat island of Houston increased 0.82±0.10°C."

† Y. Choi, H.-S. Jung, K.-Y. Nam, and W.-T. Kwon, "Adjusting urban bias in the regional mean surface temperature series of South Korea, 1968–99," *International Journal of Climatology* 23 (2003): 577–91.

‡ http://news.bbc.co.uk/1/hi/in_depth/sci_tech/2002/leicester_2002/2253636.stm. The BBC gives no scientific reference for the eight-degree claim.

§ LA population is 14,531,000; Berkeley is 6,250,000; New York is 19,345,000.

Pasadena, CA 1930–2000

Source: United States Historical Climatology Network (USHCN)

"As you see," Jennifer said, "a dramatic rise in temperature. And here is Berkeley since 1930."

Berkeley, CA 1930–2000

Source: United States Historical Climatology Network (USHCN)

"A surprisingly incomplete record. But we are using raw data, so you can see missing years. And you see a clear warming trend. Indisputable, wouldn't you agree?"

"I would," Evans said, thinking that it wasn't much of a trend—less than a degree.

"Now, here is Death Valley, one of the hottest, driest places on Earth. No urbanization has occurred here. Again, missing years."

Death Valley, CA 1933–2000

Source: United States Historical Climatology Network (USHCN)

Evans said nothing. It must be an anomaly, he thought. Jennifer put up more graphs:

McGill, NV 1930–2000

Source: United States Historical Climatology Network (USHCN)

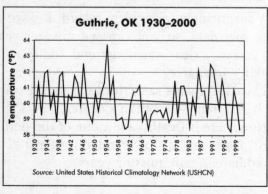

Guthrie, OK 1930–2000

Source: United States Historical Climatology Network (USHCN)

"These are stations from the Nevada desert and the Oklahoma plains," she said. "They show temperatures that are flat, or declining. And not only rural areas. Here is Boulder, Colorado. It's only of interest because NCAR is located there— the National Center for Atmospheric Research, where so much global warming research is done."

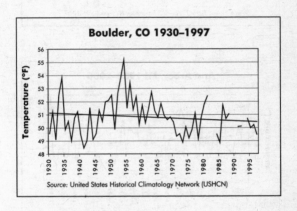

"Here are some more small cities. Truman, Missouri, where the buck stops . . ."

Source: United States Historical Climatology Network (USHCN)

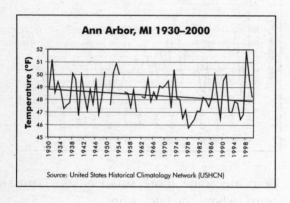

Source: United States Historical Climatology Network (USHCN)

Evans said, "You have to admit, it's not very dramatic."

"I'm not sure what you consider dramatic. Truman has gotten colder by 2.5 degrees, Greenville by 1.5 degrees, Ann Arbor by one degree since 1930. If the globe is warming, these places have been left out."

"Let's look at some bigger places," Evans said, "like Charleston."

"I have Charleston." She thumbed through her graphs.

Charleston, SC 1930–2000

Source: United States Historical Climatology Network (USHCN)

Evans said, "So, a bigger city gets warmer. What about New York?"

"I have several records from New York, city and state."

New York, NY 1930–2000

Source: United States Historical Climatology Network (USHCN)

Syracuse, NY 1930–2000

Source: United States Historical Climatology Network (USHCN)

Albany, NY 1930–2000

Source: United States Historical Climatology Network (USHCN)

Oswego, NY 1930–2000

Source: United States Historical Climatology Network (USHCN)

"As you see," Jennifer said, "New York City is warmer, but many other parts of the state, from Oswego to Albany, have become colder since 1930."

Evans was acutely aware of the cameras on him. He nodded in what he hoped was a judicious, thoughtful manner and said, "And where does this data come from?"

"From the Historical Climatology Network data set," she said. "It's a government data set, maintained at Oak Ridge National Laboratories."

"Well, it's quite interesting. But, I'd like to see

the data from Europe and Asia. This is, after all, a global phenomenon."

"Certainly," Jennifer said. She, too, was playing to the cameras. "But before we do that, I'd like your reaction to the data so far. As you can see, many places in the United States do not seem to have become warmer since 1930."

"I'm sure you cherry-picked your data," Evans said.

"To some degree. As we can be sure the defense will do."

"But the results do not surprise me," Evans said. "Weather varies locally. It always has and always will." A thought occurred to him. "By the way, why are all these graphs since 1930? Temperature records go much further back than that."

"Your point is well taken," Jennifer said. "It definitely makes a difference how far back you go. For example, here is West Point, New York, from 1931 to 2000. Trending down."

Source: United States Historical Climatology Network (USHCN)

"And here is West Point from 1900 to 2000. This time the trend is up, not down."

West Point, NY 1900–2000

Source: United States Historical Climatology Network (USHCN)

"Ah-ha," Evans said. "So you *were* massaging the data. You picked the interval of years that made you look good!"

"Absolutely," Jennifer said, nodding. "But the trick only works because temperatures in many parts of the US were warmer in the 1930s than they are today."

"It's still a trick."

"Yes, it is. The defense will not miss the opportunity to show the jury numerous examples of this trick from environmental fund-raising literature. Selecting specific years that appear to show things are getting worse."

Evans registered her insult to environmental groups. "In that case," he said, "let's not permit any tricks at all. Use the full and complete temperature record. How far back does it go?"

"At West Point, back to 1826."

"Okay. Then suppose you use that?" Evans felt confident proposing this, because it was well known that a worldwide warming trend had begun at about 1850. Every place in the world had gotten warmer since then, and the graph from West Point would reflect that.

Jennifer seemed to know it too, because she suddenly appeared very hesitant, turning away, thumbing through her stack of graphs, frowning as if she couldn't find it.

"You don't have that particular graph, do you?" he said.

"No, no. Believe me, I have it. Yes. Here." And then she pulled it out:

West Point, NY 1826–2000

Source: United States Historical Climatology Network (USHCN)

Evans took one look and saw that she had sandbagged him.

"As you predicted, this graph is quite telling," she said. "For the last one hundred seventy-four years, there has been no change in the average temperature at West Point. It was 51 degrees Fahrenheit in 1826, and it is 51 degrees in 2000."

"But that's just one record," Evans said, recovering quickly. "One of many. One of hundreds. Thousands."

"You're saying that other records will show other trends?"

"I'm sure they will. Especially using the *full* record from 1826."

"And you are correct," she said. "Different records do show different trends."

Evans sat back, satisfied with himself. Hands crossed over his chest.

"New York City, a rise of 5 degrees Fahrenheit in a hundred seventy-eight years," she said.

New York, NY 1822–2000

Source: United States Historical Climatology Network (USHCN)

"Albany, a decline of half a degree in a hundred eighty years."

Evans shrugged. "Local variations, as I said before."

"But I wonder," Jennifer said, "how these local variations fit into a theory of *global* warming. As I understand it, global warming is caused by an increase in so-called greenhouse gases, such as carbon dioxide, that trap heat in the Earth's atmosphere and prevent it from escaping into space. Is that your understanding?"

Source: United States Historical Climatology Network (USHCN)

"Yes," Evans said, grateful he did not have to summon a definition on his own.

"So, according to the theory," Jennifer said, "the atmosphere itself gets warmer, just as it would inside a greenhouse?"

"Yes."

"And these greenhouse gases affect the entire planet."

"Yes."

"And we know that carbon dioxide—the gas we all worry about—has increased the same amount everywhere in the world . . ." She pulled out another graph.*

"Yes . . ."

"And its effect is presumably the same everywhere in the world. That's why it's called *global* warming."

---

* South Pole, Mauna Loa: C. D. Keeling, T. P. Whorf, and the Carbon Dioxide Research Group, Scripps Institute of Oceanography (SIO), University of California, La Jolla, CA 92093, U.S.A.; Seychelles: Thomas J. Conway, Pieter Tans, Lee S. Waterman, National Oceanic and Atmospheric Administration, Climate Monitoring and Diagnostics Laboratory, 325 Broadway, Boulder CO 80303. See http://cdiac.esd. ornl.gov/trends/co2/contents.htm.

Source: http://cdiac.esd.ornl.gov/trends/co2/contents.htm

"Yes . . ."

"But New York and Albany are only a hundred forty miles apart. You can drive between them in three hours. Their carbon dioxide levels are identical. Yet one got a lot warmer and the other got slightly colder. Is that evidence for *global* warming?"

"Weather is local," Evans said. "Some places are warmer or colder than others. And always will be."

"But we are talking about climate, not weather. Climate is weather over a long time period."

"Yes . . ."

"So I would agree with you if both locations got warmer, albeit by different amounts. But here, one got warmer and one got colder. And as we saw, West Point—which is midway between them—remained unchanged."

Evans said, "I think the theory of global warming predicts that some places will get colder."

"Really? Why is that?"

"I'm not sure, but I read it somewhere."

"The Earth's entire atmosphere warms, and as a result some places get colder?"

"I believe so."

"As you think about it now, does that claim make sense to you?"

"No," Evans said, "but you know, climate is a complex system."

"Which means what, to you?"

"It means it's, uh, complicated. It doesn't always behave the way you think it will."

"That's certainly true," Jennifer said. "But going back to New York and Albany. The fact that these two locations are so close, yet their temperature records are so different, could lead a jury to wonder whether we're really measuring something other than a *global* effect. You would agree that in the last hundred eighty-five years, New York has grown to a city of eight million, whereas Albany has grown much less?"

"Yes," Evans said.

"And we know that the urban heat island effect makes cities hotter than the surrounding countryside."

"Yes . . ."

"And this urban heat effect is a local effect, unrelated to global warming?"

"Yes . . ."

"So, tell me: how do you know that the dramatic increase in temperature in New York is caused by global warming, and not just from an excess of concrete and skyscrapers?"

"Well." Evans hesitated. "I don't know the answer to that. But I assume it is known."

"Because if cities like New York become larger

and hotter than they were before, they will raise the average global temperature, will they not?"

"I assume they will."

"In which case, as cities expand all around the world, we might see an increase in average ground temperature simply because of urbanization. Without any global atmospheric effect at all."

"I am sure the scientists have thought of that already," Evans said. "I'm sure they can answer that."

"Yes, they can. Their answer is that they have subtracted a factor from the raw data to compensate for the urban heat effect."

"Well, there you are."

"Excuse me? Mr. Evans, you're a lawyer. Surely you are aware of the extraordinary efforts that are made in a lawsuit to be certain the evidence is untainted."

"Yes, but—"

"You don't want anybody to be able to change it."

"Yes . . ."

"But in this case, the evidence is the raw temperature data. And it is tainted by the very scientists who claim global warming is a worldwide crisis."

"Tainted? It's adjusted *downward*."

"But the question the defense will ask is, have they adjusted downward *enough*?"

"I don't know," Evans said, "this is getting very specialized and nitpicky."

"Hardly. It's a core issue. Urbanization versus

greenhouse gases as the cause of the increased average surface temperature. And the defense will have a good argument on their side," Jennifer said. "As I said before, several recent studies suggest the reduction for urban bias has, in fact, been too small.* At least one study suggests that half of the observed temperature change comes from land use alone. If that's true, then global warming in the past century is less than three tenths of a degree. Not exactly a crisis."

Evans said nothing. He tried to look intelligent for the cameras.

"Of course," Jennifer continued, "that study can be debated, too. But the point remains: as soon as anybody adjusts the data, they open themselves to the claim that their adjustment was incorrect. That's better ground for the defense. And the larger point the defense will make is that we have allowed the data to be adjusted by the very people who have the most to gain from that adjustment."

"You're saying that climate scientists are unethical?"

"I'm saying it is never a good policy for the fox to guard the hen house. Such procedures are never allowed in medicine, for example, where double-blind experimental designs are required."

"So you're saying climate scientists *are* unethical."

---

* For a summary, see Ian G. McKendry, 2003, "Applied climatology," *Progress in Physical Geography* 27, 4:597–606. "Recent studies suggest that attempts to remove the 'urban bias' from long-term climate records (and hence identify the magnitude of the enhanced greenhouse effect) may be overly simplistic."

"No, I'm saying that there are good reasons why double-blind procedures are instituted. Look: Every scientist has some idea of how his experiment is going to turn out. Otherwise he wouldn't do the experiment in the first place. He has an expectation. But expectation works in mysterious ways—and totally unconsciously. Do you know any of the studies of scientific bias?"

"No." Evans shook his head.

"Okay. Simple example. A group of genetically identical rats are sent to two different labs for testing. One lab is told that the rats were bred for intelligence and will run a maze faster than normal. The other lab is told that the rats are dumb and will run a maze slowly. Results come back— faster in one lab, slower in the other. Yet the rats are genetically identical."

"Okay, so they fudged."

"They said they didn't. Anyway, there's much more," she said. "Next example. A group of survey takers are told, Look, we know that pollsters can influence results in subtle ways. We want to avoid that. So you knock on the door, and the minute someone answers you start reading only what is on this card: 'Hello, I am doing a survey, and I am reading from this card in order not to influence you . . . et cetera.' The poll takers say nothing except what is on the card. One group of pollsters is told, this questionnaire will get seventy percent positive answers. They tell another group, you can expect thirty percent positive answers. Identical questionnaires. The results come back—seventy and thirty."

"How?" Evans said.

"It doesn't matter," she said. "All that matters is that hundreds of studies prove again and again that expectations determine outcome. People find what they think they'll find. That's the reason for 'double-blind' experiments. To eliminate bias, the experiment is divided up among different people *who do not know each other.* The people who prepare the experiment do not know the people who conduct the experiment or the people who analyze the results. These groups never communicate in any way. Their spouses and children never meet. The groups are in different universities and preferably in different countries. That's how new drugs are tested. Because that's the only way to prevent bias from creeping in."

"Okay . . ."

"So now we're talking about temperature data. It has to be adjusted in all kinds of ways. Not just for urban heat bias. Lots of other things. Stations move. They upgrade, and the new equipment may read hotter or colder than before. The equipment malfunctions and you have to decide whether to throw out certain data. You deal with lots of judgment calls in putting together the temperature record. And that's where the bias creeps in. Possibly."

"Possibly?"

"You don't know," Jennifer said, "but whenever you have one team doing all the jobs, then you're at risk for bias. If one team makes a model and also tests it and also analyzes the results, those results are at risk. They just are."

"So the temperature data are no good?"

"The temperature data are *suspect*. A decent

attorney will tear them apart. To defend them, what we intend to do is—"

Abruptly, the camera crew got up and left the room. Jennifer rested her hand on his arm. "Don't worry about any of that, the footage they shot was without sound. I just wanted it to look like a lively discussion."

"I feel foolish."

"You looked good. That's all that matters for TV."

"No," he said, leaning closer to her. "I mean, when I gave those answers, I wasn't saying what I really think. I'm, uh . . . I'm asking some—I'm changing my mind about a lot of this stuff."

"Really?"

"Yes," he said, speaking quietly. "Those graphs of temperature, for instance. They raise obvious questions about the validity of global warming."

She nodded slowly. Looking at him closely.

He said, "You, too?"

She continued to nod.

They lunched at the same Mexican restaurant as before. It was almost empty, as before; the same Sony film editors laughing at the corner table. They must come here every day, Evans thought.

But somehow everything was different, and not just because his body ached and he was on the verge of falling asleep any moment. Evans felt as if he had become a different person. And their relationship was different, too.

Jennifer ate quietly, not saying much. Evans had the sense she was waiting for him.

After a while, he said, "You know, it would be

crazy to imagine that global warming wasn't a real phenomenon."

"Crazy," she said, nodding.

"I mean, the whole world believes it."

"Yes," she said. "The whole world does. But in that war room, we think only about the jury. And the defense will have a field day with the jury."

"You mean, the example you told me?"

"Oh, it's much worse than that. We expect the defense to argue like this: Ladies and gentlemen of the jury, you've all heard the claim that something called 'global warming' is occurring because of an increase in carbon dioxide and other greenhouse gases in the atmosphere. But what you haven't been told is that carbon dioxide has increased by only a tiny amount. They'll show you a graph of increasing carbon dioxide that looks like the slope of Mount Everest. But here's the reality. Carbon dioxide has increased from 316 parts per million to 376 parts per million. *Sixty parts per million* is the total increase. Now, that's such a small change in our entire atmosphere that it is hard to imagine. How can we visualize that?"

Jennifer sat back, swung her hand wide. "Next, they'll bring out a chart showing a football field. And they'll say, Imagine the composition of the Earth's atmosphere as a football field. Most of the atmosphere is nitrogen. So, starting from the goal line, nitrogen takes you all the way to the seventy-eight-yard line. And most of what's left is oxygen. Oxygen takes you to the ninety-nine-yard line. Only one yard to go. But most of what remains is the inert gas argon. Argon brings you within three and a half inches of the goal line. That's pretty much the thickness of the chalk stripe, folks. And how much of that remaining three inches is carbon dioxide? One inch. That's how much CO_2 we have in our atmosphere. One inch in a hundred-yard football field."

She paused dramatically, then continued. "Now, ladies and gentlemen of the jury," she said, "you are told that carbon dioxide has increased in the last fifty years. Do you know how much it has increased, on our football field? It has increased by three-eighths of an inch—less than the thickness of a pencil. It's a lot more carbon dioxide, but it's a minuscule change in our total atmosphere. Yet you are asked to believe that this tiny change has driven the entire planet into a dangerous warming pattern."

Evans said, "But that's easily answered—"

"Wait," she said. "They're not done. First, raise doubts. Then, offer alternative explanations. So, now they take out that temperature chart for New York City that you saw before. A five-degree increase since 1815. And they say, back in 1815 the population of New York was a hundred twenty thousand. Today it's eight million. The city has grown by *six thousand percent*. To say nothing of all those skyscrapers and air-conditioning and concrete. Now, I ask you. Is it reasonable to believe that a city that has grown by six thousand percent is hotter because of a *tiny* increase in little old carbon dioxide around the world? Or is it hotter because it is now much, much bigger?"

She sat back in her chair.

"But it's easy to counter that argument," Evans said. "There are many examples of small things that produce big effects. A trigger represents a small part of a gun, but it's enough to fire it. And anyway, the preponderance of the evidence—"

"Peter," she said, shaking her head. "If you were on the jury and you were asked that question about New York City, what would you conclude? Global warming or too much concrete? What *do* you think, anyway?"

"I think it's probably hotter because it's a big city."

"Right."

"But you still have the sea-level argument."

"Unfortunately," she said, "the sea levels at Vanutu are not significantly elevated. Depending on the database, either they're flat or they've increased by forty millimeters. An inch and a half in thirty years. Almost nothing."

"Then you can't possibly win this case," Evans said.

"Exactly," she said. "Although I have to say your trigger argument is a nice one."

"If you can't win," Evans said, "then what is this press conference about?"

"Thank you all for coming," John Balder said, stepping up to a cluster of microphones outside the offices. Photographers' strobes flashed. "I am John Balder, and standing with me is Nicholas Drake, the president of the National Environmental Resource Fund. Here also is Jennifer Haynes, my lead counsel, and Peter Evans, of the law firm of Hassle and Black. Together we are announcing that we will be filing a lawsuit against the Environmental Protection Agency of the United States on behalf of the island nation of Vanutu, in the Pacific."

Standing in the back, Peter Evans started to bite his lip, then thought better of it. No reason to make a facial expression that might be construed as nervous.

"The impoverished people of Vanutu," Balder said, "stand to become even more impoverished by the greatest environmental threat of our times, global warming, and the danger of abrupt climate changes that will surely follow."

Evans recalled that just a few days before, Drake had called abrupt climate change a possibility on the horizon. Now it had been transformed into a certainty in less than a week.

Balder spoke in vivid terms about how the people of Vanutu were being flooded out of their ancestral homeland, emphasizing the tragedy of young children whose heritage was washing away in raging surf caused by a callous industrial giant to the north.

"It is a matter of justice for the people of Vanutu, and of the future of the entire world now threatened by abrupt weather, that we're announcing this lawsuit today."

Then he opened the floor to questions.

The first one was, "When exactly are you filing this lawsuit?"

"The issue is technically complex," Balder said. "Right now, we have in our offices forty research scientists working on our behalf day and night. When they have finished their labors, we will make our filing for injunctive relief."

"Where will you file?"

"In Los Angeles federal district court."

"What damages are you asking?" another said.

"What is the administration's response?"

"Will the court hear it?"

The questions were coming quickly now, and Balder was in his element. Evans glanced over at Jennifer, standing on the other side of the podium. She tapped her watch. Evans nodded, then looked at his own watch, made a face, and exited the podium. Jennifer was right behind him.

They went inside the warehouse and past the guards.

And Evans stared in amazement.

The lights were turned down. Most of the people Evans had seen earlier were gone. The rooms were being stripped, the furniture stacked up, the documents packed into legal storage boxes. Movers were carrying out stacks of boxes on rolling dollies. Evans said, "What's going on?"

"Our lease is up," Jennifer said.

"So you're moving?"

She shook her head. "No. We're leaving."

"What do you mean?"

"I mean, we're leaving, Peter. Looking for new jobs. This litigation is no longer being actively pursued."

Over a loudspeaker, they heard Balder say, "We fully expect to seek an injunction within the next three months. I have complete confidence in the forty brilliant men and women who are assisting us in this groundbreaking case."

Evans stepped back as movers carried a table past him. It was the same table he had been interviewed at just three hours before. Another mover followed, lugging boxes of video equipment.

"How is this going to work?" Evans said, hearing Balder over the loudspeaker. "I mean, people are going to know what's happening . . ."

"What's happening is perfectly logical," Jennifer said. "We will file a request for a preliminary injunction. Our pleading has to work its way through the system. We expect it will be rejected by the district court for jurisdiction, so we will take it to the Ninth Circuit, and then we expect to go to the Supreme Court. The litigation cannot proceed until the issue of injunction is resolved, which could take several years. Therefore we sensibly put our large research staff on hold and close our expensive offices while we wait with a skeleton legal team in place."

"Is there a skeleton team in place?"

"No. But you asked how it would be handled."

Evans watched as the boxes rolled out the back door. "Nobody ever intended to file this lawsuit, did they?"

"Let's put it this way," she said. "Balder has a remarkable winning record in the courtroom. There's only one way to build a record like that— you dump the losers long before you ever get to trial."

"So he's dumping this one?"

"Yeah. Because I guarantee you, no court is going to grant injunctive relief for excess carbon dioxide production by the American economy." She pointed to the loudspeaker. "Drake got him to emphasize abrupt climate change. That nicely dovetails with Drake's conference, which starts tomorrow."

"Yes, but—"

"Look," she said. "You know as well as I do that the whole purpose of this case was to generate publicity. They've got their press conference. There's no need to pursue it further."

She was asked by movers where to put things. Evans wandered back into the interrogation room and saw the stack of foam core graphs in the corner. He had wanted to see the ones she *hadn't* shown him, so he pulled a few out. They showed foreign weather stations around the world.

Of course, he knew that these particular charts had been chosen to prove the opposition's point. So they showed little or no warming. But still, it troubled him that there should be so many like these, from all around the world.

He saw a stack marked "Europe" and shuffled through them quickly.

There was another stack marked "Asia." He flipped through it.

"Peter?"

She was calling him.

Her own office was already packed up. She had only a few boxes of things. He helped her carry them out to her car.

"So," he said, "what're you doing now? Going back to DC and your boyfriend?"

"I don't think so," she said.

"Then what?"

"Actually, I thought I'd go with you."

"With me?"

"You're working with John Kenner, aren't you?"

Evans said, "How did you know that?"

She just smiled.

Heading out the back door, they heard the loudspeaker from the conference. Drake was talking now, thanking the press for coming, urging them to attend his forthcoming conference, and saying that the real danger from global warming was its potential for abrupt climate change.

And then he said, "Excuse me, but I regret to say, I have an extremely sad announcement to make. I have just been handed a note that says the body of my dear friend George Morton has just been found."

The full story was on the news that afternoon. The body of millionaire financier George Morton had washed up on the shore near Pismo Beach. The identification was made from clothing and from a watch on the victim's wrist. The body itself was mutilated, the result of shark attacks, the newscaster said.

The family of the philanthropist had been notified, but no date for the memorial service had been set. There was a statement from Morton's close friend Nicholas Drake, director of NERF. Drake said that Morton had devoted his life to the environmental movement and to the work of organizations like NERF, which had just recently named him their Concerned Citizen of the Year.

"If anyone was concerned about the terrible changes that are taking place around our globe, it was George Morton," Drake said. "Ever since we learned he was missing, we have been hoping against hope that he would be found in good spirits and good health. I am saddened to learn that this is not the case. I mourn the loss of my dear and dedicated friend. The world is poorer without him."

Evans was driving when Lowenstein called him on the car phone. "What're you doing?"

"Coming back from the press conference I was ordered to attend."

"Well, you're going to San Francisco."

"Why?"

"Morton's been found. Somebody has to identify the body."

"What about his daughter?"

"She's in rehab."

"What about his ex-wife? What about—"

"Evans, you're officially assigned. Make your arrangements. The forensic guys don't want to delay the autopsy so they need him ID'd before dinner."

"But—"

"Get your ass up there. I don't know what you're bitching about. Take the guy's plane, for Christ's sake. You've certainly been helping yourself to it lately, from what I hear. Now that he's dead you'd better be more careful. Oh, one more thing. Since you're not family, they'll need two people to ID him."

"Well, I can take Sarah, his secretary—"

"No. Drake wants you to take Ted Bradley."

"Why?"

"How the hell do I know? Bradley wants to go. Drake wants to indulge him, keep him happy. Bradley probably thinks there'll be news cameras there. He is an actor, after all. And he was George's close friend."

"Sort of."

"He was at the banquet table with you."

"But Sarah would be—"

"Evans, what part of this do you not understand? You're going to San Francisco and you are taking Bradley with you. Period."

Evans sighed. "Where is he?"

"He's in Sequoia. You have to stop and get him."

"Sequoia?"

"National Park. It's on the way."

"But—"

"Bradley's already been notified. My secretary will give you the number for the San Francisco morgue. Good-bye, Evans. Don't screw up."

Click.

Jennifer said, "Problem?"

"No. But I have to go to San Francisco."

"I'll come with you," she said. "Who is Sarah?"

"Morton's personal secretary. His old assistant."

"I've seen pictures of her," Jennifer said. "She doesn't look very old."

"Where did you see pictures?"

"In a magazine. They were at a tennis tournament. She's a championship tennis player, something like that?"

"I guess."

"I would have thought that since you spent so much time with Morton, you'd know her well."

"Not really," he said, shrugging. "I mean, we've spent a little time in the last few days."

"Uh-huh." She looked at him, amused. "Peter," she said. "I don't care. She's very pretty. It's only natural."

"No, no," he said, reaching for the phone. "It's

nothing like that." Desperate to put an end to this conversation, he dialed the Beverly Hills police and asked for Detective Perry. The detective was not yet back from court. Evans left a message and hung up. He turned to Jennifer. "How does it work if they issue a warrant for your arrest?"

"Criminal," she said. "Not my area. Sorry."

"Me neither."

"Somebody going to arrest you?"

"I hope not."

Then Lisa, Herb Lowenstein's chatty assistant, called. "Hi, Peter. I have the numbers for Mr. Bradley and for the San Francisco morgue. They close at eight. Can you make it by then? Herb wants to know. He's very upset."

"About what?"

"I've never seen him this way. I mean, not for a few weeks."

"What's the matter?"

"I think he's upset about George. Such a shock. And then Drake is giving him fits. He must have called five times today. And I think they were discussing you."

"Me?"

"Yes." Lisa lowered her voice, taking on a conspiratorial tone. "Herb had his door closed while he was talking, but I, uh, I heard a few things."

"Like what?" Evans said.

"Don't say anything."

"I won't."

"I mean I wasn't—I just thought that you would want to know."

"I do."

"Because there's a lot of talk here," she said,

dropping her voice even lower, "about whether you have to leave."

"Leave the firm?"

"Be, uh, let go. I thought you would want to know."

"I do. Thanks. Who's talking?"

"Well, Herb. And Don Blandings, and a couple of other senior partners. Bob and Louise. Because for some reason Nick Drake is furious with you. And somebody you are spending time with, a person named Kanner or Connor?"

"I see."

"Mr. Drake is very upset about Mr. Connor."

"Why is that?"

"He says he is a spy. For industry. For *polluters*."

"I see."

"Anyway, the feeling is Mr. Drake is an important client and you've pissed him off. Even so, they would never dare fire you if Morton were alive. But he's not, anymore. And you're gone all the time. And the police are calling here for you, which I have to tell you is *not good*. It makes everybody nervous. And then they—what are you doing with this Mr. Connor, anyway?"

"It's a long story."

"Peter. I told *you*." She sounded sulky. He knew he would have to trade information.

"Okay," he said, trying to sound reluctant. "I'm carrying out an assignment that Morton gave me, before he died."

"Really? What is it?"

"It's a secret, I can't tell you yet."

"George Morton gave you an assignment?"

"In writing," he said. Thinking: That will cool their jets.

"Wow. Really. They don't dare fire you if you're on the business of the firm."

"Lisa, I have to go."

"And if they did, you would have *such* a wrongful termination action."

"Lisa . . ."

"Okay, okay. I know you can't talk. But just . . . good luck!"

He hung up. Jennifer was smiling. "That was very skillfully done," she said.

"Thank you."

But he wasn't smiling back. As far as he was concerned, the world was closing in around him. It didn't feel good. And he was still very, very tired.

He called Sarah to arrange for the plane, but got her voice mail. He called the pilot and was told that he was in the air.

"What do you mean?"

"He's flying, right now."

"Where?"

"I can't tell you that, sir. Would you like his voice mail?"

"No," Evans said. "I need to charter a plane."

"When would you like it?"

"In half an hour. To go to San Francisco, with a stop at whatever the airport is nearest Sequoia. Returning tonight."

"I'll see what I can do."

And then fatigue overcame him. He pulled over to the side of the road and got out of the car.

Jennifer said, "What's the matter?"

"You know the way to Van Nuys?"

"Sure."

"Then you drive."

He dropped into the passenger seat and fastened his seat belt. He watched her pull into traffic, and then closed his eyes and slept.

The forest floor was dark and cool. Shafts of sunlight filtered down from the magnificent trees rising all around them. The air smelled of pine. The ground was soft underfoot.

It was a pleasant spot, with sunlight dappling the forest floor, but even so the television cameras had to turn on their lights to film the third-grade schoolchildren who sat in concentric circles around the famous actor and activist Ted Bradley. Bradley was wearing a black T-shirt that set off his makeup and his dark good looks.

"These glorious trees are your birthright," he said, gesturing all around him. "They have been standing here for centuries. Long before you were born, before your parents or your grandparents or your great-grandparents were born. Some of them, before Columbus came to America! Before the Indians came! Before anything! These trees are the oldest living things on the planet; they are the guardians of the Earth; they are wise; and they have a message for us: *Leave the planet alone.* Don't mess with it, or with us. And we must listen to them."

The kids stared open-mouthed, transfixed. The cameras were trained on Bradley.

"But now these magnificent trees—having survived the threat of fire, the threat of logging, the threat of soil erosion, the threat of acid rain—now face their greatest threat ever. Global warming. You kids know what global warming is, don't you?"

Hands went up all around the circle. "I know, I know!"

"I'm glad you do," Bradley said, gesturing for the kids to put their hands down. The only person talking today would be Ted Bradley. "But you may not know that global warming is going to cause a very sudden change in our climate. Maybe just a few months or years, and it will suddenly be much hotter or much colder. And there will be hordes of insects and diseases that will take down these wonderful trees."

"What kind of insects?" one kid asked.

"Bad ones," Bradley said. "The ones that eat trees, that worm inside them and chew them up." He wiggled his hands, suggesting the worming in progress.

"It would take an insect a long time to eat a whole tree," a girl offered.

"No, it wouldn't!" Bradley said. "That's the trouble. Because global warming means lots and lots of insects will come—a plague of insects— and they'll eat the trees fast!"

Standing to one side, Jennifer leaned close to Evans. "Do you believe this shit?"

Evans yawned. He had slept on the flight up,

and had dozed off again in the ride from the airport to this grove in Sequoia National Park. He felt groggy now, looking at Bradley. Groggy and bored.

By now the kids were fidgeting, and Bradley turned squarely to the cameras. He spoke with the easy authority he had mastered while playing the president for so many years on television. "The threat of abrupt climate change," he said, "is so devastating for mankind, and for all life on this planet, that conferences are being convened all around the world to deal with it. There is a conference in Los Angeles starting tomorrow, where scientists will discuss what we can do to mitigate this terrible threat. But if we do nothing, catastrophe looms. And these mighty, magnificent trees will be a memory, a postcard from the past, a snapshot of man's inhumanity to the natural world. We're responsible for catastrophic climate change. And only we can stop it."

He finished, with a slight turn to favor his good side, and a piercing stare from his baby blues, right into the lens.

"I have to pee-pee," one girl said.

The plane lifted off the runway and rose over the forest.

"Sorry to rush you," Evans said. "But we have to get to the morgue before six."

"No problem, no problem." Bradley smiled indulgently. After his talk, he had taken a few minutes to sign autographs for the kids. The cameras filmed that as well. He turned to Jennifer, giving her his best smile. "And what do you do, Miss Hadley?"

"I'm on the global warming legal team."

"Good, so you're one of us. How's the lawsuit going?"

"Just fine," she said, glancing at Evans.

"I get the feeling you're as brilliant as you are beautiful," Bradley said.

"Actually, no," she said. Evans could see that the actor was annoying her.

"You're being modest. It's very charming."

"I'm being honest," she said, "and telling you I don't like flattery."

"Hardly flattery, in your case," he said.

"And hardly honest, in yours," she replied.

"Believe me when I say that I genuinely admire what you're doing," Bradley said. "I can't wait for you people to stick it to the EPA. We have to keep the pressure on. That's why I did this thing with the kids. It's a sure-fire television segment for abrupt climate change. And I thought it went extremely well, didn't you?"

"Reasonably well, considering."

"Considering?"

"That it was all bullshit," Jennifer said.

Bradley's smile remained fixed, but his eyes narrowed. "I'm not sure what you're referring to," he said.

"I'm referring to all of it, Ted. The whole speech. Sequoias are sentinels and guardians of the planet? They have a message for us?"

"Well, they do—"

"They're *trees*, Ted. Big *trees*. They have about

as much of a message for mankind as an egg-plant."

"I think you are missing—"

"And they've managed to survive forest fires? Hardly—they're *dependent* on fires, because that's how they reproduce. Redwoods have tough seeds that only burst open in the heat of a fire. Fires are essential for the health of the redwood forest."

"I think," Bradley said rather stiffly, "that you may have missed my point."

"Really? What did I miss?"

"I was trying to convey—perhaps a bit lyrically—the timeless quality of these great primeval forests, and—"

"Timeless? Primeval? Do you know anything about these forests?"

"Yes. I think I do." His voice was tight. He was visibly angry now.

"Look out the window," Jennifer said, pointing to the forest as they flew above it. "How long do you think your primeval forest has looked the way it does now?"

"Obviously, for hundreds of thousands of years—"

"Not true, Ted. Human beings were here for many thousands of years before these forests ever appeared. Did you know that?"

He was clenching his jaw. He did not answer.

"Then let me lay it out for you," she said.

Twenty thousand years ago, the Ice Age glaciers receded from California, gouging out Yosemite Valley and other beauty spots as they left. As the ice walls withdrew, they left behind a gunky, damp plain with lots of lakes fed by the melting glaciers, but no vegetation at all. It was basically wet sand.

After a few thousand years, the land dried as the glaciers continued to move farther north. This region of California became arctic tundra, with tall grasses supporting little animals, like mice and squirrels. Human beings had arrived here by then, hunting the small animals and setting fires. "Okay so far?" Jennifer said. "No primeval forests yet."

"I'm listening," Ted growled. He was clearly trying to control his temper.

She continued. "At first, arctic grasses and shrubs were the only plants that could take hold in the barren glacial soil. But when they died they decomposed, and over thousands of years a layer of topsoil built up. And that initiated a sequence of plant colonization that was basically the same everywhere in post-glacial North America.

"First, lodgepole pine comes in. That's around fourteen thousand years ago. Later it's joined by spruce, hemlock, and alder—trees that are hardy but can't be first. These trees constitute the real 'primary' forest, and they dominated this landscape for the next four thousand years. Then the climate changed. It got much warmer, and all the glaciers in California melted. There were no glaciers at all in California back then. It was warm and dry, there were lots of fires, and the primary forest burned. It was replaced by a plains-type vegetation of oak trees and prairie herbs. And a few Douglas fir trees, but not many, because the climate was too dry for fir trees.

"Then, around six thousand years ago, the climate changed again. It became wetter, and the Douglas fir, hemlock, and cedar moved in and took over the land, creating the great closed-canopy forests that you see now. But someone might refer to these fir trees as a pest plant—an oversized weed—that invaded the landscape, crowding out the native plants that had been there before them. Because these big canopy forests made the ground too dark for other trees to survive. And since there were frequent fires, the closed-canopy forests were able to spread like mad. So they're not timeless, Ted. They're merely the last in line."

Bradley snorted. "They're still six thousand years old, for God's sake."

But Jennifer was relentless. "Not true," she said. "Scientists have shown that the forests continuously changed their composition. Each thousand-year period was different from the one before it. The forests changed constantly, Ted. And then, of course, there were the Indians."

"What about them?"

"The Indians were expert observers of the natural world, so they realized that old-growth forests sucked. Those forests may look impressive, but they're dead landscapes for game. So the Indians set fires, making sure the forests burned down periodically. They made sure there were only islands of old-growth forest in the midst of plains and meadows. The forests that the first Europeans saw were hardly primeval. They were *cultivated,* Ted. And it's not surprising that one hundred fifty years ago, there was less old-growth forest than there is today. The Indians were realists. Today, it's all romantic mythology."*

She sat back in her chair.

"Well, that's a very nice speech," Bradley said. "But those are technical objections. People aren't interested. And it's a good thing, because you're saying that these forests aren't really old and therefore aren't worth preserving. Whereas I say they are reminders of the beauty and power of the natural world and should be preserved at all costs. Especially from the dire threat of global warming."

Jennifer blinked. She said, "I need a drink."

"I'll join you there," Bradley said.

For Evans—who had intermittently been attempting to call Detective Perry while this discussion was taking place—the most disturbing aspect was the implication of constant change. Evans had never really focused on the idea that Indians had lived at the same time as the glaciers. Of course, he knew that this was true. He knew that early Indians had hunted the mammoth and other large mammals to extinction. But he had never considered the possibility that they would also have burned forests and changed the environment to suit their purposes.

But of course they had.

Equally disturbing was the image of so many different forests taking over, one after another.

---

* Alston Chase, *In a Dark Wood*, p. 157ff. See also p. 404ff.

Evans had never wondered what had existed before the redwood forests. He, too, had considered them primeval.

Nor had he ever thought about the landscape that the glaciers would have left behind. Thinking about it now, he realized that it probably looked like the land he had recently seen in Iceland—cold, wet, rocky, and barren. It stood to reason that generations of plants would have to grow there, building up a layer of topsoil.

But in his mind, he had always imagined a sort of animated movie in which the glaciers receded and redwood trees popped up immediately along the receding edge. The glaciers pulled away leaving redwood forest behind.

He realized now how silly that view had been.

And Evans had also noticed, in passing, how frequently Jennifer had spoken of a changing climate. First it was cold and wet, then it was warm and dry and the glaciers melted, then it was wetter again, and the glaciers came back. Changing, and changing again.

Constant change.

After a while, Bradley excused himself and went to the front of the plane to call his agent. Evans said to Jennifer, "How did you know all that stuff?"

"For the reason Bradley himself mentioned. The 'dire threat of global warming.' We had a whole team researching dire threats. Because we wanted to find everything we could to make our case as impressive as possible."

"And?"

She shook her head. "The threat of global warming," she said, "is essentially nonexistent. Even if it were a real phenomenon, it would probably result in a net benefit to most of the world."

The pilot clicked on the intercom, telling them to take their seats because they were on their final approach to San Francisco.

The anteroom was gray, cold, and smelled of disinfectant. The man behind the desk wore a lab coat. He typed at his keyboard. "Morton . . . Morton . . . Yes. George Morton. Okay. And you are . . ."

"Peter Evans. I'm Mr. Morton's attorney," Evans said.

"And I'm Ted Bradley," Ted said. He started to extend his hand, then thought better of it, pulled it back.

"Oh. Hey," the technician said. "I thought you looked familiar. You're the secretary of state."

"Actually, I'm the president."

"Right, right, the president. I knew I'd seen you before. Your wife is a drunk."

"No, actually, the secretary of state's wife is a drunk."

"Oh. I don't get to see the show that often."

"It's off the air now."

"That explains it."

"But it's in syndication in all the major markets."

Evans said, "If we could make the identification now . . ."

"Okay. Sign here, and I'll get you visitor tags."

* * *

Jennifer remained in the anteroom. Evans and Bradley walked into the morgue. Bradley looked back. "Who is she anyway?"

"She's an attorney working on the global warming team."

"I think she's a plant for industry. She's obviously some kind of extremist."

"She works right under Balder, Ted."

"Well, I can understand *that*," Bradley said, snickering. "I'd like her working under me, too. But did you listen to her, for God's sake? Old-growth forests 'suck?' That's industry talking." He leaned closer to Evans. "I think you should get rid of her."

"Get rid of her?"

"She's up to no good. Why is she with us now anyway?"

"I don't know. She wanted to come. Why are you with us, Ted?"

"I have a job to do."

The sheet draping the body was spotted with gray stains. The technician lifted it back.

"Oh Jesus," Ted Bradley said, turning quickly away.

Evans forced himself to gaze at the body. Morton had been a large man in life, and now he was even larger, his torso purple gray and bloated. The odor of decay was strong. Indenting the puffy flesh was an inch-wide ring around one wrist. Evans said, "The watch?"

"Yeah, we took it off," the technician said. "Barely got it over the hand. You need to see it?"

"Yes, I do." Evans leaned closer and stiffened his body against the smell. He wanted to look at the hands and the nails. Morton had had a childhood injury to the fourth nail on his right hand, leaving the nail dented, deformed. But one of the hands of this body was missing, and the other was gnawed and mangled. There was no way he could be sure of what he was seeing.

Behind him, Bradley said, "Are you done yet?"

"Not quite."

"Je-sus, man."

The technician said, "So, will the show go back on the air?"

"No, it's been canceled."

"Why? I liked that show."

"They should have consulted you," Bradley said.

Evans was looking at the chest now, trying to recall the pattern of chest hair that Morton had had. He'd seen him often enough in a bathing suit. But the bloating, the stretching of the skin made it difficult. He shook his head. He could not be sure it was Morton.

"Are you done yet?" Bradley said.

"Yes," Evans said.

The drape went back on, and they walked out. The technician said, "Lifeguards in Pismo made the discovery, called the police. The police ID'd him from the clothes."

"He still had clothes on?"

"Uh-huh. One leg of the pants and most of the jacket. Custom made. They called the tailor in

New York and he confirmed that they had been made for George Morton. Will you be taking his effects with you?"

"I don't know," Evans said.

"Well, you're his lawyer . . ."

"Yes, I guess I will."

"You have to sign for them."

They went back outside, where Jennifer was waiting. She was talking on her cell phone. She said, "Yes, I understand. Yes. Okay, we can do that." She flipped the phone shut when she saw them. "Finished?"

"Yes."

"And was it . . ."

"Yes," Ted said. "It was George."

Evans said nothing. He went down the hall and signed for the personal effects. The technician brought out a bag and handed it to Evans. Evans fished in it and pulled out the shreds of the tuxedo. There was a small NERF pin on the inside pocket of the jacket. He reached in and came out with the watch, a Rolex Submariner. It was the same watch Morton wore. Evans looked at the back. It was engraved GM 12–31–89. Evans nodded, put it back in the bag.

All these things belonged to George. Just touching them now made him feel inexpressibly sad.

"I guess that does it," he said. "Time to go."

They all walked back to the waiting car. After they got in, Jennifer said, "We have to make another stop."

"Oh?" Evans said.

"Yes. We have to go to the Oakland Municipal Garage."

"Why?"

"The police are waiting for us."

It was an enormous concrete structure, adjacent to a vast parking lot on the outskirts of Oakland. It was lit by harsh halogen lights. Behind the cyclone fence, most of the cars in the lot were junkers, but a few Cadillacs and Bentleys were there, too. Their limousine pulled up to the curb.

"Why are we here?" Bradley said. "I don't understand."

A policeman came to the window. "Mr. Evans? Peter Evans?"

"That's me."

"Come this way, please."

They all started to get out of the car. The cop said, "Just Mr. Evans."

Bradley sputtered, "But we are—"

"Sorry, sir. They just want Mr. Evans. You'll have to wait here."

Jennifer smiled at Bradley. "I'll keep you company."

"Great."

Evans got out of the car and followed the policeman through the metal door into the garage itself. The interior space was divided into long bays, where cars were worked on in a row. Most of the bays seemed to be given over to the repair of police cars. Evans smelled the sharp odor of acetylene torches. He sidestepped patches of motor oil and gobs of grease on the floor. He said to the cop accompanying him, "What's this about?"

"They're waiting for you, sir."

They were heading for the rear of the garage. They passed several crushed and blood-covered wrecks. Seats drenched in blood, shattered windows dark red. Some wrecks had pieces of string that stretched out from them in various directions. One wreck was being measured by a pair of technicians in blue lab coats. Another crash was being photographed by a man with a camera on a tripod.

"Is he a policeman?" Evans said.

"Nah. Lawyer. We have to let 'em in."

"So you deal with car wrecks here?"

"When it's appropriate."

They came around the corner and Evans saw Kenner standing with three plainclothes policemen, and two workers in blue lab coats. They were all standing around the crushed body of Morton's Ferrari Spyder, now raised on a hydraulic lift, with bright lights shining up at it.

"Ah, Peter," Kenner said. "Did you make the identification of George?"

"Yes."

"Good man."

Evans came forward to stand beneath the car. Various sections of the underside had been marked with yellow cloth tags. Evans said, "Okay, what's up?"

The plainclothesmen looked at one another. Then one of them began to speak. "We've been examining this Ferrari, Mr. Evans."

"I see that."

"This is the car that Mr. Morton recently bought in Monterey?"

"I believe so."

"When was that purchase made?"

"I don't know exactly." Evans tried to think back. "Not long ago. Last month or so. His assistant, Sarah, told me George had bought it."

"Who bought it?"

"She did."

"What was your involvement?"

"I had none. She merely informed me that George had bought a car."

"You didn't make the purchase or arrange insurance, anything like that?"

"No. All that would have been done by George's accountants."

"You never saw paperwork on the car?"

"No."

"And when did you first see the actual car itself?"

"The night George drove it away from the Mark Hopkins Hotel," Evans said. "The night he died."

"Did you ever see the car prior to that evening?"

"No."

"Did you hire anyone to work on the car?"

"No."

"The car was transported from Monterey to a

private garage in Sonoma, where it remained for two weeks, before being taken to San Francisco. Did you arrange the private garage?"

"No."

"The rental was in your name."

Evans shook his head. "I don't know anything about that," he said. "But Morton often put rentals and leases in the name of his accountants or attorneys, if he didn't want the owner or lessee to be publicly known."

"But if he did that, he would inform you?"

"Not necessarily."

"So you didn't know your name was being used?"

"No."

"Who worked on the car, in San Jose?"

"I have no idea."

"Because, Mr. Evans, somebody did rather extensive work on this Ferrari before Morton ever got into it. The frame was weakened at the places you see marked by the yellow tags. Anti-skid—primitive, in a vehicle this old—was disabled, and the discs were cross-loosened on the left front, right rear. Are you following me, here?"

Evans frowned.

"This car was a death trap, Mr. Evans. Someone used it to kill your client. Lethal changes were made in a garage in Sonoma. And your name is on the lease."

Downstairs in the car, Ted Bradley was grilling Jennifer Haynes. She might be pretty, but everything about her was wrong—her manner, her tough-guy attitude, and most of all her opinions.

She had said she was working on the lawsuit, and that her salary was paid by NERF, but Ted didn't think it was possible. For one thing, Ted Bradley was very publicly associated with NERF, and as a hired employee she should have known that, and she should have treated his opinions with respect.

To call the information he had shared with those kids "bullshit"—a talk he didn't have to give, a moment he had offered out of the goodness of his heart and his dedication to the environmental cause—to call that "bullshit" was outrageous. It was confrontational in the extreme. And it showed absolutely no respect. Plus, Ted knew that what he had said was true. Because, as always, NERF had given him a talking points memo listing the various things to be emphasized. And NERF would not have told him to say anything that was untrue. And the talking points said nothing about the fucking Ice Age. Everything Jennifer had said was irrelevant.

Those trees *were* magnificent. They *were* sentinels of the environment, just as the talking points claimed. In fact, he pulled the talking points out of his jacket pocket to be sure.

"I'd like to see that," Jennifer said.

"I bet you would."

"What is your problem?" she said.

See? he thought. That kind of attitude. Aggressive and confrontational.

She said, "You're one of those television stars who thinks everyone wants to touch your dick. Well, guess what, oh Big Swinging One, I don't. I think you're just an actor."

"And I think you're a plant. You're a corporate spy."

"I must not be a very good one," she said, "because you found me out."

"Because you shot your mouth off, that's why."

"It's always been my problem."

All during this conversation, Bradley felt a peculiar tension building in his chest. Women did not argue with Ted Bradley. Sometimes they were hostile for a while, but that was only because they were intimidated by him, his good looks, and his star power. They wanted to screw him, and often he'd let them. But they did not *argue* with him. This one was arguing, and it excited him and angered him in equal proportions. The tension building up inside him was almost unbearable. Her calmness, just sitting there, the direct way she looked into his eyes, the complete lack of intimidation—it was an indifference to his fame that drove him wild. All right, hell, she was beautiful.

He grabbed her face in both hands and kissed her hard on the mouth.

He could tell she liked it. To complete his dominance he stuck his tongue down her throat.

Then there was a blinding flash of pain—in his neck, his head—and he must have lost consciousness for a moment. Because the next thing he knew he was sitting on the floor of the limousine, gasping and watching blood drip all over his shirt. Ted was not sure how he had gotten there. He was not sure why he was bleeding or why his head was throbbing. Then he realized that his tongue was bleeding.

He looked up at her. She crossed her legs coolly, giving him a glimpse up her skirt, but he didn't care. He was resentful. "You bit my tongue!"

"No, asshole, you bit your own tongue."

"You assaulted me!"

She raised an eyebrow.

"You did! You assaulted me!" He looked down. "Jesus, this was a new shirt, too. From Maxfield's."

She stared at him.

"You assaulted me," he repeated.

"So sue me."

"I think I will."

"Better consult your lawyer first."

"Why?"

She nodded her head toward the front of the car. "You're forgetting the driver."

"What about him?"

"He saw it all."

"So what? You encouraged me," he said, hissing. "You were being seductive. Any guy knows the signs."

"Apparently you didn't."

"Hostile ballbreaker?" He turned and took the vodka bottle from the rack. He needed it to rinse out his mouth. He poured himself a glass, and looked back.

She was reading the talking points. She held the paper in her hands. He lunged for it. "That's not yours."

She was quick, holding the paper away from him. She raised her other hand, edge on, like a chopping knife.

"Care to try your luck again, Ted?"

"Fuck you," he said, and took a big gulp of the vodka. His tongue was on fire. What a bitch, he thought. What a goddamned bitch. Well, she'd be looking for a new job tomorrow. He'd see to that. This bimbo lawyer couldn't fuck around with Ted Bradley and get away with it.

Standing beneath the crashed Ferrari, Evans endured another ten minutes of grilling by the plainclothesmen who encircled him. Fundamentally, the story didn't make sense to him.

Evans said, "George was a good driver. If all these changes were made to the car, wouldn't he have noticed something was wrong?"

"Perhaps. But not if he was drinking heavily."

"Well, he was drinking, that's for sure."

"And who got him the drinks, Mr. Evans?"

"George got his own drinks."

"The waiter at the banquet said you were pushing drinks at Morton."

"That's not true. I was trying to limit his drinking."

Abruptly, they changed course. "Who worked on the Ferrari, Mr. Evans?"

"I have no idea."

"We know you rented a private garage outside Sonoma on Route 54. It was fairly quiet and out of the way. Any person or persons who worked on the car would have been able to come and go as they wished, without being seen. Why would you choose such a garage?"

"I didn't choose it."

"Your name is on the lease."

"How was the lease arranged?"

"By phone."

"Who paid for it?"

"It was paid in cash."

"By whom?"

"Delivered by messenger."

"You have my signature on anything? Finger-prints?"

"No. Just your name."

Evans shrugged. "Then I'm sorry, but I don't know anything about this. It's well known that I'm George Morton's attorney. Anybody could have used my name. If anything was done to this car, it was done without my knowledge."

He was thinking that they should have been asking Sarah about all this, but then, if they were good at their jobs, they'd already have talked to her.

And sure enough, she appeared from around the corner, talking on a cell phone and nodding to Kenner.

That was when Kenner stepped forward. "Okay, gentlemen. Unless you have further questions, I'll take Mr. Evans into custody on my recognizance. I don't believe he is a flight risk. He will be safe enough with me."

The cops grumbled, but in the end they agreed. Kenner handed out his card, and then he headed back toward the entrance, his arm firmly on Evans's shoulder.

Sarah followed some distance behind. The cops stayed with the Ferrari.

As they neared the door, Kenner said, "Sorry about all that. But the police didn't tell you everything. The fact is, they photographed the car from various angles and fed the shots into a computer that simulates crashes. And the computer-generated simulation didn't match the photos of the actual crash."

"I didn't know you could do that."

"Oh yes. Everybody uses computer models these days. They are *de rigueur* for the modern organization. Armed with their computer simulation, the police went back to the wreck itself, where they now decided that it had been monkeyed with. They never imagined this during their previous examinations of the wreck, but now they do. Clear example of using a computer simulation to alter your version of reality. They trusted the simulation and not the data from the ground."

"Uh-huh."

"And of course their simulation was optimized for the most common vehicle types on American roads. The computer had no ability to model the behavior of a forty-year-old, limited-production Italian racing car. They ran the simulation anyway."

Evans said, "But what's all this about a garage in Sonoma?"

Kenner shrugged. "You don't know. Sarah doesn't know. Nobody can even verify if the car was ever there. But the garage was rented—I'd guess by George himself. Though we'll never know for sure."

Back outside, Evans threw open the door to his limo and climbed in. He was astonished to see

Ted Bradley covered in blood, all down his chin and shirt front.

"What happened?"

"He slipped," Jennifer said. "And hurt himself."

On the flight back, Sarah Jones was overcome with confused feelings. First of all, she was profoundly distressed by the fact that George Morton's body had been recovered; in some part of her mind, she had been hoping against hope that he would turn up alive. Then there was the question of Peter Evans. Just as she was starting to like him—starting to see a side of him that was not wimpy, but rather tough and resilient in his own bumbling way—just as she was beginning, in fact, to have the first stirrings of feelings toward the man who had saved her life, suddenly there was this new woman, Jennifer somebody, and Peter was obviously taken with her.

And in addition, there was the arrival of Ted Bradley. Sarah had no illusions about Ted; she had seen him in action at innumerable NERF gatherings, and she had even once allowed him to work his charms on her—she was a sucker for actors—but at the last moment decided he reminded her too much of her ex. What was it about actors, anyway? They were so engaging, so personal in their approach, so intense in their feelings. It was hard to realize that they were just self-absorbed people who would do anything to get you to like them.

At least, Ted was.

And how had he been injured? Bitten his own tongue? Sarah had the feeling it had to do with this Jennifer. Undoubtedly, Ted had made a pass at her. The woman was pretty enough in a street-smart kind of way; dark hair, toughish face, compact body, muscular but skinny. A typical speeded-up New York type—in every way Sarah's opposite.

And Peter Evans was fawning over her.

Fawning.

It was sort of disgusting, but she had to admit she was disappointed personally as well. Just as she had started to like him. She sighed.

As for Bradley, he was talking to Kenner about environmental issues, showing off his extensive knowledge. And Kenner was looking at Bradley the way a python looks at a rat.

"So," Kenner said, "global warming represents a threat to the world?"

"Absolutely," Bradley said. "A threat to the whole world."

"What sort of threat are we talking about?"

"Crop failures, spreading deserts, new diseases, species extinction, all the glaciers melting, Kilimanjaro, sea-level rise, extreme weather, tornadoes, hurricanes, El Niño events—"

"That sounds extremely serious," Kenner said.

"It is," Bradley said. "It really is."

"Are you sure of your facts?"

"Of course."

"You can back your claims with references to the scientific literature?"

"Well, I can't personally, but scientists can."

"Actually, scientific studies do not support your claims. For example, crop failure—if anything, increased carbon dioxide *stimulates* plant growth. There is some evidence that this is happening. And the most recent satellite studies show the Sahara has shrunk since 1980.* As for new diseases—not true. The rate of emergence of new diseases has not changed since 1960."

"But we'll have diseases like malaria coming back to the US and Europe."

"Not according to malaria experts."[†]

Bradley snorted and folded his hands across his chest.

"Species extinction hasn't been demonstrated either. In the 1970s, Norman Myers predicted a million species would be extinct by the year 2000. Paul Ehrlich predicted that fifty percent of all species would be extinct by the year 2000. But those were just opinions.[‡] Do you know what we call opinion in the absence of evidence? We call it prejudice. Do you know how many species there are on the planet?"

---

* Fred Pearce, "Africans go back to the land as plants reclaim the desert," *New Scientist* 175, 21 September 2002, pp. 4–5. "Africa's deserts are in retreat . . . Analysis of satellite images . . . reveals that dunes are retreating right across the Sahel region . . . Vegetation is ousting sand across a swathe of land stretching . . . 6000 kilometers. . . . Analysts say the gradual greening has been happening since the mid 1980s, though has gone largely unnoticed."

† Paul Reiter, et al., "Global warming and malaria: a call for accuracy," *Lancet*, 4, no. 1 (June 2004). "Many of these much-publicized predictions are ill informed and misleading."

‡ Discussion in Lomborg, p. 252.

"No."

"Neither does anybody else. Estimates range from three million to one hundred million. Quite a range, wouldn't you say? Nobody really has any idea."*

"Your point being?"

"It's hard to know how many species are becoming extinct if you don't know how many there are in the first place. How could you tell if you were robbed if you didn't know how much money you had in your wallet to begin with? And fifteen thousand new species are described every year. By the way, do you know what the known rate of species extinction is?"

"No."

"That's because there is no known rate. Do you know how they measure numbers of species and species extinctions? Some poor bastard marks off a hectare or an acre of land and then tries to count all the bugs and animals and plants inside it. Then he comes back in ten years and counts again. But maybe the bugs have moved to an adjacent acre in the meantime. Anyway, can you imagine trying to count all the bugs in an acre of land?"

"It would be difficult."

"To put it mildly. And very inaccurate," Ken-

---

* Morjorie L. Reaka-Kudia, et al., *Biodiversity II, Understanding and Protecting our Biological Resources*, Washington: National Academies Press, 1997. "Biologists have come to recognize just how little we know about the organisms with which we share the planet Earth. In particular, attempts to determine how many species there are in total have been surprisingly fruitless." Myers: "We have no way of knowing the actual extinction rate in the tropical forests, let alone an approximate guess." In Lomborg, p. 254.

ner said, "which is the point. Now, about all the glaciers melting—not true. Some are, some aren't."*

"Nearly all of them are."

Kenner smiled thinly. "How many glaciers are we talking about?"

"Dozens."

"How many glaciers are there in the world, Ted?"

"I don't know."

"Guess."

"Maybe, uh, two hundred."

"There are more than that in California.† There are one hundred sixty thousand glaciers in the world, Ted. About sixty-seven thousand have been inventoried, but only a few have been studied with any care. There is mass balance data extending five years or more for only seventy-nine glaciers in the entire world. So, how can you say they're all melting? Nobody knows whether they are or not."‡

"Kilimanjaro is melting."

"Why is that?"

"Global warming."

"Actually, Kilimanjaro has been rapidly melt-

---

* Roger J. Braithwaite, "Glacier mass balance, the first 50 years of international monitoring," *Progress in Physical Geography* 26, no. 1 (2002): 76–95. "There is no obvious common global trend of increasing glacier melt in recent years."

† California has 497 glaciers; Raub, et al., 1980; Guyton: 108 glaciers and 401 glacierets, *Glaciers of California*, p. 115.

‡ H. Kieffer, et al., 2000, "New eyes in the sky measure glaciers and ice sheets," *EOS, Transactions, American Geophysical Union* 81: 265, 270–71. See also R. J. Braithwaite and Y. Zhang, "Relationships between interannual variability of glacier mass balance and climate," *Journal of Glaciology* 45 (2000): 456–62.

ing since the 1800s—long before global warming. The loss of the glacier has been a topic of scholarly concern for over a hundred years. And it has always been something of a mystery because, as you know, Kilimanjaro is an equatorial volcano, so it exists in a warm region. Satellite measurements of that region show no warming trend at the altitude of the Kilimanjaro glacier. So why is it melting?"

Sulking: "You tell me."

"Because of deforestation, Ted. The rain forest at the base of the mountain has been cut down, so the air blowing upward is no longer moist. Experts think that if the forest is replanted the glacier will grow again."

"That's bullshit."

"I'll give you the journal references.* Now then—sea-level rise? Was that the next threat you mentioned?"

"Yes."

"Sea level is indeed rising."

"Ah-hah!"

"As it has been for the last six thousand years, ever since the start of the Holocene. Sea level has

---

* Betsy Mason, "African Ice Under Wraps," *Nature*, 24, November 2003. "Although it's tempting to blame the ice loss on global warming, researchers think that deforestation of the mountain's foothills is the more likely culprit," http://www.nature.com/nsu/031117/031117–8.html.

Kaser, et al., "Modern glacier retreat on Kilimanjaro as evidence of climate change: Observations and facts," *International Journal of Climatology* 24: (2004): 329–39. "In recent years, Kilimanjaro and its vanishing glaciers have become an 'icon' of global warming . . . [but] processes other than air temperature control the ice recession . . . A drastic drop in atmospheric moisture at the end of the 19th century and the ensuing drier climate conditions are likely forcing glacier retreat."

been rising at the rate of ten to twenty centimeters—that's four to eight inches—every hundred years."*

"But it's rising faster now."

"Actually, not."

"Satellites prove it."

"Actually, they don't."†

"Computer models prove it's rising faster."‡

"Computer models can't *prove* anything, Ted. A prediction can't ever be proof—it hasn't happened yet. And computer models have failed to accurately predict the last ten or fifteen years. But if you want to believe in them anyway, there is no arguing with faith. Now, what was next on your list? Extreme weather—again, not true. Numerous studies show there is no increase."§

---

* See, for example, http://www.csr.utexas.edu/gmsl/main.html. "Over the last century, global sea-level change has typically been estimated from tide gauge measurements by long-term averaging. Most recent estimates of global mean sea-level rise from tide gauge measurements range from 1.7 to 2.4 mm/yr" [that is, 6" to 9" every hundred years—MC].

† Op. cit. Global mean sea-level rise as measured by satellite is 3.1 mm/yr for the last decade or slightly more than 12" a century. However, satellites show considerable variation. Thus the northern Pacific has risen, but the southern Pacific has fallen by several millimeters in recent years.

‡ Lomborg, pp. 289–90 on inadequacy of IPCC sea-level models.

§ See Henderson-Sellers, et al., 1997, "Tropical Cyclones and Global Climate Change: a post-IPCC assessment," *Bulletin of the American Meteorological Society* 79:9–38. C. Nicholls Landsea, et al. "Downward Trend in the Frequency of Intense Atlantic Hurricanes during the past five decades," *Geophysical Research Letters* 23:527–30. 1996. According to the United Nations Intergovernmental Panel on Climate Change, "Examination of meteorological data fails to support the perception [of increased frequency and severity of extreme climate events] in the context of a long-term climate change." IPCC 1995, p. 11. "Overall, there is no evidence that extreme weather events, or climate variability, has increased, in a global sense, throughout the twentieth century . . ." IPCC, *Climate Change 1995*. In the 2001 IPCC report, "No

"Look," Ted said, "you may enjoy putting me down, but the fact is, lots of people think there will be more extreme weather, including more hurricanes and tornadoes and cyclones, in the future."

"Yes, indeed, lots of people think so. But scientific studies do not bear them out.* That's why we *do* science, Ted, to see if our opinions can be verified in the real world, or whether we are just having fantasies."

"All these hurricanes are not fantasies."

Kenner sighed. He flipped open his laptop.

"What are you doing?"

"One moment," Kenner said. "Let me bring it up."

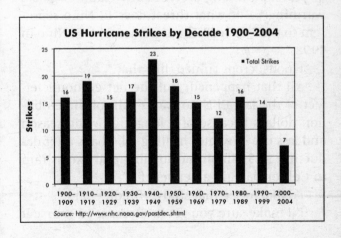

US Hurricane Strikes by Decade 1900–2004

■ Total Strikes

Strikes

| 1900–1909 | 1910–1919 | 1920–1929 | 1930–1939 | 1940–1949 | 1950–1959 | 1960–1969 | 1970–1979 | 1980–1989 | 1990–1999 | 2000–2004 |
| 16 | 19 | 15 | 17 | 23 | 18 | 15 | 12 | 16 | 14 | 7 |

Source: http://www.nhc.noaa.gov/pastdec.shtml

long-term trends evident" for tropical and extratropical storms, and no systematic changes in the "frequency of tornadoes, thunder days, or hail." *Executive summary*, p.2. For fuller discussion, see Lomborg, p. 292ff.

* Richard Feynman: "Science is what we have learned about how not to fool ourselves."

"Here is the actual data, Ted," Kenner said. "US hurricane strikes over the last hundred years are clearly not increasing. And similarly, extreme weather is not more frequent globally. The data simply do not agree with you. Now, you also mentioned El Niño events."

"Yes . . ."

"As you know, El Niño is a global weather pattern that begins when ocean temperatures along the west coast of South America remain above normal for several months. Once it's triggered, El Niño lasts about a year and a half, affecting weather around the world. El Niño occurs roughly every four years—twenty-three times in the last century. And it has been occurring for thousands of years. So it long precedes any claim of global warming.* But what threat does El Niño represent to the US, Ted? There was a major El Niño in 1998."

"Floods, crops ruined, like that."

"All that happened. But the net economic effect of the last El Niño was a gain of fifteen billion dollars because of a longer growing season and less use of winter heating oil. That's after deducting $1.5 billion for flooding and excess rain in California. Still a net benefit."

"I'd like to see that study," Bradley said.

"I'll make sure you get it.† Because of course it

---

* Lomborg, p. 292.

† Stanley A. Changnon, 1999: "Impacts of 1997–98 El Niño–Generated Weather in the United States," *Bulletin of the American Meteorological Society* 80, no. 9: pp. 1819–28. ("The net economic benefit was surprisingly positive . . . direct losses nationally were about $4 billion and the benefits were approximately $19 billion.")

also suggests that if global warming really does occur, it will probably benefit most nations of the world."

"But not *all*."

"No, Ted. Not all."

"So what exactly is your point?" Bradley said. "You're saying that we don't need to pay any attention to the environment, that we can just leave it alone and let industry pollute and everything will be hunky-dory?"

For a moment, it looked to Sarah as if Kenner would get angry, but he did not. He said, "If you oppose the death penalty, does it also mean you are in favor of doing nothing at all about crime?"

"No," Ted said.

"You can oppose the death penalty but still favor punishing criminals."

"Yes. Of course."

"Then I can say that global warming is not a threat but still favor environmental controls, can't I?"

"But it doesn't sound like you are saying that."

Kenner sighed.

Sarah was listening to this exchange, thinking Bradley wasn't really hearing what Kenner had to say. As if to prove her thoughts, Bradley continued: "Well? Aren't you saying that the environment needs no protection from us? Isn't that what you are *really* saying?"

Kenner said, "No," in a way that suggested that the conversation was over.

Sarah thought: Ted really is a fool. He has a

severely limited understanding of what he is talking about. Ted was an actor with a script, at a loss if the conversation moved away from scripted lines.

She turned away and looked toward the front of the cabin. She saw Peter talking to Jennifer, their heads together. There was a sort of intimacy in their gestures that was instantly recognizable.

She was glad when the pilot announced they were landing in Los Angeles.

Sanjong Thapa was waiting at the airport, looking worried. He and Kenner got immediately into a car and drove off. Sarah went home to her apartment. Bradley climbed into an SUV limo and left with an irritable wave. He was already on his cell phone. Peter Evans drove Jennifer to her car, which was back in Culver City. There was an awkward moment saying good-bye. He wanted to kiss her but sensed some reserve, and didn't. She promised she would call him in the morning.

He drove home, thinking of her. Sarah did not enter his mind.

It was almost midnight when Evans got back to his apartment. He was very tired and was stripping off his shirt when the phone rang. It was Janis, the exercise instructor. "Where have you *been*, you cute thing?"

"Traveling," he said.

"I have called you *every single day*," she said. "Sometimes more. Sometimes every hour."

"Uh-huh. What's up?"

"My boyfriend broke up with me."

"I'm sorry to hear that," Evans said. "Was it very—"

"Can I come over?" she said.

He sighed. "You know, Janis, I'm really tired . . ."

"I need to talk to you. I promise I won't stay, if you don't want me to. I'm only about a block away. Five minutes?"

He sighed again, louder this time. "Janis, tonight is not—"

"Okay, good, see you in five."

Click.

He sighed. She never listened, that was the trouble. He decided that when she got to his apartment, he would just tell her to leave. That's all. Just go.

Or then again, maybe he wouldn't.

Janis was uncomplicated. He was ready for an uncomplicated exchange. He pulled off his shoes and dropped them on the floor. On the other hand, he didn't want Janis around in the morning if Jennifer called. Would Jennifer call? She said she would. Did Jennifer know his home number? He wasn't sure. Maybe not.

He decided to take a shower. He might not hear Janis in the shower, so he unlocked the front door for her and headed for the bathroom. The hallway was dark and he had just a fleeting glimpse of a dark shadow before something hit him on the head, very hard. Evans yelled. The pain was intense, making him gasp, and he fell to his knees. He groaned. Someone hit him again, this time in the ear, and he fell over on his side.

Disoriented, he found himself staring at a pair of feet in dirty socks. He was being dragged into the living room. He was dropped unceremoniously on the floor. There were three men, moving around him. They had dark masks over their faces, like ski masks. One of them stepped on both his arms, pinning him down, flat on his back. Another one sat on his legs and said, "Don't talk. Don't move." A growly menacing voice.

Evans couldn't move anyway. He still felt disoriented. He looked around for the third man. He heard sloshing water. He glimpsed what looked like a plastic baggie.

"Hold him good." The third man spoke in a whisper. He crouched by Evans's shoulder, pulled up the shirtsleeve, exposing the flesh of his arm. He was wheezing softly behind the black mask. In the same whisper, he said, "You know what this is?"

He held up the baggie. The water was cloudy. Evans saw what looked like a fleshy ball, and in a panic he thought, *Oh God, they cut somebody's balls off.* But then he saw the ball moving, undulating. It was brown with white spots, about the size of a golf ball.

"You know?" the man said.

Evans shook his head.

"You will," the man whispered, and unzipped the baggie. He pushed it against the underside of Evans's arm. Evans felt wetness. The man was manipulating the baggie, squeezing the ball. Evans was trying to see, but it was hard to see exactly what was—

The ball moved. It spread, extended what looked like wings. No, not wings. It was a tiny octopus! Tiny! It could not have weighed more than a few ounces. Brownish with white rings. The man was squeezing the baggie, compressing it, pushing the little octopus toward the flesh of Evans's arm.

And then he understood.

Evans moaned and began to struggle, trying to move against his captors, but they had him firmly, and he felt the touch of the octopus, a kind of sticky sensation, like cellophane or Sticky Putty or something. He lifted his head in horror and saw that the man was snapping the baggie with his finger, trying to goad the octopus, which had wrapped itself against the skin of Evans's arm, and in a flash the rings on the octopus changed from white to blue.

The blue ring of death.

"That means he's mad." The third man holding the baggie said, "You won't feel it," but Evans did. It was a bite from the tiny beak, a single sting, almost like the sting of a needle. Evans jerked his arm and the man withdrew the baggie and sealed it again. He whispered, "Hold him good."

He went away a moment, then came back with a kitchen rag. He wiped the underside of Evans's arm, wiped the water off the floor. Still whispering, he said, "You won't feel anything for a few minutes." He walked over to the phone. "Don't try to call anybody," he said, and ripped the phone off the wall, smashing it on the floor.

The men released him. They moved quickly to the door, opened it, and were gone.

* * *

He coughed, and got to his hands and knees. He looked at his underarm; the bite looked like a dimple in the flesh, a small pink spot just at the edge of the hairs of his armpit. Nobody would ever see it.

He did not feel anything except a sort of dull tingling at the spot where the bite had occurred. His mouth was dry, but that was probably from fear. His head hurt. He reached up, felt blood, realized that they had torn open some of his stitches.

Jesus. He tried to get to his feet but his arm gave way, and he fell down again, rolling on the floor. He was still disoriented. He stared into the lights in the ceiling. His apartment had that cottage-cheese kind of ceiling. He hated that ceiling. He wanted to do something about it but it was too expensive. Anyway, he had always thought he would be moving soon. He was still disoriented. He got onto his elbows. His mouth was very dry now. It was the effect of the poison.

Some kind of a toad. No, he thought, that wasn't right. It wasn't a toad. It was a . . .

He couldn't remember.

Octopus.

That's right. It was a little octopus, hardly bigger than a thumbnail. Cute little thing.

The Indians in the Amazon used them for poison for their arrowheads. No, he thought, that was toads. No octopus in the Amazon. Or were there?

He was confused. Becoming more confused. He broke into a cold sweat. Was that part of it, too? He had to get to a phone. He might only have a few minutes of consciousness left.

He crawled to the nearest object, which was an easy chair . . . he'd had it in law school, it was pretty ratty, he had intended to get rid of it when he moved here but he hadn't gotten around to it yet . . . the living room needed a chair right in this spot . . . he'd had it re-covered in fabric his second year in law school . . . pretty dirty now . . . who had time to go shopping? With his mind racing, he pulled himself up until his chin was resting on the seat of the chair. He was gasping for breath, it felt as if he had climbed a mountain. He thought, Why am I here? Why is my chin on the chair? Then he remembered that he was trying to climb up, to sit in it.

Sit in the chair.

He got the elbow of his good arm up onto the seat and began to press himself up. Finally he was able to heave his chest onto the chair, then the rest of his body. His limbs were getting numb, and cold, and heavier by the minute. They were becoming too heavy to move. His whole body was getting heavy. He managed to get himself almost upright in the chair. There was a phone on the table beside him, but his arm was too heavy to reach for it. He tried, but he could not reach out at all now. His fingers moved slightly, but that was all. His body was very cold and very heavy.

He began to lose his balance, slowly at first and then sliding over sideways, until his chest rested on the arm of the chair and his head hung over the side. And there he stayed, unable to move. He could not lift his head. He could not move his arms. He could not even move his eyes. He stared at the fabric of the chair and the carpet on the floor and he thought, *This is the last thing I will see before I die.*

VI

BLUE

How long Peter Evans stared at the carpet he did not know. The arm of the chair pressing against his chest impeded his breathing, but it was becoming more difficult to breathe in any case. Images from his life flashed into consciousness—the basement where he played with his first computer, the blue bicycle that was stolen the same day he got it, the boxed corsage for his senior prom date, standing up in Professor Whitson's con law class, his legs shaking, while old Whitson took him apart—

"Peter? Hel-*lo?* Peter?"

—and terrorized him, they were all terrorized by Whitson, and the dinner that was the final interview for his LA job, where he spilled soup all over his shirt and the partners pretended not to notice, and—

"Peter? *Peter!* What are you doing there? Peter? Get up, Peter."

He felt hands on his shoulders, burning hot hands, and with a grunt he was hauled back into sitting position. "There, that's better." Janis peered at him, her face inches from his. "What's the matter with you? What did you take? Talk to me."

But he could not talk. He could not move at all. She was wearing a leotard top and jeans and sandals. If she moved to one side, she was out of his field of view.

"Peter?" A puzzled tone. "I think something is really wrong. Have you been doing ecstasy? Did you have a stroke? You're too young for a stroke. But it could happen, I guess. Especially with your diet. I told you no more than sixty-five grams of fat a day. If you were a vegetarian you would never have a stroke. Why don't you answer me?"

She touched his jaw, a questioning look on her face. Evans was feeling distinctly lightheaded because he could hardly breathe anymore. It was as if he had a twenty-ton stone on his chest. Even though he was sitting up, the great stone weighed on him.

He thought, *Call the hospital!*

"I don't know what to do, Peter," she said. "I just wanted to talk to you tonight, and now you're like this. I mean, I guess it's a bad time. But it's kind of scary, too. I have to be honest. I wish you would answer me. Can you answer me?"

Call the hospital!

"Maybe you'll hate me for this, but I don't know what you took that makes you this way, so I'm going to call 911 and get an ambulance. I'm really sorry and I don't want to get you into trouble, but this is freaking me out, Peter."

She went out of his field of view but he heard her picking up the phone on the table next to his chair. He thought, *Good. Hurry.*

She said, "Something is wrong with your phone."

Oh Jesus.

She stepped back into his field of view. "Your phone is not working, did you know that?"

Use your cell phone.

"Do you have your cell phone? I left mine in the car."

Go get it.

"Maybe one of the other phones in your apartment is working. You need to call your service provider, Peter. It's not safe to be without phones—what's this? Somebody tore the phone out of the wall? Have we been having a fit of pique?"

Knocking on the door. It sounded like the front door. "Hell-lo? Anybody here? Hello? Peter?" A woman's voice. He couldn't see who it was.

He heard Janis say, "Who are you?"

"Who are *you?*"

"I'm Janis. I'm Peter's friend."

"I'm Sarah. I work with Peter."

"You're tall."

"Where is Peter?" Sarah said.

"He's over there," Janis said. "Something's wrong with him."

Evans could see none of this, because he could not move his eyes. And now he saw the first gray spots that signaled the impending loss of consciousness. It took every ounce of energy he possessed to move his chest and fill his lungs the tiniest bit.

"Peter?" Sarah said.

She moved into his field of view. She looked at him.

"Are you paralyzed?" she said.

Yes! Call the hospital!

"He's sweating," Sarah said. "Cold sweats."

"He was that way when I found him," Janis said. She turned to Sarah. "What are you doing here anyway? How well do you know Peter?"

"Did you call an ambulance?" Sarah said.

"No, because my phone is in my car, and—"

"I'll do it."

Sarah flipped open her cell phone. It was the last thing Evans remembered.

**BRENTWOOD
WEDNESDAY, OCTOBER 13
1:22 A.M.**

It was late. The house was dark all around him. Nicholas Drake was sitting at his desk in his home in Brentwood, near Santa Monica. He was precisely 2.9 miles from the beach (he had recently measured it in his car), so he felt secure there. It was a good thing, too, because NERF had bought this house for him only one year before. There had been some discussion about that, because they had also bought him a townhouse in Georgetown. But Drake had pointed out that he needed a residence on the West Coast in which to entertain celebrities and important contributors.

California was, after all, the most environmentally conscious state in the nation. It had been the first to pass anti-smoking laws, almost ten years before New York or any other Eastern state did. And even when a Federal Court overturned the EPA on the issue of secondhand smoke in 1998, saying that the EPA had violated its own rules of evidence and banned a substance they had failed to prove caused any harm at all—the Federal Judge was from a tobacco state, *obviously*—even then, California did not budge. The anti-smoking laws stayed. In fact, Santa Monica was about to ban all smoking outdoors, even at the beach! Now *that* was progress!

It was easy here.

But as for getting *major* funds . . . well, that was another matter. There were some rich people in the entertainment industry who could be counted on, but for the real money in California— the investment bankers, portfolio managers, CEOs, real estate, trust funders, people with five hundred million to a couple billion, *serious* money—well, those people weren't so easy. Those people inhabited a different California. Those people belonged to golf courses that didn't allow actors to join. The big money was in the hands of pioneers and tech entrepreneurs, and they were very smart and very tough. A lot of them knew their science. Christ, a lot of them *were* scientists.

Which was why they presented such a challenge to Drake, if he wanted that bonus for making his numbers for the year. He was staring at the screen, thinking it was time for a Scotch, when a new window opened and the cursor blinked:

SCORPIO_L: Can you talk?

Speaking of dimwits, he thought. He typed:

Yes I can.

Drake shifted in his seat, adjusting the light over his desk so it would illuminate his face. He looked at the camera lens mounted just above his screen.

The window opened up. He saw Ted Bradley, sitting at his desk in his house in the San Fernando Valley.

"Well?"

"It was just as you said," Bradley said. "Evans has gone over to the dark side."

"And?"

"He was with that girl, Jennifer, who works on the lawsuit . . ."

"Jennifer Haynes?"

"Yeah. She's a wise-ass bitch."

Drake said nothing. He was listening to the sound of the voice. Bradley had been drinking again. He said, "Ted, we've talked about this before. Not everybody likes it when you come on to them."

"Yeah, they do. I mean, mostly they do."

"Ted, this is not the impression we want to make."

"Well, she insulted me."

"All right. So Jennifer Haynes was there . . ."

"She's a stooge for big oil and coal. Gotta be."

"And who else was there?"

"Sarah Jones."

"Uh-huh. She flew up to see the body?"

"I don't know why she was there. She was with a guy named Kenner, a real asshole. Another know-it-all."

"Describe him."

"Forties, dark, kind of butch. Looks military to me."

"Uh-huh. Anyone else?"

"No."

"Nobody foreign? No other people?"

"No, just the ones I described."

"Would you say that Peter Evans knew Kenner?"

"Yeah. Pretty well, I would say."

"So, it was your impression they were working together?"

"Yes. I would say very much together."

"All right, Ted," Drake said. "I like your instincts here." He watched as Bradley preened on the monitor. "I think you may be on to something. Evans could prove a problem to us."

"I'll say."

"He's been one of our trusted attorneys. Why, he was in my office just the other day, getting an assignment from me. If he's turned on us, he could do damage."

"Damn turncoat," Ted said. "He's another Bennett Arnold."

"I want you to stick close to him for the next week or so."

"My pleasure."

"Hang out with him, stay by his side. Buddy-buddy. You know."

"I got you, Nick. I'll be on him like glue."

"I'm sure he'll be at the opening of the conference later this morning," Drake said. And he thought, *Or then again, he might not make it.*

Kenner said, "I must say, it was an excellent choice. *Hapalochlaena fasciata,* the most deadly of the three species of blue-ringed octopus. So named because when it is threatened it changes color and produces bright blue rings on its skin. It's found everywhere in the coastal waters of Australia. The animal is very tiny, the bite is small and almost undetectable, and envenomation is often deadly. There is no antivenom. And a bite's not likely to be quickly recognized at a hospital in Los Angeles. Really, a masterful choice."*

Evans, who was lying in the emergency room at UCLA with a respirator on his face, just stared. He was still unable to speak. But he was no longer so frightened. Janis had gone home in a huff, mentioning something about teaching an early class. Sarah was sitting by his bed, rubbing his hand gently and looking beautiful. "Where would they have gotten one?"

---

* See S. K. Sutherland, et al., "Toxins and mode of envenomation of the common ringed or blue-banded octopus," *Med. J.Aust.* 1 (1969): 893–98. Also H. Flecker, et al., "Fatal bite from octopus," *Med. J.Aust.* 2 (1955): 329–31.

"I imagine they have several," Kenner said. "They're delicate, and don't live very long anyway. But they are captured in fairly large numbers because the Aussies are trying to make an antivenin. You probably know the Australians lead the world in deadly poisonous animals. The most poisonous snake, the most poisonous mollusk, the most poisonous fish—all from Australia or found there."

Evans thought, *Great.*

"But now of course UCLA has seen three cases. They're on it."

"Yes, we are," an intern said, coming into the room. He checked Evans's IV and his respirator. He said, "We have your preliminary blood work. It's a tetrodotoxin, like the others. You should be up and around in about three more hours. Lucky guy." He smiled winningly at Sarah, then walked out again.

"Anyway, I'm glad you're all right," Kenner said. "It would have been embarrassing to lose you."

Evans thought, *What is he talking about?* He was increasingly able to use his eye muscles, and he glanced over at Sarah. But she just smiled.

"Oh yes," Kenner said. "I need you alive, Peter. At least for a while."

Sitting in a corner of the room on his cell phone, Sanjong said, "Okay, we have some action."

Kenner said, "Is it where we thought?"

"Yes."

"What happened?"

"We just got the receipt notice. They rented an aircraft last month. A C-57 transport."

"Whew," Kenner said.

"What does that mean?" Sarah said.

"Big aircraft. They probably need it to spray."

She looked puzzled. "Spray?"

Sanjong said, "It's pretty clear they're going to disseminate AOB, ammonia-oxidizing bacteria, in large quantities. And perhaps some hydrophilic nanoparticles as well."

"To do what?"

"Control the path of a storm," Kenner said. "There's some evidence that disseminated AOB at altitude can shift a hurricane or cyclone track. Hydrophilic nanoparticles potentiate the effect. At least in theory. I don't know if it's been tried on a large system."

"They're going to control a hurricane?"

"They're going to try."

"Maybe not," Sanjong said. "Tokyo says some recent cellular and Internet traffic suggests that the project may be canceled."

"Then they don't have the initial conditions?"

"Looks like they don't, no."

Evans coughed. "Oh good," Kenner said. "You're coming around." He patted his arm. "Just rest now, Peter. Try and sleep if you can. Because, as you know, today is the big day."

"The big day?" Sarah said.

"The conference begins in about five and a half hours," Kenner said. He stood to go, then turned back to Evans. "I'm going to have Sanjong stay with you the rest of the night," he said. "I think you'll be all right here, but they've already made one attempt on your life, and I don't want them to try another."

Sanjong smiled and sat on the chair beside the bed, a stack of magazines beside him. He opened the latest issue of *Time* magazine. The cover story was "Climate Change Doomsday Ahead." He also had *Newsweek:* "Abrupt Climate Change—A New Scandal for the Administration?" And *The Economist:* "Climate Change Rears Its Ugly Head." And *Paris-Match:* "Climat: Le Nouveau Péril Américain."

Sanjong smiled cheerfully. "Just rest now," he said.

Evans closed his eyes.

At nine o'clock that morning, the invited attendees to the conference were milling around on the floor, not taking their seats. Evans was standing near the entrance, drinking coffee. He felt incredibly tired, but he was all right. He'd been a little shaky in his legs earlier, but that had passed.

The delegates were clearly academic types, many dressed casually in a manner to suggest an outdoorsy lifestyle—khakis and L.L.Bean shirts, hiking boots, Patagonia vests. "It looks like a lumberjack convention, doesn't it?" Jennifer said, standing beside Evans. "You'd never know these guys spend most of their time in front of computer monitors."

"Is that true?" Evans said.

"A lot of them, yes."

"And the hiking shoes?"

She shrugged. "The rugged look is in, at the moment."

At the podium, Nicholas Drake tapped the microphone. "Good morning, everyone," he said. "We will begin in ten minutes." Then he stepped away, and huddled with Henley.

"Waiting for the TV cameras," Jennifer said.

"They had some electrical problems this morning. Crews are still setting up."

"So, of course, everything waits for television."

At the entrance to the convention hall, there was a commotion and shouting. Evans looked over and saw an elderly man in a tweed coat and tie struggling with two security guards. "But I have been invited!" he said. "I am supposed to be here."

"Sorry, sir," the guards were saying, "your name is not on the sheet."

"But, I tell you, I have been invited!"

"Oh boy," Jennifer said, shaking her head.

"Who's that?"

"That is Professor Norman Hoffman. Ever heard of him?"

"No, why?"

"The ecology of thought? He's a famous sociologist, or should I say a notorious one. Extremely critical of environmental beliefs. A bit of a mad dog. We had him over to the war room to ask him his views. That was a mistake. The guy never shuts up. He talks a mile a minute and goes off on tangents—in every direction—and you can't turn him off. It's like a TV set that changes channels every few seconds, and there's no remote."

"No wonder they don't want him here."

"Oh yes, he would cause trouble. He already is."

Over by the entrance, the old man was struggling with the security guards. "Let go of me! How dare you! I was invited! By George Morton himself. He and I are personal friends. George Morton invited me!"

The mention of George Morton sparked something. Evans went over to the old man.

Jennifer said, "You'll be sor-ry . . ."

He shrugged. "Excuse me," he said, coming up to the guards. "I'm Mr. Morton's attorney. Can I help you?"

The old man writhed in the grip of the guards. "I'm Professor Norman Hoffman and George Morton invited me!" Up close, Evans saw that the old man was messily shaven, unkempt, his hair wild. "Why do you think I would come to this horrible convocation? For one reason only: George asked me to. He wanted my *impression* of it. Although I could have told him weeks ago: There are no surprises to be had here, I can assure you. It will unfold with all the stately ceremony of any cheap funeral."

Evans was thinking Jennifer had been right to warn him about this guy. He said politely, "Do you have a ticket, sir?"

"No, I don't have a *ticket*. I don't *need* a ticket. What don't you understand, young man? I am Professor Norman Hoffman and I am a personal friend of George Morton's. Anyway," he said, "they took my ticket."

"Who did?"

"One of those guards."

Evans said to the guards, "Did you take his ticket?"

"He didn't have a ticket."

"Do you have a stub?" Evans said to Hoffman.

"No, damn it, I do not have a *stub*. I do not need a *stub*. I do not need any of this, frankly."

"I'm sorry, Professor, but—"

"However, I managed to hold on to *this*." He gave Evans the torn corner of a ticket. It was a genuine ticket.

"Where is the rest?"

"I told you, they took it."

A guard standing to one side beckoned to Evans. Evans went over to him. The guard turned his cupped hand, revealing the rest of the ticket in his palm. "I'm sorry, sir," he said, "but Mr. Drake gave specific orders this gentleman was not to be allowed in."

"But he has a ticket," Evans said.

"Perhaps you'd like to take it up with Mr. Drake."

By now, a television crew had wandered over, drawn by the commotion. Hoffman immediately played to the cameras, struggling anew.

"Don't bother with Drake!" Hoffman yelled to Evans. "Drake won't let truth into these proceedings!" He turned to the camera. "Nicholas Drake is an immoral fraud, and these proceedings are a travesty to the poor of the world. I bear witness to the dying children of Africa and Asia! Breathing their last because of conferences like this! Fearmongers! Immoral fearmongers!" He struggled maniacally. His eyes were wild. There was spittle on his lips. He certainly appeared crazy, and the cameras switched off; the crews turned away, seemingly embarrassed. At once, Hoffman stopped his struggle. "Never mind. I've said my piece. No one is interested, as usual." He turned to his guards. "You can let me go. I have had enough of this chicanery. I cannot bear to be here another minute. Let me go!"

Evans said, "Let him go."

The guards released Hoffman. He immediately dashed into the center of the room, where a crew was now interviewing Ted Bradley. Hoffman stepped in front of Bradley and said, "This man is a pimp! He is an eco-pimp for a corrupt establishment that makes its living by spreading false fears! Don't you understand? False fears are a plague, a modern plague!"

Then the guards were on Hoffman again, dragging him bodily out of the hall. He didn't struggle this time. He just went limp, his heels scraping on the ground as he was carried out. All he said was, "Be careful, I have a bad back. You hurt me and I'll sue you for assault."

They set him outside on the curb, dusted him off, released him.

"Have a good day, sir."

"I intend to. My days are numbered."

Evans hung back with Jennifer, watching Hoffman. "I won't say I told you," Jennifer said.

"Just who is he, anyway?"

"He's a professor *emeritus* at USC. He was one of the first people to study in a rigorous statistical fashion the media and its effect on society. He's quite interesting, but as you see he has developed, uh, strong opinions."

"You think Morton really invited him here?"

"Peter, I need your help," a voice said. Evans turned and saw Drake striding toward him.

"What is it?"

"That *nut*," Drake said, nodding to Hoffman, "is probably going to go straight to the police and claim he was assaulted. We don't need that this morning. Go talk to him. See if you can calm him down."

Cautiously, Evans said, "I don't know what I can do . . ."

"Get him to explain his nutty theories," Drake said. "That'll keep him busy for *hours*."

"But then I'll miss the conf—"

"We don't need you here. We need you *there*. With the cuckoo."

There was a large crowd outside the conference center. The overflow was watching the proceedings on a big TV screen, with subtitles running underneath the speaker. Evans pushed through the gathering. "I know why you are following me," Hoffman said, when he saw Evans. "And it won't work."

"Professor—"

"You're the bright young *poseur* Nick Drake sent to put me off my purpose."

"Not at all, sir."

"Yes, you are. Don't lie to me. I don't like to be lied to."

"All right," Evans said, "it's true. I was sent by Drake."

Hoffman stopped. He seemed startled by the honesty. "I knew it. And what did he tell you to do?"

"Stop you from going to the police."

"All right then, you've succeeded. Go and tell him, I am not going to the police."

"It looks like you are."

"Oh. It *looks like* I am. You're one of those people who care what it *looks like*."

"No, sir, but you—"

"I don't care what it *looks like*. I care what *is*. Do you have any idea what is?"

"I'm not sure I follow you."

"What is your line of work?"

"I'm a lawyer."

"I should have known. Everybody is a lawyer these days. Extrapolating the statistical growth of the legal profession, by the year 2035 every single person in the United States will be a lawyer, including newborn infants. They will be *born* lawyers. What do you suppose it will be like to live in such a society?"

"Professor," Evans said, "you made some interesting comments in the hall—"

"*Interesting?* I accused them of flagrant immorality, and you call that *interesting?*"

"I'm sorry," Evans said, trying to move the discussion toward Hoffman's views. "You didn't explain why you think—"

"I do not *think* anything, young man. I *know*. That is the purpose of my research—to know things, not to surmise them. Not to theorize. Not to hypothesize. But to *know* from direct research in the field. It's a lost art in academia these days, young man—you are not *that* young—what is your name, anyway?"

"Peter Evans."

"And you work for Drake, Mr. Evans?"

"No, for George Morton."

"Well, *why didn't you say so!*" Hoffman said.

"George Morton was a great, *great* man. Come along, Mr. Evans, and I will buy you some coffee and we can talk. Do you know what I do?"

"I'm afraid I don't, sir."

"I study the ecology of thought," Hoffman said. "And how it has led to a State of Fear."

They were sitting on a bench across the street from the conference hall, just beyond the milling crowds near the entrance. It was a busy scene, but Hoffman ignored everything around him. He spoke rapidly, with great animation, moving his hands so wildly that he often slapped Evans in the chest, but he never seemed to notice.

"Ten years ago, I began with fashion and slang," he said, "the latter being of course a kind of verbal fashion. I wanted to know the determinants of change in fashion and speech. What I quickly found is that there are no identifiable determinants. Fashions change for arbitrary reasons and although there are regularities—cycles, periodicities, and correlations—these are merely descriptive, not explanatory. Are you following me?"

"I think so," Evans said.

"In any case, I realized that these periodicities and correlations could be regarded as systems in themselves. Or if you will, ecosystems. I tested that hypothesis and found it heuristically valuable. Just as there is an ecology of the natural world, in the forests and mountains and oceans, so too there is an ecology of the man-made world of mental abstractions, ideas, and thought. That is what I have studied."

"I see."

"Within modern culture, ideas constantly rise and fall. For a while everybody believes something, and then, bit by bit, they stop believing it. Eventually, no one can remember the old idea, the way no one can remember the old slang. Ideas are themselves a kind of fad, you see."

"I understand, Professor, but why—"

"Why do ideas fall out of favor, you are wondering?" Hoffman said. He was talking to himself. "The answer is simply—they do. In fashion, as in natural ecology, there are disruptions. Sharp revisions of the established order. A lightning fire burns down a forest. A different species springs up in the charred acreage. Accidental, haphazard, unexpected, abrupt change. That is what the world shows us on every side."

"Professor . . ."

"But just as ideas can change abruptly, so, too, can they hang on past their time. Some ideas continue to be embraced by the public long after scientists have abandoned them. Left brain, right brain is a perfect example. In the 1970s, it gains popularity from the work of Sperry at Caltech, who studies a specific group of brain-surgery patients. His findings have no broader meaning beyond these patients. Sperry denies any broader meaning. By 1980, it is clear that the left and right brain notion is just wrong—the two sides of the brain do not work separately in a healthy person. But in the popular culture, the concept does not die for another twenty years. People talk about it, believe it, write books about it for decades after scientists have set it aside."

"Yes, all very interesting—"

"Similarly, in environmental thought, it was widely accepted in 1960 that there is something called 'the balance of nature.' If you just left nature alone it would come into a self-maintaining state of balance. Lovely idea with a long pedigree. The Greeks believed it three thousand years ago, on the basis of nothing. Just seemed nice. However, by 1990, no scientist believes in the balance of nature anymore. The ecologists have all given it up as simply wrong. Untrue. A fantasy. They speak now of dynamic disequilibrium, of multiple equilibrium states. But they now understand that nature is *never* in balance. Never has been, never will be. On the contrary, nature is always *out of* balance, and that means—"

"Professor," Evans said, "I'd like to ask you—"

"That means that mankind, which was formerly defined as the great disrupter of the natural order, is nothing of the sort. The whole environment is being constantly disrupted all the time anyway."

"But George Morton . . ."

"Yes, yes, you wonder what I discussed with George Morton. I am coming to that. We are not off topic. Because of course, Morton wanted to know about environmental ideas. And particularly the idea of environmental crisis."

"What did you tell him?"

"If you study the media, as my graduate students and I do, seeking to find shifts in normative conceptualization, you discover something extremely interesting. We looked at transcripts of news programs of the major networks—NBC, ABC, CBS. We also looked at stories in the newspapers of New York, Washington, Miami, Los Angeles, and Seattle. We counted the frequency of certain concepts and terms used by the media. The results were very striking." He paused.

"What did you find?" Evans said, taking his cue.

"There was a major shift in the fall of 1989. Before that time, the media did not make excessive use of terms such as *crisis, catastrophe, cataclysm, plague,* or *disaster.* For example, during the 1980s, the word *crisis* appeared in news reports about as often as the word *budget.* In addition, prior to 1989, adjectives such as *dire, unprecedented, dreaded* were not common in television reports or newspaper headlines. But then it all changed."

"In what way?"

"These terms started to become more and more common. The word *catastrophe* was used five times more often in 1995 than it was in 1985. Its use doubled again by the year 2000. And the stories changed, too. There was a heightened emphasis on fear, worry, danger, uncertainty, panic."

"Why should it have changed in 1989?"

"Ah. A good question. *Critical* question. In most respects 1989 seemed like a normal year: a Soviet sub sank in Norway; Tiananmen Square in China; the *Exxon Valdez;* Salmon Rushdie sentenced to death; Jane Fonda, Mike Tyson, and Bruce Springsteen all got divorced; the Episcopal

Church hired a female bishop; Poland allowed striking unions; *Voyager* went to Neptune; a San Francisco earthquake flattened highways; and Russia, the US, France, and England all conducted nuclear tests. A year like any other. But in fact the rise in the use of the term *crisis* can be located with some precision in the autumn of 1989. And it seemed suspicious that it should coincide so closely with the fall of the Berlin Wall. Which happened on November ninth of that year."

Hoffman fell silent again, looking at Evans in a significant way. Very pleased with himself.

Evans said, "I'm sorry, Professor. I don't get it."

"Neither did we. At first we thought the association was spurious. But it wasn't. The Berlin Wall marks the collapse of the Soviet empire. And the end of the Cold War that had lasted for half a century in the West."

Another silence. Another pleased look.

"I'm sorry," Evans said finally. "I was thirteen years old then, and . . ." He shrugged. "I don't see where you are leading."

"I am leading to the notion of social control, Peter. To the requirement of every sovereign state to exert control over the behavior of its citizens, to keep them orderly and reasonably docile. To keep them driving on the right side of the road— or the left, as the case may be. To keep them paying taxes. And of course we know that social control is best managed through fear."

"Fear," Evans said.

"Exactly. For fifty years, Western nations had

maintained their citizens in a state of perpetual fear. Fear of the other side. Fear of nuclear war. The Communist menace. The Iron Curtain. The Evil Empire. And within the Communist countries, the same in reverse. Fear of us. Then, suddenly, in the fall of 1989, it was all finished. Gone, vanished. *Over.* The fall of the Berlin Wall created a vacuum of fear. Nature abhors a vacuum. Something had to fill it."

Evans frowned. "You're saying that environmental crises took the place of the Cold War?"

"That is what the evidence shows. Of course, now we have radical fundamentalism and post–9/11 terrorism to make us afraid, and those are certainly real reasons for fear, but that is not my point. My point is, there is always a cause for fear. The cause may change over time, but the fear is always with us. Before terrorism we feared the toxic environment. Before that we had the Communist menace. The point is, although the specific cause of our fear may change, we are never without the fear itself. Fear pervades society in all its aspects. Perpetually."

He shifted on the concrete bench, turning away from the crowds.

"Has it ever occurred to you how astonishing the culture of Western society really is? Industrialized nations provide their citizens with unprecedented safety, health, and comfort. Average life spans increased fifty percent in the last century. Yet modern people live in abject fear. They are afraid of strangers, of disease, of crime, of the environment. They are afraid of the homes they live in, the food they eat, the technology that surrounds them. They are in a particular panic over things they can't even see—germs, chemicals, additives, pollutants. They are timid, nervous, fretful, and depressed. And even more amazingly, they are convinced that the environment of the entire planet is being destroyed around them. Remarkable! Like the belief in witchcraft, it's an extraordinary delusion—a global fantasy worthy of the Middle Ages. Everything is going to hell, and we must all live in fear. Amazing.

"How has this world view been instilled in everybody? Because although we imagine we live in different nations—France, Germany, Japan, the US—in fact, we inhabit exactly the same state, the State of Fear. How has that been accomplished?"

Evans said nothing. He knew it wasn't necessary.

"Well, I shall tell you how," he said. "In the old days—before your time, Peter—citizens of the West believed their nation-states were dominated by something called the military-industrial complex. Eisenhower warned Americans against it in the 1960s, and after two world wars Europeans knew very well what it meant in their own countries. But the military-industrial complex is no longer the primary driver of society. In reality, for the last fifteen years we have been under the control of an entirely new complex, far more powerful and far more pervasive. I call it the politico-legal-media complex. The PLM. And it is dedicated to promoting fear in the population— under the guise of promoting safety."

"Safety is important."

"Please. Western nations are fabulously safe. Yet people do not feel they are, because of the PLM. And the PLM is powerful and stable, precisely because it unites so many institutions of society. Politicians need fears to control the population. Lawyers need dangers to litigate, and make money. The media need scare stories to capture an audience. Together, these three estates are so compelling that they can go about their business even if the scare is totally groundless. If it has no basis in fact at all. For instance, consider silicon breast implants."

Evans sighed, shaking his head. "Breast implants?"

"Yes. You will recall that breast implants were claimed to cause cancer and autoimmune diseases. Despite statistical evidence that this was not true, we saw high-profile news stories, high-profile lawsuits, high-profile political hearings. The manufacturer, Dow Corning, was hounded out of the business after paying $3.2 billion, and juries awarded huge cash payments to plaintiffs and their lawyers.

"Four years later, definitive epidemiological studies showed beyond a doubt that breast implants did not cause disease. But by then the crisis had already served its purpose, and the PLM had moved on, a ravenous machine seeking new fears, new terrors. I'm telling you, *this is the way modern society works*—by the constant creation of fear. And there is no countervailing force. There is no system of checks and balances, no restraint on the perpetual promotion of fear after fear after fear. . . ."

"Because we have freedom of speech, freedom of the press."

"That is the classic PLM answer. That's how they stay in business," Hoffman said. "But think. If it is not all right to falsely shout 'Fire!' in a crowded theater, why is it all right to shout 'Cancer!' in the pages of *The New Yorker?* When that statement is not true? We've spent more than twenty-five billion dollars to clear up the phony power-line cancer claim.* 'So what?' you say. I can see it in your face. You're thinking, we're rich, we can afford it. It's only twenty-five billion dollars. But the fact is that twenty-five billion dollars is more than the total GDP of the poorest fifty nations of the world *combined.* Half the world's population lives on two dollars a day. So that twenty-five billion would be enough to support thirty-four million people for a year. Or we could have helped all the people dying of AIDS in Africa. Instead, we piss it away on a fantasy published by a magazine whose readers take it very seriously. Trust it. It is a *stupendous* waste of money. In another world, it would be a criminal waste. One could easily imagine another Nuremberg trial—this time for the relentless squandering of Western wealth on trivialities—and complete with pictures of the dead babies in Africa and Asia that result."

---

* Estimate from the White House Science Office for all costs of the scare, including property devaluation and relocation of power lines. Cited in Park, *Voodoo Science*, p. 161. (Park was a participant in the controversy.)

He hardly paused for breath. "At the very least, we are talking about a moral outrage. Thus we can expect our religious leaders and our great humanitarian figures to cry out against this waste and the needless deaths around the world that result. But do any religious leaders speak out? No. Quite the contrary, *they join the chorus.* They promote 'What Would Jesus Drive?' As if they have forgotten that what Jesus would drive is the false prophets and fearmongers out of the temple."

He was getting quite heated now.

"We are talking about a situation that is *profoundly* immoral. It is *disgusting,* if truth be told. The PLM callously ignores the plight of the poorest and most desperate human beings on our planet in order to keep fat politicians in office, rich news anchors on the air, and conniving lawyers in Mercedes-Benz convertibles. Oh, and university professors in Volvos. Let's not forget *them.*"

"How's that?" Evans said. "What does this have to do with university professors?"

"Well, that's another discussion."

"Is there a short version?" Evans said.

"Not really. That's why headlines aren't news, Peter. But I will try to be succinct," he said. "The point is this: the world has changed in the last fifty years. We now live in the knowledge society, the information society, whatever you want to call it. And it has had enormous impact on our universities.

"Fifty years ago, if you wanted to lead what

was then called 'the life of the mind,' meaning to be an intellectual, to live by your wits, you had to work in a university. The society at large had no place for you. A few newspaper reporters, a few magazine journalists could be considered as living by their wits, but that was about it. Universities attracted those who willingly gave up worldly goods to live a cloistered intellectual life, teaching timeless values to the younger generation. Intellectual work was the exclusive province of the university.

"But today, whole sectors of society live the life of the mind. Our entire economy is based on intellectual work, now. Thirty-six percent of workers are knowledge workers. That's more than are employed in manufacturing. And when professors decided they would no longer teach young people, but leave that task to their graduate students who knew much less than they did and spoke English poorly—when that happened, the universities were thrown into crisis. What good were they anymore? They had lost their exclusive hold on the life of the mind. They no longer taught the young. Only so many theoretical texts on the semiotics of Foucault could be published in any single year. What was to become of our universities? What relevance did they have in the modern era?"

He stood up, as if energized by this question. Then abruptly, he sat down again.

"What happened," he continued, "is the universities transformed themselves in the 1980s. Formerly bastions of intellectual freedom in a world of Babbittry, formerly the locus of sexual freedom and experimentation, they now became the most restrictive environments in modern society. Because they had a new role to play. They became the creators of new fears for the PLM. Universities today are factories of fear. They invent all the new terrors and all the new social anxieties. All the new restrictive codes. Words you can't say. Thoughts you can't think. They produce a steady stream of new anxieties, dangers, and social terrors to be used by politicians, lawyers, and reporters. Foods that are bad for you. Behaviors that are unacceptable. Can't smoke, can't swear, can't screw, can't *think*. These institutions have been stood on their heads in a generation. It is really quite extraordinary.

"The modern State of Fear could never exist without universities feeding it. There is a peculiar neo-Stalinist mode of thought that is required to support all this, and it can thrive only in a restrictive setting, behind closed doors, without due process. In our society, only universities have created that—so far. The notion that these institutions are *liberal* is a cruel joke. They are fascist to the core, I'm telling you."

He broke off and pointed down the walkway. "Who is this fellow pushing toward us through the crowd? He looks oddly familiar."

Evans said, "That's Ted Bradley, the actor."

"Where have I seen him?"

"He plays the president on television."

"Oh yes. *Him*."

Ted came to a halt in front of them, panting.

"Peter," he said, "I've been looking everywhere for you. Is your cell phone on?"

"No, because—"

"Sarah has been trying to reach you. She says it's important. We have to leave town right away. And bring your passport."

Evans said, "We? What does this have to do with you?"

"I'm coming with you," Ted said.

As they started to walk away, Hoffman clutched at Evans's sleeve, holding him back. He had a new thought. "We haven't talked about *involution*," he said.

"Professor—"

"It is the next step in the development of nation-states. Indeed it is already happening. You must see the irony. After all, twenty-five billion dollars and ten years later the same rich elitists who were terrified of power-line cancer are buying magnets to strap to their ankles or put on their mattresses—imported Japanese magnets are the best, the most expensive—in order to enjoy the *healthful effects of magnetic fields*. The same magnetic fields—only now they can't get enough of them!"

"Professor," Evans said, "I have to go."

"Why don't these people just lie back against a TV screen? Snuggle up to a kitchen appliance? All the things that terrified them before."

"We'll talk later," Evans said, pulling his arm away.

"They even sell magnets in the *health* magazines!

Healthy living through magnetic fields! Insanity! No one remembers even a few years ago! George Orwell. No memory!"

"Who is that guy?" Bradley said, as they headed off. "He seems a little wound up, doesn't he?"

"The record of catastrophe is contained within the ice cores," the speaker said, droning on at the podium. He was Russian and spoke with a heavy accent. "These ice cores from Greenland show that, in the last one hundred thousand years, there have been four abrupt climate change events. Some have occurred very quickly, in a few years. While the mechanisms by which these events occurred are still being studied, they demonstrate that there can be 'trigger' effects in climate, whereby small changes—including man-made changes— can produce catastrophically large effects. We have seen a foretaste of such effects in recent days with the calving of the world's largest iceberg, and the terrible loss of life from the flash flood in the American Southwest. And it is no difficulty to predict we will see more—"

He paused, as Drake hurried up onto the stage, whispered in his ear, then stepped down again, looking at his watch.

"Uh, I must beg the forgiveness of you," the speaker said. "I seem to have brought up an out-dated version of my remarks. Word processors!

That was a part from an old talk from 2001. What I wanted to say was that the calving of the iceberg in 2001—larger than many American states—and the dangerously unseasonal weather around the world, including the sunny Southwest, portends further climate instability. It is just beginning."

Sarah Jones, standing in the back, was talking with Ann Garner, the wife of a prominent Hollywood lawyer and a major contributor to NERF. Ann was emphatic as always, and talking nonstop.

"I'll tell you what I heard," Ann was saying. "I heard there is an industry-sponsored campaign to discredit NGOs. Industry is afraid of the growing power of the environmental movement and they are desperate, *desperate* to stop it. We have had our modest successes in recent years, and it is driving them crazy, and—"

"I'm sorry," Sarah said. "Just a minute, Ann." She turned to look at the Russian speaker at the podium. *What did he say?* she thought.

She walked quickly to the press table, where reporters were lined up with their laptops open. They were getting real-time transcripts of the conference.

She looked over the shoulder of Ben Lopez, the reporter for the *Los Angeles Times*. Ben didn't mind; he had been after her for months.

"Hi ya, sweet thing."

"Hi, Ben. Mind if I look at something?"

She touched the mouse, scrolling up the screen.

"Sure, be my guest. Nice perfume."
She read:

CAN BE TRIGGER EFFECTS IN CLIMATE, WHEREBY SMALL CHANGES
INCLUDING MAN-MADE CHANGES CAN PRODUCE CATASTROPHICALLY
LARGE EFFECTS. WE HAVE HAD A FORETASTE OF SUCH EFFECTS ~~IN
RECENT DAYS WITH THE CALVING OF THE WORLD'S LARGEST ICEBERG
AND THE TERRIBLE LOSS OF LIFE FROM THE FLASH FLOOD IN THE
AMERICAN SOUTHWEST. AND IT IS NO DIFFICULTY TO PREDICT WE
WILL SEE MORE~~

While she watched, the text changed, the
strikeout disappearing, and replaced with new
text:

CAN BE TRIGGER EFFECTS IN CLIMATE, WHEREBY SMALL CHANGES
INCLUDING MAN-MADE CHANGES CAN PRODUCE CATASTROPHICALLY
LARGE EFFECTS. WE HAVE HAD A FORETASTE OF SUCH EFFECTS WITH
THE CALVING OF THE ICEBERG IN 2001 LARGER THAN MANY AMERI-
CAN STATES AND THE DANGEROUSLY UNSEASONAL WEATHER AROUND
THE WORLD INCLUDING THE SUNNY SOUTHWEST PORTENDS FUR-
THER CLIMATE INSTABILITY

"Holy shit," she said.
"Something wrong?" Ben said.
"Did you see what he said?"
"Yeah. Poor guy. Probably has jet lag to beat
hell. And obviously, he's struggling with English . . ."
The original remarks were gone. The record
was corrected. But there was no doubt about it:
*the Russian had known in advance about the iceberg
and the flash flood.* It was written into his speech.

And somebody had forgotten to tell him, when he got off the plane, that it never happened.

He knew in advance.

But now the record was corrected, the remarks stricken. She glanced at the video camera in the back, recording the proceedings. No doubt the remarks would disappear from the video record as well.

The son of a bitch knew in advance.

"Hey," Ben said, "I don't know what you're so upset about. Clue me in, will you?"

"Later," she said. "I promise." She patted his shoulder, and went back to Ann.

"So," Ann said, "what we are facing is an industry-promoted campaign, well orchestrated, well financed, pervasive and ultra right-wing, that is intent on destroying the environmental movement that stands in its way."

After what she had just seen, Sarah was in no mood to put up with this blather. "Ann," she said. "Did it ever cross your mind you might be paranoid?"

"No. Anyway, even paranoids have enemies."

"How many industry executives serve on the NERF board right now?" Sarah said.

"Uh, not that many."

Sarah knew that there were thirty board members, of whom twelve were industry figures. This was the case with all modern environmental groups. They had all had industry representatives over the last twenty years.

"Did you ask your corporate board members about this secret industry campaign?"

"No," she said. She was looking at Sarah oddly.

"Do you think," Sarah said, "that it is possible that NGOs like NERF could be the ones who are engaged in a secret campaign?"

"What are you talking about?" Ann said, stiffening. "Sarah. We're the good guys."

"Are we?"

"Yes. We are," Ann said. "What's going on with you, Sarah?"

In the parking lot outside the convention hall, Sanjong Thapa sat in the car with his laptop on his knees. He had easily hacked the WiFi network used by the journalists and was receiving the conference transcript, which was instantaneously saved. He had done it that way because he was afraid he might be discovered and locked out at any moment, but now it meant that he had the complete transcript, including the revisions. Kenner, he thought, was going to love this.

On another screen, Sanjong was monitoring the satellite images from the western Atlantic, off the coast of Florida. A large high-pressure mass was beginning to rotate, forming the ragged beginnings of a hurricane. Clearly an event was scheduled around a hurricane, but for some reason it had been abandoned.

And now he was tracking other investigative leads. In particular, Kenner was concerned about a small research submarine known as DOEV/2, and the tender ship *AV Scorpio*. That submarine and its tender ship had been leased by CanuCo, a natural gas corporation based in Calgary, to conduct research in the South Pacific, looking for undersea gas deposits. The tender had sailed to Port Moresby, New Guinea, some two months before, and had subsequently left that harbor and had been spotted near Bougainville, in the Solomon Islands.

Nothing of great interest there, until it became known that CanuCo was not a registered Canadian corporation, and that it had no assets other than a website and web address. The owner of the site was CanuCo Leasing Corp, another nonexistent company. The lease payments had been made from a Cayman Island account and paid in euros. The name of the account was Seismic Services, also in Calgary, and sharing the same postal address as CanuCo.

They were obviously the same entity. And it was Seismic Services that had originally attempted to lease a submarine. And presumably had later caused the death of Nat Damon in Vancouver.

Now there were agencies in Washington searching satellite maps, trying to find the *AV Scorpio*, somewhere in the Solomon Island chain. But the Solomons had scattered cloud cover, and the satellite passes had not yet revealed the ship's location.

That in itself was worrisome. It suggested that the ship had already hidden itself in some way, perhaps by going into a covered dock.

Somewhere in the South Pacific.

And it was a big ocean.

Equally worrisome was the fact that the tender had sailed first to Vancouver, where it had taken on thirty tons of "industrial equipment," in five-ton cartons. The Canadian government had thought the company was illegally transporting automobiles in the cartons, so they opened one. The customs officers instead found some complex equipment that they listed as "diesel generators."

Generators!

Sanjong didn't know what was in those cartons, but he was sure they weren't diesel generators. Because you didn't have to go to Vancouver to get a bunch of generators. So it was worrisome—

"Hey! You!"

He looked up and saw two security guards walking across the parking lot toward his car. Obviously his WiFi hack had been detected. It was time to go. He turned the key in the ignition and drove away, waving cheerfully to the security guards as he passed them.

"Sarah? What's going on? You're just staring into space."

"Nothing, Ann." Sarah shook her head. "Just thinking."

"About what? And what do you mean about my being paranoid?" Ann put her hand on Sarah's arm. "Really. I'm a little concerned about you."

Sarah thought, *And I'm concerned about you.*

In truth, it was Sarah who was feeling a distinct paranoid chill. She looked around the room, and her eyes met Drake's. He was staring at her, studying her from across the room. For how long? Had he seen her quick dash to the reporters' desk? Had he deduced the meaning of it? Did he know she knew?

"Sarah," Ann said, shaking her arm.

"Listen," Sarah said. "I'm really sorry, but I have to go."

"Sarah. I'm worried about you."

"I'll be fine." She started to leave the room.

"I'll just come with you," Ann said, falling into step with her.

"I'd rather you didn't."

"I'm concerned for your welfare."

"I think I need to be alone for a while," Sarah said.

"Is that any way to treat a friend?" Ann said. "I insist, darling. You need a little mothering, I can see that. And I'm here for you."

Sarah sighed.

Nicholas Drake watched as Sarah left the room. Ann was sticking with her, just as he had asked. Ann was dedicated and tenacious. Sarah would be no match for her, unless she elected to turn and literally run. But if she did that . . . well, they would have to take stronger action. These were critical times, and sometimes strong action was essential. Just as in wartime.

But Drake suspected dire action would not prove necessary. True, Kenner had managed to disrupt the first two events, but only because ELF was a bunch of amateurs. Their brand of do-it-yourself schoolboy spontaneity was unsuited to the demands of modern media. Drake had said that to Henley a dozen times. Henley shrugged it off; he was concerned about deniability. Well, NERF could certainly deny they knew these clowns. What a bunch of fuckups!

But this last event was different. It had been planned far more carefully—it had to be—and it was in professional hands. Kenner would never be able to disrupt it. He could not even get there in time, Drake thought. And between Ted Bradley and Ann, Drake had lots of eyes and ears on that team as they progressed. And just to be sure, he had other surprises in store for Kenner as well.

He flipped open his phone and dialed Henley. "We've got them covered," he said.

"Good."

"Where are you?"

"I am about to deliver the news to V.," Henley said. "I am pulling up to his house now."

Through binoculars, Kenner watched as the silver Porsche convertible pulled into the driveway of the beach house. A tall, dark man in a blue golf shirt and tan slacks got out. He wore a baseball cap and dark glasses, but Kenner recognized him at once as Henley, the head of PR for NERF.

That closed the circle, he thought. He put the binoculars down on the fence and paused to consider the implications.

"Do you know who he is, sir?" the young FBI agent said, standing by his side. He was just a kid, no more than twenty-five.

"Yes," Kenner said. "I know who he is."

They were standing on the cliffs of Santa Monica, overlooking the beach and the ocean. The beach here was several hundred yards wide, from the shore to the bike path. Then a line of houses, packed close together along the coast highway. Then six lanes of roaring traffic.

Even though they abutted the highway, the houses were phenomenally expensive—twenty or thirty million dollars each, it was said, and perhaps much more. They were inhabited by some of the wealthiest people in California.

Henley was putting up the cloth top on his Porsche. He moved in a precise, almost fussy way. Then he went to the gate and buzzed it. The house he was entering was ultra-modern, curving shapes of glass. It glistened like a jewel in the morning sun.

Henley went inside. The gate closed behind him.

"But you don't care about people *entering* the house," the FBI agent said.

"That's right," Kenner said. "I don't."

"You don't want a list, or a record of who—"

"No."

"But it might prove—"

"No," Kenner said. The kid was trying to be helpful, but it was annoying. "I don't care about any of that. I just want to know when they all leave."

"Like, if they go on vacation or something?"

"Yes," Kenner said.

"What if they leave a maid behind?"

"They won't," Kenner said.

"Actually, sir, I'm pretty sure they will. These guys always leave somebody to watch the house."

"No," Kenner said. "This house will clear out. Everybody will go."

The kid frowned. "Whose house is it, anyway?"

"It belongs to a man named V. Allen Willy," Kenner said. He might as well tell him. "He's a philanthropist."

"Uh-huh. What is he, mixed up in the mob or something?"

"You might say," Kenner said. "Sort of a protection racket."

"It figures," the kid said. "Nobody makes that much money without a story behind it, you know what I mean?"

Kenner said he did. In fact, V. Allen Willy's story was as typically American as Horatio Alger's. Al Willy had started a chain of inexpensive clothing stores, taking clothes sewn in Third World sweatshops and selling them in Western cities for thirty times the cost. After ten years, he sold his company for $400 million. Soon after, he became (by his own definition) a radical socialist, a crusader for a sustainable world, and an advocate for environmental justice.

The exploitations he had found so profitable he now attacked with the money he had made from them. He was fiery and righteous, and with the V. added to his name, memorable too. However, his attacks often led companies to pull out of their Third World factories, which were then taken over by Chinese corporations that paid local workers even less than before. Thus, by any sensible account, V. Allen Willy was exploiting workers twice—once to make his fortune, and a second time to assuage his guilty conscience at their expense. He was a strikingly handsome man and not stupid, just an egotistical and impractical do-gooder. Currently, he was said to be writing a book on the precautionary principle.

He had also started the V. Allen Willy Foundation, which supported the cause of environmental

justice through dozens of organizations, including
NERF. And he was important enough to rate a
personal visit from Henley himself.

"So he's a rich environmentalist?" the FBI kid
said.

"That's right," Kenner said.

The kid nodded. "Okay," he said. "But I still
don't get it. What makes you think a rich guy
would leave his house empty?"

"I can't tell you that," Kenner said. "But he
will. And I want to know the minute it happens."
He handed the agent a card. "Call this number."

The kid looked at the card. "That's it?"

"That's it," Kenner said.

"And when is this going to happen?"

"Soon," Kenner said.

His phone buzzed. He flipped it open. It was a
text message from Sanjong.

THEY FOUND AV SCORPIO.

"I have to go," Kenner said.

"Nonsense," Ted Bradley said, sitting back in the passenger seat as Evans drove to Van Nuys. "You can't have all the fun, Pietro. I know you've been going on these secret excursions for the last week. I'm coming, too."

"You can't come, Ted," Evans said. "They won't allow it."

"Let me worry about that, okay?" he said, grinning.

Evans thought: What's going on? Bradley was staying so close, he was practically holding his hand. He refused to leave him alone.

Evans's cell phone rang. It was Sarah.

"Where are you?" she said.

"Almost to the airport. I have Ted with me."

"Uh-huh," she said, in the vague tone that meant she couldn't talk. "Well, I just talked to the pilots, and there seems to be a problem."

"What kind of a problem?"

"Legal," she said.

"What does that mean?" Evans said. But even as he spoke, he was turning off the road toward the gate leading to the runway, and he could see for himself.

Herb Lowenstein was standing there with eight security guards. And it looked like they were sealing the doors to Morton's jet.

Evans went through the gate and got out of the car. "What's going on, Herb?"

"The aircraft is being sealed," Herb said, "as required by law."

"What law?"

"George Morton's estate is now in probate, in case you've forgotten, and the contents of said estate, including all bank accounts and real property, must be sealed pending federal evaluation and assessing of death taxes. This aircraft will remain sealed until the conclusion of that evaluation. Six to nine months from now."

At that moment, Kenner pulled up in a town car. He introduced himself, shook hands with Lowenstein. "So it's a matter of probate," he said.

"That's right," Lowenstein said.

Kenner said, "I'm surprised to hear you say that."

"Why? George Morton is deceased."

"Is he? I hadn't heard."

"They found his body yesterday. Evans and Bradley went up and made the identification."

"And the medical examiner concurred?"

Lowenstein hesitated fractionally. "I presume so."

"You presume? Surely you've received documentation from the medical examiner to that effect. The autopsy was performed last night."

"I presume—I believe that we have the documentation."

"May I see it?"

"I believe it is at the office."

Kenner said, "May I see it?"

"That would merely cause unnecessary delay of my work here." Lowenstein turned to Evans. "Did you or did you not make a positive identification of Morton's body?"

"I did," Evans said.

"And you, Ted?"

"Yeah," Bradley said. "I did. It was him, all right. It was George. Poor guy."

Kenner said to Lowenstein, "I'd still like to see the medical examiner's notification."

Lowenstein snorted. "You have no basis for such a request, and I formally deny it. I am the senior attorney in charge of the estate. I am his designated executor, and I have already told you that my office has the documentation in hand."

"I heard you," Kenner said. "But I seem to remember that to falsely declare probate is fraud. That could be quite serious for an officer of the court such as you."

"Look," Lowenstein said, "I don't know what your game is—"

"I merely want to see the document," Kenner said calmly. "There's a fax machine in the flight office, right there." He pointed to the building, near the airplane. "You can have the document sent over in a few seconds and resolve this matter without difficulty. Or, barring that, you can call the medical examiner's office in San Francisco and confirm that they have, in fact, made a positive identification."

"But we are in the presence of two eyewitnesses who—"

"These are the days of DNA testing," Kenner said, looking at his watch. "I recommend that you make the calls." He turned to the security officers. "You can open the aircraft."

The security officers looked nonplussed. "Mr. Lowenstein?"

"Just a minute, just a goddamned minute," Lowenstein said, and stalked off toward the office, putting his cell phone to his ear as he went.

"Open the plane," Kenner said. He flipped open his wallet and showed the guards his badge.

"Yes, sir," they said.

Another car pulled up, and Sarah got out with Ann Garner. Ann said, "What's the fuss?"

"Just a little misunderstanding," Kenner said. He introduced himself to her.

"I know who you are," she said, with barely concealed hostility.

"I thought you might," Kenner said, smiling.

"And I have to say," she continued, "it's guys like you—smart and unscrupulous and immoral—who have made our environment the polluted mess that it now is. So let's just get that on the table right away. I don't like you, Mr. Kenner. I don't like you personally, and I don't like what you do in the world, and I don't like anything you stand for."

"Interesting," Kenner said. "Perhaps some day you and I could have a detailed and specific conversation about exactly what is wrong with our environment, and exactly who is responsible for making it a polluted mess."

"Whenever you want," she said, angrily.

"Good. You have legal training?"

"No."

"Scientific training?"

"No."

"What is your background?"

"I worked as a documentary film producer. Before I quit to raise my family."

"Ah."

"But I am very dedicated to the environment, and I have been all my life," she said. "I read everything. I read the 'Science' section of the *New York Times* every Tuesday *cover to cover*, of course *The New Yorker*, and the *New York Review*. I am extremely well informed."

"Well then," Kenner said, "I look forward to our conversation."

The pilots were driving up to the gate; they waited while it opened. "I think we can leave in a few minutes," Kenner said. He turned to Evans. "Why don't you confirm that that is all right with Mr. Lowenstein."

"Okay," Evans said, and headed toward the flight office.

"Just so you know," Ann said, "we're going with you. I am, and so is Ted."

"That will be delightful," Kenner said.

Inside the flight office, Evans found Lowenstein hunched over a phone in the back room reserved for pilots. "But I'm telling you, the guy isn't going for it, he wants documentation," Lowenstein said. And then after a pause, "Look, Nick, I'm not going to lose my license over this one. The guy's got a law degree from Harvard."

Evans knocked on the door. "Everything okay for us to leave?"

"Just a minute," Lowenstein said into the phone. He put his hand over the receiver. "You're going to leave now?"

"That's right. Unless you have the document . . ."

"It seems there is some confusion about the exact status of Morton's estate."

"Then we're going, Herb."

"Okay, okay."

He turned back to the phone. "They're leaving, Nick," he said. "You want to stop them, do it yourself."

In the cabin, everyone was sitting down. Kenner went around passing out sheets of paper. "What's this?" Bradley said, with a glance to Ann.

"It's a release," Kenner said.

Ann was reading aloud, "'. . . not liable in the event of death, serious bodily injury, disability, dismemberment'—*dismemberment?*"

"That's right," Kenner said. "You need to understand that where we are going is extremely dangerous. I strongly advise both of you not to come. But if you insist on ignoring my advice, you need to sign that."

"Where are we going?" Bradley said.

"I can't tell you that until the plane is in the air."

"Why is it dangerous?"

"Do you have a problem signing the form?" Kenner said.

"No. Hell." Bradley scrawled his signature.

"Ann?"

Ann hesitated, bit her lip, and signed.

The pilot closed the doors. The engines whined as they taxied up the runway. The flight attendant asked what they would like to drink.

"Puligny-Montrachet," Evans said.

Ann said, "Where are we going?"

"To an island off the coast of New Guinea."

"Why?"

"There is a problem," Kenner said, "that has to be dealt with."

"You want to be any more specific?"

"Not right now."

The plane rose above the cloud layer in Los Angeles, and turned west, over the Pacific.

Sarah felt relieved when Jennifer Haynes went to the front of the cabin to take a nap, falling instantly asleep. But she found it awkward to have Ann and Ted onboard. Conversation in the cabin was stilted; Kenner was not saying much. Ted was drinking heavily. He said to Ann, "Just so you know, Mr. Kenner doesn't believe in anything that normal people believe in. Not even global warming. Or Kyoto."

"Of course he doesn't believe in Kyoto," Ann said. "He's an industry hit man. Representing coal and oil interests."

Kenner said nothing. He just handed her his card.

"Institute for Risk Analysis," Ann read aloud. "That's a new one. I'll add it to the list of phony right-wing fronts."

Kenner said nothing.

"Because it's *all* disinformation," Ann said. "The studies, the press releases, the flyers, websites, the organized campaigns, the big-money smears. Let me tell you, industry was *thrilled* when the US didn't sign Kyoto."

Kenner rubbed his chin, and said nothing.

Ann said, "We're the world's largest polluter, and our government doesn't give a damn."

Kenner smiled blandly.

"So now the United States is an international pariah, isolated from the rest of the world and justifiably despised because we failed to sign the Kyoto Protocol to attack a global problem."

She continued to goad him in this way, and finally, it seemed, he had had enough. "Tell me about Kyoto, Ann," he said. "Why should we have signed it?"

"Why? Because we have a moral obligation to join the rest of the civilized world in reducing carbon emissions to below 1990 levels."

"What effect would that treaty have?"

"The whole world knows that. It would reduce global temperatures in the year 2100."

"By how much?"

"I don't know what you're driving at."

"Don't you? The answer is well known. The effect of Kyoto would be to reduce warming by .04 degrees Celsius in the year 2100. Four hundredths of a degree. Do you dispute that outcome?"

"I certainly do. Four what? Hundredths of a degree? That's ridiculous."

"So you don't believe that would be the effect of the Kyoto Protocol?"

"Well, maybe because the United States didn't sign it—"

"No, that would be the effect if we *did* sign it. Four hundredths of a degree."

"No," she said, shaking her head. "I don't believe that's true."

"The figure has been published a number of

times in scientific journals. I can give you the references."*

Raising his glass, Bradley said to Ann, "This guy is real big on references."

"As opposed to rhetoric," Kenner said, nodding. "Yes. I am."

Bradley belched. "Four hundredths of a degree? In a hundred years? What a bunch of bullshit."

"One could say so."

"I just did," Bradley said.

"But Kyoto's a first step," Ann said, "that's the point. Because if you believe in the precautionary principle, as I do—"

"I didn't think the purpose of Kyoto was to take a first step," Kenner said. "I thought the purpose was to reduce global warming."

"Well, it is."

"Then why make a treaty that won't accomplish that? That won't, in effect, do anything at all?"

"It's a first step, as I said."

"Tell me: do you think it's *possible* to reduce carbon dioxide?"

"Of course. There are a host of alternative energy sources just waiting to be adopted. Wind power, solar, waste, geothermal—"

"Tom Wigley and a panel of seventeen scientists and engineers from around the world made a careful study and concluded it is not possible.

---

* Most recently, *Nature* 22 (October 2003): 395–741, stated, with Russia signed on, temperature affected by Kyoto would be −.02 degrees C by 2050. IPCC models estimate more, but none exceed .15 C. Lomborg, p. 302. Wigley, 1998: "Global warming reductions are small, .08–.28 C."

Their paper was published in *Science*. They said there is no known technology capable of reducing carbon emissions, or even holding them to levels many times higher than today. They conclude that wind, solar, and even nuclear power will not be sufficient to solve the problem. They say totally new and undiscovered technology is required."*

"That's crazy," Ann said. "Amory Lovins laid it all out twenty years ago. Wind and solar, conservation, energy efficiency. There's no problem."

"Apparently there is. Lovins predicted that thirty-five percent of US power would come from alternative energy by the year 2000. The actual figure turned out to be six percent."

"Not enough subsidies."

"No country in the world produces thirty-five percent renewable energy, Ann."

"But countries like Japan do much better than we do."

Kenner said, "Japan is five percent renewable. Germany is five percent. England two percent."

"Denmark."

"Eight percent."

"Well," she said, "it just means we have more work to do."

"No question about that. Wind farms chop birds to pieces, so they might not be so popular. But solar panels would work. Silent, efficient . . ."

---

* Martin Hoffert, et al., "Advanced Technology Paths to Global Climate Stability: Energy for a Greenhouse Planet," *Science* 298 (Nov. 1, 2002): 981–87. "Energy sources that can produce 100 to 300% of present world power consumption without greenhouse emissions do not exist."

"Solar is great," she said.

"Yes," Kenner said. "And all we need is about twenty-seven thousand square kilometers of panels to do the job. Just cover the state of Massachusetts with solar panels and we'd be done. Of course by 2050 our energy needs will triple, so maybe New York would be a better choice."

"Or Texas. Nobody I know cares about Texas," Ann said.

"Well, there you are," Kenner said. "Cover ten percent of Texas, and you're in business. Although," he added, "Texans would probably prefer to cover Los Angeles first."

"You're making a joke."

"Not at all. Let's settle on Nevada. It's all desert anyway. But I'm curious to hear about your personal experience with alternative energy. What about you yourself, Ann? Have you adopted alternative sources?"

"Yes. I have solar heating for my swimming pool. The maid drives a hybrid."

"What do you drive?"

"Well, I need a bigger car for the kids."

"How big?"

"Well, I drive an SUV. Sometimes."

"What about your residence? You have solar panels for your electricity?"

"Well, I had consultants come to the house. Only, Jerry—my husband—says it's too expensive to install. But I'm working on him."

"And your appliances . . ."

"Every single one is Energystar. Every one."

"That's good. And how large is your family?"

"I have two boys. Seven and nine."

"Wonderful. How big is your house?"

"I don't know exactly."

"How many square feet?"

She hesitated.

"Ah hell, tell him, Ann," Bradley said. "She has a *huge* fucking house. Must be ten, fifteen thousand square feet. Absolutely *beautiful*. And the grounds! Got to be an acre, acre and a half. Sprinklers going day and night. And such gorgeous landscaping—she has fund-raisers there all the time. Always wonderful events."

Kenner looked at her.

"Twelve thousand," Ann said. "Square feet."

"For four people?" Kenner said.

"Well, my mother-in-law lives with us, sometimes. And of course the maid in the back."

"And do you have a second home?" Kenner said.

"Shit, she's got *two*," Bradley said. "Got a *fabulous* place in Aspen, and a great house in Maine as well."

"That we inherited," Ann said. "My husband—"

"And that apartment in London," Bradley said, "is that yours or your husband's company or what?"

"The company."

Kenner said, "How about travel? You use private jets?"

"Well, I mean we don't *own* one, but we catch rides, whatever. We go when people are going anyway. We fill the plane up. Which is a *good* thing."

"Of course," Kenner said. "But I must admit I'm a little confused about the philosophy—"

"Hey," she said, suddenly angry. "I live in a milieu where I have to keep up a certain standard. It's necessary for my husband's business, and—anyway, where do you live?"

"I have an apartment in Cambridge."

"How big?"

"Nine hundred square feet. I do not own a car. I fly coach."

"I don't believe you," she said.

"I think you'd better," Bradley said. "This guy knows what he's—"

"Shut up, Ted," Ann said. "You're drunk."

"Not yet, I'm not," he said, looking wounded.

"I'm not judging you, Ann," Kenner said quietly. "I know you're a dedicated advocate. I'm just trying to figure out what your real position is on the environment."

"My position is human beings are heating the planet and poisoning the planet and we have a moral obligation to the biosphere—to all the plants and animals that are being destroyed, and to the unborn generations of human beings—to keep these catastrophic changes from taking place." She sat back, nodding her head.

"So our moral obligation is to others—other plants, animals, and other people."

"Exactly."

"We need to do what is in their interest?"

"What is in the interest of all of us."

"Conceivably their interest is not the same as ours. Conflict of interest is the usual case."

"Every creature has a right to live on the planet."

"Surely you don't believe that," Kenner said.

"I do. I'm not speciesist. Every living creature."

"Even the malaria parasite?"

"Well, it *is* part of nature."

"Then do you oppose the elimination of polio and smallpox? They were part of nature, too."

"Well, I would have to say it's part of the arrogant pattern of mankind, changing the world to suit his purposes. A testosterone-driven impulse, not shared by women—"

"You didn't answer me," Kenner said. "Do you oppose the elimination of polio and smallpox?"

"You're playing with words."

"Hardly. Is changing the world to suit one's purposes unnatural?"

"Of course. It is interfering with nature."

"Ever seen a termite mound? A beaver dam? Those creatures change the environment dramatically, affecting many other creatures. Are they interfering with nature?"

"The world is not in danger," she said, "from termite mounds."

"Arguably it is. The total weight of termites exceeds the total weight of all the humans in the world. A thousand times greater, in fact. Do you know how much methane termites produce? And methane is a more potent greenhouse gas than carbon dioxide."

"I can't continue this," Ann said. "You enjoy arguing. I don't. I just want to make the world a better place. I'm going to go read a magazine now." She went to the front of the plane and sat down, her back to Kenner.

Sarah stayed where she was. "Her intentions are good," she said.

"And her information is bad," Kenner said. "A prescription for disaster."

Ted Bradley roused himself. He had watched the debate between Kenner and Ann. He liked Ann. He was pretty sure he had gone to bed with her; when he was drinking, he sometimes couldn't remember, but he had a vaguely fond memory of Ann, and he assumed that was the reason for it.

"I think you're being harsh," Bradley said, in his presidential tone. "Why should you call someone like Ann 'a prescription for disaster?' She cares very much about these issues. She has devoted her life to them, really. She cares."

"So what?" Kenner said. "*Caring* is irrelevant. Desire to do good is irrelevant. All that counts is *knowledge* and *results*. She doesn't have the knowledge—and, worse, she doesn't know it. Human beings don't know how to do the things she believes ought to be done."

"Like what?"

"Like managing the environment. We don't know how to do that."

"What are you talking about?" Bradley said, throwing his hands in the air. "This is nonsense. Of course we can manage the environment."

"Really? Do you know anything about the history of Yellowstone Park? The first national park?"

"I've been there."

"That's not what I asked."

"Could you just get to the point?" Bradley said. "It's pretty late for Q-and-A, Professor. You know what I mean?"

"All right, then," Kenner said. "I'll tell you."

Yellowstone Park, he explained, was the first wilderness to be set aside as a natural preserve anywhere in the world. The region around the Yellowstone River in Wyoming had long been recognized for its wondrous scenic beauty. Lewis and Clark sang its praises. Artists like Bierstadt and Moran painted it. And the new Northern Pacific Railroad wanted a scenic attraction to draw tourists west. So in 1872, in part because of railroad pressure, President Ulysses Grant set aside two million acres and created Yellowstone National Park.

There was only one problem, unacknowledged then and later. No one had any experience trying to preserve wilderness. There had never been any need to do it before. And it was assumed to be much easier than it proved to be.

When Theodore Roosevelt visited the park in 1903, he saw a landscape teeming with game. There were thousands of elk, buffalo, black bear, deer, mountain lions, grizzlies, coyotes, wolves, and bighorn sheep. By that time there were rules in place to keep things as they were. Soon after that, the Park Service was formed, a new bureaucracy whose sole job was to maintain the park in its original condition.

Yet within ten years, the teeming landscape

that Roosevelt saw was gone forever. And the reason for this was the park managers—charged with keeping the park in pristine condition—had taken a series of steps that they thought were in the best interest of preserving the park and its animals. But they were wrong.

"Well," Bradley said, "our knowledge has increased with time . . ."

"No, it hasn't," Kenner said. "That's my point. It's a perpetual claim that we know more today, and it's not borne out by what actually happened."

Which was this: the early park managers mistakenly believed that elk were about to become extinct. So they tried to increase the elk herds within the park by eliminating predators. To that end, they shot and poisoned all the wolves in the park. And they prohibited Indians from hunting in the park, though Yellowstone was a traditional hunting ground.

Protected, the elk herds exploded, and ate so much of certain trees and grasses that the ecology of the area began to change. The elk ate the trees that the beavers used to make dams, so the beavers vanished. That was when the managers discovered beavers were vital to the overall water management of the region.

When the beavers disappeared, the meadows dried up; the trout and otter vanished; soil erosion increased; and the park ecology changed even further.

By the 1920s it had become abundantly clear there were too many elk, so the rangers began to shoot them by the thousands. But the change in plant ecology seemed to be permanent; the old mix of trees and grasses did not return.

It also became increasingly clear that the Indian hunters of old had exerted a valuable ecological influence on the park lands by keeping down the numbers of elk, moose, and bison. This belated recognition came as part of a more general understanding that native Americans had strongly shaped the "untouched wilderness" that the first white men saw—or thought they were seeing—when they first arrived in the New World. The "untouched wilderness" was nothing of the sort. Human beings on the North American continent had exerted a huge influence on the environment for thousands of years—burning plains grasses, modifying forests, thinning specific animal populations, and hunting others to extinction.

In retrospect, the rule forbidding Indians from hunting was seen as a mistake. But it was just one of many mistakes that continued to be made in an unbroken stream by park managers. Grizzlies were protected, then killed off. Wolves were killed off, then brought back. Animal research involving field study and radio collars was halted, then resumed after certain species were declared endangered. A policy of fire prevention was instituted, with no understanding of the regenerative effects of fire. When the policy was finally reversed, thousands of acres burned so hotly that the ground was sterilized, and the forests did not grow back without reseeding. Rainbow trout were introduced in the 1970s, soon killing off the native cutthroat species.

And on and on.

And on.

"So what you have," Kenner said, "is a history of ignorant, incompetent, and disastrously intrusive intervention, followed by attempts to repair the intervention, followed by attempts to repair the damage caused by the repairs, as dramatic as any oil spill or toxic dump. Except in this case there is no evil corporation or fossil fuel economy to blame. This disaster was caused by environmentalists charged with protecting the wilderness, who made one dreadful mistake after another—and, along the way, proved how little they understood the environment they intended to protect."

"This is absurd," Bradley said. "To preserve a wilderness, you just preserve it. You leave it alone and let the balance of nature take over. That's all that is required."

"Absolutely wrong," Kenner said. "Passive protection—leaving things alone—doesn't preserve the status quo in a wilderness, any more than it does in your backyard. The world is alive, Ted. Things are constantly in flux. Species are winning, losing, rising, falling, taking over, being pushed back. Merely setting aside wilderness doesn't freeze it in its present state, any more than locking your children in a room will prevent them from growing up. Ours is a changing world, and if you want to preserve a piece of land in a particular state, you have to decide what that state is, and then actively, even aggressively, manage it."

"But you said we don't know how to do that."

"Correct. We don't. Because any action you

take causes change in the environment, Ted. And any change hurts some plant or animal. It's inevitable. Preserving old-growth forest to help the spotted owl means Kirtland's warbler and other species are deprived of the new-growth forest they prefer. There is no free lunch."

"But—"

"No buts, Ted. Name an action that had only positive consequences."

"Okay, I will. Banning CFCs for the ozone layer."

"That harmed Third World people by eliminating cheap refrigerants so that their food spoiled more often and more of them died of food poisoning."

"But the ozone layer is more important—"

"Perhaps to you. They might disagree. But we're talking about whether you can take an action that does not have harmful consequences."

"Okay. Solar panels. Water recycling systems for houses."

"Enables people to put houses in remote wilderness areas where formerly they could not because of lack of water and power. Invades wilderness and thus endangers species that were previously unmolested."

"Banning DDT."

"Arguably the greatest tragedy of the twentieth century. DDT was the best agent against mosquitoes, and despite the rhetoric there was nothing anywhere near as good or as safe. Since the ban, two million people a year have died unnecessarily from malaria, mostly children. All together, the ban has caused more than fifty million needless deaths.* Banning DDT killed more people than Hitler, Ted. And the environmental movement pushed hard for it."[†]

"But DDT was a carcinogen."

"No, it wasn't. And everybody knew it at the time of the ban."[‡]

"It was unsafe."

"Actually, it was so safe you could eat it. People did just that for two years, in one experiment.[§] After the ban, it was replaced by parathion, which is *really* unsafe. More than a hundred farm workers died in the months after the DDT ban, because they were unaccustomed to handling really toxic pesticides."[¶]

"We disagree about all this."

"Only because you lack the relevant facts, or are unwilling to face up to the consequences of the actions of organizations you support. Banning DDT will someday be seen as a scandalous blunder."

"DDT was never banned."

"You're right. Countries were just told that if they used it, they wouldn't get foreign aid." Kenner shook his head. "But the unarguable point, based on UN statistics, is that before the DDT ban, malaria had become almost a minor illness. Fifty thousand deaths a year worldwide. A few years

---

* Some estimates put the number at 30 million deaths.

[†] Full discussion of DDT in Wildavsky, 1994, pp. 55–80.

[‡] Sweeney Committee, 25 April 1972, "DDT is not a carcinogenic hazard to man." Ruckelshaus banned it two months later, saying, DDT "poses a carcinogenic risk" to man. He never read the Sweeney report.

[§] Hayes, 1969.

[¶] John Noble Wilford, "Deaths from DDT Successor Stir Concern," *New York Times*, 21 August 1970, p. 1; Wildavsky, 1996, p. 73.

later, it was once again a global scourge. Fifty million people have died since the ban, Ted. Once again, there can be no action without harm."

A long silence followed. Ted shifted in his seat, started to speak, then closed his mouth again. Finally he said, "Okay. Fine." He adopted his most lofty, presidential manner. "You have persuaded me. I grant you the point. So?"

"So the real question with any environmental action is, do the benefits outweigh the harm? Because there is always harm."

"Okay, okay. So?"

"When do you hear any environmental group speak that way? Never. They're all absolutists. They go before judges arguing that regulations should be imposed with no consideration of costs at all.* The requirement that regulations show a cost-benefit was imposed on them by the courts after a period of wretched excess. Environmentalists screamed bloody murder about cost-benefit requirements and they're still screaming. They don't want people to know how much their forays into regulation actually cost society and the world. The most egregious example was the benzene regulations in the late 1980s that were so expensive for so little benefit that they ended up costing twenty billion dollars for every year of life saved.† Do you agree with that regulation?"

---

* Case references in Sunstein, pp. 200–1.

† See the Harvard Center for Risk Analysis study: Tengs, et al., 1995. For full discussion, see Lomborg, p. 338ff. He concludes: "When we ignore the cost of our environmental decisions . . . on other areas . . . we are in reality committing statistical murder." He puts the number of unnecessary dead at 60,000 per year in the US alone.

"Well, when you put it in those terms, no."

"What other terms are there, Ted, besides the truth? Twenty billion dollars *to save one year of life*. That was the cost of the regulation. Should you support organizations that push for such wasteful regulation?"

"No."

"The lead benzene lobbying group in Congress was NERF. Are you going to resign from its board?"

"Of course not."

Kenner just nodded slowly. "And there we have it."

Sanjong was pointing to the computer screen, and Kenner came over, sliding into the seat next to him. The screen showed an aerial image of a tropical island, heavily forested, and a broad curving bay of blue water. The photo seemed to be taken from a low-flying airplane. Around the bay were four weathered wood shacks.

"Those are new," Sanjong said. "They went up in the last twenty-four hours."

"They look old."

"Yes, but they're not. Close inspection suggests that they are artificial. They may be made out of plastic instead of wood. The largest one appears to be a residence, and the other three house equipment."

"What kind of equipment?" Kenner said.

"Nothing has been visible in the photographs. The equipment was probably offloaded at night. But I went back and got a decent description from

Hong Kong customs. The equipment consists of three hypersonic cavitation generators. Mounted in carbon matrix resonant impact assembly frames."

"Hypersonic cavitation equipment is for sale?"

"They got it. I don't know how."

Kenner and Sanjong were huddled together, speaking in low tones. Evans drifted over, leaned in close. "What's a hypersonic whatever-it-is?" he said quietly.

"Cavitation generator," Kenner said. "It's a high-energy acoustic device the size of a small truck that produces a radially symmetric cavitation field."

Evans looked blank.

"Cavitation," Sanjong explained, "refers to the formation of bubbles in a substance. When you boil water, that's cavitation. You can boil water with sound, too, but in this case the generators are designed to induce cavitation fields in a solid."

Evans said, "What solid?"

"The earth," Kenner said.

"I don't get it," Evans said. "They're going to make bubbles in the ground, like boiling water?"

"Something like that, yes."

"Why?"

They were interrupted by the arrival of Ann Garner. "Is this a boys-only meeting?" she said. "Or can anyone sit in?"

"Of course," Sanjong said, tapping the keyboard. The screen showed a dense array of graphs. "We were just reviewing the carbon dioxide levels of ice cores taken from Vostok and from North GRIP in Greenland."

"You guys can't keep me in the dark forever, you know," Ann said. "Sooner or later we will land this plane. And then I'm going to find out what you're really up to."

"That's true," Kenner said.

"Why not tell me now?"

Kenner just shook his head.

The pilot clicked the radio. "Check your seat belts, please," he said. "Prepare for landing in Honolulu."

Ann said, "Honolulu!"

"Where did you think we were going?"

"I thought—"

And then she broke off.

Sarah thought: *She knows where we are going.*

While they refueled at Honolulu, a customs inspector came onboard and asked to see their passports. He seemed amused by the presence of Ted Bradley, whom he referred to as "Mr. President"; Bradley in turn was pleased by the attention from a man in uniform.

After the customs officer checked their passports, he said to the group, "Your destination is filed as Gareda in the Solomon Islands. I just want to make sure you're aware of the travel advisory for Gareda. Most embassies have warned visitors against going there in view of the current conditions."

"What current conditions?" Ann said.

"There are rebels active on the island. There have been a number of murders. The Australian army went in last year and captured most of the rebels, but not all. There have been three murders in the last week, including two foreigners. One of the corpses was, uh, mutilated. And the head was taken."

"What?"

"The head was taken. Not while he was alive."

Ann turned to Kenner. "That's where we are going? Gareda?"

Kenner nodded slowly.

"What do you mean, the head was taken?"

"Presumably, it was for the skull."

"The skull," she repeated. "So . . . you're talking about headhunters . . ."

Kenner nodded.

"I'm getting off this plane," she said, and gathering up her handbag, walked down the stairs.

Jennifer was just waking up. "What's her problem?"

"She doesn't like good-byes," Sanjong said.

Ted Bradley was stroking his chin in what he imagined was a thoughtful manner. He said, "A foreigner had his head cut off?"

"Apparently, it was worse than that," the customs officer said.

"Jesus. What's worse than that?" Bradley said, laughing.

The customs officer said, "The situation on the ground is not entirely clear. The reports are conflicting."

Bradley stopped laughing. "No. Seriously: I want to know. What's worse than beheading?"

There was a brief silence.

"They ate him," Sanjong said.

Bradley rocked back in his chair. "They *ate* him?"

The customs officer nodded. "Parts of him," he said. "At least, that's the report."

"Holy shit," Bradley said. "Which parts? Never mind, I don't want to know. Jesus Christ. They *ate* the guy."

Kenner looked at him. "You don't have to go, Ted," he said. "You can leave, too."

"I have to admit, I'm thinking about it," he said, in his judicious, presidential tone. "Getting eaten is not a distinguished end to a career. Think of any of the greats. Think of Elvis—eaten. John Lennon—eaten. I mean, it's not how we want to be remembered." He fell silent, lowering his chin to his chest, sunk deep in thought, then raising it again. It was a gesture he'd done a hundred times on television. "But, no," he said finally. "I'll accept the danger. If you're going, I'm going."

"We're going," Kenner said.

It was nine hours flight time to Kontag Airport in Gareda. The cabin was dark; most of them slept. Kenner as usual stayed awake, sitting in the back with Sanjong, talking quietly.

Peter Evans woke up about four hours into the flight. His toes still burned from the Antarctic episode and his back was very sore from his being bounced around in the flash flood. But the pain in his toes reminded him that he was supposed to check them daily, to see if they were becoming infected. He got up and went to the back of the plane, where Kenner was sitting. He pulled off his socks and inspected his toes.

"Sniff 'em," Kenner said.

"What?"

"Smell them. You have any gangrene, you'll smell it first. They hurt?"

"Burn. Mostly just at night."

Kenner nodded. "You'll be all right. I think you'll keep them all."

Evans sat back, thinking how strange it was to have a conversation about losing his toes. Somehow it made his back hurt more. He went into the bathroom at the back of the plane and rummaged through the drawers looking for painkillers. All they had was Advil, so he took that, then came back.

"That was a clever story you arranged in Honolulu," he said. "Too bad it didn't work on Ted."

Kenner just stared.

"It's not a story," Sanjong said. "There were three murders yesterday."

"Oh. And they ate somebody?"

"That was the report."

"Oh," Evans said.

Going forward into the dark cabin, Evans saw Sarah sitting up. She whispered, "Can't sleep?"

"No. A little achy. You?"

"Yeah. Toes hurt. From the frostbite."

"Me, too."

She nodded toward the galley. "Any food back there?"

"I think so."

She got up, headed back. He trailed after her. She said, "The tops of my ears hurt, too."

"Mine are okay," he said.

She rummaged around, found some cold pasta. She held a plate out to him. He shook his head. She spooned out a plate for herself and began to eat. "So, how long have you known Jennifer?"

"I don't really know her," he said. "I just met her recently, at the law office."

"Why is she coming with us?"

"I think she knows Kenner."

"She does," Kenner said, from his chair.

"How?"

"She's my niece."

"Really?" Sarah said. "How long has she been your nie—never mind. I'm sorry. It's late."

"She's my sister's kid. Her parents died in a plane crash when she was eleven."

"Oh."

"She's been on her own a lot."

"Oh."

Evans looked at Sarah and thought once again that it was a kind of trick, how she could get up from sleeping and appear beautiful, and perfect. And she had on that perfume that had driven him quietly crazy from the moment he first smelled it.

"Well," Sarah said. "She seems very nice."

"I don't, uh, there's nothing . . ."

"It's fine," she said. "You don't have to pretend with me, Peter."

"I'm not pretending," he said, leaning slightly closer, smelling her perfume.

"Yes, you are." She moved away from him, and sat down opposite Kenner. "What happens when we get to Gareda?" she said.

The thing about her, Evans thought, was that she had the most chilling ability to instantly behave as if he did not exist. Right now she was not looking at him; she was focusing all her attention on Kenner, talking with apparent concentration to Kenner and behaving as if no one else were there.

Was that supposed to be provocative? he thought. Was that supposed to be a turn-on, to get him excited and start the chase? Because it didn't make him feel that way at all. It pissed him off.

He wanted to slap his hand down on the counter, make a big noise, and say, "Hel-lo! Earth to Sarah!" Or something like that.

But somehow he thought that that would make things worse. He could imagine her annoyed glance. *You're such a baby.* Something like that. It made him long for somebody uncomplicated, the way Janis was uncomplicated. Just a great body and a voice you could tune out. That was exactly what he needed now.

He gave a long sigh.

She heard it, glanced up at him, and then patted the seat beside her. "Come sit here, Peter," she said, "and join the conversation." And she gave him a big, dazzling smile.

He thought: *I am very confused.*

"This is Resolution Bay," Sanjong said, holding out his computer screen. It showed the bay, then zoomed back to show a map of the entire island. "It's on the northeast side of the island. The airport is on the west coast. It's about twenty-five miles away."

The island of Gareda looked like a big avocado immersed in the water, with jagged edges along the shore. "There is a mountain spine running along the center of the island," Sanjong said. "In places, it's three thousand feet high. The jungle in the interior of the island is very dense, essentially impenetrable, unless you follow the roads or one of the footpaths through the jungle. But we can't make our way cross country."

"So we take a road," Sarah said.

"Maybe," Sanjong said. "But the rebels are

known to be in this area here—" he circled the center of the island with his finger "—and they have split up in two or possibly three groups. Their exact locations are not known. They have taken over this small village here, Pavutu, near the north coast. That seems to be their headquarters. And they presumably have roadblocks up, and probably patrols on the jungle paths."

"Then how do we get to Resolution Bay?"

Kenner said, "By helicopter, if we can. I've arranged for one, but this is not the most reliable part of the world. If we can't do that, we'll head out by car. See how far we can get. But at this point we just don't know how we're going to do it."

Evans said, "And when we get to Resolution Bay?"

"There are four new structures on the beach. We have to take them down and dismantle the machinery inside. Make them inoperable. We also have to find their submarine tender and dismantle the submarine."

"What submarine?" Sarah said.

"They leased a small two-man research sub. It's been in the region for the last two weeks."

"Doing what?"

"We're pretty sure we know now. The whole Solomon Island chain of more than nine hundred islands is located within a very active geological part of the world in terms of plate tectonics. The Solomons are a part of the world where plates crunch together. That's why they have many volcanoes there, and so many earthquakes. It's a very unstable region. The Pacific Plate collides and slides under the Oldowan Java Plateau. The result is the Solomon Trench, a huge undersea feature that curves in an arc all along the northern side of the island chain. It's very deep, between two thousand and six thousand feet. The trench is just north of Resolution Bay, too."

"So it's an active geological region with a deep trench," Evans said. "I still don't see the game."

"Lot of undersea volcanoes, lot of slope debris, and therefore the potential for landslides," Kenner said.

"Landslides." Evans rubbed his eyes. It was late.

"Undersea landslides," Kenner said.

Sarah said, "They're trying to cause an undersea landslide?"

"We think so. Somewhere along the slope of the Solomon Trench. Probably at the five-hundred- to one-thousand-foot depth."

Evans said, "And what would that do? An undersea landslide?"

Kenner said to Sanjong, "Show them the big map." Sanjong brought up a map of the entire Pacific basin, from Siberia to Chile, Australia to Alaska.

"Okay," Kenner said. "Now draw a straight line out from Resolution Bay and see where it takes you."

"California!"

"Right. In about eleven hours."

Evans frowned. "An undersea landslide . . ."

"Displaces an enormous volume of water very quickly. That is the most common way a tsunami is formed. Once propagated, the wave front will travel right across the Pacific at five hundred miles an hour."

"Holy shit," Evans said. "How big a wave are we talking?"

"Actually, it's a series, what's called a wave train. The undersea landslide in Alaska in 1952 generated a wave forty-seven feet high. But the height of this one is impossible to anticipate because wave height is a function of the shoreline it hits. In parts of California it could be up to sixty feet high. A six-story building."

"Oh boy," Sarah said.

"And how much time do we have before they do this?" Evans said.

"The conference runs two more days. The wave will take a day to cross the Pacific. So . . ."

"We have one day."

"At most, yes. One day to land, make our way to Resolution Bay, and stop them."

"Stop who?" Ted Bradley said, yawning and coming back toward them. "Je-sus! Do I have a headache or what! How about a little hair of the dog?" He paused, stared at the group, looking from face to face. "Hey, what's going on here? You guys look like I interrupted a funeral."

Three hours later, the sun came up and the plane began its descent. Now it was flying low, passing over green forested islands fringed in an unearthly pale blue. They saw few roads and few towns, mostly small villages.

Ted Bradley looked out the window. "Isn't it beautiful?" he said. "Truly unspoiled paradise. This is what is vanishing in our world."

Seated opposite him, Kenner said nothing. He, too, was staring out the window.

"Don't you think the problem," Bradley said, "is that we have lost contact with nature?"

"No," Kenner said. "I think the problem is I don't see many roads."

"Don't you think," Bradley said, "that's because it's the white man, not the natives, who wants to conquer nature, to beat it into submission?"

"No, I don't think that."

"I do," Bradley said. "I find that people who live closer to the earth, in their villages, surrounded by nature, that those people have a natural ecological sense and a feeling for the fitness of it all."

"Spent a lot of time in villages, Ted?" Kenner said.

"As a matter of fact, yes. I shot a picture in Zimbabwe and another one in Botswana. I know what I am talking about."

"Uh-huh. You stayed in villages all that time?"

"No, I stayed in hotels. I had to, for insurance. But I had a lot of experiences in villages. There is no question that village life is best and ecologically soundest. Frankly, I think everyone in the world should live that way. And certainly, we should not be encouraging village people to industrialize. That's the problem."

"I see. So you want to stay in a hotel, but you want everybody else to stay in a village."

"No, you're not hearing—"

"Where do you live now, Ted?" Kenner said.

"Sherman Oaks."

"Is that a village?"

"No. Well, it's a sort of a village, I suppose you could say . . . But I have to be in LA for my work," Bradley said. "I don't have a choice."

"Ted, have you ever stayed in a Third World village? Even for one night?"

Bradley shifted in his seat. "As I said before, I spent a lot of time in the villages while we were shooting. I know what I'm talking about."

"If village life is so great, why do you think people want to leave?"

"They shouldn't leave. That's my point."

"You know better than they do?" Kenner said.

Bradley paused, then blurted: "Well, frankly, if you must know, yes. I do know better. I have the benefit of education and broader experience. And

I know firsthand the dangers of industrial society and how it is making the whole world sick. So, yes, I think I do know what is best for them. Certainly I know what is ecologically best for the planet."

"I have a problem," Kenner said, "with other people deciding what is in my best interest when they don't live where I do, when they don't know the local conditions or the local problems I face, when they don't even live in the same country as I do, but they still feel—in some far-off Western city, at a desk in some glass skyscraper in Brussels or Berlin or New York—they still feel that they know the solution to all my problems and how I should live my life. I have a problem with that."

"What's your problem?" Bradley said. "I mean, look: You don't seriously believe everybody on the planet should do whatever they want, do you? That would be terrible. These people need help and guidance."

"And you're the one to give it? To 'these people'?"

"Okay, so it's not politically correct to talk this way. But do you want all these people to have the same horrific, wasteful living standard that we do in America and, to a lesser extent, Europe?"

"I don't see you giving it up."

"No," Ted said, "but I conserve where I can. I recycle. I support a carbon-neutral lifestyle. The point is, if all these other people industrialize, it will add a terrible, terrible burden of global pollution to the planet. That should not happen."

"I got mine, but you can't have yours?"

"It's a question of facing realities," Bradley said.

"Your realities. Not theirs."

At that point, Sanjong beckoned to Kenner. "Excuse me," Kenner said, and got up.

"Walk away if you want," Bradley said, "but you know I speak truth!" He gestured to the flight attendant and held up his glass. "Just one more, sweetie. One more for the road."

Sanjong said, "The helicopter's not there yet."

"What's the matter?"

"It was coming over from another island. They've closed the air space because they're worried the rebels have surface-to-air missiles."

Kenner frowned. "How long until we land?"

"Ten minutes."

"Keep your fingers crossed."

Abandoned, Ted Bradley slid to the other side of the plane, to sit with Peter Evans. "Isn't it gorgeous?" he said. "Look at that water. Crystalline and pure. Look at the depth of that blue. Look at those beautiful villages, in the heart of nature."

Evans was staring out the window but saw only poverty. The villages were clusters of corrugated tin shacks, the roads red mud ruts. The people looked poorly dressed and moved slowly. There was a depressing, disconsolate feeling about them. He imagined sickness, disease, infant death . . .

"Gorgeous," Bradley said. "Pristine! I can't wait to get down there. This is as good as a vacation!

Did anyone here know the Solomons were so beautiful?"

From the front, Jennifer said, "Inhabited by headhunters, for most of history."

"Yes, well, that's all in the past," Bradley said. "If it ever existed at all. I mean, all that talk about cannibalism. Everybody knows it is not true. I read a book by some professor.* There never were any cannibals, anywhere in the world. It's all a big myth. Another example of the way the white man demonizes people of color. When Columbus came to the West Indies, he thought they told him there were cannibals there, but it wasn't true. I forget the details. There are no cannibals anywhere. Just a myth. Why are you staring at me that way?"

Evans turned. Bradley was talking to Sanjong, who was indeed staring.

"Well?" Bradley said. "You're giving me a look. Okay, buddy boy. Does that mean you disagree with me?"

"You're truly a fool," Sanjong said, in an astonished voice. "Have you ever been to Sumatra?"

"Can't say that I have."

"New Guinea?"

"No. Always wanted to go, buy some tribal art. Great stuff."

"Borneo?"

"No, but I always wanted to go there, too. That Sultan What's his name, he did a great job remodeling the Dorchester in London—"

"Well," Sanjong said, "if you go to Borneo you

---

* William Arens, *The Man-Eating Myth*.

will see the Dyak longhouses where they still display the skulls of the people they killed."

"Oh, that's just tourist-attraction stuff."

"In New Guinea, they had a disease called *kuru*, transmitted by eating the brains of their enemies."

"That's not true."

"Gajdusek won a Nobel Prize for it. They were eating brains, all right."

"But that was a long time ago."

"Sixties. Seventies."

"You guys just like to tell scare stories," Bradley said, "at the expense of the indigenous people of the world. Come on, face the facts, human beings are not cannibals."*

Sanjong blinked. He looked at Kenner. Kenner shrugged.

"Absolutely beautiful down there," Bradley said, looking out the window. "And it looks like we're going to land."

---

* Cannibalism in the American southwest: http://www.nature.com/ nature/fow/000907.html; Richard A. Marlar, Leonard L. Banks, Brian R. Billman, Patricia M. Lambert, and Jennifer Marlar, "Biochemical evidence of cannibalism at a prehistoric Puebloan site in southwestern Colorado," *Nature* 407, 74078 (7 Sept. 2000). Among Celts in England: http://www.bris.ac.uk/Depts/Info-Office/news/archive/cannibal .htm. Among Neanderthals: http://news.bbc.co.uk/1/hi/sci/tech/462048 .stm; same issue, Jared M. Diamond, "Archeology, talk of cannibalism" ("Incontrovertible evidence of cannibalism has been found at a 900-year-old site in the southwestern United States. Why do horrified critics deny that many societies have found cannibalism acceptable?").

VII

RESOLUTION

Kotak Field was sticky with humid heat. They walked to the small open shack that was marked KASTOM in roughly painted letters. To one side of the building was a wooden fence and a gate marked with a red handprint and a sign that said, NOGOT ROT.

"Ah, nougat rot," Bradley said. "Must be a local tooth problem."

"Actually," Sanjong said, "the red hand means kapu. 'Forbidden.' The sign says 'No Got Right,' which is Pidgin for 'You don't have permission to pass.'"

"Huh. I see."

Evans found the heat almost unbearable. He was tired after the long plane ride, and anxious about what lay ahead of them. Alongside him, Jennifer walked casually, seemingly fresh and energetic. "You're not tired?" Evans said to her.

"I slept on the plane."

He looked back at Sarah. She, too, seemed to have plenty of energy, striding forward.

"Well, I'm pretty tired."

"You can sleep in the car," Jennifer said. She

didn't seem very interested in his condition. He found it a little irritating.

And it was certainly debilitatingly hot and humid. By the time they reached the customs house, Evans's shirt was soaked. His hair was wet. Sweat was dripping off his nose and chin onto the papers he was supposed to fill out. The ink from the pen ran in the puddles of his sweat. He glanced up at the customs officer, a dark, muscular man with curly hair and wearing pressed white trousers and a white shirt. His skin was dry; he looked almost cool. He met Evans's eyes, and smiled. *"Oh, waitman, dis no taim bilong san. You tumas hotpela."*

Evans nodded. "Yes, true," he said. He had no idea what the man had said.

Sanjong translated. "It's not even the hot time of summer. But you're too much hot. You *tumas hot.* Ya?"

"He got that right. Where'd you learn Pidgin?"

"New Guinea. I worked there a year."

"Doing what?"

But Sanjong was hurrying on with Kenner, who was waving to a young man who had driven up in a Land Rover. The man jumped out. He was dark, wearing tan shorts and a T-shirt. His shoulders were covered in tattoos. His grin was infectious. "Hey, Jon Kanner! *Hamamas klok!*" He pounded his chest with his fist and hugged Kenner.

"He has a happy heart," Sanjong said. "They know each other."

The newcomer was introduced all around as Henry, with no other name. "Hanri!" he said, grinning broadly, pumping their hands. Then he turned to Kenner.

"I understand there is trouble with the helicopter," Kenner said.

"What? No *trabel. Me got klostu long.*" He laughed. "It's just over there, my friend," he said, in perfectly accented British English.

"Good," Kenner said, "we were worried."

"Yas, but serious Jon. We better *hariyap. Mi yet harim planti yangpelas, krosim, pasim birua, got plenti masket, noken stap gut, ya?*"

Evans had the impression Henry was speaking Pidgin so the rest of them would not understand.

Kenner nodded. "I heard that, too," he said. "Lots of rebels here. They're mostly young boys? And angry? And well armed. Figures."

"I worry for the helicopter, my friend."

"Why? Do you know something about the pilot?"

"Yes, I do."

"Why? Who is the pilot?"

Henry giggled, and slapped Kenner on the back. "I am!"

"Well, then, we should go."

They all started down the road, away from the airfield. The jungle rose up on both sides of the road. The air buzzed with the sound of cicadas. Evans looked back with longing at the beautiful white Gulfstream jet, poised on the runway against a blue sky. The pilots in their white shirts and black trousers were checking the wheels. He wondered if he would ever see the airplane again.

Kenner was saying, "And we heard, Henry, some people were killed?"

Henry made a face. "No just killed, Jon. *Olpela.* Ya?"

"So we heard."

"Ya. *Distru.*"

So it was true. "The rebels did it?"

Henry nodded. "Oh! this new *chif,* him name Sambuca, like a drink. Don't ask why this name. Him crazy man, Jon. *Longlong man tru.* Everything back to *olpela* for dis guy. Old ways are better. *Allatime allatime.*"

"Well, the old ways are better," Ted Bradley said, trudging along behind, "if you ask me."

Henry turned. "You got cell phones, you got computers, you got antibiotics, medicines, hospitals. And you say the old ways are better?"

"Yes, because they are," Bradley said. "They were more human, they allowed more of the human texture to life. Believe me, if you ever had a chance to experience these so-called modern miracles yourself, you would know that they're not so great—"

"I got a degree at the University of Melbourne," Henry said. "So I have some familiarity."

"Oh, well, then," Bradley said. And under his breath, he muttered, "Might have told me. Asshole."

"By the way," Henry said, "take my advice, don't do that here. Don't talk under your breath."

"Why not?"

"In this country, some *pelas* think it means you've been possessed by a demon and they'll get scared. And they might kill you."

"I see. Charming."

"So, in this country, if you have something to say, you speak up!"

"I'll remember that."

* * *

Sarah walked alongside Bradley, but she was not listening to the conversation. Henry was a character, caught between worlds, sometimes speaking in an Oxbridge accent, sometimes dropping into Pidgin. It didn't bother her.

She was looking at the jungle. The air on the road was hot and still, trapped between the huge trees that rose up on both sides of the path. The trees were forty, fifty feet high, covered in twisted vines. And at ground level, in the darkness beneath the canopy above, huge ferns grew so thickly they presented an impenetrable barrier, a solid green wall.

She thought: You could walk five feet into that and get lost forever. You'd never find your way out again.

Along the road were the rusted hulks of long-abandoned cars, windshields smashed, chassis crumpled and corroded brown and yellow. As she walked past she saw ripped upholstery, old dashboards with clocks and speedometers ripped out, leaving gaping holes.

They turned right onto a side path and she saw the helicopter ahead. She gasped. It was beautiful, painted green with a crisp white stripe, the metal blades and struts gleaming. Everybody commented on it.

"Yes, the outside is good," Henry said. "But I think the inside, the engine, maybe is not so good." He wiggled his hand. "So so."

"Great," Bradley said. "Speaking for myself, I'd prefer it the other way around."

They opened the doors to get in. In the back

were stacks of wooden crates, with sawdust. They smelled of grease. "I got the supplies you wanted," he said to Kenner.

"And enough ammunition?"

"Oh ya. All things you asked for."

"Then we can go," Kenner said.

In the back, Sarah buckled her belt. She put on headphones. The engines whined, and the blades spun faster. The helicopter shuddered as it started to lift off. "We have too many people," Henry said, "so we will have to hope for the best! Cross your fingers!"

And giggling maniacally, he lifted off into the blue sky.

TO RESOLUTION
THURSDAY, OCTOBER 14
9:02 A.M.

The jungle slid beneath them, mile after mile of dense canopy forest. In places, wisps of mist clung to the trees, particularly at the higher altitudes. Sarah was surprised at how mountainous the island was, how rugged the terrain. She saw no roads at all. From time to time, they passed over a small village in a jungle clearing. Otherwise, nothing but miles of trees. Henry was flying due north, intending to drop them off along the coast a few miles west of Resolution Bay.

"Charming villages," Ted Bradley said, as they flew over another one. "What do the people grow here?"

"Nothing. Land's no good here. They work the copper mines," Henry said.

"Oh, that's too bad."

"Not if you live here. Biggest money they ever saw. People kill to work in the mines. What I mean to say is, they kill. Some murders occur every year."

Bradley was shaking his head. "Terrible. Just terrible. But look down there," he said, pointing. "There's a village has actual thatched huts. Is that the old style, the old way of doing things, still kept alive?"

"No man," Henry said. "That's a rebel village. That's *new* style. Big thatch *haus*, very impressive, big house for *chif*." He explained that Sambuca had instructed the people in every village to build these huge, three-story structures of thatch, complete with ladders going up to high walkways at the third level. The idea was to give rebels a view over the jungle, so they could see the arrival of Australian troops.

But in the old days, Henry said, the people never had such buildings in Gareda. The architecture was low and open, erected mostly to protect against rain and let smoke out. There was no need for high buildings, which were impractical since they would blow down in the next cyclone anyway. "But Sambuca, he wants them now, so he makes the *yangpelas*, the young fellows, build them. There may be six or eight on this island now, in rebel territory."

"So we're going over rebel territory now?" Bradley said.

"So far, so good," Henry said. And he giggled again. "Not so long now, we'll see the coast in four, five minutes and—Oh damn shit!"

"What?" They were skimming the forest canopy.

"I made a big mistake."

"What mistake?" Bradley said.

"Tumas longwe es."

"You're too far east?" Kenner said.

"Damn shit. Damn damn shit. Hang on!" Henry banked the helicopter steeply, but not before they all glimpsed a huge clearing, with four of the enormous thatch structures interspersed with the more common houses of wood and corrugated tin. There were a half-dozen trucks clustered in the muddy center of the clearing. Some of the trucks had machine guns mounted on their backs.

"What is this?" Bradley said, looking down. "This is much bigger than the others—"

"This Pavutu! Rebel headquarters!"

And then the clearing was gone, the helicopter moving swiftly away. Henry was breathing hard. They could hear his breath over the earphones.

Kenner said nothing. He was staring intently at Henry.

"Well, I think we're all right," Bradley said. "It looks like they didn't see us."

"Oh yeah," Henry said. "Nice wish."

"Why?" Bradley said. "Even if they did see us—what can they do?"

"They have radios," Henry said. "They're not stupid, these *yangpelas*."

"What do you mean?"

"They want this helicopter."

"Why? Can they fly it?"

"*Orait orait!* Yes! Because they want me, too." Henry explained that for months now, no helicopters had been allowed on the island. This one had been brought over only because Kenner had pulled some very important strings. But it was specifically not to fall into rebel hands.

"Well, they probably think we're going south," Bradley said. "I mean, we are, aren't we?"

"These boys know better," Henry said. "They know."

"They know what?" Bradley said.

Kenner said, "The ELF would have had to buy off the rebels in order to land on the island. So the rebels know there's something going on at Resolution Bay. When they saw this helicopter, they knew where it was going."

"These boys aren't stupid," Henry said again.

"I never said they were," Bradley protested.

"Ya. But you think it. I know you, *waitman*. This in the back of your tongue. You think it."

"I promise you, I did not," Bradley said. "Really. I have no such feelings at all. You simply didn't understand me."

"Ya," Henry said.

Sarah was sitting in the middle of the second seat, wedged between Ted and Jennifer. Peter and Sanjong were behind in the little backseat, with all the boxes. She couldn't really see out the windows, so she had trouble following the discussion. She wasn't sure what it was all about.

So she asked Jennifer. "Do you understand what's going on?"

Jennifer nodded. "As soon as the rebels saw the helicopter they knew it was going to Resolution. Now, whatever we do, they'll be expecting it to show up in that area. They have radios, and they're in different groups scattered around. They can keep an eye on us. And they'll be there when we land."

"I am very sorry," Henry said. "So very sorry."

"Never mind," Kenner said. His voice was neutral.

"What do we do now?" Henry said.

Kenner said, "Continue exactly as planned. Go north and put us down on the coast."

There was no mistaking the urgency in his voice.

In the backseat, pushed up against Sanjong, smelling the grease that coated the machine guns, Peter Evans wondered where this urgency came from. He looked at his watch. It was nine in the morning, which meant that of their original twenty-four hours, only twenty remained. But this was a small island, and it should allow plenty of time—

And then he had a thought. "Wait a minute," he said. "What time is it in Los Angeles?"

Sanjong said, "They're on the other side of the dateline. Twenty-seven hours behind."

"No, I mean elapsed time. Actual time difference."

"Six hours."

"And you calculated a transit time of what?"

"Thirteen hours," Sanjong said.

"I think we made a mistake," Evans said, biting his lip. He wasn't sure how much he should say in front of Henry. And indeed, Sanjong was shaking his head, indicating *not now*.

But they *had* made a mistake. There was no doubt about it. Assuming that Drake wanted the tidal wave to hit on the last day of the conference, he would surely want it to happen during the morning. That would provide the most visible disaster. And it would allow the whole afternoon for discussion and media interviews afterward. Every television camera in America would be at that conference, talking to the scientists who just happened to be there. It would create a gigantic media event.

So, Evans thought, assume the wave was to hit Los Angeles no later than noon tomorrow.

Subtract thirteen hours for the wave front to cross the Pacific.

That meant the wave had to be propagated at eleven P.M. Los Angeles time. Which meant that the local time in Gareda would be . . . five P.M.

Five P.M. *today*.

They didn't have a day to stop this thing from happening.

They had just eight hours.

So that was the reason for Kenner's urgency. That was why he was going ahead with his plan, despite the new problem. He had no choice, and he knew it. He had to land on the coast somewhere very near Resolution. There wasn't enough time to do anything else.

Even though it was possible they were heading right into a trap.

Leaving the forest behind, the helicopter burst out over blue water and turned around, going east. Evans saw a narrow sandy beach with patches of ragged lava rock, and mangrove swamps clinging to the water's edge. The helicopter swung low and followed the beach, heading east.

"How far from Resolution are we?" Kenner said.

"Five, six kilometers," Henry said.

"And how far from Pavutu?"

"Maybe ten kilometers, on a mud track."

"Okay," Kenner said. "Let's find a place to put down."

"There's a good place I know maybe one kilometer ahead."

"Fine. Go there."

Evans was thinking. Five kilometers walking on a beach, that was about three miles, should take them an hour and a half at most. They could make it to Resolution Bay well before noon. That would give them—

"This the spot," Henry said. A finger of rugged lava protruded into the ocean. Centuries of waves had smoothed it enough to make a landing possible.

"Do it," Kenner said.

The helicopter circled, prepared to descend. Evans was looking out over at the dense wall of jungle, where it met the beach. He saw tire tracks in the sand and a sort of gap in the trees that was probably a road. And those tire tracks—

"Say listen," Evans said. "I think—"

Sanjong jabbed him in the ribs. Hard.

Evans grunted.

"What is it, Peter?" Kenner said.

"Uh, nothing."

"We're going down," Henry said. The helicopter descended smoothly, slowly settling onto the lava. Waves lapped at the edge of the rock pad. It was peaceful. Kenner looked out the bubble canopy, scanning the area.

"Okay? This good spot?" Henry said. He seemed

nervous now that they were down. "I don't want to stay so long, Jon. Because maybe they come soon . . ."

"Yeah, I understand."

Kenner cracked open the door, then paused.

"So, alla okay. Jon?"

"Just fine, Henry. Very nice spot. Get out and open this back door for us, will you?"

"Yeah, Jon, I think you can get it—"

"*Get out!*" And with astonishing swiftness there was a gun jammed against Henry's head. Henry sputtered and moaned in fear as he fumbled with his door. "But Jon, I need to stay inside, Jon—"

"You've been a bad boy, Henry," Kenner said.

"You going to shoot me now, Jon?"

"Not now," Kenner said, and abruptly he shoved him out. Henry tumbled onto the sharp lava, howling in pain. Kenner slid over to the pilot's seat and shut the door. Immediately Henry was up, pounding on the canopy, his eyes wild. He was terrified.

"Jon! Jon! Please, Jon!"

"Sorry, Henry." Kenner pushed the stick, and the helicopter began to rise into the air. They had not climbed twenty feet before a dozen men emerged from the jungle all along the beach and began firing at them with rifles. Kenner swung out over the ocean, going north, away from the island. Looking back, they could see Henry standing forlorn on the lava. Some of the men were running toward him. He threw up his hands.

"Little shit," Bradley said. "He would have gotten us killed."

"He may still," Kenner said.

They flew due north, over open water.

"So what do we do now," Sarah said, "land on the other side of the bay? Walk in from the other side?"

"No," Kenner said. "That's what they'll expect us to do."

"So, then . . ."

"We wait a few minutes and go back to the western side, same as before."

"They won't be expecting that?"

"They may. We'll go to a different spot."

"Farther away from the bay?"

"No. Closer."

"Won't ELF hear us?"

"Doesn't matter. By now, they know we're coming."

In the back, Sanjong was breaking open the wooden cases and reaching for the guns. He stopped abruptly.

"Bad news," he said.

"What?"

"No guns." He pushed a lid higher. "These crates contain ammunition. But no guns."

"That little bastard," Bradley said.

"What do we do now?" Sarah said.

"We go in anyway," Kenner said.

He turned the helicopter and, skimming the water, headed back to Gareda.

The western arc of Resolution Bay consisted of a hilly, jungle-covered spine that jutted out into the water, terminating in a rocky point. The outer side of the spine flattened into a rocky plateau, some fifty feet above the beach, which curved off to the west. The plateau was protected by high overhanging trees.

That was where the helicopter now stood, covered in a camouflage tarp, overlooking the beach below. Evans glanced back at it, hoping that it would blend into the landscape, but instead it was only too obviously visible, especially when seen from above. The group was now already fifty feet above it, as they scrambled and clawed up the jungle slope that rose steeply from the beach. It was surprisingly tough going. They were climbing single file, and had to be careful because the ground underfoot was muddy. Bradley had already slipped, and slid some ten yards down. His whole left side was covered in black mud. And Evans could see that there was a fat leech on the back of his neck, but he decided not to point it out just then.

No one spoke. The team of six climbed in silence, trying to make as little noise as possible. Despite their best efforts, they were fairly noisy, the undergrowth crackling beneath their feet, small branches snapping as they reached to pull themselves up.

Kenner was somewhere farther ahead, leading the way. Evans couldn't see him. Sanjong was bringing up the rear. He had a rifle slung over his shoulder; he had brought it with him and assembled it from a small briefcase in the copter. Kenner carried a pistol. The rest of them were unarmed.

The air was still, wet, and stupefyingly hot. The jungle buzzed, an incessant background drone of insects. Halfway up the slope, it began to rain, lightly at first and then a stupendous tropical downpour. In a moment they were drenched. Water streamed down the hillside. It was slipperier than ever.

Now they were two hundred feet above the beach, and the prospect of losing footing was clearly nervous-making. Peter looked up at Sarah, who was just ahead of him. She moved with her usual agility and grace. She seemed to be dancing up the hillside.

There were times, he thought, huffing his way along, when he really resented her.

And Jennifer, who was ahead of Sarah, was climbing with equal ease. She hardly reached for the tree limbs, though Evans was grabbing for them constantly, feeling panic as his fingers slipped on the fungus-covered bark. Watching Jennifer, he had the sense that she was almost too good at this, too skilled. Going up this treacherous jungle hill, she radiated a kind of indifference, as if it were all to be expected. It was the attitude of an Army Ranger, or the member of some elite force, tough, experienced, conditioned. Unusual, he thought, for a lawyer. More than unusual. But then, she was Kenner's niece.

And farther up was Bradley, with the leech on his neck. He was muttering and cursing and grunting with every step. Finally Jennifer punched him, then held a finger to her lips: be quiet. Bradley nodded, and though he clearly disliked taking advice from her, he was silent from then on.

At around three hundred feet they felt the stirring of a breeze, and soon after, they climbed onto the crest of the ridge. The foliage was so thick they could not see down into Resolution Bay below, but they could hear the shouts of working men and the intermittent rumble of machinery. Briefly, there was a kind of electronic hum, a sound that started softly, then built quickly until in a few moments it seemed literally to fill the air, and to make Evans's eardrums ache.

Then the sound was gone.

Evans looked at Kenner.

Kenner just nodded.

Sanjong climbed a tree, scaling it quickly. From his vantage point, he could look down on the valley. He came back down, and pointed to a hill leading down to the bay. He shook his head: too steep at this point. He indicated they should circle around, and descend on a more gentle slope.

So they started out, following the ridge around the bay. Most of the time they could see nothing but the six-foot-tall ferns dripping with water. After half an hour, there was a sudden break in the foliage, and they had a panoramic view of Resolution Bay spread out below them.

The bay was about a mile wide, and had structures set at intervals on the sand. The largest one was to the far right, at the eastern edge of the bay. Three others of equal size were arranged at intervals, making a sort of triangle in the western section of the bay.

Evans could see there was something funny about the houses, though. Something odd about the wood that was used. He squinted.

Sanjong nudged him. He wiggled his hand in the air.

Evans looked. Yes, it was true. The wooden structures were moving, fluttering in the air.

They were tents.

Tents made to look like wooden structures. And pretty good ones, too. It was no wonder they had fooled the aerial survey, Evans thought.

As they watched, men emerged from one or another of the tents and shouted to others down the beach. They were speaking English, but it was difficult to make out what they were saying at this distance. Most of it seemed to be technical.

Sanjong nudged Evans again. Evans saw him make a kind of pyramid with three fingers. Then he began to wiggle the fingers.

So, apparently they were tuning the generators in the tent. Or something like that.

The others in the group did not seem to be interested in the details. They were breathing hard, catching their breaths in the soft breeze, and staring down at the bay. And probably thinking, as Evans was, that there were a lot of men down there. At least eight or ten. All in jeans and work shirts.

"Christ, there's a lot of those bastards," Bradley muttered.

Jennifer nudged him hard in the ribs.

He mouthed: Oh, sorry.

She shook her head. She mouthed: You'll get us killed.

Bradley made a face. He clearly thought she was being melodramatic.

Then, from the jungle below them, they heard a cough.

They froze.

They waited in silence. They heard the buzz of cicadas, the occasional call of distant birds.

It came again, the same soft cough. As if the person was trying not to make noise.

Sanjong crouched down, listening hard. The cough came a third time, and to Evans there was the strangest sensation of familiarity about it. It reminded him of his grandfather, who had had heart failure when Evans was a kid. His grandfather used to cough like that, in the hospital. Weakly. Little coughs.

Now there was silence. They had not heard the cougher move away—if he had, he was truly noiseless—but the sound stopped.

Kenner looked at his watch. They waited five

minutes, then he signaled for them to continue moving east, curving around the bay.

Just as they were leaving, they heard the cough once more. This time, there were three, in succession: *uh uh uh*. Then nothing.

Kenner signaled. Move out.

They had not gone a hundred yards when they came upon a path. It was a clear trail, even though the overhanging branches hung low. It must be an animal trail, Evans thought, wondering vaguely what kind of animals they might be. There were probably feral pigs here. There were pigs everywhere. He vaguely remembered stories of people being surprised by pigs, gored by the tusks of an aggressive boar that charged out of the underbrush—

The first thing he heard, however, was a mechanical *click*. He knew instantly what it was: the sound of a gun being cocked.

The entire group froze, strung out in single file. Nobody moved.

Another *click*.

And another. *Click!*

Evans looked around quickly. He saw nobody. It seemed they were alone in the jungle.

Then he heard a voice: *"Dai. Nogot sok, waitman. Indai. Stopim!"*

Evans had no idea what it meant, but the meaning was clear enough to them all. Nobody moved.

From the bushes ahead, a young boy emerged. He was wearing boots without socks, green shorts, a "Madonna World Tour" T-shirt, and a baseball cap that said "Perth Glory." A half-smoked cigarette stub hung from his lips. He had an ammunition belt over one shoulder and a machine gun slung over the other shoulder. He was five feet tall and could not have been more than ten or eleven. He pointed his gun with casual insolence. *"Okay, waitman. You prisner biulong me, savve? Bookim dano!"* And he jerked his thumb, indicating they should move forward. *"Gohet!"*

For a moment, they were all too astonished to move. Then, from the jungle on both sides of the path, other boys emerged.

Bradley said, "What is this, the lost boys?"

Without expression, one of the kids slammed the butt of his rifle into Bradley's stomach. Bradley gasped and went down.

"Stopim waitman bilong toktok."

"Oh, Jesus," Bradley said, rolling on the ground.

The kid hit him again, this time in the head, and kicked him hard. Bradley moaned.

"Antap! Antap!" the kid said, gesturing for him to get up. When Bradley didn't respond, the kid kicked him again. *"Antap!"*

Sarah went over and helped Bradley to his feet. Bradley was coughing. Sarah was smart enough not to say anything.

"Oh, nais mari," the kid said. Then he pushed her away from Bradley.

"Antap!"

But as they trudged forward, one of the kids went over to Bradley, and squeezed the back of his arm, the triceps. He laughed. *"Taiis gut!"*

Evans felt a chill, as the words sank in. These

boys were speaking a version of English. He could decipher it, if he thought about it a little, and played the words back in his head. *Nais mari* was "Nice Mary." Maybe Mary was a word for woman. *Antap* was "And up."

And *taiis gut* was "Taste good."

They walked single file through the jungle, the kids at their side. Kenner was in the lead, then Ted, who was bleeding from his head, and Sarah, and Jennifer. Then Evans.

Evans glanced over his shoulder.

Sanjong was not behind him.

All he saw was another ragged kid with a rifle. *"Antap! Antap!"*

The kid made a threatening gesture with his rifle.

Evans turned, and hurried forward.

There was something chilling about being herded by children. Except these weren't children. He was only too aware of the cold look in their eyes. They had seen a lot in their lives. They lived in another world. It was not Evans's world.

But he was now in theirs.

Up ahead, he saw a pair of jeeps at the side of a muddy road.

He looked at his watch. It was ten o'clock.

Seven hours to go.

But somehow it didn't seem important anymore.

The kids pushed them into the jeeps, and then they drove off, down a muddy track, into the dark and trackless interior of the jungle.

PAVUTU
THURSDAY, OCTOBER 14
11:02 A.M.

There were times, Sarah thought, when she really did not want to be a woman. That was how she felt as she was driven into the muddy village of Pavutu, the rebel stronghold, in the back of an open jeep. The village seemed to be populated almost entirely by men, who came yelling into the clearing to see who had arrived. But there were women, too, including older women who stared at her height and her hair, and then came up and poked at her, as if she might not be real.

Jennifer, who was shorter and darker, stood beside her and attracted no attention at all. Nevertheless, they were herded together into one of the huge thatch houses. Inside the house was a large open space, a kind of central room, three stories high. There was a ladder made of wood leading up to a series of landings, going all the way to the top, where there was a kind of catwalk and a viewing area. In the center of the room was a fire, and at the fire sat a heavyset man with pale skin and a dark beard. He wore sunglasses and had a sort of beret with the Jamaican flag on it.

This, it seemed, was Sambuca. They were shoved in front of him, and he leered at them, but it was clear to Sarah—she had an instinct for these things—that he was not interested in them. He was interested in Ted, and in Peter. Kenner he inspected briefly, then looked away.

"*Killim.*"

They pushed Kenner out the door, poking him with the butts of their rifles. They were clearly excited at the prospect of executing him.

"*No nau,*" Sambuca said, in a growl. "*Behain.*"

It took Sarah a moment to translate in her head. Not now. Behind. Which must mean later on, she thought. So Kenner had a reprieve, at least for a while.

Sambuca turned and stared at the others in the room.

"*Meris,*" he said, with a dismissive wave. "*Goapim meri behain.*"

Sarah had the distinct impression, from the grins on the faces of the boys, that they were being given the freedom to do with the two women what they wanted. Go up 'em. She and Jennifer were led off to a back room.

Sarah remained calm. Of course she knew things were bad. But they were not bad yet. She was noticing that Jennifer did not appear to be shaken in the least. She had the same flat, uninterested expression that she might have if she was walking toward a company cocktail party.

The boys took the two women into a thatched room at the back of the larger building. There were two posts sunk in the earthen floor. One of the kids took out a pair of handcuffs and cuffed Jennifer to one post, her hands behind her back. Then he cuffed Sarah to the other post in the same way. Then another kid reached up and squeezed Sarah's tit, smiled knowingly, and walked out of the room.

"Charming," Jennifer said, when they were alone. "You all right?"

"So far, yes." There were drums starting to beat from somewhere outside, in the courtyard between the thatch buildings.

"Good," Jennifer said. "It's not over yet."

"Sanjong is—"

"Right. He is."

"But we came a long way in the jeeps."

"Yes. At least two or three miles. I tried to see the odometer, but it was spattered with mud. But on foot, even running, it'll take him a while."

"He had a rifle."

"Yes."

"Can you get free?"

Jennifer shook her head. "It's too tight."

Through the open door, they saw Bradley and Evans being led away to another room. They glimpsed the two men only for a moment. Not long after, Kenner followed. He glanced into their room, giving what seemed to Sarah a meaningful look.

But she couldn't be sure.

Jennifer sat down on the bare earth, leaning back against the pole. She said, "Might as well sit down. It could be a long night." Sarah sat down, too.

A moment later, a young boy looked in and saw that they were sitting. He came into the room, looked at their handcuffs, and then walked out again.

Outside, the drums were louder. People must

have been starting to gather, because the women could hear shouts and murmurs.

"Going to be a ceremony," Jennifer said. "And I'm afraid I know what it is."

In the next room, Evans and Kenner were also handcuffed around two posts. Because there was not a third post, Ted Bradley was handcuffed and left seated on the ground. His head was no longer bleeding, but he had a huge bruise over his left eye. And he looked distinctly frightened. But his eyelids were drooping, as if he might fall asleep.

"What's your impression of village life so far, Ted?" Kenner said. "Still think it's the best way to live?"

"This isn't village life. This is savagery."

"It's all part of it."

"No, it's not. These young kids, that fat creepy guy . . . this is lunacy. This is everything gone wrong."

"You just don't get it, do you?" Kenner said. "You think civilization is some horrible, polluting human invention that separates us from the state of nature. But civilization doesn't separate us from nature, Ted. Civilization *protects* us from nature: Because what you see right now, all around you—this *is* nature."

"Oh no. No, no. Humans are kind, cooperative . . ."

"Horseshit, Ted."

"There are genes for altruism."

"Wishful thinking, Ted."

"All cruelty springs from weakness."

"Some people *like* cruelty, Ted."

"Leave him alone," Evans said.

"Why should I? Come on, Ted. Aren't you going to answer me?"

"Oh, fuck you," Ted said. "Maybe we're all going to get killed here by these juvenile delinquent creeps, but I want you to know, if it's the last fucking thing I say in my life, that you are a major and unrelenting asshole, Kenner. You bring out the worst in everybody. You're a pessimist, you're an obstructionist, you're against all progress, against everything that is good and noble. You are a right-wing pig in . . . in . . . in whatever the fuck you are wearing. Whatever those clothes are. Where's your gun?"

"I dropped it."

"Where?"

"Back in the jungle."

"You think Sanjong has it?"

"I hope so."

"Is he coming to get us?"

Kenner shook his head. "He's doing the job we came to do."

"You mean he's going to the bay."

"Yes."

"So nobody is coming to get us?"

"No, Ted. Nobody."

"We're fucked," he said. "We're fucking *fucked*. I can't believe it." And he started to cry.

Two boys entered the room, carrying two heavy hemp ropes. They attached one rope to each of Bradley's wrists, tying them firmly. Then they walked out again.

The drums beat louder.

Out in the center of the village, people took up a rhythmic chant.

Jennifer said, "Can you see out the door from where you are?"

"Yes."

"Keep an eye out. Tell me if someone is coming."

"All right," Sarah said.

She glanced back and saw that Jennifer had arched her back and was gripping the pole between her hands. She had also bent her legs so her soles touched the wood, and proceeded to shimmy up the pole at a remarkable speed, like an acrobat. She got to the top, raised her cuffed hands clear of the top of the pole, and then jumped lightly to the ground.

"Anybody?" she said.

"No . . . How'd you learn to do that?"

"Keep looking out the door."

Jennifer slid back against her pole again, as if she were still handcuffed to it.

"Anybody yet?"

"No, not yet."

Jennifer sighed. "We need one of those kids to come in," she said. "Soon."

Outside, Sambuca was giving a speech, screaming brief phrases that were each answered by a shout from the crowd. Their leader was building them up, working them into a frenzy. Even in Ted's room, they could feel it building.

Bradley was curled in fetal position, crying softly.

Two men came in, much older than the boys. They unlocked his handcuffs. They lifted him to his feet. Each man took a rope. Together they led him outside.

A moment later, the crowd roared.

"Hey, cutie pie," Jennifer said, when a boy stuck his head in the door. She grinned. "You like what you see, cutie pie?" She shifted her pelvis suggestively.

The boy looked suspicious at first, but he came deeper into the room. He was older than the others, maybe fourteen or fifteen, and he was bigger. He was carrying a rifle and wore a knife on his belt.

"You want to have some fun? Want to let me go?" Jennifer said, smiling with a little pout. "You understand me? My arms hurt, baby. Want to have fun?"

He gave a laugh, sort of a gurgle from deep in his throat. He moved toward her and pushed her legs open, then crouched down in front of her.

"Oh, let me go first, please . . ."

"*No meri,*" he said, laughing and shaking his head. He knew he could have her while she remained cuffed to the pole. He was kneeling between her legs, fumbling with his shorts, but it was clumsy holding the gun, so he set the gun down.

What happened next was very fast. Jennifer

arched her back and kicked her legs up, clipping the kid under the chin, snapping his head back. She continued the motion, crunching into a ball, swinging her arms under her hips and butt and then up her legs, so now her hands were in front of her instead of behind. As the kid staggered to his feet, she slammed him in the side of the head with both hands. He went down on his knees. She dove on him, knocking him over, and pounded his head into the ground. Then she pulled the knife off his belt and cut his throat.

She sat on his body while he shivered and spasmed and the blood poured from his throat and onto the bare earth. It seemed to take a long time. When the body was finally motionless, she got off him, and rifled through his pockets.

Sarah watched the whole thing, her mouth open.

"Damn it," Jennifer said. "Damn it."

"What's the matter?"

"He doesn't have the key!"

She rolled the body over, grunting with the effort. She got blood on her arms from the flowing throat. She paid no attention to it.

"Where are the damn keys?"

"Maybe the other kid has it."

"Which one cuffed us?"

"I don't remember," Sarah said. "I was confused." She was staring at the body, looking at all the blood.

"Hey," Jennifer said, "get over it. You know what these guys are going to do? They're going to beat us up, gang-bang us, and then kill us. Fuck 'em. We kill as many as we can and try to get out of here alive. But *I need the damn key!*"

Sarah struggled to her feet.

"Good idea," Jennifer said. She came over and crouched down in front of Sarah.

"What?"

"Stand on my back and shimmy up. Get yourself off the pole. And hurry."

Outside, the crowd was screaming and roaring, a constant and ugly sound.

Ted Bradley blinked in the bright sunlight. He was disoriented by pain and fear and by the sight that greeted his eyes: two lines of old women, forming a corridor for him to walk down, all applauding him wildly. In fact, beyond the old women was a sea of faces—dark-skinned men and young girls and kids hardly waist high. And they were all yelling and cheering. Dozens of people, crowded together.

They were cheering him!

Despite himself, Ted smiled. It was a weak smile, sort of a half-smile, because he was tired and hurt, but he knew from experience that it would convey just the right hint of subtle pleasure at their response. As he was carried forward by the two men, he nodded and smiled. He allowed his smile to become broader.

At the far end of the women was Sambuca himself—but he, too, was applauding wildly, his hands high in the air, a broad smile on his face.

Ted didn't know what was happening here, but obviously he had misunderstood the meaning of the whole thing. Either that or they had figured out who he was and now thought better of their original plan. It wouldn't be the first time. The women were cheering so loudly as he was carried forward, their mouths gaping with excitement, that he tried to shake off the men who were holding him, he tried to walk unaided. And he did!

But now that he was closer he noticed that the applauding women had heavy sticks resting against their hips as they cheered. Some had baseball bats and some lengths of metal pipe. And as he came closer they continued to shout, but they picked up their bats and sticks and began to strike him, heavy blows on the face and shoulders and body. The pain was instant and incredible, and he sank down to the ground, but immediately the men with the ropes hauled him up again, and dragged him while the women beat him and screamed and beat him. And the pain streaked through his body and he felt a vague detachment, an emptiness, but still the blows came, merciless, again and again.

And finally, barely conscious, he came to the end of the line of women and saw a pair of poles. The men quickly tied his arms to the two poles in a way that kept him upright. And now the crowd fell silent. His head was bowed, he saw blood dripping from his head onto the ground. And he saw two naked feet appear in his line of vision, and the blood spattered on the feet, and someone lifted his head.

It was Sambuca, though Bradley could barely focus on his face. The world was gray and faint.

But he saw that Sambuca was grinning at him, revealing a row of yellow pointed teeth. And then Sambuca held up a knife so Ted could see it, and smiled again, and with two fingers grabbed the flesh of Ted's cheek and sliced it off with the knife.

There was no pain, surprisingly no pain but it made him dizzy to see Sambuca hold up the bloody chunk of his cheek and, grinning, open his mouth and take a bite. The blood ran down Sambuca's chin as he chewed, grinning all the while. Bradley's head was spinning now. He was nauseated and terrified and revolted, and he felt a pain at his chest. He looked down to see a young boy of eight or nine cutting flesh from his underarm with a pocket knife. And a woman raced forward, screaming for the others to get out of the way, and she hacked a slice from the back of his forearm. And then the whole crowd was upon him, and the knives were everywhere, and they were cutting and yelling and cutting and yelling and he saw one knife move toward his eyes, and felt his trousers tugged down, and he knew nothing more.

Evans listened to the crowd cheering and yelling. Somehow he knew what was happening. He looked at Kenner. But Kenner just shook his head.

There was nothing to do. No help was coming. There was no way out.

The door opened, and two boys appeared. They carried two heavy hemp ropes, now visibly soaked in blood. They walked up to Evans and carefully knotted the ropes to his hands. Evans felt his heart start to pound.

The boys finished and left the room.

Outside, the crowd was roaring.

"Don't worry," Kenner said. "They'll let you wait a while. There's still hope."

"Hope for *what?*" Evans said in a burst of anger.

Kenner shook his head. "Just . . . hope."

Jennifer was waiting for the next kid to come in the room. He did, finally, and took one look at the fallen boy and began to bolt, but Jennifer had her arms around his neck. She yanked him back into the room with her hands over his mouth so he couldn't scream and she made a sudden, quick twist and let him fall to the ground. He wasn't dead, but he would be there a while.

But in that moment when she had looked outside, she had seen the keys.

They were out in the thatch passageway, on a bench across the hall.

There were two guns in the room now, but there was no point in firing them. It would just bring everybody on them. Jennifer didn't want to look outside again. She heard murmuring voices. She couldn't be sure whether they were coming from the next room or from the hallway. She couldn't make a mistake.

She leaned back against the wall by the door and moaned. Softly at first, and then louder, because the crowd was still very noisy. She moaned and moaned.

Nobody came.

Did she dare to look out?

She took a breath and waited.

Evans was trembling. The blood-soaked ropes were cold on his wrists. He couldn't stand the waiting. He felt like he was going to pass out. Outside the crowd was slowly becoming quieter. They were settling down. He knew what that meant. Soon it would be time for the next victim.

Then he heard a quiet sound.

It was a man coughing. Softly, insistently.

Kenner understood first. "In here," he said loudly.

There was a whacking sound as a machete blade poked through the thatched wall. Evans turned. He saw the slash in the wall widen, and a thick, brown hand reached in to pull the slash wider open still. A heavily bearded face peered through the gash at them.

For a moment Evans did not recognize him, but then the man put his finger to his lips, and there was something in the gesture that was familiar, and Evans suddenly saw past the beard.

"George!"

It was George Morton.

Alive.

Morton stepped through into the room. "Keep it down," he hissed.

"You took your sweet time," Kenner said, turning so Morton could unlock his cuffs. Morton gave Kenner a pistol. Then it was Evans's turn. With a click, his hands were free. Evans tugged at the hemp ropes, trying to get them off his wrists. But they were securely tied.

Morton whispered, "Where are the others?"

Kenner pointed to the room next door. He took the machete from Morton. "You take Peter. I'll get the girls."

With the machete, Kenner stepped out into the hallway.

Morton grabbed Evans by the arm. Evans jerked his head.

"Let's go."

"But—"

"Do as he says, kid."

They stepped through the slash in the wall, and into the jungle beyond.

Kenner moved down the empty hallway. There were openings at both ends. He could be surprised at any moment. If the alarm went up, they were all dead. He saw the keys on the bench, picked them up, and went to the door of the women's room. Looking into the room, he saw that the poles were abandoned. He didn't see either of the women.

Staying outside, he tossed the keys into the room.

"It's me," he whispered.

A moment later, he saw Jennifer scramble from her hiding place behind the door to grab the keys. In a few seconds she and Sarah had both unlocked each other. They grabbed the boys' guns and started for the door.

Too late. From around the corner three heavy-set young men were coming toward Kenner. They all carried machine guns. They were talking and laughing, not paying attention.

Kenner slipped into the women's room. He pressed back against the wall, gestured for the two women to go back to the poles. They made it just in time as the men entered the room. Jennifer said, "Hi, guys," with a big smile. At that moment, the men registered the two fallen boys and the blood-soaked earth, but it was too late. Kenner took one; Jennifer got the second with her knife. The third was almost out the door when Kenner hit him with the butt of the gun. There was the crack of skull. He went down hard.

It was time to go.

Out in the courtyard, the crowd was growing restless. Sambuca squinted. The first *waitman* was long dead, the body cooling at his feet, no longer as appetizing as he was before. And those in the crowd who had not tasted glory were clamoring for their piece, for the next opportunity. The women were resting their bats and pipes on their shoulders, talking in small clusters, waiting for the game to continue.

Where was the next man?

Sambuca barked an order, and three men ran toward the thatch building.

It was a long, muddy slide down the steep hill, but Evans didn't mind. He was following Morton, who seemed to know his way around the jungle very well. They fell to the bottom, landing in a shallow running stream, the water pale brown with peat. Morton signaled for him to follow, and ran splashing down the streambed. Morton had lost a lot of weight; his body was trim and fit, his face tight, hard looking.

Evans said, "We thought you were dead."

"Don't talk. Just go. They'll be after us in a minute."

And even as he spoke, Evans could hear someone sliding down the hillside after them. He turned and ran down the stream, slipping over wet rocks, falling, getting up and running again.

Kenner came down the hillside with the two women right behind him. They banged against gnarled roots and protruding brambles as they slid down, but it was still the fastest way to get away from the village. He could see from the streaks in the mud ahead of him that Morton had gone that way, too. And he was sure that he had no more than a minute's head start before the alarm was sounded.

They came crashing down through the last of the undergrowth to the streambed. They heard gunshots from the village above. So their escape had already been discovered.

The bay, Kenner knew, was off to the left. He told the others to go ahead, running in the streambed.

"What about you?" Sarah said.

"I'll be with you in a minute."

The women headed off, moving surprisingly quickly. Kenner eased back to the muddy track, raised his gun, and waited. It was only a few seconds before the first of the rebels came down the slope. He fired three quick bursts. The bodies caught in the gnarled branches. One tumbled all the way to the streambed.

Kenner waited.

The men above would expect him to run now. So he waited. Sure enough, in a couple of minutes he heard them starting down again. They were noisy—frightened kids. He fired again, and heard screams. But he didn't think he'd hit anything. They were just screams of fear.

But from now on, he was sure they would take a different route down. And it would be slower.

Kenner turned and ran.

Sarah and Jennifer were moving fast through the water when a bullet whined past Sarah's ear. "Hey," she shouted. "It's us!"

"Oh, sorry," Morton said, as they caught up to him.

"Which way?" Jennifer said.

Morton pointed downstream.

They ran.

Evans looked for his watch, but one of the kids had taken it from him. His wrist was bare. But Morton had a watch. "What time is it?" Evans asked him.

"Three-fifteen."

They had less than two hours remaining.

"How far to the bay?"

"Maybe another hour," Morton said, "if we go cross jungle. And we must. Those boys are fearsome trackers. Many times they've almost gotten me. They know I'm here, but so far I've eluded them."

"How long have you been here?"

"Nine days. Seems like nine years."

Running down a streambed, they crouched low beneath overhanging branches. Evans's thighs burned. His knees ached. But somehow it didn't matter to him. For some reason, the pain felt like an affirmation. He didn't care about the heat or the bugs or the leeches that he knew were all over his ankles and legs. He was just glad to be alive.

"We turn here," Morton said. He left the streambed, dashing off to the right, scrambling over big boulders, and then crashing into dense, waist-high ferns.

"Any snakes in here?" Sarah said.

"Yeah, plenty," Morton said. "But I don't worry about them."

"What do you worry about?"

"Plenti pukpuk."

"And they are?"

"Crocodiles."

And he plunged onward, vanishing into dense foliage.

"Great," Evans said.

Kenner stopped in the middle of the river. Something was wrong. Until now, he had seen signs of previous runners in the stream. Bits of mud on rocks, wet finger marks or shoe prints, or disturbed algae. But for the last few minutes, nothing.

The others had left the stream.

He'd missed where.

Morton would make sure of that, he thought. Morton would know a good place to leave the river where their exit wouldn't be noticed. Probably somewhere with ferns and swampy, marshy grass between boulders on riverbanks—grass that would be spongy underfoot and would spring back at once.

Kenner had missed it.

He turned around and headed upstream, moving slowly. He knew that if he didn't find their tracks, he couldn't leave the river. He would be sure to get lost. And if he stayed in the river too long, the kids would find him. And they'd kill him.

There was one hour left, now. Morton crouched among the mangroves and rocks near the center of Resolution Bay. The others were clustered around him. The water lapped softly against the sand, a few feet away.

"This is what I know," he said, speaking low. "The submarine tender is hidden under a camouflage tarp at the east end of the bay. You can't see it from here. They have been sending the submarine down every day for a week. The sub has limited battery power, so it can stay at depth for only an hour at a time. But it seems pretty clear they are placing a kind of cone-shaped explosive that depends on accurately timed detonation—"

"They had them in Antarctica," Sarah said.

"All right, then you know. Here, they're intended to trigger an underwater avalanche. Judging how long the sub stays down, I figure they are placing them at about the ninety-meter level, which happens to be the most efficient level for tsunami-causing avalanches."

"What about the tents up here?" Evans said.

"It seems they're taking no chances. Either they don't have enough cone explosives or they don't trust them to do the job, because they have placed something called hypersonic cavitation generators in the tents. They're big pieces of equipment about the size of a small truck. Diesel powered, make a lot of noise when they fire them up to test them, which they've been doing for days. They moved the tents several times, just a foot or two each time, so I assume there's some critical issue about placement. Maybe they're focusing the beams, or whatever it is those things generate. I'm not entirely clear about what they do. But apparently they're important for creating the landslide."

Sarah said, "And what do we do?"

"There's no way we can stop them," Morton said. "We are only four—five, if Kenner makes it, which he doesn't seem to be doing. There are thirteen of them. Seven on the ship and six on shore. All armed with automatic weapons."

"But we have Sanjong," Evans said. "Don't forget him."

"That Nepali guy? I'm sure the rebels got him. There were gunshots about an hour ago along the ridge where they first found you. I was a few yards below, just before they picked you up. I tried to signal you by coughing, but . . ." He shrugged, turned back to the beach. "Anyway. Assuming the three cavitation generators are meant to work together to create some effect on the underwater slope, I figure our best chance is to take one of the generators out—or maybe two of them. That would disrupt their plan or at least weaken the effect."

Jennifer said, "Can we cut the power supply?"

Morton shook his head. "They're self-powered. Diesel attached to the main units."

"Battery ignition?"

"No. Solar panels. They're autonomous."

"Then we have to take out the guys running the units."

"Yes. And they've been alerted to our presence. As you can see, there's one standing outside each tent, guarding it, and they've got a sentry somewhere up on that ridge." He pointed to the western slope. "We can't see where he is, but I assume he is watching the whole bay."

"So? Big deal. Let him watch," Jennifer said. "I say we just take out all these guys in the tents, and trash the machines. We've got enough weapons here to do the job, and—" She paused. She had removed the magazine from her rifle; it was empty. "Better check your loads."

There was a moment of fumbling. They were all shaking their heads. Evans had four rounds. Sarah had two. Morton's rifle had none. "Those guys had practically no ammo . . ."

"And we don't either." Jennifer took a long breath. "This is going to be a little tougher without weapons." She edged forward and looked out on the beach, squinting in the bright light. "There's ten yards between the jungle and those tents. Open beach, no cover. If we charge the tents we'll never make it."

"What about a distraction?"

"I don't know what it could be. There's one guy outside each tent and one guy inside. They both armed?"

Morton nodded. "Automatic weapons."

"Not good," she said. "Not good at all."

Kenner splashed down the river, looking hard left and right. He had not gone more than a hundred yards when he saw the faint imprint of a wet hand on a boulder. The damp print had almost dried. He looked more closely. He saw the grass at the edge of the stream had been trampled.

This was where they had left the stream.

He set out, heading toward the bay. Morton obviously knew his way around. This was another streambed, but much smaller. Kenner noticed with some unease that it sloped downward fairly steeply. That was a bad sign. But it was a passable route through the jungle. Somewhere up ahead, he heard the barking of a dog. It sounded like the dog was hoarse, or sick, or something.

Kenner hurried ahead, ducking beneath the branches.

He had to get to the others, before it was too late.

Morton heard the barking and frowned.

"What's the matter?" Jennifer said. "The rebels chasing us with dogs?"

"No. That's not a dog."

"It didn't really sound like a dog."

"It's not. They've learned a trick in this part of the world. They bark like a dog, and then when the dogs come out, they eat them."

"Who does?"

"Crocs. That's a crocodile you hear. Somewhere behind us."

Out on the beach, they heard the sudden rumbling of automobile engines. Peering forward through the mangroves, they saw three jeeps coming from the east side of the bay, rumbling across the sand toward them.

"What's this?" Evans said.

"They've been practicing this," Morton said. "All week. Watch. One stops at each tent. See? Tent one . . . tent two . . . tent three. They all stop. They all keep the motors running. All pointed west."

"What's west?"

"There's a dirt track, goes up the hill about a hundred yards and then dead-ends."

"Something used to be up there?"

"No. They cut the road themselves. First thing they did when they got here." Morton looked toward the eastern curve of the bay. "Usually by this time, the ship has pulled out, and moved into deep water. But it's not doing it yet."

"Uh-oh," Evans said.

"What is it?"

"I think we've forgotten something."

"What's that?"

"We've been worried about this tsunami wave heading toward the California coast. But a landslide would suck water downward, right? And then it would rise back up again. But that's kind of like dropping this pebble into this ditch." He dropped a pebble into a muddy puddle at their feet. "And the wave the pebble generates . . . is circular."

"It goes in all directions . . ."

"Oh no," Sarah said.

"Oh yes. All directions, including back to this coast. The tsunami will hit here, too. And fast. How far offshore is the Solomon Trench?"

Morton shrugged. "I don't know. Maybe two miles. I really don't know, Peter."

"If these waves travel five hundred miles an hour," Evans said, "then that means it gets to this coast in . . ."

"Twenty-four seconds," Sarah said.

"Right. That's how much time we have to get out of here, once the undersea landslide begins. Twenty-four seconds."

With a sudden chugging rumble, they heard the first diesel generator come to life. Then the second, then the third. All three were running.

Morton glanced at his watch. "This is it," he said. "They've started."

And now they heard an electronic whine, faint at first but rapidly building to a deep electronic hum. It filled the air.

"Those're the cavitators," Morton said. "Kicking in."

Jennifer slung her rifle over her shoulder. "Let's get ready."

Sanjong slid silently from the branches of the overhanging tree, onto the deck of the *AV Scorpion*. The forty-foot ship must have a very shallow draft, because it was pulled up close to the peninsula on the eastern side, so that the huge jungle trees overhung it. The ship couldn't really be seen from the beach; Sanjong had only realized that it was there when he heard the crackle of radios coming from the jungle.

He crouched in the stern, hiding behind the winch that raised the submarine, listening. He heard voices from all sides, it seemed like. He guessed that there were six or seven men onboard. But what he wanted was to find the timing detonators. He guessed that they were in the pilothouse, but he couldn't be sure. And between his hiding place and the pilothouse was a long expanse of open deck.

He looked at the mini-sub hanging above him. It was bright blue, about seven feet long, with a bubble canopy, now raised. The sub was raised and lowered into the water by the winch.

And the winch . . .

He looked for the control panel. He knew it had to be nearby because the operator would have to be able to see the submarine as it was lowered. Finally he saw it: a closed metal box on the other side of the ship. He crept over, opened the box, and looked at the buttons. There were six, marked with arrows in all directions. Like a big keypad.

He pressed the down arrow.

With a rumble, the winch began to lower the submarine into the water.

An alarm began to sound.

He heard running feet.

He ducked back into a doorway and waited.

* * *

From the beach, they faintly heard the sound of an alarm over the rumble of the generators and the cavitation hum. Evans looked around. "Where's it coming from?"

"It must be from the ship, over there."

Out on the beach, the men heard it, too. They were standing in pairs by the entrance to the tents, pointing. Wondering what to do.

And then, from the jungle behind them, a sudden burst of machine-gun fire opened up. The men on the beach were alarmed now, swinging their guns, looking this way and that.

"Screw it," Jennifer said, taking Evans's rifle. "This is it. It won't get any better."

And firing, she ran out onto the beach.

The crocodile had charged Kenner with frightening speed. He had little more than a glimpse of huge white jaws open wide and thrashing water before he fired with his machine gun. The jaw smashed down, just missing his leg; the animal writhed, twisted, and attacked again, jaws closing on a low-hanging branch.

The bullets hadn't done anything. Kenner turned and ran, sprinting down the streambed.

The croc roared behind him.

Jennifer was running across the sand, heading for the nearest tent. She went about ten yards before two bullets struck her left leg and knocked her down. She fell onto hot sand, still firing as she fell. She saw the guard at the entrance to the tent drop. She knew he was dead.

Evans came up behind her and started to

crouch down. She shouted, "Keep going! Go!" Evans ran forward, toward the tent.

On the ship, the men halted the descent of the submarine, stopping the winch. Now they could hear the gunshots coming from the beach. They had all rushed to the starboard side of the ship, and now they were looking over the railing, trying to see what was going on.

Sanjong went down the deck on the port side. No one was there. He came to the cabin. There was a big board there, dense with electronics. A man in shorts and a T-shirt was crouched over it, making adjustments. At the top of the board were three rows of lights, marked with numerals.

The timing board.

For the undersea detonations.

Sarah and Morton were sprinting along the edge of the beach, staying close to the jungle, as they headed for the second tent. The man outside the tent saw them almost at once and was firing bursts of machine-gun fire at them, but he must have been very nervous, Sarah thought, because he wasn't hitting them. Branches and leaves snapped all around them from the bullets. And with every step, they were getting close enough for Sarah to fire back. She was carrying Morton's pistol. At twenty yards, she stopped and leaned against the nearest tree trunk. She held her arm stiffly and aimed. The first shot missed. The second one hit the man outside the tent in the right shoulder, and he dropped his gun in the sand. Morton saw it, and left the forest, running across the sand toward the tent. The man was struggling to get up. Sarah shot again.

And then Morton disappeared inside the tent. And she heard two quick gunshots and a scream of pain.

She ran.

Evans was inside the tent. He faced a wall of chugging machinery, a huge complex of twisting pipes and vents, ending in a flat, round plate eight feet wide, set about two feet above the surface of the sand. The generator was about seven feet high; all the metal was hot to the touch. The noise was deafening. He didn't see anybody there. Holding his rifle ready—painfully aware that the magazine was empty—he swung around the first corner, then the second.

And then he saw him.

It was Bolden. The guy from the Antarctic. He was working at a control panel, adjusting big knobs while he looked at a shaded LCD screen and a row of dials. He was so preoccupied, he didn't even notice Evans at first.

Evans felt a burst of pure rage. If his gun had been loaded he would have shot him. Bolden's gun was leaning against the wall of the tent. He needed both hands to adjust the controls.

Evans shouted. Bolden turned. Evans gestured for him to put up his hands.

Bolden charged.

Morton had just stepped into the tent when the first bullet struck his ear and the second hit his shoulder. He screamed in pain and fell to his knees. The movement saved his life because the next bullet whined past his forehead, ripping through the tent cloth. He was lying on the ground next to the chugging machinery when the gunman came around, holding his rifle ready. He was a twentyish man, bearded, grim, all business. He aimed at Morton.

And then he fell against the machine, blood hissing as it splattered on hot metal. Sarah was standing inside the tent, firing her pistol once, twice, three times, lowering her arm each time as the man fell. She turned to Morton.

"I forgot you were a good shot," he said.

"You okay?" she said. He nodded. "Then how do I turn this thing off?"

Evans grunted as Bolden smashed into his body. The two men stumbled back against the tent fabric, then forward again. Evans brought the butt of his gun down on Bolden's back, but it had no effect. He kept trying to hit him in the head, but only connected with his back. Bolden, for his part, seemed to be trying to drive Evans out of the tent.

The two men fell to the ground. The machinery was thumping above them. And now Evans realized what Bolden was trying to do.

He was trying to push Evans under the plate. Even by being near the edge, Evans could feel the air vibrating intensely. The air was much hotter here.

Bolden hit Evans in the head, and his sunglasses went flying across the ground, beneath the flat plate. Instantly, they shattered. Then the frames crumpled.

Then they pulverized.

Vanished into nothing.

Evans watched with horror. And little by little, Bolden was pushing him closer to the edge, closer, closer . . .

Evans struggled, with the sudden strength of desperation. Abruptly, he kicked up.

Bolden's face mashed against hot metal. He howled. His cheek was smoking and black. Evans kicked again, and got out from beneath him. Got to his feet. Standing over Bolden, he kicked him hard in the ribs, as hard as he could. He tried to kill him.

That's for Antarctica.

Bolden grabbed Evans's leg on the next kick, and Evans went down. But he kicked once more as he fell, hitting Bolden in the head, and with the impact, Bolden rolled once.

And rolled under the plate.

His body was half under, half out. It began to shake, to vibrate. Bolden opened his mouth to scream but there was no sound. Evans kicked him a final time, and the body went entirely under.

By the time Evans had dropped to his hands and knees, to look under the plate, nothing was there. Just a haze of acrid smoke.

He got to his feet, and went outside.

Glancing over her shoulder, Jennifer ripped her blouse with her teeth and tore a strip of cloth for a tourniquet. She didn't think an artery had been hit, but there was a lot of blood on one leg and a lot of blood in the sand, and she was feeling a little dizzy.

She had to keep watching because there was one more tent, and if the guys from that tent showed up . . .

She spun, raising her gun as a figure emerged from the forest.

It was John Kenner. She lowered the gun.

He ran toward her.

Sanjong fired into the glass in front of the control deck, but nothing happened. The glass didn't even shatter. Bulletproof glass, he thought in surprise. The technician inside looked up in shock. By then Sanjong was moving toward the door.

The technician reached for the control switches. Sanjong fired twice, once hitting the technician, once aiming for the control panel.

But it was too late. Across the top of the panel, red lights flashed, one after another. The undersea detonations were taking place.

Automatically, a loud alarm began to sound, like a submarine claxon. The men on the other side of the ship were shouting, terror in their voices, and with good reason, Sanjong thought.

The tsunami had been generated.

It was only a matter of seconds now before it would hit them.

The air was filled with sound.

Evans ran from the tent. Directly ahead he saw Kenner lifting Jennifer in his arms. Kenner was shouting something, but Evans couldn't hear. He could vaguely see that Jennifer was soaked in blood. Evans ran for the jeep, jumped in, and drove it over to Kenner.

Kenner put Jennifer in the back. She was breathing shallowly. Directly ahead, they saw Sarah helping Morton into the other jeep. Kenner had to shout over the noise. For a minute Evans couldn't understand.

Then he realized what Kenner was saying. "Sanjong! Where is Sanjong!"

Evans shook his head. "Morton says he's dead! Rebels!"

"Do you know for sure?"

"No!"

Kenner looked back down the beach.

"Drive!"

Sarah was in the car, trying to hold Morton up-right and drive at the same time. But she had to let go of him to shift gears, and as soon as she did he'd flop over against her shoulder. He was wheezing, breathing with difficulty. She suspected that his lung was punctured. She was distracted, trying to count in her head. She thought it was already ten seconds since the landslide.

Which meant they had fifteen seconds to get up the hill.

Sanjong leapt from the ship to the trees on the shore. He grabbed a handful of leaves and branches. He scrambled down to the ground and began to climb the hill frantically. On the ship, the men saw him, and they jumped, too, trying to follow him.

Sanjong guessed that they all had half a minute before the first wave struck. It would be the smallest wave, but it would still probably be five meters high. The runup—the splash on the hillside—could be another five meters. That meant he had to scramble at least thirty feet up the muddy slope in the next thirty seconds.

He knew he would never make it.

He couldn't do it.

He climbed anyway.

Sarah drove up the muddy track, the jeep slipping precariously on the incline. Beside her, Morton was not saying anything and his skin had turned an ugly blue gray. She yelled, "Hold on, George! Hold on! Just a little!" The jeep fishtailed in the mud, and Sarah howled in panic. She downshifted, grinding gears, got control, and continued up. In the rearview mirror, she saw Evans behind her.

In her mind, she was counting:

Eighteen.

Nineteen.

Twenty.

From the third tent on the beach, two men with machine guns jumped into the last remaining jeep. They drove up the hill after Evans, firing at him as they drove. Kenner was firing back. The bullets shattered Evans's windshield. Evans slowed.

"Keep driving!" Kenner yelled. "Go!"

Evans couldn't really see. Where the windshield wasn't shattered it was spattered with mud. He kept moving his head, trying to see the route ahead.

"Go!" Kenner yelled.

The bullets were whizzing around them.

Kenner was shooting at the tires of the jeep behind them. He hit them, and the jeep lurched over onto its side. The two men fell out into the mud. They scrambled to their feet, limping. They were only about fifteen feet above the beach.

Not high enough.

Kenner looked back at the ocean.

He saw the wave coming toward the shore.

It was enormous, as wide as the eye could see, a foaming line of surf, a white arc spreading as it came toward the beach. It was not a very high wave, but it grew as it came ashore, rising up, rising higher . . .

The jeep lurched to a halt.

"Why did you stop?" Kenner yelled.

"It's the end of the damn road!" Evans shouted.

The wave was now about fifteen feet high.

With a roar of surf, the wave struck the beach and raced inland toward them.

To Evans, it seemed as if everything was happening in slow motion—the big wave churning white, boiling over the sand, and somehow keeping its crest all the way across the beach, and into the jungle, completely covering the green landscape in white as the water boiled up the slope toward them.

He couldn't take his eyes off it, because it seemed never to lose its power, but just kept coming. Farther down the muddy track the two men were scrambling away from their fallen jeep, and then they were covered in white water and gone from sight.

The wave rushed up the slope another four or five feet, then suddenly slowed, receded, sweeping back. It left behind no trace of the men or their jeep. The jungle trees were ragged, many uprooted.

The wave slid back into the ocean, farther and farther away, exposing the beach far out to sea, before it finally died away, and the ocean was gentle again.

"That's the first," Kenner said. "The next ones will be bigger."

* * *

Sarah was holding Morton upright, trying to keep him comfortable. His lips were a terrible blue color and his skin was cold, but he seemed to be alert. He wasn't talking, but he was watching the water.

"Hang on, George," she said.

He nodded. He was mouthing something.

"What is it? What are you saying?"

She read his lips. A weak grin.

Wouldn't miss it if it was the last thing I did.

The next wave came in.

From a distance, it looked exactly like the first, but as it neared the shore they could see that it was noticeably bigger, half again as large as the first, and the roar as it smashed into the beach was like an explosion. A vast sheet of water raced up the hill toward them, coming much higher than before.

They were almost a hundred feet away. The wave had come a good sixty feet up the slope.

"The next one will be bigger," Kenner said.

The sea was quiet for several minutes. Evans turned to Jennifer. "Listen," he said, "do you want me to—"

She wasn't there. For a moment he thought she had fallen out of the jeep. Then he saw she had fallen on the floor, where she lay curled in pain. Her face and shoulder were soaked in blood.

"Jennifer?"

Kenner grabbed Evans's hand, pushed it back gently. He shook his head. "Those guys in the jeep," he said. "She was okay until then." Evans was stunned. He felt dizzy. He looked at her. "Jennifer?"

Her eyes were closed. She was hardly breathing.

"Turn away," Kenner said. "She'll make it or she won't."

The next wave was coming in.

There was nowhere they could go. They had reached the end of the track. They were surrounded by jungle. They just waited, and watched the water rush up in a hissing, terrifying wall toward them. The wave had already broken. This was just surge rushing up the hillside, but it was still a wall of water nine or ten feet high.

Sarah was sure it was going to take them all, but the wave lost energy just a few yards away, thinning and slowing, and then sliding back down to the ocean.

Kenner looked at his watch. "We have a few minutes," he said. "Let's do what we can."

"What do you mean?" Sarah said.

"I mean, climb as high as we can."

"There's another wave?"

"At least."

"Bigger?"

"Yes."

Five minutes passed. They scrambled up the hillside another twenty yards. Kenner was carrying Jennifer's bleeding body. By now she had lost consciousness. Evans and Sarah were helping Morton, who was moving with great difficulty.

Finally, Evans picked Morton up and carried him piggyback style.

"Glad you lost some weight," Evans said.

Morton, not speaking, just patted him on the shoulder.

Evans staggered up the hill.

The next wave came in.

When it receded, their jeeps had vanished. The spot where they had been parked was littered with the trunks of uprooted trees. They stared, very tired. They argued: Was that the fourth wave or the fifth? No one could remember. They decided it must have been the fourth.

"What do we do?" Sarah said to Kenner.

"We climb."

Eight minutes later, the next wave came in. It was smaller than the one before. Evans was too tired to do anything but stare at it. Kenner was trying to stop Jennifer's bleeding, but her skin was an ugly pale gray and her lips were blue. Down at the beach, there was no sign of human activity at all. The tents were gone. The generators were gone. There was nothing but piled-up debris, tree branches, pieces of wood, seaweed, foam.

"What's that?" Sarah said.

"What?"

"Someone is shouting."

They looked across to the opposite side of the bay. Someone was waving to them.

"It's Sanjong," Kenner said. "Son of a bitch." He grinned. "I hope he's smart enough to stay where he is. It'll take him a couple of hours to get across the debris. Let's go see if our helicopter is still there or if the wave took it. Then we'll go pick him up."

Eight thousand miles to the east, it was the middle of the night in Golden, Colorado, when the computers of the National Earthquake Information Center registered an atypical seismic disturbance originating from the Pacific basin, just north of the Solomon Islands, and measuring 6.3 Richter. That was a strong quake, but not unusually strong. The peculiar characteristics of the disturbance led the computer to categorize it as an "anomalous event," a fairly common designation for seismic events in that part of the world, where three tectonic plates met in strange overlapping patterns.

The NEIC computers assessed the earthquake as lacking the relatively slow movement associated with tsunamis, and thus did not classify it as a "tsunami-generating event." However, in the South Pacific, this designation was being reexamined, following the devastating New Guinea earthquake of 1998—the single most destructive tsunami of the twentieth century—which also did not have the classic slow tsunami profile. Thus, as a precaution, the computers flagged the earthquake to the sensors of the MORN, the

Mid-Ocean Relay Network, operating out of Hilo, Hawaii.

Six hours later, mid-ocean buoys detected a nine-inch rise in the ocean level consistent with a tsunami wave train. Because of the great depth of the mid-ocean, tsunamis often raised the sea level only a few inches. On this particular evening, ships in the area felt nothing at all as the big wave front passed beneath them. Nevertheless, the buoys felt it, and triggered an alarm.

It was the middle of the night in Hawaii when the computers pinged and the screens came up. The network manager, Joe Ohiri, had been dozing. He got up, poured himself a cup of coffee and inspected the data. It was clearly a tsunami profile, though one that appeared to be losing force in its ocean passage. Hawaii was of course in its path, but this wave would strike the south shore of the islands, a relative rarity. Ohiri made a quick wave-force calculation, was unimpressed with the results, and so sent a routine notification to civil defense units on all the inhabited islands. It began "This is an information message . . ." and finished with the usual boilerplate about the alert being based on preliminary information. Ohiri knew that nobody would pay much attention to it. Ohiri also notified the West Coast and Alaska Warning Centers, because the wave train was due to strike the coast in early mid-morning of the following day.

Five hours later, the DART buoys off the coast of California and Alaska detected the passage of a tsunami train, now further weakened. Computers calculated the velocity and wave force and recommended no action. This meant that the message went out to the local stations as a tsunami information bulletin, not an alert:

> BASED ON LOCATION AND MAGNITUDE THE EARTHQUAKE WAS NOT SUFFICIENT TO GENERATE A TSUNAMI DAMAGING TO CALIFORNIA–OREGON–WASHINGTON–BRITISH COLUMBIA OR ALASKA. SOME AREAS MAY EXPERIENCE SMALL SEA LEVEL CHANGES.

Kenner, who was monitoring the messages on his computer, shook his head when he saw this. "Nick Drake is not going to be a happy man today." It was Kenner's hypothesis that they had needed the cavitation generators to extend the effect of the underwater detonations, and to create the relatively long-lasting landslide that would have produced a truly powerful ocean-crossing tsunami. That had been thwarted.

Ninety minutes later, the much-weakened tsunami train struck the beaches of California. It consisted of a set of five waves averaging six feet in height that excited surfers briefly, but passed unnoticed by everyone else.

Belatedly, Kenner was notified that the FBI had been attempting to reach him for the past twelve hours. It turned out that V. Allen Willy had vacated his beach house at two A.M. local time. This was less than an hour after the events in Resolution Bay had taken place, and more than ten hours prior to the tsunami notification.

Kenner suspected that Willy had gotten cold feet, and had been unwilling to wait. But it was an important and telling mistake. Kenner called the agent and started proceedings to subpoena Willy's phone records.

None of them was allowed to leave the island for the next three days. There were formalities, forms, interrogations. There were problems with emergency care for Morton's collapsed lung and Jennifer's massive blood loss. Morton wanted to be taken to Sydney for surgery, but he was not allowed to leave because he had been reported as a missing person in America. Although he complained bitterly about witch doctors, a very good surgeon trained in Melbourne took care of his lung in Gareda Town. But Jennifer had not been able to wait for that surgeon; she had needed three transfusions during five hours of surgery to remove the bullets in her upper body, and then she was on a respirator, near death for the next forty-eight hours. But at the end of the second day she opened her eyes, pulled off her oxygen mask, and said to Evans, sitting at her bedside, "Stop looking so gloomy. I'm here, for God's sake." Her voice was weak, but she was smiling.

Then there were problems about their contact with the rebels. There were problems about the fact that one of their party had disappeared, the famous actor Ted Bradley. They all told the story of what had happened to Bradley, but there was no way to corroborate it. So the police made them tell it again.

And suddenly, abruptly, unaccountably, they were allowed to leave. Their papers were in order. Their passports were returned. There was no difficulty. They could leave whenever they wanted.

Evans slept most of the way to Honolulu. After the plane refueled and took off again, he sat up and talked to Morton and the others. Morton was explaining what had happened on the night of his car crash.

"There was obviously a problem with Nick and what he was doing with his money. NERF was not doing good things. Nick was very angry—dangerously angry. He threatened me, and I took him at his word. I had established the link between his organization and ELF, and he was threatened, to put it mildly. Kenner and I thought he would try to kill me. Well, he did try. With that girl at the coffee shop, that morning in Beverly Hills."

"Oh yes." Evans remembered Sarah had mentioned it. "But how did you stage that car crash? It was so incredibly dangerous—"

"What, do you think I'm crazy?" Morton said. "I never crashed."

"What do you mean?"

"I kept right on driving, that night."

"But." Evans fell silent, shaking his head. "I don't get it."

"Yes, you do," Sarah said. "Because I let it slip to you, by accident. Before George called me and told me to keep my mouth shut about it."

It came back to him then. The conversation from days ago. He hadn't paid much attention at the time. Sarah had said:

*He told me to buy a new Ferrari from a guy in
Monterey and have it shipped to San Francisco.*

When Evans expressed surprise that George
was buying another Ferrari:

*I know. How many Ferraris can one man use? And
this one doesn't seem up to his usual standard. From
the e-mail pictures it looks kind of beat up.*

And then she said:

*The Ferrari he bought is a 1972 365 GTS Daytona
Spyder. He already has one, Peter. It's like he doesn't
know . . .*

"Oh, I knew all right," Morton said. "What a
waste of money. The car was a piece of crap. And
then I had to fly a couple of Hollywood prop guys
up to Sonoma to beat the hell out of it and make
it look like a crash. Then they flat-bedded it out
that night, set it on the road, fired up the smoke
pots . . ."

"And you drove right past a wreck that was
already in place," Evans said.

"Yes," Morton said, nodding. "Drove right
around the corner. Pulled off the road, climbed
up the hill, and watched you guys."

"You son of a bitch."

"I'm sorry," Morton said, "but we needed real
emotion to distract the police from the problems."

"What problems?"

"Ice-cold engine block, for one," Kenner said.
"That engine hadn't run for days. One of the cops
noticed it was cold while the car was being put
on the truck. He came back and asked you the
time of the accident, all of that. I was concerned
they would figure it out."

"But they didn't," Morton said.

"No. They knew something was wrong. But I don't think they ever guessed identical Ferraris."

"No one in his right mind," Morton said, "would intentionally destroy a 1972 365 GTS. Even a crappy one."

Morton was smiling, but Evans was angry. "Somebody could have told me—"

"No," Kenner said. "We needed you to work Drake. Like the cell phone."

"What about it?"

"The cell phone was a very low-quality bug. We needed Drake to suspect that you were part of the investigation. We needed him pressured."

"Well, it worked. That's why I got poisoned in my apartment, isn't it?" Evans said. "You guys were willing to take a lot of risks with my life."

"It turned out all right," Kenner said.

"You did this car crash to pressure Drake?"

"And to get me free," Morton said. "I needed to go down to the Solomons and find out what they were doing. I knew Nick would save the best for last. Although if they had been able to modify that hurricane—that was the third stunt they planned—so that it hit Miami, that would have been spectacular."

"Fuck you, George," Evans said.

"I'm sorry it had to be this way," Kenner said.

"And fuck you, too."

Then Evans got up and went to the front of the plane. Sarah was sitting alone. He was so angry he refused to speak to her. He spent the next hour staring out the window. Finally, she began talking quietly to him, and at the end of half an hour, they embraced.

*   *   *

Evans slept for a while, restless, his body sore. He couldn't find a comfortable position to rest. Intermittently, he would wake up, groggy. One time he thought he heard Kenner talking to Sarah.

Let's remember where we live, Kenner was saying. We live on the third planet from a medium-size sun. Our planet is five billion years old, and it has been changing constantly all during that time. The Earth is now on its third atmosphere.

The first atmosphere was helium and hydrogen. It dissipated early on, because the planet was so hot. Then, as the planet cooled, volcanic eruptions produced a second atmosphere of steam and carbon dioxide. Later the water vapor condensed, forming the oceans that cover most of the planet. Then, around three billion years ago, some bacteria evolved to consume carbon dioxide and excrete a highly toxic gas, oxygen. Other bacteria released nitrogen. The atmospheric concentration of these gases slowly increased. Organisms that could not adapt died out.

Meanwhile, the planet's land masses, floating on huge tectonic plates, eventually came together in a configuration that interfered with the circulation of ocean currents. It began to get cold for the first time. The first ice appeared two billion years ago.

And for the last seven hundred thousand years, our planet has been in a geological ice age, characterized by advancing and retreating glacial ice. No one is entirely sure why, but ice now covers the planet every hundred thousand years, with smaller advances every twenty thousand or so. The last advance was twenty thousand years ago, so we're due for the next one.

And even today, after five billion years, our planet remains amazingly active. We have five hundred volcanoes, and an eruption every two weeks. Earthquakes are continuous: a million and a half a year, a moderate Richter 5 quake every six hours, a big earthquake every ten days. Tsunamis race across the Pacific Ocean every three months.

Our atmosphere is as violent as the land beneath it. At any moment there are one thousand five hundred electrical storms across the planet. Eleven lightning bolts strike the ground each second. A tornado tears across the surface every six hours. And every four days, a giant cyclonic storm, hundreds of miles in diameter, spins over the ocean and wreaks havoc on the land.

The nasty little apes that call themselves human beings can do nothing except run and hide. For these same apes to imagine they can stabilize this atmosphere is arrogant beyond belief. They can't control the climate.

The reality is, they run from the storms.

"What do we do now?"

"I'll tell you what we do," Morton said. "You work for me. I'm starting a new environmental organization. I have to think of a name. I don't want one of these pretentious names with the words *world* and *resource* and *defense* and *wildlife* and *fund* and *preservation* and *wilderness* in them. You can string those words together in any combination. World Wildlife Preservation Fund. Wilderness Resource Defense Fund. Fund for the Defense of World Resources. Anyway, those fake names are all taken. I need something plain and new. Something honest. I was thinking of 'Study the Problem And Fix It.' Except the acronym doesn't work. But maybe that's a plus. We will have scientists and field researchers and economists and engineers—and one lawyer."

"What would this organization do?"

"There is so much to do! For example: Nobody knows how to manage wilderness. We would set aside a wide variety of wilderness tracts and run them under different management strategies. Then we'd ask outside teams to assess how we are doing, and modify the strategies. And then do it again. A true iterative process, externally assessed. Nobody's ever done that. And in the end we'll have a body of knowledge about how to manage different terrains. Not preserve them. You can't preserve them. They're going to change all the time, no matter what. But you could manage them—if you knew how to do it. Which nobody does. That's one big area. Management of complex environmental systems."

"Okay . . ."

"Then we'd do developing-world problems. The biggest cause of environmental destruction is poverty. Starving people can't worry about pollution. They worry about food. Half a billion people are starving in the world right now. More than half a billion without clean water. We need to design delivery systems that really work, test them, have them verified by outsiders, and once we know they work, replicate them."

"It sounds difficult."

"It's difficult if you are a government agency or an ideologue. But if you just want to study the problem and fix it, you can. And this would be entirely private. Private funding, private land. No bureaucrats. Administration is five percent of staff and resources. Everybody is out working. We'd run environmental research as a business. And cut the crap."

"Why hasn't somebody done it?"

"Are you kidding? Because it's radical. Face the facts, all these environmental organizations are thirty, forty, fifty years old. They have big buildings, big obligations, big staffs. They may trade on their youthful dreams, but the truth is, they're now part of the establishment. And the establishment works to preserve the status quo. It just does."

"Okay. What else?"

"Technology assessment. Third world countries can leapfrog. They skip telephone lines and go right to cellular. But nobody is doing decent technology assessment in terms of what works and how to balance the inevitable drawbacks. Wind power's great, unless you're a bird. Those things are giant bird guillotines. Maybe we should build them anyway. But people don't know how to think about this stuff. They just posture and pontificate. Nobody tests. Nobody does field research. Nobody dares to solve the problems—because the solution might contradict your philosophy, and for most people clinging to beliefs is more important than succeeding in the world."

"Really?"

"Trust me. When you're my age, you'll know it is true. Next, how about recreational land use— multipurpose land use. It's a rat's nest. Nobody has figured out how to do it, and it's so hot, so fierce that good people just give up and quit, or vanish in a blizzard of lawsuits. But that doesn't help. The answer probably lies in a range of solutions. It may be necessary to designate certain areas for one or another use. But everybody lives on the same planet. Some people like opera, some people like Vegas. And there's a lot of people that like Vegas."

"Anything else?"

"Yes. We need a new mechanism to fund research. Right now, scientists are in exactly the same position as Renaissance painters, commissioned to make the portrait the patron wants done. And if they are smart, they'll make sure their work subtly flatters the patron. Not overtly. Subtly. This is not a good system for research into those areas of science that affect policy. Even worse, the system works against problem solving. Because if you solve a problem, your funding ends. All that's got to change."

"How?"

"I have some ideas. Make scientists blind to their funding. Make assessment of research blind. We can have major policy-oriented research carried out by multiple teams doing the same work. Why not, if it's really important? We'll push to change how journals report research. Publish the article *and* the peer reviews in the same issue. That'll clean up everybody's act real fast. Get the journals out of politics. Their editors openly take sides on certain issues. Bad dogs."

Evans said, "Anything else?"

"New labels. If you read some authors who say, 'We find that anthropogenic greenhouse gases and sulphates have had a detectable influence on sea-level pressure' it sounds like they went into the world and measured something. Actually, they just ran a simulation. They talk as if simulations were real-world data. They're not. That's a problem that has to be fixed. I favor a stamp: WARNING: COMPUTER SIMULATION—MAY BE ERRONEOUS and UNVERIFIABLE. Like on cigarettes. Put the same stamp on newspaper articles, and in the corner of newscasts. WARNING: SPECULATION—MAY BE FACT-FREE. Can you see that peppered all over the front pages?"

"Anything else?" Evans was smiling now.

"There are a few more things," Morton said, "but those are the major points. It's going to be very difficult. It's going to be uphill all the way. We'll be opposed, sabotaged, denigrated. We'll be called terrible names. The establishment will not like it. Newspapers will sneer. But, eventually, money will start to flow to us because we'll show results. And then everybody will shut up. And then we will get lionized, which is the most dangerous time of all."

"And?"

"By then, I'm long dead. You and Sarah will have run the organization for twenty years. And your final job will be to disband it, before it becomes another tired old environmental organization spouting outmoded wisdom, wasting resources, and doing more harm than good."

"I see," Evans said. "And when it's disbanded?"

"You'll find a bright young person and try to excite him or her to do what really needs to be done in the next generation."

Evans looked at Sarah.

She shrugged. "Unless you have a better idea," she said.

Half an hour before they reached the California coast, they saw the spreading brown haze hanging over the ocean. It grew thicker and darker as they approached land. Soon they saw the lights of the city, stretching away for miles. It was blurred by the atmosphere above.

"It looks a bit like hell, doesn't it," Sarah said. "Hard to think we're going to land in that."

"We have a lot of work to do," Morton said.

The plane descended smoothly toward Los Angeles.

AUTHOR'S MESSAGE

A novel such as *State of Fear*, in which so many divergent views are expressed, may lead the reader to wonder where, exactly, the author stands on these issues. I have been reading environmental texts for three years, in itself a hazardous undertaking. But I have had an opportunity to look at a lot of data, and to consider many points of view. I conclude:

- We know astonishingly little about every aspect of the environment, from its past history, to its present state, to how to conserve and protect it. In every debate, all sides overstate the extent of existing knowledge and its degree of certainty.

- Atmospheric carbon dioxide is increasing, and human activity is the probable cause.

- We are also in the midst of a natural warming trend that began about 1850, as we emerged from a four-hundred-year cold spell known as the "Little Ice Age."

- Nobody knows how much of the present warming trend might be a natural phenomenon.

- Nobody knows how much of the present warming trend might be man-made.

- Nobody knows how much warming will occur in the next century. The computer models vary by 400 percent, de facto proof that nobody knows. But if I had to guess—the only thing anyone is doing, really—I would guess the increase will be 0.812436 degrees C. There is no evidence that my guess about the state of the world one hundred years from now is any better or worse than anyone else's. (We can't "assess" the future, nor can we "predict" it. These are euphemisms. We can only guess. An informed guess is just a guess.)

- I suspect that part of the observed surface warming will ultimately be attributable to human activity. I suspect that the principal human effect will come from land use, and that the atmospheric component will be minor.

- Before making expensive policy decisions on the basis of climate models, I think it is reasonable to require that those models predict future temperatures accurately for a period of ten years. Twenty would be better.

- I think for anyone to believe in impending resource scarcity, after two hundred years of such false alarms, is kind of weird. I don't know whether such a belief today is best ascribed to ignorance of history, sclerotic dogmatism, unhealthy love of Malthus, or simple pigheadedness, but it is evidently a hardy perennial in human calculation.

- There are many reasons to shift away from fossil fuels, and we will do so in the next century without legislation, financial incentives, carbon-conservation programs, or the interminable yammering of fearmongers. So far as I know, nobody had to ban horse transport in the early twentieth century.

- I suspect the people of 2100 will be much richer than we are, consume more energy, have a smaller global population, and enjoy more wilderness than we have today. I don't think we have to worry about them.

- The current near-hysterical preoccupation with safety is at best a waste of resources and a crimp on the human spirit, and at worst an invitation to totalitarianism. Public education is desperately needed.

- I conclude that most environmental "principles" (such as sustainable development or the precautionary principle) have the effect of preserving the economic advantages of the West and thus constitute modern imperialism toward the developing world. It is a nice way of saying, "We got ours and we don't want you to get yours, because you'll cause too much pollution."

- The "precautionary principle," properly applied, forbids the precautionary principle. It is self-contradictory. The precautionary principle therefore cannot be spoken of in terms that are too harsh.

- I believe people are well intentioned. But I have great respect for the corrosive influence of bias, systematic distortions of thought, the power of rationalization, the guises of self-interest, and the inevitability of unintended consequences.

- I have more respect for people who change their views after acquiring new information than for those who cling to views they held thirty years ago. The world changes. Ideologues and zealots don't.

- In the thirty-five-odd years since the environmental movement came into existence, science has undergone a major revolution. This revolution has brought new understanding of nonlinear dynamics, complex systems, chaos theory, catastrophe theory. It has transformed the way we think about evolution and ecology. Yet these no-longer-new ideas have hardly penetrated the thinking of environmental activists, which seems oddly fixed in the concepts and rhetoric of the 1970s.

- We haven't the foggiest notion how to preserve what we term "wilderness," and we had better study it in the field and learn how to do so. I see no evidence that we are conducting such research in a humble, rational, and systematic way. I therefore hold little hope for wilderness management in the twenty-first century. I blame environmental organizations every bit as much as developers and strip miners. There is no difference in outcomes between greed and incompetence.

- We need a new environmental movement, with new goals and new organizations. We need more people working in the field, in the actual environment, and fewer people behind computer screens. We need more scientists and many fewer lawyers.

- We cannot hope to manage a complex system such as the environment through litigation. We can only change its state temporarily—usually by preventing something—with eventual results that we cannot predict and ultimately cannot control.

- Nothing is more inherently political than our shared physical environment, and nothing is more ill served by allegiance to a single political party. Precisely because the environment is shared it cannot be managed by one faction according to its own economic or aesthetic preferences. Sooner or later, the opposing faction will take power, and previous policies will be reversed. Stable management of the environment requires recognition that all preferences have their place: snowmobilers and fly fishermen, dirt bikers and hikers, developers and preservationists. These preferences are at odds, and their incompatibility cannot be avoided. But resolving incompatible goals is a true function of politics.

- We desperately need a nonpartisan, blinded funding mechanism to conduct research to determine appropriate policy. Scientists are only too aware whom they are working for. Those who fund research—whether a drug company, a government agency, or an environmental organization—always have a particular outcome in mind. Research funding is almost never open-ended or open-minded. Scientists know that continued funding depends on delivering the results the funders desire. As a result, environmental organization "studies" are every bit as biased and suspect as industry "studies." Government "studies" are similarly biased according to who is running the department or administration at the time. No faction should be given a free pass.

- I am certain there is too much certainty in the world.

- I personally experience a profound pleasure being in nature. My happiest days each year are those I spend in wilderness. I wish natural environments to be preserved for future generations. I am not satisfied they will be preserved in sufficient quantities, or with sufficient skill. I conclude that the "exploiters of the environment" include environmental organizations, government organizations, and big business. All have equally dismal track records.

- Everybody has an agenda. Except me.

APPENDIX I
Why Politicized Science Is Dangerous

Imagine that there is a new scientific theory that warns of an impending crisis, and points to a way out.

This theory quickly draws support from leading scientists, politicians, and celebrities around the world. Research is funded by distinguished philanthropies, and carried out at prestigious universities. The crisis is reported frequently in the media. The science is taught in college and high school classrooms.

I don't mean global warming. I'm talking about another theory, which rose to prominence a century ago.

Its supporters included Theodore Roosevelt, Woodrow Wilson, and Winston Churchill. It was approved by Supreme Court justices Oliver Wendell Holmes and Louis Brandeis, who ruled in its favor. The famous names who supported it included Alexander Graham Bell, inventor of the telephone; activist Margaret Sanger; botanist Luther Burbank; Leland Stanford, founder of Stanford University; the novelist H. G. Wells; the playwright George Bernard Shaw; and hundreds of others. Nobel Prize winners gave support.

Research was backed by the Carnegie and Rocke-feller Foundations. The Cold Springs Harbor Institute was built to carry out this research, but important work was also done at Harvard, Yale, Princeton, Stanford, and Johns Hopkins. Legislation to address the crisis was passed in states from New York to California.

These efforts had the support of the National Academy of Sciences, the American Medical Association, and the National Research Council. It was said that if Jesus were alive, he would have supported this effort.

All in all, the research, legislation, and molding of public opinion surrounding the theory went on for almost half a century. Those who opposed the theory were shouted down and called reactionary, blind to reality, or just plain ignorant. But in hindsight, what is surprising is that so few people objected.

Today, we know that this famous theory that gained so much support was actually pseudoscience. The crisis it claimed was nonexistent. And the actions taken in the name of this theory were morally and criminally wrong. Ultimately, they led to the deaths of millions of people.

The theory was eugenics, and its history is so dreadful—and, to those who were caught up in it, so embarrassing—that it is now rarely discussed. But it is a story that should be well known to every citizen, so that its horrors are not repeated.

The theory of eugenics postulated a crisis of the gene pool leading to the deterioration of the human race. The best human beings were not breeding as rapidly as the inferior ones—the foreigners, immigrants, Jews, degenerates, the unfit, and the "feeble minded." Francis Galton, a respected British scientist, first speculated about this area, but his ideas were taken far beyond anything he intended. They were adopted by science-minded Americans, as well as those who had no interest in science but who were worried about the immigration of inferior races early in the twentieth century—"dangerous human pests" who represented "the rising tide of imbeciles" and who were polluting the best of the human race.

The eugenicists and the immigrationists joined forces to put a stop to this. The plan was to identify individuals who were feeble-minded—Jews were agreed to be largely feeble-minded, but so were many foreigners, as well as blacks—and stop them from breeding by isolation in institutions or by sterilization.

As Margaret Sanger said, "Fostering the good-for-nothing at the expense of the good is an extreme cruelty ... there is no greater curse to posterity than that of bequeathing them an increasing population of imbeciles." She spoke of the burden of caring for "this dead weight of human waste."

Such views were widely shared. H. G. Wells spoke against "ill-trained swarms of inferior citizens." Theodore Roosevelt said that "Society has no business to permit degenerates to reproduce their kind." Luther Burbank: "Stop permitting criminals and weaklings to reproduce." George Bernard Shaw said that only eugenics could save mankind.

There was overt racism in this movement, exemplified by texts such as *The Rising Tide of Color Against White World Supremacy*, by American author Lothrop Stoddard. But, at the time, racism was considered an unremarkable aspect of the effort to attain a marvelous goal—the improvement of humankind in the future. It was this avant-garde notion that attracted the most liberal and progressive minds of a generation. California was one of twenty-nine American states to pass laws allowing sterilization, but it proved the most forward-looking and enthusiastic—more sterilizations were carried out in California than anywhere else in America.

Eugenics research was funded by the Carnegie Foundation, and later by the Rockefeller Foundation. The latter was so enthusiastic that even after the center of the eugenics effort moved to Germany, and involved the gassing of individuals from mental institutions, the Rockefeller Foundation continued to finance German researchers at a very high level. (The foundation was quiet about it, but they were still funding research in 1939, only months before the onset of World War II.)

Since the 1920s, American eugenicists had been jealous because the Germans had taken leadership of the movement away from them. The Germans were admirably progressive. They set up ordinary-looking houses where "mental defectives" were brought and interviewed one at a time, before being led into a back room, which was, in fact, a gas chamber. There, they were gassed with carbon monoxide, and their bodies disposed of in a crematorium located on the property.

Eventually, this program was expanded into a vast network of concentration camps located near railroad lines, enabling the efficient transport and killing of ten million undesirables.

After World War II, nobody was a eugenicist, and nobody had ever been a eugenicist. Biographers of the celebrated and the powerful did not dwell on the attractions of this philosophy to their subjects, and sometimes did not mention it at all. Eugenics ceased to be a subject for college classrooms, although some argue that its ideas continue to have currency in disguised form.

But in retrospect, three points stand out. First, despite the construction of Cold Springs Harbor Laboratory, despite the efforts at universities and the pleadings of lawyers, there was no scientific basis for eugenics. In fact, nobody at that time knew what a gene really was. The movement was able to proceed because it employed vague terms never rigorously defined. "Feeble-mindedness" could mean anything from poverty and illiteracy to epilepsy. Similarly, there was no clear definition of "degenerate" or "unfit."

Second, the eugenics movement was really a social program masquerading as a scientific one. What drove it was concern about immigration and racism and undesirable people moving into one's neighborhood or country. Once again, vague terminology helped conceal what was really going on.

Third, and most distressing, the scientific establishment in both the United States and Germany did not mount any sustained protest. Quite the contrary. In Germany scientists quickly fell into line with the program. Modern German researchers have gone back to review Nazi documents from the 1930s. They expected to find directives telling scientists what research should be done. But none were necessary. In the words of Ute Deichman, "Scientists, including those who were not members of the [Nazi] party, helped to get funding for their work through their modified behavior and direct cooperation with the state." Deichman speaks of the "active role of scientists themselves in regard to Nazi race policy . . . where [research] was aimed at confirming the racial doctrine . . . no external pressure can be documented." German scientists adjusted their research interests to the new policies. And those few who did not adjust disappeared.

A second example of politicized science is quite different in character, but it exemplifies the hazards of government ideology controlling the work of science, and of uncritical media promoting false concepts. Trofim Denisovich Lysenko was a self-promoting peasant who, it was said, "solved the problem of fertilizing the fields without fertilizers and minerals." In 1928 he claimed to have invented a procedure called vernalization, by which seeds were moistened and chilled to enhance the later growth of crops.

Lysenko's methods never faced a rigorous test, but his claim that his treated seeds passed on their characteristics to the next generation represented a revival of Lamarckian ideas at a time when the rest of the world was embracing Mendelian genetics. Josef Stalin was drawn to Lamarckian ideas, which implied a future unbounded by hereditary constraints; he also wanted improved agricultural production. Lysenko promised both, and became the darling of a Soviet media that was on the lookout for stories about clever peasants who had developed revolutionary procedures.

Lysenko was portrayed as a genius, and he milked his celebrity for all it was worth. He was especially skillful at denouncing his opponents. He used questionnaires from farmers to prove that vernalization increased crop yields, and thus avoided any direct tests. Carried on a wave of state-sponsored enthusiasm, his rise was rapid. By 1937, he was a member of the Supreme Soviet.

By then, Lysenko and his theories dominated Russian biology. The result was famines that killed millions, and purges that sent hundreds of dissenting Soviet scientists to the gulags or the firing squads. Lysenko was aggressive in attacking genetics, which was finally banned as "bourgeois pseudo-science" in 1948. There was never any basis for Lysenko's ideas, yet he controlled Soviet research for thirty years. Lysenkoism ended in the 1960s, but Russian biology still has not entirely recovered from that era.

Now we are engaged in a great new theory, that once again has drawn the support of politicians, scientists, and celebrities around the world. Once again, the theory is promoted by major foundations. Once again, the research is carried out at prestigious universities. Once again, legislation is passed and social programs are urged in its name. Once again, critics are few and harshly dealt with.

Once again, the measures being urged have little basis in fact or science. Once again, groups with other agendas are hiding behind a movement that appears high-minded. Once again, claims of moral superiority are used to justify extreme actions. Once again, the fact that some people are hurt is shrugged off because an abstract cause is said to be greater than any human consequences. Once again, vague terms like *sustainability* and *generational justice*—terms that have no agreed definition—are employed in the service of a new crisis.

I am not arguing that global warming is the same as eugenics. But the similarities are not superficial. And I do claim that open and frank discussion of the data, and of the issues, is being suppressed. Leading scientific journals have taken strong editorial positions on the side of global warming, which, I argue, they have no business doing. Under the circumstances, any scientist who has doubts understands clearly that they will be wise to mute their expression.

One proof of this suppression is the fact that so many of the outspoken critics of global warming are retired professors. These individuals are no longer seeking grants, and no longer have to face colleagues whose grant applications and career advancement may be jeopardized by their criticisms.

In science, the old men are usually wrong. But in politics, the old men are wise, counsel caution, and in the end are often right.

The past history of human belief is a cautionary tale. We have killed thousands of our fellow human beings because we believed they had signed a contract with the devil, and had become witches. We still kill more than a thousand people each year for witchcraft. In my view, there is only one hope for humankind to emerge from what Carl Sagan called "the demon-haunted world" of our past. That hope is science.

But as Alston Chase put it, "when the search for truth is confused with political advocacy, the pursuit of knowledge is reduced to the quest for power."

That is the danger we now face. And that is why the intermixing of science and politics is a bad combination, with a bad history. We must remember the history, and be certain that what we present to the world as knowledge is disinterested and honest.

APPENDIX II
Sources of Data for Graphs

World temperature data has been taken from the Goddard Institute for Space Studies, Columbia University, New York (GISS); the Jones, et al. data set from the Climate Research Unit, University of East Anglia, Norwich, UK (CRU); and the Global Historical Climatology Network (GHCN) maintained by the National Climatic Data Center (NCDC) and the Carbon Dioxide Information and Analysis Center (CDIAC) of Oak Ridge National Laboratory, Oak Ridge, Tennessee.

The GISS station page is not easy to find from their home page, but it is found at http://www.giss.nasa.gov/data/update/gistemp/station data/. **Note: Shortly after the hardcover publication of this book, GISS changed its website to show less data. The station data no longer goes back before 1880, and thus heightens the appearance of a steady rise in temperature.**

The Jones data set reference is P. D. Jones, D. E. Parker, T. J. Osborn, and K. R. Briffa, 1999. Global and hemispheric temperature anomolies—land

and marine instrument records. In *Trends: A Compendium of Data on Global Change.* Carbon Dioxide Information Analysis Center, Oak Ridge National Laboratory, US Department of Energy, Oak Ridge, Tennessee.

Global Historical Climatology Network is maintained at NCDC and CDIAC of Oak Ridge National Laboratory. The home page is http://cdiac.esd.ornl.gov/ghcn/ghcn.html.

Temperature data for the United States comes from the United States Historical Climatology Network (USHCN) maintained at NCDC and CDIAC of Oak Ridge National Laboratory, which states: "We recommend using USHCN whenever possible for long-term climate analyses. . . ."

The USHCN home page is http://www.ncdc.noaa.gov/oa/climate/research/ushcn/ushcn.html.

The reference is D. R. Easterling, T. R. Karl, E. H. Mason, P. Y. Hughes, D. P. Bowman, R. C. Daniels, and T. A. Boden (eds.). 1996. *United States Historical Climatology Network (US HCN) Monthly Temperature and Precipitation Data.* ORNL/CDIAC-87, NDP-019/R3. Carbon Dioxide Information Analysis Center, Oak Ridge National Laboratory, Oak Ridge, Tennessee.

Graphs are generated in Microsoft Excel from tabular data provided on the websites.

The satellite images are from NASA (http://datasystem.earthkam.ucsd.edu). The rendering of the globe image on the part-opener pages is adapted from NASA (http://earthobservatory.nasa.gov/Observatory/Datasets/tsurf.tovs.html).

BIBLIOGRAPHY

What follows is a list of books and journal articles I found most useful in preparing this novel. I found the texts by Beckerman, Chase, Huber, Lomborg, and Wildavsky to be particularly revealing.

Environmental science is a contentious and intensely politicized field. No reader should assume that any author listed below agrees with the views I express in this book. Quite the contrary: many of them disagree strongly. I am presenting these references to assist those readers who would like to review my thinking and arrive at their own conclusions.

Aber, John D., and Jerry M. Melillo. *Terrestrial Ecosystems*. San Francisco: Harcourt Academic Press, 2001. A standard textbook.

Abrupt Climate Change: Inevitable Surprises (Report of the Committee on Abrupt Climate Change, National Research Council). Washington, DC: National Academy Press, 2002. The text concludes that abrupt climate change might occur sometime in the future, triggered by mechanisms not yet understood, and that in the meantime more research is needed. Surely no one could object.

Adam, Barbara, Ulrich Beck, and Jost Van Loon. *The Risk Society and Beyond.* London: Sage Publications, 2000.

Altheide, David L. *Creating Fear, News and the Construction of Crisis.* New York: Aldine de Gruyter, 2002. A book about fear and its expanding place in public life. Overlong and repetitive, but addressing a highly significant subject. Some of the statistical analyses are quite amazing.

Anderson, J. B. and J. T. Andrews. "Radiocarbon Constraints on Ice Sheet Advance and Retreat in the Weddell Sea, Antarctica." *Geology* 27 (1999): 179–82.

Anderson, Terry L., and Donald R. Leal. *Free Market Environmentalism.* New York: Palgrave (St. Martin's Press), 2001. The authors argue government management of environmental resources has a poor track record in the former Soviet Union, and in the Western democracies as well. They make the case for the superiority of private and market-based management of environmental resources. Their case histories are particularly interesting.

Arens, William. *The Man-Eating Myth.* New York: Oxford, 1979.

Arquilla, John, and David Ronfeldt, eds. *In Athena's Camp: Preparing for Conflict in the Information Age.* Santa Monica, Calif.: RAND National Defense Research Institute, 1997. See particularly part III on the advent of netwar and its implications.

Aunger, Robert, ed. *Darwinizing Culture*. New York: Oxford University Press, 2000. See especially the last three chapters, which devastate the trendy concept of memes. There is no better example of the way that trendy quasi-scientific ideas can gain currency even in the face of preexisting evidence that they are baseless. And the text serves as a model for the expression of brisk disagreement without ad hominem characterization.

Beck, Ulrich. *Risk Society: Towards a New Modernity*. Trans. Mark Ritter. London: Sage, 1992. This highly influential text by a German sociologist presents a fascinating redefinition of the modern state as protector against industrial society, instead of merely the ground upon which it is built.

Beckerman, Wilfred. *A Poverty of Reason: Sustainable Development and Economic Growth*. Oakland, Calif.: Independent Institute, 2003. A short, witty, stinging review of sustainability, climate change, and the precautionary principle by an Oxford economist and former member of the Royal Commission on Environmental Pollution who cares more about the poor of the world than he does the elitist egos of Western environmentalists. Clearly argued and fun to read.

Bennett, W. Lance. *News: The Politics of Illusion*. New York: Addison-Wesley, 2003.

Black, Edwin. *War Against the Weak: Eugenics and America's Campaign to Create a Master Race*. New York: Four Walls, 2003. The history of the eugenics movement in America and Germany is an unpleasant story, and perhaps for that reason, most texts present it confusingly. This book is an admirably clear narrative.

Bohm, R. "Urban bias in temperature time series—a case study for the city of Vienna, Austria." *Climatic Change* 38 (1998): 113–28.

Braithwaite, Roger J. "Glacier mass balance: The first 50 years of international monitoring." *Progress in Physical Geography* 26, no. 1 (2002): 76–95.

Braithwaite, R. J., and Y. Zhang. "Relationships between interannual variability of glacier mass balance and climate." *Journal of Glaciology* 45 (2000): 456–62.

Briggs, Robin. *Witches and Neighbors: The Social and Cultural Context of European Witchcraft*. New York: HarperCollins, 1996.

Brint, Steven. "Professionals and the Knowledge Economy: Rethinking the Theory of the Postindustrial Society." *Current Sociology* 49, no. 1 (July 2001): 101–32.

Brower, Michael, and Warren Leon. *The Consumer's Guide to Effective Environmental Choices: Practical Advice from the Union of Concerned Scientists*. New York: Three Rivers Press, 1999. Of particular interest for its advice on mundane decisions: paper vs. plastic shopping bags (plastic), cloth vs. disposable diapers (disposable). On broader issues, the analysis is extremely vague and exemplifies the difficulties of determining "sustainable development" that are pointed out by Wilfred Beckerman.

Carson, Rachel. *Silent Spring*. Boston: Houghton Mifflin, 1962. I am old enough to remember reading this poetic persuasive text with alarm and excitement when it was first published; it was clear even then that it would change the world. With the passage of time Carson's text appears more flawed and more overtly polemical. It is, to be blunt, about one-third right and two-thirds wrong. Carson is particularly to be faulted for her specious promotion of the idea that most cancer is caused by the environment. This fear remains in general circulation decades later.

Castle, Terry. "Contagious Folly." In Chandler, Davidson, and Harootunian, *Questions of Evidence.*

Chandler, James, Arnold I. Davidson, and Harry Harootunian. *Questions of Evidence: Proof, Practice and Persuasion Across the Disciplines.* Chicago: University of Chicago Press, 1993.

Changnon, Stanley A. "Impacts of 1997–98 El Niño-Generated Weather in the United States." *Bulletin of the American Meteorological Society* 80, no. 9, (1999): 1819–28.

Chapin, F. Stuart, Pamela A. Matson, and Harold A. Mooney. *Principles of Terrestrial Ecosystems Ecology.* New York: Springer-Verlag, 2002. Clearer and with more technical detail than most ecology texts.

Chase, Alston. *In a Dark Wood: The Fight over Forests and the Myths of Nature.* New Brunswick, N.J.: Transaction Publishers, 2001. Essential reading. This book is a history of the conflict over the forests of the Northwest, a cheerless and distressing story. As a former professor of philosophy, the author is one of the few writers in the environmental field who shows the slightest interest in ideas—where they come from, what consequences have flowed from them in the historical past, and therefore what consequences are likely to flow from them now. Chase discusses such notions as the mystic vision of wilderness and the balance of nature from the standpoint of both science and philosophy. He is contemptuous of much conventional wisdom and the muddle-headed attitudes he calls "California cosmology." The book is long and sometimes rambling, but extremely rewarding.

———. *Playing God in Yellowstone: The Destruction of America's First National Park*. New York: Atlantic, 1986. Essential reading. Arguably the first and clearest critique of ever-changing environmental beliefs and their practical consequences. Anyone who assumes we know how to manage wilderness areas needs to read this sobering history of the century-long mismanagement of Yellowstone, the first national park. Chase's text has been reviled in some quarters, but to my knowledge, never seriously disputed.

Chen, L., W. Zhu, X. Zhou, and Z. Zhou, "Characteristics of the heat island effect in Shanghai and its possible mechanism." *Advances in Atmospheric Sciences* 20 (2003): 991-1001.

Choi, Y., H.-S. Jung, K.-Y. Nam, and W.-T. Kwon, "Adjusting urban bias in the regional mean surface temperature series of South Korea, 1968–99." *International Journal of Climatology* 23 (2003): 577–91.

Christianson, Gale E. *Greenhouse: The 200-Year Story of Global Warming*. New York: Penguin, 1999.

Chylek, P., J. E. Box, and G. Lesins. "Global Warming and the Greenland Ice Sheet." *Climatic Change* 63 (2004): 201–21.

Comiso, J. C. "Variability and Trends in Antarctic Surface Temperatures From *in situ* and Satellite Infrared Measurements." *Journal of Climate* 13 (2000): 1674–96.

Cook, Timothy E. *Governing with the News: The News Media as a Political Institution*. Chicago: University of Chicago Press, 1998.

Cooke, Roger M. *Experts in Uncertainty*. New York: Oxford University Press, 1991.

Davis, Ray Jay, and Lewis Grant. *Weather Modification Technology and Law*. AAAS Selected Symposium. Boulder, Col.: Westview Press, Inc., 1978. Of historical interest only.

Deichmann, Ute. *Biologist Under Hitler*, tr. Thomas Dunlap. Cambridge, Mass.: Harvard University Press, 1996. Difficult in structure, disturbing in content.

Doran, P. T., J. C. Priscu, W. B. Lyons, J. E. Walsh, A. G. Fountain, D. M. McKnight, D. L. Moorhead, R. A. Virginia, D. H. Wall, G. D. Clow, C. H. Fritsen, C. P. McKay, and A. N. Parsons. "Antarctic Climate Cooling and Terrestrial Ecosystem Response." *Nature* 415 (2002): 517–20.

Dörner, Dietrich. *The Logic of Failure: Recognizing and Avoiding Error in Complex Situations*. Cambridge, Mass.: Perseus, 1998. What prevents human beings from successfully managing the natural environment and other complex systems? Dozens of pundits have weighed in with their unsubstantiated opinions. Dörner, a cognitive psychologist, performed experiments and found out. Using computer simulations of complex environments, he invited intellectuals to improve the situation. They often made it worse. Those who did well gathered information before acting, thought systemically, reviewed progress, and corrected their course often. Those who did badly clung to their theories, acted too quickly, did not correct course, and blamed others when things went wrong. Dörner concludes that our failures in managing complex systems do not represent any inherent lack of human capability. Rather they reflect bad habits of thought and lazy procedures.

Dowie, Mark. *Losing Ground: American Environmentalism at the Close of the Twentieth Century.* Cambridge, Mass.: MIT Press, 1995. A former editor of *Mother Jones* concludes that the American environmental movement has lost relevance through compromise and capitulation. Well written, but weakly documented, the book is most interesting for the frame of mind it conveys—an uncompromising posture that rarely specifies what solutions would be satisfactory. This makes the text essentially nonscientific in its outlook and its implications, and all the more interesting for that.

Drake, Frances. *Global Warming: The Science of Climate Change.* New York: Oxford University Press, 2000. This well-written overview for college students can be read by any interested reader.

Drucker, Peter. *Post-Capitalist Society.* New York: Harper Business, 1993.

Eagleton, Terry. *Ideology: An Introduction.* New York: Verso, 1991.

Edgerton, Robert B. *Sick Societies: Challenging the Myth of Primitive Harmony.* New York: Free Press, 1992. An excellent summary of the evidence disputing the notion of the noble savage that goes on to consider whether cultures adopt maladaptive beliefs and practices. The author concludes that all cultures do so. The text also attacks the currently trendy academic notion of "unconscious" problem-solving, in which primitive cultures are assumed to be acting in an ecologically sound fashion, even when they appear wasteful and destructive. Edgerton argues they aren't doing anything of the sort—they *are* wasteful and destructive.

Edwards, Paul N., and Stephen Schneider. "The 1995 IPCC Report: Broad Consensus or 'Scientific Cleansing'?" *EcoFable/Ecoscience* 1, no. 1 (1997): 3–9. A spirited argument in defense of changes to the 1995 IPCC report by Ben Santer. However, the article focuses on the controversy that resulted and does not review in detail the changes to the text that were made. Thus the paper talks about the controversy without examining its substance.

Einarsson, Porleifur. *Geology of Iceland.* Trans. Georg Douglas. Reykjavík: Mal og menning, 1999. Surely one of the clearest geology textbooks ever written. The author is professor of geology at the University of Iceland.

Etheridge, D. M., et al. "Natural and anthropogenic

changes in atmospheric CO_2 over the last 1000 years from air in Antarctic ice and firn." *Journal of Geophysical Research* 101 (1996): 4115–28.

Fagan, Brian. *The Little Ice Age: How Climate Made History 1300–1850*. New York: Basic Books, 2000. Our experience of climate is limited to the span of our lives. The degree to which climate has varied in the past, and even in historical times, is hard for anyone to conceive. This book, by an archaeologist who writes extremely well, makes clear through historical detail how much warmer—and colder—it has been during the last thousand years.

Feynman, Richard. *The Character of Physical Law*. Cambridge, Mass.: MIT Press, 1965. Feynman exemplifies the crispness of thought in physics as compared with the mushy subjectivity of fields such as ecology or climate research.

Finlayson-Pitts, Barbara J., and James N. Pitts, Jr. *Chemistry of the Upper and Lower Atmosphere: Theory, Experiments, and Applications*. New York: Academic Press, 2000. A clear text that can be read by anyone with a good general science background.

Fisher, Andy. *Radical Ecopsychology: Psychology in the Service of Life*. Albany, N.Y.: State University of New York Press, 2002. An astonishing text by a psychotherapist. In my opinion, the greatest problem for all observers of the world is to determine whether their perceptions are genuine and verifiable or whether they are merely the projections of inner feelings. This book says it doesn't matter. The text consists almost entirely of unsubstantiated opinions about human nature and our interaction with the natural world. Anecdotal, egotistical, and wholly tautological, it is a dazzling example of unbridled fantasy. It can stand in for a whole literature of related texts in which feeling-expression masquerades as fact.

Flecker, H., and B. C. Cotton. "Fatal bite from octopus." *Medical Journal of Australia* 2 (1955): 329–31.

Forrester, Jay W. *Principles of Systems.* Waltham, Mass.: Wright-Allen Press, 1971. Some day Forrester will be acknowledged as one of the most important scientists of the twentieth century. He is one of the first, and surely the most influential, researcher to model complex systems on the computer. He did groundbreaking studies of everything from high-tech corporate behavior to urban renewal, and he was the first to get any inkling of how difficult it is to manage complex systems. His work was an early inspiration for the attempts to model the world that ultimately became the Club of Rome's *Limits of Growth.* But the Club didn't understand the most fundamental principles behind Forrester's work.

Forsyth, Tim. *Critical Political Ecology: The Politics of Environmental Science.* New York: Routledge, 2003. A careful but often critical examination of environmental orthodoxy by a lecturer in environment and development at the London School of Economics. The text contains many important insights I have not seen elsewhere, including the consequences of the IPCC emphasis on computer models (as opposed to other forms of data) and the question of how many environmental effects are usefully regarded as "global." However, the author adopts much of the postmodernist critique of science, and thus refers to certain "laws" of science, when few scientists would grant them such status.

Freeze, R. Allan. *The Environmental Pendulum: A Quest for the Truth about Toxic Chemicals, Human Health, and Environmental Protection.* Berkeley, Calif.: University of California Press, 2000. A university professor with on-the-ground experience dealing with toxic waste sites has written a cranky and highly informative book detailing his experiences and views. One of the few books by a person who is not only academically qualified but experienced in the field. His opinions are complex and sometimes seemingly contradictory. But that's reality.

Furedi, Frank. *Culture of Fear: Risk-taking and the Morality of Low Expectation.* New York: Continuum, 2002. As Western societies become more affluent and safer, as life expectancy has steadily increased, one might expect the populations to become relaxed and secure. The opposite has happened: Western societies have become panic-stricken and hysterically risk averse. The pattern is evident in everything from environmental issues to the vastly increased supervision of children. This text by a British sociologist discusses why.

Gelbspan, Ross. *The Heat Is On: The Climate Crisis, the Cover-Up, the Prescription.* Cambridge, Mass.: Perseus, 1998. A reporter who has written extensively on environmental matters presents the classic doomsday scenarios well. Penn and Teller characterize him in scatological terms.

Gilovitch, Thomas, Dale Griffin, and Daniel Kahneman, eds. *Heuristics and Biases: The Psychology of Intuitive Judgment.* Cambridge, UK: Cambridge University Press, 2002. Psychologists have created a substantial body of experimental data on human decision making since the 1950s. It has been well replicated and makes essential reading for anyone who wants to understand how people make decisions and how they think about the decisions that others make. The entire volume is compelling (though sometimes disheartening), and articles of particular interest are listed separately.

Glassner, Barry. *The Culture of Fear.* New York: Basic Books, 1999. Debunks fearmongering with precision and calmness.

Glimcher, Paul W. *Decisions, Uncertainty, and the Brain.* Cambridge, Mass.: MIT Press, 2003.

Glynn, Kevin. *Tabloid Culture.* Durham, N.C.: Duke University Press, 2000.

Goldstein, William M., and Robin M. Hogarth, eds. *Research on Judgment and Decision Making.* Cambridge, UK: Cambridge University Press, 1997.

Gross, Paul R., and Norman Leavitt. *Higher Superstition: The Academic Left and Its Quarrels with Science.* Baltimore: Johns Hopkins University Press, 1994. See chapter 6, "The Gates of Eden" for a discussion of environmentalism in the context of current postmodern academic criticism.

Guyton, Bill. *Glaciers of California*. Berkeley, Calif.: University of California Press, 1998. An elegant gem of a book.

Hadley Center. "Climate Change, Observations and Predictions, Recent Research on Climate Change Science from the Hadley Center," December 2003. Obtainable at *www.metoffice.com*. In sixteen pages the Hadley Center presents the most important arguments relating to climate science and the predictions for future warming from computer models. Beautifully written, and illustrated with graphic sophistication, it easily surpasses other climate science websites and constitutes the best brief introduction for the interested reader.

Hansen, James E., Makiko Sato, Andrew Lacis, Reto Ruedy, Ina Tegen, and Elaine Matthews. "Climate Forcings in the Industrial Era." *Proceedings of the National Academy of Sciences* 95 (October 1998): 12753–58.

Hansen, James E. and Makiko Sato, "Trends of Measured Climate Forcing Agents." *Proceedings of the National Academy of Sciences* 98 (December 2001): 14778–83.

Hayes, Wayland Jackson. "Pesticides and Human Toxicity." *Annals of the New York Academy of Sciences* 160 (1969): 40–54.

Henderson-Sellers, et al. "Tropical cyclones and global climate change: A post-IPCC assessment." *Bulletin of the American Meteorological Society* 79 (1997): 9–38.

Hoffert, Martin, Ken Caldeira, Gregory Benford, David R. Criswell, Christopher Green, Howard Herzog, Atul K. Jain, Haroon S. Kheshgi, Klaus

S. Lackner, John S. Lewis, H. Douglas Light-foot, Wallace Manheimer, John C. Mankins, Michael E. Mauel, L. John Perkins, Michael E. Schlesinger, Tyler Volk, and Tom M. L. Wigley. "Advanced Technology Paths to Global Climate Stability: Energy for a Greenhouse Planet." *Science* 298 (1 November 2001): 981–87.

Horowitz, Daniel. *The Anxieties of Affluence.* Amherst, Mass.: University of Massachusetts Press, 2004.

Houghton, John. *Global Warming, the Complete Briefing.* Cambridge, UK: Cambridge University Press, 1997. Sir John is a leading figure in the IPCC and a world-renowned spokesperson for climate change. He presents a clear statement of the predictions of the global circulation models for future climate. He draws principally from IPCC reports, which this text summarizes and explains. Skip the first chapter, which is scattered and vague, unlike the rest of the book.

Huber, Peter, *Hard Green: Saving the Environment from the Environmentalists, a Conservative Manifesto.* New York: Basic Books, 1999. I read dozens of books on the environment, most quite similar in tone and content. This was the first one that made me sit up and pay serious attention. It's not like the others, to put it mildly. Huber holds an engineering degree from MIT and a law degree from Harvard; he has clerked for Ruth Bader Ginsburg and Sandra Day O'Connor; he is a fellow at the conservative Manhattan Institute. His book criticizes modern environmental thought in both its underlying attitudes and its scientific claims. The text is quick, funny, informed, and relentless. It can be difficult to follow and demands an informed reader. But anyone who clings to the environmental views that evolved in the 1980s and 1990s must answer the arguments of this book.

Inadvertent Climate Modification, Report of the Study of Man's Impact on Climate (SMIC). Cambridge, Mass.: MIT Press, 1971. A fascinating early attempt to model climate and predict human interaction with it.

IPCC. *Aviation and the Global Atmosphere.* Intergovernmental Panel on Climate Change. Cambridge, UK: Cambridge University Press, 1999.

———. *Climate Change 1992: The Supplementary Report to the IPCC Scientific Assessment.* Intergovernmental Panel of Climate Change. Cambridge, UK: Cambridge University Press, 1992.

———. *Climate Change 1995: Economic and Social Dimensions of Climate Change.* Intergovernmental Panel of Climate Change. Cambridge, UK: Cambridge University Press, 1996.

———. *Climate Change 1995: Impacts, Adaptation and Mitigation of Climate Change Scientific/Technical Analysis.* Contribution of Working Group II to the Second Assessment Report of the IPCC. Intergovernmental Panel of Climate Change. Cambridge, UK: Cambridge University Press, 1996.

———. *Climate Change 1995: The Science of Climate Change.* Intergovernmental Panel of Climate Change. Cambridge, UK: Cambridge University Press, 1996.

———. *Climate Change 2001: Impacts, Adaptation, and Vulnerability.* Intergovernmental Panel of Climate Change. Cambridge, UK: Cambridge University Press, 2001.

———. *Climate Change 2001: Synthesis Report.* Intergovernmental Panel of Climate Change. Cambridge, UK: Cambridge University Press, 2001.

———. *Climate Change 2001: The Scientific Basis.* Cambridge, UK: Cambridge University Press, 2001.

———. *Climate Change: The IPCC Response Strategies.* Intergovernmental Panel of Climate Change. Washington, DC: Island Press, 1991.

———. *Emissions Scenarios.* Intergovernmental Panel of Climate Change. Cambridge, UK: Cambridge University Press, 2000.

———. *Land Use, Land-Use Change, and Forestry.* Intergovernmental Panel of Climate Change. Cambridge, UK: Cambridge University Press, 2000.

———. *The Regional Impacts of Climate Change: An Assessment of Vulnerability.* Intergovernmental Panel on Climate Change. Cambridge, UK: Cambridge University Press, 1998.

Jacob, Daniel J. *Introduction to Atmospheric Chemistry.* Princeton, N.J.: Princeton University Press, 1999.

Joravsky, David. *The Lysenko Affair.* Chicago: University of Chicago Press, 1970. A readable account of this depressing episode.

Joughin, I., and S. Tulaczyk. "Positive Mass Balance of the Ross Ice Streams, West Antarctica." *Science* 295 (2002): 476–80.

Kahneman, Daniel, and Amos Tversky, eds. *Choices, Values and Frames*. Cambridge, UK: Cambridge University Press, 2000. The authors are responsible for a revolution in our understanding of the psychology behind human decision-making. The history of the environmental movement is characterized by some very positive decisions made on the basis of inadequate information, and some unfortunate decisions made despite good information that argued against the decision. This book sheds light on how such things happen.

Kalnay, Eugenia, and Ming Cai. "Impact of Urbanization and Land-Use on Climate." *Nature* 423 (29 May 2003): 528–31. "Our estimate of .27 C mean surface warming per century due to land use changes is at least twice as high as previous estimates based on urbanization alone." The authors later report a calculation error, raising their estimate [*Nature* 23 (4 September 2003): 102]. "The corrected estimate of the trend in daily mean temperature due to land use changes is .35 C per century."

Kaser, Georg, Douglas R. Hardy, Thomas Molg, Raymond S. Bradley, and Tharsis M. Hyera. "Modern Glacier Retreat on Kilimanjaro as Evidence of Climate Change: Observations and Facts." *International Journal of Climatology* 24 (2004): 329–39.

Kieffer, H., J. S. Kargel, R. Barry, R. Bindschadler, M. Bishop, D. MacKinnon, A. Ohmura, B. Raup, M. Antoninetti, J. Bamber, M. Braun, I. Brown, D. Cohen, L. Copland, J. DueHagen, R. V. Engeset, B. Fitzharris, K. Fujita, W. Haeberli,

J. O. Hagen, D. Hall, M. Hoelzle, M. Johansson, A. Kaab, M. Koenig, V. Konovalov, M. Maisch, F. Paul, F. Rau, N. Reeh, E. Rignot, A. Rivera, M. Ruyter de Wildt, T. Scambos, J. Schaper, G. Scharfen, J. Shroder, O. Solomina, D. Thompson, K. Van der Veen, T. Wohlleben, and N. Young. "New eyes in the sky measure glaciers and ice sheets." *EOS, Transactions, American Geophysical Union* 81, no. 265 (2000): 270–71.

Kline, Wendy. *Building a Better Race: Gender, Sexuality and Eugenics from the Turn of the Century to the Baby Boom.* Berkeley, Calif.: University of California Press, 2001.

Koshland, Daniel J. "Credibility in Science and the Press." *Science* 254 (1 Nov. 1991): 629. Bad science reporting takes its toll; the former head of the American Association for the Advancement of Science complains about it.

Kraus, Nancy, Trorbjorn Malmfors, and Paul Slovic. "Intuitive Toxicology: Expert and Lay Judgments of Chemical Risks." In *Slovic,* 2000. The extent to which uninformed opinion should be given a place in decision making is highlighted by the question of whether ordinary people have an intuitive sense of what in their environment is harmful—whether they are, in the words of these authors, intuitive toxicologists. As I read the data, they aren't.

Krech, Shepard. *The Ecological Indian: Myth and History.* New York: Norton, 1999. An anthropologist carefully reviews the data indicating that native Americans were not the exemplary ecologists of yore. Also reviews recent changes in ecological science.

Kuhl, Stevan. *The Nazi Connection: Eugenics, American Racism, and German National Socialism*. New York: Oxford University Press, 1994.

Kuran, Timur. *Private Truths, Public Lies: The Social Consequences of Preference Falsification*. Cambridge, Mass.: Harvard University Press, 1995.

Landsea, C., N. Nicholls, W. Gray, and L. Avila. "Downward Trend in the Frequency of Intense Atlantic Hurricanes During the Past Five Decades." *Geophysical Research Letters* 23 (1996): 527–30.

Landsea, Christopher W., and John A. Knaff. "How Much Skill Was There in Forecasting the Very Strong 1997–98 El Niño?" *Bulletin of the American Meteorological Society* 81, no. 9 (September 2000): 2017–19. Authors found the older, simpler models performed best. "The use of more complex, physically realistic dynamical models does not automatically provide more reliable forecasts . . . . [Our findings] may be surprising given the general perception that seasonal El Niño forecasts from dynamical models have been quite successful and may even be considered a solved problem." They discuss in detail that the models did not, in fact, predict well. Yet "others are using the supposed success in dynamical El Niño forecasting to support other agendas . . . one could even have less confidence in anthropogenic global studies because of the lack of skill in predicting El Niño. . . . The bottom line is that the successes in forecasting have been overstated (sometimes drastically) and misapplied in other areas."

Lave, Lester B. "Benefit-Cost Analysis: Do the Benefits Exceed the Costs?" In Robert W. Hahn, ed., *Risks, Costs, and Lives Saved: Getting Better Results from Regulation.* New York: Oxford University Press, 1996. A critical review of problems in cost-benefit analysis by an economist who supports the tool but acknowledges that opponents sometimes have a point.

Lean, Judith, and David Rind. "Climate Forcing by Changing Solar Radiation." *Journal of Climate* 11 (December 1988): 3069–94. How much does the sun affect climate? These authors suggest about half the observed surface warming since 1900 and one-third of the warming since 1970 may be attributed to the sun. But there are uncertainties here. "Present inability to adequately specify climate forcing by changing solar radiation has implications for policy making regarding anthropogenic global change, which must be detected against natural climate variability."

LeBlanc, Steven A., and Katherine E. Register. *Constant Battles.* New York: St. Martin's Press, 2003. The myth of the noble savage and the Edenic past dies hard. LeBlanc is one of the handful of archaeologists who have given close scrutiny to evidence for past warfare and has worked to revise an academic inclination to see a peaceful past. LeBlanc argues that primitive societies fought constantly and brutally.

Levack, Brian P. *The Witch-Hunt in Early Modern Europe.* Second Edition. London: Longman, 1995. In the sixteenth century, the educated elites of Europe believed that certain human beings had made contracts with the devil. They believed that witches gathered to perform horrific rites, and that they flew across the sky in the night. On the basis of these beliefs, these elites tortured countless people, and killed 50,000 to 60,000 of their countrymen, mostly old women. However, they also killed men and children, and sometimes (because it was thought unseemly to burn a child) they imprisoned the children until he or she was old enough to be executed. Most of the extensive literature on witchcraft (including the present volume) does not in my view fully come to grips with the truth of this period. The fact that so many people were executed for a fantasy—and despite the reservations of prominent skeptics—carries a lesson that we must always bear in mind. The consensus of the intelligentsia is not necessarily correct, no matter how many believe it, or for how many years the belief is held. It may still be wrong. In fact, it may be *very* wrong. And we must never forget it. Because it will happen again. And indeed it has.

Lilla, Mark. *The Reckless Mind: Intellectuals in Politics.* New York: New York Review of Books, 2001. This razor-sharp text focuses on twentieth-century philosophers but serves as a reminder of the intellectual's temptation "to succumb to the allure of an idea, to allow passion to blind us to its tyrannical potential."

Lindzen, Richard S. "Do Deep Ocean Temperature Records Verify Models?" *Geophysical Research Letters* 29, no. 0 (2002): 10.1029/2001GL014360.

Changes in ocean temperature cannot be taken as a verification of GCMs, computer climate models.

———. "The Press Gets It Wrong: Our Report Doesn't Support the Kyoto Treaty." *Wall Street Journal,* 11 June 2001. This brief essay by a distinguished MIT professor summarizes one example of the way the media misinterprets scientific reports on climate. In this case, the National Academy of Sciences report on climate change, widely claimed to say what it did not. Lindzen was one of eleven authors of the report. http://opinionjournal.com/editorial/feature.html?id=95000606

Lindzen, R. S., and K. Emanuel. "The Greenhouse Effect." In *Encyclopedia of Global Change, Environmental Change and Human Society. Volume 1.* Andrew S. Goudie, ed., New York: Oxford University Press, 2002, pp. 562–66. What exactly is the greenhouse effect everybody talks about but nobody ever explains in any detail? A brief, clear summary.

Liu, J., J. A. Curry, and D. G. Martinson. "Interpretation of Recent Antarctic Sea Ice Variability." *Geophysical Research Letters* 31 (2004): 10.1029/2003 GL018732.

Lomborg, Bjorn. *The Skeptical Environmentalist.* Cambridge, UK: Cambridge University Press, 2002. By now, many people know the story behind this text: The author, a Danish statistician and Greenpeace activist, set out to disprove the views of the late Julian Simon, an economist who claimed that dire environmental fears were wrong and that the world was actually improving. To Lomborg's surprise, he found that Simon was mostly right. Lomborg's text is crisp, calm, clean, devastating to established dogma. Since publication, the author has been subjected to relentless ad hominem attacks, which can only mean his conclusions are unobjectionable in any serious scientific way. Throughout the long controversy, Lomborg has behaved in exemplary fashion. Sadly, his critics have not. Special mention must go to the *Scientific American*, which was particularly reprehensible. All in all, the treatment accorded Lomborg can be viewed as a confirmation of the postmodern critique of science as just another power struggle. A sad episode for science.

Lovins, Amory B. *Soft Energy Paths: Toward a Durable Peace*. New York: Harper and Row, 1977. Perhaps the most important advocate for alternative energy wrote this anti-nuclear energy text in the 1970s for Friends of the Earth, elaborating on an influential essay he wrote for *Foreign Affairs* the year before. The resulting text can be seen as a major link in the chain of events and thinking that set the US on a different energy path from the nations of Europe. Lovins is trained as a physicist and is a MacArthur Fellow.

McKendry, Ian G. "Applied Climatology." *Progress in Physical Geography* 27, no. 4 (2003): 597–606. "Recent studies suggest that attempts to remove the 'urban bias' from long-term climate records (and hence identify the magnitude of the enhanced greenhouse effect) may be overly simplistic. This will likely continue to be a contentious issue. . . ."

Manes, Christopher. *Green Rage: Radical Environmentalism and the Unmaking of Civilization.* Boston: Little Brown, 1990. Not to be missed.

Man's Impact on the Global Environment, Assessments and Recommendations for Action, Report of the Study of Critical Environmental Problems (SCEP). Cambridge, Mass.: MIT Press, 1970. The text predicts carbon dioxide levels of 370 ppm in the year 2000 and a surface-temperature increase of .5 C as a result. The actual figures were 360 ppm and .3 C—far more accurate than predictions made fifteen years later, using lots more computer power.

Marlar, Richard A., et al. "Biochemical evidence of cannibalism at a prehistoric Puebloan site in southwestern Colorado." *Nature* 407, 74078, 7 Sept. 2000.

Martin, Paul S. "Prehistoric Overkill: The Global Model." In *Quaternary Extinctions: A Prehistoric Revolution.* Paul S. Martin and Richard G. Klein, eds. Tucson, Ariz.: University of Arizona Press, 1984, 354–403.

Mason, Betsy. "African Ice Under Wraps." *Nature online publication,* 24 November 2003.

Matthews, Robert A. J. "Facts versus factions: The use and abuse of subjectivity in scientific research." In Morris, *Rethinking Risk,* pp. 247–82. A physicist argues "the failure of the scientific community to take decisive action over the flaws in standard statistical methods, and the resulting waste of resources spent on futile attempts to replicate claims based on them, constitute a major scientific scandal." The book also contains an impressive list of major scientific developments held back by the subjective prejudice of scientists. So much for the reliability of the "consensus" of scientists.

Meadows, Donella H., Dennis L. Meadows, Jorgen Randers, and William W. Behrens III. *The Limits to Growth: A Report for the Club of Rome's Project on the Predicament of Mankind.* New York: New American Library, 1972. It is a shame this book is out of print, because it was hugely influential in its day, and it set the tone ("the predicament of mankind") for much that followed. To read it now is to be astonished at how primitive were the techniques for assessing the state of the world, and how incautious the predictions of future trends. Many of the graphs have no axes, and are therefore just pictures of technical-looking curves. In retrospect, the text is notable not so much for its errors of prediction as for its consistent tone of urgent overstatement bordering on hysteria. The conclusion: "Concerted international measures and joint long-term planning will be necessary on a scale and scope without precedent. Such an effort calls for joint endeavor by all peoples, whatever their culture, economic system, or level of development. . . . This supreme effort is . . . founded on a basic change of values and goals at individual, national and world levels." And so forth.

Medvedev, Zhores A. *The Rise and Fall of T. D. Lysenko.* New York: Columbia University Press, 1969. Extremely difficult to read.

Michaels, Patrick J., and Robert C. Balling, Jr. *The Satanic Gases: Clearing the Air about Global Warming.* Washington, DC: Cato, 2000. These skeptical authors have a sense of humor and a clear style. Use of graphs is unusually good. The Cato Institute is a pro–free market organization with libertarian overtones.

Morris, Julian, ed. *Rethinking Risk and the Precautionary Principle.* Oxford, UK: Butterworth/ Heinemann, 2000. A broad-ranging critique that discusses, for example, how precautionary thinking has harmed children's development.

Nye, David E. *Consuming Power,* Cambridge, Mass.: MIT Press, 1998. America consumes more power per capita than any other country, and Nye is the most knowledgeable scholar about the history of American technology. He draws markedly different conclusions from those less informed. This text is scathing about determinist views of technology. It has clear implications for the validity of IPCC "scenarios."

Oleary, Rosemary, Robert F. Durant, Daniel J. Fiorino, and Paul S. Weiland. *Managing for the Environment: Understanding the Legal, Organizational, and Policy Challenges.* New York: Wiley and Sons, 1999. A much-needed compendium that sometimes covers too much in too little detail.

Ordover, Nancy. *American Eugenics: Race, Queer Anatomy, and the Science of Nationalism.* Minneapolis, Minn.: University of Minnesota Press, 2003. Fascinating in content, confusing in structure, difficult to read, but uncompromising. The author insists on the culpability of both the left and right in the eugenics movement, both in the past and in the present day.

Pagels, Heinz R. *The Dreams of Reason: Computers and the Rise of the Sciences of Complexity.* New York: Simon and Schuster, 1988. The study of complexity represents a true revolution in science, albeit a rather old revolution. This delightful book is seventeen years old, written when the revolution was exciting and new. One would think seventeen years would be enough time for the understanding of complexity and nonlinear dynamics to revise the thinking of environmental activists. But evidently not.

Park, Robert. *Voodoo Science: The Road from Foolishness to Fraud.* New York: Oxford University Press, 2000. The author is a professor of physics and a director of the American Physical Society. His book is especially good on the "Currents of Death" EMF/powerline/cancer controversy, in which he was involved (as a skeptic).

Parkinson, C. L. "Trends in the Length of the Southern Ocean Sea-Ice Season, 1979–99." *Annals of Glaciology* 34 (2002): 435–40.

Parsons, Michael L. *Global Warming: The Truth Behind the Myth,* New York: Plenum, 1995. A skeptical review of data by a professor of health sciences (and therefore not a climate scientist). Outsider's analysis of data.

Pearce, Fred, "Africans go back to the land as plants reclaim the desert." *New Scientist* 175 (21 September 2002): 4–5.

Penn and Teller. *Bullshit!* Showtime series. Brisk, amusing attacks on conventional wisdom and sacred cows. The episode in which a young woman signs up environmentalists to ban "dihydrogen monoxide" (better known as water) is especially funny. "Dihydrogen monoxide," she explains, "is found in lakes and rivers, it remains on fruits and vegetables after they're washed, it makes you sweat . . ." And the people sign up. Another episode on recycling is the clearest brief explanation of what is right and wrong about this practice.

Pepper, David. *Modern Environmentalism: An Introduction*. London: Routledge, 1996. A detailed account of the multiple strands of environmental philosophy by a sympathetic observer. Along with the quite different work of Douglas and Wildavsky, this book considers why mutually incompatible views of nature are held by different groups, and why compromise among them is so unlikely. It also makes clear the extent to which environmental views encompass beliefs about how human society should be structured. The author is a professor of geography and writes well.

Petit, J. R., J. Jouzel, D. Raynaud, N. I. Barkov, J.-M. Barnola, I. Basile, M. Bender, J. Chappellaz, M. Davis, G. Delaygue, M. Delmotte, V. M. Kotlyakov, M. Legrand, V. Y. Lipenkov, C. Lorius, L. Pepin, C. Ritz, E. Saltzman, and M. Stievenard. "1999. Climate and atmospheric history of the past 420,000 years from the Vostok ice core, Antarctica." *Nature* 399: 429–36.

Pielou, E. C. *After the Ice Age: The Return of Life to Glaciated North America*. Chicago: University of

Chicago Press, 1991. A wonderful book, a model of its kind. Explains how life returned as the glaciers receded twenty thousand years ago, and how scientists analyze the data to arrive at their conclusions. Along the way, an excellent reminder of how dramatically our planet has changed in the geologically recent past.

Ponte, Lowell. *The Cooling.* Englewood, N.J.: Prentice-Hall, 1972. The most highly praised of the books from the 1970s that warned of an impending ice age. (The cover asks: "Has the next ice age already begun? Can we survive it?") Contains a chapter on how we might modify the global climate to prevent excessive cooling. A typical quote: "We simply cannot afford to gamble against this possibility by ignoring it. We cannot risk inaction. Those scientists who say we are entering a period of climatic instability [i.e., unpredictability] are acting irresponsibly. The indications that our climate can soon change for the worse are too strong to be reasonably ignored" (p. 237).

Pritchard, James A. *Preserving Yellowstone's Natural Conditions: Science and the Perception of Nature.* Lincoln, Neb.: University of Nebraska Press, 1999. Balance of evidence that elk have changed habitat. Also the nonequilibrium paradigm.

Pronin, Emily, Carolyn Puccio, and Lee Rosh. "Understanding Misunderstanding: Social Psychological Perspectives." In Gilovitch, et al., pp. 636–65. A cool assessment of human disagreement.

Rasool, S. I., and S. H. Schneider. "Atmospheric Carbon Dioxide and Aerosols: Effects of Large Increases on Global Climate." *Science* (11 July 1971): 138–41. An example of the research in the 1970s that suggested that human influence on climate was leading to cooling, not warming. The authors state that increasing carbon dioxide in the atmosphere will not raise temperature as much as increasing aerosols will reduce it. "An increase by only a factor of 4 in global aerosol background concentration may be sufficient to reduce the surface temperature by as much as 3.5 K . . . believed to be sufficient to trigger an ice age."

Raub, W. D., A. Post, C. S. Brown, and M. F. Meier. "Perennial ice masses of the Sierra Nevada, California." *Proceedings of the International Assoc. of Hydrological Science*, no. 126 (1980): 33–34. Cited in Guyton, 1998.

Reference Manual on Scientific Evidence, Federal Judicial Center. Washington, DC: US Government Printing Office, 1994. After years of abuse, the Federal Courts in the US established detailed guidelines for the admissibility of various kinds of scientific testimony and scientific evidence. This volume runs 634 pages.

Reiter, Paul, Christopher J. Tomas, Peter M. Atkinson, Simon I. Hay, Sarah E. Randolph, David J. Rogers, G. Dennis Shanks, Robert W. Snow, and Andrew Spielman. "Global Warming and Malaria: A Call for Accuracy." *Lancet* 4, no. 1 (June 2004).

Rice, Glen E., and Steven A. LeBlanc, eds. *Deadly Landscape*. Salt Lake City, Utah: University of

Utah Press, 2001. More evidence for a strife-filled human past.

Roberts, Leslie R. "Counting on Science at EPA." *Science* 249 (10 August 1990): 616–18. An important brief report on how the EPA ranks risks. Essentially it does what the public wants, not what the EPA experts advise. This is sometimes but not always a bad thing.

Roszak, Theodore. *The Voice of the Earth.* New York: Simon and Schuster, 1992. Roszak is often at the leading edge of emerging social movements, and here he gives an early insight into a blend of ecology and psychology that has since become widespread, even though it is essentially pure feeling without objective foundation. Nevertheless, ecopsychology has become a guiding light in the minds of many people, particularly those without scientific training. My own view is that the movement projects the dissatisfactions of contemporary society onto a natural world that is so seldom experienced that it serves as a perfect projection screen. One must also recall the blunt view of Richard Feynman: "We have learned from much experience that all philosophical intuitions about what nature is going to do fail."

Russell, Jeffrey B. *A History of Witchcraft, Sorcerers, Heretics and Pagans.* London: Thames and Hudson Ltd., 1980. Lest we forget.

Salzman, Jason. *Making the News: A Guide for Activists and Non-Profits.* Boulder, Col.: Westview Press, 2003.

Santer, B. D., K. E. Taylor, T. M. L. Wigley, T. C.

Johns, P. D. Jones, D. J. Karoly, J. F. B. Mitchell, A. H. Oort, J. E. Penner, V. Ramaswamy, M. D. Schwarzkopf, R. J. Stouffer, and S. Tett. "A Search for Human Influences on the Thermal Structure of the Atmosphere." *Nature* 382 (4 July 1996): 39–46. "It is likely that [temperature change in the free atmosphere] is partially due to human activities, though many uncertainties remain, particularly relating to estimates of natural variability." One year after the 1995 IPCC statement that a human effect on climate had been discerned, this article by several IPCC scientists shows considerably more caution about such a claim.

Schullery, Paul. *Searching for Yellowstone: Ecology and Wonder in the Last Wilderness.* New York: Houghton Mifflin, 1997. The author was for many years an employee of the Forest Service and takes a more benign approach to events at Yellowstone than others do.

Scott, James C. *Seeing Like a State: How Certain Schemes to Improve the Human Condition Have Failed.* New Haven, Conn.: Yale University Press, 1998. An extraordinary and original book that reminds us how seldom academic thought is genuinely fresh.

Shrader-Frechette, K. S. *Risk and Rationality: Philosophical Foundations for Populist Reforms.* Berkeley, Calif.: University of California Press, 1991.

Singer, S. Fred. *Hot Talk, Cold Science: Global Warming's Unfinished Debate.* Oakland, Calif.: Independent Institute, 1998. Singer is among the most visible of global warming skeptics. A retired professor of environmental science who has held a number of government posts, including Director of Weather Satellite Service and Director for the Center for Atmospheric and Space Sciences, he is a far more qualified advocate for his views than his critics admit. They usually attempt to portray him as a sort of eccentric nutcase. This book is only seventy-two pages long, and the reader may judge for himself.

Slovic, Paul, ed. *The Perception of Risk.* London: Earthscan, 2000. Slovic has been influential in emphasizing that the concept of "risk" entails not only expert opinion but also the feelings and fears of the population at large. In a democracy, such popular opinions must be addressed in policy making. I take a tougher stance. I believe ignorance is best addressed by education, not by unneeded or wasteful regulation. Unfortunately, the evidence is that we spend far too much soothing false or minor fears.

Stott, Philip, and Sian Sullivan, eds. *Political Ecology: Science, Myth and Power.* London: Arnold, 2000. Focused on Africa. Stott is now retired, witty, and runs an amusing skeptical blog.

Streutker, D. R. "Satellite-measured growth of the urban heat island of Houston, Texas." *Remote Sensing of Environment* 85 (2003): 282–89. "Between 1987 and 1999, the mean nighttime surface temperature heat island of Houston increased 0.82 ± 0.10 °C."

Sunstein, Cass R. *Risk and Reason: Safety, Law, and the Environment.* New York: Cambridge University Press, 2002. A law professor examines major environmental issues from the standpoint of cost-benefit analysis and concludes that new mechanisms for assessing regulations are needed if we are to break free of the current pattern of "hysteria and neglect"—in which we aggressively regulate minor risks while ignoring more significant ones. The detailed chapter on arsenic levels is particularly revealing for anyone wishing to understand the difficulties that rational regulation faces in a highly politicized world.

Sutherland, S. K., and W. R. Lane. "Toxins and mode of envenomation of the common ringed or blue-banded octopus." *Medical Journal Australia* 1 (1969): 893–98.

Tengs, Tammo O., Miriam E. Adams, Joseph S. Plitskin, Dana Gelb Safran, Joanna E. Siegel, Milton C. Weinstein, and John D. Graham. "Five hundred life-saving interventions and their cost effectiveness." *Risk Analysis* 15, no. 3 (1995): 369–90. The Harvard School of Public Health is dismissed in some quarters as a right-wing institution. But this influential and disturbing study by the Harvard Center for Risk Analysis of the costs of regulation has not been disputed. It implies that a great deal of regulatory effort is wasted, and wasteful.

Thomas, Keith. *Man and the Natural World: Changing Attitudes in England 1500–1800*. New York: Oxford University Press, 1983. Are environmental attitudes a matter of fashion? Thomas's delightful book charts changing perceptions of nature from a locus of danger, to a subject of worshipful appreciation, and finally to the beloved wilderness of elite aesthetes.

Thompson, D. W. J., and S. Solomon. "Interpretation of Recent Southern Hemisphere Climate Change." *Science* 296 (2002): 895–99.

Tommasi, Mariano, and Kathryn Lerulli, eds. *The New Economics of Human Behavior*. Cambridge, UK: Cambridge University Press, 1995.

US Congress. *Final Report of the Advisory Committee on Weather Control*. United States Congress. Hawaii: University Press of the Pacific, 2003.

Victor, David G. "Climate of Doubt: The imminent collapse of the Kyoto Protocol on global warming may be a blessing in disguise. The treaty's architecture is fatally flawed." *The Sciences* (Spring 2001): 18–23. Victor is a fellow at the Council on Foreign Relations and an advocate of carbon emission controls who argues that "prudence demands action to check the rise in greenhouse gases, but the Kyoto Protocol is a road to nowhere."

Viscusi, Kip. *Fatal Tradeoffs: Public and Private Responsibilities for Risk*. New York: Oxford University Press, 1992. Start at section III.

———. *Rational Risk Policy*. Oxford: Clarendon, 1998. The author is a professor of law and economics at Harvard.

Vyas, N. K., M. K. Dash, S. M. Bhandari, N. Khare, A. Mitra, and P. C. Pandey. "On the Secular Trends in Sea Ice Extent over the Antarctic Region Based on OCEANSAT-1 MSMR Observations." *International Journal of Remote Sensing* 24 (2003): 2277–87.

Wallack, Lawrence, Katie Woodruff, Lori Dorfman, and Iris Diaz. *News for a Change: An Advo-*

cate's Guide to Working with the Media. London: Sage Publications, 1999.

Weart, Spencer R. *The Discovery of Global Warming.* Cambridge, Mass.: Harvard University Press, 2003.

West, Darrell M. *The Rise and Fall of the Media Establishment.* New York: Bedford/St. Martin's Press, 2001.

White, Geoffrey M. *Identity Through History: Living Stories in a Solomon Islands Society.* Cambridge, UK: Cambridge University Press, 1991.

Wigley, Tom. "Global Warming Protocol: CO_2, CH_4 and climate implications." *Geophysical Research Letters* 25, no. 13 (1 July 1998): 2285–88.

Wildavsky, Aaron. *But Is It True? A Citizen's Guide to Environmental Health and Safety Issues.* Cambridge: Harvard University Press, 1995. A professor of political science and public policy at Berkeley turned his students loose to research both the history and the scientific status of major environmental issues: DDT, Alar, Love Canal, asbestos, the ozone hole, global warming, acid rain. The book is an excellent resource for a more complete discussion of these issues than is usually provided. For example, the author devotes twenty-five pages to the history of the DDT ban, twenty pages to Alar, and so on. Wildavsky concludes that nearly all environmental claims have been either untrue or wildly overstated.

———. *Searching for Safety.* New Brunswick, N.J.: Transaction, 1988. If we want a safe society and a safe life, how should we go about getting it? A good-humored exploration of strategies for safety in industrial society. Drawing on data from a wide range of disciplines, Wildavsky argues that resilience is a better strategy than anticipation, and that anticipatory strategies (such as the precautionary principle) favor the social elite over the mass of poorer people.

Winsor, P. "Arctic Sea Ice Thickness Remained Constant During the 1990s." *Geophysical Research Letters* 28, no. 6 (March 2001): 1039–41.

Read on for an excerpt from

MICHAEL CRICHTON'S
NEXT

Available from HarperCollins Publishers

Vasco Borden, forty-nine, tugged at the lapels of his suit and straightened his tie as he walked down the plush carpeted hallway. He wasn't used to wearing a suit, though he had had this one, in navy, specially tailored to minimize the muscular bulk of his body. Borden was big, six-four, two-forty, an ex–football player who worked as a private investigator and fugitive-recovery specialist. And right now, Vasco was following his man, a thirty-year-old balding postdoc, a fugitive from MicroProteonomics of Cambridge, Mass., as he headed right for the main room of the conference.

The BioChange 2006 Conference, enthusiastically entitled "Make It Happen Now!" was being held at the Venetian hotel in Las Vegas. The two thousand attendees represented all sorts of biotech workers, including investors, HR officers who hired scientists, technology transfer officers, CEOs, and intellectual property attorneys. In one way or another, nearly every biotech company in America was represented here.

It was the perfect place for the fugitive to meet his contact. The fugitive looked like a dink; he had an innocent face and a little soul patch on his chin; he slouched when he walked and gave the impression of timidity and ineptitude. But the fact was, he'd made off with twelve transgenic embryos in a cryogenic dewar and transported them across country to this conference, where he intended to turn them over to whomever he was working for.

It wouldn't be the first time a postdoc got tired of working on salary. Or the last.

The fugitive went over to the check-in table to get his conference card to drape around his neck. Vasco hung by the entrance, slipping his own card over his head. He'd come prepared for this. He pretended to look at the event roster.

The big speeches were all in the main ballroom. Seminars were scheduled for such topics as "Fine-Tune Your Recruiting Process," and "Winning Strategies to Keep Research Talent," "Executive and Equity Compensation," "Corporate Governance and the SEC," "Patent Office Trends," and "Investor Angels: Boon or Curse?" and, finally, "Trade Secrets Piracy: Protect Yourself Now!"

Much of Vasco's work involved high-tech firms. He had been to these conferences before. Either they were about science or business. This one was business.

The fugitive, whose name was Eddie Tolman, walked past him into the ballroom. Vasco followed. Tolman went down a few rows and dropped into a seat with no one nearby. Vasco slipped into the row behind and sat a little to one side. The Tolman kid checked his cell phone for text messages, then seemed to relax, and looked up to listen to the speech.

Vasco wondered why.

The man at the podium was one of the most famous venture capitalists in California, a legend in high-tech investment, Jack B. Watson. Watson's face was blown up large on the screen behind him, his trademark suntan and striking good looks magnified to fill the room. Watson was a young-looking fifty-two, and assiduously cultivated his reputation as a capitalist with a conscience. That appellation had carried him through a succession of ruthless business deals: all the media ever showed were his appearances at charter schools, or handing out scholarships for underprivileged kids.

But in this room, Vasco knew, Watson's reputation for tough deal making would be foremost in everyone's mind. He wondered if Watson was ruthless enough to acquire a dozen transgenic embryos by illicit means. He probably was.

However, at the moment, Watson was cheerleading: "Biotechnology is booming. We are poised to see the greatest growth of any industry since computers thirty years ago. The largest biotech company, Amgen, in Los Angeles, employs seven thousand people. Federal grants to universities exceed four billion a year on campuses from New York to San Francisco, Boston to Miami. Venture capitalists invest in biotech companies at a rate of five billion a year. The lure of magnificent cures made possible by stem cells, cytokines, and proteonomics is drawing the brightest talent

to the field. And with a global population growing older by the minute, our future is brighter
than ever. And that's not all!

"We've reached the point where we can stick it
to Big Pharma—and we will. Those massive,
bloated companies need us and they know it.
They need genes, they need technology. They're
the past. We're the future. We're where the
money is!"

That drew huge applause. Vasco shifted his
bulk in his seat. The audience was applauding,
even though they knew that this son of a bitch
would cut their company to pieces in a second if
it suited his bottom line.

"Of course, we face obstacles to our progress.
Some people—however well intentioned they
think they are—choose to stand in the way of
human betterment. They don't want the paralyzed to walk, the cancer patient to thrive, the
sick child to live and play. These people have
their reasons for objecting. Religious, ethical, or
even 'practical.' But whatever their reasons, they
are on the side of death. And they will not triumph!"

More thunderous applause. Vasco glanced at
the fugitive, Tolman. The kid was checking his
phone again. Evidently waiting for a message.
And waiting impatiently.

Did that mean the contact was late?

That was sure to make Tolman nervous. Because somewhere, Vasco knew, this kid had
stashed a stainless steel thermos of liquid nitrogen that held the embryos. It wasn't in the kid's

room. Vasco had already searched it. And five days had passed since Tolman left Cambridge. The coolant wouldn't last forever. And if the embryos thawed, they would be worthless. So unless Tolman had a way to top up his LN2, by now he must be anxious to retrieve his container, and hand it over to his buyer.

It had to happen soon.

Within an hour, Vasco was sure of it.

"Of course, people will try to obstruct progress," Watson said, from the podium. "Even our best companies find themselves embroiled in pointless, unproductive litigation. One of my startups, BioGen, in Los Angeles, is in court right now because some guy named Burnet thinks he doesn't need to honor the contracts he himself signed. Because now he's changed his mind. Burnet is trying to block medical progress unless we pay him. An extortionist whose daughter is the lawyer handling the case for him. Keeping it in the family." Watson smiled.

"But we will win the Burnet case. Because progress cannot be stopped!"

At that, Watson threw both hands up in the air, waving to the audience as applause filled the room. He almost acts like a candidate, Vasco thought. Is that what Watson was aiming for? The guy certainly had enough money to get elected. Being rich was essential in American politics these days. Pretty soon—

He looked over, and saw that the Tolman kid was gone.

The seat was empty.

Shit!

"Progress is our mission, our sacred calling," Watson cried. "Progress to vanquish disease! Progress to halt aging, banish dementia, extend life! A life free of disease, decay, pain, and fear! The great dream of humanity—made real at last!"

Vasco Borden wasn't listening. He was heading down the row toward the side aisle, scanning the exit doors. A couple of people leaving, nobody looking like Tolman. The guy couldn't have gotten away, there was—

He looked back just in time to see Tolman moving slowly up the center aisle. The kid was looking at his cell phone again.

"Sixty billion this year. Two hundred billion next year. Five hundred billion in five years! That is the future of our industry, and that is the prospect we bring to all mankind!"

The crowd suddenly rose to its feet, giving Watson a standing ovation, and for a moment Vasco could no longer see Tolman at all.

But only for a moment—now Tolman was making for the center exit. Vasco turned away, slipping through the side door and out into the lobby, just as Tolman came blinking into the bright lobby light.

Tolman glanced at his watch and headed down the far corridor, past big glass windows that looked out on the red brick campanile of San Marco, re-created by the Venetian hotel and lit brilliantly at night. He was going toward the swimming pool area, or perhaps the courtyard. This time of night those spaces would be crowded.

Vasco stayed close.

This was it, he thought.

In the ballroom, Jack Watson paced back and forth, smiling and waving to the cheering crowd. "Thank you, that's very kind, thank you . . ." ducking his head a little each time he said it. Just the right amount of modesty.

Rick Diehl snorted in disgust as he watched. Diehl was backstage, taking it all in on a little black-and-white monitor. Diehl was the thirty-four-year-old CEO of BioGen Research, a struggling startup in Los Angeles, and this performance by his most important outside investor filled him with unease. Because Diehl knew that despite the cheerleading, and the press releases with smiling black kids, at the end of the day, Jack Watson was a true bastard. As someone put it, "The best I can say about Watson is, he's not a sadist. He's just a first-class son of a bitch."

Diehl had accepted funding from Watson with the greatest reluctance. He wished he didn't need it. Diehl's wife was wealthy, and he had started BioGen with her money. His first venture as CEO had been to bid on a cell line being licensed by UCLA. It was the so-called Burnet cell line, developed from a man named Frank Burnet, whose body produced powerful cancer-fighting chemicals called cytokines.

Diehl hadn't really expected to land the license, but he did, and suddenly he faced the prospect of gearing up for FDA approval for clinical trials. The cost of clinical trials started at a million dollars, and went rapidly to ten million a pop, not counting downstream costs and after-marketing expenses. He could no longer rely solely on his wife's money. He needed outside financing.

That was when he discovered just how risky venture capitalists considered cytokines to be. Many cytokines, such as interleukins, had taken years to come to market. And many others were known to be dangerous, even deadly, to patients. And then Frank Burnet had brought a lawsuit, casting doubt on BioGen's ownership of the cell line. Diehl had trouble getting investors to even meet with him. In the end, he had to accept smiling, suntanned Jack Watson.

But Watson, Diehl knew, wanted nothing less than to take over BioGen and throw Rick Diehl out on his ass.

"Jack! Fantastic speech! Fantastic!" Rick extended his hand, as Watson came backstage at last.

"Yeah. Glad you liked it." Watson didn't shake his hand. Instead, he unclipped his wireless transmitter and dropped it in Diehl's palm. "Take care of this, Rick."

"Sure, Jack."

"Your wife here?"

"No, Karen couldn't make it." Diehl shrugged. "Thing with the kids."

"I'm sorry she missed this speech," Watson said.

"I'll see she gets the DVD," Diehl said.

"But we got the bad news out there," Watson said. "That's the point. Everybody now knows there's a lawsuit, they know Burnet is a bad guy, and they know we're on top of it. That's the important thing. The company's now perfectly positioned."

Diehl said, "Is *that* why you agreed to give the speech?"

Watson stared at him. "You think I *want* to come to Vegas? Christ." He unclipped the microphone, handed it to Diehl. "Take care of this, too."

"Sure, Jack."

And Jack Watson turned and walked away from him without another word. Rick Diehl shivered. Thank God for Karen's money, he thought. Because without it, he'd be doomed.

Passing through the arches of the Doge's Palace, Vasco Borden moved into the courtyard, following his fugitive, Eddie Tolman, through the nighttime crowd. He heard his earpiece crackle. That would be his assistant, Dolly, in another part of the hotel. He touched his ear. "Go," he said.

"Baldy boy Tolman has reserved some entertainment."

"Is that right?"

"That's right, he—"

"Hold on," Vasco said. "Just hold that thought."

Up ahead, he was seeing something he could not believe. From the right side of the courtyard, he saw Jack B. Watson, accompanied by a beautiful, slinky, dark-haired woman, merging with the crowd. Watson was famous for always being accompanied by gorgeous women. They all worked for him, they were all smart, and they were all stunning.

The woman didn't surprise Vasco. What surprised him was that Jack Watson was heading directly toward Eddie Tolman, the fugitive. That made no sense at all. Even if Tolman were doing a deal with Watson, the famous investor would never meet him face-to-face. And certainly never in public. But there they were, on a collision course in the crowded Venetian courtyard, right before his eyes.

What the hell? He couldn't believe it was going to happen.

But then the slinky woman stumbled a bit, and stopped. She was wearing a short, skintight dress and heels. She leaned on Watson's shoulder, bent her knee, showing plenty of leg, and inspected her shoe. She adjusted her heel strap, stood up again, and smiled at Watson. And Vasco glanced away from them and saw that Tolman was gone.

But now Watson and the woman crossed Vasco's own path, passing so close to him that he could smell her perfume, and he heard Watson murmur something to her, and she squeezed his arm and put her head on his shoulder as they walked. The romantic couple.

Was all that an accident? Had it happened on purpose? Had they made him? He pressed his earpiece.

"Dolly. I lost him."

"No prob. I got him." He glanced up. She was

on the second floor, watching everything below. "Was that Jack Watson that just walked by?"

"Yeah. I thought maybe . . ."

"No, no," Dolly said. "I can't imagine Watson's involved in this. Not his style. I mean, Baldy boy is heading for his room because he has an appointment. That's what I was telling you. He got some entertainment."

"Namely?"

"Russian girl. Apparently he only likes Russians. Tall ones."

"Anybody we know?"

"No, but I have a little information. And I got cameras in his suite."

"How'd you do that?" He was smiling.

"Let's just say Venetian security isn't what it used to be. Cheaper, too."

Irina Katayeva, twenty-two, knocked on the door. In her left hand she held a bottle of wine, encased in a velvet gift bag with drawstrings at the top. A guy of about thirty answered the door, smiled. He wasn't attractive.

"Are you Eddie?"

"That's right. Come on in."

"I brought this for you, from the hotel safe." She handed him the wine.

Watching all this on his little handheld video monitor, Vasco said, "She gave it to him in the hallway. Where it would be seen on the security monitor. Why didn't she wait until she was in the room?"

"Maybe she was told to do it that way," Dolly said.

"She must be six feet. What do we know about her?"

"Good English. Four years in this country. Studying at the university."

"Works at the hotel?"

"No."

"So, non-pro?" Vasco said.

"This is Nevada," Dolly said.

On the monitor, the Russian girl went into the room and the door closed. Vasco turned the tuning dial on his video monitor, picked up one of the inside cameras. The kid had a big suite, close to two thousand square feet, done in the Venetian style. The girl nodded and smiled.

"Nice. Nice room."

"Yeah. So, you want a drink?"

She shook her head. "I don't really have time." She reached behind her back and unzipped the dress, left it hanging from her shoulders. She turned around, pretending to be puzzled, allowing him to see her bare back all the way down to her buttocks. "Which way is the bedroom?"

"This way, baby."

As they went into the bedroom, Vasco again turned the dials. He saw the bedroom just as she was saying, "I don't know anything about your business, and I don't want to know. Business is *so* boring." She let the dress fall. She stepped out of it and lay down on the bed, naked now except for high heels. She kicked them off. "I don't think you need a drink," she said. "And I know I don't."

Tolman threw himself on her, landing with a kind of thud. She grunted and tried to smile. "Easy, boy." He was panting, gasping. He reached

for her hair, to caress her. "Leave the hair alone,"
she said. She twisted away. "Just lie down," she
said, "and let me make you happy."

"Aw, hell," Vasco said, staring at the tiny screen.
"Do you believe that? He ain't even a minute-
man. When a woman looks like that, you'd
think—"

"Never mind," Dolly said, over the headset.
"She's getting dressed now."

"So she is," he said. "And rather hurriedly,
too."

"She's supposed to give him half an hour. And
if he paid her, I didn't see it."

"Me neither. But he's getting dressed, too."

"Something's up," Dolly said. "She's walking
out the door."

Vasco thumbed the tuner, trying to change to
a different camera. All he got was static. "I can't
see shit."

"She's leaving. He's still there. No, wait . . . he's
leaving, too."

"Yeah?"

"Yeah. And he's taking the wine bottle with
him."

"Okay," Vasco said. "And where's he going with
it?"

Frozen embryos in liquid nitrogen were transported in a special stainless steel thermos lined
with borosilicate glass called a dewar. Dewars
were mostly big affairs, shaped like milk jugs, but
you could get them as small as a liter. A dewar
didn't have the shape of a wine bottle, because

they had a wide-mouth cap, but it would be about the same size. And would fit in a wine sack for sure.

"He must be carrying it," Vasco said. "It must be in the sack."

"I figure," Dolly said. "You see 'em yet?"

"Yeah, I do."

Vasco picked up the couple on the ground floor, near the gondola stand. They walked arm in arm, the guy carrying the wine bottle in the crook of his arm, keeping it upright. It was an awkward way to carry it, and they made an odd-looking pair—the beautiful girl and the diffident, slouchy guy. They walked along the canal, hardly glancing at the shops as they passed them.

"On their way to a meeting," Vasco said.

"I see 'em," Dolly said. Vasco looked down the crowded street and saw Dolly at the far end. Dolly was twenty-eight, and completely ordinary-looking. Dolly could be anybody: an accountant, girlfriend, secretary, assistant. She could always pass. Tonight she was dressed Vegas-style, teased blond hair and a sparkly dress with cleavage. She was a little overweight, which made the impression perfect. Vasco had been with her for four years now, and they worked well as a team. In private life, they got along only okay. She hated that he smoked cigars in bed.

"Heading for the hall," Dolly said. "No, they're doubling back."

The main hall was a huge oval passageway, high gilded ceiling, soft lights, marble pillars. It dwarfed the crowds that moved through it. Vasco hung back. "Change their mind? Or they made us?"

"I think they're being careful."

"Well, this is the big moment." Because even more than catching the fugitive, they had to know whom he was turning the embryos over to. Obviously someone at the conference.

"Won't be long now," Dolly said.

Rick Diehl was walking back and forth along the shops by the gondola canal, holding his cell phone in his hand. He ignored the stores, which were filled with expensive stuff of the sort he never wanted. Diehl had grown up as the third son of a Baltimore physician. All the other boys went to medical school and became obstetricians, like their father. Diehl refused, and went into medical research. Family pressure eventually drove him to move West. He did genetic research at UCSF for a while, but he was more intrigued by the entrepreneurial culture among the universities in San Francisco. It seemed like every professor worth his salt had either started his own company or was sitting on the boards of several biotech firms. At lunch, the conversation was all about tech transfer, cross-licensing, milestone payments, buyouts and payouts, foreground and background IPRs.

By then Karen, Rick's wife, had come into a substantial inheritance, and he realized he had enough capital to get started. The Bay Area was crowded with firms; there was intense competition for space and hiring. He decided to go to the area north of Los Angeles, where Amgen had set up their huge facility. Diehl built a terrific modern plant, put bright research teams in place, and was on his way. His father and brothers came to visit. They were duly impressed.

But . . . why wasn't she calling him back? He looked at his watch. It was nine o'clock. The kids should be in bed by now. And Karen should be home. The maid said she had gone out an hour before, she didn't know where. But Karen never left without her cell phone. She must have it with her. Why wasn't she calling him back?

He didn't understand it, and it just made him nervous as hell. Here he was, alone in this damn city, with more beautiful women per square foot than he had ever seen in his life. True, they were plastic, lots of surgery, but they were also sexy as hell.

Up ahead, he saw a schlumpy guy walking with a tall chick who was striding along on spike heels, and she was just a knockout: black hair, smooth skin, and a hot, lean body. The schlumpy guy must have paid for her, but even so, he clearly didn't appreciate her. He was clutching his wine bottle like it was a baby, and appeared so nervous he was almost sweating.

But that girl . . . Jesus, she was hot. Hot, hot . . .

Why the hell, he thought, wasn't Karen calling him back?

"Hey," Vasco said. "Looky look. It's that BioGen guy. Walking around like he has nothing to do."

"I see him," Dolly said. She was about a block ahead of him.

"Nope, never mind."

Tolman and the Russian girl walked right past

the BioGen guy, who did nothing but flip open his phone and dial. What was his name? Diehl. Vasco had heard something about him. Started a company on his wife's dough, and now maybe she was in control of their marriage. Something like that. Rich broad, old Eastern family, lots of money. Those broads could wear the pants.

"Restaurant," Dolly said. "They're going in that Terrazo place."

Il Terrazzo Antico was a two-story restaurant with glassed-in balconies. The décor was whore-house modern, gilded everything. Pillars, ceiling, walls: every surface covered with decoration. Made Vasco jumpy just to look at it.

The couple walked in, right past the reservation desk, heading for a side table. And at the table, Vasco saw a heavyset guy who looked like a thug, dark-skinned and heavy-browed, and the thug was looking at the Russian girl and practically licking his lips.

Tolman marched right up to the table and spoke to the dark-skinned man. The guy looked puzzled. He didn't invite them to sit. Vasco thought, *Something's wrong*. The Russian girl had stepped back a pace.

At that moment a flash went off. Dolly had snapped a picture. The Tolman kid looked, took it all in, and bolted.

"Shit, Dolly!"

Vasco started running after Tolman, who was heading deeper into the restaurant. A waiter held up his hands. "Sir, excuse me—"

Vasco knocked him flat, kept right on going. Tolman was ahead, moving slower than he might, because he was trying not to shake his precious wine bottle. But he didn't know where he was going anymore. He didn't know the restaurant; he was just running. *Whang* through swinging doors, into the kitchen, Vasco right after him. Everybody was yelling at them, and some of the cooks were waving knives, but Tolman pushed on, apparently convinced there was some sort of rear entrance to the kitchen.

There wasn't. He was trapped. He looked around wildly. Vasco slowed. He flashed one of his badges, in an official-looking wallet. "Citizen's arrest," he said. Tolman cowered back by two walk-in freezers and a narrow door with a slim vertical window. Tolman went through the narrow door and it closed behind him.

A light blinked by the door.

It was a service elevator.

Shit. "Where does this go?"

"Second floor."

"Anywhere else?"

"No, just second floor."

Vasco pressed his earpiece. "Dolly?"

"I'm on it," she said. He heard her panting, as she ran upstairs.

Vasco positioned himself in front of the elevator door and waited. He pressed the button to bring the elevator down.

"I'm at the elevator now," Dolly said. "I saw him; he went back down."

"That's a tiny elevator," Vasco said.

"I know."

"If he's really got liquid nitrogen with him, he shouldn't be in there." A couple of years back,

Vasco had chased a fugitive into a laboratory-supply warehouse. The guy had nearly suffocated after he locked himself in a closet.

The elevator came down. As soon as it stopped, Vasco yanked the handle to open it, but Tolman must have pushed an emergency switch, because the door wouldn't open. Vasco could see the wine sack on the floor. The velvet had been pushed down to reveal the stainless steel rim of the dewar.

And the top was off. White steam around the opening.

Through the glass, Tolman stared at him, wild-eyed. "Come out, son," Vasco said. "Don't be foolish."

Tolman shook his head.

"It's dangerous," Vasco said. "You know it's dangerous."

But the kid pushed a button, and the elevator started back up.

Vasco had a bad feeling.

The kid knew, all right. He knew exactly what he was doing.

"He's up here," Dolly said, standing on the second floor. "But the door won't open. No, he's going down again."

"Go back to the table," Vasco said to her. "Let him go."

She realized at once what he was talking about. She hurried back down the plush red velvet staircase to the ground floor. She was not surprised to see that the table where the thuggish man had sat was now empty. No thug. No beautiful Russian girl. Just a hundred-dollar bill tucked under a glass. He'd paid in cash, of course.

And vanished.

Vasco was now surrounded by three hotel security guys, all talking at once. Standing half a head above them he yelled for quiet. "One thing," he said. "How do we get the elevator open?"

"He must have hit the override."

"How do we get it *open*?"

"We have to kill the power to it."

"Will that open it?"

"No, but then we can wedge it open, once it's stopped."

"How long will that take?"

"Maybe ten, fifteen minutes. Doesn't matter, this guy isn't going anyplace."

"Yes, he is," Vasco said.

The security guy laughed. "Where the hell can he go?"

The elevator came down again. Tolman was on his knees, holding the glass door shut.

"Get up," Vasco said. "Get up, get up. Come on, son, it's not worth it, stand up!"

Suddenly, Tolman's eyes rolled up into his head and he fell onto his back. The elevator started to rise.

"What the hell?" one of the security men said. "Who is he, anyway?"

Ah shit, Vasco thought.

The kid had pushed some override that had jammed the elevator circuits. It took them forty minutes to get the doors open and haul him out.

He was long since dead, of course. The instant he fell, he was immersed in 100 percent nitrogen atmosphere, from the liquid nitrogen that was streaming from the dewar. Because nitrogen was heavier than air, it progressively filled the elevator from the bottom up. Once the kid flopped on his back, he was already unconscious, and he would have died within a minute.

The security guys wanted to know what was in the dewar, which was no longer smoking. Vasco got some gloves and pulled out the long metal stick. There was nothing there, just a series of empty clips where the embryos should have been. The embryos had been removed.

"You mean to say he killed himself?" one of the security men said.

"That's right," Vasco said. "He worked in an embryology lab. He knew about the danger of liquid nitrogen in a confined space." Nitrogen caused more laboratory fatalities than any other chemical. Half the people who died were trying to rescue co-workers who had collapsed in confined spaces.

"It was his way out of a bad situation," Vasco said.

Later, driving home with him, Dolly said, "So what happened to the embryos?"

Vasco shook his head. "No idea. The kid never got them."

"You think the girl took them? Before she went to his room?"

"Somebody took them." Vasco sighed. "The hotel doesn't know her?"

"They reviewed security cameras. They don't know her."

"And her student status?"

"University had her as a student last year. She didn't enroll this year."

"So she's vanished."

"Yeah," Dolly said. "Her, the dark-skinned guy, the embryos. Everything vanished."

"I'd like to know how all this goes together," Vasco said.

"Maybe it doesn't," Dolly said.

"Wouldn't be the first time," Vasco said. Up ahead, he saw the neon of a roadhouse in the desert. He pulled over. He needed a drink.

Praise for *A Thousand Splendid Suns*

'Hosseini vividly brings home what life is like for women . . . he makes the Afghans come alive as loving, feeling individuals'
Guardian

'If he cut his teeth by writing about his countrymen, it is the plight of Afghanistan's women that has brought him to realise his full powers as a novelist' *The Times*

'A beautifully crafted and disturbing story . . . As unforgettable as *The Kite Runner*, this novel places us in Afghanistan with an open heart' Isabel Allende

'The story pounds along at such a pace, it threatens to leap from the page' *Metro*

'A historical romance, in which attention remains deliberately focused on the women . . . grippingly told' *Daily Telegraph*

'*A Thousand Splendid Suns* has all the particularity of a novel and all the force of a fable . . . it reads, in many ways, like an old-fashioned romantic adventure' *Mail on Sunday*

'Hosseini has done it again . . . *A Thousand Splendid Suns* is a triumph. In Khaled Hosseini, Afghanistan has at last found a voice' *Financial Times*

'Impossible to resist' *Entertainment Weekly*

'It's the soul-stirring connection between two victimised women that gives this novel its battered heart' *People*

'What keeps this novel vivid and compelling is Hosseini's eye for the textures of daily life and his ability to portray a full range of human emotions' *Los Angeles Times*

'I loved this book – I couldn't put it down and read it in one sitting' Fiona Bruce

'Love may not be the first thing that comes to mind when you consider the war-ravaged landscape of Afghanistan. But that is the emotion – subterranean, powerful, beautiful, illicit and infinitely patient – that suffuses the pages' *O, the Oprah Magazine*

'Absolutely read it' *More*

'The story of the sacrifices necessary to sustain hope and joy, and the power of love to overcome fear. Splendid indeed'
New York Daily News

'Hosseini has an extraordinary storytelling ability . . . you would want to be a statue not to be moved by this story'
Irish Independent

'The hope is this: Despite the unjust cruelties of our world, the heroines of *A Thousand Splendid Suns* do endure, both on the page and in our imagination' *Miami Herald*

'Just as heartrending, just as powerful' *Evening Standard* Books to Brighten Up Your Summer

'You will find yourself unable to break from the narrative, gasping as you turn the page, weeping at the predicament of Mariam and Laila . . . powerful and moving' *Good Book Guide*

'A riveting read' *Financial Times* Summer Books

'A novel that bears testament to the power of love . . . deeply moving' *Sunday Express*

A THOUSAND
SPLENDID SUNS

Khaled Hosseini

BLOOMSBURY
LONDON · NEW DELHI · NEW YORK · SYDNEY

BY THE SAME AUTHOR

The Kite Runner
And The Mountains Echoed

First published in Great Britain 2007
This paperback edition published 2013

Copyright © 2007 by ATSS Publications, LLC

Translation of the poem 'Kabul' by Josephine Barry Davis

The moral right of the author has been asserted

Bloomsbury Publishing Plc,
50 Bedford Square, London WC1B 3DP

Bloomsbury Publishing is a trademark of Bloomsbury Plc

Bloomsbury Publishing, London, New Delhi, New York and Sydney

A CIP catalogue record for this book
is available from the British Library

Paperback ISBN 978 1 4088 4444 1

10 9 8 7 6

Printed and bound in India by Thomson Press India Ltd.

www.bloomsbury.com/khaledhosseini

This book is dedicated to Haris and Farah,
both the *noor* of my eyes, and to the women of Afghanistan.

PART ONE

1.

Mariam was five years old the first time she heard the word *harami*.

It happened on a Thursday. It must have, because Mariam remembered that she had been restless and pre-occupied that day, the way she was only on Thursdays, the day when Jalil visited her at the *kolba*. To pass the time until the moment that she would see him at last, crossing the knee-high grass in the clearing and waving, Mariam had climbed a chair and taken down her mother's Chinese tea set. The tea set was the sole relic that Mariam's mother, Nana, had of her own mother, who had died when Nana was two. Nana cherished each blue-and-white porcelain piece, the graceful curve of the pot's spout, the hand-painted finches and chrysanthemums, the dragon on the sugar bowl, meant to ward off evil.

It was this last piece that slipped from Mariam's fingers, that fell to the wooden floorboards of the *kolba* and shattered.

When Nana saw the bowl, her face flushed red and her

3

upper lip shivered, and her eyes, both the lazy one and the good, settled on Mariam in a flat, unblinking way. Nana looked so mad that Mariam feared the *jinn* would enter her mother's body again. But the *jinn* didn't come, not that time. Instead, Nana grabbed Mariam by the wrists, pulled her close, and, through gritted teeth, said, "You are a clumsy little *harami*. This is my reward for everything I've endured. An heirloom-breaking, clumsy little *harami*."

At the time, Mariam did not understand. She did not know what this word *harami*—bastard—meant. Nor was she old enough to appreciate the injustice, to see that it is the creators of the *harami* who are culpable, not the *harami*, whose only sin is being born. Mariam *did* surmise, by the way Nana said the word, that it was an ugly, loathsome thing to be a *harami*, like an insect, like the scurrying cockroaches Nana was always cursing and sweeping out of the *kolba*.

Later, when she was older, Mariam did understand. It was the way Nana uttered the word—not so much saying it as spitting it at her—that made Mariam feel the full sting of it. She understood then what Nana meant, that a *harami* was an unwanted thing; that she, Mariam, was an illegitimate person who would never have legitimate claim to the things other people had, things such as love, family, home, acceptance.

Jalil never called Mariam this name. Jalil said she was his little flower. He was fond of sitting her on his lap and telling her stories, like the time he told her that Herat, the city where Mariam was born, in 1959, had once been the cradle of Persian culture, the home of writers, painters, and Sufis.

"You couldn't stretch a leg here without poking a poet in the ass," he laughed.

Jalil told her the story of Queen Gauhar Shad, who had raised the famous minarets as her loving ode to Herat back in the fifteenth century. He described to her the green wheat fields of Herat, the orchards, the vines pregnant with plump grapes, the city's crowded, vaulted bazaars.

"There is a pistachio tree," Jalil said one day, "and beneath it, Mariam jo, is buried none other than the great poet Jami." He leaned in and whispered, "Jami lived over five hundred years ago. He did. I took you there once, to the tree. You were little. You wouldn't remember."

It was true. Mariam didn't remember. And though she would live the first fifteen years of her life within walking distance of Herat, Mariam would never see this storied tree. She would never see the famous minarets up close, and she would never pick fruit from Herat's orchards or stroll in its fields of wheat. But whenever Jalil talked like this, Mariam would listen with enchantment. She would admire Jalil for his vast and worldly knowledge. She would quiver with pride to have a father who knew such things.

"What rich lies!" Nana said after Jalil left. "Rich man telling rich lies. He never took you to any tree. And don't let him charm you. He betrayed us, your beloved father. He cast us out. He cast us out of his big fancy house like we were nothing to him. He did it happily."

Mariam would listen dutifully to this. She never dared say to Nana how much she disliked her talking this way about Jalil. The truth was that around Jalil, Mariam did not feel at all like a *harami*. For an hour or two every Thursday, when Jalil came to see her, all smiles and gifts and endearments, Mariam felt deserving of all the beauty and bounty that life had to give. And, for this, Mariam loved Jalil.

EVEN IF SHE had to share him.

Jalil had three wives and nine children, nine legitimate children, all of whom were strangers to Mariam. He was one of Herat's wealthiest men. He owned a cinema, which Mariam had never seen, but at her insistence Jalil had described it to her, and so she knew that the façade was made of blue-and-tan terra-cotta tiles, that it had private balcony seats and a trellised ceiling. Double swinging doors opened into a tiled lobby, where posters of Hindi films were encased in glass displays. On Tuesdays, Jalil said one day, kids got free ice cream at the concession stand.

Nana smiled demurely when he said this. She waited until he had left the *kolba*, before snickering and saying, "The children of strangers get ice cream. What do you get, Mariam? Stories of ice cream."

In addition to the cinema, Jalil owned land in Karokh, land in Farah, three carpet stores, a clothing shop, and a black 1956 Buick Roadmaster. He was one of Herat's best-connected men, friend of the mayor and the provincial governor. He had a cook, a driver, and three house-keepers.

Nana had been one of the housekeepers. Until her belly began to swell.

When that happened, Nana said, the collective gasp of Jalil's family sucked the air out of Herat. His in-laws swore blood would flow. The wives demanded that he throw her out. Nana's own father, who was a lowly stone carver in the nearby village of Gul Daman, disowned her. Disgraced, he packed his things and boarded a bus to Iran, never to be seen or heard from again.

"Sometimes," Nana said early one morning, as she was feeding the chickens outside the *kolba*, "I wish my father had had the stomach to sharpen one of his knives and do the honorable thing. It might have been better for me." She tossed another handful of seeds into the coop, paused, and looked at Mariam. "Better for you too, maybe. It would have spared you the grief of knowing that you are what you are. But he was a coward, my father. He

6

didn't have the *dil*, the heart, for it."

Jalil didn't have the *dil* either, Nana said, to do the honorable thing. To stand up to his family, to his wives and in-laws, and accept responsibility for what he had done. Instead, behind closed doors, a face-saving deal had quickly been struck. The next day, he had made her gather her few things from the servants' quarters, where she'd been living, and sent her off.

"You know what he told his wives by way of defense? That I *forced* myself on him. That it was my fault. *Didi?* You see? This is what it means to be a woman in this world."

Nana put down the bowl of chicken feed. She lifted Mariam's chin with a finger.

"Look at me, Mariam."

Reluctantly, Mariam did.

Nana said, "Learn this now and learn it well, my daughter: Like a compass needle that points north, a man's accusing finger always finds a woman. Always. You remember that, Mariam."

2.

To Jalil and his wives, I was a pokeroot. A mugwort. You too. And you weren't even born yet."

"What's a mugwort?" Mariam asked.

"A weed," Nana said. "Something you rip out and toss aside."

Mariam frowned internally. Jalil didn't treat her as a weed. He never had. But Mariam thought it wise to suppress this protest.

"Unlike weeds, I had to be replanted, you see, given food and water. On account of you. That was the deal Jalil made with his family."

Nana said she had refused to live in Herat.

"For what? To watch him drive his *kinchini* wives around town all day?"

She said she wouldn't live in her father's empty house either, in the village of Gul Daman, which sat on a steep hill two kilometers north of Herat. She said she wanted to live somewhere removed, detached, where neighbors wouldn't stare at her belly, point at her, snicker, or, worse yet, assault her with insincere kindnesses.

"And, believe me," Nana said, "it was a relief to your father having me out of sight. It suited him just fine."

It was Muhsin, Jalil's eldest son by his first wife, Khadija, who suggested the clearing. It was on the outskirts of Gul Daman. To get to it, one took a rutted, uphill dirt track that branched off the main road between Herat and Gul Daman. The track was flanked on either side by knee-high grass and speckles of white and bright yellow flowers. The track snaked uphill and led to a flat field where poplars and cottonwoods soared and wild bushes grew in clusters. From up there, one could make out the tips of the rusted blades of Gul Daman's windmill, on the left, and, on the right, all of Herat spread below. The path ended perpendicular to a wide, trout-filled stream, which rolled down from the Safid-koh mountains surrounding Gul Daman. Two hundred yards upstream, toward the mountains, there was a circular grove of weeping willow trees. In the center, in the shade of the willows, was the clearing.

Jalil went there to have a look. When he came back, Nana said, he sounded like a warden bragging about the clean walls and shiny floors of his prison.

"And so, your father built us this rathole."

NANA HAD ALMOST married once, when she was fifteen. The suitor had been a boy from Shindand, a young parakeet seller. Mariam knew the story from Nana herself, and, though Nana dismissed the episode, Mariam could tell by the wistful light in her eyes that she had been happy. Perhaps for the only time in her life, during those days leading up to her wedding, Nana had been genuinely happy.

As Nana told the story, Mariam sat on her lap and pictured her mother being fitted for a wedding dress. She imagined her on horseback, smiling shyly behind a veiled green gown, her palms painted red with henna, her hair parted with silver dust, the braids held together by tree sap. She saw musicians blowing the *shahnai* flute and banging on *dohol* drums, street children hooting and giving chase.

Then, a week before the wedding date, a *jinn* had entered Nana's body. This required no description to Mariam. She had witnessed it enough times with her own eyes: Nana collapsing suddenly, her body tightening, becoming rigid, her eyes rolling back, her arms and legs shaking as if something were throttling her from the inside, the froth at the corners of her mouth, white, sometimes pink with blood. Then the drowsiness, the frightening disorientation, the incoherent mumbling.

When the news reached Shindand, the parakeet seller's family called off the wedding.

"They got spooked" was how Nana put it.

The wedding dress was stashed away. After that, there were no more suitors.

IN THE CLEARING, Jalil and two of his sons, Farhad and Muhsin, built the small kolba where Mariam would live the first fifteen years of her life. They raised it with sun-dried bricks and plastered it with mud and handfuls of straw. It had two sleeping cots, a wooden table, two straight-backed chairs, a window, and shelves nailed to the walls where Nana placed clay pots and her beloved Chinese tea set. Jalil put in a new cast-iron stove for the winter and stacked logs of chopped wood behind the *kolba*. He added a tandoor outside for making bread and a chicken coop with a fence around it. He brought a few sheep, built them a feeding trough. He had Farhad and Muhsin dig a deep hole a hundred yards outside the circle of willows and built an outhouse over it.

Jalil could have hired laborers to build the *kolba*, Nana said, but he didn't.

"His idea of penance."

IN NANA'S ACCOUNT of the day that she gave birth to Mariam, no one came to help. It happened on a damp, overcast day in the spring of 1959, she said, the twenty-sixth year of King Zahir Shah's mostly uneventful forty-year reign. She said that Jalil hadn't bothered to summon a doctor, or even a midwife, even though he knew that the *jinn* might enter her body and cause her to have one of her fits in the act of delivering. She lay all alone on the *kolba*'s floor, a knife by her side, sweat drenching her body.

"When the pain got bad, I'd bite on a pillow and scream into it until I was hoarse. And still no one came to wipe my face or give me a drink of water. And you, Mariam jo, you were in no rush. Almost two days you made me lay on that cold, hard floor. I didn't eat or sleep, all I did was push and pray that you would come out."

"I'm sorry, Nana."

"I cut the cord between us myself. That's why I had a knife."

"I'm sorry."

Nana always gave a slow, burdened smile here, one of lingering recrimination or reluctant forgiveness, Mariam could never tell. It did not occur to young Mariam to ponder the unfairness of apologizing for the manner of her own birth.

By the time it *did* occur to her, around the time she turned ten, Mariam no longer believed this story of her birth. She believed Jalil's version, that though he'd been away he'd arranged for Nana to be taken to a hospital in Herat where she had been tended to by a doctor. She had lain on a clean, proper bed in a well-lit room. Jalil shook his head with sadness when Mariam told him about the knife.

Mariam also came to doubt that she had made her mother suffer for two full days.

"They told me it was all over within under an hour," Jalil said. "You were a good daughter, Mariam jo. Even in birth you were a good daughter."

"He wasn't even there!" Nana spat. "He was in Takht-e-Safar, horseback riding with his precious friends."

When they informed him that he had a new daughter, Nana said, Jalil had shrugged, kept brushing his horse's mane, and stayed in Takht-e-Safar another two weeks.

"The truth is, he didn't even hold you until you were a month old. And then only to look down once, comment on your longish face, and hand you back to me."

Mariam came to disbelieve this part of the story as well. Yes, Jalil admitted, he had been horseback riding in Takht-e-Safar, but, when they gave him the news, he had not shrugged. He had hopped on the saddle and ridden back to Herat. He had bounced her in his arms, run his thumb over her flaky eyebrows, and hummed a lullaby. Mariam did not picture Jalil saying that her face was long, though it was true that it was long.

Nana said she was the one who'd picked the name Mariam because it had been the name of her mother. Jalil said he chose the name because Mariam, the tuberose, was a lovely flower.

"Your favorite?" Mariam asked.

"Well, one of," he said and smiled.

3.

One of Mariam's earliest memories was the sound of a wheelbarrow's squeaky iron wheels bouncing over rocks. The wheelbarrow came once a month, filled with rice, flour, tea, sugar, cooking oil, soap, toothpaste. It was pushed by two of Mariam's half brothers, usually Muhsin and Ramin, sometimes Ramin and Farhad. Up the dirt track, over rocks and pebbles, around holes and bushes, the boys took turns pushing until they reached the stream. There, the wheelbarrow had to be emptied and the items hand-carried across the water. Then the boys would transfer the wheelbarrow across the stream and load it up again. Another two hundred yards of pushing followed, this time through tall, dense grass and around thickets of shrubs. Frogs leaped out of their way. The brothers waved mosquitoes from their sweaty faces.

"He has servants," Mariam said. "He could send a servant."

"His idea of penance," Nana said.

The sound of the wheelbarrow drew Mariam and Nana

13

outside. Mariam would always remember Nana the way she looked on Ration Day: a tall, bony, barefoot woman leaning in the doorway, her lazy eye narrowed to a slit, arms crossed in a defiant and mocking way. Her short-cropped, sunlit hair would be uncovered and uncombed. She would wear an ill-fitting gray shirt buttoned to the throat. The pockets were filled with walnut-sized rocks.

The boys sat by the stream and waited as Mariam and Nana transferred the rations to the *kolba*. They knew better than to get any closer than thirty yards, even though Nana's aim was poor and most of the rocks landed well short of their targets. Nana yelled at the boys as she carried bags of rice inside, and called them names Mariam didn't understand. She cursed their mothers, made hateful faces at them. The boys never returned the insults.

Mariam felt sorry for the boys. How tired their arms and legs must be, she thought pityingly, pushing that heavy load. She wished she were allowed to offer them water. But she said nothing, and if they waved at her she didn't wave back. Once, to please Nana, Mariam even yelled at Muhsin, told him he had a mouth shaped like a lizard's ass—and was consumed later with guilt, shame, and fear that they would tell Jalil. Nana, though, laughed so hard, her rotting front tooth in full display, that Mariam thought she would lapse into one of her fits. She looked at Mariam when she was done and said, "You're a good daughter."

When the barrow was empty, the boys scuffled back and pushed it away. Mariam would wait and watch them disappear into the tall grass and flowering weeds.

"Are you coming?"

"Yes, Nana."

"They laugh at you. They do. I hear them."

"I'm coming."

"You don't believe me?"

"Here I am."

"You know I love you, Mariam jo."

IN THE MORNINGS, they awoke to the distant bleating of sheep and the high-pitched toot of a flute as Gul Daman's shepherds led their flock to graze on the grassy hillside. Mariam and Nana milked the goats, fed the hens, and collected eggs. They made bread together. Nana showed her how to knead dough, how to kindle the tandoor and slap the flattened dough onto its inner walls. Nana taught her to sew too, and to cook rice and all the different toppings: *shalqam* stew with turnip, spinach *sabzi*, cauliflower with ginger.

Nana made no secret of her dislike for visitors—and, in fact, people in general—but she made exceptions for a select few. And so there was Gul Daman's leader, the village *arbab*, Habib Khan, a small-headed, bearded man with a large belly who came by once a month or so, tailed by a servant, who carried a chicken, sometimes a pot of *kichiri* rice, or a basket of dyed eggs, for Mariam.

Then there was a rotund, old woman that Nana called Bibi jo, whose late husband had been a stone carver and friends with Nana's father. Bibi jo was invariably accompanied by one of her six brides and a grandchild or two. She limped and huffed her way across the clearing and made a great show of rubbing her hip and lowering herself, with a pained sigh, onto the chair that Nana pulled up for her. Bibi jo too always brought Mariam something, a box of *dishlemeh* candy, a basket of quinces. For Nana, she first brought complaints about her failing health, and then gossip from Herat and Gul Daman, delivered at length and with gusto, as her daughter-in-law sat listening quietly and dutifully behind her.

But Mariam's favorite, other than Jalil of course, was Mullah Faizullah, the elderly village Koran tutor, its *akhund*. He came by once or twice a week from Gul Daman to teach Mariam the five daily *namaz* prayers and tutor her in Koran recitation, just as he had taught Nana when she'd been a little girl. It was Mullah Faizullah who had taught Mariam to read, who had patiently looked over her shoulder as her lips worked the words soundlessly, her index finger lingering beneath each word, pressing until the nail bed went white, as though she could squeeze the meaning out of the symbols. It was Mullah Faizullah who had held her hand, guided the pencil in it along the rise of each *alef*, the curve of each *beh*, the three dots of each *seh*.

He was a gaunt, stooping old man with a toothless smile and a white beard that dropped to his navel. Usually, he came alone to the *kolba*, though sometimes with his russet-haired son Hamza, who was a few years older than Mariam. When he showed up at the *kolba*, Mariam kissed Mullah Faizullah's hand—which felt like kissing a set of twigs covered with a thin layer of skin—and he kissed the top of her brow before they sat inside for the day's lesson. After, the two of them sat outside the *kolba*, ate pine nuts and sipped green tea, watched the bulbul birds darting from tree to tree. Sometimes they went for walks among the bronze fallen leaves and alder bushes, along the stream and toward the mountains. Mullah Faizullah twirled the beads of his *tasbeh* rosary as they strolled, and, in his quivering voice, told Mariam stories of all the things he'd seen in his youth, like the two-headed snake he'd found in Iran, on Isfahan's Thirty-three Arch Bridge, or the watermelon he had split once outside the Blue Mosque in Mazar, to find the seeds forming the words *Allah* on one half, *Akbar* on the other.

Mullah Faizullah admitted to Mariam that, at times, he did not understand the meaning of the Koran's words. But he said he liked the enchanting sounds the Arabic words made as they rolled off his tongue. He said they comforted him, eased his heart.

"They'll comfort you too, Mariam jo," he said. "You can summon them in your time of need, and they won't fail you. God's words will never betray you, my girl."

Mullah Faizullah listened to stories as well as he told them. When Mariam spoke, his attention never wavered. He nodded slowly and smiled with a look of gratitude, as if he had been granted a coveted privilege. It was easy to tell Mullah Faizullah things that Mariam didn't dare tell Nana.

One day, as they were walking, Mariam told him that she wished she would be allowed to go to school.

"I mean a real school, *akhund* sahib. Like in a class-room. Like my father's other kids."

Mullah Faizullah stopped.

The week before, Bibi jo had brought news that Jalil's daughters Saideh and Naheed were going to the Mehri School for girls in Herat. Since then, thoughts of class-rooms and teachers had rattled around Mariam's head, images of notebooks with lined pages, columns of num-bers, and pens that made dark, heavy marks. She pictured herself in a classroom with other girls her age. Mariam longed to place a ruler on a page and draw important-looking lines.

"Is that what you want?" Mullah Faizullah said, looking at her with his soft, watery eyes, his hands behind his stooping back, the shadow of his turban falling on a patch of bristling buttercups.

"Yes."

"And you want me to ask your mother for permission."

Mariam smiled. Other than Jalil, she thought there was no one in the world who understood her better than her old tutor.

"Then what can I do? God, in His wisdom, has given us each weaknesses, and foremost among my many is that I

17

am powerless to refuse you, Mariam jo," he said, tapping her cheek with one arthritic finger.

But later, when he broached Nana, she dropped the knife with which she was slicing onions. "What for?"

"If the girl wants to learn, let her, my dear. Let the girl have an education."

"Learn? Learn what, Mullah sahib?" Nana said sharply. "What is there to learn?" She snapped her eyes toward Mariam.

Mariam looked down at her hands.

"What's the sense schooling a girl like you? It's like shining a spittoon. And you'll learn nothing of value in those schools. There is only one, only one skill a woman like you and me needs in life, and they don't teach it in school. Look at me."

"You should not speak like this to her, my child," Mullah Faizullah said.

"Look at me."

Mariam did.

"Only one skill. And it's this: *tahamul.* Endure."

"Endure what, Nana?"

"Oh, don't you fret about *that,*" Nana said. "There won't be any shortage of things."

She went on to say how Jalil's wives had called her an ugly, lowly stone carver's daughter. How they'd made her wash laundry outside in the cold until her face went numb and her fingertips burned.

"It's our lot in life, Mariam. Women like us. We endure. It's all we have. Do you understand? Besides, they'll laugh at you in school. They will. They'll call you *harami.* They'll say the most terrible things about you. I won't have it."

Mariam nodded.

"And no more talk about school. You're all I have. I won't lose you to them. Look at me. No more talk about school."

"Be reasonable. Come now. If the girl wants—" Mullah Faizullah began.

"And you, *akhund* sahib, with all due respect, you should know better than to encourage these foolish ideas of hers. If you really care about her, then you make her see that she belongs here at home with her mother. There is nothing out there for her. Nothing but rejection and heartache. I know, *akhund* sahib. I *know*."

4.

Mariam loved having visitors at the *kolba*. The village *arbab* and his gifts, Bibi jo and her aching hip and endless gossiping, and, of course, Mullah Faizullah. But there was no one, no one, that Mariam longed to see more than Jalil.

The anxiety set in on Tuesday nights. Mariam would sleep poorly, fretting that some business entanglement would prevent Jalil from coming on Thursday, that she would have to wait a whole other week to see him. On Wednesdays, she paced outside, around the *kolba,* tossed chicken feed absentmindedly into the coop. She went for aimless walks, picking petals from flowers and batting at the mosquitoes nibbling on her arms. Finally, on Thursdays, all she could do was sit against a wall, eyes glued to the stream, and wait. If Jalil was running late, a terrible dread filled her bit by bit. Her knees would weaken, and she would have to go somewhere and lie down.

Then Nana would call, "And there he is, your father. In all his glory."

20

Mariam would leap to her feet when she spotted him hopping stones across the stream, all smiles and hearty waves. Mariam knew that Nana was watching her, gauging her reaction, and it always took effort to stay in the doorway, to wait, to watch him slowly make his way to her, to not run to him. She restrained herself, patiently watched him walk through the tall grass, his suit jacket slung over his shoulder, the breeze lifting his red necktie.

When Jalil entered the clearing, he would throw his jacket on the tandoor and open his arms. Mariam would walk, then finally run, to him, and he would catch her under the arms and toss her up high. Mariam would squeal.

Suspended in the air, Mariam would see Jalil's upturned face below her, his wide, crooked smile, his widow's peak, his cleft chin—a perfect pocket for the tip of her pinkie—his teeth, the whitest in a town of rotting molars. She liked his trimmed mustache, and she liked that no matter the weather he always wore a suit on his visits—dark brown, his favorite color, with the white triangle of a handkerchief in the breast pocket—and cuff links too, and a tie, usually red, which he left loosened. Mariam could see herself too, reflected in the brown of Jalil's eyes: her hair billowing, her face blazing with excitement, the sky behind her.

Nana said that one of these days he would miss, that she, Mariam, would slip through his fingers, hit the ground, and break a bone. But Mariam did not believe that Jalil would drop her. She believed that she would always land safely into her father's clean, well-manicured hands.

They sat outside the *kolba*, in the shade, and Nana served them tea. Jalil and she acknowledged each other with an uneasy smile and a nod. Jalil never brought up Nana's rock throwing or her cursing.

Despite her rants against him when he wasn't around,

21

Nana was subdued and mannerly when Jalil visited. Her hair was always washed. She brushed her teeth, wore her best *hijab* for him. She sat quietly on a chair across from him, hands folded on her lap. She did not look at him directly and never used coarse language around him. When she laughed, she covered her mouth with a fist to hide the bad tooth.

Nana asked about his businesses. And his wives too. When she told him that she had heard, through Bibi jo, that his youngest wife, Nargis, was expecting her third child, Jalil smiled courteously and nodded.

"Well. You must be happy," Nana said. "How many is that for you, now? Ten, is it, *mashallah*? Ten?"

Jalil said yes, ten.

"Eleven, if you count Mariam, of course."

Later, after Jalil went home, Mariam and Nana had a small fight about this. Mariam said she had tricked him.

After tea with Nana, Mariam and Jalil always went fishing in the stream. He showed her how to cast her line, how to reel in the trout. He taught her the proper way to gut a trout, to clean it, to lift the meat off the bone in one motion. He drew pictures for her as they waited for a strike, showed her how to draw an elephant in one stroke without ever lifting the pen off the paper. He taught her rhymes. Together they sang:

Lili lili birdbath,
Sitting on a dirt path,
Minnow sat on the rim and drank,
Slipped, and in the water she sank.

Jalil brought clippings from Herat's newspaper, *Ittifaq-i Islam*, and read from them to her. He was Mariam's link, her proof that there existed a world at large, beyond the *kolba*, beyond Gul Daman and Herat too, a world of presidents with unpronounceable names, and trains and museums and soccer, and rockets that orbited the earth and landed on the moon, and, every Thursday, Jalil brought a piece of that world with him to the *kolba*.

He was the one who told her in the summer of 1973, when Mariam was fourteen, that King Zahir Shah, who had ruled from Kabul for forty years, had been overthrown in a bloodless coup.

"His cousin Daoud Khan did it while the king was in Italy getting medical treatment. You remember Daoud Khan, right? I told you about him. He was prime minister in Kabul when you were born. Anyway, Afghanistan is no longer a monarchy, Mariam. You see, it's a republic now, and Daoud Khan is the president. There are rumors that the socialists in Kabul helped him take power. Not that he's a socialist himself, mind you, but that they helped him. That's the rumor anyway."

Mariam asked him what a socialist was and Jalil began to explain, but Mariam barely heard him.

"Are you listening?"

"I am."

He saw her looking at the bulge in his coat's side pocket. "Ah. Of course. Well. Here, then. Without further ado . . ."

He fished a small box from his pocket and gave it to her. He did this from time to time, bring her small presents. A carnelian bracelet cuff one time, a choker with lapis lazuli beads another. That day, Mariam opened the box and found a leaf-shaped pendant, tiny coins etched with moons and stars hanging from it.

"Try it on, Mariam jo."

She did. "What do you think?"

Jalil beamed. "I think you look like a queen."

After he left, Nana saw the pendant around Mariam's

neck.

"Nomad jewelry," she said. "I've seen them make it. They melt the coins people throw at them and make jewelry. Let's see him bring you gold next time, your precious father. Let's see him."

When it was time for Jalil to leave, Mariam always stood in the doorway and watched him exit the clearing, deflated at the thought of the week that stood, like an immense, immovable object, between her and his next visit. Mariam always held her breath as she watched him go. She held her breath and, in her head, counted seconds. She pretended that for each second that she didn't breathe, God would grant her another day with Jalil.

At night, Mariam lay in her cot and wondered what his house in Herat was like. She wondered what it would be like to live with him, to see him every day. She pictured herself handing him a towel as he shaved, telling him when he nicked himself. She would brew tea for him. She would sew on his missing buttons. They would take walks in Herat together, in the vaulted bazaar where Jalil said you could find anything you wanted. They would ride in his car, and people would point and say, "There goes Jalil Khan with his daughter." He would show her the famed tree that had a poet buried beneath it.

One day soon, Mariam decided, she would tell Jalil these things. And when he heard, when he saw how much she missed him when he was gone, he would surely take her with him. He would bring her to Herat, to live in his house, just like his other children.

5.

"I know what I want," Mariam said to Jalil.

It was the spring of 1974, the year Mariam turned fifteen. The three of them were sitting outside the *kolba,* in a patch of shade thrown by the willows, on folding chairs arranged in a triangle.

"For my birthday . . . I know what I want."

"You do?" said Jalil, smiling encouragingly.

Two weeks before, at Mariam's prodding, Jalil had let on that an American film was playing at his cinema. It was a special kind of film, what he'd called a cartoon. The entire film was a series of drawings, he said, thousands of them, so that when they were made into a film and projected onto a screen you had the illusion that the drawings were moving. Jalil said the film told the story of an old, childless toymaker who is lonely and desperately wants a son. So he carves a puppet, a boy, who magically comes to life. Mariam had asked him to tell her more, and Jalil said that the old man and his puppet had all sorts of adventures, that there was a place called Pleasure Island, and

25

bad boys who turned into donkeys. They even got swallowed by a whale at the end, the puppet and his father. Mariam had told Mullah Faizullah all about this film.

"I want you to take me to your cinema," Mariam said now. "I want to see the cartoon. I want to see the puppet boy."

With this, Mariam sensed a shift in the atmosphere. Her parents stirred in their seats. Mariam could feel them exchanging looks.

"That's not a good idea," said Nana. Her voice was calm, had the controlled, polite tone she used around Jalil, but Mariam could feel her hard, accusing glare.

Jalil shifted on his chair. He coughed, cleared his throat.

"You know," he said, "the picture quality isn't that good. Neither is the sound. And the projector's been malfunctioning recently. Maybe your mother is right. Maybe you can think of another present, Mariam jo."

"Aneh," Nana said. "You see? Your father agrees."

BUT LATER, at the stream, Mariam said, "Take me."

"I'll tell you what," Jalil said. "I'll send someone to pick you up and take you. I'll make sure they get you a good seat and all the candy you want."

"Nay. I want *you* to take me."

"Mariam jo—"

"And I want you to invite my brothers and sisters too. I want to meet them. I want us all to go, together. It's what I want."

Jalil sighed. He was looking away, toward the mountains.

Mariam remembered him telling her that on the screen a human face looked as big as a house, that when a car crashed up there you felt the metal twisting in your bones. She pictured herself sitting in the private balcony seats,

26

lapping at ice cream, alongside her siblings and Jalil. "It's what I want," she said.

Jalil looked at her with a forlorn expression.

"Tomorrow. At noon. I'll meet you at this very spot. All right? Tomorrow?"

"Come here," he said. He hunkered down, pulled her to him, and held her for a long, long time.

AT FIRST, Nana paced around the *kolba*, clenching and unclenching her fists.

"Of all the daughters I could have had, why did God give me an ungrateful one like you? Everything I endured for you! How dare you! How dare you abandon me like this, you treacherous little *harami*!"

Then she mocked.

"What a stupid girl you are! You think you matter to him, that you're wanted in his house? You think you're a daughter to him? That he's going to take you in? Let me tell you something. A man's heart is a wretched, wretched thing, Mariam. It isn't like a mother's womb. It won't bleed, it won't stretch to make room for you. I'm the only one who loves you. I'm all you have in this world, Mariam, and when I'm gone you'll have nothing. You'll have nothing. You *are* nothing!"

Then she tried guilt.

"I'll die if you go. The *jinn* will come, and I'll have one of my fits. You'll see, I'll swallow my tongue and die. Don't leave me, Mariam jo. Please stay. I'll die if you go."

Mariam said nothing.

"You know I love you, Mariam jo."

Mariam said she was going for a walk.

She feared she might say hurtful things if she stayed: that she knew the *jinn* was a lie, that Jalil had told her that what Nana had was a disease with a name and that pills could make it better. She might have asked Nana

27

why she refused to see Jalil's doctors, as he had insisted she do, why she wouldn't take the pills he'd bought for her. If she could articulate it, she might have said to Nana that she was tired of being an instrument, of being lied to, laid claim to, used. That she was sick of Nana twisting the truths of their life and making her, Mariam, another of her grievances against the world.

You're afraid, Nana, she might have said. *You're afraid that I might find the happiness you never had. And you don't want me to be happy. You don't want a good life for me. You're the one with the wretched heart.*

THERE WAS A LOOKOUT, on the edge of the clearing, where Mariam liked to go. She sat there now, on dry, warm grass. Herat was visible from here, spread below her like a child's board game: the Women's Garden to the north of the city, Char-suq Bazaar and the ruins of Alexander the Great's old citadel to the south. She could make out the minarets in the distance, like the dusty fingers of giants, and the streets that she imagined were milling with people, carts, mules. She saw swallows swooping and circling overhead. She was envious of these birds. They had been to Herat. They had flown over its mosques, its bazaars. Maybe they had landed on the walls of Jalil's home, on the front steps of his cinema.

She picked up ten pebbles and arranged them vertically, in three columns. This was a game that she played privately from time to time when Nana wasn't looking. She put four pebbles in the first column, for Khadija's children, three for Afsoon's, and three in the third column for Nargis's children. Then she added a fourth column. A solitary, eleventh pebble.

THE NEXT MORNING, Mariam wore a cream-colored dress that fell to her knees, cotton trousers, and a green *hijab* over her hair. She agonized a bit over the *hijab*, its being green and not matching the dress, but it would have to do—moths had eaten holes into her white one.

She checked the clock. It was an old hand-wound clock with black numbers on a mint green face, a present from Mullah Faizullah. It was nine o'clock. She wondered where Nana was. She thought about going outside and looking for her, but she dreaded the confrontation, the aggrieved looks. Nana would accuse her of betrayal. She would mock her for her mistaken ambitions.

Mariam sat down. She tried to make time pass by drawing an elephant in one stroke, the way Jalil had shown her, over and over. She became stiff from all the sitting but wouldn't lie down for fear that her dress would wrinkle.

When the hands finally showed eleven-thirty, Mariam pocketed the eleven pebbles and went outside. On her way to the stream, she saw Nana sitting on a chair, in the shade, beneath the domed roof of a weeping willow. Mariam couldn't tell whether Nana saw her or not.

At the stream, Mariam waited by the spot they had agreed on the day before. In the sky, a few gray, cauliflower-shaped clouds drifted by. Jalil had taught her that gray clouds got their color by being so dense that their top parts absorbed the sunlight and cast their own shadow along the base. *That's what you see, Mariam jo,* he had said, *the dark in their underbelly.*

Some time passed.

Mariam went back to the *kolba*. This time, she walked around the west-facing periphery of the clearing so she wouldn't have to pass by Nana. She checked the clock. It was almost one o'clock.

He's a businessman, Mariam thought. *Something has come up.*

She went back to the stream and waited awhile longer. Blackbirds circled overhead, dipped into the grass

29

somewhere. She watched a caterpillar inching along the foot of an immature thistle.

She waited until her legs were stiff. This time, she did not go back to the *kolba*. She rolled up the legs of her trousers to the knees, crossed the stream, and, for the first time in her life, headed down the hill for Herat.

NANA WAS WRONG about Herat too. No one pointed. No one laughed. Mariam walked along noisy, crowded, cypress-lined boulevards, amid a steady stream of pedestrians, bicycle riders, and mule-drawn *garis*, and no one threw a rock at her. No one called her a *harami*. Hardly anyone even looked at her. She was, unexpectedly, marvelously, an ordinary person here.

For a while, Mariam stood by an oval-shaped pool in the center of a big park where pebble paths crisscrossed. With wonder, she ran her fingers over the beautiful marble horses that stood along the edge of the pool and gazed down at the water with opaque eyes. She spied on a cluster of boys who were setting sail to paper ships. Mariam saw flowers everywhere, tulips, lilies, petunias, their petals awash in sunlight. People walked along the paths, sat on benches and sipped tea.

Mariam could hardly believe that she was here. Her heart was battering with excitement. She wished Mullah Faizullah could see her now. How daring he would find her. How brave! She gave herself over to the new life that awaited her in this city, a life with a father, with sisters and brothers, a life in which she would love and be loved back, without reservation or agenda, without shame.

Sprightly, she walked back to the wide thoroughfare near the park. She passed old vendors with leathery faces sitting under the shade of plane trees, gazing at her impassively behind pyramids of cherries and mounds of grapes. Barefoot boys gave chase to cars and buses, waving bags of quinces. Mariam stood at a street corner and watched the passersby, unable to understand how they could be so indifferent to the marvels around them.

After a while, she worked up the nerve to ask the elderly owner of a horse-drawn *gari* if he knew where Jalil, the cinema's owner, lived. The old man had plump cheeks and wore a rainbow-striped *chapan*. "You're not from Herat, are you?" he said companionably. "Everyone knows where Jalil Khan lives."

"Can you point me?"

He opened a foil-wrapped toffee and said, "Are you alone?"

"Yes."

"Climb on. I'll take you."

"I can't pay you. I don't have any money."

He gave her the toffee. He said he hadn't had a ride in two hours and he was planning on going home anyway. Jalil's house was on the way.

Mariam climbed onto the *gari*. They rode in silence, side by side. On the way there, Mariam saw herb shops, and open-fronted cubbyholes where shoppers bought oranges and pears, books, shawls, even falcons. Children played marbles in circles drawn in dust. Outside teahouses, on carpet-covered wooden platforms, men drank tea and smoked tobacco from hookahs.

The old man turned onto a wide, conifer-lined street. He brought his horse to a stop at the midway point.

"There. Looks like you're in luck, *dokhtar jo*. That's his car."

Mariam hopped down. He smiled and rode on.

MARIAM HAD NEVER before touched a car. She ran her fingers along the hood of Jalil's car, which was black, shiny, with glittering wheels in which Mariam saw a flattened, widened version of herself. The seats were made of white leather. Behind the steering wheel, Mariam saw round glass panels with needles behind them.

For a moment, Mariam heard Nana's voice in her head, mocking, dousing the deep-seated glow of her hopes. With shaky legs, Mariam approached the front door of the house. She put her hands on the walls. They were so tall, so foreboding, Jalil's walls. She had to crane her neck to see where the tops of cypress trees protruded over them from the other side. The treetops swayed in the breeze, and she imagined they were nodding their welcome to her. Mariam steadied herself against the waves of dismay passing through her.

A barefoot young woman opened the door. She had a tattoo under her lower lip.

"I'm here to see Jalil Khan. I'm Mariam. His daughter."

A look of confusion crossed the girl's face. Then, a flash of recognition. There was a faint smile on her lips now, and an air of eagerness about her, of anticipation. "Wait here," the girl said quickly.

She closed the door.

A few minutes passed. Then a man opened the door. He was tall and square-shouldered, with sleepy-looking eyes and a calm face.

"I'm Jalil Khan's chauffeur," he said, not unkindly.

"His what?"

"His driver. Jalil Khan is not here."

"I see his car," Mariam said.

"He's away on urgent business."

"When will he be back?"

"He didn't say."

Mariam said she would wait.

He closed the gates. Mariam sat, and drew her knees to her chest. It was early evening already, and she was getting hungry. She ate the *gari* driver's toffee. A while later, the driver came out again.

"You need to go home now," he said. "It'll be dark in less than an hour."

"I'm used to the dark."

"It'll get cold too. Why don't you let me drive you home? I'll tell him you were here."

Mariam only looked at him.

"I'll take you to a hotel, then. You can sleep comfortably there. We'll see what we can do in the morning."

"Let me in the house."

"I've been instructed not to. Look, no one knows when he's coming back. It could be days."

Mariam crossed her arms.

The driver sighed and looked at her with gentle reproach.

Over the years, Mariam would have ample occasion to think about how things might have turned out if she had let the driver take her back to the *kolba*. But she didn't. She spent the night outside Jalil's house. She watched the sky darken, the shadows engulf the neighboring house-fronts. The tattooed girl brought her some bread and a plate of rice, which Mariam said she didn't want. The girl left it near Mariam. From time to time, Mariam heard footsteps down the street, doors swinging open, muffled greetings. Electric lights came on, and windows glowed dimly. Dogs barked. When she could no longer resist the hunger, Mariam ate the plate of rice and the bread. Then she listened to the crickets chirping from gardens. Overhead, clouds slid past a pale moon.

In the morning, she was shaken awake. Mariam saw that during the night someone had covered her with a blanket.

It was the driver shaking her shoulder.

"This is enough. You've made a scene. *Bas.* It's time to go."

Mariam sat up and rubbed her eyes. Her back and neck were sore. "I'm going to wait for him."

"Look at me," he said. "Jalil Khan says that I need to take you back now. Right now. Do you understand? Jalil Khan says so."

He opened the rear passenger door to the car. "*Bia.* Come on," he said softly.

"I want to see him," Mariam said. Her eyes were tearing over.

The driver sighed. "Let me take you home. Come on, *dokhtar jo.*"

Mariam stood up and walked toward him. But then, at the last moment, she changed direction and ran to the front gates. She felt the driver's fingers fumbling for a grip at her shoulder. She shed him and burst through the open gates.

In the handful of seconds that she was in Jalil's garden, Mariam's eyes registered seeing a gleaming glass structure with plants inside it, grape vines clinging to wooden trellises, a fishpond built with gray blocks of stone, fruit trees, and bushes of brightly colored flowers everywhere. Her gaze skimmed over all of these things before they found a face, across the garden, in an upstairs window. The face was there for only an instant, a flash, but long enough. Long enough for Mariam to see the eyes widen, the mouth open. Then it snapped away from view. A hand appeared and frantically pulled at a cord. The curtains fell shut.

Then a pair of hands buried into her armpits and she was lifted off the ground. Mariam kicked. The pebbles spilled from her pocket. Mariam kept kicking and crying as she was carried to the car and lowered onto the cold leather of the backseat.

THE DRIVER TALKED in a muted, consoling tone as he drove. Mariam did not hear him. All during the ride, as she bounced in the backseat, she cried. They were tears of grief, of anger, of disillusionment. But mainly tears of a

34

deep, deep shame at how foolishly she had given herself over to Jalil, how she had fretted over what dress to wear, over the mismatching *hijab*, walking all the way here, refusing to leave, sleeping on the street like a stray dog. And she was ashamed of how she had dismissed her mother's stricken looks, her puffy eyes. Nana, who had warned her, who had been right all along.

Mariam kept thinking of his face in the upstairs window. He let her sleep on the street. *On the street.* Mariam cried lying down. She didn't sit up, didn't want to be seen. She imagined all of Herat knew this morning how she'd disgraced herself. She wished Mullah Faizullah were here so she could put her head on his lap and let him comfort her.

After a while, the road became bumpier and the nose of the car pointed up. They were on the uphill road between Herat and Gul Daman.

What would she say to Nana, Mariam wondered. How would she apologize? How could she even face Nana now?

The car stopped and the driver helped her out. "I'll walk you," he said.

She let him guide her across the road and up the track. There was honeysuckle growing along the path, and milkweed too. Bees were buzzing over twinkling wildflowers. The driver took her hand and helped her cross the stream. Then he let go, and he was talking about how Herat's famous one hundred and twenty days' winds would start blowing soon, from midmorning to dusk, and how the sand flies would go on a feeding frenzy, and then suddenly he was standing in front of her, trying to cover her eyes, pushing her back the way they had come and saying, "Go back! No. Don't look now. Turn around! Go back!"

But he wasn't fast enough. Mariam saw. A gust of wind blew and parted the drooping branches of the weeping willow like a curtain, and Mariam caught a glimpse of what was beneath the tree: the straight-backed chair, overturned. The rope dropping from a high branch. Nana dangling at the end of it.

6.

They buried Nana in a corner of the cemetery in Gul Daman. Mariam stood beside Bibi jo, with the women, as Mullah Faizullah recited prayers at the graveside and the men lowered Nana's shrouded body into the ground.

Afterward, Jalil walked Mariam to the *kolba*, where, in front of the villagers who accompanied them, he made a great show of tending to Mariam. He collected a few of her things, put them in a suitcase. He sat beside her cot, where she lay down, and fanned her face. He stroked her forehead, and, with a woebegone expression on his face, asked if she needed *anything? anything?*—he said it like that, twice.

"I want Mullah Faizullah," Mariam said.

"Of course. He's outside. I'll get him for you."

It was when Mullah Faizullah's slight, stooping figure appeared in the *kolba*'s doorway that Mariam cried for the first time that day.

"Oh, Mariam jo."

He sat next to her and cupped her face in his hands. "You go on and cry, Mariam jo. Go on. There is no shame in it. But remember, my girl, what the Koran says, 'Blessed is He in Whose hand is the kingdom, and He Who has power over all things, Who created death and life that He may try you.' The Koran speaks the truth, my girl. Behind every trial and every sorrow that He makes us shoulder, God has a reason."

But Mariam could not hear comfort in God's words. Not that day. Not then. All she could hear was Nana saying, *I'll die if you go. I'll just die.* All she could do was cry and cry and let her tears fall on the spotted, paper-thin skin of Mullah Faizullah's hands.

On the ride to his house, Jalil sat in the backseat of his car with Mariam, his arm draped over her shoulder.

"You can stay with me, Mariam jo," he said. "I've asked them already to clean a room for you. It's upstairs. You'll like it, I think. You'll have a view of the garden."

For the first time, Mariam could hear him with Nana's ears. She could hear so clearly now the insincerity that had always lurked beneath, the hollow, false assurances. She could not bring herself to look at him.

When the car stopped before Jalil's house, the driver opened the door for them and carried Mariam's suitcase. Jalil guided her, one palm cupped around each of her shoulders, through the same gates outside of which, two days before, Mariam had slept on the sidewalk waiting for him. Two days before—when Mariam could think of nothing in the world she wanted more than to walk in this garden with Jalil—felt like another lifetime. How could her life have turned upside down so quickly, Mariam asked herself. She kept her gaze to the ground, on her feet, stepping on the gray stone path. She was aware of the presence of people in the garden, murmuring, stepping aside, as she and Jalil walked past. She sensed the weight of eyes on her, looking down from the windows upstairs.

Inside the house too, Mariam kept her head down. She walked on a maroon carpet with a repeating blue-and-yellow octagonal pattern, saw out of the corner of her eye the marble bases of statues, the lower halves of vases, the frayed ends of richly colored tapestries hanging from walls. The stairs she and Jalil took were wide and covered with a similar carpet, nailed down at the base of each step. At the top of the stairs, Jalil led her to the left, down another long, carpeted hallway. He stopped by one of the doors, opened it, and let her in.

"Your sisters Niloufar and Atieh play here sometimes," Jalil said, "but mostly we use this as a guest room. You'll be comfortable here, I think. It's nice, isn't it?"

The room had a bed with a green-flowered blanket knit in a tightly woven, honeycomb design. The curtains, pulled back to reveal the garden below, matched the blanket. Beside the bed was a three-drawer chest with a flower vase on it. There were shelves along the walls, with framed pictures of people Mariam did not recognize. On one of the shelves, Mariam saw a collection of identical wooden dolls, arranged in a line in order of decreasing size.

Jalil saw her looking. "*Matryoshka* dolls. I got them in Moscow. You can play with them, if you want. No one will mind."

Mariam sat down on the bed.

"Is there anything you want?" Jalil said.

Mariam lay down. Closed her eyes. After a while, she heard him softly shut the door.

EXCEPT FOR WHEN she had to use the bathroom down the hall, Mariam stayed in the room. The girl with the tattoo, the one who had opened the gates to her, brought her meals on a tray: lamb kebab, *sabzi*, *aush* soup. Most of it went uneaten. Jalil came by several times a day, sat on the bed beside her, asked her if she was all right.

"You could eat downstairs with the rest of us," he said, but without much conviction. He understood a little too readily when Mariam said she preferred to eat alone.

From the window, Mariam watched impassively what she had wondered about and longed to see for most of her life: the comings and goings of Jalil's daily life. Servants rushed in and out of the front gates. A gardener was always trimming bushes, watering plants in the green-house. Cars with long, sleek hoods pulled up on the street. From them emerged men in suits, in *chapan*s and caracul hats, women in *hijab*s, children with neatly combed hair. And as Mariam watched Jalil shake these strangers' hands, as she saw him cross his palms on his chest and nod to their wives, she knew that Nana had spoken the truth. She did not belong here.

But where do I belong? What am I going to do now?

I'm all you have in this world, Mariam, and when I'm gone you'll have nothing. You'll have nothing. You are nothing!

Like the wind through the willows around the *kolba*, gusts of an inexpressible blackness kept passing through Mariam.

On Mariam's second full day at Jalil's house, a little girl came into the room.

"I have to get something," she said.

Mariam sat up on the bed and crossed her legs, pulled the blanket on her lap.

The girl hurried across the room and opened the closet door. She fetched a square-shaped gray box.

"You know what this is?" she said. She opened the box. "It's called a gramophone. *Gramo. Phone.* It plays records.

You know, music. A gramophone."

"You're Niloufar. You're eight."

The little girl smiled. She had Jalil's smile and his dimpled chin. "How did you know?"

Mariam shrugged. She didn't say to this girl that she'd once named a pebble after her.

"Do you want to hear a song?"

Mariam shrugged again.

Niloufar plugged in the gramophone. She fished a small record from a pouch beneath the box's lid. She put it on, lowered the needle. Music began to play.

> *I will use a flower petal for paper,*
> *And write you the sweetest letter,*
> *You are the sultan of my heart,*
> *the sultan of my heart.*

"Do you know it?"

"No."

"It's from an Iranian film. I saw it at my father's cinema. Hey, do you want to see something?"

Before Mariam could answer, Niloufar had put her palms and forehead to the ground. She pushed with her soles and then she was standing upside down, on her head, in a three-point stance.

"Can you do that?" she said thickly.

"No."

Niloufar dropped her legs and pulled her blouse back down. "I could teach you," she said, pushing hair from her flushed brow. "So how long will you stay here?"

"I don't know."

"My mother says you're not really my sister like you say you are."

"I never said I was," Mariam lied.

"She says you did. I don't care. What I mean is, I don't

41

mind if you did say it, or if you are my sister. I don't mind."

Mariam lay down. "I'm tired now."

"My mother says a *jinn* made your mother hang herself."

"You can stop that now," Mariam said, turning to her side. "The music, I mean."

Bibi jo came to see her that day too. It was raining by the time she came. She lowered her large body onto the chair beside the bed, grimacing.

"This rain, Mariam jo, it's murder on my hips. Just murder, I tell you. I hope . . . Oh, now, come here, child. Come here to Bibi jo. Don't cry. There, now. You poor thing. *Tsk.* You poor, poor thing."

That night, Mariam couldn't sleep for a long time. She lay in bed looking at the sky, listening to the footsteps below, the voices muffled by walls and the sheets of rain punishing the window. When she did doze off, she was startled awake by shouting. Voices downstairs, sharp and angry. Mariam couldn't make out the words. Someone slammed a door.

The next morning, Mullah Faizullah came to visit her. When she saw her friend at the door, his white beard and his amiable, toothless smile, Mariam felt tears stinging the corners of her eyes again. She swung her feet over the side of the bed and hurried over. She kissed his hand as always and he her brow. She pulled him up a chair.

He showed her the Koran he had brought with him and opened it. "I figured no sense in skipping our routine, eh?"

"You know I don't need lessons anymore, Mullah sahib. You taught me every *surrah* and *ayat* in the Koran years ago."

He smiled, and raised his hands in a gesture of surrender. "I confess, then. I've been found out. But I can think of worse excuses to visit you."

"You don't need excuses. Not you."

"You're kind to say that, Mariam jo."

He passed her his Koran. As he'd taught her, she kissed it three times—touching it to her brow between each kiss—and gave it back to him.

"How are you, my girl?"

"I keep," Mariam began. She had to stop, feeling like a rock had lodged itself in her throat. "I keep thinking of what she said to me before I left. She—"

"*Nay, nay, nay.*" Mullah Faizullah put his hand on her knee. "Your mother, may Allah forgive her, was a troubled and unhappy woman, Mariam jo. She did a terrible thing to herself. To herself, to you, and also to Allah. He will forgive her, for He is all-forgiving, but Allah is saddened by what she did. He does not approve of the taking of life, be it another's or one's own, for He says that life is sacred. You see—" He pulled his chair closer, took Mariam's hand in both of his own. "You see, I knew your mother before you were born, when she was a little girl, and I tell you that she was unhappy then. The seed for what she did was planted long ago, I'm afraid. What I mean to say is that this was not your fault. It wasn't your fault, my girl."

"I shouldn't have left her. I should have—"

"You stop that. These thoughts are no good, Mariam jo. You hear me, child? No good. They will destroy you. It wasn't your fault. It wasn't your fault. No."

Mariam nodded, but as desperately as she wanted to she could not bring herself to believe him.

ONE AFTERNOON, a week later, there was a knock on the door, and a tall woman walked in. She was fair-skinned, had reddish hair and long fingers.

"I'm Afsoon," she said. "Niloufar's mother. Why don't you wash up, Mariam, and come downstairs?"

Mariam said she would rather stay in her room.

"No, *na fahmidi*, you don't understand. You *need* to come down. We have to talk to you. It's important."

7.

They sat across from her, Jalil and his wives, at a long, dark brown table. Between them, in the center of the table, was a crystal vase of fresh marigolds and a sweating pitcher of water. The red-haired woman who had introduced herself as Niloufar's mother, Afsoon, was sitting on Jalil's right. The other two, Khadija and Nargis, were on his left. The wives each had on a flimsy black scarf, which they wore not on their heads but tied loosely around the neck like an afterthought. Mariam, who could not imagine that they would wear black for Nana, pictured one of them suggesting it, or maybe Jalil, just before she'd been summoned.

Afsoon poured water from the pitcher and put the glass before Mariam on a checkered cloth coaster. "Only spring and it's warm already," she said. She made a fanning motion with her hand.

"Have you been comfortable?" Nargis, who had a small chin and curly black hair, asked. "We hope you've been comfortable. This . . . ordeal . . . must be very hard for you. So difficult."

The other two nodded. Mariam took in their plucked eyebrows, the thin, tolerant smiles they were giving her. There was an unpleasant hum in Mariam's head. Her throat burned. She drank some of the water.

Through the wide window behind Jalil, Mariam could see a row of flowering apple trees. On the wall beside the window stood a dark wooden cabinet. In it was a clock, and a framed photograph of Jalil and three young boys holding a fish. The sun caught the sparkle in the fish's scales. Jalil and the boys were grinning.

"Well," Afsoon began. "I—that is, we—have brought you here because we have some very good news to give you."

Mariam looked up.

She caught a quick exchange of glances between the women over Jalil, who slouched in his chair looking unseeingly at the pitcher on the table. It was Khadija, the oldest-looking of the three, who turned her gaze to Mariam, and Mariam had the impression that this duty too had been discussed, agreed upon, before they had called for her.

"You have a suitor," Khadija said.

Mariam's stomach fell. "A what?" she said through suddenly numb lips.

"A *khastegar*. A suitor. His name is Rasheed," Khadija went on. "He is a friend of a business acquaintance of your father's. He's a Pashtun, from Kandahar originally, but he lives in Kabul, in the Deh-Mazang district, in a two-story house that he owns."

Afsoon was nodding. "And he does speak Farsi, like us, like you. So you won't have to learn Pashto."

Mariam's chest was tightening. The room was reeling up and down, the ground shifting beneath her feet.

"He's a shoemaker," Khadija was saying now. "But not some kind of ordinary street-side *moochi*, no, no. He has his own shop, and he is one of the most sought-after shoemakers in Kabul. He makes them for diplomats, members of the presidential family—that class of people. So you see, he will have no trouble providing for you."

Mariam fixed her eyes on Jalil, her heart somersaulting in her chest. "Is this true? What she's saying, is it true?"

But Jalil wouldn't look at her. He went on chewing the corner of his lower lip and staring at the pitcher.

"Now he *is* a little older than you," Afsoon chimed in. "But he can't be more than . . . forty. Forty-five at the most. Wouldn't you say, Nargis?"

"Yes. But I've seen nine-year-old girls given to men twenty years older than your suitor, Mariam. We all have. What are you, fifteen? That's a good, solid marrying age for a girl." There was enthusiastic nodding at this. It did not escape Mariam that no mention was made of her half sisters Saideh or Naheed, both her own age, both students in the Mehri School in Herat, both with plans to enroll in Kabul University. Fifteen, evidently, was not a good, solid marrying age for them.

"What's more," Nargis went on, "he too has had a great loss in his life. His wife, we hear, died during childbirth ten years ago. And then, three years ago, his son drowned in a lake."

"It's very sad, yes. He's been looking for a bride the last few years but hasn't found anyone suitable."

"I don't want to," Mariam said. She looked at Jalil. "I don't want this. Don't make me." She hated the sniffling, pleading tone of her voice but could not help it.

"Now, be reasonable, Mariam," one of the wives said.

Mariam was no longer keeping track of who was saying what. She went on staring at Jalil, waiting for him to speak up, to say that none of this was true.

"You can't spend the rest of your life here."

"Don't you want a family of your own?"

"Yes. A home, children of your own?"

"You have to move on."

"True that it would be preferable that you marry a local, a Tajik, but Rasheed is healthy, and interested in you. He has a home and a job. That's all that really matters, isn't it? And Kabul is a beautiful and exciting city. You may not get another opportunity this good."

Mariam turned her attention to the wives.

"I'll live with Mullah Faizullah," she said. "He'll take me in. I know he will."

"That's no good," Khadija said. "He's old and so . . ." She searched for the right word, and Mariam knew then that what she really wanted to say was *He's so close.* She understood what they meant to do. *You may not get another opportunity this good.* And neither would they. They had been disgraced by her birth, and this was their chance to erase, once and for all, the last trace of their husband's scandalous mistake. She was being sent away because she was the walking, breathing embodiment of their shame.

"He's so old and weak," Khadija eventually said. "And what will you do when he's gone? You'd be a burden to his family."

As you are now to us. Mariam almost *saw* the unspoken words exit Khadija's mouth, like foggy breath on a cold day.

Mariam pictured herself in Kabul, a big, strange, crowded city that, Jalil had once told her, was some six hundred and fifty kilometers to the east of Herat. *Six hundred and fifty kilometers.* The farthest she'd ever been from the *kolba* was the two-kilometer walk she'd made to Jalil's house. She pictured herself living there, in Kabul, at the other end of that unimaginable distance, living in a stranger's house where she would have to concede to his moods and his issued demands. She would have to clean after this man, Rasheed, cook for him, wash his clothes. And there would be other chores as well—Nana had told her what husbands did to their wives. It was the thought of these intimacies in particular, which she imagined as painful acts of perversity, that filled her with dread and made her break out in a sweat.

She turned to Jalil again. "Tell them. Tell them you won't let them do this."

"Actually, your father has already given Rasheed his answer," Afsoon said. "Rasheed is here, in Herat; he has come all the way from Kabul. The *nikka* will be tomorrow morning, and then there is a bus leaving for Kabul at noon."

"Tell them!" Mariam cried.

The women grew quiet now. Mariam sensed that they were watching him too. Waiting. A silence fell over the room. Jalil kept twirling his wedding band, with a bruised, helpless look on his face. From inside the cabinet, the clock ticked on and on.

"Jalil jo?" one of the women said at last.

Jalil's eyes lifted slowly, met Mariam's, lingered for a moment, then dropped. He opened his mouth, but all that came forth was a single, pained groan.

"Say something," Mariam said.

Then Jalil did, in a thin, threadbare voice. "Goddamn it, Mariam, don't do this to me," he said as though he was the one to whom something was being done.

And, with that, Mariam felt the tension vanish from the room.

As Jalil's wives began a new—and more sprightly—round of reassuring, Mariam looked down at the table. Her eyes traced the sleek shape of the table's legs, the sinuous curves of its corners, the gleam of its reflective, dark brown surface. She noticed that every time she breathed out, the surface fogged, and she disappeared from her father's table.

Afsoon escorted her back to the room upstairs. When Afsoon closed the door, Mariam heard the rattling of a key as it turned in the lock.

8.

In the morning, Mariam was given a long-sleeved, dark green dress to wear over white cotton trousers. Afsoon gave her a green *hijab* and a pair of matching sandals.

She was taken to the room with the long, brown table, except now there was a bowl of sugar-coated almond candy in the middle of the table, a Koran, a green veil, and a mirror. Two men Mariam had never seen before—witnesses, she presumed—and a mullah she did not recognize were already seated at the table.

Jalil showed her to a chair. He was wearing a light brown suit and a red tie. His hair was washed. When he pulled out the chair for her, he tried to smile encouragingly. Khadija and Afsoon sat on Mariam's side of the table this time.

The mullah motioned toward the veil, and Nargis arranged it on Mariam's head before taking a seat. Mariam looked down at her hands.

"You can call him in now," Jalil said to someone.

Mariam smelled him before she saw him. Cigarette

smoke and thick, sweet cologne, not faint like Jalil's. The scent of it flooded Mariam's nostrils. Through the veil, from the corner of her eye, Mariam saw a tall man, thick-bellied and broad-shouldered, stooping in the doorway. The size of him almost made her gasp, and she had to drop her gaze, her heart hammering away. She sensed him lingering in the doorway. Then his slow, heavy-footed movement across the room. The candy bowl on the table clinked in tune with his steps. With a thick grunt, he dropped on a chair beside her. He breathed noisily.

The mullah welcomed them. He said this would not be a traditional *nikka*.

"I understand that Rasheed *agha* has tickets for the bus to Kabul that leaves shortly. So, in the interest of time, we will bypass some of the traditional steps to speed up the proceedings."

The mullah gave a few blessings, said a few words about the importance of marriage. He asked Jalil if he had any objections to this union, and Jalil shook his head. Then the mullah asked Rasheed if he indeed wished to enter into a marriage contract with Mariam. Rasheed said, "Yes." His harsh, raspy voice reminded Mariam of the sound of dry autumn leaves crushed underfoot.

"And do you, Mariam jan, accept this man as your husband?"

Mariam stayed quiet. Throats were cleared.

"She does," a female voice said from down the table.

"Actually," the mullah said, "she herself has to answer. And she should wait until I ask three times. The point is, he's seeking her, not the other way around."

He asked the question two more times. When Mariam didn't answer, he asked it once more, this time more force-fully. Mariam could feel Jalil beside her shifting on his seat, could sense feet crossing and uncrossing beneath the table. There was more throat clearing. A small, white hand reached out and flicked a bit of dust off the table.

"Mariam," Jalil whispered.

"Yes," she said shakily.

A mirror was passed beneath the veil. In it, Mariam saw her own face first, the archless, unshapely eyebrows, the flat hair, the eyes, mirthless green and set so closely together that one might mistake her for being cross-eyed. Her skin was coarse and had a dull, spotty appearance. She thought her brow too wide, the chin too narrow, the lips too thin. The overall impression was of a long face, a triangular face, a bit houndlike. And yet Mariam saw that, oddly enough, the whole of these unmemorable parts made for a face that was not pretty but, somehow, not unpleasant to look at either.

In the mirror, Mariam had her first glimpse of Rasheed: the big, square, ruddy face; the hooked nose; the flushed cheeks that gave the impression of sly cheerfulness; the watery, bloodshot eyes; the crowded teeth, the front two pushed together like a gabled roof; the impossibly low hairline, barely two finger widths above the bushy eyebrows; the wall of thick, coarse, salt-and-pepper hair.

Their gazes met briefly in the glass and slid away.

This is the face of my husband, Mariam thought.

They exchanged the thin gold bands that Rasheed fished from his coat pocket. His nails were yellow-brown, like the inside of a rotting apple, and some of the tips were curling, lifting. Mariam's hands shook when she tried to slip the band onto his finger, and Rasheed had to help her. Her own band was a little tight, but Rasheed had no trouble forcing it over her knuckles.

"There," he said.

"It's a pretty ring," one of the wives said. "It's lovely, Mariam."

"All that remains now is the signing of the contract," the mullah said.

Mariam signed her name—the *meem,* the *reh,* the *ya,* and the *meem* again—conscious of all the eyes on her hand. The next time Mariam signed her name to a document, twenty-seven years later, a mullah would again be present.

"You are now husband and wife," the mullah said. "*Tabreek.* Congratulations."

RASHEED WAITED in the multicolored bus. Mariam could not see him from where she stood with Jalil, by the rear bumper, only the smoke of his cigarette curling up from the open window. Around them, hands shook and farewells were said. Korans were kissed, passed under. Barefoot boys bounced between travelers, their faces invisible behind their trays of chewing gum and cigarettes.

Jalil was busy telling her that Kabul was so beautiful, the Moghul emperor Babur had asked that he be buried there. Next, Mariam knew, he'd go on about Kabul's gardens, and its shops, its trees, and its air, and, before long, she would be on the bus and he would walk alongside it, waving cheerfully, unscathed, spared.

Mariam could not bring herself to allow it.

"I used to worship you," she said.

Jalil stopped in midsentence. He crossed and uncrossed his arms. A young Hindi couple, the wife cradling a boy, the husband dragging a suitcase, passed between them. Jalil seemed grateful for the interruption. They excused themselves, and he smiled back politely.

"On Thursdays, I sat for hours waiting for you. I worried myself sick that you wouldn't show up."

"It's a long trip. You should eat something." He said he could buy her some bread and goat cheese.

"I thought about you all the time. I used to pray that you'd live to be a hundred years old. I didn't know. I didn't know that you were ashamed of me."

Jalil looked down, and, like an overgrown child, dug at something with the toe of his shoe.

"You were ashamed of me."

"I'll visit you," he muttered. "I'll come to Kabul and see you. We'll—"

"No. No," she said. "Don't come. I won't see you. Don't you come. I don't want to hear from you. Ever. *Ever.*"

He gave her a wounded look.

"It ends here for you and me. Say your good-byes."

"Don't leave like this," he said in a thin voice.

"You didn't even have the decency to give me the time to say good-bye to Mullah Faizullah."

She turned and walked around to the side of the bus. She could hear him following her. When she reached the hydraulic doors, she heard him behind her.

"Mariam jo."

She climbed the stairs, and though she could spot Jalil out of the corner of her eye walking parallel to her she did not look out the window. She made her way down the aisle to the back, where Rasheed sat with her suitcase between his feet. She did not turn to look when Jalil's palms pressed on the glass, when his knuckles rapped and rapped on it. When the bus jerked forward, she did not turn to see him trotting alongside it. And when the bus pulled away, she did not look back to see him receding, to see him disappear in the cloud of exhaust and dust.

Rasheed, who took up the window and middle seat, put his thick hand on hers.

"There now, girl. There. There," he said. He was squinting out the window as he said this, as though something more interesting had caught his eye.

9.

It was early evening the following day by the time they arrived at Rasheed's house.

"We're in Deh-Mazang," he said. They were outside, on the sidewalk. He had her suitcase in one hand and was unlocking the wooden front gate with the other. "In the south and west part of the city. The zoo is nearby, and the university too."

Mariam nodded. Already she had learned that, though she could understand him, she had to pay close attention when he spoke. She was unaccustomed to the Kabuli dialect of his Farsi, and to the underlying layer of Pashto accent, the language of his native Kandahar. He, on the other hand, seemed to have no trouble understanding her Herati Farsi.

Mariam quickly surveyed the narrow, unpaved road along which Rasheed's house was situated. The houses on this road were crowded together and shared common walls, with small, walled yards in front buffering them from the street. Most of the homes had flat roofs and were made of burned brick, some of mud the same dusty color as the mountains that ringed the city. Gutters separated the sidewalk from the road on both sides and flowed with muddy water. Mariam saw small mounds of flyblown garbage littering the street here and there. Rasheed's house had two stories. Mariam could see that it had once been blue.

When Rasheed opened the front gate, Mariam found herself in a small, unkempt yard where yellow grass struggled up in thin patches. Mariam saw an outhouse on the right, in a side yard, and, on the left, a well with a hand pump, a row of dying saplings. Near the well was a tool-shed, and a bicycle leaning against the wall.

"Your father told me you like to fish," Rasheed said as they were crossing the yard to the house. There was no backyard, Mariam saw. "There are valleys north of here. Rivers with lots of fish. Maybe I'll take you someday."

He unlocked the front door and let her into the house.

Rasheed's house was much smaller than Jalil's, but, compared to Mariam and Nana's *kolba*, it was a mansion. There was a hallway, a living room downstairs, and a kitchen in which he showed her pots and pans and a pressure cooker and a kerosene *ishtop*. The living room had a pistachio green leather couch. It had a rip down its side that had been clumsily sewn together. The walls were bare. There was a table, two cane-seat chairs, two folding chairs, and, in the corner, a black, cast-iron stove.

Mariam stood in the middle of the living room, looking around. At the *kolba*, she could touch the ceiling with her fingertips. She could lie in her cot and tell the time of day by the angle of sunlight pouring through the window. She knew how far her door would open before its hinges creaked. She knew every splinter and crack in each of the thirty wooden floorboards. Now all those familiar things were gone. Nana was dead, and she was here, in a strange city, separated from the life she'd known by valleys and chains of snow-capped mountains and entire deserts. She was in a stranger's house, with all its different rooms and its smell of cigarette smoke, with its unfamiliar cupboards full of unfamiliar utensils, its heavy, dark green curtains, and a ceiling she knew she could not reach. The space of it suffocated Mariam. Pangs of longing bore into her, for Nana, for Mullah Faizullah, for her old life.

Then she was crying.

"What's this crying about?" Rasheed said crossly. He reached into the pocket of his pants, uncurled Mariam's fingers, and pushed a handkerchief into her palm. He lit himself a cigarette and leaned against the wall. He watched as Mariam pressed the handkerchief to her eyes.

"Done?"

Mariam nodded.

"Sure?"

"Yes."

He took her by the elbow then and led her to the living-room window.

"This window looks north," he said, tapping the glass with the crooked nail of his index finger. "That's the Asmai mountain directly in front of us—see?—and, to the left, is the Ali Abad mountain. The university is at the foot of it. Behind us, east, you can't see from here, is the Shir Darwaza mountain. Every day, at noon, they shoot a cannon from it. Stop your crying, now. I mean it."

Mariam dabbed at her eyes.

"That's one thing I can't stand," he said, scowling, "the sound of a woman crying. I'm sorry. I have no patience for it."

"I want to go home," Mariam said.

Rasheed sighed irritably. A puff of his smoky breath hit Mariam's face. "I won't take that personally. This time."

Again, he took her by the elbow, and led her upstairs.

There was a narrow, dimly lit hallway there and two bedrooms. The door to the bigger one was ajar. Through it Mariam could see that it, like the rest of the house, was sparsely furnished: bed in the corner, with a brown blanket and a pillow, a closet, a dresser. The walls were bare except for a small mirror. Rasheed closed the door.

"This is my room."

He said she could take the guest room. "I hope you don't mind. I'm accustomed to sleeping alone."

Mariam didn't tell him how relieved she was, at least about this.

The room that was to be Mariam's was much smaller than the room she'd stayed in at Jalil's house. It had a bed, an old, gray-brown dresser, a small closet. The window looked into the yard and, beyond that, the street below. Rasheed put her suitcase in a corner.

Mariam sat on the bed.

"You didn't notice," he said. He was standing in the doorway, stooping a little to fit. "Look on the windowsill. You know what kind they are? I put them there before leaving for Herat."

Only now Mariam saw a basket on the sill. White tuberoses spilled from its sides.

"You like them? They please you?"

"Yes."

"You can thank me then."

"Thank you. I'm sorry. *Tashakor*—"

"You're shaking. Maybe I scare you. Do I scare you? Are you frightened of me?"

Mariam was not looking at him, but she could hear something slyly playful in these questions, like a needling. She quickly shook her head in what she recognized as her first lie in their marriage.

"No? That's good, then. Good for you. Well, this is your home now. You're going to like it here. You'll see. Did I tell you we have electricity? Most days and every night?"

He made as if to leave. At the door, he paused, took a long drag, crinkled his eyes against the smoke. Mariam thought he was going to say something. But he didn't. He closed the door, left her alone with her suitcase and her flowers.

10.

The first few days, Mariam hardly left her room. She was awakened every dawn for prayer by the distant cry of *azan*, after which she crawled back into bed. She was still in bed when she heard Rasheed in the bathroom, washing up, when he came into her room to check on her before he went to his shop. From her window, she watched him in the yard, securing his lunch in the rear carrier pack of his bicycle, then walking his bicycle across the yard and into the street. She watched him pedal away, saw his broad, thick-shouldered figure disappear around the turn at the end of the street.

For most of the days, Mariam stayed in bed, feeling adrift and forlorn. Sometimes she went downstairs to the kitchen, ran her hands over the sticky, grease-stained counter, the vinyl, flowered curtains that smelled like burned meals. She looked through the ill-fitting drawers, at the mismatched spoons and knives, the colander and chipped, wooden spatulas, these would-be instruments of her new daily life, all of it reminding her of the havoc that had struck her life, making her feel uprooted, displaced, like an intruder on someone else's life.

At the *kolba*, her appetite had been predictable. Here, her stomach rarely growled for food. Sometimes she took a plate of leftover white rice and a scrap of bread to the living room, by the window. From there, she could see the roofs of the one-story houses on their street. She could see into their yards too, the women working laundry lines and shooing their children, chickens pecking at dirt, the shovels and spades, the cows tethered to trees.

She thought longingly of all the summer nights that she and Nana had slept on the flat roof of the *kolba*, looking at the moon glowing over Gul Daman, the night so hot their shirts would cling to their chests like a wet leaf to a window. She missed the winter afternoons of reading in the *kolba* with Mullah Faizullah, the clink of icicles falling on her roof from the trees, the crows cawing outside from snow-burdened branches.

Alone in the house, Mariam paced restlessly, from the kitchen to the living room, up the steps to her room and down again. She ended up back in her room, doing her prayers or sitting on the bed, missing her mother, feeling nauseated and homesick.

It was with the sun's westward crawl that Mariam's anxiety really ratcheted up. Her teeth rattled when she thought of the night, the time when Rasheed might at last decide to do to her what husbands did to their wives. She lay in bed, wracked with nerves, as he ate alone downstairs.

He always stopped by her room and poked his head in.

"You can't be sleeping already. It's only seven. Are you awake? Answer me. Come, now."

He pressed on until, from the dark, Mariam said, "I'm here."

He slid down and sat in her doorway. From her bed, she could see his large-framed body, his long legs, the smoke swirling around his hook-nosed profile, the amber tip of his cigarette brightening and dimming.

He told her about his day. A pair of loafers he had custom-made for the deputy foreign minister—who, Rasheed said, bought shoes only from him. An order for sandals from a Polish diplomat and his wife. He told her of the superstitions people had about shoes: that putting them on a bed invited death into the family, that a quarrel would follow if one put on the left shoe first.

"Unless it was done unintentionally on a Friday," he said. "And did you know it's supposed to be a bad omen to tie shoes together and hang them from a nail?"

Rasheed himself believed none of this. In his opinion, superstitions were largely a female preoccupation.

He passed on to her things he had heard on the streets, like how the American president Richard Nixon had resigned over a scandal.

Mariam, who had never heard of Nixon, or the scandal that had forced him to resign, did not say anything back. She waited anxiously for Rasheed to finish talking, to crush his cigarette, and take his leave. Only when she'd heard him cross the hallway, heard his door open and close, only then would the metal fist gripping her belly let go.

Then one night he crushed his cigarette and instead of saying good night leaned against the doorway.

"Are you ever going to unpack that thing?" he said, motioning with his head toward her suitcase. He crossed his arms. "I figured you might need some time. But this is absurd. A week's gone and . . . Well, then, as of tomorrow morning I expect you to start behaving like a wife. *Fahmidi?* Is that understood?"

Mariam's teeth began to chatter.

"I need an answer."

"Yes."

"Good," he said. "What did you think? That this is a hotel? That I'm some kind of hotelkeeper? Well, it . . . Oh. Oh. *La illah u ilillah.* What did I say about the crying, Mariam? What did I say to you about the crying?"

THE NEXT MORNING, after Rasheed left for work, Mariam unpacked her clothes and put them in the dresser. She drew a pail of water from the well and, with a rag, washed the windows of her room and the windows to the living room downstairs. She swept the floors, beat the cobwebs fluttering in the corners of the ceiling. She opened the windows to air the house.

She set three cups of lentils to soak in a pot, found a knife and cut some carrots and a pair of potatoes, left them too to soak. She searched for flour, found it in the back of one of the cabinets behind a row of dirty spice jars, and made fresh dough, kneading it the way Nana had shown her, pushing the dough with the heel of her hand, folding the outer edge, turning it, and pushing it away again. Once she had floured the dough, she wrapped it in a moist cloth, put on a *hijab,* and set out for the communal tandoor.

Rasheed had told her where it was, down the street, a left then a quick right, but all Mariam had to do was follow the flock of women and children who were headed the same way. The children Mariam saw, chasing after their mothers or running ahead of them, wore shirts patched and patched again. They wore trousers that looked too big or too small, sandals with ragged straps that flapped back and forth. They rolled discarded old bicycle tires with sticks.

Their mothers walked in groups of three or four, some in burqas, others not. Mariam could hear their high-pitched chatter, their spiraling laughs. As she walked with her head down, she caught bits of their banter, which seemingly always had to do with sick children or lazy, ungrateful husbands.

As if the meals cook themselves.

Wallah o billah, *never a moment's rest!*

And he says to me, I swear it, it's true, he actually says to me . . .

This endless conversation, the tone plaintive but oddly cheerful, flew around and around in a circle. On it went, down the street, around the corner, in line at the tandoor. Husbands who gambled. Husbands who doted on their mothers and wouldn't spend a rupiah on them, the wives. Mariam wondered how so many women could suffer the same miserable luck, to have married, all of them, such dreadful men. Or was this a wifely game that she did not know about, a daily ritual, like soaking rice or making dough? Would they expect her soon to join in?

In the tandoor line, Mariam caught sideways glances shot at her, heard whispers. Her hands began to sweat. She imagined they all knew that she'd been born a *harami,* a source of shame to her father and his family. They all knew that she'd betrayed her mother and disgraced herself.

With a corner of her *hijab,* she dabbed at the moisture above her upper lip and tried to gather her nerves.

For a few minutes, everything went well.

Then someone tapped her on the shoulder. Mariam turned around and found a light-skinned, plump woman wearing a *hijab,* like her. She had short, wiry black hair and a good-humored, almost perfectly round face. Her lips were much fuller than Mariam's, the lower one slightly droopy, as though dragged down by the big, dark mole just below the lip line. She had big greenish eyes that shone at

Mariam with an inviting glint.

"You're Rasheed jan's new wife, aren't you?" the woman said, smiling widely. "The one from Herat. You're so young! Mariam jan, isn't it? My name is Fariba. I live on your street, five houses to your left, the one with the green door. This is my son Noor."

The boy at her side had a smooth, happy face and wiry hair like his mother's. There was a patch of black hairs on the lobe of his left ear. His eyes had a mischievous, reckless light in them. He raised his hand. *"Salaam, Khala* jan."

"Noor is ten. I have an older boy too, Ahmad."

"He's thirteen," Noor said.

"Thirteen going on forty." The woman Fariba laughed. "My husband's name is Hakim," she said. "He's a teacher here in Deh-Mazang. You should come by sometime, we'll have a cup—"

And then suddenly, as if emboldened, the other women pushed past Fariba and swarmed Mariam, forming a circle around her with alarming speed.

"So you're Rasheed jan's young bride—"

"How do you like Kabul?"

"I've been to Herat. I have a cousin there."

"Do you want a boy or a girl first?"

"The minarets! Oh, what beauty! What a gorgeous city!"

"Boy is better, Mariam jan, they carry the family name—"

"Bah! Boys get married and run off. Girls stay behind and take care of you when you're old."

"We heard you were coming."

"Have twins. One of each! Then everyone's happy."

Mariam backed away. She was hyperventilating. Her ears buzzed, her pulse fluttered, her eyes darted from one face to another. She backed away again, but there was nowhere to go to—she was in the center of a circle. She spotted Fariba, who was frowning, who saw that she was in distress.

"Let her be!" Fariba was saying. "Move aside, let her be! You're frightening her!"

Mariam clutched the dough close to her chest and pushed through the crowd around her.

"Where are you going, *hamshira*?"

She pushed until somehow she was in the clear and then she ran up the street. It wasn't until she'd reached the intersection that she realized she'd run the wrong way. She turned around and ran back in the other direction, head down, tripping once and scraping her knee badly, then up again and running, bolting past the women.

"What's the matter with you?"

"You're bleeding, *hamshira*!"

Mariam turned one corner, then the other. She found the correct street but suddenly could not remember which was Rasheed's house. She ran up then down the street, panting, near tears now, began trying doors blindly. Some were locked, others opened only to reveal unfamiliar yards, barking dogs, and startled chickens. She pictured Rasheed coming home to find her still searching this way, her knee bleeding, lost on her own street. Now she did start crying. She pushed on doors, muttering panicked prayers, her face moist with tears, until one opened, and she saw, with relief, the outhouse, the well, the toolshed. She slammed the door behind her and turned the bolt. Then she was on all fours, next to the wall, retching. When she was done, she crawled away, sat against the wall, with her legs splayed before her. She had never in her life felt so alone.

WHEN RASHEED CAME HOME that night, he brought with him a brown paper bag. Mariam was disappointed that he did not notice the clean windows, the swept floors, the missing cobwebs. But he did look pleased that she had already set his dinner plate, on a clean *sofrah* spread on the living-room floor.

"I made *daal*," Mariam said.

"Good. I'm starving."

She poured water for him from the *aftawa* to wash his hands with. As he dried with a towel, she put before him a steaming bowl of *daal* and a plate of fluffy white rice. This was the first meal she had cooked for him, and Mariam wished she had been in a better state when she made it. She'd still been shaken from the incident at the tandoor as she'd cooked, and all day she had fretted about the *daal*'s consistency, its color, worried that he would think she'd stirred in too much ginger or not enough turmeric.

He dipped his spoon into the gold-colored *daal*.

Mariam swayed a bit. What if he was disappointed or angry? What if he pushed his plate away in displeasure?

"Careful," she managed to say. "It's hot."

Rasheed pursed his lips and blew, then put the spoon into his mouth.

"It's good," he said. "A little undersalted but good. Maybe better than good, even."

Relieved, Mariam looked on as he ate. A flare of pride caught her off guard. She had done well—*maybe better than good, even*—and it surprised her, this thrill she felt over his small compliment. The day's earlier unpleasantness receded a bit.

"Tomorrow is Friday," Rasheed said. "What do you say I show you around?"

"Around Kabul?"

"No. Calcutta."

Mariam blinked.

"It's a joke. Of course Kabul. Where else?" He reached

into the brown paper bag. "But first, something I have to tell you."

He fished a sky blue burqa from the bag. The yards of pleated cloth spilled over his knees when he lifted it. He rolled up the burqa, looked at Mariam.

"I have customers, Mariam, men, who bring their wives to my shop. The women come uncovered, they talk to me directly, look me in the eye without shame. They wear makeup and skirts that show their knees. Sometimes they even put their feet in front of me, the women do, for measurements, and their husbands stand there and watch. They allow it. They think nothing of a stranger touching their wives' bare feet! They think they're being modern men, intellectuals, on account of their education, I suppose. They don't see that they're spoiling their own *nang* and *namoos,* their honor and pride."

He shook his head.

"Mostly, they live in the richer parts of Kabul. I'll take you there. You'll see. But they're here too, Mariam, in this very neighborhood, these soft men. There's a teacher living down the street, Hakim is his name, and I see his wife Fariba all the time walking the streets alone with nothing on her head but a scarf. It embarrasses me, frankly, to see a man who's lost control of his wife."

He fixed Mariam with a hard glare.

"But I'm a different breed of man, Mariam. Where I come from, one wrong look, one improper word, and blood is spilled. Where I come from, a woman's face is her husband's business only. I want you to remember that. Do you understand?"

Mariam nodded. When he extended the bag to her, she took it.

The earlier pleasure over his approval of her cooking had evaporated. In its stead, a sensation of shrinking. This man's will felt to Mariam as imposing and immovable as

69

the Safid-koh mountains looming over Gul Daman.

Rasheed passed the paper bag to her. "We have an understanding, then. Now, let me have some more of that *daal*."

11.

Mariam had never before worn a burqa. Rasheed had to help her put it on. The padded headpiece felt tight and heavy on her skull, and it was strange seeing the world through a mesh screen. She practiced walking around her room in it and kept stepping on the hem and stumbling. The loss of peripheral vision was unnerving, and she did not like the suffocating way the pleated cloth kept pressing against her mouth.

"You'll get used to it," Rasheed said. "With time, I bet you'll even like it."

They took a bus to a place Rasheed called the Shar-e-Nau Park, where children pushed each other on swings and slapped volleyballs over ragged nets tied to tree trunks. They strolled together and watched boys fly kites, Mariam walking beside Rasheed, tripping now and then on the burqa's hem. For lunch, Rasheed took her to eat in a small kebab house near a mosque he called the Haji Yaghoub. The floor was sticky and the air smoky. The walls smelled faintly of raw meat and the music, which Rasheed described to her as *logari,* was loud. The cooks were thin boys who fanned skewers with one hand and swatted gnats with the other. Mariam, who had never been inside a restaurant, found it odd at first to sit in a crowded room with so many strangers, to lift her burqa to put morsels of food into her mouth. A hint of the same anxiety as the day at the tandoor stirred in her stomach, but Rasheed's presence was of some comfort, and, after a while, she did not mind so much the music, the smoke, even the people. And the burqa, she learned to her surprise, was also comforting. It was like a one-way window. Inside it, she was an observer, buffered from the scrutinizing eyes of strangers. She no longer worried that people knew, with a single glance, all the shameful secrets of her past.

On the streets, Rasheed named various buildings with authority; this is the American Embassy, he said, that the Foreign Ministry. He pointed to cars, said their names and where they were made: Soviet Volgas, American Chevrolets, German Opels.

"Which is your favorite?" he asked.

Mariam hesitated, pointed to a Volga, and Rasheed laughed.

Kabul was far more crowded than the little that Mariam had seen of Herat. There were fewer trees and fewer *garis* pulled by horses, but more cars, taller buildings, more traffic lights and more paved roads. And everywhere Mariam heard the city's peculiar dialect: "Dear" was *jan* instead of *jo,* "sister" became *hamshira* instead of *hamshireh,* and so on.

From a street vendor, Rasheed bought her ice cream. It was the first time she'd eaten ice cream and Mariam had never imagined that such tricks could be played on a palate. She devoured the entire bowl, the crushed-pistachio topping, the tiny rice noodles at the bottom. She marveled at the bewitching texture, the lapping sweetness of it.

They walked on to a place called Kocheh-Morgha, Chicken Street. It was a narrow, crowded bazaar in a neighborhood that Rasheed said was one of Kabul's wealthier ones.

"Around here is where foreign diplomats live, rich businessmen, members of the royal family—that sort of people. Not like you and me."

"I don't see any chickens," Mariam said.

"That's the one thing you can't find on Chicken Street." Rasheed laughed.

The street was lined with shops and little stalls that sold lambskin hats and rainbow-colored *chapan*s. Rasheed stopped to look at an engraved silver dagger in one shop, and, in another, at an old rifle that the shopkeeper assured Rasheed was a relic from the first war against the British.

"And I'm Moshe Dayan," Rasheed muttered. He half smiled, and it seemed to Mariam that this was a smile meant only for her. A private, married smile.

They strolled past carpet shops, handicraft shops, pastry shops, flower shops, and shops that sold suits for men and dresses for women, and, in them, behind lace curtains, Mariam saw young girls sewing buttons and ironing collars. From time to time, Rasheed greeted a shopkeeper he knew, sometimes in Farsi, other times in Pashto. As they shook hands and kissed on the cheek, Mariam stood a few feet away. Rasheed did not wave her over, did not introduce her.

He asked her to wait outside an embroidery shop. "I know the owner," he said. "I'll just go in for a minute, say my *salaam*."

Mariam waited outside on the crowded sidewalk. She watched the cars crawling up Chicken Street, threading through the horde of hawkers and pedestrians, honking at children and donkeys who wouldn't move. She watched the bored-looking merchants inside their tiny stalls, smoking, or spitting into brass spittoons, their faces emerging from the shadows now and then to peddle textiles and fur-collared *poostin* coats to passersby.

But it was the women who drew Mariam's eyes the most.

The women in this part of Kabul were a different breed from the women in the poorer neighborhoods—like the one where she and Rasheed lived, where so many of the women covered fully. These women were—what was the word Rasheed had used?—"modern." Yes, modern Afghan women married to modern Afghan men who did not mind that their wives walked among strangers with makeup on their faces and nothing on their heads. Mariam watched them cantering uninhibited down the street, sometimes with a man, sometimes alone, sometimes with rosy-cheeked children who wore shiny shoes and watches with leather bands, who walked bicycles with high-rise handle-bars and gold-colored spokes—unlike the children in Deh-Mazang, who bore sand-fly scars on their cheeks and rolled old bicycle tires with sticks.

These women were all swinging handbags and rustling skirts. Mariam even spotted one smoking behind the wheel of a car. Their nails were long, polished pink or orange, their lips red as tulips. They walked in high heels, and quickly, as if on perpetually urgent business. They wore dark sunglasses, and, when they breezed by, Mariam caught a whiff of their perfume. She imagined that they all had university degrees, that they worked in office build-ings, behind desks of their own, where they typed and smoked and made important telephone calls to important people. These women mystified Mariam. They made her aware of her own lowliness, her plain looks, her lack of aspirations, her ignorance of so many things.

Then Rasheed was tapping her on the shoulder and handing her something.

"Here."

It was a dark maroon silk shawl with beaded fringes and edges embroidered with gold thread.

"Do you like it?"

Mariam looked up. Rasheed did a touching thing then. He blinked and averted his gaze.

Mariam thought of Jalil, of the emphatic, jovial way in which he'd pushed his jewelry at her, the overpowering cheerfulness that left room for no response but meek gratitude. Nana had been right about Jalil's gifts. They had been halfhearted tokens of penance, insincere, corrupt gestures meant more for his own appeasement than hers. This shawl, Mariam saw, was a true gift.

"It's beautiful," she said.

THAT NIGHT, Rasheed visited her room again. But instead of smoking in the doorway, he crossed the room and sat beside her where she lay on the bed. The springs creaked as the bed tilted to his side.

There was a moment of hesitation, and then his hand was on her neck, his thick fingers slowly pressing the knobs in the back of it. His thumb slid down, and now it was stroking the hollow above her collarbone, then the flesh beneath it. Mariam began shivering. His hand crept lower still, lower, his fingernails catching in the cotton of her blouse.

"I can't," she croaked, looking at his moonlit profile, his thick shoulders and broad chest, the tufts of gray hair protruding from his open collar.

His hand was on her right breast now, squeezing it hard through the blouse, and she could hear him breathing deeply through the nose.

He slid under the blanket beside her. She could feel his hand working at his belt, at the drawstring of her trousers. Her own hands clenched the sheets in fistfuls. He rolled on top of her, wriggled and shifted, and she let out a whimper. Mariam closed her eyes, gritted her teeth.

The pain was sudden and astonishing. Her eyes sprang open. She sucked air through her teeth and bit on the knuckle of her thumb. She slung her free arm over Rasheed's back and her fingers dug at his shirt.

Rasheed buried his face into her pillow, and Mariam stared, wide-eyed, at the ceiling above his shoulder, shivering, lips pursed, feeling the heat of his quick breaths on her shoulder. The air between them smelled of tobacco, of the onions and grilled lamb they had eaten earlier. Now and then, his ear rubbed against her cheek, and she knew from the scratchy feel that he had shaved it.

When it was done, he rolled off her, panting. He dropped his forearm over his brow. In the dark, she could see the blue hands of his watch. They lay that way for a while, on their backs, not looking at each other.

"There is no shame in this, Mariam," he said, slurring a little. "It's what married people do. It's what the Prophet himself and his wives did. There is no shame."

A few moments later, he pushed back the blanket and left the room, leaving her with the impression of his head on her pillow, leaving her to wait out the pain down below, to look at the frozen stars in the sky and a cloud that draped the face of the moon like a wedding veil.

12.

Ramadan came in the fall that year, 1974. For the first time in her life, Mariam saw how the sighting of the new crescent moon could transform an entire city, alter its rhythm and mood. She noticed a drowsy hush overtaking Kabul. Traffic became languid, scant, even quiet. Shops emptied. Restaurants turned off their lights, closed their doors. Mariam saw no smokers on the streets, no cups of tea steaming from window ledges. And at *iftar,* when the sun dipped in the west and the cannon fired from the Shir Darwaza mountain, the city broke its fast, and so did Mariam, with bread and a date, tasting for the first time in her fifteen years the sweetness of sharing in a communal experience.

Except for a handful of days, Rasheed didn't observe the fast. The few times he did, he came home in a sour mood. Hunger made him curt, irritable, impatient. One night, Mariam was a few minutes late with dinner, and he started eating bread with radishes. Even after Mariam put the rice and the lamb and okra *qurma* in front of him, he wouldn't touch it. He said nothing, and went on chewing the bread, his temples working, the vein on his forehead, full and angry. He went on chewing and staring ahead, and when Mariam spoke to him he looked at her without seeing her face and put another piece of bread into his mouth.

Mariam was relieved when Ramadan ended.

Back at the *kolba,* on the first of three days of Eid-ul-Fitr celebration that followed Ramadan, Jalil would visit Mariam and Nana. Dressed in suit and tie, he would come bearing Eid presents. One year, he gave Mariam a wool scarf. The three of them would sit for tea and then Jalil would excuse himself.

"Off to celebrate Eid with his real family," Nana would say as he crossed the stream and waved.

Mullah Faizullah would come too. He would bring Mariam chocolate candy wrapped in foil, a basketful of dyed boiled eggs, cookies. After he was gone, Mariam would climb one of the willows with her treats. Perched on a high branch, she would eat Mullah Faizullah's chocolates and drop the foil wrappers until they lay scattered about the trunk of the tree like silver blossoms. When the chocolate was gone, she would start in on the cookies, and, with a pencil, she would draw faces on the eggs he had brought her now. But there was little pleasure in this for her. Mariam dreaded Eid, this time of hospitality and ceremony, when families dressed in their best and visited each other. She would imagine the air in Herat crackling with merriness, and high-spirited, bright-eyed people showering each other with endearments and goodwill. A forlornness would descend on her like a shroud then and would lift only when Eid had passed.

This year, for the first time, Mariam saw with her eyes the Eid of her childhood imaginings.

Rasheed and she took to the streets. Mariam had never

walked amid such liveliness. Undaunted by the chilly weather, families had flooded the city on their frenetic rounds to visit relatives. On their own street, Mariam saw Fariba and her son Noor, who was dressed in a suit. Fariba, wearing a white scarf, walked beside a small-boned, shy-looking man with eyeglasses. Her older son was there too—Mariam somehow remembered Fariba saying his name, Ahmad, at the tandoor that first time. He had deep-set, brooding eyes, and his face was more thoughtful, more solemn, than his younger brother's, a face as sugges-tive of early maturity as his brother's was of lingering boy-ishness. Around Ahmad's neck was a glittering ALLAH pendant.

Fariba must have recognized her, walking in burqa beside Rasheed. She waved, and called out, *"Eid mubarak!"*

From inside the burqa, Mariam gave her a ghost of a nod.

"So you know that woman, the teacher's wife?" Rasheed said.

Mariam said she didn't.

"Best you stay away. She's a nosy gossiper, that one. And the husband fancies himself some kind of educated intel-lectual. But he's a mouse. Look at him. Doesn't he look like a mouse?"

They went to Shar-e-Nau, where kids romped about in new shirts and beaded, brightly colored vests and com-pared Eid gifts. Women brandished platters of sweets. Mariam saw festive lanterns hanging from shopwindows, heard music blaring from loudspeakers. Strangers called out *"Eid mubarak"* to her as they passed.

That night they went to *Chaman,* and, standing behind Rasheed, Mariam watched fireworks light up the sky, in flashes of green, pink, and yellow. She missed sitting with Mullah Faizullah outside the *kolba,* watching the fireworks explode over Herat in the distance, the sudden bursts of color reflected in her tutor's soft, cataract-riddled eyes. But, mostly, she missed Nana. Mariam wished her mother were alive to see this. To see *her,* amid all of it. To see at last that contentment and beauty were not unattainable things. Even for the likes of them.

THEY HAD Eid visitors at the house. They were all men, friends of Rasheed's. When a knock came, Mariam knew to go upstairs to her room and close the door. She stayed there, as the men sipped tea downstairs with Rasheed, smoked, chatted. Rasheed had told Mariam that she was not to come down until the visitors had left.

Mariam didn't mind. In truth, she was even flattered. Rasheed saw sanctity in what they had together. Her honor, her *namoos,* was something worth guarding to him. She felt prized by his protectiveness. Treasured and significant.

On the third and last day of Eid, Rasheed went to visit some friends. Mariam, who'd had a queasy stomach all night, boiled some water and made herself a cup of green tea sprinkled with crushed cardamom. In the living room, she took in the aftermath of the previous night's Eid visits: the overturned cups, the half-chewed pumpkin seeds stashed between mattresses, the plates crusted with the outline of last night's meal. Mariam set about cleaning up the mess, marveling at how energetically lazy men could be.

She didn't mean to go into Rasheed's room. But the cleaning took her from the living room to the stairs, and then to the hallway upstairs and to his door, and, the next thing she knew, she was in his room for the first time, sitting on his bed, feeling like a trespasser.

She took in the heavy, green drapes, the pairs of polished shoes lined up neatly along the wall, the closet door, where the gray paint had chipped and showed the wood beneath. She spotted a pack of cigarettes atop the dresser beside his bed. She put one between her lips and stood before the small oval mirror on the wall. She puffed air into the mirror and made ash-tapping motions. She put it back. She could never manage the seamless grace with which Kabuli women smoked. On her, it looked coarse, ridiculous.

Guiltily, she slid open the top drawer of his dresser.

She saw the gun first. It was black, with a wooden grip and a short muzzle. Mariam made sure to memorize which way it was facing before she picked it up. She turned it over in her hands. It was much heavier than it looked. The grip felt smooth in her hand, and the muzzle was cold. It was disquieting to her that Rasheed owned something whose sole purpose was to kill another person. But surely he kept it for their safety. Her safety.

Beneath the gun were several magazines with curling corners. Mariam opened one. Something inside her dropped. Her mouth gaped of its own will.

On every page were women, beautiful women, who wore no shirts, no trousers, no socks or underpants. They wore nothing at all. They lay in beds amid tumbled sheets and gazed back at Mariam with half-lidded eyes. In most of the pictures, their legs were apart, and Mariam had a full view of the dark place between. In some, the women were prostrated as if—God forbid this thought—in *sujda* for prayer. They looked back over their shoulders with a look of bored contempt.

Mariam quickly put the magazine back where she'd found it. She felt drugged. Who were these women? How could they allow themselves to be photographed this way? Her stomach revolted with distaste. Was this what he did then, those nights that he did not visit her room? Had she been a disappointment to him in this particular regard? And what about all his talk of honor and propriety, his disapproval of the female customers, who, after all, were only showing him their feet to get fitted for shoes? *A woman's face,* he'd said, *is her husband's business only.* Surely the women on these pages had husbands, some of them must. At the least, they had brothers. If so, why did Rasheed insist that *she* cover when he thought nothing of looking at the private areas of other men's wives and sisters?

Mariam sat on his bed, embarrassed and confused. She cupped her face with her hands and closed her eyes. She breathed and breathed until she felt calmer.

Slowly, an explanation presented itself. He was a man, after all, living alone for years before she had moved in. His needs differed from hers. For her, all these months later, their coupling was still an exercise in tolerating pain. His appetite, on the other hand, was fierce, sometimes bordering on the violent. The way he pinned her down, his hard squeezes at her breasts, how furiously his hips worked. He was a man. All those years without a woman. Could she fault him for being the way God had created him?

Mariam knew that she could never talk to him about this. It was unmentionable. But was it unforgivable? She only had to think of the other man in her life. Jalil, a husband of three and father of nine at the time, having relations with Nana out of wedlock. Which was worse, Rasheed's magazine or what Jalil had done? And what entitled her anyway, a villager, a *harami,* to pass judgment?

Mariam tried the bottom drawer of the dresser.

It was there that she found a picture of the boy, Yunus. It was black-and-white. He looked four, maybe five. He was wearing a striped shirt and a bow tie. He was a handsome little boy, with a slender nose, brown hair, and dark, slightly sunken eyes. He looked distracted, as though something had caught his eye just as the camera had flashed.

Beneath that, Mariam found another photo, also black-and-white, this one slightly more grainy. It was of a seated woman and, behind her, a thinner, younger Rasheed, with black hair. The woman was beautiful. Not as beautiful as the women in the magazine, perhaps, but beautiful. Certainly more beautiful than her, Mariam. She had a delicate chin and long, black hair parted in the center. High cheekbones and a gentle forehead. Mariam pictured her own face, her thin lips and long chin, and felt a flicker of jealousy.

She looked at this photo for a long time. There was something vaguely unsettling about the way Rasheed seemed to loom over the woman. His hands on her shoulders. His savoring, tight-lipped smile and her unsmiling, sullen face. The way her body tilted forward subtly, as though she were trying to wriggle free of his hands.

Mariam put everything back where she'd found it.

Later, as she was doing laundry, she regretted that she had sneaked around in his room. For what? What thing of substance had she learned about him? That he owned a gun, that he was a man with the needs of a man? And she shouldn't have stared at the photo of him and his wife for as long as she had. Her eyes had read meaning into what was random body posture captured in a single moment of time.

What Mariam felt now, as the loaded clotheslines bounced heavily before her, was sorrow for Rasheed. He too had had a hard life, a life marked by loss and sad turns of fate. Her thoughts returned to his boy Yunus, who had once built snowmen in this yard, whose feet had pounded these same stairs. The lake had snatched him from Rasheed, swallowed him up, just as a whale had swallowed the boy's namesake prophet in the Koran. It pained Mariam—it pained her considerably—to picture Rasheed panic-stricken and helpless, pacing the banks of the lake and pleading with it to spit his son back onto dry land. And she felt for the first time a kinship with her husband. She told herself that they would make good companions after all.

13.

On the bus ride home from the doctor, the strangest thing was happening to Mariam. Everywhere she looked, she saw bright colors: on the drab, gray concrete apartments, on the tin-roofed, open-fronted stores, in the muddy water flowing in the gutters. It was as though a rainbow had melted into her eyes.

Rasheed was drumming his gloved fingers and humming a song. Every time the bus bucked over a pothole and jerked forward, his hand shot protectively over her belly.

"What about Zalmai?" he said. "It's a good Pashtun name."

"What if it's a girl?" Mariam said.

"I think it's a boy. Yes. A boy."

A murmur was passing through the bus. Some passengers were pointing at something and other passengers were leaning across seats to see.

"Look," said Rasheed, tapping a knuckle on the glass. He was smiling. "There. See?"

On the streets, Mariam saw people stopping in their tracks. At traffic lights, faces emerged from the windows of cars, turned upward toward the falling softness. What was it about a season's first snowfall, Mariam wondered, that was so entrancing? Was it the chance to see something as yet unsoiled, untrodden? To catch the fleeting grace of a new season, a lovely beginning, before it was trampled and corrupted?

"If it's a girl," Rasheed said, "and it isn't, but, if it *is* a girl, then you can choose whatever name you want."

MARIAM AWOKE the next morning to the sound of sawing and hammering. She wrapped a shawl around her and went out into the snow-blown yard. The heavy snowfall of the previous night had stopped. Now only a scattering of light, swirling flakes tickled her cheeks. The air was windless and smelled like burning coal. Kabul was eerily silent, quilted in white, tendrils of smoke snaking up here and there.

She found Rasheed in the toolshed, pounding nails into a plank of wood. When he saw her, he removed a nail from the corner of his mouth.

"It was going to be a surprise. He'll need a crib. You weren't supposed to see until it was done."

Mariam wished he wouldn't do that, hitch his hopes to its being a boy. As happy as she was about this pregnancy, his expectation weighed on her. Yesterday, Rasheed had gone out and come home with a suede winter coat for a boy, lined inside with soft sheepskin, the sleeves embroidered with fine red and yellow silk thread.

Rasheed lifted a long, narrow board. As he began to saw it in half, he said the stairs worried him. "Something will have to be done about them later, when he's old enough to climb." The stove worried him too, he said. The knives and forks would have to be stowed somewhere out of reach.

"You can't be too careful. Boys are reckless creatures."

Mariam pulled the shawl around her against the chill.

THE NEXT MORNING, Rasheed said he wanted to invite his friends for dinner to celebrate. All morning, Mariam cleaned lentils and moistened rice. She sliced eggplants for *borani,* and cooked leeks and ground beef for *aushak.* She swept the floor, beat the curtains, aired the house, despite the snow that had started up again. She arranged mattresses and cushions along the walls of the living room, placed bowls of candy and roasted almonds on the table.

She was in her room by early evening before the first of the men arrived. She lay in bed as the hoots and laughter and bantering voices downstairs began to mushroom. She couldn't keep her hands from drifting to her belly. She thought of what was growing there, and happiness rushed in like a gust of wind blowing a door wide open. Her eyes watered.

Mariam thought of her six-hundred-and-fifty-kilometer bus trip with Rasheed, from Herat in the west, near the border with Iran, to Kabul in the east. They had passed small towns and big towns, and knots of little villages that kept springing up one after another. They had gone over mountains and across raw-burned deserts, from one province to the next. And here she was now, over those boulders and parched hills, with a home of her own, a husband of her own, heading toward one final, cherished province: Motherhood. How delectable it was to think of this baby, *her* baby, *their* baby. How glorious it was to know that her love for it already dwarfed anything she had ever felt as a human being, to know that there was no need any longer for pebble games.

Downstairs, someone was tuning a harmonium. Then the clanging of a hammer tuning a tabla. Someone cleared his throat. And then there was whistling and clapping and yipping and singing.

Mariam stroked the softness of her belly. *No bigger than a fingernail,* the doctor had said.

I'm going to be a mother, she thought.

"I'm going to be a mother," she said. Then she was laughing to herself, and saying it over and over, relishing the words.

When Mariam thought of this baby, her heart swelled inside of her. It swelled and swelled until all the loss, all the grief, all the loneliness and self-abasement of her life washed away. This was why God had brought her here, all the way across the country. She knew this now. She remembered a verse from the Koran that Mullah Faizullah had taught her: *And Allah is the East and the West, therefore wherever you turn there is Allah's purpose* . . . She laid down her prayer rug and did *namaz.* When she was done, she cupped her hands before her face and asked God not to let all this good fortune slip away from her.

It was Rasheed's idea to go to the *hamam.* Mariam had never been to a bathhouse, but he said there was nothing finer than stepping out and taking that first breath of cold air, to feel the heat rising from the skin.

In the women's *hamam,* shapes moved about in the steam around Mariam, a glimpse of a hip here, the contour of a shoulder there. The squeals of young girls, the grunts of old women, and the trickling of bathwater echoed between the walls as backs were scrubbed and hair soaped. Mariam sat in the far corner by herself, working on her heels with a pumice stone, insulated by a wall of steam from the passing shapes.

Then there was blood and she was screaming.

The sound of feet now, slapping against the wet cobblestones. Faces peering at her through the steam. Tongues clucking.

Later that night, in bed, Fariba told her husband that when she'd heard the cry and rushed over she'd found Rasheed's wife shriveled into a corner, hugging her knees, a pool of blood at her feet.

"You could hear the poor girl's teeth rattling, Hakim, she was shivering so hard."

When Mariam had seen her, Fariba said, she had asked in a high, supplicating voice, *It's normal, isn't it? Isn't it? Isn't it normal?*

ANOTHER BUS RIDE with Rasheed. Snowing again. Falling thick this time. It was piling in heaps on sidewalks, on roofs, gathering in patches on the bark of straggly trees. Mariam watched the merchants plowing snow from their storefronts. A group of boys was chasing a black dog. They waved sportively at the bus. Mariam looked over to Rasheed. His eyes were closed. He wasn't humming. Mariam reclined her head and closed her eyes too. She wanted out of her cold socks, out of the damp wool sweater that was prickly against her skin. She wanted away from this bus.

At the house, Rasheed covered her with a quilt when she lay on the couch, but there was a stiff, perfunctory air about this gesture.

"What kind of answer is that?" he said again. "That's what a mullah is supposed to say. You pay a doctor his fee, you want a better answer than 'God's will.' "

Mariam curled up her knees beneath the quilt and said he ought to get some rest.

"God's will," he simmered.

He sat in his room smoking cigarettes all day.

Mariam lay on the couch, hands tucked between her knees, watched the whirlpool of snow twisting and spinning outside the window. She remembered Nana saying once that each snowflake was a sigh heaved by an aggrieved woman somewhere in the world. That all the sighs drifted up the sky, gathered into clouds, then broke into tiny pieces that fell silently on the people below.

As a reminder of how women like us suffer, she'd said. *How quietly we endure all that falls upon us.*

14.

The grief kept surprising Mariam. All it took to unleash it was her thinking of the unfinished crib in the toolshed or the suede coat in Rasheed's closet. The baby came to life then and she could hear it, could hear its hungry grunts, its gurgles and jabbering. She felt it sniffing at her breasts. The grief washed over her, swept her up, tossed her upside down. Mariam was dumbfounded that she could miss in such a crippling manner a being she had never even seen.

Then there were days when the dreariness didn't seem quite as unrelenting to Mariam. Days when the mere thought of resuming the old patterns of her life did not seem so exhausting, when it did not take enormous efforts of will to get out of bed, to do her prayers, to do the wash, to make meals for Rasheed.

Mariam dreaded going outside. She was envious, suddenly, of the neighborhood women and their wealth of children. Some had seven or eight and didn't understand how fortunate they were, how blessed that their children had flourished in their wombs, lived to squirm in their arms and take the milk from their breasts. Children that they had not bled away with soapy water and the bodily filth of strangers down some bathhouse drain. Mariam resented them when she overheard them complaining about misbehaving sons and lazy daughters.

A voice inside her head tried to soothe her with well-intended but misguided consolation.

You'll have others, Inshallah. *You're young. Surely you'll have many other chances.*

But Mariam's grief wasn't aimless or unspecific. Mariam grieved for *this* baby, this particular child, who had made her so happy for a while.

Some days, she believed that the baby had been an undeserved blessing, that she was being punished for what she had done to Nana. Wasn't it true that she might as well have slipped that noose around her mother's neck herself? Treacherous daughters did not deserve to be mothers, and this was just punishment. She had fitful dreams, of Nana's *jinn* sneaking into her room at night, burrowing its claws into her womb, and stealing her baby. In these dreams, Nana cackled with delight and vindication.

Other days, Mariam was besieged with anger. It was Rasheed's fault for his premature celebration. For his foolhardy faith that she was carrying a boy. Naming the baby as he had. Taking God's will for granted. His fault, for making her go to the bathhouse. Something there, the steam, the dirty water, the soap, something there had caused this to happen. No. Not Rasheed. *She* was to blame. She became furious with herself for sleeping in the wrong position, for eating meals that were too spicy, for not eating enough fruit, for drinking too much tea.

It was God's fault, for taunting her as He had. For not granting her what He had granted so many other women. For dangling before her, tantalizingly, what He knew would give her the greatest happiness, then pulling it away.

But it did no good, all this fault laying, all these harangues of accusations bouncing in her head. It was *kofr*, sacrilege, to think these thoughts. Allah was not spiteful. He was not a petty God. Mullah Faizullah's words whispered in her head: *Blessed is He in Whose hand is the kingdom, and He Who has power over all things, Who created death and life that He may try you.*

Ransacked with guilt, Mariam would kneel and pray for forgiveness for these thoughts.

MEANWHILE, a change had come over Rasheed ever since the day at the bathhouse. Most nights when he came home, he hardly talked anymore. He ate, smoked, went to bed, sometimes came back in the middle of the night for a brief and, of late, quite rough session of coupling. He was more apt to sulk these days, to fault her cooking, to complain about clutter around the yard or point out even minor uncleanliness in the house. Occasionally, he took her around town on Fridays, like he used to, but on the sidewalks he walked quickly and always a few steps ahead of her, without speaking, unmindful of Mariam who almost had to run to keep up with him. He wasn't so ready with a laugh on these outings anymore. He didn't buy her sweets or gifts, didn't stop and name places to her as he used to. Her questions seemed to irritate him.

One night, they were sitting in the living room listening to the radio. Winter was passing. The stiff winds that plastered snow onto the face and made the eyes water had calmed. Silvery fluffs of snow were melting off the branches of tall elms and would be replaced in a few weeks with stubby, pale green buds. Rasheed was shaking his foot absently to the tabla beat of a Hamahang song, his eyes crinkled against cigarette smoke.

"Are you angry with me?" Mariam asked.

Rasheed said nothing. The song ended and the news came on. A woman's voice reported that President Daoud Khan had sent yet another group of Soviet consultants back to Moscow, to the expected displeasure of the Kremlin.

"I worry that you are angry with me."

Rasheed sighed.

"Are you?"

His eyes shifted to her. "Why would I be angry?"

"I don't know, but ever since the baby—"

"Is that the kind of man you take me for, after everything I've done for you?"

"No. Of course not."

"Then stop pestering me!"

"I'm sorry. *Bebakhsh*, Rasheed. I'm sorry."

He crushed out his cigarette and lit another. He turned up the volume on the radio.

"I've been thinking, though," Mariam said, raising her voice so as to be heard over the music.

Rasheed sighed again, more irritably this time, turned down the volume once more. He rubbed his forehead wearily. "What now?"

"I've been thinking, that maybe we should have a proper burial. For the baby, I mean. Just us, a few prayers, nothing more."

Mariam had been thinking about it for a while. She didn't want to forget this baby. It didn't seem right, not to mark this loss in some way that was permanent.

"What for? It's idiotic."

"It would make me feel better, I think."

"Then *you* do it," he said sharply. "I've already buried one son. I won't bury another. Now, if you don't mind, I'm trying to listen."

He turned up the volume again, leaned his head back and closed his eyes.

One sunny morning that week, Mariam picked a spot in the yard and dug a hole.

"In the name of Allah and with Allah, and in the name of the messenger of Allah upon whom be the blessings and peace of Allah," she said under her breath as her shovel bit into the ground. She placed the suede coat that Rasheed had bought for the baby in the hole and shoveled dirt over it.

"You make the night to pass into the day and You make the day to pass into the night, and You bring forth the living from the dead and You bring forth the dead from the living, and You give sustenance to whom You please without measure."

She patted the dirt with the back of the shovel. She squatted by the mound, closed her eyes.

Give sustenance, Allah.

Give sustenance to me.

15.

APRIL 1978

On April 17, 1978, the year Mariam turned nineteen, a man named Mir Akbar Khyber was found murdered. Two days later, there was a large demonstration in Kabul. Everyone in the neighborhood was in the streets talking about it. Through the window, Mariam saw neighbors milling about, chatting excitedly, transistor radios pressed to their ears. She saw Fariba leaning against the wall of her house, talking with a woman who was new to Deh-Mazang. Fariba was smiling, and her palms were pressed against the swell of her pregnant belly. The other woman, whose name escaped Mariam, looked older than Fariba, and her hair had an odd purple tint to it. She was holding a little boy's hand. Mariam knew the boy's name was Tariq, because she had heard this woman on the street call after him by that name.

Mariam and Rasheed didn't join the neighbors. They listened in on the radio as some ten thousand people poured into the streets and marched up and down Kabul's government district. Rasheed said that Mir Akbar Khyber had been a prominent communist, and that his supporters were blaming the murder on President Daoud Khan's government. He didn't look at her when he said this. These days, he never did anymore, and Mariam wasn't ever sure if she was being spoken to.

"What's a communist?" she asked.

Rasheed snorted, and raised both eyebrows. "You don't know what a communist is? Such a simple thing. Everyone knows. It's common knowledge. You don't . . . Bah. I don't know why I'm surprised." Then he crossed his ankles on the table and mumbled that it was someone who believed in Karl Marxist.

"Who's Karl Marxist?"

Rasheed sighed.

On the radio, a woman's voice was saying that Taraki, the leader of the Khalq branch of the PDPA, the Afghan communist party, was in the streets giving rousing speeches to demonstrators.

"What I meant was, what do they want?" Mariam asked. "These communists, what is it that they believe?"

Rasheed chortled and shook his head, but Mariam thought she saw uncertainty in the way he crossed his arms, the way his eyes shifted. "You know nothing, do you? You're like a child. Your brain is empty. There is no information in it."

"I ask because—"

"*Chup ko*. Shut up."

Mariam did.

It wasn't easy tolerating him talking this way to her, to bear his scorn, his ridicule, his insults, his walking past her like she was nothing but a house cat. But after four years of marriage, Mariam saw clearly how much a woman could tolerate when she was afraid. And Mariam *was* afraid. She lived in fear of his shifting moods, his volatile temperament, his insistence on steering even mundane exchanges down a confrontational path that, on occasion, he would resolve with punches, slaps, kicks, and sometimes try to make amends for with polluted apologies and sometimes not.

In the four years since the day at the bathhouse, there had been six more cycles of hopes raised then dashed, each loss, each collapse, each trip to the doctor more crushing for Mariam than the last. With each disappointment, Rasheed had grown more remote and resentful. Now nothing she did pleased him. She cleaned the house, made sure he always had a supply of clean shirts, cooked him his favorite dishes. Once, disastrously, she even bought makeup and put it on for him. But when he came home, he took one look at her and winced with such distaste that she rushed to the bathroom and washed it all off, tears of shame mixing with soapy water, rouge, and mascara.

Now Mariam dreaded the sound of him coming home in the evening. The key rattling, the creak of the door— these were sounds that set her heart racing. From her bed, she listened to the *click-clack* of his heels, to the muffled shuffling of his feet after he'd shed his shoes. With her ears, she took inventory of his doings: chair legs dragged across the floor, the plaintive squeak of the cane seat when he sat, the clinking of spoon against plate, the flutter of newspaper pages flipped, the slurping of water. And as her heart pounded, her mind wondered what excuse he would use that night to pounce on her. There was always something, some minor thing that would infuriate him, because no matter what she did to please him, no matter how thoroughly she submitted to his wants and demands, it wasn't enough. She could not give him his son back. In this most essential way, she had failed him—seven times she had failed him—and now she was nothing but a burden to him. She could see it in the way he looked at her, *when* he looked at her. She was a burden to him.

"What's going to happen?" she asked him now.

Rasheed shot her a sidelong glance. He made a sound between a sigh and a groan, dropped his legs from the table, and turned off the radio. He took it upstairs to his room. He closed the door.

ON APRIL 27, Mariam's question was answered with crackling sounds and intense, sudden roars. She ran barefoot down to the living room and found Rasheed already by the window, in his undershirt, his hair disheveled, palms pressed to the glass. Mariam made her way to the window next to him. Overhead, she could see military planes zooming past, heading north and east. Their deafening shrieks hurt her ears. In the distance, loud booms resonated and sudden plumes of smoke rose to the sky.

"What's going on, Rasheed?" she said. "What is all this?"

"God knows," he muttered. He tried the radio and got only static.

"What do we do?"

Impatiently, Rasheed said, "We wait."

LATER IN THE DAY, Rasheed was still trying the radio as Mariam made rice with spinach sauce in the kitchen. Mariam remembered a time when she had enjoyed, even looked forward to, cooking for Rasheed. Now cooking was an exercise in heightened anxiety. The *qurma*s were always too salty or too bland for his taste. The rice was judged either too greasy or too dry, the bread declared too doughy or too crispy. Rasheed's faultfinding left her stricken in the kitchen with self-doubt.

When she brought him his plate, the national anthem was playing on the radio.

"I made *sabzi*," she said.

"Put it down and be quiet."

After the music faded, a man's voice came on the radio. He announced himself as Air Force Colonel Abdul Qader. He reported that earlier in the day the rebel Fourth Armored Division had seized the airport and key intersections in the city. Kabul Radio, the ministries of Communication and the Interior, and the Foreign Ministry building had also been captured. Kabul was in the hands of the people now, he said proudly. Rebel MiGs had attacked the Presidential Palace. Tanks had broken into the premises, and a fierce battle was under way there. Daoud's loyalist forces were all but defeated, Abdul Qader said in a reassuring tone.

Days later, when the communists began the summary executions of those connected with Daoud Khan's regime, when rumors began floating about Kabul of eyes gouged and genitals electrocuted in the Pol-e-Charkhi Prison, Mariam would hear of the slaughter that had taken place at the Presidential Palace. Daoud Khan *had* been killed, but not before the communist rebels had killed some twenty members of his family, including women and grandchildren. There would be rumors that he had taken his own life, that he'd been gunned down in the heat of battle; rumors that he'd been saved for last, made to watch the massacre of his family, then shot.

Rasheed turned up the volume and leaned in closer.

"A revolutionary council of the armed forces has been established, and our *watan* will now be known as the Democratic Republic of Afghanistan," Abdul Qader said. "The era of aristocracy, nepotism, and inequality is over, fellow *hamwatan*s. We have ended decades of tyranny. Power is now in the hands of the masses and freedom-loving people. A glorious new era in the history of our country is afoot. A new Afghanistan is born. We assure you that you have nothing to fear, fellow Afghans. The new regime will maintain the utmost respect for principles, both Islamic and democratic. This is a time of rejoicing and celebration."

Rasheed turned off the radio.

"So is this good or bad?" Mariam asked.

"Bad for the rich, by the sound of it," Rasheed said. "Maybe not so bad for us."

Mariam's thoughts drifted to Jalil. She wondered if the communists would go after him, then. Would they jail him? Jail his sons? Take his businesses and properties from him?

"Is this warm?" Rasheed said, eyeing the rice.

"I just served it from the pot."

He grunted, and told her to hand him a plate.

DOWN THE STREET, as the night lit up in sudden flashes of red and yellow, an exhausted Fariba had propped herself up on her elbows. Her hair was matted with sweat, and droplets of moisture teetered on the edge of her upper lip. At her bedside, the elderly midwife, Wajma, watched as Fariba's husband and sons passed around the infant. They were marveling at the baby's light hair, at her pink cheeks and puckered, rosebud lips, at the slits of jade green eyes moving behind her puffy lids. They smiled at each other when they heard her voice for the first time, a cry that started like the mewl of a cat and exploded into a healthy, full-throated yowl. Noor said her eyes were like gemstones. Ahmad, who was the most religious member of the family, sang the *azan* in his baby sister's ear and blew in her face three times.

"Laila it is, then?" Hakim asked, bouncing his daughter.

"Laila it is," Fariba said, smiling tiredly. "Night Beauty. It's perfect."

RASHEED MADE a ball of rice with his fingers. He put it in his mouth, chewed once, then twice, before grimacing and spitting it out on the *sofrah*.

"What's the matter?" Mariam asked, hating the apologetic tone of her voice. She could feel her pulse quickening, her skin shrinking.

"What's the matter?" he mewled, mimicking her. "What's the matter is that you've done it again."

"But I boiled it five minutes more than usual."

"That's a bold lie."

"I swear—"

He shook the rice angrily from his fingers and pushed the plate away, spilling sauce and rice on the *sofrah*. Mariam watched as he stormed out of the living room, then out of the house, slamming the door on his way out.

Mariam kneeled to the ground and tried to pick up the grains of rice and put them back on the plate, but her hands were shaking badly, and she had to wait for them to stop. Dread pressed down on her chest. She tried taking a few deep breaths. She caught her pale reflection in the darkened living-room window and looked away.

Then she heard the front door opening, and Rasheed was back in the living room.

"Get up," he said. "Come here. Get up."

He snatched her hand, opened it, and dropped a handful of pebbles into it.

"Put these in your mouth."

"What?"

"Put. These. In your mouth."

"Stop it, Rasheed, I'm—"

His powerful hands clasped her jaw. He shoved two fingers into her mouth and pried it open, then forced the cold, hard pebbles into it. Mariam struggled against him, mumbling, but he kept pushing the pebbles in, his upper lip curled in a sneer.

"Now chew," he said.

Through the mouthful of grit and pebbles, Mariam

102

mumbled a plea. Tears were leaking out of the corners of her eyes.

"CHEW!" he bellowed. A gust of his smoky breath slammed against her face.

Mariam chewed. Something in the back of her mouth cracked.

"Good," Rasheed said. His cheeks were quivering. "Now you know what your rice tastes like. Now you know what you've given me in this marriage. Bad food, and nothing else."

Then he was gone, leaving Mariam to spit out pebbles, blood, and the fragments of two broken molars.

PART TWO

16.

Nine-year-old Laila rose from bed, as she did most mornings, hungry for the sight of her friend Tariq. This morning, however, she knew there would be no Tariq sighting.

"How long will you be gone?" she'd asked when Tariq had told her that his parents were taking him south, to the city of Ghazni, to visit his paternal uncle.

"Thirteen days."

"Thirteen days?"

"It's not so long. You're making a face, Laila."

"I am not."

"You're not going to cry, are you?"

"I am not going to cry! Not over you. Not in a thousand years."

She'd kicked at his shin, not his artificial but his real one, and he'd playfully whacked the back of her head.

Thirteen days. Almost two weeks. And, just five days in, Laila had learned a fundamental truth about time: Like the accordion on which Tariq's father sometimes played old Pashto songs, time stretched and contracted depending on Tariq's absence or presence.

Downstairs, her parents were fighting. Again. Laila knew the routine: Mammy, ferocious, indomitable, pacing and ranting; Babi, sitting, looking sheepish and dazed, nodding obediently, waiting for the storm to pass. Laila closed her door and changed. But she could still hear them. She could still hear *her.* Finally, a door slammed. Pounding footsteps. Mammy's bed creaked loudly. Babi, it seemed, would survive to see another day.

"Laila!" he called now. "I'm going to be late for work!"

"One minute!"

Laila put on her shoes and quickly brushed her shoulder-length, blond curls in the mirror. Mammy always told Laila that she had inherited her hair color—as well as her thick-lashed, turquoise green eyes, her dimpled cheeks, her high cheekbones, and the pout of her lower lip, which Mammy shared—from her great-grandmother, Mammy's grandmother. *She was a* pari, *a stunner,* Mammy said. *Her beauty was the talk of the valley. It skipped two generations of women in our family, but it sure didn't bypass you, Laila.* The valley Mammy referred to was the Panjshir, the Farsi-speaking Tajik region one hundred kilometers northeast of Kabul. Both Mammy and Babi, who were first cousins, had been born and raised in Panjshir; they had moved to Kabul back in 1960 as hopeful, bright-eyed newlyweds when Babi had been admitted to Kabul University.

Laila scrambled downstairs, hoping Mammy wouldn't come out of her room for another round. She found Babi kneeling by the screen door.

"Did you see this, Laila?"

The rip in the screen had been there for weeks. Laila hunkered down beside him. "No. Must be new."

"That's what I told Fariba." He looked shaken, reduced,

as he always did after Mammy was through with him. "She says it's been letting in bees."

Laila's heart went out to him. Babi was a small man, with narrow shoulders and slim, delicate hands, almost like a woman's. At night, when Laila walked into Babi's room, she always found the downward profile of his face burrowing into a book, his glasses perched on the tip of his nose. Sometimes he didn't even notice that she was there. When he did, he marked his page, smiled a close-lipped, companionable smile. Babi knew most of Rumi's and Hafez's *ghazal*s by heart. He could speak at length about the struggle between Britain and czarist Russia over Afghanistan. He knew the difference between a stalactite and a stalagmite, and could tell you that the distance between the earth and the sun was the same as going from Kabul to Ghazni one and a half million times. But if Laila needed the lid of a candy jar forced open, she had to go to Mammy, which felt like a betrayal. Ordinary tools befuddled Babi. On his watch, squeaky door hinges never got oiled. Ceilings went on leaking after he plugged them. Mold thrived defiantly in kitchen cabinets. Mammy said that before he left with Noor to join the jihad against the Soviets, back in 1980, it was Ahmad who had dutifully and competently minded these things.

"But if you have a book that needs urgent reading," she said, "then Hakim is your man."

Still, Laila could not shake the feeling that at one time, before Ahmad and Noor had gone to war against the Soviets—before Babi had *let* them go to war—Mammy too had thought Babi's bookishness endearing, that, once upon a time, she too had found his forgetfulness and ineptitude charming.

"So what is today?" he said now, smiling coyly. "Day five? Or is it six?"

"What do I care? I don't keep count," Laila lied,

shrugging, loving him for remembering. Mammy had no idea that Tariq had left.

"Well, his flashlight will be going off before you know it," Babi said, referring to Laila and Tariq's nightly signaling game. They had played it for so long it had become a bedtime ritual, like brushing teeth.

Babi ran his finger through the rip. "I'll patch this as soon as I get a chance. We'd better go." He raised his voice and called over his shoulder, "We're going now, Fariba! I'm taking Laila to school. Don't forget to pick her up!"

Outside, as she was climbing on the carrier pack of Babi's bicycle, Laila spotted a car parked up the street, across from the house where the shoemaker, Rasheed, lived with his reclusive wife. It was a Benz, an unusual car in this neighborhood, blue with a thick white stripe bisecting the hood, the roof, and the trunk. Laila could make out two men sitting inside, one behind the wheel, the other in the back.

"Who are they?" she said.

"It's not our business," Babi said. "Climb on, you'll be late for class."

Laila remembered another fight, and, that time, Mammy had stood over Babi and said in a mincing way, *That's your business, isn't it, cousin? To make nothing your business. Even your own sons going to war. How I pleaded with you. But you buried your nose in those cursed books and let our sons go like they were a pair of* harami*s.*

Babi pedaled up the street, Laila on the back, her arms wrapped around his belly. As they passed the blue Benz, Laila caught a fleeting glimpse of the man in the backseat: thin, white-haired, dressed in a dark brown suit, with a white handkerchief triangle in the breast pocket. The only other thing she had time to notice was that the car had Herat license plates.

They rode the rest of the way in silence, except at the turns, where Babi braked cautiously and said, "Hold on, Laila. Slowing down. Slowing down. There."

IN CLASS THAT DAY, Laila found it hard to pay attention, between Tariq's absence and her parents' fight. So when the teacher called on her to name the capitals of Romania and Cuba, Laila was caught off guard.

The teacher's name was Shanzai, but, behind her back, the students called her Khala Rangmaal, Auntie Painter, referring to the motion she favored when she slapped students—palm, then back of the hand, back and forth, like a painter working a brush. Khala Rangmaal was a sharp-faced young woman with heavy eyebrows. On the first day of school, she had proudly told the class that she was the daughter of a poor peasant from Khost. She stood straight, and wore her jet-black hair pulled tightly back and tied in a bun so that, when Khala Rangmaal turned around, Laila could see the dark bristles on her neck. Khala Rangmaal did not wear makeup or jewelry. She did not cover and forbade the female students from doing it. She said women and men were equal in every way and there was no reason women should cover if men didn't.

She said that the Soviet Union was the best nation in the world, along with Afghanistan. It was kind to its workers, and its people were all equal. Everyone in the Soviet Union was happy and friendly, unlike America, where crime made people afraid to leave their homes. And everyone in Afghanistan would be happy too, she said, once the antiprogressives, the backward bandits, were defeated.

"That's why our Soviet comrades came here in 1979. To lend their neighbor a hand. To help us defeat these brutes who want our country to be a backward, primitive nation. And you must lend your own hand, children. You must report anyone who might know about these rebels. It's your duty. You must listen, then report. Even if it's your parents, your uncles or aunts. Because none of them loves you as much as your country does. Your country comes first, remember! I will be proud of you, and so will your country."

On the wall behind Khala Rangmaal's desk was a map of the Soviet Union, a map of Afghanistan, and a framed photo of the latest communist president, Najibullah, who, Babi said, had once been the head of the dreaded KHAD, the Afghan secret police. There were other photos too, mainly of young Soviet soldiers shaking hands with peasants, planting apple saplings, building homes, always smiling genially.

"Well," Khala Rangmaal said now, "have I disturbed your daydreaming, *Inqilabi* Girl?"

This was her nickname for Laila, Revolutionary Girl, because she'd been born the night of the April coup of 1978—except Khala Rangmaal became angry if anyone in her class used the word *coup*. What had happened, she insisted, was an *inqilab,* a revolution, an uprising of the working people against inequality. *Jihad* was another forbidden word. According to her, there wasn't even a war out there in the provinces, just skirmishes against trouble-makers stirred by people she called foreign provocateurs. And certainly no one, *no one,* dared repeat in her presence the rising rumors that, after eight years of fighting, the Soviets were losing this war. Particularly now that the American president, Reagan, had started shipping the Mujahideen Stinger Missiles to down the Soviet helicopters, now that Muslims from all over the world were joining the cause: Egyptians, Pakistanis, even wealthy Saudis, who left their millions behind and came to Afghanistan to fight the jihad.

"Bucharest. Havana," Laila managed.

"And are those countries our friends or not?"

"They are, *moalim* sahib. They are friendly countries."

Khala Rangmaal gave a curt nod.

WHEN SCHOOL LET OUT, Mammy again didn't show up like she was supposed to. Laila ended up walking home with two of her classmates, Giti and Hasina.

Giti was a tightly wound, bony little girl who wore her hair in twin ponytails held by elastic bands. She was always scowling, and walking with her books pressed to her chest, like a shield. Hasina was twelve, three years older than Laila and Giti, but had failed third grade once and fourth grade twice. What she lacked in smarts Hasina made up for in mischief and a mouth that, Giti said, ran like a sewing machine. It was Hasina who had come up with the Khala Rangmaal nickname.

Today, Hasina was dispensing advice on how to fend off unattractive suitors. "Foolproof method, guaranteed to work. I give you my word."

"This is stupid. I'm too young to have a suitor!" Giti said.

"You're not too young."

"Well, no one's come to ask for *my* hand."

"That's because you have a beard, my dear."

Giti's hand shot up to her chin, and she looked with alarm to Laila, who smiled pityingly—Giti was the most humorless person Laila had ever met—and shook her head with reassurance.

"Anyway, you want to know what to do or not, ladies?"

"Go ahead," Laila said.

"Beans. No less than four cans. On the evening the toothless lizard comes to ask for your hand. But the timing, ladies, the timing is everything. You have to suppress the fireworks 'til it's time to serve him his tea."

"I'll remember that," Laila said.

"So will he."

Laila could have said then that she didn't need this advice because Babi had no intention of giving her away anytime soon. Though Babi worked at Silo, Kabul's gigantic bread factory, where he labored amid the heat and the humming machinery stoking the massive ovens and mill grains all day, he was a university-educated man. He'd been a high school teacher before the communists fired him—this was shortly after the coup of 1978, about a year and a half before the Soviets had invaded. Babi had made it clear to Laila from a young age that the most important thing in his life, after her safety, was her schooling.

I know you're still young, but I want you to understand and learn this now, he said. *Marriage can wait, education cannot. You're a very, very bright girl. Truly, you are. You can be anything you want, Laila. I know this about you. And I also know that when this war is over, Afghanistan is going to need you as much as its men, maybe even more. Because a society has no chance of success if its women are uneducated, Laila. No chance.*

But Laila didn't tell Hasina that Babi had said these things, or how glad she was to have a father like him, or how proud she was of his regard for her, or how determined she was to pursue her education just as he had his. For the last two years, Laila had received the *awal numra* certificate, given yearly to the top-ranked student in each grade. She said nothing of these things to Hasina, though, whose own father was an ill-tempered taxi driver who in two or three years would almost certainly give her away. Hasina had told Laila, in one of her infrequent serious moments, that it had already been decided that she would marry a first cousin who was twenty years older than her and owned an auto shop in Lahore. *I've seen him twice,* Hasina had said. *Both times he ate with his mouth open.*

"Beans, girls," Hasina said. "You remember that. Unless, of course"—here she flashed an impish grin and nudged Laila with an elbow—"it's your young handsome, one-legged prince who comes knocking. Then . . ."

Laila slapped the elbow away. She would have taken offense if anyone else had said that about Tariq. But she knew that Hasina wasn't malicious. She mocked—it was what she did—and her mocking spared no one, least of all herself.

"You shouldn't talk that way about people!" Giti said.

"What people is that?"

"People who've been injured because of war," Giti said earnestly, oblivious to Hasina's toying.

"I think Mullah Giti here has a crush on Tariq. I knew it! Ha! But he's already spoken for, don't you know? Isn't he, Laila?"

"I do not have a crush. On anyone!"

They broke off from Laila, and, still arguing this way, turned in to their street.

Laila walked alone the last three blocks. When she was on her street, she noticed that the blue Benz was still parked there, outside Rasheed and Mariam's house. The elderly man in the brown suit was standing by the hood now, leaning on a cane, looking up at the house.

That was when a voice behind Laila said, "Hey. Yellow Hair. Look here."

Laila turned around and was greeted by the barrel of a gun.

17.

The gun was red, the trigger guard bright green. Behind the gun loomed Khadim's grinning face. Khadim was eleven, like Tariq. He was thick, tall, and had a severe underbite. His father was a butcher in Deh-Mazang, and, from time to time, Khadim was known to fling bits of calf intestine at passersby. Sometimes, if Tariq wasn't nearby, Khadim shadowed Laila in the schoolyard at recess, leering, making little whining noises. One time, he'd tapped her on the shoulder and said, *You're so very pretty, Yellow Hair. I want to marry you.*

Now he waved the gun. "Don't worry," he said. "This won't show. Not on *your* hair."

"Don't you do it! I'm warning you."

"What are you going to do?" he said. "Sic your cripple on me? 'Oh, Tariq jan. Oh, won't you come home and save me from the *badmash*!' "

Laila began to backpedal, but Khadim was already pumping the trigger. One after another, thin jets of warm water struck Laila's hair, then her palm when she

116

raised it to shield her face.

Now the other boys came out of their hiding, laughing, cackling.

An insult Laila had heard on the street rose to her lips. She didn't really understand it—couldn't quite picture the logistics of it—but the words packed a fierce potency, and she unleashed them now.

"Your mother eats cock!"

"At least she's not a loony like yours," Khadim shot back, unruffled. "At least my father's not a sissy! And, by the way, why don't you smell your hands?"

The other boys took up the chant. "Smell your hands! Smell your hands!"

Laila did, but she knew even before she did, what he'd meant about it not showing in her hair. She let out a high-pitched yelp. At this, the boys hooted even harder.

Laila turned around and, howling, ran home.

SHE DREW WATER from the well, and, in the bathroom, filled a basin, tore off her clothes. She soaped her hair, frantically digging fingers into her scalp, whimpering with disgust. She rinsed with a bowl and soaped her hair again. Several times, she thought she might throw up. She kept mewling and shivering, as she rubbed and rubbed the soapy washcloth against her face and neck until they reddened.

This would have never happened if Tariq had been with her, she thought as she put on a clean shirt and fresh trousers. Khadim wouldn't have dared. Of course, it wouldn't have happened if Mammy had shown up like she was supposed to either. Sometimes Laila wondered why Mammy had even bothered having her. People, she believed now, shouldn't be allowed to have new children if they'd already given away all their love to their old ones. It wasn't fair. A fit of anger claimed her. Laila went to her room, collapsed on her bed.

When the worst of it had passed, she went across the hallway to Mammy's door and knocked. When she was younger, Laila used to sit for hours outside this door. She would tap on it and whisper Mammy's name over and over, like a magic chant meant to break a spell: *Mammy, Mammy, Mammy, Mammy* . . . But Mammy never opened the door. She didn't open it now. Laila turned the knob and walked in.

Sometimes Mammy had good days. She sprang out of bed bright-eyed and playful. The droopy lower lip stretched upward in a smile. She bathed. She put on fresh clothes and wore mascara. She let Laila brush her hair, which Laila loved doing, and pin earrings through her earlobes. They went shopping together to Mandaii Bazaar. Laila got her to play snakes and ladders, and they ate shavings from blocks of dark chocolate, one of the few things they shared a common taste for. Laila's favorite part of Mammy's good days was when Babi came home, when she and Mammy looked up from the board and grinned at him with brown teeth. A gust of contentment puffed through the room then, and Laila caught a momentary glimpse of the tenderness, the romance, that had once bound her parents back when this house had been crowded and noisy and cheerful.

Mammy sometimes baked on her good days and invited neighborhood women over for tea and pastries. Laila got to lick the bowls clean, as Mammy set the table with cups and napkins and the good plates. Later, Laila would take her place at the living-room table and try to break into the conversation, as the women talked boisterously and drank tea and complimented Mammy on her baking. Though there was never much for her to say, Laila liked to sit and listen in because at these gatherings she was treated

118

to a rare pleasure: She got to hear Mammy speaking affectionately about Babi.

"What a first-rate teacher he was," Mammy said. "His students loved him. And not only because he wouldn't beat them with rulers, like other teachers did. They respected him, you see, because he respected *them*. He was marvelous."

Mammy loved to tell the story of how she'd proposed to him.

"I was sixteen, he was nineteen. Our families lived next door to each other in Panjshir. Oh, I had the crush on him, *hamshiras*! I used to climb the wall between our houses, and we'd play in his father's orchard. Hakim was always scared that we'd get caught and that my father would give him a slapping. 'Your father's going to give me a slapping,' he'd always say. He was so cautious, so serious, even then. And then one day I said to him, I said, 'Cousin, what will it be? Are you going to ask for my hand or are you going to make me come *khastegari* to you?' I said it just like that. You should have seen the face on him!"

Mammy would slap her palms together as the women, and Laila, laughed.

Listening to Mammy tell these stories, Laila knew that there had been a time when Mammy always spoke this way about Babi. A time when her parents did not sleep in separate rooms. Laila wished she hadn't missed out on those times.

Inevitably, Mammy's proposal story led to matchmaking schemes. When Afghanistan was free from the Soviets and the boys returned home, they would need brides, and so, one by one, the women paraded the neighborhood girls who might or might not be suitable for Ahmad and Noor. Laila always felt excluded when the talk turned to her brothers, as though the women were discussing a beloved film that only she hadn't seen. She'd been two years old when Ahmad and Noor had left Kabul for Panjshir up north, to join Commander Ahmad Shah Massoud's forces and fight the jihad. Laila hardly remembered anything at all about them. A shiny ALLAH pendant around Ahmad's neck. A patch of black hairs on one of Noor's ears. And that was it.

"What about Azita?"

"The rugmaker's daughter?" Mammy said, slapping her cheek with mock outrage. "She has a thicker mustache than Hakim!"

"There's Anahita. We hear she's top in her class at Zarghoona."

"Have you seen the teeth on that girl? Tombstones. She's hiding a graveyard behind those lips."

"How about the Wahidi sisters?"

"Those two dwarfs? No, no, no. Oh, no. Not for my sons. Not for my sultans. They deserve better."

As the chatter went on, Laila let her mind drift, and, as always, it found Tariq.

MAMMY HAD PULLED the yellowish curtains. In the darkness, the room had a layered smell about it: sleep, unwashed linen, sweat, dirty socks, perfume, the previous night's leftover *qurma*. Laila waited for her eyes to adjust before she crossed the room. Even so, her feet became entangled with items of clothing that littered the floor.

Laila pulled the curtains open. At the foot of the bed was an old metallic folding chair. Laila sat on it and watched the unmoving blanketed mound that was her mother.

The walls of Mammy's room were covered with pictures of Ahmad and Noor. Everywhere Laila looked, two strangers smiled back. Here was Noor mounting a tricycle. Here was Ahmad doing his prayers, posing beside a sundial Babi and he had built when he was twelve. And there they were, her brothers, sitting back to back beneath the old pear tree in the yard.

Beneath Mammy's bed, Laila could see the corner of Ahmad's shoe box protruding. From time to time, Mammy showed her the old, crumpled newspaper clippings in it, and pamphlets that Ahmad had managed to collect from insurgent groups and resistance organizations headquartered in Pakistan. One photo, Laila remembered, showed a man in a long white coat handing a lollipop to a legless little boy. The caption below the photo read: *Children are the intended victims of Soviet land mine campaign*. The article went on to say that the Soviets also liked to hide explosives inside brightly colored toys. If a child picked it up, the toy exploded, tore off fingers or an entire hand. The father could not join the jihad then; he'd have to stay home and care for his child. In another article in Ahmad's box, a young Mujahid was saying that the Soviets had dropped gas on his village that burned people's skin and blinded them. He said he had seen his mother and sister running for the stream, coughing up blood.

"Mammy."

The mound stirred slightly. It emitted a groan.

"Get up, Mammy. It's three o'clock."

Another groan. A hand emerged, like a submarine periscope breaking surface, and dropped. The mound moved more discernibly this time. Then the rustle of blankets as layers of them shifted over each other. Slowly, in stages, Mammy materialized: first the slovenly hair, then the white, grimacing face, eyes pinched shut against the light, a hand groping for the headboard, the sheets sliding down as she pulled herself up, grunting. Mammy made an effort to look up, flinched against the light, and her head drooped over her chest.

"How was school?" she muttered.

So it would begin. The obligatory questions, the perfunctory answers. Both pretending. Unenthusiastic partners, the two of them, in this tired old dance.

"School was fine," Laila said.

"Did you learn anything?"

"The usual."

"Did you eat?"

"I did."

"Good."

Mammy raised her head again, toward the window. She winced and her eyelids fluttered. The right side of her face was red, and the hair on that side had flattened. "I have a headache."

"Should I fetch you some aspirin?"

Mammy massaged her temples. "Maybe later. Is your father home?"

"It's only three."

"Oh. Right. You said that already." Mammy yawned. "I was dreaming just now," she said, her voice only a bit louder than the rustle of her nightgown against the sheets. "Just now, before you came in. But I can't remember it now. Does that happen to you?"

"It happens to everybody, Mammy."

"Strangest thing."

"I should tell you that while you were dreaming, a boy shot piss out of a water gun on my hair."

"Shot what? What was that? I'm sorry."

"Piss. Urine."

"That's . . . that's terrible. God. I'm sorry. Poor you. I'll have a talk with him first thing in the morning. Or maybe with his mother. Yes, that would be better, I think."

"I haven't told you who it was."

"Oh. Well, who was it?"

"Never mind."

"You're angry."

"You were supposed to pick me up."

"I was," Mammy croaked. Laila could not tell whether this was a question. Mammy began picking at her hair. This was one of life's great mysteries to Laila, that Mammy's picking had not made her bald as an egg. "What about . . . What's his name, your friend, Tariq? Yes, what about him?"

"He's been gone for a week."

"Oh." Mammy sighed through her nose. "Did you wash?"

"Yes."

"So you're clean, then." Mammy turned her tired gaze to the window. "You're clean, and everything is fine."

Laila stood up. "I have homework now."

"Of course you do. Shut the curtains before you go, my love," Mammy said, her voice fading. She was already sinking beneath the sheets.

As Laila reached for the curtains, she saw a car pass by on the street tailed by a cloud of dust. It was the blue Benz with the Herat license plate finally leaving. She followed it with her eyes until it vanished around a turn, its back window twinkling in the sun.

"I won't forget tomorrow," Mammy was saying behind her. "I promise."

"You said that yesterday."

"You don't know, Laila."

"Know what?" Laila wheeled around to face her mother. "What don't I know?"

Mammy's hand floated up to her chest, tapped there. "In *here*. What's in *here*." Then it fell flaccid. "You just don't know."

18.

A week passed, but there was still no sign of Tariq. Then another week came and went.

To fill the time, Laila fixed the screen door that Babi still hadn't got around to. She took down Babi's books, dusted and alphabetized them. She went to Chicken Street with Hasina, Giti, and Giti's mother, Nila, who was a seamstress and sometime sewing partner of Mammy's. In that week, Laila came to believe that of all the hardships a person had to face none was more punishing than the simple act of waiting.

Another week passed.

Laila found herself caught in a net of terrible thoughts.

He would never come back. His parents had moved away for good; the trip to Ghazni had been a ruse. An adult scheme to spare the two of them an upsetting farewell.

A land mine had gotten to him again. The way it did in 1981, when he was five, the last time his parents took him south to Ghazni. That was shortly after Laila's third birthday. He'd been lucky that time, losing only a leg; lucky that he'd survived at all.

Her head rang and rang with these thoughts.

Then one night Laila saw a tiny flashing light from down the street. A sound, something between a squeak and a gasp, escaped her lips. She quickly fished her own flashlight from under the bed, but it wouldn't work. Laila banged it against her palm, cursed the dead batteries. But it didn't matter. He was back. Laila sat on the edge of her bed, giddy with relief, and watched that beautiful, yellow eye winking on and off.

ON HER WAY to Tariq's house the next day, Laila saw Khadim and a group of his friends across the street. Khadim was squatting, drawing something in the dirt with a stick. When he saw her, he dropped the stick and wiggled his fingers. He said something and there was a round of chuckles. Laila dropped her head and hurried past.

"What did you *do*?" she exclaimed when Tariq opened the door. Only then did she remember that his uncle was a barber.

Tariq ran his hand over his newly shaved scalp and smiled, showing white, slightly uneven teeth.

"Like it?"

"You look like you're enlisting in the army."

"You want to feel?" He lowered his head.

The tiny bristles scratched Laila's palm pleasantly. Tariq wasn't like some of the other boys, whose hair concealed cone-shaped skulls and unsightly lumps. Tariq's head was perfectly curved and lump-free.

When he looked up, Laila saw that his cheeks and brow had sunburned.

"What took you so long?" she said.

"My uncle was sick. Come on. Come inside."

He led her down the hallway to the family room. Laila loved everything about this house. The shabby old rug in the family room, the patchwork quilt on the couch, the ordinary clutter of Tariq's life: his mother's bolts of fabric, her sewing needles embedded in spools, the old magazines, the accordion case in the corner waiting to be cracked open.

"Who is it?"

It was his mother calling from the kitchen.

"Laila," he answered.

He pulled her a chair. The family room was brightly lit and had double windows that opened into the yard. On the sill were empty jars in which Tariq's mother pickled eggplant and made carrot marmalade.

"You mean our *aroos,* our daughter-in-law," his father announced, entering the room. He was a carpenter, a lean, white-haired man in his early sixties. He had gaps between his front teeth, and the squinty eyes of someone who had spent most of his life outdoors. He opened his arms and Laila went into them, greeted by his pleasant and familiar smell of sawdust. They kissed on the cheek three times.

"You keep calling her that and she'll stop coming here," Tariq's mother said, passing by them. She was carrying a tray with a large bowl, a serving spoon, and four smaller bowls on it. She set the tray on the table. "Don't mind the old man." She cupped Laila's face. "It's good to see you, my dear. Come, sit down. I brought back some water-soaked fruit with me."

The table was bulky and made of a light, unfinished wood—Tariq's father had built it, as well as the chairs. It was covered with a moss green vinyl tablecloth with little magenta crescents and stars on it. Most of the living-room wall was taken up with pictures of Tariq at various ages. In some of the very early ones, he had two legs.

"I heard your brother was sick," Laila said to Tariq's father, dipping a spoon into her bowl of soaked raisins, pistachios, and apricots.

He was lighting a cigarette. "Yes, but he's fine now, *shokr e Khoda,* thanks to God."

"Heart attack. His second," Tariq's mother said, giving her husband an admonishing look.

Tariq's father blew smoke and winked at Laila. It struck her again that Tariq's parents could easily pass for his grandparents. His mother hadn't had him until she'd been well into her forties.

"How is your father, my dear?" Tariq's mother said, looking on over her bowl.

As long as Laila had known her, Tariq's mother had worn a wig. It was turning a dull purple with age. It was pulled low on her brow today, and Laila could see the gray hairs of her sideburns. Some days, it rode high on her forehead. But, to Laila, Tariq's mother never looked pitiable in it. What Laila saw was the calm, self-assured face beneath the wig, the clever eyes, the pleasant, unhurried manners.

"He's fine," Laila said. "Still at Silo, of course. He's fine."

"And your mother?"

"Good days. Bad ones too. The same."

"Yes," Tariq's mother said thoughtfully, lowering her spoon into the bowl. "How hard it must be, how terribly hard, for a mother to be away from her sons."

"You're staying for lunch?" Tariq said.

"You have to," said his mother. "I'm making *shorwa.*"

"I don't want to be a *mozahem.*"

"Imposing?" Tariq's mother said. "We leave for a couple of weeks and you turn polite on us?"

"All right, I'll stay," Laila said, blushing and smiling.

"It's settled, then."

The truth was, Laila loved eating meals at Tariq's house as much as she disliked eating them at hers. At Tariq's, there was no eating alone; they always ate as a family. Laila liked the violet plastic drinking glasses they used and the quarter lemon that always floated in the water pitcher. She liked how they started each meal with a bowl of fresh yogurt, how they squeezed sour oranges on everything, even their yogurt, and how they made small, harmless jokes at each other's expense.

Over meals, conversation always flowed. Though Tariq and his parents were ethnic Pashtuns, they spoke Farsi when Laila was around for her benefit, even though Laila more or less understood their native Pashto, having learned it in school. Babi said that there were tensions between their people—the Tajiks, who were a minority, and Tariq's people, the Pashtuns, who were the largest ethnic group in Afghanistan. *Tajiks have always felt slighted,* Babi had said. *Pashtun kings ruled this country for almost two hundred and fifty years, Laila, and Tajiks for all of nine months, back in 1929.*

And you, Laila had asked, *do you feel slighted, Babi?*

Babi had wiped his eyeglasses clean with the hem of his shirt. *To me, it's nonsense—and very dangerous nonsense at that—all this talk of I'm Tajik and you're Pashtun and he's Hazara and she's Uzbek. We're all Afghans, and that's all that should matter. But when one group rules over the others for so long . . . There's contempt. Rivalry. There is. There always has been.*

Maybe so. But Laila never felt it in Tariq's house, where these matters never even came up. Her time with Tariq's family always felt natural to Laila, effortless, uncomplicated by differences in tribe or language, or by the personal spites and grudges that infected the air at her own home.

"How about a game of cards?" Tariq said.

"Yes, go upstairs," his mother said, swiping disapprovingly

at her husband's cloud of smoke. "I'll get the *shorwa* going."

They lay on their stomachs in the middle of Tariq's room and took turns dealing for *panjpar*. Pedaling air with his foot, Tariq told her about his trip. The peach saplings he had helped his uncle plant. A garden snake he had captured.

This room was where Laila and Tariq did their homework, where they built playing-card towers and drew ridiculous portraits of each other. If it was raining, they leaned on the windowsill, drinking warm, fizzy orange Fanta, and watched the swollen rain droplets trickle down the glass.

"All right, here's one," Laila said, shuffling. "What goes around the world but stays in a corner?"

"Wait." Tariq pushed himself up and swung his artificial left leg around. Wincing, he lay on his side, leaning on his elbow. "Hand me that pillow." He placed it under his leg. "There. That's better."

Laila remembered the first time he'd shown her his stump. She'd been six. With one finger, she had poked the taut, shiny skin just below his left knee. Her finger had found little hard lumps there, and Tariq had told her they were spurs of bone that sometimes grew after an amputation. She'd asked him if his stump hurt, and he said it got sore at the end of the day, when it swelled and didn't fit the prosthesis like it was supposed to, like a finger in a thimble. *And sometimes it gets rubbed. Especially when it's hot. Then I get rashes and blisters, but my mother has creams that help. It's not so bad.*

Laila had burst into tears.

What are you crying for? He'd strapped his leg back on. *You asked to see it, you* giryanok, *you crybaby! If I'd known you were going to bawl, I wouldn't have shown you.*

"A stamp," he said.

"What?"

"The riddle. The answer is a stamp. We should go to the zoo after lunch."

"You knew that one. Did you?"

"Absolutely not."

"You're a cheat."

"And you're envious."

"Of what?"

"My masculine smarts."

"Your *masculine* smarts? Really? Tell me, who always wins at chess?"

"I let you win." He laughed. They both knew that wasn't true.

"And who failed math? Who do you come to for help with your math homework even though you're a grade ahead?"

"I'd be two grades ahead if math didn't bore me."

"I suppose geography bores you too."

"How did you know? Now, shut up. So are we going to the zoo or not?"

Laila smiled. "We're going."

"Good."

"I missed you."

There was a pause. Then Tariq turned to her with a half-grinning, half-grimacing look of distaste. "What's the *matter* with you?"

How many times had she, Hasina, and Giti said those same three words to each other, Laila wondered, said it without hesitation, after only two or three days of not seeing each other? *I missed you, Hasina. Oh, I missed you too.* In Tariq's grimace, Laila learned that boys differed from girls in this regard. They didn't make a show of friendship. They felt no urge, no need, for this sort of talk. Laila imagined it had been this way for her brothers too. Boys, Laila came to see, treated friendship the way they treated the sun: its existence undisputed; its radiance best enjoyed, not beheld directly.

"I was trying to annoy you," she said.

He gave her a sidelong glance. "It worked."

But she thought his grimace softened. And she thought that maybe the sunburn on his cheeks deepened momentarily.

LAILA DIDN'T MEAN to tell him. She'd, in fact, decided that telling him would be a very bad idea. Someone would get hurt, because Tariq wouldn't be able to let it pass. But when they were on the street later, heading down to the bus stop, she saw Khadim again, leaning against a wall. He was surrounded by his friends, thumbs hooked in his belt loops. He grinned at her defiantly.

And so she told Tariq. The story spilled out of her mouth before she could stop it.

"He did what?"

She told him again.

He pointed to Khadim. "Him? He's the one? You're sure?"

"I'm sure."

Tariq clenched his teeth and muttered something to himself in Pashto that Laila didn't catch. "You wait here," he said, in Farsi now.

"No, Tariq—"

He was already crossing the street.

Khadim was the first to see him. His grin faded, and he pushed himself off the wall. He unhooked his thumbs from the belt loops and made himself more upright, taking on a self-conscious air of menace. The others followed his gaze.

Laila wished she hadn't said anything. What if they banded together? How many of them were there—ten? eleven? twelve? What if they hurt him?

Then Tariq stopped a few feet from Khadim and his band. There was a moment of consideration, Laila thought, maybe a change of heart, and, when he bent down, she imagined he would pretend his shoelace had come undone and walk back to her. Then his hands went to work, and she understood.

The others understood too when Tariq straightened up, standing on one leg. When he began hopping toward Khadim, then charging him, his unstrapped leg raised high over his shoulder like a sword.

The boys stepped aside in a hurry. They gave him a clear path to Khadim.

Then it was all dust and fists and kicks and yelps.

Khadim never bothered Laila again.

THAT NIGHT, as most nights, Laila set the dinner table for two only. Mammy said she wasn't hungry. On those nights that she was, she made a point of taking a plate to her room before Babi even came home. She was usually asleep or lying awake in bed by the time Laila and Babi sat down to eat.

Babi came out of the bathroom, his hair—peppered white with flour when he'd come home—washed clean now and combed back.

"What are we having, Laila?"

"Leftover *aush* soup."

"Sounds good," he said, folding the towel with which he'd dried his hair. "So what are we working on tonight? Adding fractions?"

"Actually, converting fractions to mixed numbers."

"Ah. Right."

Every night after dinner, Babi helped Laila with her homework and gave her some of his own. This was only to keep Laila a step or two ahead of her class, not because he disapproved of the work assigned by the school—the

132

propaganda teaching notwithstanding. In fact, Babi thought that the one thing the communists had done right—or at least intended to—ironically, was in the field of education, the vocation from which they had fired him. More specifically, the education of women. The government had sponsored literacy classes for all women. Almost two-thirds of the students at Kabul University were women now, Babi said, women who were studying law, medicine, engineering.

Women have always had it hard in this country, Laila, but they're probably more free now, under the communists, and have more rights than they've ever had before, Babi said, always lowering his voice, aware of how intolerant Mammy was of even remotely positive talk of the communists. *But it's true,* Babi said, *it's a good time to be a woman in Afghanistan. And you can take advantage of that, Laila. Of course, women's freedom—* here, he shook his head ruefully—*is also one of the reasons people out there took up arms in the first place.*

By "out there," he didn't mean Kabul, which had always been relatively liberal and progressive. Here in Kabul, women taught at the university, ran schools, held office in the government. No, Babi meant the tribal areas, especially the Pashtun regions in the south or in the east near the Pakistani border, where women were rarely seen on the streets and only then in burqa and accompanied by men. He meant those regions where men who lived by ancient tribal laws had rebelled against the communists and their decrees to liberate women, to abolish forced marriage, to raise the minimum marriage age to sixteen for girls. There, men saw it as an insult to their centuries-old tradition, Babi said, to be told by the government—and a godless one at that—that their daughters had to leave home, attend school, and work alongside men.

God forbid that should happen! Babi liked to say sarcastically. Then he would sigh, and say, *Laila, my love, the only enemy an Afghan cannot defeat is himself.*

Babi took his seat at the table, dipped bread into his bowl of *aush*.

Laila decided that she would tell him about what Tariq had done to Khadim, over the meal, before they started in on fractions. But she never got the chance. Because, right then, there was a knock at the door, and, on the other side of the door, a stranger with news.

19.

I need to speak to your parents, *dokhtar jan*," he said when Laila opened the door. He was a stocky man, with a sharp, weather-roughened face. He wore a potato-colored coat, and a brown wool *pakol* on his head.

"Can I tell them who's here?"

Then Babi's hand was on Laila's shoulder, and he gently pulled her from the door.

"Why don't you go upstairs, Laila. Go on."

As she moved toward the steps, Laila heard the visitor say to Babi that he had news from Panjshir. Mammy was in the room now too. She had one hand clamped over her mouth, and her eyes were skipping from Babi to the man in the *pakol*.

Laila peeked from the top of the stairs. She watched the stranger sit down with her parents. He leaned toward them. Said a few muted words. Then Babi's face was white, and getting whiter, and he was looking at his hands, and Mammy was screaming, screaming, and tearing at her hair.

*   *   *

THE NEXT MORNING, the day of the *fatiha,* a flock of neighborhood women descended on the house and took charge of preparations for the *khatm* dinner that would take place after the funeral. Mammy sat on the couch the whole morning, her fingers working a handkerchief, her face bloated. She was tended to by a pair of sniffling women who took turns patting Mammy's hand gingerly, like she was the rarest and most fragile doll in the world. Mammy did not seem aware of their presence.

Laila kneeled before her mother and took her hands. "Mammy."

Mammy's eyes drifted down. She blinked.

"We'll take care of her, Laila jan," one of the women said with an air of self-importance. Laila had been to funerals before where she had seen women like this, women who relished all things that had to do with death, official consolers who let no one trespass on their self-appointed duties.

"It's under control. You go on now, girl, and do something else. Leave your mother be."

Shooed away, Laila felt useless. She bounced from one room to the next. She puttered around the kitchen for a while. An uncharacteristically subdued Hasina and her mother came. So did Giti and her mother. When Giti saw Laila, she hurried over, threw her bony arms around her, and gave Laila a very long, and surprisingly strong, embrace. When she pulled back, tears had pooled in her eyes. "I am so sorry, Laila," she said. Laila thanked her. The three girls sat outside in the yard until one of the women assigned them the task of washing glasses and stacking plates on the table.

Babi too kept walking in and out of the house aimlessly, looking, it seemed, for something to do.

"Keep him away from me." That was the only time Mammy said anything all morning.

Babi ended up sitting alone on a folding chair in the hallway, looking desolate and small. Then one of the women told him he was in the way there. He apologized and disappeared into his study.

THAT AFTERNOON, the men went to a hall in Karteh-Seh that Babi had rented for the *fatiha*. The women came to the house. Laila took her spot beside Mammy, next to the living-room entrance where it was customary for the family of the deceased to sit. Mourners removed their shoes at the door, nodded at acquaintances as they crossed the room, and sat on folding chairs arranged along the walls. Laila saw Wajma, the elderly midwife who had delivered her. She saw Tariq's mother too, wearing a black scarf over the wig. She gave Laila a nod and a slow, sad, close-lipped smile.

From a cassette player, a man's nasal voice chanted verses from the Koran. In between, the women sighed and shifted and sniffled. There were muted coughs, murmurs, and, periodically, someone let out a theatrical, sorrow-drenched sob.

Rasheed's wife, Mariam, came in. She was wearing a black *hijab*. Strands of her hair strayed from it onto her brow. She took a seat along the wall across from Laila.

Next to Laila, Mammy kept rocking back and forth. Laila drew Mammy's hand into her lap and cradled it with both of hers, but Mammy did not seem to notice.

"Do you want some water, Mammy?" Laila said in her ear. "Are you thirsty?"

But Mammy said nothing. She did nothing but sway back and forth and stare at the rug with a remote, spirit-less look.

Now and then, sitting next to Mammy, seeing the drooping, woebegone looks around the room, the magnitude of the disaster that had struck her family would register with Laila. The possibilities denied. The hopes dashed.

But the feeling didn't last. It was hard to feel, *really* feel, Mammy's loss. Hard to summon sorrow, to grieve the deaths of people Laila had never really thought of as alive in the first place. Ahmad and Noor had always been like lore to her. Like characters in a fable. Kings in a history book.

It was Tariq who was real, flesh and blood. Tariq, who taught her cusswords in Pashto, who liked salted clover leaves, who frowned and made a low, moaning sound when he chewed, who had a light pink birthmark just beneath his left collarbone shaped like an upside-down mandolin.

So she sat beside Mammy and dutifully mourned Ahmad and Noor, but, in Laila's heart, her true brother was alive and well.

20.

The ailments that would hound Mammy for the rest of her days began. Chest pains and headaches, joint aches and night sweats, paralyzing pains in her ears, lumps no one else could feel. Babi took her to a doctor, who took blood and urine, shot X-rays of Mammy's body, but found no physical illness.

Mammy lay in bed most days. She wore black. She picked at her hair and gnawed on the mole below her lip. When Mammy was awake, Laila found her staggering through the house. She always ended up in Laila's room, as though she would run into the boys sooner or later if she just kept walking into the room where they had once slept and farted and fought with pillows. But all she ran into was their absence. And Laila. Which, Laila believed, had become one and the same to Mammy.

The only task Mammy never neglected was her five daily *namaz* prayers. She ended each *namaz* with her head hung low, hands held before her face, palms up, muttering a prayer for God to bring victory to the Mujahideen. Laila had to shoulder more and more of the chores. If she didn't tend to the house, she was apt to find clothes, shoes, open rice bags, cans of beans, and dirty dishes strewn about everywhere. Laila washed Mammy's dresses and changed her sheets. She coaxed her out of bed for baths and meals. She was the one who ironed Babi's shirts and folded his pants. Increasingly, she was the cook.

Sometimes, after she was done with her chores, Laila crawled into bed next to Mammy. She wrapped her arms around her, laced her fingers with her mother's, buried her face in her hair. Mammy would stir, murmur something. Inevitably, she would start in on a story about the boys.

One day, as they were lying this way, Mammy said, "Ahmad was going to be a leader. He had the charisma for it. People three times his age listened to him with respect, Laila. It was something to see. And Noor. Oh, my Noor. He was always making sketches of buildings and bridges. He was going to be an architect, you know. He was going to transform Kabul with his designs. And now they're both *shaheed*, my boys, both martyrs."

Laila lay there and listened, wishing Mammy would notice that *she*, Laila, hadn't become *shaheed*, that she was alive, here, in bed with her, that she had hopes and a future. But Laila knew that her future was no match for her brothers' past. They had overshadowed her in life. They would obliterate her in death. Mammy was now the curator of their lives' museum and she, Laila, a mere visitor. A receptacle for their myths. The parchment on which Mammy meant to ink their legends.

"The messenger who came with the news, he said that when they brought the boys back to camp, Ahmad Shah Massoud personally oversaw the burial. He said a prayer for them at the gravesite. That's the kind of brave young men your brothers were, Laila, that Commander Massoud himself, the Lion of Panjshir, God bless him, would over-see their burial."

Mammy rolled onto her back. Laila shifted, rested her head on Mammy's chest.

"Some days," Mammy said in a hoarse voice, "I listen to that clock ticking in the hallway. Then I think of all the ticks, all the minutes, all the hours and days and weeks and months and years waiting for me. All of it without them. And I can't breathe then, like someone's stepping on my heart, Laila. I get so weak. So weak I just want to collapse somewhere."

"I wish there was something I could do," Laila said, meaning it. But it came out sounding broad, perfunctory, like the token consolation of a kind stranger.

"You're a good daughter," Mammy said, after a deep sigh. "And I haven't been much of a mother to you."

"Don't say that."

"Oh, it's true. I know it and I'm sorry for it, my love."

"Mammy?"

"Mm."

Laila sat up, looking down at Mammy. There were gray strands in Mammy's hair now. And it startled Laila how much weight Mammy, who'd always been plump, had lost. Her cheeks had a sallow, drawn look. The blouse she was wearing drooped over her shoulders, and there was a gap-ing space between her neck and the collar. More than once Laila had seen the wedding band slide off Mammy's finger.

"I've been meaning to ask you something."

"What is it?"

"You wouldn't . . ." Laila began.

She'd talked about it to Hasina. At Hasina's suggestion, the two of them had emptied the bottle of aspirin in the gutter, hidden the kitchen knives and the sharp kebab skewers beneath the rug under the couch. Hasina had found a rope in the yard. When Babi couldn't find his razors, Laila had to tell him of her fears. He dropped on the edge of the couch, hands between his knees. Laila waited for some kind of reassurance from him. But all she got was a bewildered, hollow-eyed look.

"You wouldn't . . . Mammy I worry that—"

"I thought about it the night we got the news," Mammy said. "I won't lie to you, I've thought about it since too. But, no. Don't worry, Laila. I want to see my sons' dream come true. I want to see the day the Soviets go home disgraced, the day the Mujahideen come to Kabul in victory. I want to be there when it happens, when Afghanistan is free, so the boys see it too. They'll see it through my eyes."

Mammy was soon asleep, leaving Laila with dueling emotions: reassured that Mammy meant to live on, stung that *she* was not the reason. *She* would never leave her mark on Mammy's heart the way her brothers had, because Mammy's heart was like a pallid beach where Laila's footprints would forever wash away beneath the waves of sorrow that swelled and crashed, swelled and crashed.

21.

The driver pulled his taxi over to let pass another long convoy of Soviet jeeps and armored vehicles. Tariq leaned across the front seat, over the driver, and yelled, *"Pajalusta! Pajalusta!"*

A jeep honked and Tariq whistled back, beaming and waving cheerfully. "Lovely guns!" he yelled. "Fabulous jeeps! Fabulous army! Too bad you're losing to a bunch of peasants firing slingshots!"

The convoy passed. The driver merged back onto the road.

"How much farther?" Laila asked.

"An hour at the most," the driver said. "Barring any more convoys or checkpoints."

They were taking a day trip, Laila, Babi, and Tariq. Hasina had wanted to come too, had begged her father, but he wouldn't allow it. The trip was Babi's idea. Though he could hardly afford it on his salary, he'd hired a driver for the day. He wouldn't disclose anything to Laila about their destination except to say that, with it, he was contributing to her education.

They had been on the road since five in the morning. Through Laila's window, the landscape shifted from snow-capped peaks to deserts to canyons and sun-scorched outcroppings of rocks. Along the way, they passed mud houses with thatched roofs and fields dotted with bundles of wheat. Pitched out in the dusty fields, here and there, Laila recognized the black tents of Koochi nomads. And, frequently, the carcasses of burned-out Soviet tanks and wrecked helicopters. This, she thought, was Ahmad and Noor's Afghanistan. This, here in the provinces, was where the war was being fought, after all. Not in Kabul. Kabul was largely at peace. Back in Kabul, if not for the occasional bursts of gunfire, if not for the Soviet soldiers smoking on the sidewalks and the Soviet jeeps always bumping through the streets, war might as well have been a rumor.

It was late morning, after they'd passed two more checkpoints, when they entered a valley. Babi had Laila lean across the seat and pointed to a series of ancient-looking walls of sun-dried red in the distance.

"That's called Shahr-e-Zohak. The Red City. It used to be a fortress. It was built some nine hundred years ago to defend the valley from invaders. Genghis Khan's grandson attacked it in the thirteenth century, but he was killed. It was Genghis Khan himself who then destroyed it."

"And that, my young friends, is the story of our country, one invader after another," the driver said, flicking cigarette ash out the window. "Macedonians. Sassanians. Arabs. Mongols. Now the Soviets. But we're like those walls up there. Battered, and nothing pretty to look at, but still standing. Isn't that the truth, *badar*?"

"Indeed it is," said Babi.

*   *   *

Half an hour later, the driver pulled over.

"Come on, you two," Babi said. "Come outside and have a look."

They got out of the taxi. Babi pointed. "There they are. Look."

Tariq gasped. Laila did too. And she knew then that she could live to be a hundred and she would never again see a thing as magnificent.

The two Buddhas were enormous, soaring much higher than she had imagined from all the photos she'd seen of them. Chiseled into a sun-bleached rock cliff, they peered down at them, as they had nearly two thousand years before, Laila imagined, at caravans crossing the valley on the Silk Road. On either side of them, along the overhanging niche, the cliff was pocked with myriad caves.

"I feel so small," Tariq said.

"You want to climb up?" Babi said.

"Up the statues?" Laila asked. "We can do that?"

Babi smiled and held out his hand. "Come on."

The climb was hard for Tariq, who had to hold on to both Laila and Babi as they inched up a winding, narrow, dimly lit staircase. They saw shadowy caves along the way, and tunnels honeycombing the cliff every which way.

"Careful where you step," Babi said. His voice made a loud echo. "The ground is treacherous."

In some parts, the staircase was open to the Buddha's cavity.

"Don't look down, children. Keep looking straight ahead."

As they climbed, Babi told them that Bamiyan had once been a thriving Buddhist center until it had fallen under Islamic Arab rule in the ninth century. The sandstone cliffs were home to Buddhist monks who carved caves in them to use as living quarters and as sanctuary for weary traveling pilgrims. The monks, Babi said, painted beautiful frescoes along the walls and roofs of their caves.

"At one point," he said, "there were five thousand monks living as hermits in these caves."

Tariq was badly out of breath when they reached the top. Babi was panting too. But his eyes shone with excitement.

"We're standing atop its head," he said, wiping his brow with a handkerchief. "There's a niche over here where we can look out."

They inched over to the craggy overhang and, standing side by side, with Babi in the middle, gazed down on the valley.

"Look at this!" said Laila.

Babi smiled.

The Bamiyan Valley below was carpeted by lush farming fields. Babi said they were green winter wheat and alfalfa, potatoes too. The fields were bordered by poplars and criss-crossed by streams and irrigation ditches, on the banks of which tiny female figures squatted and washed clothes. Babi pointed to rice paddies and barley fields draping the slopes. It was autumn, and Laila could make out people in bright tunics on the roofs of mud brick dwellings laying out the harvest to dry. The main road going through the town was poplar-lined too. There were small shops and teahouses and street-side barbers on either side of it. Beyond the village, beyond the river and the streams, Laila saw foothills, bare and dusty brown, and, beyond those, as beyond everything else in Afghanistan, the snowcapped Hindu Kush.

The sky above all of this was an immaculate, spotless blue.

"It's so quiet," Laila breathed. She could see tiny sheep and horses but couldn't hear their bleating and whinnying.

"It's what I always remember about being up here,"

Babi said. "The silence. The peace of it. I wanted you to experience it. But I also wanted you to see your country's heritage, children, to learn of its rich past. You see, some things I can teach you. Some you learn from books. But there are things that, well, you just have to *see* and *feel*."

"Look," said Tariq.

They watched a hawk, gliding in circles above the village.

"Did you ever bring Mammy up here?" Laila asked.

"Oh, many times. Before the boys were born. After too. Your mother, she used to be adventurous then, and . . . so *alive*. She was just about the liveliest, happiest person I'd ever met." He smiled at the memory. "She had this laugh. I swear it's why I married her, Laila, for that laugh. It bulldozed you. You stood no chance against it."

A wave of affection overcame Laila. From then on, she would always remember Babi this way: reminiscing about Mammy, with his elbows on the rock, hands cupping his chin, his hair ruffled by the wind, eyes crinkled against the sun.

"I'm going to look at some of those caves," Tariq said.

"Be careful," said Babi.

"I will, *Kaka jan*," Tariq's voice echoed back.

Laila watched a trio of men far below, talking near a cow tethered to a fence. Around them, the trees had started to turn, ochre and orange, scarlet red.

"I miss the boys too, you know," Babi said. His eyes had welled up a tad. His chin was trembling. "I may not . . . With your mother, both her joy and sadness are extreme. She can't hide either. She never could. Me, I suppose I'm different. I tend to . . . But it broke me too, the boys dying. I miss them too. Not a day passes that I . . . It's very hard, Laila. So very hard." He squeezed the inner corners of his eyes with his thumb and forefinger. When he tried to talk, his voice broke. He pulled his lips over his teeth and waited. He took a long, deep breath, looked at her. "But I'm glad I have you. Every day, I thank God for you. Every single day. Sometimes, when your mother's having one of her really dark days, I feel like you're all I have, Laila."

Laila drew closer to him and rested her cheek up against his chest. He seemed slightly startled—unlike Mammy, he rarely expressed his affection physically. He planted a brisk kiss on the top of her head and hugged her back awkwardly. They stood this way for a while, looking down on the Bamiyan Valley.

"As much as I love this land, some days I think about leaving it," Babi said.

"Where to?"

"Anyplace where it's easy to forget. Pakistan first, I suppose. For a year, maybe two. Wait for our paperwork to get processed."

"And then?"

"And then, well, it *is* a big world. Maybe America. Somewhere near the sea. Like California."

Babi said the Americans were a generous people. They would help them with money and food for a while, until they could get on their feet.

"I would find work, and, in a few years, when we had enough saved up, we'd open a little Afghan restaurant. Nothing fancy, mind you, just a modest little place, a few tables, some rugs. Maybe hang some pictures of Kabul. We'd give the Americans a taste of Afghan food. And with your mother's cooking, they'd line up and down the street.

"And you, you would continue going to school, of course. You know how I feel about that. That would be our absolute top priority, to get you a good education, high school then college. But in your free time, *if* you wanted to, you could help out, take orders, fill water pitchers, that sort of thing."

Babi said they would hold birthday parties at the restaurant, engagement ceremonies, New Year's get-togethers. It would turn into a gathering place for other Afghans who, like them, had fled the war. And, late at night, after everyone had left and the place was cleaned up, they would sit for tea amid the empty tables, the three of them, tired but thankful for their good fortune.

When Babi was done speaking, he grew quiet. They both did. They knew that Mammy wasn't going anywhere. Leaving Afghanistan had been unthinkable to her while Ahmad and Noor were still alive. Now that they were *shaheed*, packing up and running was an even worse affront, a betrayal, a disavowal of the sacrifice her sons had made.

How can you think of it? Laila could hear her saying. *Does their dying mean nothing to you, cousin? The only solace I find is in knowing that I walk the same ground that soaked up their blood. No. Never.*

And Babi would never leave without her, Laila knew, even though Mammy was no more a wife to him now than she was a mother to Laila. For Mammy, he would brush aside this daydream of his the way he flicked specks of flour from his coat when he got home from work. And so they would stay. They would stay until the war ended. And they would stay for whatever came after war.

Laila remembered Mammy telling Babi once that she had married a man who had no convictions. Mammy didn't understand. She didn't understand that if she looked into a mirror, she would find the one unfailing conviction of his life looking right back at her.

LATER, after they'd eaten a lunch of boiled eggs and potatoes with bread, Tariq napped beneath a tree on the banks of a gurgling stream. He slept with his coat neatly folded into a pillow, his hands crossed on his chest. The driver went to the village to buy almonds. Babi sat at the foot of a thick-trunked acacia tree reading a paperback. Laila knew the book; he'd read it to her once. It told the story of an old fisherman named Santiago who catches an enormous fish. But by the time he sails his boat to safety, there is nothing left of his prize fish; the sharks have torn it to pieces.

Laila sat on the edge of the stream, dipping her feet into the cool water. Overhead, mosquitoes hummed and cottonwood seeds danced. A dragonfly whirred nearby. Laila watched its wings catch glints of sunlight as it buzzed from one blade of grass to another. They flashed purple, then green, orange. Across the stream, a group of local Hazara boys were picking patties of dried cow dung from the ground and stowing them into burlap sacks tethered to their backs. Somewhere, a donkey brayed. A generator sputtered to life.

Laila thought again about Babi's little dream. *Somewhere near the sea.*

There was something she hadn't told Babi up there atop the Buddha: that, in one important way, she was glad they couldn't go. She would miss Giti and her pinch-faced earnestness, yes, and Hasina too, with her wicked laugh and reckless clowning around. But, mostly, Laila remembered all too well the inescapable drudgery of those four weeks without Tariq when he had gone to Ghazni. She remembered all too well how time had dragged without him, how she had shuffled about feeling waylaid, out of balance. How could she ever cope with his permanent absence?

Maybe it was senseless to want to be near a person so badly here in a country where bullets had shredded her own brothers to pieces. But all Laila had to do was picture Tariq going at Khadim with his leg and then nothing in the world seemed more sensible to her.

*   *   *

SIX MONTHS LATER, in April 1988, Babi came home with big news.

"They signed a treaty!" he said. "In Geneva. It's official! They're leaving. Within nine months, there won't be any more Soviets in Afghanistan!"

Mammy was sitting up in bed. She shrugged.

"But the communist regime is staying," she said. "Najibullah is the Soviets' puppet president. He's not going anywhere. No, the war will go on. This is not the end."

"Najibullah won't last," said Babi.

"They're leaving, Mammy! They're actually leaving!"

"You two celebrate if you want to. But I won't rest until the Mujahideen hold a victory parade right here in Kabul."

And, with that, she lay down again and pulled up the blanket.

22.

JANUARY 1989

One cold, overcast day in January 1989, three months before Laila turned eleven, she, her parents, and Hasina went to watch one of the last Soviet convoys exit the city. Spectators had gathered on both sides of the thoroughfare outside the Military Club near Wazir Akbar Khan. They stood in muddy snow and watched the line of tanks, armored trucks, and jeeps as light snow flew across the glare of the passing headlights. There were heckles and jeers. Afghan soldiers kept people off the street. Every now and then, they had to fire a warning shot.

Mammy hoisted a photo of Ahmad and Noor high over her head. It was the one of them sitting back-to-back under the pear tree. There were others like her, women with pictures of their *shaheed* husbands, sons, brothers held high.

Someone tapped Laila and Hasina on the shoulder. It was Tariq.

"Where did you get that thing?" Hasina exclaimed.

"I thought I'd come dressed for the occasion." Tariq

said. He was wearing an enormous Russian fur hat, complete with earflaps, which he had pulled down. "How do I look?"

"Ridiculous," Laila laughed.

"That's the idea."

"Your parents came here with you dressed like this?"

"They're home, actually," he said.

The previous fall, Tariq's uncle in Ghazni had died of a heart attack, and, a few weeks later, Tariq's father had suffered a heart attack of his own, leaving him frail and tired, prone to anxiety and bouts of depression that overtook him for weeks at a time. Laila was glad to see Tariq like this, like his old self again. For weeks after his father's illness, Laila had watched him moping around, heavy-faced and sullen.

The three of them stole away while Mammy and Babi stood watching the Soviets. From a street vendor, Tariq bought them each a plate of boiled beans topped with thick cilantro chutney. They ate beneath the awning of a closed rug shop, then Hasina went to find her family.

On the bus ride home, Tariq and Laila sat behind her parents. Mammy was by the window, staring out, clutching the picture against her chest. Beside her, Babi was impassively listening to a man who was arguing that the Soviets might be leaving but that they would send weapons to Najibullah in Kabul.

"He's their puppet. They'll keep the war going through him, you can bet on that."

Someone in the next aisle voiced his agreement.

Mammy was muttering to herself, long-winded prayers that rolled on and on until she had no breath left and had to eke out the last few words in a tiny, high-pitched squeak.

THEY WENT TO Cinema Park later that day, Laila and Tariq, and had to settle for a Soviet film that was dubbed, to unintentionally comic effect, in Farsi. There was a merchant ship, and a first mate in love with the captain's daughter. Her name was Alyona. Then came a fierce storm, lightning, rain, the heaving sea tossing the ship. One of the frantic sailors yelled something. An absurdly calm Afghan voice translated: "My dear sir, would you kindly pass the rope?"

At this, Tariq burst out cackling. And, soon, they both were in the grips of a hopeless attack of laughter. Just when one became fatigued, the other would snort, and off they would go on another round. A man sitting two rows up turned around and shushed them.

There was a wedding scene near the end. The captain had relented and let Alyona marry the first mate. The newlyweds were smiling at each other. Everyone was drinking vodka.

"I'm never getting married," Tariq whispered.

"Me neither," said Laila, but not before a moment of nervous hesitation. She worried that her voice had betrayed her disappointment at what he had said. Her heart galloping, she added, more forcefully this time, "Never."

"Weddings are stupid."

"All the fuss."

"All the money spent."

"For what?"

"For clothes you'll never wear again."

"Ha!"

"If I ever *do* get married," Tariq said, "they'll have to make room for three on the wedding stage. Me, the bride, and the guy holding the gun to my head."

The man in the front row gave them another admonishing look.

On the screen, Alyona and her new husband locked lips.

Watching the kiss, Laila felt strangely conspicuous all at once. She became intensely aware of her heart thumping, of the blood thudding in her ears, of the shape of Tariq beside her, tightening up, becoming still. The kiss dragged on. It seemed of utmost urgency to Laila, suddenly, that she not stir or make a noise. She sensed that Tariq was observing her—one eye on the kiss, the other on her—as she was observing *him*. Was he listening to the air whooshing in and out of her nose, she wondered, waiting for a subtle faltering, a revealing irregularity, that would betray her thoughts?

And what would it be like to kiss him, to feel the fuzzy hair above his lip tickling her own lips?

Then Tariq shifted uncomfortably in his seat. In a strained voice, he said, "Did you know that if you fling snot in Siberia, it's a green icicle before it hits the ground?"

They both laughed, but briefly, nervously, this time. And when the film ended and they stepped outside, Laila was relieved to see that the sky had dimmed, that she wouldn't have to meet Tariq's eyes in the bright daylight.

23.

APRIL 1992

Three years passed.

In that time, Tariq's father had a series of strokes. They left him with a clumsy left hand and a slight slur to his speech. When he was agitated, which happened frequently, the slurring got worse.

Tariq outgrew his leg again and was issued a new leg by the Red Cross, though he had to wait six months for it.

As Hasina had feared, her family took her to Lahore, where she was made to marry the cousin who owned the auto shop. The morning that they took her, Laila and Giti went to Hasina's house to say good-bye. Hasina told them that the cousin, her husband-to-be, had already started the process to move them to Germany, where his brothers lived. Within the year, she thought, they would be in Frankfurt. They cried then in a three-way embrace. Giti was inconsolable. The last time Laila ever saw Hasina, she was being helped by her father into the crowded backseat of a taxi.

The Soviet Union crumbled with astonishing swiftness. Every few weeks, it seemed to Laila, Babi was coming home with news of the latest republic to declare independence. Lithuania. Estonia. Ukraine. The Soviet flag was lowered over the Kremlin. The Republic of Russia was born.

In Kabul, Najibullah changed tactics and tried to portray himself as a devout Muslim. "Too little and far too late," said Babi. "You can't be the chief of KHAD one day and the next day pray in a mosque with people whose relatives you tortured and killed." Feeling the noose tightening around Kabul, Najibullah tried to reach a settlement with the Mujahideen but the Mujahideen balked.

From her bed, Mammy said, "Good for them." She kept her vigils for the Mujahideen and waited for her parade. Waited for her sons' enemies to fall.

AND, EVENTUALLY, they did. In April 1992, the year Laila turned fourteen.

Najibullah surrendered at last and was given sanctuary in the UN compound near Darulaman Palace, south of the city.

The jihad was over. The various communist regimes that had held power since the night Laila was born were all defeated. Mammy's heroes, Ahmad's and Noor's brothers-in-war, had won. And now, after more than a decade of sacrificing everything, of leaving behind their families to live in mountains and fight for Afghanistan's sovereignty, the Mujahideen were coming to Kabul, in flesh, blood, and battle-weary bone.

Mammy knew all of their names.

There was Dostum, the flamboyant Uzbek commander, leader of the Junbish-i-Milli faction, who had a reputation for shifting allegiances. The intense, surly Gulbuddin Hekmatyar, leader of the Hezb-e-Islami faction, a Pashtun who had studied engineering and once killed a Maoist

student. Rabbani, Tajik leader of the Jamiat-e-Islami faction, who had taught Islam at Kabul University in the days
of the monarchy. Sayyaf, a Pashtun from Paghman with
Arab connections, a stout Muslim and leader of the
Ittehad-i-Islami faction. Abdul Ali Mazari, leader of the
Hizb-e-Wahdat faction, known as Baba Mazari among his
fellow Hazaras, with strong Shi'a ties to Iran.

And, of course, there was Mammy's hero, Rabbani's ally,
the brooding, charismatic Tajik commander Ahmad Shah
Massoud, the Lion of Panjshir. Mammy had nailed up a
poster of him in her room. Massoud's handsome, thoughtful face, eyebrow cocked and trademark *pakol* tilted, would
become ubiquitous in Kabul. His soulful black eyes would
gaze back from billboards, walls, storefront windows, from
little flags mounted on the antennas of taxicabs.

For Mammy, this was the day she had longed for. This
brought to fruition all those years of waiting.

At last, she could end her vigils, and her sons could rest
in peace.

THE DAY AFTER Najibullah surrendered, Mammy rose
from bed a new woman. For the first time in the five years
since Ahmad and Noor had become *shaheed,* she didn't
wear black. She put on a cobalt blue linen dress with white
polka dots. She washed the windows, swept the floor, aired
the house, took a long bath. Her voice was shrill with mer-
riment.

"A party is in order," she declared.

She sent Laila to invite neighbors. "Tell them we're
having a big lunch tomorrow!"

In the kitchen, Mammy stood looking around, hands
on her hips, and said, with friendly reproach, "What have
you done to my kitchen, Laila? *Wooy.* Everything is in a different place."

She began moving pots and pans around, theatrically,

as though she were laying claim to them anew, restaking her territory, now that she was back. Laila stayed out of her way. It was best. Mammy could be as indomitable in her fits of euphoria as in her attacks of rage. With unsettling energy, Mammy set about cooking: *aush* soup with kidney beans and dried dill, *kofta*, steaming hot *mantu* drenched with fresh yogurt and topped with mint.

"You're plucking your eyebrows," Mammy said, as she was opening a large burlap sack of rice by the kitchen counter.

"Only a little."

Mammy poured rice from the sack into a large black pot of water. She rolled up her sleeves and began stirring.

"How is Tariq?"

"His father's been ill," Laila said.

"How old is he now anyway?"

"I don't know. Sixties, I guess."

"I meant Tariq."

"Oh. Sixteen."

"He's a nice boy. Don't you think?"

Laila shrugged.

"Not really a boy anymore, though, is he? Sixteen. Almost a man. Don't you think?"

"What are you getting at, Mammy?"

"Nothing," Mammy said, smiling innocently. "Nothing. It's just that you . . . Ah, nothing. I'd better not say anyway."

"I see you want to," Laila said, irritated by this circuitous, playful accusation.

"Well." Mammy folded her hands on the rim of the pot. Laila spotted an unnatural, almost rehearsed, quality to the way she said "Well" and to this folding of hands. She feared a speech was coming.

"It was one thing when you were little kids running around. No harm in that. It was charming. But now. Now. I notice you're wearing a bra, Laila."

Laila was caught off guard.

"And you could have told me, by the way, about the bra. I didn't know. I'm disappointed you didn't tell me." Sensing her advantage, Mammy pressed on. "Anyway, this isn't about me or the bra. It's about you and Tariq. He's a boy, you see, and, as such, what does he care about reputation? But you? The reputation of a girl, especially one as pretty as you, is a delicate thing, Laila. Like a mynah bird in your hands. Slacken your grip and away it flies."

"And what about all your wall climbing, the sneaking around with Babi in the orchards?" Laila said, pleased with her quick recovery.

"We were cousins. And we married. Has this boy asked for your hand?"

"He's a friend. A *rafiq*. It's not like that between us," Laila said, sounding defensive, and not very convincing. "He's like a brother to me," she added, misguidedly. And she knew, even before a cloud passed over Mammy's face and her features darkened, that she'd made a mistake.

"*That* he is not," Mammy said flatly. "You will not liken that one-legged carpenter's boy to your brothers. There is *no one* like your brothers."

"I didn't say he . . . That's not how I meant it."

Mammy sighed through the nose and clenched her teeth.

"Anyway," she resumed, but without the coy lightheartedness of a few moments ago, "what I'm trying to say is that if you're not careful, people will talk."

Laila opened her mouth to say something. It wasn't that Mammy didn't have a point. Laila knew that the days of innocent, unhindered frolicking in the streets with Tariq had passed. For some time now, Laila had begun to sense a new strangeness when the two of them were out in public. An awareness of being looked at, scrutinized, whispered about, that Laila had never felt before. And *wouldn't* have felt even now but for one fundamental fact: She had fallen for Tariq. Hopelessly and desperately. When he was near, she couldn't help but be consumed with the most scandalous thoughts, of his lean, bare body entangled with hers. Lying in bed at night, she pictured him kissing her belly, wondered at the softness of his lips, at the feel of his hands on her neck, her chest, her back, and lower still. When she thought of him this way, she was overtaken with guilt, but also with a peculiar, warm sensation that spread upward from her belly until it felt as if her face were glowing pink.

No. Mammy had a point. More than she knew, in fact. Laila suspected that some, if not most, of the neighbors were already gossiping about her and Tariq. Laila had noticed the sly grins, was aware of the whispers in the neighborhood that the two of them were a couple. The other day, for instance, she and Tariq were walking up the street together when they'd passed Rasheed, the shoemaker, with his burqa-clad wife, Mariam, in tow. As he'd passed by them, Rasheed had playfully said, "If it isn't Laili and Majnoon," referring to the star-crossed lovers of Nezami's popular twelfth-century romantic poem—a Farsi version of *Romeo and Juliet*, Babi said, though he added that Nezami had written his tale of ill-fated lovers four centuries before Shakespeare.

Mammy had a point.

What rankled Laila was that Mammy hadn't earned the right to make it. It would have been one thing if Babi had raised this issue. But Mammy? All those years of aloofness, of cooping herself up and not caring where Laila went and whom she saw and what she thought . . . It was unfair. Laila felt like she was no better than these pots and pans, something that could go neglected, then laid claim to, at will, whenever the mood struck.

But this was a big day, an important day, for all of them. It would be petty to spoil it over this. In the spirit of things, Laila let it pass.

"I get your point," she said.

"Good!" Mammy said. "That's resolved, then. Now, where is Hakim? Where, oh where, is that sweet little husband of mine?"

IT WAS A dazzling, cloudless day, perfect for a party. The men sat on rickety folding chairs in the yard. They drank tea and smoked and talked in loud bantering voices about the Mujahideen's plan. From Babi, Laila had learned the outline of it: Afghanistan was now called the Islamic State of Afghanistan. An Islamic Jihad Council, formed in Peshawar by several of the Mujahideen factions, would oversee things for two months, led by Sibghatullah Mojadidi. This would be followed then by a leadership council led by Rabbani, who would take over for four months. During those six months, a *loya jirga* would be held, a grand council of leaders and elders, who would form an interim government to hold power for two years, leading up to democratic elections.

One of the men was fanning skewers of lamb sizzling over a makeshift grill. Babi and Tariq's father were playing a game of chess in the shade of the old pear tree. Their faces were scrunched up in concentration. Tariq was sitting at the board too, in turns watching the match, then listening in on the political chat at the adjacent table.

The women gathered in the living room, the hallway, and the kitchen. They chatted as they hoisted their babies and expertly dodged, with minute shifts of their hips, the children tearing after each other around the house. An Ustad Sarahang *ghazal* blared from a cassette player.

Laila was in the kitchen, making carafes of *dogh* with Giti. Giti was no longer as shy, or as serious, as before. For several months now, the perpetual severe scowl had cleared from her brow. She laughed openly these days, more frequently, and—it struck Laila—a bit flirtatiously. She had done away with the drab ponytails, let her hair grow, and streaked it with red highlights. Laila learned eventually that the impetus for this transformation was an eighteen-year-old boy whose attention Giti had caught. His name was Sabir, and he was a goalkeeper on Giti's older brother's soccer team.

"Oh, he has the most handsome smile, and this thick, thick black hair!" Giti had told Laila. No one knew about their attraction, of course. Giti had secretly met him twice for tea, fifteen minutes each time, at a small teahouse on the other side of town, in Taimani.

"He's going to ask for my hand, Laila! Maybe as early as this summer. Can you believe it? I swear I can't stop thinking about him."

"What about school?" Laila had asked. Giti had tilted her head and given her a *We both know better* look.

By the time we're twenty, Hasina used to say, *Giti and I, we'll have pushed out four, five kids each. But you, Laila, you'll make us two dummies proud. You're going to be somebody. I know one day I'll pick up a newspaper and find your picture on the front page.*

Giti was beside Laila now, chopping cucumbers, with a dreamy, far-off look on her face.

Mammy was nearby, in her brilliant summer dress, peeling boiled eggs with Wajma, the midwife, and Tariq's mother.

"I'm going to present Commander Massoud with a picture of Ahmad and Noor," Mammy was saying to Wajma as Wajma nodded and tried to look interested and sincere.

"He personally oversaw the burial. He said a prayer at their grave. It'll be a token of thanks for his decency." Mammy cracked another boiled egg. "I hear he's a reflective, honorable man. I think he would appreciate it."

All around them, women bolted in and out of the kitchen, carried out bowls of *qurma*, platters of *mastawa*, loaves of bread, and arranged it all on the *sofrah* spread on the living-room floor.

Every once in a while, Tariq sauntered in. He picked at this, nibbled on that.

"No men allowed," said Giti.

"Out, out, out," cried Wajma.

Tariq smiled at the women's good-humored shooing. He seemed to take pleasure in not being welcome here, in infecting this female atmosphere with his half-grinning, masculine irreverence.

Laila did her best not to look at him, not to give these women any more gossip fodder than they already had. So she kept her eyes down and said nothing to him, but she remembered a dream she'd had a few nights before, of his face and hers, together in a mirror, beneath a soft, green veil. And grains of rice, dropping from his hair, bouncing off the glass with a *tink*.

Tariq reached to sample a morsel of veal cooked with potatoes.

"Ho bacha!" Giti slapped the back of his hand. Tariq stole it anyway and laughed.

He stood almost a foot taller than Laila now. He shaved. His face was leaner, more angular. His shoulders had broadened. Tariq liked to wear pleated trousers, black shiny loafers, and short-sleeve shirts that showed off his newly muscular arms—compliments of an old, rusty set of barbells that he lifted daily in his yard. His face had lately adopted an expression of playful contentiousness. He had taken to a self-conscious cocking of his head when he spoke, slightly to the side, and to arching one eyebrow when he laughed. He let his hair grow and had fallen into the habit of tossing the floppy locks often and unnecessarily. The corrupt half grin was a new thing too.

The last time Tariq was shooed out of the kitchen, his mother caught Laila stealing a glance at him. Laila's heart jumped, and her eyes fluttered guiltily. She quickly occupied herself with tossing the chopped cucumber into the pitcher of salted, watered-down yogurt. But she could sense Tariq's mother watching, her knowing, approving half smile.

The men filled their plates and glasses and took their meals to the yard. Once they had taken their share, the women and children settled on the floor around the *sofrah* and ate.

It was after the *sofrah* was cleared and the plates were stacked in the kitchen, when the frenzy of tea making and remembering who took green and who black started, that Tariq motioned with his head and slipped out the door.

Laila waited five minutes, then followed.

She found him three houses down the street, leaning against the wall at the entrance of a narrow-mouthed alley between two adjacent houses. He was humming an old Pashto song, by Ustad Awal Mir:

Da ze ma ziba watan,
da ze ma dada watan.
This is our beautiful land,
this is our beloved land.

And he was smoking, another new habit, which he'd picked up from the guys Laila spotted him hanging around with these days. Laila couldn't stand them, these new friends of Tariq's. They all dressed the same way, pleated trousers, and tight shirts that accentuated their arms and chest. They all wore too much cologne, and they all smoked. They strutted around the neighborhood in groups, joking, laughing loudly, sometimes even calling after girls, with identical stupid, self-satisfied grins on their faces. One of Tariq's friends, on the basis of the most passing of resemblances to Sylvester Stallone, insisted he be called Rambo.

"Your mother would kill you if she knew about your smoking," Laila said, looking one way, then the other, before slipping into the alley.

"But she doesn't," he said. He moved aside to make room.

"That could change."

"Who is going to tell? You?"

Laila tapped her foot. "Tell your secret to the wind, but don't blame it for telling the trees."

Tariq smiled, the one eyebrow arched. "Who said that?"

"Khalil Gibran."

"You're a show-off."

"Give me a cigarette."

He shook his head no and crossed his arms. This was a new entry in his repertoire of poses: back to the wall, arms crossed, cigarette dangling from the corner of his mouth, his good leg casually bent.

"Why not?"

"Bad for you," he said.

"And it's not bad for you?"

"I do it for the girls."

"What girls?"

He smirked. "They think it's sexy."

"It's not."

"No?"

"I assure you."

"Not sexy?"

"You look *khila,* like a half-wit."

"That hurts," he said.

"What girls anyway?"

"You're jealous."

"I'm indifferently curious."

"You can't be both." He took another drag and squinted through the smoke. "I'll bet they're talking about us now."

In Laila's head, Mammy's voice rang out. *Like a mynah bird in your hands. Slacken your grip and away it flies.* Guilt bore its teeth into her. Then Laila shut off Mammy's voice. Instead, she savored the way Tariq had said *us.* How thrilling, how conspiratorial, it sounded coming from him. And how reassuring to hear him say it like that—casually, naturally. *Us.* It acknowledged their connection, crystallized it.

"And what are they saying?"

"That we're canoeing down the River of Sin," he said. "Eating a slice of Impiety Cake."

"Riding the Rickshaw of Wickedness?" Laila chimed in.

"Making Sacrilege *Qurma.*"

They both laughed. Then Tariq remarked that her hair was getting longer. "It's nice," he said.

Laila hoped she wasn't blushing. "You changed the subject."

"From what?"

"The empty-headed girls who think you're sexy."

"You know."

"Know what?"

"That I only have eyes for you."

Laila swooned inside. She tried to read his face but was met by a look that was indecipherable: the cheerful, cretinous grin at odds with the narrow, half-desperate look in his eyes. A clever look, calculated to fall precisely at the midpoint between mockery and sincerity.

Tariq crushed his cigarette with the heel of his good foot. "So what do you think about all this?"

"The party?"

"Who's the half-wit now? I meant the Mujahideen, Laila. Their coming to Kabul."

"Oh."

She started to tell him something Babi had said, about the troublesome marriage of guns and ego, when she heard a commotion coming from the house. Loud voices. Screaming.

Laila took off running. Tariq hobbled behind her.

There was a melee in the yard. In the middle of it were two snarling men, rolling on the ground, a knife between them. Laila recognized one of them as a man from the table who had been discussing politics earlier. The other was the man who had been fanning the kebab skewers. Several men were trying to pull them apart. Babi wasn't among them. He stood by the wall, at a safe distance from the fight, with Tariq's father, who was crying.

From the excited voices around her, Laila caught snippets that she put together: The fellow at the politics table, a Pashtun, had called Ahmad Shah Massoud a traitor for "making a deal" with the Soviets in the 1980s. The kebab man, a Tajik, had taken offense and demanded a retraction. The Pashtun had refused. The Tajik had said that if not for Massoud, the other man's sister would still be "giving it" to Soviet soldiers. They had come to blows. One of them had then brandished a knife; there was disagreement as to who.

With horror, Laila saw that Tariq had thrown himself into the scuffle. She also saw that some of the peacemakers were now throwing punches of their own. She thought she spotted a second knife.

Later that evening, Laila thought of how the melee had toppled over, with men falling on top of one another, amid yelps and cries and shouts and flying punches, and, in the middle of it, a grimacing Tariq, his hair disheveled, his leg come undone, trying to crawl out.

*   *   *

IT WAS DIZZYING how quickly everything unraveled.

The leadership council was formed prematurely. It elected Rabbani president. The other factions cried nepotism. Massoud called for peace and patience.

Hekmatyar, who had been excluded, was incensed. The Hazaras, with their long history of being oppressed and neglected, seethed.

Insults were hurled. Fingers pointed. Accusations flew. Meetings were angrily called off and doors slammed. The city held its breath. In the mountains, loaded magazines snapped into Kalashnikovs.

The Mujahideen, armed to the teeth but now lacking a common enemy, had found the enemy in each other.

Kabul's day of reckoning had come at last.

And when the rockets began to rain down on Kabul, people ran for cover. Mammy did too, literally. She changed into black again, went to her room, shut the curtains, and pulled the blanket over her head.

24.

"It's the whistling," Laila said to Tariq, "the damn whistling, I hate more than anything."

Tariq nodded knowingly.

It wasn't so much the whistling itself, Laila thought later, but the seconds between the start of it and impact. The brief and interminable time of feeling suspended. The not knowing. The waiting. Like a defendant about to hear the verdict.

Often it happened at dinner, when she and Babi were at the table. When it started, their heads snapped up. They listened to the whistling, forks in midair, unchewed food in their mouths. Laila saw the reflection of their half-lit faces in the pitch-black window, their shadows unmoving on the wall. The whistling. Then the blast, blissfully elsewhere, followed by an expulsion of breath and the knowledge that they had been spared for now while somewhere else, amid cries and choking clouds of smoke, there was a scrambling, a bare-handed frenzy of digging, of pulling from the debris, what remained of a sister, a brother, a grandchild.

But the flip side of being spared was the agony of wondering who hadn't. After every rocket blast, Laila raced to the street, stammering a prayer, certain that, this time, surely this time, it was Tariq they would find buried beneath the rubble and smoke.

At night, Laila lay in bed and watched the sudden white flashes reflected in her window. She listened to the rattling of automatic gunfire and counted the rockets whining overhead as the house shook and flakes of plaster rained down on her from the ceiling. Some nights, when the light of rocket fire was so bright a person could read a book by it, sleep never came. And, if it did, Laila's dreams were suffused with fire and detached limbs and the moaning of the wounded.

Morning brought no relief. The muezzin's call for *namaz* rang out, and the Mujahideen set down their guns, faced west, and prayed. Then the rugs were folded, the guns loaded, and the mountains fired on Kabul, and Kabul fired back at the mountains, as Laila and the rest of the city watched as helpless as old Santiago watching the sharks take bites out of his prize fish.

EVERYWHERE LAILA WENT, she saw Massoud's men. She saw them roam the streets and every few hundred yards stop cars for questioning. They sat and smoked atop tanks, dressed in their fatigues and ubiquitous *pakol*s. They peeked at passersby from behind stacked sandbags at intersections.

Not that Laila went out much anymore. And, when she did, she was always accompanied by Tariq, who seemed to relish this chivalric duty.

"I bought a gun," he said one day. They were sitting outside, on the ground beneath the pear tree in Laila's yard. He showed her. He said it was a semiautomatic, a Beretta. To Laila, it merely looked black and deadly.

"I don't like it," she said. "Guns scare me."

Tariq turned the magazine over in his hand.

"They found three bodies in a house in Karteh-Seh last week," he said. "Did you hear? Sisters. All three raped. Their throats slashed. Someone had bitten the rings off their fingers. You could tell, they had teeth marks—"

"I don't want to hear this."

"I don't mean to upset you," Tariq said. "But I just . . . I feel better carrying this."

He was her lifeline to the streets now. He heard the word of mouth and passed it on to her. Tariq was the one who told her, for instance, that militiamen stationed in the mountains sharpened their marksmanship—and settled wagers over said marksmanship—by shooting civilians down below, men, women, children, chosen at random. He told her that they fired rockets at cars but, for some reason, left taxis alone—which explained to Laila the recent rash of people spraying their cars yellow.

Tariq explained to her the treacherous, shifting boundaries within Kabul. Laila learned from him, for instance, that this road, up to the second acacia tree on the left, belonged to one warlord; that the next four blocks, ending with the bakery shop next to the demolished pharmacy, was another warlord's sector; and that if she crossed that street and walked half a mile west, she would find herself in the territory of yet another warlord and, therefore, fair game for sniper fire. And this was what Mammy's heroes were called now. Warlords. Laila heard them called *tofangdar* too. Riflemen. Others still called them Mujahideen, but, when they did, they made a face—a sneering, distasteful face—the word reeking of deep aversion and deep scorn. Like an insult.

Tariq snapped the magazine back into his handgun.

"Do you have it in you?" Laila said.

"To what?"

"To use this thing. To kill with it."

Tariq tucked the gun into the waist of his denims. Then he said a thing both lovely and terrible. "For you," he said. "I'd kill with it for you, Laila."

He slid closer to her and their hands brushed, once, then again. When Tariq's fingers tentatively began to slip into hers, Laila let them. And when suddenly he leaned over and pressed his lips to hers, she let him again.

At that moment, all of Mammy's talk of reputations and mynah birds sounded immaterial to Laila. Absurd, even. In the midst of all this killing and looting, all this ugliness, it was a harmless thing to sit here beneath a tree and kiss Tariq. A small thing. An easily forgivable indulgence. So she let him kiss her, and when he pulled back she leaned in and kissed *him*, heart pounding in her throat, her face tingling, a fire burning in the pit of her belly.

IN JUNE OF THAT YEAR, 1992, there was heavy fighting in West Kabul between the Pashtun forces of the warlord Sayyaf and the Hazaras of the Wahdat faction. The shelling knocked down power lines, pulverized entire blocks of shops and homes. Laila heard that Pashtun militiamen were attacking Hazara households, breaking in and shooting entire families, execution style, and that Hazaras were retaliating by abducting Pashtun civilians, raping Pashtun girls, shelling Pashtun neighborhoods, and killing indiscriminately. Every day, bodies were found tied to trees, sometimes burned beyond recognition. Often, they'd been shot in the head, had had their eyes gouged out, their tongues cut out.

Babi tried again to convince Mammy to leave Kabul.

"They'll work it out," Mammy said. "This fighting is temporary. They'll sit down and figure something out."

"Fariba, all these people *know* is war," said Babi. "They learned to walk with a milk bottle in one hand and a gun in the other."

"Who are *you* to say?" Mammy shot back. "Did you fight jihad? Did you abandon everything you had and risk your life? If not for the Mujahideen, we'd still be the Soviets' servants, remember. And now you'd have us betray them!"

"We aren't the ones doing the betraying, Fariba."

"You go, then. Take your daughter and run away. Send me a postcard. But peace is coming, and I, for one, am going to wait for it."

The streets became so unsafe that Babi did an unthinkable thing: He had Laila drop out of school.

He took over the teaching duties himself. Laila went into his study every day after sundown, and, as Hekmatyar launched his rockets at Massoud from the southern outskirts of the city, Babi and she discussed the *ghazals* of Hafez and the works of the beloved Afghan poet Ustad Khalilullah Khalili. Babi taught her to derive the quadratic equation, showed her how to factor polynomials and plot parametric curves. When he was teaching, Babi was transformed. In his element, amid his books, he looked taller to Laila. His voice seemed to rise from a calmer, deeper place, and he didn't blink nearly as much. Laila pictured him as he must have been once, erasing his blackboard with graceful swipes, looking over a student's shoulder, fatherly and attentive.

But it wasn't easy to pay attention. Laila kept getting distracted.

"What is the area of a pyramid?" Babi would ask, and all Laila could think of was the fullness of Tariq's lips, the heat of his breath on her mouth, her own reflection in his hazel eyes. She'd kissed him twice more since the time beneath the tree, longer, more passionately, and, she thought, less clumsily. Both times, she'd met him secretly in the dim alley where he'd smoked a cigarette the day of Mammy's lunch party. The second time, she'd let him touch her breast.

"Laila?"

"Yes, Babi."

"Pyramid. Area. Where are you?"

"Sorry, Babi. I was, uh . . . Let's see. Pyramid. Pyramid. One-third the area of the base times the height."

Babi nodded uncertainly, his gaze lingering on her, and Laila thought of Tariq's hands, squeezing her breast, sliding down the small of her back, as the two of them kissed and kissed.

ONE DAY THAT same month of June, Giti was walking home from school with two classmates. Only three blocks from Giti's house, a stray rocket struck the girls. Later that terrible day, Laila learned that Nila, Giti's mother, had run up and down the street where Giti was killed, collecting pieces of her daughter's flesh in an apron, screeching hysterically. Giti's decomposing right foot, still in its nylon sock and purple sneaker, would be found on a rooftop two weeks later.

At Giti's *fatiha,* the day after the killings, Laila sat stunned in a roomful of weeping women. This was the first time that someone whom Laila had known, been close to, loved, had died. She couldn't get around the unfathomable reality that Giti wasn't alive anymore. Giti, with whom Laila had exchanged secret notes in class, whose fingernails she had polished, whose chin hair she had plucked with tweezers. Giti, who was going to marry Sabir the goalkeeper. Giti was dead. *Dead.* Blown to pieces. At last, Laila began to weep for her friend. And all the tears that she hadn't been able to shed at her brothers' funeral came pouring down.

25.

Laila could hardly move, as though cement had solidified in every one of her joints. There was a conversation going on, and Laila knew that she was at one end of it, but she felt removed from it, as though she were merely eavesdropping. As Tariq talked, Laila pictured her life as a rotted rope, snapping, unraveling, the fibers detaching, falling away.

It was a hot, muggy afternoon that August of 1992, and they were in the living room of Laila's house. Mammy had had a stomachache all day, and, minutes before, despite the rockets that Hekmatyar was launching from the south, Babi had taken her to see a doctor. And here was Tariq now, seated beside Laila on the couch, looking at the ground, hands between his knees.

Saying that he was leaving.

Not the neighborhood. Not Kabul. But Afghanistan altogether.

Leaving.

Laila was struck blind.

"Where? Where will you go?"

"Pakistan first. Peshawar. Then I don't know. Maybe Hindustan. Iran."

"How long?"

"I don't know."

"I mean, how long have you known?"

"A few days. I was going to tell you, Laila, I swear, but I couldn't bring myself to. I knew how upset you'd be."

"When?"

"Tomorrow."

"Tomorrow?"

"Laila, look at me."

"Tomorrow."

"It's my father. His heart can't take it anymore, all this fighting and killing."

Laila buried her face in her hands, a bubble of dread filling her chest.

She should have seen this coming, she thought. Almost everyone she knew had packed their things and left. The neighborhood had been all but drained of familiar faces, and now, only four months after fighting had broken out between the Mujahideen factions, Laila hardly recognized anybody on the streets anymore. Hasina's family had fled in May, off to Tehran. Wajma and her clan had gone to Islamabad that same month. Giti's parents and her siblings left in June, shortly after Giti was killed. Laila didn't know where they had gone—she heard a rumor that they had headed for Mashad, in Iran. After people left, their homes sat unoccupied for a few days, then either militiamen took them or strangers moved in.

Everyone was leaving. And now Tariq too.

"And my mother is not a young woman anymore," he was saying. "They're so afraid all the time. Laila, look at me."

"You should have told me."

"Please look at me."

A groan came out of Laila. Then a wail. And then she was crying, and when he went to wipe her cheek with the pad of his thumb she swiped his hand away. It was selfish and irrational, but she was furious with him for abandoning her, Tariq, who was like an extension of her, whose shadow sprung beside hers in every memory. How could he leave her? She slapped him. Then she slapped him again and pulled at his hair, and he had to take her by the wrists, and he was saying something she couldn't make out, he was saying it softly, reasonably, and, somehow, they ended up brow to brow, nose to nose, and she could feel the heat of his breath on her lips again.

And when, suddenly, he leaned in, she did too.

IN THE COMING DAYS and weeks, Laila would scramble frantically to commit it all to memory, what happened next. Like an art lover running out of a burning museum, she would grab whatever she could—a look, a whisper, a moan—to salvage from perishing, to preserve. But time is the most unforgiving of fires, and she couldn't, in the end, save it all. Still, she had these: that first, tremendous pang of pain down below. The slant of sunlight on the rug. Her heel grazing the cold hardness of his leg, lying beside them, hastily unstrapped. Her hands cupping his elbows. The upside-down, mandolin-shaped birthmark beneath his collarbone, glowing red. His face hovering over hers. His black curls dangling, tickling her lips, her chin. The terror that they would be discovered. The disbelief at their own boldness, their courage. The strange and indescribable pleasure, interlaced with the pain. And the look, the myriad of *looks,* on Tariq: of apprehension, tenderness, apology, embarrassment, but mostly, mostly, of hunger.

THERE WAS FRENZY AFTER. Shirts hurriedly buttoned, belts buckled, hair finger-combed. They sat, then, they sat

178

beside each other, smelling of each other, faces flushed pink, both of them stunned, both of them speechless before the enormity of what had just happened. What they had done.

Laila saw three drops of blood on the rug, *her* blood, and pictured her parents sitting on this couch later, oblivious to the sin that she had committed. And now the shame set in, and the guilt, and, upstairs, the clock ticked on, impossibly loud to Laila's ears. Like a judge's gavel pounding again and again, condemning her.

Then Tariq said, "Come with me."

For a moment, Laila almost believed that it could be done. She, Tariq, and his parents, setting out together. Packing their bags, climbing aboard a bus, leaving behind all this violence, going to find blessings, or trouble, and whichever came they would face it together. The bleak isolation awaiting her, the murderous loneliness, it didn't have to be.

She could go. They could be together.

They would have more afternoons like this.

"I want to marry you, Laila."

For the first time since they were on the floor, she raised her eyes to meet his. She searched his face. There was no playfulness this time. His look was one of conviction, of guileless yet ironclad earnestness.

"Tariq—"

"Let me marry you, Laila. Today. We could get married today."

He began to say more, about going to a mosque, finding a mullah, a pair of witnesses, a quick *nikka* . . .

But Laila was thinking of Mammy, as obstinate and uncompromising as the Mujahideen, the air around her choked with rancor and despair, and she was thinking of Babi, who had long surrendered, who made such a sad, pathetic opponent to Mammy.

Sometimes . . . I feel like you're all I have, Laila.

These were the circumstances of her life, the inescapable truths of it.

"I'll ask Kaka Hakim for your hand. He'll give us his blessing, Laila, I know it."

He was right. Babi would. But it would shatter him.

Tariq was still speaking, his voice hushed, then high, beseeching, then reasoning; his face hopeful, then stricken.

"I can't," Laila said.

"Don't say that. I love you."

"I'm sorry—"

"I love you."

How long had she waited to hear those words from him? How many times had she dreamed them uttered? There they were, spoken at last, and the irony crushed her.

"It's my father I can't leave," Laila said. "I'm all he has left. His heart couldn't take it either."

Tariq knew this. He knew she could not wipe away the obligations of her life any more than he could his, but it went on, his pleadings and her rebuttals, his proposals and her apologies, his tears and hers.

In the end, Laila had to make him leave.

At the door, she made him promise to go without goodbyes. She closed the door on him. Laila leaned her back against it, shaking against his pounding fists, one arm gripping her belly and a hand across her mouth, as he spoke through the door and promised that he would come back, that he would come back for her. She stood there until he tired, until he gave up, and then she listened to his uneven footsteps until they faded, until all was quiet, save for the gunfire cracking in the hills and her own heart thudding in her belly, her eyes, her bones.

26.

It was, by far, the hottest day of the year. The mountains trapped the bone-scorching heat, stifled the city like smoke. Power had been out for days. All over Kabul, electric fans sat idle, almost mockingly so.

Laila was lying still on the living-room couch, sweating through her blouse. Every exhaled breath burned the tip of her nose. She was aware of her parents talking in Mammy's room. Two nights ago, and again last night, she had awakened and thought she heard their voices downstairs. They were talking every day now, ever since the bullet, ever since the new hole in the gate.

Outside, the far-off *boom* of artillery, then, more closely, the stammering of a long string of gunfire, followed by another.

Inside Laila too a battle was being waged: guilt on one side, partnered with shame, and, on the other, the conviction that what she and Tariq had done was not sinful; that it had been natural, good, beautiful, even inevitable, spurred by the knowledge that they might never see each other again.

Laila rolled to her side on the couch now and tried to remember something: At one point, when they were on the floor, Tariq had lowered his forehead on hers. Then he had panted something, either *Am I hurting you?* or *Is this hurting you?*

Laila couldn't decide which he had said.

Am I hurting you?

Is this hurting you?

Only two weeks since he had left, and it was already happening. Time, blunting the edges of those sharp memories. Laila bore down mentally. What had he said? It seemed vital, suddenly, that she know.

Laila closed her eyes. Concentrated.

With the passing of time, she would slowly tire of this exercise. She would find it increasingly exhausting to conjure up, to dust off, to resuscitate once again what was long dead. There would come a day, in fact, years later, when Laila would no longer bewail his loss. Or not as relentlessly; not nearly. There would come a day when the details of his face would begin to slip from memory's grip, when overhearing a mother on the street call after her child by Tariq's name would no longer cut her adrift. She would not miss him as she did now, when the ache of his absence was her unremitting companion—like the phantom pain of an amputee.

Except every once in a long while, when Laila was a grown woman, ironing a shirt or pushing her children on a swing set, something trivial, maybe the warmth of a carpet beneath her feet on a hot day or the curve of a stranger's forehead, would set off a memory of that afternoon together. And it would all come rushing back. The spontaneity of it. Their astonishing imprudence. Their clumsiness. The pain of the act, the pleasure of it, the sadness of it. The heat of their entangled bodies.

It would flood her, steal her breath.

But then it would pass. The moment would pass. Leave her deflated, feeling nothing but a vague restlessness.

She decided that he had said *Am I hurting you?* Yes. That was it. Laila was happy that she'd remembered.

Then Babi was in the hallway, calling her name from the top of the stairs, asking her to come up quickly.

"She's agreed!" he said, his voice tremulous with suppressed excitement. "We're leaving, Laila. All three of us. We're leaving Kabul."

IN MAMMY'S ROOM, the three of them sat on the bed. Outside, rockets were zipping across the sky as Hekmatyar's and Massoud's forces fought and fought. Laila knew that somewhere in the city someone had just died, and that a pall of black smoke was hovering over some building that had collapsed in a puffing mass of dust. There would be bodies to step around in the morning. Some would be collected. Others not. Then Kabul's dogs, who had developed a taste for human meat, would feast.

All the same, Laila had an urge to run through those streets. She could barely contain her own happiness. It took effort to sit, to not shriek with joy. Babi said they would go to Pakistan first, to apply for visas. Pakistan, where Tariq was! Tariq was only gone seventeen days, Laila calculated excitedly. If only Mammy had made up her mind seventeen days earlier, they could have left together. She would have been with Tariq right now! But that didn't matter now. They were going to Peshawar—she, Mammy, and Babi—and they would find Tariq and his parents there. Surely they would. They would process their paperwork together. Then, who knew? Who knew? Europe? America? Maybe, as Babi was always saying, somewhere near the sea . . .

Mammy was half lying, half sitting against the headboard. Her eyes were puffy. She was picking at her hair.

Three days before, Laila had gone outside for a breath of air. She'd stood by the front gates, leaning against them, when she'd heard a loud crack and something had zipped by her right ear, sending tiny splinters of wood flying before her eyes. After Giti's death, and the thousands of rounds fired and myriad rockets that had fallen on Kabul, it was the sight of that single round hole in the gate, less than three fingers away from where Laila's head had been, that shook Mammy awake. Made her see that one war had cost her two children already; this latest could cost her her remaining one.

From the walls of the room, Ahmad and Noor smiled down. Laila watched Mammy's eyes bouncing now, guiltily, from one photo to the other. As if looking for their consent. Their blessing. As if asking for forgiveness.

"There's nothing left for us here," Babi said. "Our sons are gone, but we still have Laila. We still have each other, Fariba. We can make a new life."

Babi reached across the bed. When he leaned to take her hands, Mammy let him. On her face, a look of concession. Of resignation. They held each other's hands, lightly, and then they were swaying quietly in an embrace. Mammy buried her face in his neck. She grabbed a handful of his shirt.

For hours that night, the excitement robbed Laila of sleep. She lay in bed and watched the horizon light up in garish shades of orange and yellow. At some point, though, despite the exhilaration inside and the crack of artillery fire outside, she fell asleep.

And dreamed.

They are on a ribbon of beach, sitting on a quilt. It's a chilly, overcast day, but it's warm next to Tariq under the blanket draped over their shoulders. She can see cars parked behind a low fence of chipped white paint beneath a row of windswept palm trees. The wind makes her eyes water and buries their shoes in sand, hurls knots of dead grass from the curved ridges of one dune to another. They're watching sailboats bob in the distance. Around them, seagulls squawk and shiver in the wind. The wind whips up another spray of sand off the shallow, windward slopes. There is a noise then like a chant, and she tells him something Babi had taught her years before about singing sand.

He rubs at her eyebrow, wipes grains of sand from it. She catches a flicker of the band on his finger. It's identical to hers—gold with a sort of maze pattern etched all the way around.

It's true, she tells him. *It's the friction, of grain against grain. Listen.* He does. He frowns. They wait. They hear it again. A groaning sound, when the wind is soft, when it blows hard, a mewling, high-pitched chorus.

BABI SAID THEY should take only what was absolutely necessary. They would sell the rest.

"That should hold us in Peshawar until I find work."

For the next two days, they gathered items to be sold. They put them in big piles.

In her room, Laila set aside old blouses, old shoes, books, toys. Looking under her bed, she found a tiny yellow glass cow Hasina had passed to her during recess in fifth grade. A miniature-soccer-ball key chain, a gift from Giti. A little wooden zebra on wheels. A ceramic astronaut she and Tariq had found one day in a gutter. She'd been six and he eight. They'd had a minor row, Laila remembered, over which one of them had found it.

Mammy too gathered her things. There was a reluctance in her movements, and her eyes had a lethargic, faraway look in them. She did away with her good plates, her napkins, all her jewelry—save for her wedding band—and most of her old clothes.

"You're not selling this, are you?" Laila said, lifting Mammy's wedding dress. It cascaded open onto her lap. She touched the lace and ribbon along the neckline, the hand-sewn seed pearls on the sleeves.

Mammy shrugged and took it from her. She tossed it brusquely on a pile of clothes. Like ripping off a Band-Aid in one stroke, Laila thought.

It was Babi who had the most painful task.

Laila found him standing in his study, a rueful expression on his face as he surveyed his shelves. He was wearing a secondhand T-shirt with a picture of San Francisco's red bridge on it. Thick fog rose from the whitecapped waters and engulfed the bridge's towers.

"You know the old bit," he said. "You're on a deserted island. You can have five books. Which do you choose? I never thought I'd actually have to."

"We'll have to start you a new collection, Babi."

"Mm." He smiled sadly. "I can't believe I'm leaving Kabul. I went to school here, got my first job here, became a father in this town. It's strange to think that I'll be sleeping beneath another city's skies soon."

"It's strange for me too."

"All day, this poem about Kabul has been bouncing around in my head. Saib-e-Tabrizi wrote it back in the seventeenth century, I think. I used to know the whole poem, but all I can remember now is two lines:

*"One could not count the moons that shimmer on her roofs,
Or the thousand splendid suns that hide behind her walls."*

Laila looked up, saw he was weeping. She put an arm around his waist. "Oh, Babi. We'll come back. When this war is over. We'll come back to Kabul, *inshallah.* You'll see."

*   *   *

ON THE THIRD MORNING, Laila began moving the piles of things to the yard and depositing them by the front door. They would fetch a taxi then and take it all to a pawnshop.

Laila kept shuffling between the house and the yard, back and forth, carrying stacks of clothes and dishes and box after box of Babi's books. She should have been exhausted by noon, when the mound of belongings by the front door had grown waist high. But, with each trip, she knew that she was that much closer to seeing Tariq again, and, with each trip, her legs became more sprightly, her arms more tireless.

"We're going to need a big taxi."

Laila looked up. It was Mammy calling down from her bedroom upstairs. She was leaning out the window, resting her elbows on the sill. The sun, bright and warm, caught in her graying hair, shone on her drawn, thin face. Mammy was wearing the same cobalt blue dress she had worn the day of the lunch party four months earlier, a youthful dress meant for a young woman, but, for a moment, Mammy looked to Laila like an old woman. An old woman with stringy arms and sunken temples and slow eyes rimmed by darkened circles of weariness, an altogether different creature from the plump, round-faced woman beaming radiantly from those grainy wedding photos.

"Two big taxis," Laila said.

She could see Babi too, in the living room stacking boxes of books atop each other.

"Come up when you're done with those," Mammy said. "We'll sit down for lunch. Boiled eggs and leftover beans."

"My favorite," Laila said.

She thought suddenly of her dream. She and Tariq on a quilt. The ocean. The wind. The dunes.

What had it sounded like, she wondered now, the singing sands?

187

Laila stopped. She saw a gray lizard crawl out of a crack in the ground. Its head shot side to side. It blinked. Darted under a rock.

Laila pictured the beach again. Except now the singing was all around. And growing. Louder and louder by the moment, higher and higher. It flooded her ears. Drowned everything else out. The gulls were feathered mimes now, opening and closing their beaks noiselessly, and the waves were crashing with foam and spray but no roar. The sands sang on. Screaming now. A sound like . . . a tinkling?

Not a tinkling. No. A whistling.

Laila dropped the books at her feet. She looked up to the sky. Shielded her eyes with one hand.

Then a giant roar.

Behind her, a flash of white.

The ground lurched beneath her feet.

Something hot and powerful slammed into her from behind. It knocked her out of her sandals. Lifted her up. And now she was flying, twisting and rotating in the air, seeing sky, then earth, then sky, then earth. A big burning chunk of wood whipped by. So did a thousand shards of glass, and it seemed to Laila that she could see each individual one flying all around her, flipping slowly end over end, the sunlight catching in each. Tiny, beautiful rainbows.

Then Laila struck the wall. Crashed to the ground. On her face and arms, a shower of dirt and pebbles and glass. The last thing she was aware of was seeing something thud to the ground nearby. A bloody chunk of something. On it, the tip of a red bridge poking through thick fog.

SHAPES MOVING ABOUT. A fluorescent light shines from the ceiling above. A woman's face appears, hovers over hers.

Laila fades back to the dark.

ANOTHER FACE. This time a man's. His features seem broad and droopy. His lips move but make no sound. All Laila hears is ringing.

The man waves his hand at her. Frowns. His lips move again.

It hurts. It hurts to breathe. It hurts everywhere.

A glass of water. A pink pill.

Back to the darkness.

THE WOMAN AGAIN. Long face, narrow-set eyes. She says something. Laila can't hear anything but the ringing. But she can see the words, like thick black syrup, spilling out of the woman's mouth.

Her chest hurts. Her arms and legs hurt.

All around, shapes moving.

Where is Tariq?

Why isn't he here?

Darkness. A flock of stars.

BABI AND SHE, perched somewhere high up. He is pointing to a field of barley. A generator comes to life.

The long-faced woman is standing over her looking down.

It hurts to breathe.

Somewhere, an accordion playing.

Mercifully, the pink pill again. Then a deep hush. A deep hush falls over everything.

PART THREE

27.

Mariam

D o you know who I am?"

The girl's eyes fluttered.

"Do you know what has happened?"

The girl's mouth quivered. She closed her eyes. Swallowed. Her hand grazed her left cheek. She mouthed something.

Mariam leaned in closer.

"This ear," the girl breathed. "I can't hear."

FOR THE FIRST WEEK, the girl did little but sleep, with help from the pink pills Rasheed paid for at the hospital. She murmured in her sleep. Sometimes she spoke gibberish, cried out, called out names Mariam did not recognize. She wept in her sleep, grew agitated, kicked the blankets off, and then Mariam had to hold her down. Sometimes she retched and retched, threw up everything Mariam fed her.

When she wasn't agitated, the girl was a sullen pair of

eyes staring from under the blanket, breathing out short little answers to Mariam and Rasheed's questions. Some days she was childlike, whipped her head side to side, when Mariam, then Rasheed, tried to feed her. She went rigid when Mariam came at her with a spoon. But she tired easily and submitted eventually to their persistent badgering. Long bouts of weeping followed surrender.

Rasheed had Mariam rub antibiotic ointment on the cuts on the girl's face and neck, and on the sutured gashes on her shoulder, across her forearms and lower legs. Mariam dressed them with bandages, which she washed and recycled. She held the girl's hair back, out of her face, when she had to retch.

"How long is she staying?" she asked Rasheed.

"Until she's better. Look at her. She's in no shape to go. Poor thing."

It was Rasheed who found the girl, who dug her out from beneath the rubble.

"Lucky I was home," he said to the girl. He was sitting on a folding chair beside Mariam's bed, where the girl lay. "Lucky for you, I mean. I dug you out with my own hands. There was a scrap of metal this big—" Here, he spread his thumb and index finger apart to show her, at least doubling, in Mariam's estimation, the actual size of it. "This big. Sticking right out of your shoulder. It was really embedded in there. I thought I'd have to use a pair of pliers. But you're all right. In no time, you'll be *nau socha*. Good as new."

It was Rasheed who salvaged a handful of Hakim's books.

"Most of them were ash. The rest were looted, I'm afraid."

He helped Mariam watch over the girl that first week. One day, he came home from work with a new blanket and pillow. Another day, a bottle of pills.

"Vitamins," he said.

It was Rasheed who gave Laila the news that her friend Tariq's house was occupied now.

"A gift," he said. "From one of Sayyaf's commanders to three of his men. A gift. Ha!"

The three *men* were actually boys with suntanned, youthful faces. Mariam would see them when she passed by, always dressed in their fatigues, squatting by the front door of Tariq's house, playing cards and smoking, their Kalashnikovs leaning against the wall. The brawny one, the one with the self-satisfied, scornful demeanor, was the leader. The youngest was also the quietest, the one who seemed reluctant to wholeheartedly embrace his friends' air of impunity. He had taken to smiling and tipping his head *salaam* when Mariam passed by. When he did, some of his surface smugness dropped away, and Mariam caught a glint of humility as yet uncorrupted.

Then one morning rockets slammed into the house. They were rumored later to have been fired by the Hazaras of Wahdat. For some time, neighbors kept finding bits and pieces of the boys.

"They had it coming," said Rasheed.

THE GIRL WAS extraordinarily lucky, Mariam thought, to escape with relatively minor injuries, considering the rocket had turned her house into smoking rubble. And so, slowly, the girl got better. She began to eat more, began to brush her own hair. She took baths on her own. She began taking her meals downstairs, with Mariam and Rasheed.

But then some memory would rise, unbidden, and there would be stony silences or spells of churlishness. Withdrawals and collapses. Wan looks. Nightmares and sudden attacks of grief. Retching.

And sometimes regrets.

"I shouldn't even be here," she said one day.

Mariam was changing the sheets. The girl watched from the floor, her bruised knees drawn up against her chest.

"My father wanted to take out the boxes. The books. He said they were too heavy for me. But I wouldn't let him. I was so eager. I should have been the one inside the house when it happened."

Mariam snapped the clean sheet and let it settle on the bed. She looked at the girl, at her blond curls, her slender neck and green eyes, her high cheekbones and plump lips. Mariam remembered seeing her on the streets when she was little, tottering after her mother on the way to the tandoor, riding on the shoulders of her brother, the younger one, with the patch of hair on his ear. Shooting marbles with the carpenter's boy.

The girl was looking back as if waiting for Mariam to pass on some morsel of wisdom, to say something encouraging. But what wisdom did Mariam have to offer? What encouragement? Mariam remembered the day they'd buried Nana and how little comfort she had found when Mullah Faizullah had quoted the Koran for her. *Blessed is He in Whose hand is the kingdom, and He Who has power over all things, Who created death and life that He may try you.* Or when he'd said of her own guilt, *These thoughts are no good, Mariam jo. They will destroy you. It wasn't your fault. It wasn't your fault.*

What could she say to this girl that would ease her burden?

As it turned out, Mariam didn't have to say anything. Because the girl's face twisted, and she was on all fours then saying she was going to be sick.

"Wait! Hold on. I'll get a pan. Not on the floor. I just cleaned . . . Oh. Oh. *Khodaya.* God."

THEN ONE DAY, about a month after the blast that killed the girl's parents, a man came knocking. Mariam opened the door. He stated his business.

"There is a man here to see you," Mariam said.

The girl raised her head from the pillow.

"He says his name is Abdul Sharif."

"I don't know any Abdul Sharif."

"Well, he's here asking for you. You need to come down and talk to him."

28.

Laila

Laila sat across from Abdul Sharif, who was a thin, small-headed man with a bulbous nose pocked with the same cratered scars that pitted his cheeks. His hair, short and brown, stood on his scalp like needles in a pincushion.

"You'll have to forgive me, *hamshira*," he said, adjusting his loose collar and dabbing at his brow with a handkerchief. "I still haven't quite recovered, I fear. Five more days of these, what are they called . . . sulfa pills."

Laila positioned herself in her seat so that her right ear, the good one, was closest to him. "Were you a friend of my parents?"

"No, no," Abdul Sharif said quickly. "Forgive me." He raised a finger, took a long sip of the water that Mariam had placed in front of him.

"I should begin at the beginning, I suppose." He dabbed at his lips, again at his brow. "I am a businessman. I own clothing stores, mostly men's clothing. *Chapans*, hats, *tumban*s, suits, ties—you name it. Two stores here in Kabul, in Taimani and Shar-e-Nau, though I just sold those. And two in Pakistan, in Peshawar. That's where my warehouse is as well. So I travel a lot, back and forth. Which, these days"—he shook his head and chuckled tiredly—"let's just say that it's an adventure.

"I was in Peshawar recently, on business, taking orders, going over inventory, that sort of thing. Also to visit my family. We have three daughters, *alhamdulellah*. I moved them and my wife to Peshawar after the Mujahideen began going at each other's throats. I won't have their names added to the *shaheed* list. Nor mine, to be honest. I'll be joining them there very soon, *inshallah*.

"Anyway, I was supposed to be back in Kabul the Wednesday before last. But, as luck would have it, I came down with an illness. I won't bother you with it, *hamshira*, suffice it to say that when I went to do my private business, the simpler of the two, it felt like passing chunks of broken glass. I wouldn't wish it on Hekmatyar himself. My wife, Nadia jan, Allah bless her, she begged me to see a doctor. But I thought I'd beat it with aspirin and a lot of water. Nadia jan insisted and I said no, back and forth we went. You know the saying *A stubborn ass needs a stubborn driver*. This time, I'm afraid, the ass won. That would be me."

He drank the rest of this water and extended the glass to Mariam. "If it's not too much *zahmat*."

Mariam took the glass and went to fill it.

"Needless to say, I should have listened to her. She's always been the more sensible one, God give her a long life. By the time I made it to the hospital, I was burning with a fever and shaking like a *beid* tree in the wind. I could barely stand. The doctor said I had blood poisoning. She said two or three more days and I would have made my wife a widow.

"They put me in a special unit, reserved for really sick

people, I suppose. Oh, *tashakor.*" He took the glass from Mariam and from his coat pocket produced a large white pill. "The *size* of these things."

Laila watched him swallow his pill. She was aware that her breathing had quickened. Her legs felt heavy, as though weights had been tethered to them. She told herself that he wasn't done, that he hadn't told her anything as yet. But he would go on in a second, and she resisted an urge to get up and leave, leave before he told her things she didn't want to hear.

Abdul Sharif set his glass on the table.

"That's where I met your friend, Mohammad Tariq Walizai."

Laila's heart sped up. Tariq in a hospital? A special unit? *For really sick people?*

She swallowed dry spit. Shifted on her chair. She had to steel herself. If she didn't, she feared she would come unhinged. She diverted her thoughts from hospitals and special units and thought instead about the fact that she hadn't heard Tariq called by his full name since the two of them had enrolled in a Farsi winter course years back. The teacher would call roll after the bell and say his name like that—Mohammad Tariq Walizai. It had struck her as comically officious then, hearing his full name uttered.

"What happened to him I heard from one of the nurses," Abdul Sharif resumed, tapping his chest with a fist as if to ease the passage of the pill. "With all the time I've spent in Peshawar, I've become pretty proficient in Urdu. Anyway, what I gathered was that your friend was in a lorry full of refugees, twenty-three of them, all headed for Peshawar. Near the border, they were caught in cross fire. A rocket hit the lorry. Probably a stray, but you never know with these people, you never know. There were only six survivors, all of them admitted to the same unit. Three died within twenty-four hours. Two of them lived—sisters, as I understood it—

and had been discharged. Your friend Mr. Walizai was the last. He'd been there for almost three weeks by the time I arrived."

So he was alive. But how badly had they hurt him? Laila wondered frantically. How badly? Badly enough to be put in a special unit, evidently. Laila was aware that she had started sweating, that her face felt hot. She tried to think of something else, something pleasant, like the trip to Bamiyan to see the Buddhas with Tariq and Babi. But instead an image of Tariq's parents presented itself: Tariq's mother trapped in the lorry, upside down, screaming for Tariq through the smoke, her arms and chest on fire, the wig melting into her scalp . . .

Laila had to take a series of rapid breaths.

"He was in the bed next to mine. There were no walls, only a curtain between us. So I could see him pretty well."

Abdul Sharif found a sudden need to toy with his wedding band. He spoke more slowly now.

"Your friend, he was badly—very badly—injured, you understand. He had rubber tubes coming out of him everywhere. At first—" He cleared his throat. "At first, I thought he'd lost both legs in the attack, but a nurse said no, only the right, the left one was on account of an old injury. There were internal injuries too. They'd operated three times already. Took out sections of intestines, I don't remember what else. And he was burned. Quite badly. That's all I'll say about that. I'm sure you have your fair share of nightmares, *hamshira*. No sense in me adding to them."

Tariq was legless now. He was a torso with two stumps. *Legless.* Laila thought she might collapse. With deliberate, desperate effort, she sent the tendrils of her mind out of this room, out the window, away from this man, over the street outside, over the city now, and its flat-topped houses and bazaars, its maze of narrow streets turned to sand castles.

"He was drugged up most of the time. For the pain, you understand. But he had moments when the drugs were wearing off when he was clear. In pain but clear of mind. I would talk to him from my bed. I told him who I was, where I was from. He was glad, I think, that there was a *hamwatan* next to him.

"I did most of the talking. It was hard for him to. His voice was hoarse, and I think it hurt him to move his lips. So I told him about my daughters, and about our house in Peshawar and the veranda my brother-in-law and I are building out in the back. I told him I had sold the stores in Kabul and that I was going back to finish up the paperwork. It wasn't much. But it occupied him. At least, I like to think it did.

"Sometimes he talked too. Half the time, I couldn't make out what he was saying, but I caught enough. He described where he'd lived. He talked about his uncle in Ghazni. And his mother's cooking and his father's carpentry, him playing the accordion.

"But, mostly, he talked about you, *hamshira*. He said you were—how did he put it—his earliest memory. I think that's right, yes. I could tell he cared a great deal about you. *Balay*, that much was plain to see. But he said he was glad you weren't there. He said he didn't want you seeing him like that."

Laila's feet felt heavy again, anchored to the floor, as if all her blood had suddenly pooled down there. But her mind was far away, free and fleet, hurtling like a speeding missile beyond Kabul, over craggy brown hills and over deserts ragged with clumps of sage, past canyons of jagged red rock and over snowcapped mountains . . .

"When I told him I was going back to Kabul, he asked me to find you. To tell you that he was thinking of you.

That he missed you. I promised him I would. I'd taken quite a liking to him, you see. He was a decent sort of boy, I could tell."

Abdul Sharif wiped his brow with the handkerchief.

"I woke up one night," he went on, his interest in the wedding band renewed, "I think it was night anyway, it's hard to tell in those places. There aren't any windows. Sunrise, sundown, you just don't know. But I woke up, and there was some sort of commotion around the bed next to mine. You have to understand that I was full of drugs myself, always slipping in and out, to the point where it was hard to tell what was real and what you'd dreamed up. All I remember is, doctors huddled around the bed, calling for this and that, alarms bleeping, syringes all over the ground.

"In the morning, the bed was empty. I asked a nurse. She said he fought valiantly."

Laila was dimly aware that she was nodding. She'd known. Of course she'd known. She'd known the moment she had sat across from this man why he was here, what news he was bringing.

"At first, you see, at first I didn't think you even existed," he was saying now. "I thought it was the morphine talking. Maybe I even *hoped* you didn't exist; I've always dreaded bearing bad news. But I promised him. And, like I said, I'd become rather fond of him. So I came by here a few days ago. I asked around for you, talked to some neighbors. They pointed to this house. They also told me what had happened to your parents. When I heard about that, well, I turned around and left. I wasn't going to tell you. I decided it would be too much for you. For anybody."

Abdul Sharif reached across the table and put a hand on her kneecap. "But I came back. Because, in the end, I think he would have wanted you to know. I believe that. I'm so sorry. I wish . . ."

Laila wasn't listening anymore. She was remembering the day the man from Panjshir had come to deliver the news of Ahmad's and Noor's deaths. She remembered Babi, white-faced, slumping on the couch, and Mammy, her hand flying to her mouth when she heard. Laila had watched Mammy come undone that day and it had scared her, but she hadn't felt any true sorrow. She hadn't understood the awfulness of her mother's loss. Now another stranger bringing news of another death. Now *she* was the one sitting on the chair. Was this her penalty, then, her punishment for being aloof to her own mother's suffering?

Laila remembered how Mammy had dropped to the ground, how she'd screamed, torn at her hair. But Laila couldn't even manage that. She could hardly move. She could hardly move a muscle.

She sat on the chair instead, hands limp in her lap, eyes staring at nothing, and let her mind fly on. She let it fly on until it found the place, the good and safe place, where the barley fields were green, where the water ran clear and the cottonwood seeds danced by the thousands in the air; where Babi was reading a book beneath an acacia and Tariq was napping with his hands laced across his chest, and where she could dip her feet in the stream and dream good dreams beneath the watchful gaze of gods of ancient, sun-bleached rock.

29.

Mariam

I'm so sorry," Rasheed said to the girl, taking his bowl of *mastawa* and meatballs from Mariam without looking at her. "I know you were very close . . . *friends* . . . the two of you. Always together, since you were kids. It's a terrible thing, what's happened. Too many young Afghan men are dying this way."

He motioned impatiently with his hand, still looking at the girl, and Mariam passed him a napkin.

For years, Mariam had looked on as he ate, the muscles of his temples churning, one hand making compact little rice balls, the back of the other wiping grease, swiping stray grains, from the corners of his mouth. For years, he had eaten without looking up, without speaking, his silence condemning, as though some judgment were being passed, then broken only by an accusatory grunt, a disapproving cluck of his tongue, a one-word command for more bread, more water.

Now he ate with a spoon. Used a napkin. Said *lotfan*

when asking for water. And talked. Spiritedly and incessantly.

"If you ask me, the Americans armed the wrong man in Hekmatyar. All the guns the CIA handed him in the eighties to fight the Soviets. The Soviets are gone, but he still has the guns, and now he's turning them on innocent people like your parents. And he calls this jihad. What a farce! What does jihad have to do with killing women and children? Better the CIA had armed Commander Massoud."

Mariam's eyebrows shot up of their own will. *Commander* Massoud? In her head, she could hear Rasheed's rants against Massoud, how he was a traitor and a communist. But, then, Massoud was a Tajik, of course. Like Laila.

"Now, *there* is a reasonable fellow. An honorable Afghan. A man genuinely interested in a peaceful resolution."

Rasheed shrugged and sighed.

"Not that they give a damn in America, mind you. What do they care that Pashtuns and Hazaras and Tajiks and Uzbeks are killing each other? How many Americans can even tell one from the other? Don't expect help from them, I say. Now that the Soviets have collapsed, we're no use to them. We served our purpose. To them, Afghanistan is a *kenarab,* a shit hole. Excuse my language, but it's true. What do you think, Laila jan?"

The girl mumbled something unintelligible and pushed a meatball around in her bowl.

Rasheed nodded thoughtfully, as though she'd said the most clever thing he'd ever heard. Mariam had to look away.

"You know, your father, God give him peace, your father and I used to have discussions like this. This was before you were born, of course. On and on we'd go about politics. About books too. Didn't we, Mariam? You remember."

Mariam busied herself taking a sip of water.

"Anyway, I hope I am not boring you with all this talk of politics."

Later, Mariam was in the kitchen, soaking dishes in soapy water, a tightly wound knot in her belly.

It wasn't so much *what* he said, the blatant lies, the contrived empathy, or even the fact that he had not raised a hand to her, Mariam, since he had dug the girl out from under those bricks.

It was the *staged* delivery. Like a performance. An attempt on his part, both sly and pathetic, to impress. To charm.

And suddenly Mariam knew that her suspicions were right. She understood with a dread that was like a blinding whack to the side of her head that what she was witnessing was nothing less than a courtship.

WHEN SHE'D at last worked up the nerve, Mariam went to his room.

Rasheed lit a cigarette, and said, "Why not?"

Mariam knew right then that she was defeated. She'd half expected, half hoped, that he would deny everything, feign surprise, maybe even outrage, at what she was implying. She might have had the upper hand then. She might have succeeded in shaming him. But it stole her grit, his calm acknowledgment, his matter-of-fact tone.

"Sit down," he said. He was lying on his bed, back to the wall, his thick, long legs splayed on the mattress. "Sit down before you faint and cut your head open."

Mariam felt herself drop onto the folding chair beside his bed.

"Hand me that ashtray, would you?" he said.

Obediently, she did.

Rasheed had to be sixty or more now—though Mariam, and in fact Rasheed himself did not know his exact age. His hair had gone white, but it was as thick and coarse as ever. There was a sag now to his eyelids and the skin of his neck, which was wrinkled and leathery. His cheeks hung a bit more than they used to. In the mornings, he stooped just a tad. But he still had the stout shoulders, the thick torso, the strong hands, the swollen belly that entered the room before any other part of him did.

On the whole, Mariam thought that he had weathered the years considerably better than she.

"We need to legitimize this situation," he said now, balancing the ashtray on his belly. His lips scrunched up in a playful pucker. "People will talk. It looks dishonorable, an unmarried young woman living here. It's bad for my reputation. And hers. And yours, I might add."

"Eighteen years," Mariam said. "And I never asked you for a thing. Not one thing. I'm asking now."

He inhaled smoke and let it out slowly. "She can't just *stay* here, if that's what you're suggesting. I can't go on feeding her and clothing her and giving her a place to sleep. I'm not the Red Cross, Mariam."

"But this?"

"What of it? What? She's too young, you think? She's fourteen. Hardly a child. You were fifteen, remember? My mother was fourteen when she had me. Thirteen when she married."

"I . . . I don't want this," Mariam said, numb with contempt and helplessness.

"It's not your decision. It's hers and mine."

"I'm too old."

"She's too young, you're too old. This is nonsense."

"I *am* too old. Too old for you to do this to me," Mariam said, balling up fistfuls of her dress so tightly her hands shook. "For you, after all these years, to make me an *ambagh.*"

"Don't be so dramatic. It's a common thing and you know it. I have friends who have two, three, four wives.

208

Your own father had three. Besides, what I'm doing now most men I know would have done long ago. You know it's true."

"I won't allow it."

At this, Rasheed smiled sadly.

"There *is* another option," he said, scratching the sole of one foot with the calloused heel of the other. "She can leave. I won't stand in her way. But I suspect she won't get far. No food, no water, not a rupiah in her pockets, bullets and rockets flying everywhere. How many days do you suppose she'll last before she's abducted, raped, or tossed into some roadside ditch with her throat slit? Or all three?"

He coughed and adjusted the pillow behind his back.

"The roads out there are unforgiving, Mariam, believe me. Bloodhounds and bandits at every turn. I wouldn't like her chances, not at all. But let's say that by some miracle she gets to Peshawar. What then? Do you have any idea what those camps are like?"

He gazed at her from behind a column of smoke.

"People living under scraps of cardboard. TB, dysentery, famine, crime. And that's before winter. Then it's frostbite season. Pneumonia. People turning to icicles. Those camps become frozen graveyards.

"Of course," he made a playful, twirling motion with his hand, "she could keep warm in one of those Peshawar brothels. Business is booming there, I hear. A beauty like her ought to bring in a small fortune, don't you think?"

He set the ashtray on the nightstand and swung his legs over the side of the bed.

"Look," he said, sounding more conciliatory now, as a victor could afford to. "I knew you wouldn't take this well. I don't really blame you. But this is for the best. You'll see. Think of it this way, Mariam. I'm giving *you* help around the house and *her* a sanctuary. A home and a husband. These days, times being what they are, a woman needs a husband. Haven't you noticed all the widows sleeping on the streets? They would kill for this chance. In fact, this is . . . Well, I'd say this is downright charitable of me."

He smiled.

"The way I see it, I deserve a medal."

LATER, in the dark, Mariam told the girl.

For a long time, the girl said nothing.

"He wants an answer by this morning," Mariam said.

"He can have it now," the girl said. "My answer is yes."

30.

Laila

The next day, Laila stayed in bed. She was under the blanket in the morning when Rasheed poked his head in and said he was going to the barber. She was still in bed when he came home late in the afternoon, when he showed her his new haircut, his new used suit, blue with cream pinstripes, and the wedding band he'd bought her.

Rasheed sat on the bed beside her, made a great show of slowly undoing the ribbon, of opening the box and plucking out the ring delicately. He let on that he'd traded in Mariam's old wedding ring for it.

"She doesn't care. Believe me. She won't even notice."

Laila pulled away to the far end of the bed. She could hear Mariam downstairs, the hissing of her iron.

"She never wore it anyway," Rasheed said.

"I don't want it," Laila said, weakly. "Not like this. You have to take it back."

"Take it back?" An impatient look flashed across his face and was gone. He smiled. "I had to add some cash too—quite a lot, in fact. This is a better ring, twenty-two-karat gold. Feel how heavy? Go on, feel it. No?" He closed the box. "How about flowers? That would be nice. You like flowers? Do you have a favorite? Daisies? Tulips? Lilacs? No flowers? Good! I don't see the point myself. I just thought . . . Now, I know a tailor here in Deh-Mazang. I was thinking we could take you there tomorrow, get you fitted for a proper dress."

Laila shook her head.

Rasheed raised his eyebrows.

"I'd just as soon—" Laila began.

He put a hand on her neck. Laila couldn't help wincing and recoiling. His touch felt like wearing a prickly old wet wool sweater with no undershirt.

"Yes?"

"I'd just as soon we get it done."

Rasheed's mouth opened, then spread in a yellow, toothy grin. "Eager," he said.

BEFORE ABDUL SHARIF'S VISIT, Laila had decided to leave for Pakistan. Even after Abdul Sharif came bearing his news, Laila thought now, she might have left. Gone somewhere far from here. Detached herself from this city where every street corner was a trap, where every alley hid a ghost that sprang at her like a jack-in-the-box. She might have taken the risk.

But, suddenly, leaving was no longer an option.

Not with this daily retching.

This new fullness in her breasts.

And the awareness, somehow, amid all of this turmoil, that she had missed a cycle.

Laila pictured herself in a refugee camp, a stark field with thousands of sheets of plastic strung to makeshift poles flapping in the cold, stinging wind. Beneath one of these makeshift tents, she saw her baby, Tariq's baby, its temples wasted, its jaws slack, its skin mottled, bluish gray. She pictured its tiny body washed by strangers, wrapped in a tawny shroud, lowered into a hole dug in a patch of windswept land under the disappointed gaze of vultures.

How could she run now?

Laila took grim inventory of the people in her life. Ahmad and Noor, dead. Hasina, gone. Giti, dead. Mammy, dead. Babi, dead. Now Tariq . . .

But, miraculously, something of her former life remained, her last link to the person that she had been before she had become so utterly alone. A part of Tariq still alive inside her, sprouting tiny arms, growing translucent hands. How could she jeopardize the only thing she had left of him, of her old life?

She made her decision quickly. Six weeks had passed since her time with Tariq. Any longer and Rasheed would grow suspicious.

She knew that what she was doing was dishonorable. Dishonorable, disingenuous, and shameful. And spectacularly unfair to Mariam. But even though the baby inside her was no bigger than a mulberry, Laila already saw the sacrifices a mother had to make. Virtue was only the first.

She put a hand on her belly. Closed her eyes.

LAILA WOULD REMEMBER the muted ceremony in bits and fragments. The cream-colored stripes of Rasheed's suit. The sharp smell of his hair spray. The small shaving nick just above his Adam's apple. The rough pads of his tobacco-stained fingers when he slid the ring on her. The pen. Its not working. The search for a new pen. The contract. The signing, his sure-handed, hers quavering. The prayers. Noticing, in the mirror, that Rasheed had trimmed his eyebrows.

And, somewhere in the room, Mariam watching. The air choking with her disapproval.

Laila could not bring herself to meet the older woman's gaze.

LYING BENEATH HIS cold sheets that night, she watched him pull the curtains shut. She was shaking even before his fingers worked her shirt buttons, tugged at the drawstring of her trousers. He was agitated. His fingers fumbled endlessly with his own shirt, with undoing his belt. Laila had a full view of his sagging breasts, his protruding belly button, the small blue vein in the center of it, the tufts of thick white hair on his chest, his shoulders, and upper arms. She felt his eyes crawling all over her.

"God help me, I think I love you," he said.

Through chattering teeth, she asked him to turn out the lights.

Later, when she was sure that he was asleep, Laila quietly reached beneath the mattress for the knife she had hidden there earlier. With it, she punctured the pad of her index finger. Then she lifted the blanket and let her finger bleed on the sheets where they had lain together.

31.

Mariam

In the daytime, the girl was no more than a creaking bedspring, a patter of footsteps overhead. She was water splashing in the bathroom, or a teaspoon clinking against glass in the bedroom upstairs. Occasionally, there were sightings: a blur of billowing dress in the periphery of Mariam's vision, scurrying up the steps, arms folded across the chest, sandals slapping the heels.

But it was inevitable that they would run into each other. Mariam passed the girl on the stairs, in the narrow hallway, in the kitchen, or by the door as she was coming in from the yard. When they met like this, an awkward tension rushed into the space between them. The girl gathered her skirt and breathed out a word or two of apology, and, as she hurried past, Mariam would chance a sidelong glance and catch a blush. Sometimes she could smell Rasheed on her. She could smell his sweat on the girl's skin, his tobacco, his appetite. Sex, mercifully, was a closed chapter in her own life. It had been for some time, and now even the thought of those laborious sessions of lying beneath Rasheed made Mariam queasy in the gut.

At night, however, this mutually orchestrated dance of avoidance between her and the girl was not possible. Rasheed said they were a family. He insisted they were, and families had to eat together, he said.

"What is this?" he said, his fingers working the meat off a bone—the spoon-and-fork charade was abandoned a week after he married the girl. "Have I married a pair of statues? Go on, Mariam, *gap bezan,* say something to her. Where are your manners?"

Sucking marrow from a bone, he said to the girl, "But you mustn't blame her. She is quiet. A blessing, really, because, *wallah,* if a person hasn't got much to say she might as well be stingy with words. We are city people, you and I, but she is *dehati.* A village girl. Not even a village girl. No. She grew up in a *kolba* made of mud *outside* the village. Her father put her there. Have you told her, Mariam, have you told her that you are a *harami*? Well, she is. But she is not without qualities, all things considered. You will see for yourself, Laila jan. She is sturdy, for one thing, a good worker, and without pretensions. I'll say it this way: If she were a car, she would be a Volga."

Mariam was a thirty-three-year-old woman now, but that word, *harami,* still had sting. Hearing it still made her feel like she was a pest, a cockroach. She remembered Nana pulling her wrists. *You are a clumsy little* harami. *This is my reward for everything I've endured. An heirloom-breaking clumsy little* harami.

"You," Rasheed said to the girl, "you, on the other hand, would be a Benz. A brand-new, first-class, shiny Benz. *Wah wah.* But. But." He raised one greasy index finger. "One must take certain . . . cares . . . with a Benz. As a matter of respect for its beauty and craftsmanship, you see. Oh, you must be thinking that I am crazy, *diwana,* with all this talk of automobiles. I am not saying you are cars. I am merely making a point."

For what came next, Rasheed put down the ball of rice he'd made back on the plate. His hands dangled idly over his meal, as he looked down with a sober, thoughtful expression.

"One mustn't speak ill of the dead much less the *shaheed*. And I intend no disrespect when I say this, I want you to know, but I have certain . . . reservations . . . about the way your parents—Allah, forgive them and grant them a place in paradise—about their, well, their leniency with you. I'm sorry."

The cold, hateful look the girl flashed Rasheed at this did not escape Mariam, but he was looking down and did not notice.

"No matter. The point is, I am your husband now, and it falls on me to guard not only *your* honor but *ours,* yes, our *nang* and *namoos.* That is the husband's burden. You let me worry about that. Please. As for you, you are the queen, the *malika,* and this house is your palace. Anything you need done you ask Mariam and she will do it for you. Won't you, Mariam? And if you fancy something, I will get it for you. You see, that is the sort of husband I am.

"All I ask in return, well, it is a simple thing. I ask that you avoid leaving this house without my company. That's all. Simple, no? If I am away and you need something urgently, I mean *absolutely* need it and it cannot wait for me, then you can send Mariam and she will go out and get it for you. You've noticed a discrepancy, surely. Well, one does not drive a Volga and a Benz in the same manner. That would be foolish, wouldn't it? Oh, I also ask that when we are out together, that you wear a burqa. For your own protection, naturally. It is best. So many lewd men in this town now. Such vile intentions, so eager to dishonor even a married woman. So. That's all."

He coughed.

"I should say that Mariam will be my eyes and ears when I am away." Here, he shot Mariam a fleeting look that was as hard as a steel-toed kick to the temple. "Not that I am mistrusting. Quite the contrary. Frankly, you strike me as far wiser than your years. But you are still a young woman, Laila jan, a *dokhtar e jawan,* and young women can make unfortunate choices. They can be prone to mischief. Anyway, Mariam will be accountable. And if there is a slipup . . ."

On and on he went. Mariam sat watching the girl out of the corner of her eye as Rasheed's demands and judgments rained down on them like the rockets on Kabul.

ONE DAY, Mariam was in the living room folding some shirts of Rasheed's that she had plucked from the clothesline in the yard. She didn't know how long the girl had been standing there, but, when she picked up a shirt and turned around, she found her standing by the doorway, hands cupped around a glassful of tea.

"I didn't mean to startle you," the girl said. "I'm sorry."

Mariam only looked at her.

The sun fell on the girl's face, on her large green eyes and her smooth brow, on her high cheekbones and the appealing, thick eyebrows, which were nothing like Mariam's own, thin and featureless. Her yellow hair, uncombed this morning, was middle-parted.

Mariam could see in the stiff way the girl clutched the cup, the tightened shoulders, that she was nervous. She imagined her sitting on the bed working up the nerve.

"The leaves are turning," the girl said companionably. "Have you seen? Autumn is my favorite. I like the smell of it, when people burn leaves in their gardens. My mother, she liked springtime the best. You knew my mother?"

"Not really."

The girl cupped a hand behind her ear. "I'm sorry?"

Mariam raised her voice. "I said no. I didn't know your mother."

"Oh."

"Is there something you want?"

"Mariam jan, I want to . . . About the things he said the other night—"

"I have been meaning to talk to you about it." Mariam broke in.

"Yes, please," the girl said earnestly, almost eagerly. She took a step forward. She looked relieved.

Outside, an oriole was warbling. Someone was pulling a cart; Mariam could hear the creaking of its hinges, the bouncing and rattling of its iron wheels. There was the sound of gunfire not so far away, a single shot followed by three more, then nothing.

"I won't be your servant," Mariam said. "I won't."

The girl flinched. "No. Of course not!"

"You may be the palace *malika* and me a *dehati*, but I won't take orders from you. You can complain to him and he can slit my throat, but I won't do it. Do you hear me? I won't be your servant."

"No! I don't expect—"

"And if you think you can use your looks to get rid of me, you're wrong. I was here first. I won't be thrown out. I won't have you cast me out."

"It's not what I want," the girl said weakly.

"And I see your wounds are healed up now. So you can start doing your share of the work in this house—"

The girl was nodding quickly. Some of her tea spilled, but she didn't notice. "Yes, that's the other reason I came down, to thank you for taking care of me—"

"Well, I wouldn't have," Mariam snapped. "I wouldn't have fed you and washed you and nursed you if I'd known you were going to turn around and steal my husband."

"Steal—"

"I will still cook and wash the dishes. You will do the laundry and the sweeping. The rest we will alternate daily. And one more thing. I have no use for your company. I don't want it. What I want is to be alone. You will leave me be, and I will return the favor. That's how we will get on. Those are the rules."

When she was done speaking, her heart was hammering and her mouth felt parched. Mariam had never before spoken in this manner, had never stated her will so forcefully. It ought to have felt exhilarating, but the girl's eyes had teared up and her face was drooping, and what satisfaction Mariam found from this outburst felt meager, somehow illicit.

She extended the shirts toward the girl.

"Put them in the *almari*, not the closet. He likes the whites in the top drawer, the rest in the middle, with the socks."

The girl set the cup on the floor and put her hands out for the shirts, palms up. "I'm sorry about all of this," she croaked.

"You should be," Mariam said. "You should be sorry."

32.

Laila

Laila remembered a gathering once, years before at the house, on one of Mammy's good days. The women had been sitting in the garden, eating from a platter of fresh mulberries that Wajma had picked from the tree in her yard. The plump mulberries had been white and pink, and some the same dark purple as the bursts of tiny veins on Wajma's nose.

"You heard how his son died?" Wajma had said, energetically shoveling another handful of mulberries into her sunken mouth.

"He drowned, didn't he?" Nila, Giti's mother, said. "At Ghargha Lake, wasn't it?"

"But did you know, did you know that Rasheed . . ." Wajma raised a finger, made a show of nodding and chewing and making them wait for her to swallow. "Did you know that he used to drink *sharab* back then, that he was crying drunk that day? It's true. Crying drunk, is what I heard. And that was midmorning. By noon, he had passed out on a lounge chair. You could have fired the noon cannon next to his ear and he wouldn't have batted an eyelash."

Laila remembered how Wajma had covered her mouth, burped; how her tongue had gone exploring between her few remaining teeth.

"You can imagine the rest. The boy went into the water unnoticed. They spotted him a while later, floating face-down. People rushed to help, half trying to wake up the boy, the other half the father. Someone bent over the boy, did the . . . the mouth-to-mouth thing you're supposed to do. It was pointless. They could all see that. The boy was gone."

Laila remembered Wajma raising a finger and her voice quivering with piety. "This is why the Holy Koran forbids *sharab*. Because it always falls on the sober to pay for the sins of the drunk. So it does."

It was this story that was circling in Laila's head after she gave Rasheed the news about the baby. He had immediately hopped on his bicycle, ridden to a mosque, and prayed for a boy.

That night, all during the meal, Laila watched Mariam push a cube of meat around her plate. Laila was there when Rasheed sprang the news on Mariam in a high, dramatic voice—Laila had never before witnessed such cheerful cruelty. Mariam's lashes fluttered when she heard. A flush spread across her face. She sat sulking, looking desolate.

After, Rasheed went upstairs to listen to his radio, and Laila helped Mariam clear the *sofrah*.

"I can't imagine what you are now," Mariam said, picking grains of rice and bread crumbs, "if you were a Benz before."

Laila tried a more lighthearted tactic. "A train? Maybe a big jumbo jet."

Mariam straightened up. "I hope you don't think this excuses you from chores."

Laila opened her mouth, thought better of it. She reminded herself that Mariam was the only innocent party in this arrangement. Mariam and the baby.

Later, in bed, Laila burst into tears.

What was the matter? Rasheed wanted to know, lifting her chin. Was she ill? Was it the baby, was something wrong with the baby? No?

Was Mariam mistreating her?

"That's it, isn't it?"

"No."

"*Wallah o billah,* I'll go down and teach her a lesson. Who does she think she is, that *harami,* treating you—"

"No!"

He was getting up already, and she had to grab him by the forearm, pull him back down. "Don't! No! She's been decent to me. I need a minute, that's all. I'll be fine."

He sat beside her, stroking her neck, murmuring. His hand slowly crept down to her back, then up again. He leaned in, flashed his crowded teeth.

"Let's see, then," he purred, "if I can't help you feel better."

FIRST, the trees—those that hadn't been cut down for firewood—shed their spotty yellow-and-copper leaves. Then came the winds, cold and raw, ripping through the city. They tore off the last of the clinging leaves, and left the trees looking ghostly against the muted brown of the hills. The season's first snowfall was light, the flakes no sooner fallen than melted. Then the roads froze, and snow gathered in heaps on the rooftops, piled halfway up frost-caked windows. With snow came the kites, once the rulers of Kabul's winter skies, now timid trespassers in territory claimed by streaking rockets and fighter jets.

Rasheed kept bringing home news of the war, and Laila was baffled by the allegiances that Rasheed tried to explain to her. Sayyaf was fighting the Hazaras, he said. The Hazaras were fighting Massoud.

"And he's fighting Hekmatyar, of course, who has the support of the Pakistanis. Mortal enemies, those two, Massoud and Hekmatyar. Sayyaf, he's siding with Massoud. And Hekmatyar supports the Hazaras for now."

As for the unpredictable Uzbek commander Dostum, Rasheed said no one knew where he would stand. Dostum had fought the Soviets in the 1980s alongside the Mujahideen but had defected and joined Najibullah's communist puppet regime after the Soviets had left. He had even earned a medal, presented by Najibullah himself, before defecting once again and returning to the Mujahideen's side. For the time being, Rasheed said, Dostum was supporting Massoud.

In Kabul, particularly in western Kabul, fires raged, and black palls of smoke mushroomed over snow-clad buildings. Embassies closed down. Schools collapsed. In hospital waiting rooms, Rasheed said, the wounded were bleeding to death. In operating rooms, limbs were being amputated without anesthesia.

"But don't worry," he said. "You're safe with me, my flower, my *gul*. Anyone tries to harm you, I'll rip out their liver and make them eat it."

That winter, everywhere Laila turned, walls blocked her way. She thought longingly of the wide-open skies of her childhood, of her days of going to *buzkashi* tournaments with Babi and shopping at Mandaii with Mammy, of her days of running free in the streets and gossiping about boys with Giti and Hasina. Her days of sitting with Tariq in a bed of clover on the banks of a stream somewhere, trading riddles and candy, watching the sun go down.

But thinking of Tariq was treacherous because, before

she could stop, she saw him lying on a bed, far from home, tubes piercing his burned body. Like the bile that kept burning her throat these days, a deep, paralyzing grief would come rising up Laila's chest. Her legs would turn to water. She would have to hold on to something.

Laila passed that winter of 1992 sweeping the house, scrubbing the pumpkin-colored walls of the bedroom she shared with Rasheed, washing clothes outside in a big copper *lagaan*. Sometimes she saw herself as if hovering above her own body, saw herself squatting over the rim of the *lagaan*, sleeves rolled up to the elbows, pink hands wringing soapy water from one of Rasheed's undershirts. She felt lost then, casting about, like a shipwreck survivor, no shore in sight, only miles and miles of water.

When it was too cold to go outside, Laila ambled around the house. She walked, dragging a fingernail along the wall, down the hallway, then back, down the steps, then up, her face unwashed, hair uncombed. She walked until she ran into Mariam, who shot her a cheerless glance and went back to slicing the stem off a bell pepper and trimming strips of fat from meat. A hurtful silence would fill the room, and Laila could almost see the wordless hostility radiating from Mariam like waves of heat rising from asphalt. She would retreat back to her room, sit on the bed, and watch the snow falling.

RASHEED TOOK HER to his shoe shop one day.

When they were out together, he walked alongside her, one hand gripping her by the elbow. For Laila, being out in the streets had become an exercise in avoiding injury. Her eyes were still adjusting to the limited, gridlike visibility of the burqa, her feet still stumbling over the hem. She walked in perpetual fear of tripping and falling, of breaking an ankle stepping into a pothole. Still, she found some comfort in the anonymity that the burqa provided. She wouldn't be recognized this way if she ran into an old acquaintance of hers. She wouldn't have to watch the surprise in their eyes, or the pity or the glee, at how far she had fallen, at how her lofty aspirations had been dashed.

Rasheed's shop was bigger and more brightly lit than Laila had imagined. He had her sit behind his crowded workbench, the top of which was littered with old soles and scraps of leftover leather. He showed her his hammers, demonstrated how the sandpaper wheel worked, his voice ringing high and proud.

He felt her belly, not through the shirt but under it, his fingertips cold and rough like bark on her distended skin. Laila remembered Tariq's hands, soft but strong, the tortuous, full veins on the backs of them, which she had always found so appealingly masculine.

"Swelling so quickly," Rasheed said. "It's going to be a big boy. My son will be a *pahlawan*! Like his father."

Laila pulled down her shirt. It filled her with fear when he spoke like this.

"How are things with Mariam?"

She said they were fine.

"Good. Good."

She didn't tell him that they'd had their first true fight.

It had happened a few days earlier. Laila had gone to the kitchen and found Mariam yanking drawers and slamming them shut. She was looking, Mariam said, for the long wooden spoon she used to stir rice.

"Where did you put it?" she said, wheeling around to face Laila.

"Me?" Laila said. "I didn't take it. I hardly come in here."

"I've noticed."

"Is that an accusation? It's how you wanted it,

remember. You said you would make the meals. But if you want to switch—"

"So you're saying it grew little legs and walked out. *Teep, teep, teep, teep.* Is that what happened, *degeh*?"

"I'm saying . . ." Laila said, trying to maintain control. Usually, she could will herself to absorb Mariam's derision and finger-pointing. But her ankles had swollen, her head hurt, and the heartburn was vicious that day. "I am saying that maybe you've misplaced it."

"Misplaced it?" Mariam pulled a drawer. The spatulas and knives inside it clanked. "How long have you been here, a few months? I've lived in this house for nineteen years, *dokhtar jo*. I have kept *that* spoon in *this* drawer since you were shitting your diapers."

"Still," Laila said, on the brink now, teeth clenched, "it's possible you put it somewhere and forgot."

"And it's possible *you* hid it somewhere, to aggravate me."

"You're a sad, miserable woman," Laila said.

Mariam flinched, then recovered, pursed her lips. "And you're a whore. A whore and a *dozd*. A thieving whore, that's what you are!"

Then there was shouting. Pots raised though not hurled. They'd called each other names, names that made Laila blush now. They hadn't spoken since. Laila was still shocked at how easily she'd come unhinged, but, the truth was, part of her had liked it, had liked how it felt to scream at Mariam, to curse at her, to have a target at which to focus all her simmering anger, her grief.

Laila wondered, with something like insight, if it wasn't the same for Mariam.

After, she had run upstairs and thrown herself on Rasheed's bed. Downstairs, Mariam was still yelling, "Dirt on your head! Dirt on your head!" Laila had lain on the bed, groaning into the pillow, missing her parents

227

suddenly and with an overpowering intensity she hadn't felt since those terrible days just after the attack. She lay there, clutching handfuls of the bedsheet, until, suddenly, her breath caught. She sat up, hands shooting down to her belly.

The baby had just kicked for the first time.

33.

Mariam

Early one morning the next spring, of 1993, Mariam stood by the living-room window and watched Rasheed escort the girl out of the house. The girl was tottering forward, bent at the waist, one arm draped protectively across the taut drum of her belly, the shape of which was visible through her burqa. Rasheed, anxious and overly attentive, was holding her elbow, directing her across the yard like a traffic policeman. He made a *Wait here* gesture, rushed to the front gate, then motioned for the girl to come forward, one foot propping the gate open. When she reached him, he took her by the hand, helped her through the gate. Mariam could almost hear him say, *"Watch your step, now, my flower, my gul."*

They came back early the next evening.

Mariam saw Rasheed enter the yard first. He let the gate go prematurely, and it almost hit the girl on the face. He crossed the yard in a few, quick steps. Mariam detected a shadow on his face, a darkness underlying the coppery light of dusk. In the house, he took off his coat, threw it on the couch. Brushing past Mariam, he said in a brusque voice, "I'm hungry. Get supper ready."

The front door to the house opened. From the hallway, Mariam saw the girl, a swaddled bundle in the hook of her left arm. She had one foot outside, the other inside, against the door, to prevent it from springing shut. She was stooped over and was grunting, trying to reach for the paper bag of belongings that she had put down in order to open the door. Her face was grimacing with effort. She looked up and saw Mariam.

Mariam turned around and went to the kitchen to warm Rasheed's meal.

"It's like someone is ramming a screwdriver into my ear," Rasheed said, rubbing his eyes. He was standing in Mariam's door, puffy-eyed, wearing only a *tumban* tied with a floppy knot. His white hair was straggly, pointing every which way. "This crying. I can't stand it."

Downstairs, the girl was walking the baby across the floor, trying to sing to her.

"I haven't had a decent night's sleep in two months," Rasheed said. "And the room smells like a sewer. There's shit cloths lying all over the place. I stepped on one just the other night."

Mariam smirked inwardly with perverse pleasure.

"Take her outside!" Rasheed yelled over his shoulder. "Can't you take her outside?"

The singing was suspended briefly. "She'll catch pneumonia!"

"It's summertime!"

"What?"

Rasheed clenched his teeth and raised his voice. "I said, It's warm out!"

"I'm not taking her outside!"

The singing resumed.

"Sometimes, I swear, sometimes I want to put that thing in a box and let her float down Kabul River. Like baby Moses."

Mariam never heard him call his daughter by the name the girl had given her, Aziza, the Cherished One. It was always *the baby*, or, when he was really exasperated, *that thing*.

Some nights, Mariam overheard them arguing. She tiptoed to their door, listened to him complain about the baby—always the baby—the insistent crying, the smells, the toys that made him trip, the way the baby had hijacked Laila's attentions from him with constant demands to be fed, burped, changed, walked, held. The girl, in turn, scolded him for smoking in the room, for not letting the baby sleep with them.

There were other arguments waged in voices pitched low.

"The doctor said six weeks."

"Not yet, Rasheed. No. Let go. Come on. Don't do that."

"It's been two months."

"*Ssht.* There. You woke up the baby." Then more sharply, "*Khosh shodi?* Happy now?"

Mariam would sneak back to her room.

"Can't you help?" Rasheed said now. "There must be something you can do."

"What do I know about babies?" Mariam said.

"Rasheed! Can you bring the bottle? It's sitting on the *almari*. She won't feed. I want to try the bottle again."

The baby's screeching rose and fell like a cleaver on meat.

Rasheed closed his eyes. "That thing is a warlord. Hekmatyar. I'm telling you, Laila's given birth to Gulbuddin Hekmatyar."

MARIAM WATCHED AS the girl's days became consumed with cycles of feeding, rocking, bouncing, walking. Even when the baby napped, there were soiled diapers to scrub and leave to soak in a pail of the disinfectant that the girl had insisted Rasheed buy for her. There were fingernails to trim with sandpaper, coveralls and pajamas to wash and hang to dry. These clothes, like other things about the baby, became a point of contention.

"What's the matter with them?" Rasheed said.

"They're boys' clothes. For a *bacha*."

"You think she knows the difference? I paid good money for those clothes. And another thing, I don't care for that tone. Consider that a warning."

Every week, without fail, the girl heated a black metal brazier over a flame, tossed a pinch of wild rue seeds in it, and wafted the *espandi* smoke in her baby's direction to ward off evil.

Mariam found it exhausting to watch the girl's lolloping enthusiasm—and had to admit, if only privately, to a degree of admiration. She marveled at how the girl's eyes shone with worship, even in the mornings when her face drooped and her complexion was waxy from a night's worth of walking the baby. The girl had fits of laughter when the baby passed gas. The tiniest changes in the baby enchanted her, and everything it did was declared spectacular.

"Look! She's reaching for the rattle. How clever she is."

"I'll call the newspapers," said Rasheed.

Every night, there were demonstrations. When the girl insisted he witness something, Rasheed tipped his chin upward and cast an impatient, sidelong glance down the blue-veined hook of his nose.

"Watch. Watch how she laughs when I snap my fingers. There. See? Did you see?"

Rasheed would grunt, and go back to his plate. Mariam remembered how the girl's mere presence used to overwhelm him. Everything she said used to please him, intrigue him, make him look up from his plate and nod with approval.

The strange thing was, the girl's fall from grace ought to have pleased Mariam, brought her a sense of vindication. But it didn't. It didn't. To her own surprise, Mariam found herself pitying the girl.

It was also over dinner that the girl let loose a steady stream of worries. Topping the list was pneumonia, which was suspected with every minor cough. Then there was dysentery, the specter of which was raised with every loose stool. Every rash was either chicken pox or measles.

"You should not get so attached," Rasheed said one night.

"What do you mean?"

"I was listening to the radio the other night. Voice of America. I heard an interesting statistic. They said that in Afghanistan one out of four children will die before the age of five. That's what they said. Now, they—What? What? Where are you going? Come back here. Get back here this instant!"

He gave Mariam a bewildered look. "What's the matter with her?"

That night, Mariam was lying in bed when the bickering started again. It was a hot, dry summer night, typical of the month of *Saratan* in Kabul. Mariam had opened her window, then shut it when no breeze came through to temper the heat, only mosquitoes. She could feel the heat rising from the ground outside, through the wheat brown, splintered planks of the outhouse in the yard, up through the walls and into her room.

Usually, the bickering ran its course after a few minutes,

but half an hour passed and not only was it still going on, it was escalating. Mariam could hear Rasheed shouting now. The girl's voice, underneath his, was tentative and shrill. Soon the baby was wailing.

Then Mariam heard their door open violently. In the morning, she would find the doorknob's circular impression in the hallway wall. She was sitting up in bed when her own door slammed open and Rasheed came through.

He was wearing white underpants and a matching undershirt, stained yellow in the underarms with sweat. On his feet he wore flip-flops. He held a belt in his hand, the brown leather one he'd bought for his *nikka* with the girl, and was wrapping the perforated end around his fist.

"It's your doing. I know it is," he snarled, advancing on her.

Mariam slid out of her bed and began backpedaling. Her arms instinctively crossed over her chest, where he often struck her first.

"What are you talking about?" she stammered.

"Her denying me. You're teaching her to."

Over the years, Mariam had learned to harden herself against his scorn and reproach, his ridiculing and reprimanding. But this fear she had no control over. All these years and still she shivered with fright when he was like this, sneering, tightening the belt around his fist, the creaking of the leather, the glint in his bloodshot eyes. It was the fear of the goat, released in the tiger's cage, when the tiger first looks up from its paws, begins to growl.

Now the girl was in the room, her eyes wide, her face contorted.

"I should have known that you'd corrupt her," Rasheed spat at Mariam. He swung the belt, testing it against his own thigh. The buckle jingled loudly.

"Stop it, *bas!*" the girl said. "Rasheed, you can't do this."

"Go back to the room."

Mariam backpedaled again.

"No! Don't do this!"

"Now!"

Rasheed raised the belt again and this time came at Mariam.

Then an astonishing thing happened: The girl lunged at him. She grabbed his arm with both hands and tried to drag him down, but she could do no more than dangle from it. She did succeed in slowing Rasheed's progress toward Mariam.

"Let go!" Rasheed cried.

"You win. You win. Don't do this. Please, Rasheed, no beating! Please don't do this."

They struggled like this, the girl hanging on, pleading, Rasheed trying to shake her off, keeping his eyes on Mariam, who was too stunned to do anything.

In the end, Mariam knew that there would be no beating, not that night. He'd made his point. He stayed that way a few moments longer, arm raised, chest heaving, a fine sheen of sweat filming his brow. Slowly, Rasheed lowered his arm. The girl's feet touched ground and still she wouldn't let go, as if she didn't trust him. He had to yank his arm free of her grip.

"I'm on to you," he said, slinging the belt over his shoulder. "I'm on to you both. I won't be made an *ahmaq,* a fool, in my own house."

He threw Mariam one last, murderous stare, and gave the girl a shove in the back on the way out.

When she heard their door close, Mariam climbed back into bed, buried her head beneath the pillow, and waited for the shaking to stop.

                              *   *   *

THREE TIMES THAT NIGHT, Mariam was awakened from sleep. The first time, it was the rumble of rockets in the west, coming from the direction of Karteh-Char. The second time, it was the baby crying downstairs, the girl's shushing, the clatter of spoon against milk bottle. Finally, it was thirst that pulled her out of bed.

Downstairs, the living room was dark, save for a bar of moonlight spilling through the window. Mariam could hear the buzzing of a fly somewhere, could make out the outline of the cast-iron stove in the corner, its pipe jutting up, then making a sharp angle just below the ceiling.

On her way to the kitchen, Mariam nearly tripped over something. There was a shape at her feet. When her eyes adjusted, she made out the girl and her baby lying on the floor on top of a quilt.

The girl was sleeping on her side, snoring. The baby was awake. Mariam lit the kerosene lamp on the table and hunkered down. In the light, she had her first real close-up look at the baby, the tuft of dark hair, the thick-lashed hazel eyes, the pink cheeks, and lips the color of ripe pomegranate.

Mariam had the impression that the baby too was examining her. She was lying on her back, her head tilted sideways, looking at Mariam intently with a mixture of amusement, confusion, and suspicion. Mariam wondered if her face might frighten her, but then the baby squealed happily and Mariam knew that a favorable judgment had been passed on her behalf.

"*Shh,*" Mariam whispered. "You'll wake up your mother, half deaf as she is."

The baby's hand balled into a fist. It rose, fell, found a spastic path to her mouth. Around a mouthful of her own hand, the baby gave Mariam a grin, little bubbles of spittle shining on her lips.

                                 236

"Look at you. What a sorry sight you are, dressed like a damn boy. And all bundled up in this heat. No wonder you're still awake."

Mariam pulled the blanket off the baby, was horrified to find a second one beneath, clucked her tongue, and pulled that one off too. The baby giggled with relief. She flapped her arms like a bird.

"Better, *nay*?"

As Mariam was pulling back, the baby grabbed her pinkie. The tiny fingers curled themselves tightly around it. They felt warm and soft, moist with drool.

"*Gunuh,*" the baby said.

"All right, *bas,* let go."

The baby hung on, kicked her legs again.

Mariam pulled her finger free. The baby smiled and made a series of gurgling sounds. The knuckles went back to the mouth.

"What are you so happy about? Huh? What are you smiling at? You're not so clever as your mother says. You have a brute for a father and a fool for a mother. You wouldn't smile so much if you knew. No you wouldn't. Go to sleep, now. Go on."

Mariam rose to her feet and walked a few steps before the baby started making the *eh, eh, eh* sounds that Mariam knew signaled the onset of a hearty cry. She retraced her steps.

"What is it? What do you want from me?"

The baby grinned toothlessly.

Mariam sighed. She sat down and let her finger be grabbed, looked on as the baby squeaked, as she flexed her plump legs at the hips and kicked air. Mariam sat there, watching, until the baby stopped moving and began snoring softly.

Outside, mockingbirds were singing blithely, and, once in a while, when the songsters took flight, Mariam could see their wings catching the phosphorescent blue of moonlight beaming through the clouds. And though her throat was parched with thirst and her feet burned with pins and needles, it was a long time before Mariam gently freed her finger from the baby's grip and got up.

34.

Laila

Of all earthly pleasures, Laila's favorite was lying next to Aziza, her baby's face so close that she could watch her big pupils dilate and shrink. Laila loved running her finger over Aziza's pleasing, soft skin, over the dimpled knuckles, the folds of fat at her elbows. Sometimes she lay Aziza down on her chest and whispered into the soft crown of her head things about Tariq, the father who would always be a stranger to Aziza, whose face Aziza would never know. Laila told her of his aptitude for solving riddles, his trickery and mischief, his easy laugh.

"He had the prettiest lashes, thick like yours. A good chin, a fine nose, and a round forehead. Oh, your father was handsome, Aziza. He was perfect. Perfect, like you are."

But she was careful never to mention him by name.

Sometimes she caught Rasheed looking at Aziza in the most peculiar way. The other night, sitting on the bedroom floor, where he was shaving a corn from his foot, he said quite casually, "So what was it like between you two?"

Laila had given him a puzzled look, as though she didn't understand.

"Laili and Majnoon. You and the *yaklenga*, the cripple. What was it you had, he and you?"

"He was my friend," she said, careful that her voice not shift too much in key. She busied herself making a bottle. "You know that."

"I don't know *what* I know." Rasheed deposited the shavings on the windowsill and dropped onto the bed. The springs protested with a loud creak. He splayed his legs, picked at his crotch. "And as . . . *friends*, did the two of you ever do anything out of order?"

"Out of order?"

Rasheed smiled lightheartedly, but Laila could feel his gaze, cold and watchful. "Let me see, now. Well, did he ever give you a kiss? Maybe put his hand where it didn't belong?"

Laila winced with, she hoped, an indignant air. She could feel her heart drumming in her throat. "He was like a *brother* to me."

"So he was a friend or a brother?"

"Both. He—"

"Which was it?"

"He was like both."

"But brothers and sisters are creatures of curiosity. Yes. Sometimes a brother lets his sister see his pecker, and a sister will—"

"You sicken me," Laila said.

"So there was nothing."

"I don't want to talk about this anymore."

Rasheed tilted his head, pursed his lips, nodded. "People gossiped, you know. I remember. They said all sorts of things about you two. But you're saying there was nothing."

240

She willed herself to glare at him.

He held her eyes for an excruciatingly long time in an unblinking way that made her knuckles go pale around the milk bottle, and it took all that Laila could muster to not falter.

She shuddered at what he would do if he found out that she had been stealing from him. Every week, since Aziza's birth, she pried his wallet open when he was asleep or in the outhouse and took a single bill. Some weeks, if the wallet was light, she took only a five-afghani bill, or nothing at all, for fear that he would notice. When the wallet was plump, she helped herself to a ten or a twenty, once even risking two twenties. She hid the money in a pouch she'd sewn in the lining of her checkered winter coat.

She wondered what he would do if he knew that she was planning to run away next spring. Next summer at the latest. Laila hoped to have a thousand afghanis or more stowed away, half of which would go to the bus fare from Kabul to Peshawar. She would pawn her wedding ring when the time drew close, as well as the other jewelry that Rasheed had given her the year before when she was still the *malika* of his palace.

"Anyway," he said at last, fingers drumming his belly, "I can't be blamed. I am a husband. These are the things a husband wonders. But he's lucky he died the way he did. Because if he was here now, if I got my hands on him . . ." He sucked through his teeth and shook his head.

"What happened to not speaking ill of the dead?"

"I guess some people can't be dead enough," he said.

Two DAYS LATER, Laila woke up in the morning and found a stack of baby clothes, neatly folded, outside her bedroom door. There was a twirl dress with little pink fishes sewn around the bodice, a blue floral wool dress with matching socks and mittens, yellow pajamas with carrot-colored polka dots, and green cotton pants with a dotted ruffle on the cuff.

"There is a rumor," Rasheed said over dinner that night, smacking his lips, taking no notice of Aziza or the pajamas Laila had put on her, "that Dostum is going to change sides and join Hekmatyar. Massoud will have his hands full then, fighting those two. And we mustn't forget the Hazaras." He took a pinch of the pickled eggplant Mariam had made that summer. "Let's hope it's just that, a rumor. Because if that happens, this war," he waved one greasy hand, "will seem like a Friday picnic at Paghman."

Later, he mounted her and relieved himself with wordless haste, fully dressed save for his *tumban,* not removed but pulled down to the ankles. When the frantic rocking was over, he rolled off her and was asleep in minutes.

Laila slipped out of the bedroom and found Mariam in the kitchen squatting, cleaning a pair of trout. A pot of rice was already soaking beside her. The kitchen smelled like cumin and smoke, browned onions and fish.

Laila sat in a corner and draped her knees with the hem of her dress.

"Thank you," she said.

Mariam took no notice of her. She finished cutting up the first trout and picked up the second. With a serrated knife, she clipped the fins, then turned the fish over, its underbelly facing her, and sliced it expertly from the tail to the gills. Laila watched her put her thumb into its mouth, just over the lower jaw, push it in, and, in one downward stroke, remove the gills and the entrails.

"The clothes are lovely."

"I had no use for them," Mariam muttered. She dropped the fish on a newspaper smudged with slimy, gray juice and sliced off its head. "It was either your daughter or the moths."

"Where did you learn to clean fish like that?"

"When I was a little girl, I lived by a stream. I used to catch my own fish."

"I've never fished."

"Not much to it. It's mostly waiting."

Laila watched her cut the gutted trout into thirds. "Did you sew the clothes yourself?"

Mariam nodded.

"When?"

Mariam rinsed sections of fish in a bowl of water. "When I was pregnant the first time. Or maybe the second time. Eighteen, nineteen years ago. Long time, anyhow. Like I said, I never had any use for them."

"You're a really good *khayat*. Maybe you can teach me."

Mariam placed the rinsed chunks of trout into a clean bowl. Drops of water dripping from her fingertips, she raised her head and looked at Laila, looked at her as if for the first time.

"The other night, when he . . . Nobody's ever stood up for me before," she said.

Laila examined Mariam's drooping cheeks, the eyelids that sagged in tired folds, the deep lines that framed her mouth—she saw these things as though she too were looking at someone for the first time. And, for the first time, it was not an adversary's face Laila saw but a face of grievances unspoken, burdens gone unprotested, a destiny submitted to and endured. If she stayed, would this be her own face, Laila wondered, twenty years from now?

"I couldn't let him," Laila said. "I wasn't raised in a household where people did things like that."

"*This* is your household now. You ought to get used to it."

"Not to *that*. I won't."

"He'll turn on you too, you know," Mariam said, wiping her hands dry with a rag. "Soon enough. And you gave him a daughter. So, you see, your sin is even less forgivable than mine."

Laila rose to her feet. "I know it's chilly outside, but what do you say we sinners have us a cup of *chai* in the yard?"

Mariam looked surprised. "I can't. I still have to cut and wash the beans."

"I'll help you do it in the morning."

"And I have to clean up here."

"We'll do it together. If I'm not mistaken, there's some *halwa* left over. Awfully good with *chai*."

Mariam put the rag on the counter. Laila sensed anxiety in the way she tugged at her sleeves, adjusted her *hijab*, pushed back a curl of hair.

"The Chinese say it's better to be deprived of food for three days than tea for one."

Mariam gave a half smile. "It's a good saying."

"It is."

"But I can't stay long."

"One cup."

They sat on folding chairs outside and ate *halwa* with their fingers from a common bowl. They had a second cup, and when Laila asked her if she wanted a third Mariam said she did. As gunfire cracked in the hills, they watched the clouds slide over the moon and the last of the season's fireflies charting bright yellow arcs in the dark. And when Aziza woke up crying and Rasheed yelled for Laila to come up and shut her up, a look passed between Laila and Mariam. An unguarded, knowing look. And in this fleeting, wordless exchange with Mariam, Laila knew that they were not enemies any longer.

35.

Mariam

From that night on, Mariam and Laila did their chores together. They sat in the kitchen and rolled dough, chopped green onions, minced garlic, offered bits of cucumber to Aziza, who banged spoons nearby and played with carrots. In the yard, Aziza lay in a wicker bassinet, dressed in layers of clothing, a winter muffler wrapped snugly around her neck. Mariam and Laila kept a watchful eye on her as they did the wash, Mariam's knuckles bumping Laila's as they scrubbed shirts and trousers and diapers.

Mariam slowly grew accustomed to this tentative but pleasant companionship. She was eager for the three cups of *chai* she and Laila would share in the yard, a nightly ritual now. In the mornings, Mariam found herself looking forward to the sound of Laila's cracked slippers slapping the steps as she came down for breakfast and to the tinkle of Aziza's shrill laugh, to the sight of her eight little teeth, the milky scent of her skin. If Laila and Aziza slept in, Mariam became anxious waiting. She washed dishes that didn't need washing. She rearranged cushions in the living room. She dusted clean windowsills. She kept herself occupied until Laila entered the kitchen, Aziza hoisted on her hip.

When Aziza first spotted Mariam in the morning, her eyes always sprang open, and she began mewling and squirming in her mother's grip. She thrust her arms toward Mariam, demanding to be held, her tiny hands opening and closing urgently, on her face a look of both adoration and quivering anxiety.

"What a scene you're making," Laila would say, releasing her to crawl toward Mariam. "What a scene! Calm down. Khala Mariam isn't going anywhere. There she is, your aunt. See? Go on, now."

As soon as she was in Mariam's arms, Aziza's thumb shot into her mouth and she buried her face in Mariam's neck.

Mariam bounced her stiffly, a half-bewildered, half-grateful smile on her lips. Mariam had never before been wanted like this. Love had never been declared to her so guilelessly, so unreservedly.

Aziza made Mariam want to weep.

"Why have you pinned your little heart to an old, ugly hag like me?" Mariam would murmur into Aziza's hair. "Huh? I am nobody, don't you see? A *dehati*. What have I got to give you?"

But Aziza only muttered contentedly and dug her face in deeper. And when she did that, Mariam swooned. Her eyes watered. Her heart took flight. And she marveled at how, after all these years of rattling loose, she had found in this little creature the first true connection in her life of false, failed connections.

EARLY THE FOLLOWING YEAR, in January 1994, Dostum *did* switch sides. He joined Gulbuddin Hekmatyar, and took up position near Bala Hissar, the old citadel walls that loomed over the city from the Koh-e-Shirdawaza mountains. Together, they fired on Massoud and Rabbani forces at the Ministry of Defense and the Presidential Palace. From either side of the Kabul River, they released rounds of artillery at each other. The streets became littered with bodies, glass, and crumpled chunks of metal. There was looting, murder, and, increasingly, rape, which was used to intimidate civilians and reward militiamen. Mariam heard of women who were killing themselves out of fear of being raped, and of men who, in the name of honor, would kill their wives or daughters if they'd been raped by the militia.

Aziza shrieked at the thumping of mortars. To distract her, Mariam arranged grains of rice on the floor, in the shape of a house or a rooster or a star, and let Aziza scatter them. She drew elephants for Aziza the way Jalil had shown her, in one stroke, without ever lifting the tip of the pen.

Rasheed said civilians were getting killed daily, by the dozens. Hospitals and stores holding medical supplies were getting shelled. Vehicles carrying emergency food supplies were being barred from entering the city, he said, raided, shot at. Mariam wondered if there was fighting like this in Herat too, and, if so, how Mullah Faizullah was coping, if he was still alive, and Bibi jo too, with all her sons, brides, and grandchildren. And, of course, Jalil. Was he hiding out, Mariam wondered, as she was? Or had he taken his wives and children and fled the country? She hoped Jalil was somewhere safe, that he'd managed to get away from all of this killing.

For a week, the fighting forced even Rasheed to stay home. He locked the door to the yard, set booby traps, locked the front door too and barricaded it with the couch. He paced the house, smoking, peering out the window, cleaning his gun, loading and loading it again. Twice, he fired his weapon into the street claiming he'd seen someone trying to climb the wall.

"They're forcing young boys to join," he said. "The Mujahideen are. In plain daylight, at gunpoint. They drag boys right off the streets. And when soldiers from a rival militia capture these boys, they torture them. I heard they electrocute them—it's what I heard—that they crush their balls with pliers. They make the boys lead them to their homes. Then they break in, kill their fathers, rape their sisters and mothers."

He waved his gun over his head. "Let's see them try to break into my house. I'll crush *their* balls! I'll blow their heads off! Do you know how lucky you two are to have a man who's not afraid of Shaitan himself?"

He looked down at the ground, noticed Aziza at his feet. "Get off my heels!" he snapped, making a shooing motion with his gun. "Stop following me! And you can stop twirling your wrists like that. I'm not picking you up. Go on! Go on before you get stepped on."

Aziza flinched. She crawled back to Mariam, looking bruised and confused. In Mariam's lap, she sucked her thumb cheerlessly and watched Rasheed in a sullen, pensive way. Occasionally, she looked up, Mariam imagined, with a look of wanting to be reassured.

But when it came to fathers, Mariam had no assurances to give.

MARIAM WAS RELIEVED when the fighting subsided again, mostly because they no longer had to be cooped up with Rasheed, with his sour temper infecting the household. And he'd frightened her badly waving that loaded gun near Aziza.

One day that winter, Laila asked to braid Mariam's hair.

Mariam sat still and watched Laila's slim fingers in the mirror tighten her plaits, Laila's face scrunched in concentration. Aziza was curled up asleep on the floor. Tucked under her arm was a doll Mariam had hand-stitched for her. Mariam had stuffed it with beans, made it a dress with tea-dyed fabric and a necklace with tiny empty thread spools through which she'd threaded a string.

Then Aziza passed gas in her sleep. Laila began to laugh, and Mariam joined in. They laughed like this, at each other's reflection in the mirror, their eyes tearing, and the moment was so natural, so effortless, that suddenly Mariam started telling her about Jalil, and Nana, and the *jinn*. Laila stood with her hands idle on Mariam's shoulders, eyes locked on Mariam's face in the mirror. Out the words came, like blood gushing from an artery. Mariam told her about Bibi jo, Mullah Faizullah, the humiliating trek to Jalil's house, Nana's suicide. She told about Jalil's wives, and the hurried *nikka* with Rasheed, the trip to Kabul, her pregnancies, the endless cycles of hope and disappointment, Rasheed's turning on her.

After, Laila sat at the foot of Mariam's chair. Absently, she removed a scrap of lint entangled in Aziza's hair. A silence ensued.

"I have something to tell you too," Laila said.

MARIAM DID NOT SLEEP that night. She sat in bed, watched the snow falling soundlessly.

Seasons had come and gone; presidents in Kabul had been inaugurated and murdered; an empire had been defeated; old wars had ended and new ones had broken out. But Mariam had hardly noticed, hardly cared. She had passed these years in a distant corner of her mind. A dry, barren field, out beyond wish and lament, beyond dream and disillusionment. There, the future did not matter. And the past held only this wisdom: that love was a damaging mistake, and its accomplice, hope, a treacherous illusion. And whenever those twin poisonous flowers began to sprout in the parched land of that field,

249

Mariam uprooted them. She uprooted them and ditched them before they took hold.

But somehow, over these last months, Laila and Aziza—a *harami* like herself, as it turned out—had become extensions of her, and now, without them, the life Mariam had tolerated for so long suddenly seemed intolerable.

We're leaving this spring, Aziza and I. Come with us, Mariam.

The years had not been kind to Mariam. But perhaps, she thought, there were kinder years waiting still. A new life, a life in which she would find the blessings that Nana had said a *harami* like her would never see. Two new flowers had unexpectedly sprouted in her life, and, as Mariam watched the snow coming down, she pictured Mullah Faizullah twirling his *tasbeh* beads, leaning in and whispering to her in his soft, tremulous voice, *But it is God Who has planted them, Mariam jo. And it is His will that you tend to them. It is His will, my girl.*

36.

Laila

As daylight steadily bleached darkness from the sky that spring morning of 1994, Laila became certain that Rasheed knew. That, any moment now, he would drag her out of bed and ask whether she'd really taken him for such a *khar,* such a donkey, that he wouldn't find out. But *azan* rang out, and then the morning sun was falling flat on the rooftops and the roosters were crowing and nothing out of the ordinary happened.

She could hear him now in the bathroom, the tapping of his razor against the edge of the basin. Then downstairs, moving about, heating tea. The keys jingled. Now he was crossing the yard, walking his bicycle.

Laila peered through a crack in the living-room curtains. She watched him pedal away, a big man on a small bicycle, the morning sun glaring off the handlebars.

"Laila?"

Mariam was in the doorway. Laila could tell that she hadn't slept either. She wondered if Mariam too had been seized all night by bouts of euphoria and attacks of mouth-drying anxiety.

"We'll leave in half an hour," Laila said.

IN THE BACKSEAT of the taxi, they did not speak. Aziza sat on Mariam's lap, clutching her doll, looking with wide-eyed puzzlement at the city speeding by.

"Ona!" she cried, pointing to a group of little girls skipping rope. "Mayam! *Ona.*"

Everywhere she looked, Laila saw Rasheed. She spotted him coming out of barbershops with windows the color of coal dust, from tiny booths that sold partridges, from battered, open-fronted stores packed with old tires piled from floor to ceiling.

She sank lower in her seat.

Beside her, Mariam was muttering a prayer. Laila wished she could see her face, but Mariam was in burqa—they both were—and all she could see was the glitter of her eyes through the grid.

This was Laila's first time out of the house in weeks, discounting the short trip to the pawnshop the day before—where she had pushed her wedding ring across a glass counter, where she'd walked out thrilled by the finality of it, knowing there was no going back.

All around her now, Laila saw the consequences of the recent fighting whose sounds she'd heard from the house. Homes that lay in roofless ruins of brick and jagged stone, gouged buildings with fallen beams poking through the holes, the charred, mangled husks of cars, upended, sometimes stacked on top of each other, walls pocked by holes of every conceivable caliber, shattered glass everywhere. She saw a funeral procession marching toward a mosque, a black-clad old woman at the rear tearing at her hair. They passed a cemetery littered with rock-piled graves and ragged *shaheed* flags fluttering in the breeze.

Laila reached across the suitcase, wrapped her fingers around the softness of her daughter's arm.

AT THE Lahore Gate bus station, near Pol Mahmood Khan in East Kabul, a row of buses sat idling along the curbside. Men in turbans were busy heaving bundles and crates onto bus tops, securing suitcases down with ropes. Inside the station, men stood in a long line at the ticket booth. Burqa-clad women stood in groups and chatted, their belongings piled at their feet. Babies were bounced, children scolded for straying too far.

Mujahideen militiamen patrolled the station and the curbside, barking curt orders here and there. They wore boots, *pakol*s, dusty green fatigues. They all carried Kalashnikovs.

Laila felt watched. She looked no one in the face, but she felt as though every person in this place knew, that they were looking on with disapproval at what she and Mariam were doing.

"Do you see anybody?" Laila asked.

Mariam shifted Aziza in her arms. "I'm looking."

This, Laila had known, would be the first risky part, finding a man suitable to pose with them as a family member. The freedoms and opportunities that women had enjoyed between 1978 and 1992 were a thing of the past now— Laila could still remember Babi saying of those years of communist rule, *It's a good time to be a woman in Afghanistan, Laila.* Since the Mujahideen takeover in April 1992, Afghanistan's name had been changed to the Islamic State of Afghanistan. The Supreme Court under Rabbani was filled now with hardliner mullahs who did away with the communist-era decrees that empowered women and instead passed rulings based on Shari'a, strict Islamic laws that ordered women to cover, forbade their travel without a male relative, punished adultery with stoning. Even if the actual enforcement of these laws was sporadic at best. *But they'd enforce them on us more,* Laila had said to Mariam, *if they weren't so busy killing each other. And us.*

The second risky part of this trip would come when they actually arrived in Pakistan. Already burdened with nearly two million Afghan refugees, Pakistan had closed its borders to Afghans in January of that year. Laila had heard that only those with visas would be admitted. But the border was porous—always had been—and Laila knew that thousands of Afghans were still crossing into Pakistan either with bribes or by proving humanitarian grounds—and there were always smugglers who could be hired. *We'll find a way when we get there,* she'd told Mariam.

"How about him?" Mariam said, motioning with her chin.

"He doesn't look trustworthy."

"And him?"

"Too old. And he's traveling with two other men."

Eventually, Laila found him sitting outside on a park bench, with a veiled woman at his side and a little boy in a skullcap, roughly Aziza's age, bouncing on his knees. He was tall and slender, bearded, wearing an open-collared shirt and a modest gray coat with missing buttons.

"Wait here," she said to Mariam. Walking away, she again heard Mariam muttering a prayer.

When Laila approached the young man, he looked up, shielded the sun from his eyes with a hand.

"Forgive me, brother, but are you going to Peshawar?"

"Yes," he said, squinting.

"I wonder if you can help us. Can you do us a favor?"

He passed the boy to his wife. He and Laila stepped away.

"What is it, *hamshira*?"

She was encouraged to see that he had soft eyes, a kind face.

She told him the story that she and Mariam had agreed on. She was a *biwa,* she said, a widow. She and her mother and daughter had no one left in Kabul. They were going to Peshawar to stay with her uncle.

"You want to come with my family," the young man said.

"I know it's *zahmat* for you. But you look like a decent brother, and I—"

"Don't worry, *hamshira.* I understand. It's no trouble. Let me go and buy your tickets."

"Thank you, brother. This is *sawab,* a good deed. God will remember."

She fished the envelope from her pocket beneath the burqa and passed it to him. In it was eleven hundred afghanis, or about half of the money she'd stashed over the past year plus the sale of the ring. He slipped the envelope in his trouser pocket.

"Wait here."

She watched him enter the station. He returned half an hour later.

"It's best I hold on to your tickets," he said. The bus leaves in one hour, at eleven. We'll all board together. My name is Wakil. If they ask—and they shouldn't—I'll tell them you're my cousin."

Laila gave him their names, and he said he would remember.

"Stay close," he said.

They sat on the bench adjacent to Wakil and his family's. It was a sunny, warm morning, the sky streaked only by a few wispy clouds hovering in the distance over the hills. Mariam began feeding Aziza a few of the crackers she'd remembered to bring in their rush to pack. She offered one to Laila.

"I'll throw up," Laila laughed. "I'm too excited."

"Me too."

"Thank you, Mariam."

"For what?"

"For this. For coming with us," Laila said. "I don't think I could do this alone."

"You won't have to."

"We're going to be all right, aren't we, Mariam, where we're going?"

Mariam's hand slid across the bench and closed over hers. "The Koran says Allah is the East and the West, therefore wherever you turn there is Allah's purpose."

"Bov!" Aziza cried, pointing to a bus. "Mayam, *bov!*"

"I see it, Aziza jo," Mariam said. "That's right, *bov*. Soon we're all going to ride on a *bov*. Oh, the things you're going to see."

Laila smiled. She watched a carpenter in his shop across the street sawing wood, sending chips flying. She watched the cars bolting past, their windows coated with soot and grime. She watched the buses growling idly at the curb, with peacocks, lions, rising suns, and glittery swords painted on their sides.

In the warmth of the morning sun, Laila felt giddy and bold. She had another of those little sparks of euphoria, and when a stray dog with yellow eyes limped by, Laila leaned forward and pet its back.

A few minutes before eleven, a man with a bullhorn called for all passengers to Peshawar to begin boarding. The bus doors opened with a violent hydraulic hiss. A parade of travelers rushed toward it, scampering past each other to squeeze through.

Wakil motioned toward Laila as he picked up his son.

"We're going," Laila said.

Wakil led the way. As they approached the bus, Laila saw faces appear in the windows, noses and palms pressed to the glass. All around them, farewells were yelled.

A young militia soldier was checking tickets at the bus door.

"Bov!" Aziza cried.

Wakil handed tickets to the soldier, who tore them in half and handed them back. Wakil let his wife board first. Laila saw a look pass between Wakil and the militiaman. Wakil, perched on the first step of the bus, leaned down and said something in his ear. The militiaman nodded.

Laila's heart plummeted.

"You two, with the child, step aside," the soldier said.

Laila pretended not to hear. She went to climb the steps, but he grabbed her by the shoulder and roughly pulled her out of the line. "You too," he called to Mariam. "Hurry up! You're holding up the line."

"What's the problem, brother?" Laila said through numb lips. "We have tickets. Didn't my cousin hand them to you?"

He made a *Shh* motion with his finger and spoke in a low voice to another guard. The second guard, a rotund fellow with a scar down his right cheek, nodded.

"Follow me," this one said to Laila.

"We have to board this bus," Laila cried, aware that her voice was shaking. "We have tickets. Why are you doing this?"

"You're not going to get on this bus. You might as well accept that. You will follow me. Unless you want your little girl to see you dragged."

As they were led to a truck, Laila looked over her shoulder and spotted Wakil's boy at the rear of the bus. The boy saw her too and waved happily.

AT THE POLICE STATION at Torabaz Khan Intersection, they were made to sit apart, on opposite ends of a long, crowded corridor, between them a desk, behind which a man smoked one cigarette after another and clacked occasionally on a typewriter. Three hours passed this way. Aziza tottered from Laila to Mariam, then back. She played with a paper clip that the man at the desk gave her. She finished the crackers. Eventually, she fell asleep in Mariam's lap.

At around three o'clock, Laila was taken to an interview room. Mariam was made to wait with Aziza in the corridor.

The man sitting on the other side of the desk in the interview room was in his thirties and wore civilian clothes—black suit, tie, black loafers. He had a neatly trimmed beard, short hair, and eyebrows that met. He stared at Laila, bouncing a pencil by the eraser end on the desk.

"We know," he began, clearing his throat and politely covering his mouth with a fist, "that you have already told one lie today, *hamshira*. The young man at the station was not your cousin. He told us as much himself. The question is whether you will tell more lies today. Personally, I advise you against it."

"We were going to stay with my uncle," Laila said. "That's the truth."

The policeman nodded. "The *hamshira* in the corridor, she's your mother?"

"Yes."

"She has a Herati accent. You don't."

"She was raised in Herat, I was born here in Kabul."

"Of course. And you are widowed? You said you were. My condolences. And this uncle, this *kaka*, where does he live?"

"In Peshawar."

"Yes, you said that." He licked the point of his pencil and poised it over a blank sheet of paper. "But where in Peshawar? Which neighborhood, please? Street name, sector number."

Laila tried to push back the bubble of panic that was coming up her chest. She gave him the name of the only street she knew in Peshawar—she'd heard it mentioned once, at the party Mammy had thrown when the Mujahideen had first come to Kabul—"Jamrud Road."

"Oh, yes. Same street as the Pearl Continental Hotel. He might have mentioned it."

Laila seized this opportunity and said he had. "That very same street, yes."

"Except the hotel is on Khyber Road."

Laila could hear Aziza crying in the corridor. "My daughter's frightened. May I get her, brother?"

"I prefer 'Officer.' And you'll be with her shortly. Do you have a telephone number for this uncle?"

"I do. I did. I . . ." Even with the burqa between them, Laila was not buffered from his penetrating eyes. "I'm so upset, I seem to have forgotten it."

He sighed through his nose. He asked for the uncle's name, his wife's name. How many children did he have? What were their names? Where did he work? How old was he? His questions left Laila flustered.

He put down his pencil, laced his fingers together, and leaned forward the way parents do when they want to convey something to a toddler. "You do realize, *hamshira*, that it is a crime for a woman to run away. We see a lot of it. Women traveling alone, claiming their husbands have died. Sometimes they're telling the truth, most times not. You can be imprisoned for running away, I assume you understand that, *nay*?"

"Let us go, Officer . . ." She read the name on his lapel tag. "Officer Rahman. Honor the meaning of your name and show compassion. What does it matter to you to let a mere two women go? What's the harm in releasing us? We are not criminals."

"I can't."

"I beg you, please."

"It's a matter of *qanoon, hamshira*, a matter of law," Rahman said, injecting his voice with a grave, self-important

259

tone. "It is my responsibility, you see, to maintain order."

In spite of her distraught state, Laila almost laughed. She was stunned that he'd used that word in the face of all that the Mujahideen factions had done—the murders, the lootings, the rapes, the tortures, the executions, the bombings, the tens of thousands of rockets they had fired at each other, heedless of all the innocent people who would die in the cross fire. *Order.* But she bit her tongue.

"If you send us back," she said instead, slowly, "there is no saying what he will do to us."

She could see the effort it took him to keep his eyes from shifting. "What a man does in his home is his business."

"What about the law, *then,* Officer Rahman?" Tears of rage stung her eyes. "Will you be there to maintain order?"

"As a matter of policy, we do not interfere with private family matters, *hamshira.*"

"Of course you don't. When it benefits the man. And isn't this a 'private family matter,' as you say? Isn't it?"

He pushed back from his desk and stood up, straightened his jacket. "I believe this interview is finished. I must say, *hamshira,* that you have made a very poor case for yourself. Very poor indeed. Now, if you would wait outside I will have a few words with your . . . whoever she is."

Laila began to protest, then to yell, and he had to summon the help of two more men to have her dragged out of his office.

Mariam's interview lasted only a few minutes. When she came out, she looked shaken.

"He asked so many questions," she said. "I'm sorry, Laila jo. I am not smart like you. He asked so many questions, I didn't know the answers. I'm sorry."

"It's not your fault, Mariam," Laila said weakly. "It's mine. It's all my fault. Everything is my fault."

*   *   *

It was past six o'clock when the police car pulled up in front of the house. Laila and Mariam were made to wait in the backseat, guarded by a Mujahid soldier in the passenger seat. The driver was the one who got out of the car, who knocked on the door, who spoke to Rasheed. It was he who motioned for them to come.

"Welcome home," the man in the front seat said, lighting a cigarette.

"You," he said to Mariam. "You wait here."

Mariam quietly took a seat on the couch.

"You two, upstairs."

Rasheed grabbed Laila by the elbow and pushed her up the steps. He was still wearing the shoes he wore to work, hadn't yet changed to his flip-flops, taken off his watch, hadn't even shed his coat yet. Laila pictured him as he must have been an hour, or maybe minutes, earlier, rushing from one room to another, slamming doors, furious and incredulous, cursing under his breath.

At the top of the stairs, Laila turned to him.

"She didn't want to do it," she said. "I made her do it. She didn't want to go—"

Laila didn't see the punch coming. One moment she was talking and the next she was on all fours, wide-eyed and red-faced, trying to draw a breath. It was as if a car had hit her at full speed, in the tender place between the lower tip of the breastbone and the belly button. She realized she had dropped Aziza, that Aziza was screaming. She tried to breathe again and could only make a husky, choking sound. Dribble hung from her mouth.

Then she was being dragged by the hair. She saw Aziza lifted, saw her sandals slip off, her tiny feet kicking. Hair was ripped from Laila's scalp, and her eyes watered with pain. She saw his foot kick open the door to Mariam's room, saw Aziza flung onto the bed. He let go of Laila's hair, and she felt the toe of his shoe connect with her left buttock. She howled with pain as he slammed the door shut. A key rattled in the lock.

Aziza was still screaming. Laila lay curled up on the floor, gasping. She pushed herself up on her hands, crawled to where Aziza lay on the bed. She reached for her daughter.

Downstairs, the beating began. To Laila, the sounds she heard were those of a methodical, familiar proceeding. There was no cursing, no screaming, no pleading, no surprised yelps, only the systematic business of beating and being beaten, the *thump, thump* of something solid repeatedly striking flesh, something, someone, hitting a wall with a thud, cloth ripping. Now and then, Laila heard running footsteps, a wordless chase, furniture turning over, glass shattering, then the thumping once more.

Laila took Aziza in her arms. A warmth spread down the front of her dress when Aziza's bladder let go.

Downstairs, the running and chasing finally stopped. There was a sound now like a wooden club repeatedly slapping a side of beef.

Laila rocked Aziza until the sounds stopped, and, when she heard the screen door creak open and slam shut, she lowered Aziza to the ground and peeked out the window. She saw Rasheed leading Mariam across the yard by the nape of her neck. Mariam was barefoot and doubled over. There was blood on his hands, blood on Mariam's face, her hair, down her neck and back. Her shirt had been ripped down the front.

"I'm so sorry, Mariam," Laila cried into the glass.

She watched him shove Mariam into the toolshed. He went in, came out with a hammer and several long planks of wood. He shut the double doors to the shed, took a key from his pocket, worked the padlock. He tested the doors, then went around the back of the shed and fetched a ladder.

A few minutes later, his face was in Laila's window, nails tucked in the corner of his mouth. His hair was disheveled. There was a swath of blood on his brow. At the sight of him, Aziza shrieked and buried her face in Laila's armpit.

Rasheed began nailing boards across the window.

THE DARK WAS TOTAL, impenetrable and constant, without layer or texture. Rasheed had filled the cracks between the boards with something, put a large and immovable object at the foot of the door so no light came from under it. Something had been stuffed in the keyhole.

Laila found it impossible to tell the passage of time with her eyes, so she did it with her good ear. *Azan* and crowing roosters signaled morning. The sounds of plates clanking in the kitchen downstairs, the radio playing, meant evening.

The first day, they groped and fumbled for each other in the dark. Laila couldn't see Aziza when she cried, when she went crawling.

"Aishee," Aziza mewled. *"Aishee."*

"Soon." Laila kissed her daughter, aiming for the forehead, finding the crown of her head instead. "We'll have milk soon. You just be patient. Be a good, patient little girl for Mammy, and I'll get you some *aishee.*"

Laila sang her a few songs.

Azan rang out a second time and still Rasheed had not given them any food, and, worse, no water. That day, a thick, suffocating heat fell on them. The room turned into a pressure cooker. Laila dragged a dry tongue over her lips, thinking of the well outside, the water cold and fresh. Aziza kept crying, and Laila noticed with alarm that when she wiped her cheeks her hands came back dry. She stripped the clothes off Aziza, tried to find something to fan her with, settled for blowing on her until she became light-headed. Soon, Aziza stopped crawling around. She slipped in and out of sleep.

Several times that day, Laila banged her fists against the walls, used up her energy screaming for help, hoping that a neighbor would hear. But no one came, and her shrieking only frightened Aziza, who began to cry again, a weak, croaking sound. Laila slid to the ground. She thought guiltily of Mariam, beaten and bloodied, locked in this heat in the toolshed.

Laila fell asleep at some point, her body baking in the heat. She had a dream that she and Aziza had run into Tariq. He was across a crowded street from them, beneath the awning of a tailor's shop. He was sitting on his haunches and sampling from a crate of figs. *That's your father,* Laila said. *That man there, you see him? He's your real* baba. She called his name, but the street noise drowned her voice, and Tariq didn't hear.

She woke up to the whistling of rockets streaking overhead. Somewhere, the sky she couldn't see erupted with blasts and the long, frantic hammering of machine-gun fire. Laila closed her eyes. She woke again to Rasheed's heavy footsteps in the hallway. She dragged herself to the door, slapped her palms against it.

"Just one glass, Rasheed. Not for me. Do it for her. You don't want her blood on your hands."

He walked past.

She began to plead with him. She begged for forgiveness, made promises. She cursed him.

His door closed. The radio came on.

The muezzin called *azan* a third time. Again the heat. Aziza became even more listless. She stopped crying, stopped moving altogether.

Laila put her ear over Aziza's mouth, dreading each

264

time that she would not hear the shallow whooshing of breath. Even this simple act of lifting herself made her head swim. She fell asleep, had dreams she could not remember. When she woke up, she checked on Aziza, felt the parched cracks of her lips, the faint pulse at her neck, lay down again. They would die here, of that Laila was sure now, but what she really dreaded was that she would outlast Aziza, who was young and brittle. How much more could Aziza take? Aziza would die in this heat, and Laila would have to lie beside her stiffening little body and wait for her own death. Again she fell asleep. Woke up. Fell asleep. The line between dream and wakefulness blurred.

It wasn't roosters or *azan* that woke her up again but the sound of something heavy being dragged. She heard a rattling. Suddenly, the room was flooded with light. Her eyes screamed in protest. Laila raised her head, winced, and shielded her eyes. Through the cracks between her fingers, she saw a big, blurry silhouette standing in a rectangle of light. The silhouette moved. Now there was a shape crouching beside her, looming over her, and a voice by her ear.

"You try this again and I will find you. I swear on the Prophet's name that I will find you. And, when I do, there isn't a court in this godforsaken country that will hold me accountable for what I will do. To Mariam first, then to her, and you last. I'll make you watch. You understand me? *I'll make you watch.*"

And, with that, he left the room. But not before delivering a kick to the flank that would have Laila pissing blood for days.

37.

Mariam
SEPTEMBER 1996

Two and a half years later, Mariam awoke on the morning of September 27 to the sounds of shouting and whistling, firecrackers and music. She ran to the living room, found Laila already at the window, Aziza mounted on her shoulders. Laila turned and smiled.

"The Taliban are here," she said.

MARIAM HAD FIRST heard of the Taliban two years before, in October 1994, when Rasheed had brought home news that they had overthrown the warlords in Kandahar and taken the city. They were a guerrilla force, he said, made up of young Pashtun men whose families had fled to Pakistan during the war against the Soviets. Most of them had been raised—some even born—in refugee camps along the Pakistani border, and in Pakistani madrasas, where they were schooled in *Shari'a* by mullahs. Their leader was a mysterious, illiterate, one-eyed recluse named Mullah Omar, who, Rasheed said with some amusement, called himself *Ameer-ul-Mumineen*, Leader of the Faithful.

"It's true that these boys have no *risha*, no roots," Rasheed said, addressing neither Mariam nor Laila. Ever since the failed escape, two and a half years ago, Mariam knew that she and Laila had become one and the same being to him, equally wretched, equally deserving of his distrust, his disdain and disregard. When he spoke, Mariam had the sense that he was having a conversation with himself, or with some invisible presence in the room, who, unlike her and Laila, was worthy of his opinions.

"They may have no past," he said, smoking and looking up at the ceiling. "They may know nothing of the world or this country's history. Yes. And, compared to them, Mariam here might as well be a university professor. Ha! All true. But look around you. What do you see? Corrupt, greedy Mujahideen commanders, armed to the teeth, rich off heroin, declaring jihad on one another and killing everyone in between—that's what. At least the Taliban are pure and incorruptible. At least they're decent Muslim boys. *Wallah*, when they come, they will clean up this place. They'll bring peace and order. People won't get shot anymore going out for milk. No more rockets! Think of it."

For two years now, the Taliban had been making their way toward Kabul, taking cities from the Mujahideen, ending factional war wherever they'd settled. They had captured the Hazara commander Abdul Ali Mazari and executed him. For months, they'd settled in the southern outskirts of Kabul, firing on the city, exchanging rockets with Ahmad Shah Massoud. Earlier in that September of 1996, they had captured the cities of Jalalabad and Sarobi.

The Taliban had one thing the Mujahideen did not, Rasheed said. They were united.

"Let them come," he said. "I, for one, will shower them with rose petals."

*   *   *

THEY WENT OUT that day, the four of them, Rasheed lead-ing them from one bus to the next, to greet their new world, their new leaders. In every battered neighborhood, Mariam found people materializing from the rubble and moving into the streets. She saw an old woman wasting handfuls of rice, tossing it at passersby, a drooping, tooth-less smile on her face. Two men were hugging by the remains of a gutted building, in the sky above them the whistle, hiss, and pop of a few firecrackers set off by boys perched on rooftops. The national anthem played on cas-sette decks, competing with the honking of cars.

"Look, Mayam!" Aziza pointed to a group of boys run-ning down Jadeh Maywand. They were pounding their fists into the air and dragging rusty cans tied to strings. They were yelling that Massoud and Rabbani had withdrawn from Kabul.

Everywhere, there were shouts: *Allah-u-akbar!*

Mariam saw a bedsheet hanging from a window on Jadeh Maywand. On it, someone had painted three words in big, black letters: ZENDA BAAD TALIBAN! Long live the Taliban!

As they walked the streets, Mariam spotted more signs—painted on windows, nailed to doors, billowing from car antennas—that proclaimed the same.

MARIAM SAW HER first of the Taliban later that day, at Pashtunistan Square, with Rasheed, Laila, and Aziza. A melee of people had gathered there. Mariam saw people craning their necks, people crowded around the blue fountain in the center of the square, people perched on its dry bed. They were trying to get a view of the end of the square, near the old Khyber Restaurant.

Rasheed used his size to push and shove past the onlookers, and led them to where someone was speaking through a loudspeaker.

When Aziza saw, she let out a shriek and buried her face in Mariam's burqa.

The loudspeaker voice belonged to a slender, bearded young man who wore a black turban. He was standing on some sort of makeshift scaffolding. In his free hand, he held a rocket launcher. Beside him, two bloodied men hung from ropes tied to traffic-light posts. Their clothes had been shredded. Their bloated faces had turned purple-blue.

"I know him," Mariam said, "the one on the left."

A young woman in front of Mariam turned around and said it was Najibullah. The other man was his brother. Mariam remembered Najibullah's plump, mustachioed face, beaming from billboards and storefront windows during the Soviet years.

She would later hear that the Taliban had dragged Najibullah from his sanctuary at the UN headquarters near Darulaman Palace. That they had tortured him for hours, then tied his legs to a truck and dragged his lifeless body through the streets.

"He killed many, many Muslims!" the young Talib was shouting through the loudspeaker. He spoke Farsi with a Pashto accent, then would switch to Pashto. He punctuated his words by pointing to the corpses with his weapon. "His crimes are known to everybody. He was a communist and a *kafir*. This is what we do with infidels who commit crimes against Islam!"

Rasheed was smirking.

In Mariam's arms, Aziza began to cry.

THE FOLLOWING DAY, Kabul was overrun by trucks. In Khair khana, in Shar-e-Nau, in Karteh-Parwan, in Wazir Akbar Khan and Taimani, red Toyota trucks weaved through the streets. Armed bearded men in black turbans sat in their beds. From each truck, a loudspeaker blared announcements, first in Farsi, then Pashto. The same message played from loudspeakers perched atop mosques, and on the radio, which was now known as the Voice of *Shari'a.* The message was also written in flyers, tossed into the streets. Mariam found one in the yard.

Our watan *is now known as the Islamic Emirate of Afghanistan. These are the laws that we will enforce and you will obey:*

All citizens must pray five times a day. If it is prayer time and you are caught doing something other, you will be beaten.

All men will grow their beards. The correct length is at least one clenched fist beneath the chin. If you do not abide by this, you will be beaten.

All boys will wear turbans. Boys in grade one through six will wear black turbans, higher grades will wear white. All boys will wear Islamic clothes. Shirt collars will be buttoned.

Singing is forbidden.

Dancing is forbidden.

Playing cards, playing chess, gambling, and kite flying are forbidden.

Writing books, watching films, and painting pictures are forbidden.

If you keep parakeets, you will be beaten. Your birds will be killed.

If you steal, your hand will be cut off at the wrist. If you steal again, your foot will be cut off.

If you are not Muslim, do not worship where you can be seen by Muslims. If you do, you will be beaten and imprisoned. If you are caught trying to convert a Muslim to your faith, you will be executed.

Attention women:

You will stay inside your homes at all times. It is not proper for women to wander aimlessly about the streets. If you go outside, you must be accompanied by a mahram, *a male relative. If you are caught alone on the street, you will be beaten and sent home.*

You will not, under any circumstance, show your face. You will cover with burqa when outside. If you do not, you will be severely beaten.

Cosmetics are forbidden.

Jewelry is forbidden.

You will not wear charming clothes.

You will not speak unless spoken to.

You will not make eye contact with men.

You will not laugh in public. If you do, you will be beaten.

You will not paint your nails. If you do, you will lose a finger.

Girls are forbidden from attending school. All schools for girls will be closed immediately.

Women are forbidden from working.

If you are found guilty of adultery, you will be stoned to death.

Listen. Listen well. Obey. Allah-u-akbar.

Rasheed turned off the radio. They were sitting on the living-room floor, eating dinner less than a week after they'd seen Najibullah's corpse hanging by a rope.

"They can't make half the population stay home and do nothing," Laila said.

"Why not?" Rasheed said. For once, Mariam agreed with him. He'd done the same to her and Laila, in effect, had he not? Surely Laila saw that.

"This isn't some village. This is *Kabul.* Women here used to practice law and medicine; they held office in the

271

government—"

Rasheed grinned. "Spoken like the arrogant daughter of a poetry-reading university man that you are. How urbane, how Tajik, of you. You think this is some new, radical idea the Taliban are bringing? Have you ever lived outside of your precious little shell in Kabul, my *gul*? Ever cared to visit the *real* Afghanistan, the south, the east, along the tribal border with Pakistan? No? I have. And I can tell you that there are many places in this country that have always lived this way, or close enough anyhow. Not that you would know."

"I refuse to believe it," Laila said. "They're not serious."

"What the Taliban did to Najibullah looked serious to me," Rasheed said. "Wouldn't you agree?"

"He was a communist! He was the head of the Secret Police."

Rasheed laughed.

Mariam heard the answer in his laugh: that in the eyes of the Taliban, being a communist and the leader of the dreaded KHAD made Najibullah only *slightly* more contemptible than a woman.

38.

Laila

Laila was glad, when the Taliban went to work, that Babi wasn't around to witness it. It would have crippled him.

Men wielding pickaxes swarmed the dilapidated Kabul Museum and smashed pre-Islamic statues to rubble—that is, those that hadn't already been looted by the Mujahideen. The university was shut down and its students sent home. Paintings were ripped from walls, shredded with blades. Television screens were kicked in. Books, except the Koran, were burned in heaps, the stores that sold them closed down. The poems of Khalili, Pajwak, Ansari, Haji Dehqan, Ashraqi, Beytaab, Hafez, Jami, Nizami, Rumi, Khayyám, Beydel, and more went up in smoke.

Laila heard of men being dragged from the streets, accused of skipping *namaz*, and shoved into mosques. She learned that Marco Polo Restaurant, near Chicken Street, had been turned into an interrogation center. Sometimes screaming was heard from behind its black-painted windows. Everywhere, the Beard Patrol roamed the streets in Toyota trucks on the lookout for clean-shaven faces to bloody.

They shut down the cinemas too. Cinema Park. Ariana. Aryub. Projection rooms were ransacked and reels of films set to fire. Laila remembered all the times she and Tariq had sat in those theaters and watched Hindi films, all those melodramatic tales of lovers separated by some tragic turn of fate, one adrift in some faraway land, the other forced into marriage, the weeping, the singing in fields of marigolds, the longing for reunions. She remembered how Tariq would laugh at her for crying at those films.

"I wonder what they've done to my father's cinema," Mariam said to her one day. "If it's still there, that is. Or if he still owns it."

Kharabat, Kabul's ancient music ghetto, was silenced. Musicians were beaten and imprisoned, their *rubab*s, *tamboura*s, and harmoniums trampled upon. The Taliban went to the grave of Tariq's favorite singer, Ahmad Zahir, and fired bullets into it.

"He's been dead for almost twenty years," Laila said to Mariam. "Isn't dying once enough?"

RASHEED WASN'T BOTHERED much by the Taliban. All he had to do was grow a beard, which he did, and visit the mosque, which he also did. Rasheed regarded the Taliban with a forgiving, affectionate kind of bemusement, as one might regard an erratic cousin prone to unpredictable acts of hilarity and scandal.

Every Wednesday night, Rasheed listened to the Voice of *Shari'a* when the Taliban would announce the names of those scheduled for punishment. Then, on Fridays, he went to Ghazi Stadium, bought a Pepsi, and watched the spectacle. In bed, he made Laila listen as he described with a queer sort of exhilaration the hands he'd seen severed, the lashings, the hangings, the beheadings.

"I saw a man today slit the throat of his brother's murderer," he said one night, blowing halos of smoke.

"They're savages," Laila said.

"You think?" he said. "Compared to what? The Soviets killed a million people. Do you know how many people the Mujahideen killed in Kabul alone these last four years? Fifty thousand. *Fifty thousand!* Is it so insensible, by comparison, to chop the hands off a few thieves? Eye for an eye, tooth for a tooth. It's in the Koran. Besides, tell me this: If someone killed Aziza, wouldn't you want the chance to avenge her?"

Laila shot him a disgusted look.

"I'm making a point," he said.

"You're just like them."

"It's an interesting eye color she has, Aziza. Don't you think? It's neither yours nor mine."

Rasheed rolled over to face her, gently scratched her thigh with the crooked nail of his index finger.

"Let me explain," he said. "If the fancy should strike me—and I'm not saying it will, but it could—it could—I would be within my rights to give Aziza away. How would you like that? Or I could go to the Taliban one day, just walk in and say that I have my suspicions about you. That's all it would take. Whose word do you think they would believe? What do you think they'd do to you?"

Laila pulled her thigh from him.

"Not that I would," he said. "I wouldn't. *Nay.* Probably not. You know me."

"You're despicable," Laila said.

"That's a big word," Rasheed said. "I've always disliked that about you. Even when you were little, when you were running around with that cripple, you thought you were so

275

clever, with your books and poems. What good are all your smarts to you now? What's keeping you off the streets, your smarts or me? I'm despicable? Half the women in this city would kill to have a husband like me. They would *kill* for it."

He rolled back and blew smoke toward the ceiling.

"You like big words? I'll give you one: perspective. That's what I'm doing here, Laila. Making sure you don't lose perspective."

What turned Laila's stomach the rest of the night was that every word Rasheed had uttered, every last one, was true.

But, in the morning, and for several mornings after that, the queasiness in her gut persisted, then worsened, became something dismayingly familiar.

ONE COLD, overcast afternoon soon after, Laila lay on her back on the bedroom floor. Mariam was napping with Aziza in her room.

In Laila's hands was a metal spoke she had snapped with a pair of pliers from an abandoned bicycle wheel. She'd found it in the same alley where she had kissed Tariq years back. For a long time, Laila lay on the floor, sucking air through her teeth, legs parted.

She'd adored Aziza from the moment when she'd first suspected her existence. There had been none of this self-doubt, this uncertainty. What a terrible thing it was, Laila thought now, for a mother to fear that she could not summon love for her own child. What an unnatural thing. And yet she had to wonder, as she lay on the floor, her sweaty hands poised to guide the spoke, if indeed she could ever love Rasheed's child as she had Tariq's.

In the end, Laila couldn't do it.

It wasn't the fear of bleeding to death that made her drop the spoke, or even the idea that the act was damnable—which she suspected it was. Laila dropped the spoke because she could not accept what the Mujahideen readily had: that sometimes in war innocent life had to be taken. Her war was against Rasheed. The baby was blameless. And there had been enough killing already. Laila had seen enough killing of innocents caught in the cross fire of enemies.

39.

Mariam
SEPTEMBER 1997

This hospital no longer treats women," the guard barked. He was standing at the top of the stairs, looking down icily on the crowd gathered in front of Malalai Hospital.

A loud groan rose from the crowd.

"But this is a women's hospital!" a woman shouted behind Mariam. Cries of approval followed this.

Mariam shifted Aziza from one arm to the other. With her free arm, she supported Laila, who was moaning, and had her own arm flung around Rasheed's neck.

"Not anymore," the Talib said.

"My wife is having a baby!" a heavyset man yelled. "Would you have her give birth here on the street, brother?"

Mariam had heard the announcement, in January of that year, that men and women would be seen in different hospitals, that all female staff would be discharged from Kabul's hospitals and sent to work in one central facility.

No one had believed it, and the Taliban hadn't enforced the policy. Until now.

"What about Ali Abad Hospital?" another man cried.

The guard shook his head.

"Wazir Akbar Khan?"

"Men only," he said.

"What are we supposed to do?"

"Go to Rabia Balkhi," the guard said.

A young woman pushed forward, said she had already been there. They had no clean water, she said, no oxygen, no medications, no electricity. "There is nothing there."

"That's where you go," the guard said.

There were more groans and cries, an insult or two. Someone threw a rock.

The Talib lifted his Kalashnikov and fired rounds into the air. Another Talib behind him brandished a whip.

The crowd dispersed quickly.

The waiting room at Rabia Balkhi was teeming with women in burqas and their children. The air stank of sweat and unwashed bodies, of feet, urine, cigarette smoke, and antiseptic. Beneath the idle ceiling fan, children chased each other, hopping over the stretched-out legs of dozing fathers.

Mariam helped Laila sit against a wall from which patches of plaster shaped like foreign countries had slid off. Laila rocked back and forth, hands pressing against her belly.

"I'll get you seen, Laila jo. I promise."

"Be quick," said Rasheed.

Before the registration window was a horde of women, shoving and pushing against each other. Some were still holding their babies. Some broke from the mass and charged the double doors that led to the treatment rooms. An armed Talib guard blocked their way, sent them back.

Mariam waded in. She dug in her heels and burrowed against the elbows, hips, and shoulder blades of strangers. Someone elbowed her in the ribs, and she elbowed back. A hand made a desperate grab at her face. She swatted it away. To propel herself forward, Mariam clawed at necks, at arms and elbows, at hair, and, when a woman nearby hissed, Mariam hissed back.

Mariam saw now the sacrifices a mother made. Decency was but one. She thought ruefully of Nana, of the sacrifices that she too had made. Nana, who could have given her away, or tossed her in a ditch somewhere and run. But she hadn't. Instead, Nana had endured the shame of bearing a *harami*, had shaped her life around the thankless task of raising Mariam and, in her own way, of loving her. And, in the end, Mariam had chosen Jalil over her. As she fought her way with impudent resolve to the front of the melee, Mariam wished she had been a better daughter to Nana. She wished she'd understood then what she understood now about motherhood.

She found herself face-to-face with a nurse, who was covered head to toe in a dirty gray burqa. The nurse was talking to a young woman, whose burqa headpiece had soaked through with a patch of matted blood.

"My daughter's water broke and the baby won't come," Mariam called.

"*I'm* talking to her!" the bloodied young woman cried. "Wait your turn!"

The whole mass of them swayed side to side, like the tall grass around the *kolba* when the breeze swept across the clearing. A woman behind Mariam was yelling that her girl had broken her elbow falling from a tree. Another woman cried that she was passing bloody stools.

"Does she have a fever?" the nurse asked. It took Mariam a moment to realize she was being spoken to.

"No," Mariam said.

"Bleeding?"

"No."

"Where is she?"

Over the covered heads, Mariam pointed to where Laila was sitting with Rasheed.

"We'll get to her," the nurse said.

"How long?" Mariam cried. Someone had grabbed her by the shoulders and was pulling her back.

"I don't know," the nurse said. She said they had only two doctors and both were operating at the moment.

"She's in pain," Mariam said.

"Me too!" the woman with the bloodied scalp cried. "Wait your turn!"

Mariam was being dragged back. Her view of the nurse was blocked now by shoulders and the backs of heads. She smelled a baby's milky burp.

"Take her for a walk," the nurse yelled. "And wait."

It was dark outside when a nurse finally called them in. The delivery room had eight beds, on which women moaned and twisted tended to by fully covered nurses. Two of the women were in the act of delivering. There were no curtains between the beds. Laila was given a bed at the far end, beneath a window that someone had painted black. There was a sink nearby, cracked and dry, and a string over the sink from which hung stained surgical gloves. In the middle of the room Mariam saw an aluminum table. The top shelf had a soot-colored blanket on it; the bottom shelf was empty.

One of the women saw Mariam looking.

"They put the live ones on the top," she said tiredly.

The doctor, in a dark blue burqa, was a small, harried woman with birdlike movements. Everything she said came out sounding impatient, urgent.

"First baby." She said it like that, not as a question but as a statement.

"Second," Mariam said.

Laila let out a cry and rolled on her side. Her fingers closed against Mariam's.

"Any problems with the first delivery?"

"No."

"You're the mother?"

"Yes," Mariam said.

The doctor lifted the lower half of her burqa and produced a metallic, cone-shaped instrument. She raised Laila's burqa and placed the wide end of the instrument on her belly, the narrow end to her own ear. She listened for almost a minute, switched spots, listened again, switched spots again.

"I have to feel the baby now, *hamshira*."

She put on one of the gloves hung by a clothespin over the sink. She pushed on Laila's belly with one hand and slid the other inside. Laila whimpered. When the doctor was done, she gave the glove to a nurse, who rinsed it and pinned it back on the string.

"Your daughter needs a caesarian. Do you know what that is? We have to open her womb and take the baby out, because it is in the breech position."

"I don't understand," Mariam said.

The doctor said the baby was positioned so it wouldn't come out on its own. "And too much time has passed as is. We need to go to the operating room now."

Laila gave a grimacing nod, and her head drooped to one side.

"There *is* something I have to tell you," the doctor said. She moved closer to Mariam, leaned in, and spoke in a lower, more confidential tone. There was a hint of embarrassment in her voice now.

"What is she saying?" Laila groaned. "Is something

wrong with the baby?"

"But how will she stand it?" Mariam said.

The doctor must have heard accusation in this question, judging by the defensive shift in her tone.

"You think I want it this way?" she said. "What do you want me to do? They won't give me what I need. I have no X-ray either, no suction, no oxygen, not even simple antibiotics. When NGOs offer money, the Taliban turn them away. Or they funnel the money to the places that cater to men."

"But, Doctor sahib, isn't there something you can give her?" Mariam asked.

"What's going on?" Laila moaned.

"You can buy the medicine yourself, but—"

"Write the name," Mariam said. "You write it down and I'll get it."

Beneath the burqa, the doctor shook her head curtly. "There is no time," she said. "For one thing, none of the nearby pharmacies have it. So you'd have to fight through traffic from one place to the next, maybe all the way across town, with little likelihood that you'd ever find it. It's almost eight-thirty now, so you'll probably get arrested for breaking curfew. Even if you find the medicine, chances are you can't afford it. Or you'll find yourself in a bidding war with someone just as desperate. There is no time. This baby needs to come out now."

"Tell me what's going on!" Laila said. She had propped herself up on her elbows.

The doctor took a breath, then told Laila that the hospital had no anesthetic.

"But if we delay, you will lose your baby."

"Then cut me open," Laila said. She dropped back on the bed and drew up her knees. "Cut me open and give me my baby."

*   *   *

INSIDE THE OLD, DINGY operating room, Laila lay on a gurney bed as the doctor scrubbed her hands in a basin. Laila was shivering. She drew in air through her teeth every time the nurse wiped her belly with a cloth soaked in a yellow-brown liquid. Another nurse stood at the door. She kept cracking it open to take a peek outside.

The doctor was out of her burqa now, and Mariam saw that she had a crest of silvery hair, heavy-lidded eyes, and little pouches of fatigue at the corners of her mouth.

"They want us to operate in burqa," the doctor explained, motioning with her head to the nurse at the door. "She keeps watch. She sees them coming; I cover."

She said this in a pragmatic, almost indifferent, tone, and Mariam understood that this was a woman far past outrage. Here was a woman, she thought, who had understood that she was lucky to even be working, that there was always something, something else, that they could take away.

There were two vertical, metallic rods on either side of Laila's shoulders. With clothespins, the nurse who'd cleansed Laila's belly pinned a sheet to them. It formed a curtain between Laila and the doctor.

Mariam positioned herself behind the crown of Laila's head and lowered her face so their cheeks touched. She could feel Laila's teeth rattling. Their hands locked together.

Through the curtain, Mariam saw the doctor's shadow move to Laila's left, the nurse to the right. Laila's lips had stretched all the way back. Spit bubbles formed and popped on the surface of her clenched teeth. She made quick, little hissing sounds.

The doctor said, "Take heart, little sister."

She bent over Laila.

Laila's eyes snapped open. Then her mouth opened. She held like this, held, held, shivering, the cords in her neck stretched, sweat dripping from her face, her fingers crushing Mariam's.

Mariam would always admire Laila for how much time passed before she screamed.

40.

Laila

FALL 1999

It was Mariam's idea to dig the hole. One morning, she pointed to a patch of soil behind the toolshed. "We can do it here," she said. "This is a good spot."

They took turns striking the ground with a spade, then shoveling the loose dirt aside. They hadn't planned on a big hole, or a deep one, so the work of digging shouldn't have been as demanding as it turned out. It was the drought, started in 1998, in its second year now, that was wreaking havoc everywhere. It had hardly snowed that past winter and didn't rain at all that spring. All over the country, farmers were leaving behind their parched lands, selling off their goods, roaming from village to village looking for water. They moved to Pakistan or Iran. They settled in Kabul. But water tables were low in the city too, and the shallow wells had dried up. The lines at the deep wells were so long, Laila and Mariam would spend hours waiting their turn. The Kabul River, without its yearly spring floods, had turned bone-dry. It was a public toilet now, nothing in it but human waste and rubble.

So they kept swinging the spade and striking, but the sun-blistered ground had hardened like a rock, the dirt unyielding, compressed, almost petrified.

Mariam was forty now. Her hair, rolled up above her face, had a few stripes of gray in it. Pouches sagged beneath her eyes, brown and crescent-shaped. She'd lost two front teeth. One fell out, the other Rasheed knocked out when she'd accidentally dropped Zalmai. Her skin had coarsened, tanned from all the time they were spending in the yard sitting beneath the brazen sun. They would sit and watch Zalmai chase Aziza.

When it was done, when the hole was dug, they stood over it and looked down.

"It should do," Mariam said.

Zalmai was two now. He was a plump little boy with curly hair. He had small brownish eyes, and a rosy tint to his cheeks, like Rasheed, no matter the weather. He had his father's hairline too, thick and half-moon-shaped, set low on his brow.

When Laila was alone with him, Zalmai was sweet, good-humored, and playful. He liked to climb Laila's shoulders, play hide-and-seek in the yard with her and Aziza. Sometimes, in his calmer moments, he liked to sit on Laila's lap and have her sing to him. His favorite song was "Mullah Mohammad Jan." He swung his meaty little feet as she sang into his curly hair and joined in when she got to the chorus, singing what words he could make with his raspy voice:

Come and let's go to Mazar, Mullah Mohammad jan,
To see the fields of tulips, o beloved companion.

Laila loved the moist kisses Zalmai planted on her cheeks, loved his dimpled elbows and stout little toes. She loved tickling him, building tunnels with cushions and pillows for him to crawl through, watching him fall asleep in her arms with one of his hands always clutching her ear. Her stomach turned when she thought of that afternoon, lying on the floor with the spoke of a bicycle wheel between her legs. How close she'd come. It was unthinkable to her now that she could have even entertained the idea. Her son was a blessing, and Laila was relieved to discover that her fears had proved baseless, that she loved Zalmai with the marrow of her bones, just as she did Aziza.

But Zalmai worshipped his father, and, because he did, he was transformed when his father was around to dote on him. Zalmai was quick then with a defiant cackle or an impudent grin. In his father's presence, he was easily offended. He held grudges. He persisted in mischief in spite of Laila's scolding, which he never did when Rasheed was away.

Rasheed approved of all of it. "A sign of intelligence," he said. He said the same of Zalmai's recklessness—when he swallowed, then pooped, marbles; when he lit matches; when he chewed on Rasheed's cigarettes.

When Zalmai was born, Rasheed had moved him into the bed he shared with Laila. He had bought him a new crib and had lions and crouching leopards painted on the side panels. He'd paid for new clothes, new rattles, new bottles, new diapers, even though they could not afford them and Aziza's old ones were still serviceable. One day, he came home with a battery-run mobile, which he hung over Zalmai's crib. Little yellow-and-black bumblebees dangled from a sunflower, and they crinkled and squeaked when squeezed. A tune played when it was turned on.

"I thought you said business was slow," Laila said.

"I have friends I can borrow from," he said dismissively.

"How will you pay them back?"

"Things will turn around. They always do. Look, he

likes it. See?"

Most days, Laila was deprived of her son. Rasheed took him to the shop, let him crawl around under his crowded workbench, play with old rubber soles and spare scraps of leather. Rasheed drove in his iron nails and turned the sandpaper wheel, and kept a watchful eye on him. If Zalmai toppled a rack of shoes, Rasheed scolded him gently, in a calm, half-smiling way. If he did it again, Rasheed put down his hammer, sat him up on his desk, and talked to him softly.

His patience with Zalmai was a well that ran deep and never dried.

They came home together in the evening, Zalmai's head bouncing on Rasheed's shoulder, both of them smelling of glue and leather. They grinned the way people who share a secret do, slyly, like they'd sat in that dim shoe shop all day not making shoes at all but devising secret plots. Zalmai liked to sit beside his father at dinner, where they played private games, as Mariam, Laila, and Aziza set plates on the *sofrah*. They took turns poking each other on the chest, giggling, pelting each other with bread crumbs, whispering things the others couldn't hear. If Laila spoke to them, Rasheed looked up with displeasure at the unwelcome intrusion. If she asked to hold Zalmai—or, worse, if Zalmai reached for her—Rasheed glowered at her.

Laila walked away feeling stung.

THEN ONE NIGHT, a few weeks after Zalmai turned two, Rasheed came home with a television and a VCR. The day had been warm, almost balmy, but the evening was cooler and already thickening into a starless, chilly night.

He set it down on the living-room table. He said he'd bought it on the black market.

"Another loan?" Laila asked.

"It's a Magnavox."

Aziza came into the room. When she saw the TV, she ran to it.

"Careful, Aziza jo," said Mariam. "Don't touch."

Aziza's hair had become as light as Laila's. Laila could see her own dimples on her cheeks. Aziza had turned into a calm, pensive little girl, with a demeanor that to Laila seemed beyond her six years. Laila marveled at her daughter's manner of speech, her cadence and rhythm, her thoughtful pauses and intonations, so adult, so at odds with the immature body that housed the voice. It was Aziza who with lighthearted authority had taken it upon herself to wake Zalmai every day, to dress him, feed him his breakfast, comb his hair. She was the one who put him down to nap, who played even-tempered peacemaker to her volatile sibling. Around him, Aziza had taken to giving an exasperated, queerly adult headshake.

Aziza pushed the TV's POWER button. Rasheed scowled, snatched her wrist and set it on the table, not gently at all.

"This is Zalmai's TV," he said.

Aziza went over to Mariam and climbed in her lap. The two of them were inseparable now. Of late, with Laila's blessing, Mariam had started teaching Aziza verses from the Koran. Aziza could already recite by heart the surah of *ikhlas*, the surah of *fatiha*, and already knew how to perform the four *ruqats* of morning prayer.

It's all I have to give her, Mariam had said to Laila, *this knowledge, these prayers. They're the only true possession I've ever had.*

Zalmai came into the room now. As Rasheed watched with anticipation, the way people wait the simple tricks of street magicians, Zalmai pulled on the TV's wire, pushed the buttons, pressed his palms to the blank screen. When he lifted them, the condensed little palms faded from the glass. Rasheed smiled with pride, watched as Zalmai kept pressing his palms and lifting them, over and over.

The Taliban had banned television. Videotapes had been gouged publicly, the tapes ripped out and strung on fence posts. Satellite dishes had been hung from lamp-posts. But Rasheed said just because things were banned didn't mean you couldn't find them.

"I'll start looking for some cartoon videos tomorrow," he said. "It won't be hard. You can buy anything in underground bazaars."

"Then maybe you'll buy us a new well," Laila said, and this won her a scornful gaze from him.

It was later, after another dinner of plain white rice had been consumed and tea forgone again on account of the drought, after Rasheed had smoked a cigarette, that he told Laila about his decision.

"No," Laila said.

He said he wasn't asking.

"I don't care if you are or not."

"You would if you knew the full story."

He said he had borrowed from more friends than he let on, that the money from the shop alone was no longer enough to sustain the five of them. "I didn't tell you earlier to spare you the worrying."

"Besides," he said, "you'd be surprised how much they can bring in."

Laila said no again. They were in the living room. Mariam and the children were in the kitchen. Laila could hear the clatter of dishes, Zalmai's high-pitched laugh, Aziza saying something to Mariam in her steady, reasonable voice.

"There will be others like her, younger even," Rasheed said. "Everyone in Kabul is doing the same."

Laila told him she didn't care what other people did with their children.

"I'll keep a close eye on her," Rasheed said, less patiently now. "It's a safe corner. There's a mosque across

291

the street."

"I won't let you turn my daughter into a street beggar!" Laila snapped.

The slap made a loud smacking sound, the palm of his thick-fingered hand connecting squarely with the meat of Laila's cheek. It made her head whip around. It silenced the noises from the kitchen. For a moment, the house was perfectly quiet. Then a flurry of hurried footsteps in the hallway before Mariam and the children were in the living room, their eyes shifting from her to Rasheed and back.

Then Laila punched him.

It was the first time she'd struck anybody, discounting the playful punches she and Tariq used to trade. But those had been open-fisted, more pats than punches, self-consciously friendly, comfortable expressions of anxieties that were both perplexing and thrilling. They would aim for the muscle that Tariq, in a professorial voice, called the *deltoid*.

Laila watched the arch of her closed fist, slicing through the air, felt the crinkle of Rasheed's stubbly, coarse skin under her knuckles. It made a sound like dropping a rice bag to the floor. She hit him hard. The impact actually made him stagger two steps backward.

From the other side of the room, a gasp, a yelp, and a scream. Laila didn't know who had made which noise. At the moment, she was too astounded to notice or care, waiting for her mind to catch up with what her hand had done. When it did, she believed she might have smiled. She might have *grinned* when, to her astonishment, Rasheed calmly walked out of the room.

Suddenly, it seemed to Laila that the collective hardships of their lives—hers, Aziza's, Mariam's—simply dropped away, vaporized like Zalmai's palms from the TV screen. It seemed worthwhile, if absurdly so, to have endured all they'd endured for this one crowning moment, for this act of defiance that would end the suffering of all indignities.

Laila did not notice that Rasheed was back in the room. Until his hand was around her throat. Until she was lifted off her feet and slammed against the wall.

Up close, his sneering face seemed impossibly large. Laila noticed how much puffier it was getting with age, how many more broken vessels charted tiny paths on his nose. Rasheed didn't say anything. And, really, what could be said, what needed saying, when you'd shoved the barrel of your gun into your wife's mouth?

IT WAS THE RAIDS, the reason they were in the yard digging. Sometimes monthly raids, sometimes weekly. Of late, almost daily. Mostly, the Taliban confiscated stuff, gave a kick to someone's rear, whacked the back of a head or two. But sometimes there were public beatings, lashings of soles and palms.

"Gently," Mariam said now, her knees over the edge. They lowered the TV into the hole by each clutching one end of the plastic sheet in which it was wrapped.

"That should do it," Mariam said.

They patted the dirt when they were done, filling the hole up again. They tossed some of it around so it wouldn't look conspicuous.

"There," Mariam said, wiping her hands on her dress.

When it was safer, they'd agreed, when the Taliban cut down on their raids, in a month or two or six, or maybe longer, they would dig the TV up.

IN LAILA'S DREAM, she and Mariam are out behind the toolshed digging again. But, this time, it's Aziza they're lowering into the ground. Aziza's breath fogs the sheet of plastic in which they have wrapped her. Laila sees her panicked eyes, the whiteness of her palms as they slap and push against the sheet. Aziza pleads. Laila can't hear her screams. *Only for a while,* she calls down, *it's only for a while. It's the raids, don't you know, my love? When the raids are over, Mammy and Khala Mariam will dig you out. I promise, my love. Then we can play. We can play all you want.* She fills the shovel. Laila woke up, out of breath, with a taste of soil in her mouth, when the first granular lumps of dirt hit the plastic.

41.

Mariam

In the summer of 2000, the drought reached its third and worst year.

In Helmand, Zabol, Kandahar, villages turned into herds of nomadic communities, always moving, searching for water and green pastures for their livestock. When they found neither, when their goats and sheep and cows died off, they came to Kabul. They took to the Kareh-Ariana hillside, living in makeshift slums, packed in huts, fifteen or twenty at a time.

That was also the summer of *Titanic,* the summer that Mariam and Aziza were a tangle of limbs, rolling and giggling, Aziza insisting *she* get to be Jack.

"Quiet, Aziza jo."

"Jack! Say my name, Khala Mariam. Say it. Jack!"

"Your father will be angry if you wake him."

"Jack! And you're Rose."

It would end with Mariam on her back, surrendering, agreeing again to be Rose. "Fine, you be Jack," she relented. "You die young, and I get to live to a ripe old age."

"Yes, but I die a hero," said Aziza, "while you, Rose, you spend your entire, miserable life longing for me." Then, straddling Mariam's chest, she'd announce, "Now we must kiss!" Mariam whipped her head side to side, and Aziza, delighted with her own scandalous behavior, cackled through puckered lips.

Sometimes Zalmai would saunter in and watch this game. What did *he* get to be, he asked.

"You can be the iceberg," said Aziza.

That summer, *Titanic* fever gripped Kabul. People smuggled pirated copies of the film from Pakistan—sometimes in their underwear. After curfew, everyone locked their doors, turned out the lights, turned down the volume, and reaped tears for Jack and Rose and the passengers of the doomed ship. If there was electrical power, Mariam, Laila, and the children watched it too. A dozen times or more, they unearthed the TV from behind the toolshed, late at night, with the lights out and quilts pinned over the windows.

At the Kabul River, vendors moved into the parched riverbed. Soon, from the river's sunbaked hollows, it was possible to buy *Titanic* carpets, and *Titanic* cloth, from bolts arranged in wheelbarrows. There was *Titanic* deodorant, *Titanic* toothpaste, *Titanic* perfume, *Titanic pakora*, even *Titanic* burqas. A particularly persistent beggar began calling himself "Titanic Beggar."

"Titanic City" was born.

It's the song, they said.

No, the sea. The luxury. The ship.

It's the sex, they whispered.

Leo, said Aziza sheepishly. *It's all about Leo.*

"Everybody wants Jack," Laila said to Mariam. "That's what it is. Everybody wants Jack to rescue them from disaster. But there is no Jack. Jack is not coming back. Jack is dead."

THEN, late that summer, a fabric merchant fell asleep and forgot to put out his cigarette. He survived the fire, but his store did not. The fire took the adjacent fabric store as well, a secondhand clothing store, a small furniture shop, a bakery.

They told Rasheed later that if the winds had blown east instead of west, his shop, which was at the corner of the block, might have been spared.

THEY SOLD EVERYTHING.

First to go were Mariam's things, then Laila's. Aziza's baby clothes, the few toys Laila had fought Rasheed to buy her. Aziza watched the proceedings with a docile look. Rasheed's watch too was sold, his old transistor radio, his pair of neckties, his shoes, and his wedding ring. The couch, the table, the rug, and the chairs went too. Zalmai threw a wicked tantrum when Rasheed sold the TV.

After the fire, Rasheed was home almost every day. He slapped Aziza. He kicked Mariam. He threw things. He found fault with Laila, the way she smelled, the way she dressed, the way she combed her hair, her yellowing teeth.

"What's happened to you?" he said. "I married a *pari*, and now I'm saddled with a hag. You're turning into Mariam."

He got fired from the kebab house near Haji Yaghoub Square because he and a customer got into a scuffle. The customer complained that Rasheed had rudely tossed the bread on his table. Harsh words had passed. Rasheed had called the customer a monkey-faced Uzbek. A gun had been brandished. A skewer pointed in return. In Rasheed's version, he held the skewer. Mariam had her doubts.

Fired from the restaurant in Taimani because

customers complained about the long waits, Rasheed said the cook was slow and lazy.

"You were probably out back napping," said Laila.

"Don't provoke him, Laila jo," Mariam said.

"I'm warning you, woman," he said.

"Either that or smoking."

"I swear to God."

"You can't help being what you are."

And then he was on Laila, pummeling her chest, her head, her belly with fists, tearing at her hair, throwing her to the wall. Aziza was shrieking, pulling at his shirt; Zalmai was screaming too, trying to get him off his mother. Rasheed shoved the children aside, pushed Laila to the ground, and began kicking her. Mariam threw herself on Laila. He went on kicking, kicking Mariam now, spittle flying from his mouth, his eyes glittering with murderous intent, kicking until he couldn't anymore.

"I swear you're going to make me kill you, Laila," he said, panting. Then he stormed out of the house.

WHEN THE MONEY ran out, hunger began to cast a pall over their lives. It was stunning to Mariam how quickly alleviating hunger became the crux of their existence.

Rice, boiled plain and white, with no meat or sauce, was a rare treat now. They skipped meals with increasing and alarming regularity. Sometimes Rasheed brought home sardines in a can and brittle, dried bread that tasted like sawdust. Sometimes a stolen bag of apples, at the risk of getting his hand sawed off. In grocery stores, he carefully pocketed canned ravioli, which they split five ways, Zalmai getting the lion's share. They ate raw turnips sprinkled with salt. Limp leaves of lettuce and blackened bananas for dinner.

Death from starvation suddenly became a distinct possibility. Some chose not to wait for it. Mariam heard of a neighborhood widow who had ground some dried bread, laced it with rat poison, and fed it to all seven of her children. She had saved the biggest portion for herself.

Aziza's ribs began to push through the skin, and the fat from her cheeks vanished. Her calves thinned, and her complexion turned the color of weak tea. When Mariam picked her up, she could feel her hip bone poking through the taut skin. Zalmai lay around the house, eyes dulled and half closed, or in his father's lap limp as a rag. He cried himself to sleep, when he could muster the energy, but his sleep was fitful and sporadic. White dots leaped before Mariam's eyes whenever she got up. Her head spun, and her ears rang all the time. She remembered something Mullah Faizullah used to say about hunger when Ramadan started: *Even the snakebitten man finds sleep, but not the hungry.*

"My children are going to die," Laila said. "Right before my eyes."

"They are not," Mariam said. "I won't let them. It's going to be all right, Laila jo. I know what to do."

ONE BLISTERING-HOT DAY, Mariam put on her burqa, and she and Rasheed walked to the Intercontinental Hotel. Bus fare was an unaffordable luxury now, and Mariam was exhausted by the time they reached the top of the steep hill. Climbing the slope, she was struck by bouts of dizziness, and twice she had to stop, wait for it to pass.

At the hotel entrance, Rasheed greeted and hugged one of the doormen, who was dressed in a burgundy suit and visor cap. There was some friendly-looking talk between them. Rasheed spoke with his hand on the doorman's elbow. He motioned toward Mariam at one point, and they both looked her way briefly. Mariam thought there was something vaguely familiar about the doorman.

When the doorman went inside, Mariam and Rasheed

waited. From this vantage point, Mariam had a view of the Polytechnic Institute, and, beyond that, the old Khair khana district and the road to Mazar. To the south, she could see the bread factory, Silo, long abandoned, its pale yellow façade pocked with yawning holes from all the shelling it had endured. Farther south, she could make out the hollow ruins of Darulaman Palace, where, many years back, Rasheed had taken her for a picnic. The memory of that day was a relic from a past that no longer seemed like her own.

Mariam concentrated on these things, these landmarks. She feared she might lose her nerve if she let her mind wander.

Every few minutes, jeeps and taxis drove up to the hotel entrance. Doormen rushed to greet the passengers, who were all men, armed, bearded, wearing turbans, all of them stepping out with the same self-assured, casual air of menace. Mariam heard bits of their chatter as they vanished through the hotel's doors. She heard Pashto and Farsi, but Urdu and Arabic too.

"Meet our *real* masters," Rasheed said in a low-pitched voice. "Pakistani and Arab Islamists. The Taliban are puppets. *These* are the big players and Afghanistan is their playground."

Rasheed said he'd heard rumors that the Taliban were allowing these people to set up secret camps all over the country, where young men were being trained to become suicide bombers and jihadi fighters.

"What's taking him so long?" Mariam said.

Rasheed spat, and kicked dirt on the spit.

An hour later, they were inside, Mariam and Rasheed, following the doorman. Their heels clicked on the tiled floor as they were led across the pleasantly cool lobby. Mariam saw two men sitting on leather chairs, rifles and a coffee table between them, sipping black tea and eating from a plate of syrup-coated *jelabi,* rings sprinkled with powdered sugar. She thought of Aziza, who loved *jelabi,* and tore her gaze away.

The doorman led them outside to a balcony. From his pocket, he produced a small black cordless phone and a scrap of paper with a number scribbled on it. He told Rasheed it was his supervisor's satellite phone.

"I got you five minutes," he said. "No more."

"Tashakor," Rasheed said. "I won't forget this."

The doorman nodded and walked away. Rasheed dialed. He gave Mariam the phone.

As Mariam listened to the scratchy ringing, her mind wandered. It wandered to the last time she'd seen Jalil, thirteen years earlier, back in the spring of 1987. He'd stood on the street outside her house, leaning on a cane, beside the blue Benz with the Herat license plates and the white stripe bisecting the roof, the hood, and trunk. He'd stood there for hours, waiting for her, now and then calling her name, just as she had once called *his* name outside *his* house. Mariam had parted the curtain once, just a bit, and caught a glimpse of him. Only a glimpse, but long enough to see that his hair had turned fluffy white, and that he'd started to stoop. He wore glasses, a red tie, as always, and the usual white handkerchief triangle in his breast pocket. Most striking, he was thinner, much thinner, than she remembered, the coat of his dark brown suit drooping over his shoulders, the trousers pooling at his ankles.

Jalil had seen her too, if only for a moment. Their eyes had met briefly through a part in the curtains, as they had met many years earlier through a part in another pair of curtains. But then Mariam had quickly closed the curtains. She had sat on the bed, waited for him to leave.

She thought now of the letter Jalil had finally left at her door. She had kept it for days, beneath her pillow, picking it up now and then, turning it over in her hands. In the end, she had shredded it unopened.

And now here she was, after all these years, calling him.

Mariam regretted her foolish, youthful pride now. She wished now that she had let him in. What would have been the harm to let him in, sit with him, let him say what he'd come to say? He was her father. He'd not been a good father, it was true, but how ordinary his faults seemed now, how forgivable, when compared to Rasheed's malice, or to the brutality and violence that she had seen men inflict on one another.

She wished she hadn't destroyed his letter.

A man's deep voice spoke in her ear and informed her that she'd reached the mayor's office in Herat.

Mariam cleared her throat. "*Salaam,* brother, I am looking for someone who lives in Herat. Or he did, many years ago. His name is Jalil Khan. He lived in Shar-e-Nau and owned the cinema. Do you have any information as to his whereabouts?"

The irritation was audible in the man's voice. "This is why you call the mayor's office?"

Mariam said she didn't know who else to call. "Forgive me, brother. I know you have important things to tend to, but it is life and death, a question of life and death I am calling about."

"I don't know him. The cinema's been closed for many years."

"Maybe there's someone there who might know him, someone—"

"There is no one."

Mariam closed her eyes. "Please, brother. There are children involved. Small children."

A long sigh.

"Maybe someone there—"

"There's a groundskeeper here. I think he's lived here all of his life."

"Yes, ask him, please."

"Call back tomorrow."

Mariam said she couldn't. "I have this phone for five minutes only. I don't—"

There was a click at the other end, and Mariam thought he had hung up. But she could hear footsteps, and voices, a distant car horn, and some mechanical humming punctuated by clicks, maybe an electric fan. She switched the phone to her other ear, closed her eyes.

She pictured Jalil smiling, reaching into his pocket.

Ah. Of course. Well. Here then. Without further ado . . .

A leaf-shaped pendant, tiny coins etched with moons and stars hanging from it.

Try it on, Mariam jo.

What do you think?

I think you look like a queen.

A few minutes passed. Then footsteps, a creaking sound, and a click. "He does know him."

"He does?"

"It's what he says."

"Where is he?" Mariam said. "Does this man know where Jalil Khan is?"

There was a pause. "He says he died years ago, back in 1987."

Mariam's stomach fell. She'd considered the possibility, of course. Jalil would have been in his mid- to late seventies by now, but . . .

1987.

He was dying then. He had driven all the way from Herat to say good-bye.

She moved to the edge of the balcony. From up here, she could see the hotel's once-famous swimming pool, empty and grubby now, scarred by bullet holes and decaying tiles. And there was the battered tennis court, the ragged net lying limply in the middle of it like dead skin shed by a snake.

"I have to go now," the voice at the other end said.

"I'm sorry to have bothered you," Mariam said, weeping soundlessly into the phone. She saw Jalil waving to her, skipping from stone to stone as he crossed the stream, his pockets swollen with gifts. All the times she had held her breath for him, for God to grant her more time with him. "Thank you," Mariam began to say, but the man at the other end had already hung up.

Rasheed was looking at her. Mariam shook her head.

"Useless," he said, snatching the phone from her. "Like daughter, like father."

On their way out of the lobby, Rasheed walked briskly to the coffee table, which was now abandoned, and pocketed the last ring of *jelabi*. He took it home and gave it to Zalmai.

42.

Laila

In a paper bag, Aziza packed these things: her flowered shirt and her lone pair of socks, her mismatched wool gloves, an old, pumpkin-colored blanket dotted with stars and comets, a splintered plastic cup, a banana, her set of dice.

It was a cool morning in April 2001, shortly before Laila's twenty-third birthday. The sky was a translucent gray, and gusts of a clammy, cold wind kept rattling the screen door.

This was a few days after Laila heard that Ahmad Shah Massoud had gone to France and spoken to the European Parliament. Massoud was now in his native North, and leading the Northern Alliance, the sole opposition group still fighting the Taliban. In Europe, Massoud had warned the West about terrorist camps in Afghanistan, and pleaded with the U.S. to help him fight the Taliban.

"If President Bush doesn't help us," he had said, "these terrorists will damage the U.S. and Europe very soon."

A month before that, Laila had learned that the Taliban had planted TNT in the crevices of the giant Buddhas in Bamiyan and blown them apart, calling them objects of idolatry and sin. There was an outcry around the world, from the U.S. to China. Governments, historians, and archaeologists from all over the globe had written letters, pleaded with the Taliban not to demolish the two greatest historical artifacts in Afghanistan. But the Taliban had gone ahead and detonated their explosives inside the two-thousand-year-old Buddhas. They had chanted *Allah-u-akbar* with each blast, cheered each time the statues lost an arm or a leg in a crumbling cloud of dust. Laila remembered standing atop the bigger of the two Buddhas with Babi and Tariq, back in 1987, a breeze blowing in their sunlit faces, watching a hawk gliding in circles over the sprawling valley below. But when she heard the news of the statues' demise, Laila was numb to it. It hardly seemed to matter. How could she care about statues when her own life was crumbling dust?

Until Rasheed told her it was time to go, Laila sat on the floor in a corner of the living room, not speaking and stone-faced, her hair hanging around her face in straggly curls. No matter how much she breathed in and out, it seemed to Laila that she couldn't fill her lungs with enough air.

ON THE WAY to Karteh-Seh, Zalmai bounced in Rasheed's arms, and Aziza held Mariam's hand as she walked quickly beside her. The wind blew the dirty scarf tied under Aziza's chin and rippled the hem of her dress. Aziza was more grim now, as though she'd begun to sense, with each step, that she was being duped. Laila had not found the strength to tell Aziza the truth. She had told her that she was going to a school, a special school where the children ate and slept and didn't come home after class. Now Aziza kept pelting Laila with the same questions she had been asking for days. Did the students sleep in different rooms or all in one great big room? Would she make friends? Was she, Laila, sure that the teachers would be nice?

And, more than once, *How long do I have to stay?*

They stopped two blocks from the squat, barracks-style building.

"Zalmai and I will wait here," Rasheed said. "Oh, before I forget . . ."

He fished a stick of gum from his pocket, a parting gift, and held it out to Aziza with a stiff, magnanimous air. Aziza took it and muttered a thank-you. Laila marveled at Aziza's grace, Aziza's vast capacity for forgiveness, and her eyes filled. Her heart squeezed, and she was faint with sorrow at the thought that this afternoon Aziza would not nap beside her, that she would not feel the flimsy weight of Aziza's arm on her chest, the curve of Aziza's head pressing into her ribs, Aziza's breath warming her neck, Aziza's heels poking her belly.

When Aziza was led away, Zalmai began wailing, crying, Ziza! Ziza! He squirmed and kicked in his father's arms, called for his sister, until his attention was diverted by an organ-grinder's monkey across the street.

They walked the last two blocks alone, Mariam, Laila, and Aziza. As they approached the building, Laila could see its splintered façade, the sagging roof, the planks of wood nailed across frames with missing windows, the top of a swing set over a decaying wall.

They stopped by the door, and Laila repeated to Aziza what she had told her earlier.

"And if they ask about your father, what do you say?"

"The Mujahideen killed him," Aziza said, her mouth set with wariness.

"That's good. Aziza, do you understand?"

"Because this is a special school," Aziza said. Now that

they were here, and the building was a reality, she looked shaken. Her lower lip was quivering and her eyes threatened to well up, and Laila saw how hard she was struggling to be brave. "If we tell the truth," Aziza said in a thin, breathless voice, "they won't take me. It's a special school. I want to go home."

"I'll visit all the time," Laila managed to say. "I promise."

"Me too," said Mariam. "We'll come to see you, Aziza jo, and we'll play together, just like always. It's only for a while, until your father finds work."

"They have food here," Laila said shakily. She was glad for the burqa, glad that Aziza couldn't see how she was falling apart inside it. "Here, you won't go hungry. They have rice and bread and water, and maybe even fruit."

"But *you* won't be here. And Khala Mariam won't be with me."

"I'll come and see you," Laila said. "All the time. Look at me, Aziza. I'll come and see you. I'm your mother. If it kills me, I'll come and see you."

THE ORPHANAGE DIRECTOR was a stooping, narrow-chested man with a pleasantly lined face. He was balding, had a shaggy beard, eyes like peas. His name was Zaman. He wore a skullcap. The left lens of his eyeglasses was chipped.

As he led them to his office, he asked Laila and Mariam their names, asked for Aziza's name too, her age. They passed through poorly lit hallways where barefoot children stepped aside and watched. They had disheveled hair or shaved scalps. They wore sweaters with frayed sleeves, ragged jeans whose knees had worn down to strings, coats patched with duct tape. Laila smelled soap and talcum, ammonia and urine, and rising apprehension in Aziza, who had begun whimpering.

Laila had a glimpse of the yard: weedy lot, rickety swing set, old tires, a deflated basketball. The rooms they passed were bare, the windows covered with sheets of plastic. A boy darted from one of the rooms and grabbed Laila's elbow, and tried to climb up into her arms. An attendant, who was cleaning up what looked like a puddle of urine, put down his mop and pried the boy off.

Zaman seemed gently proprietary with the orphans. He patted the heads of some, as he passed by, said a cordial word or two to them, tousled their hair, without condescension. The children welcomed his touch. They all looked at him, Laila thought, in hope of approval.

He showed them into his office, a room with only three folding chairs, and a disorderly desk with piles of paper scattered atop it.

"You're from Herat," Zaman said to Mariam. "I can tell from your accent."

He leaned back in his chair and laced his hands over his belly, and said he had a brother-in-law who used to live there. Even in these ordinary gestures, Laila noted a laborious quality to his movements. And though he was smiling faintly, Laila sensed something troubled and wounded beneath, disappointment and defeat glossed over with a veneer of good humor.

"He was a glassmaker," Zaman said. "He made these beautiful, jade green swans. You held them up to sunlight and they glittered inside, like the glass was filled with tiny jewels. Have you been back?"

Mariam said she hadn't.

"I'm from Kandahar myself. Have you ever been to Kandahar, *hamshira*? No? It's lovely. What gardens! And the grapes! Oh, the grapes. They bewitch the palate."

A few children had gathered by the door and were peeking in. Zaman gently shooed them away, in Pashto.

"Of course I love Herat too. City of artists and writers,

Sufis and mystics. You know the old joke, that you can't stretch a leg in Herat without poking a poet in the rear."

Next to Laila, Aziza snorted.

Zaman feigned a gasp. "Ah, there. I've made you laugh, little *hamshira*. That's usually the hard part. I was worried, there, for a while. I thought I'd have to cluck like a chicken or bray like a donkey. But, there you are. And so lovely you are."

He called in an attendant to look after Aziza for a few moments. Aziza leaped onto Mariam's lap and clung to her.

"We're just going to talk, my love," Laila said. "I'll be right here. All right? Right here."

"Why don't we go outside for a minute, Aziza jo?" Mariam said. "Your mother needs to talk to Kaka Zaman here. Just for a minute. Now, come on."

When they were alone, Zaman asked for Aziza's date of birth, history of illnesses, allergies. He asked about Aziza's father, and Laila had the strange experience of telling a lie that was really the truth. Zaman listened, his expression revealing neither belief nor skepticism. He ran the orphanage on the honor system, he said. If a *hamshira* said her husband was dead and she couldn't care for her children, he didn't question it.

Laila began to cry.

Zaman put down his pen.

"I'm ashamed," Laila croaked, her palm pressed to her mouth.

"Look at me, *hamshira*."

"What kind of mother abandons her own child?"

"Look at me."

Laila raised her gaze.

"It isn't your fault. Do you hear me? Not you. It's those *savages*, those *wahshis*, who are to blame. They bring shame on me as a Pashtun. They've disgraced the name of my people. And you're not alone, *hamshira*. We get mothers like you all the time—all the time—mothers who come here who can't feed their children because the Taliban won't let them go out and make a living. So you don't blame yourself. No one here blames you. I understand." He leaned forward. "*Hamshira*. I understand."

Laila wiped her eyes with the cloth of her burqa.

"As for this place," Zaman sighed, motioning with his hand, "you can see that it's in dire state. We're always underfunded, always scrambling, improvising. We get little or no support from the Taliban. But we manage. Like you, we do what we have to do. Allah is good and kind, and Allah provides, and, as long He provides, I will see to it that Aziza is fed and clothed. That much I promise you."

Laila nodded.

"All right?"

He was smiling companionably. "But don't cry, *hamshira*. Don't let her see you cry."

Laila wiped her eyes again. "God bless you," she said thickly. "God bless you, brother."

BUT WHEN THE time for good-byes came, the scene erupted precisely as Laila had dreaded.

Aziza panicked.

All the way home, leaning on Mariam, Laila heard Aziza's shrill cries. In her head, she saw Zaman's thick, calloused hands close around Aziza's arms; she saw them pull, gently at first, then harder, then with force to pry Aziza loose from her. She saw Aziza kicking in Zaman's arms as he hurriedly turned the corner, heard Aziza screaming as though she were about to vanish from the face of the earth. And Laila saw herself running down the hallway, head down, a howl rising up her throat.

"I smell her," she told Mariam at home. Her eyes swam unseeingly past Mariam's shoulder, past the yard, the walls, to the mountains, brown as smoker's spit. "I smell her sleep smell. Do you? Do you smell it?"

"Oh, Laila jo," said Mariam. "Don't. What good is this? What good?"

AT FIRST, Rasheed humored Laila, and accompanied them—her, Mariam, and Zalmai—to the orphanage, though he made sure, as they walked, that she had an eyeful of his grievous looks, an earful of his rants over what a hardship she was putting him through, how badly his legs and back and feet ached walking to and from the orphanage. He made sure she knew how awfully put out he was.

"I'm not a young man anymore," he said. "Not that you care. You'd run me to the ground, if you had your way. But you don't, Laila. You don't have your way."

They parted ways two blocks from the orphanage, and he never spared them more than fifteen minutes. "A minute late," he said, "and I start walking. I mean it."

Laila had to pester him, plead with him, in order to spin out the allotted minutes with Aziza a bit longer. For herself, and for Mariam, who was disconsolate over Aziza's absence, though, as always, Mariam chose to cradle her own suffering privately and quietly. And for Zalmai too, who asked for his sister every day, and threw tantrums that sometimes dissolved into inconsolable fits of crying.

Sometimes, on the way to the orphanage, Rasheed stopped and complained that his leg was sore. Then he turned around and started walking home in long, steady strides, without so much as a limp. Or he clucked his tongue and said, "It's my lungs, Laila. I'm short of breath. Maybe tomorrow I'll feel better, or the day after. We'll see." He never bothered to feign a single raspy breath. Often, as he turned back and marched home, he lit a cigarette. Laila would have to tail him home, helpless, trembling with resentment and impotent rage.

Then one day he told Laila he wouldn't take her anymore. "I'm too tired from walking the streets all day," he said, "looking for work."

"Then I'll go by myself," Laila said. "You can't stop me, Rasheed. Do you hear me? You can hit me all you want, but I'll keep going there."

"Do as you wish. But you won't get past the Taliban. Don't say I didn't warn you."

"I'm coming with you," Mariam said.

Laila wouldn't allow it. "You have to stay home with Zalmai. If we get stopped . . . I don't want him to see."

And so Laila's life suddenly revolved around finding ways to see Aziza. Half the time, she never made it to the orphanage. Crossing the street, she was spotted by the Taliban and riddled with questions—*What is your name? Where are you going? Why are you alone? Where is your* mahram?—before she was sent home. If she was lucky, she was given a tongue-lashing or a single kick to the rear, a shove in the back. Other times, she met with assortments of wooden clubs, fresh tree branches, short whips, slaps, often fists.

One day, a young Talib beat Laila with a radio antenna. When he was done, he gave a final whack to the back of her neck and said, "I see you again, I'll beat you until your mother's milk leaks out of your bones."

That time, Laila went home. She lay on her stomach, feeling like a stupid, pitiable animal, and hissed as Mariam arranged damp cloths across her bloodied back and thighs. But, usually, Laila refused to cave in. She made as if she were going home, then took a different route down side streets. Sometimes she was caught, questioned, scolded—two, three, even four times in a single day. Then the whips came down and the antennas sliced through the air, and she trudged home, bloodied, without so much as a glimpse of Aziza. Soon Laila took to wearing extra layers, even in the heat, two, three sweaters beneath the burqa, for padding against the beatings.

But for Laila, the reward, if she made it past the Taliban, was worth it. She could spend as much time as she liked then—*hours,* even—with Aziza. They sat in the courtyard, near the swing set, among other children and visiting mothers, and talked about what Aziza had learned that week.

Aziza said Kaka Zaman made it a point to teach them something every day, reading and writing most days, sometimes geography, a bit of history or science, something about plants, animals.

"But we have to pull the curtains," Aziza said, "so the Taliban don't see us." Kaka Zaman had knitting needles and balls of yarn ready, she said, in case of a Taliban inspection. "We put the books away and pretend to knit."

One day, during a visit with Aziza, Laila saw a middle-aged woman, her burqa pushed back, visiting with three boys and a girl. Laila recognized the sharp face, the heavy eyebrows, if not the sunken mouth and gray hair. She remembered the shawls, the black skirts, the curt voice, how she used to wear her jet-black hair tied in a bun so that you could see the dark bristles on the back of her neck. Laila remembered this woman once forbidding the female students from covering, saying women and men were equal, that there was no reason women should cover if men didn't.

At one point, Khala Rangmaal looked up and caught her gaze, but Laila saw no lingering, no light of recognition, in her old teacher's eyes.

"They're fractures along the earth's crust," said Aziza. "They're called faults."

It was a warm afternoon, a Friday, in June of 2001. They were sitting in the orphanage's back lot, the four of them,

Laila, Zalmai, Mariam, and Aziza. Rasheed had relented this time—as he infrequently did—and accompanied the four of them. He was waiting down the street, by the bus stop.

Barefoot kids scampered about around them. A flat soccer ball was kicked around, chased after listlessly.

"And, on either side of the faults, there are these sheets of rock that make up the earth's crust," Aziza was saying.

Someone had pulled the hair back from Aziza's face, braided it, and pinned it neatly on top of her head. Laila begrudged whoever had gotten to sit behind her daughter, to flip sections of her hair one over the other, had asked her to sit still.

Aziza was demonstrating by opening her hands, palms up, and rubbing them against each other. Zalmai watched this with intense interest.

"Kectonic plates, they're called?"

"*Tectonic,*" Laila said. It hurt to talk. Her jaw was still sore, her back and neck ached. Her lip was swollen, and her tongue kept poking the empty pocket of the lower incisor Rasheed had knocked loose two days before. Before Mammy and Babi had died and her life turned upside down, Laila never would have believed that a human body could withstand this much beating, this viciously, this regularly, and keep functioning.

"Right. And when they slide past each other, they catch and slip—see, Mammy?—and it releases energy, which travels to the earth's surface and makes it shake."

"You're getting so smart," Mariam said. "So much smarter than your dumb *khala.*"

Aziza's face glowed, broadened. "You're not dumb, Khala Mariam. And Kaka Zaman says that, sometimes, the shifting of rocks is deep, deep below, and it's powerful and scary down there, but all we feel on the surface is a slight tremor. Only a slight tremor."

The visit before this one, it was oxygen atoms in the atmosphere scattering the blue light from the sun. *If the earth had no atmosphere,* Aziza had said a little breathlessly, *the sky wouldn't be blue at all but a pitch-black sea and the sun a big bright star in the dark.*

"Is Aziza coming home with us this time?" Zalmai said.

"Soon, my love," Laila said. "Soon."

Laila watched him wander away, walking like his father, stooping forward, toes turned in. He walked to the swing set, pushed an empty seat, ended up sitting on the concrete, ripping weeds from a crack.

Water evaporates from the leaves—Mammy, did you know?—the way it does from laundry hanging from a line. And that drives the flow of water up the tree. From the ground and through the roots, then all the way up the tree trunk, through the branches and into the leaves. It's called transpiration.

More than once, Laila had wondered what the Taliban would do about Kaka Zaman's clandestine lessons if they found out.

During visits, Aziza didn't allow for much silence. She filled all the spaces with effusive speech, delivered in a high, ringing voice. She was tangential with her topics, and her hands gesticulated wildly, flying up with a nervousness that wasn't like her at all. She had a new laugh, Aziza did. Not so much a laugh, really, as nervous punctuation, meant, Laila suspected, to reassure.

And there were other changes. Laila would notice the dirt under Aziza's fingernails, and Aziza would notice her noticing and bury her hands under her thighs. Whenever a kid cried in their vicinity, snot oozing from his nose, or if a kid walked by bare-assed, hair clumped with dirt, Aziza's eyelids fluttered and she was quick to explain it away. She was like a hostess embarrassed in front of her guests by the squalor of her home, the untidiness of her children.

Questions of how she was coping were met with vague

but cheerful replies.

Doing fine, Khala. I'm fine.

Do kids pick on you?

They don't, Mammy. Everyone is nice.

Are you eating? Sleeping all right?

Eating. Sleeping too. Yes. We had lamb last night. Maybe it was last week.

When Aziza spoke like this, Laila saw more than a little of Mariam in her.

Aziza stammered now. Mariam noticed it first. It was subtle but perceptible, and more pronounced with words that began with *t*. Laila asked Zaman about it. He frowned and said, "I thought she'd always done that."

They left the orphanage with Aziza that Friday afternoon for a short outing and met Rasheed, who was waiting for them by the bus stop. When Zalmai spotted his father, he uttered an excited squeak and impatiently wriggled from Laila's arms. Aziza's greeting to Rasheed was rigid but not hostile.

Rasheed said they should hurry, he had only two hours before he had to report back to work. This was his first week as a doorman for the Intercontinental. From noon to eight, six days a week, Rasheed opened car doors, carried luggage, mopped up the occasional spill. Sometimes, at day's end, the cook at the buffet-style restaurant let Rasheed bring home a few leftovers—as long as he was discreet about it—cold meatballs sloshing in oil; fried chicken wings, the crust gone hard and dry; stuffed pasta shells turned chewy; stiff, gravelly rice. Rasheed had promised Laila that once he had some money saved up, Aziza could move back home.

Rasheed was wearing his uniform, a burgundy red polyester suit, white shirt, clip-on tie, visor cap pressing down on his white hair. In this uniform, Rasheed was transformed. He looked vulnerable, pitiably bewildered, almost harmless. Like someone who had accepted without a sigh of protest the indignities life had doled out to him. Someone both pathetic and admirable in his docility.

They rode the bus to Titanic City. They walked into the riverbed, flanked on either side by makeshift stalls clinging to the dry banks. Near the bridge, as they were descending the steps, a barefoot man dangled dead from a crane, his ears cut off, his neck bent at the end of a rope. In the river, they melted into the horde of shoppers milling about, the money changers and bored-looking NGO workers, the cigarette vendors, the covered women who thrust fake antibiotic prescriptions at people and begged for money to fill them. Whip-toting, *naswar*-chewing Talibs patrolled Titanic City on the lookout for the indiscreet laugh, the unveiled face.

From a toy kiosk, between a *poosteen* coat vendor and a fake-flower stand, Zalmai picked out a rubber basketball with yellow and blue swirls.

"Pick something," Rasheed said to Aziza.

Aziza hedged, stiffened with embarrassment.

"Hurry. I have to be at work in an hour."

Aziza chose a gum-ball machine—the same coin could be inserted to get candy, then retrieved from the flap-door coin return below.

Rasheed's eyebrows shot up when the seller quoted him the price. A round of haggling ensued, at the end of which Rasheed said to Aziza contentiously, as if it were *she* who'd haggled him, "Give it back. I can't afford both."

On the way back, Aziza's high-spirited façade waned the closer they got to the orphanage. The hands stopped flying up. Her face turned heavy. It happened every time. It was Laila's turn now, with Mariam pitching in, to take up the chattering, to laugh nervously, to fill the melancholy quiet with breathless, aimless banter.

Later, after Rasheed had dropped them off and taken a

bus to work, Laila watched Aziza wave good-bye and scuff along the wall in the orphanage back lot. She thought of Aziza's stutter, and of what Aziza had said earlier about fractures and powerful collisions deep down and how sometimes all we see on the surface is a slight tremor.

"GET AWAY, YOU!" Zalmai cried.

"Hush," Mariam said. "Who are you yelling at?"

He pointed. "There. That man."

Laila followed his finger. There *was* a man at the front door of the house, leaning against it. His head turned when he saw them approaching. He uncrossed his arms. Limped a few steps toward them.

Laila stopped.

A choking noise came up her throat. Her knees weakened. Laila suddenly wanted, *needed,* to grope for Mariam's arm, her shoulder, her wrist, something, anything, to lean on. But she didn't. She didn't dare. She didn't dare move a muscle. She didn't dare breathe, or blink even, for fear that he was nothing but a mirage shimmering in the distance, a brittle illusion that would vanish at the slightest provocation. Laila stood perfectly still and looked at Tariq until her chest screamed for air and her eyes burned to blink. And, somehow, miraculously, after she took a breath, closed and opened her eyes, he was still standing there. Tariq was still standing there.

Laila allowed herself to take a step toward him. Then another. And another. And then she was running.

43.

Mariam

Upstairs, in Mariam's room, Zalmai was wound up. He bounced his new rubber basketball around for a while, on the floor, against the walls. Mariam asked him not to, but he knew that she had no authority to exert over him and so he went on bouncing his ball, his eyes holding hers defiantly. For a while, they pushed his toy car, an ambulance with bold red lettering on the sides, sending it back and forth between them across the room.

Earlier, when they had met Tariq at the door, Zalmai had clutched the basketball close to his chest and stuck a thumb in his mouth—something he didn't do anymore except when he was apprehensive. He had eyed Tariq with suspicion.

"Who is that man?" he said now. "I don't like him."

Mariam was going to explain, say something about him and Laila growing up together, but Zalmai cut her off and said to turn the ambulance around, so the front grille faced him, and, when she did, he said he wanted his basketball again.

"Where is it?" he said. "Where is the ball Baba jan got me? Where is it? I want it! I want it!" his voice rising and becoming more shrill with each word.

"It was just here," Mariam said, and he cried, "No, it's lost, I know it. I just know it's lost! Where is it? Where is it?"

"Here," she said, fetching the ball from the closet where it had rolled to. But Zalmai was bawling now and pounding his fists, crying that it wasn't the same ball, it couldn't be, because his ball was lost, and this was a fake one, where had his real ball gone? Where? Where where where?

He screamed until Laila had to come upstairs to hold him, to rock him and run her fingers through his tight, dark curls, to dry his moist cheeks and cluck her tongue in his ear.

Mariam waited outside the room. From atop the staircase, all she could see of Tariq were his long legs, the real one and the artificial one, in khaki pants, stretched out on the uncarpeted living-room floor. It was then that she realized why the doorman at the Continental had looked familiar the day she and Rasheed had gone there to place the call to Jalil. He'd been wearing a cap and sunglasses, that was why it hadn't come to her earlier. But Mariam remembered now, from nine years before, remembered him sitting downstairs, patting his brow with a handkerchief and asking for water. Now all manner of questions raced through her mind: Had the sulfa pills too been part of the ruse? Which one of them had plotted the lie, provided the convincing details? And how much had Rasheed paid Abdul Sharif—if that was even his name—to come and crush Laila with the story of Tariq's death?

44.

Laila

Tariq said that one of the men who shared his cell had a cousin who'd been publicly flogged once for painting flamingos. He, the cousin, had a seemingly incurable thing for them.

"Entire sketchbooks," Tariq said. "Dozens of oil paintings of them, wading in lagoons, sunbathing in marshlands. Flying into sunsets too, I'm afraid."

"Flamingos," Laila said. She looked at him sitting against the wall, his good leg bent at the knee. She had an urge to touch him again, as she had earlier by the front gate when she'd run to him. It embarrassed her now to think of how she'd thrown her arms around his neck and wept into his chest, how she'd said his name over and over in a slurring, thick voice. Had she acted too eagerly, she wondered, too desperately? Maybe so. But she hadn't been able to help it. And now she longed to touch him again, to prove to herself again that he was really here, that he was not a dream, an apparition.

"Indeed," he said. "Flamingos."

When the Taliban had found the paintings, Tariq said, they'd taken offense at the birds' long, bare legs. After they'd tied the cousin's feet and flogged his soles bloody, they had presented him with a choice: Either destroy the paintings or make the flamingos decent. So the cousin had picked up his brush and painted trousers on every last bird.

"And there you have it. Islamic flamingos," Tariq said.

Laughter came up, but Laila pushed it back down. She was ashamed of her yellowing teeth, the missing incisor. Ashamed of her withered looks and swollen lip. She wished she'd had the chance to wash her face, at least comb her hair.

"But he'll have the last laugh, the cousin," Tariq said. "He painted those trousers with watercolor. When the Taliban are gone, he'll just wash them off." He smiled— Laila noticed that he had a missing tooth of his own—and looked down at his hands. "Indeed."

He was wearing a *pakol* on his head, hiking boots, and a black wool sweater tucked into the waist of khaki pants. He was half smiling, nodding slowly. Laila didn't remember him saying this before, this word *indeed,* and this pensive gesture, the fingers making a tent in his lap, the nodding, it was new too. Such an adult word, such an adult gesture, and why should it be so startling? He *was* an adult now, Tariq, a twenty-five-year-old man with slow movements and a tiredness to his smile. Tall, bearded, slimmer than in her dreams of him, but with strong-looking hands, workman's hands, with tortuous, full veins. His face was still lean and handsome but not fair-skinned any longer; his brow had a weathered look to it, sunburned, like his neck, the brow of a traveler at the end of a long and wearying journey. His *pakol* was pushed back on his head, and she could see that he'd started to lose his hair. The hazel of his eyes was

323

duller than she remembered, paler, or perhaps it was merely the light in the room.

Laila thought of Tariq's mother, her unhurried manners, the clever smiles, the dull purple wig. And his father, with his squinty gaze, his wry humor. Earlier, at the door, with a voice full of tears, tripping over her own words, she'd told Tariq what she thought had happened to him and his parents, and he had shaken his head. So now she asked him how they were doing, his parents. But she regretted the question when Tariq looked down and said, a bit distractedly, "Passed on."

"I'm so sorry."

"Well. Yes. Me too. Here." He fished a small paper bag from his pocket and passed it to her. "Compliments of Alyona." Inside was a block of cheese in plastic wrap.

"Alyona. It's a pretty name." Laila tried to say this next without wavering. "Your wife?"

"My goat." He was smiling at her expectantly, as though waiting for her to retrieve a memory.

Then Laila remembered. The Soviet film. Alyona had been the captain's daughter, the girl in love with the first mate. That was the day that she, Tariq, and Hasina had watched Soviet tanks and jeeps leave Kabul, the day Tariq had worn that ridiculous Russian fur hat.

"I had to tie her to a stake in the ground," Tariq was saying. "And build a fence. Because of the wolves. In the foothills where I live, there's a wooded area nearby, maybe a quarter of a mile away, pine trees mostly, some fir, deodars. They mostly stick to the woods, the wolves do, but a bleating goat, one that likes to go wandering, that can draw them out. So the fence. The stake."

Laila asked him which foothills.

"Pir Panjal. Pakistan," he said. "Where I live is called Murree; it's a summer retreat, an hour from Islamabad. It's hilly and green, lots of trees, high above sea level. So it's cool in the summer. Perfect for tourists."

The British had built it as a hill station near their military headquarters in Rawalpindi, he said, for the Victorians to escape the heat. You could still spot a few relics of the colonial times, Tariq said, the occasional tea-room, tin-roofed bungalows, called cottages, that sort of thing. The town itself was small and pleasant. The main street was called the Mall, where there was a post office, a bazaar, a few restaurants, shops that overcharged tourists for painted glass and hand-knotted carpets. Curiously, the Mall's one-way traffic flowed in one direction one week, the opposite direction the next week.

"The locals say that Ireland's traffic is like that too in places," Tariq said. "I wouldn't know. Anyway, it's nice. It's a plain life, but I like it. I like living there."

"With your goat. With Alyona."

Laila meant this less as a joke than as a surreptitious entry into another line of talk, such as who else was there with him worrying about wolves eating goats. But Tariq only went on nodding.

"I'm sorry about your parents too," he said.

"You heard."

"I spoke to some neighbors earlier," he said. A pause, during which Laila wondered what else the neighbors had told him. "I don't recognize anybody. From the old days, I mean."

"They're all gone. There's no one left you'd know."

"I don't recognize Kabul."

"Neither do I," Laila said. "And I never left."

"MAMMY HAS A new friend," Zalmai said after dinner later that same night, after Tariq had left. "A man."

Rasheed looked up. "*Does* she, now?"

*   *   *

325

Tariq asked if he could smoke.

They had stayed awhile at the Nasir Bagh refugee camp near Peshawar, Tariq said, tapping ash into a saucer. There were sixty thousand Afghans living there already when he and his parents arrived.

"It wasn't as bad as some of the other camps like, God forbid, Jalozai," he said. "I guess at one point it was even some kind of model camp, back during the Cold War, a place the West could point to and prove to the world they weren't just funneling arms into Afghanistan."

But that had been during the Soviet war, Tariq said, the days of jihad and worldwide interest and generous funding and visits from Margaret Thatcher.

"You know the rest, Laila. After the war, the Soviets fell apart, and the West moved on. There was nothing at stake for them in Afghanistan anymore and the money dried up. Now Nasir Bagh is tents, dust, and open sewers. When we got there, they handed us a stick and a sheet of canvas and told us to build ourselves a tent."

Tariq said what he remembered most about Nasir Bagh, where they had stayed for a year, was the color brown. "Brown tents. Brown people. Brown dogs. Brown porridge."

There was a leafless tree he climbed every day, where he straddled a branch and watched the refugees lying about in the sun, their sores and stumps in plain view. He watched little emaciated boys carrying water in their jerry cans, gathering dog droppings to make fire, carving toy AK-47s out of wood with dull knives, lugging the sacks of wheat flour that no one could make bread from that held together. All around the refugee town, the wind made the tents flap. It hurled stubbles of weed everywhere, lifted kites flown from the roofs of mud hovels.

"A lot of kids died. Dysentery, TB, hunger—you name it. Mostly, that damn dysentery. God, Laila. I saw so many kids buried. There's nothing worse a person can see."

He crossed his legs. It grew quiet again between them for a while.

"My father didn't survive that first winter," he said. "He died in his sleep. I don't think there was any pain."

That same winter, he said, his mother caught pneumonia and almost died, would have died, if not for a camp doctor who worked out of a station wagon made into a mobile clinic. She would wake up all night long, feverish, coughing out thick, rust-colored phlegm. The queues were long to see the doctor, Tariq said. Everyone was shivering in line, moaning, coughing, some with shit running down their legs, others too tired or hungry or sick to make words.

"But he was a decent man, the doctor. He treated my mother, gave her some pills, saved her life that winter."

That same winter, Tariq had cornered a kid.

"Twelve, maybe thirteen years old," he said evenly. "I held a shard of glass to his throat and took his blanket from him. I gave it to my mother."

He made a vow to himself, Tariq said, after his mother's illness, that they would not spend another winter in camp. He'd work, save, move them to an apartment in Peshawar with heating and clean water. When spring came, he looked for work. From time to time, a truck came to camp early in the morning and rounded up a couple of dozen boys, took them to a field to move stones or an orchard to pick apples in exchange for a little money, sometimes a blanket, a pair of shoes. But they never wanted him, Tariq said.

"One look at my leg and it was over."

There were other jobs. Ditches to dig, hovels to build, water to carry, feces to shovel from outhouses. But young men fought over these jobs, and Tariq never stood a chance.

Then he met a shopkeeper one day, that fall of 1993.

"He offered me money to take a leather coat to Lahore.

Not a lot but enough, enough for one or maybe two months' apartment rent."

The shopkeeper gave him a bus ticket, Tariq said, and the address of a street corner near the Lahore Rail Station where he was to deliver the coat to a friend of the shop-keeper's.

"I knew already. Of course I knew," Tariq said. "He said that if I got caught, I was on my own, that I should remember that he knew where my mother lived. But the money was too good to pass up. And winter was coming again."

"How far did you get?" Laila asked.

"Not far," he said and laughed, sounding apologetic, ashamed. "Never even got on the bus. But I thought I was immune, you know, safe. As though there was some accountant up there somewhere, a guy with a pencil tucked behind his ear who kept track of these things, who tallied things up, and he'd look down and say, 'Yes, yes, he can have this, we'll let it go. He's paid some dues already, this one.' "

It was in the seams, the hashish, and it spilled all over the street when the police took a knife to the coat.

Tariq laughed again when he said this, a climbing, shaky kind of laugh, and Laila remembered how he used to laugh like this when they were little, to cloak embarrass-ment, to make light of things he'd done that were fool-hardy or scandalous.

"HE HAS A LIMP," Zalmai said.

"Is this who I *think* it is?"

"He was only visiting," Mariam said.

"Shut up, you," Rasheed snapped, raising a finger. He turned back to Laila. "Well, what do you know? Laili and Majnoon reunited. Just like old times." His face turned stony. "So you let him in. Here. In my house. You let him in. He was in here with my son."

"You duped me. You lied to me," Laila said, gritting her teeth. "You had that man sit across from me and . . . You knew I would leave if I thought he was alive."

"AND YOU DIDN'T LIE TO ME?" Rasheed roared. "You think I didn't figure it out? About your *harami*? You take me for a fool, you whore?"

THE MORE TARIQ TALKED, the more Laila dreaded the moment when he would stop. The silence that would follow, the signal that it was her turn to give account, to provide the why and how and when, to make official what he surely already knew. She felt a faint nausea whenever he paused. She averted his eyes. She looked down at his hands, at the coarse, dark hairs that had sprouted on the back of them in the intervening years.

Tariq wouldn't say much about his years in prison save that he'd learned to speak Urdu there. When Laila asked, he gave an impatient shake of his head. In this gesture, Laila saw rusty bars and unwashed bodies, violent men and crowded halls, and ceilings rotting with moldy deposits. She read in his face that it had been a place of abasement, of degradation and despair.

Tariq said his mother tried to visit him after his arrest.

"Three times she came. But I never got to see her," he said.

He wrote her a letter, and a few more after that, even though he doubted that she would receive them.

"And I wrote you."

"You did?"

"Oh, *volumes*," he said. "Your friend Rumi would have envied my production." Then he laughed again, uproariously this time, as though he was both startled at his own boldness and embarrassed by what he had let on.

Zalmai began bawling upstairs.

*   *   *

"Just like old times, then," Rasheed said. "The two of you. I suppose you let him see your face."

"She did," said Zalmai. Then, to Laila, "You did, Mammy. I saw you."

"Your son doesn't care for me much," Tariq said when Laila returned downstairs.

"I'm sorry," she said. "It's not that. He just . . . Don't mind him." Then quickly she changed the subject because it made her feel perverse and guilty to feel that about Zalmai, who was a child, a little boy who loved his father, whose instinctive aversion to this stranger was understandable and legitimate.

And I wrote you.

Volumes.

Volumes.

"How long have you been in Murree?"

"Less than a year," Tariq said.

He befriended an older man in prison, he said, a fellow named Salim, a Pakistani, a former field hockey player who had been in and out of prison for years and who was serving ten years for stabbing an undercover policeman. Every prison has a man like Salim, Tariq said. There was always someone who was cunning and connected, who worked the system and found you things, someone around whom the air buzzed with both opportunity and danger. It was Salim who had sent out Tariq's queries about his mother, Salim who had sat him down and told him, in a soft, fatherly voice, that she had died of exposure.

Tariq spent seven years in the Pakistani prison. "I got off easy," he said. "I was lucky. The judge sitting on my case, it turned out, had a brother who'd married an Afghan woman. Maybe he showed mercy. I don't know."

When Tariq's sentence was up, early in the winter of

330

2000, Salim gave him his brother's address and phone number. The brother's name was Sayeed.

"He said Sayeed owned a small hotel in Murree," Tariq said. "Twenty rooms and a lounge, a little place to cater to tourists. He said tell him I sent you."

Tariq had liked Murree as soon as he'd stepped off the bus: the snow-laden pines; the cold, crisp air; the shuttered wooden cottages, smoke curling up from chimneys.

Here was a place, Tariq had thought, knocking on Sayeed's door, a place not only worlds removed from the wretchedness he'd known but one that made even the notion of hardship and sorrow somehow obscene, unimaginable.

"I said to myself, here is a place where a man can get on."

Tariq was hired as a janitor and handyman. He did well, he said, during the one-month trial period, at half pay, that Sayeed granted him. As Tariq spoke, Laila saw Sayeed, whom she imagined narrow-eyed and ruddy-faced, standing at the reception office window watching Tariq chop wood and shovel snow off the driveway. She saw him stooping over Tariq's legs, observing, as Tariq lay beneath the sink fixing a leaky pipe. She pictured him checking the register for missing cash.

Tariq's shack was beside the cook's little bungalow, he said. The cook was a matronly old widow named Adiba. Both shacks were detached from the hotel itself, separated from the main building by a scattering of almond trees, a park bench, and a pyramid-shaped stone fountain that, in the summer, gurgled water all day. Laila pictured Tariq in his shack, sitting up in bed, watching the leafy world outside his window.

At the end of the grace period, Sayeed raised Tariq's pay to full, told him his lunches were free, gave him a wool coat, and fitted him for a new leg. Tariq said he'd wept at the man's kindness.

With his first month's full salary in his pocket, Tariq had gone to town and bought Alyona.

"Her fur is perfectly white," Tariq said, smiling. "Some mornings, when it's snowed all night, you look out the window and all you see of her is two eyes and a muzzle."

Laila nodded. Another silence ensued. Upstairs, Zalmai had begun bouncing his ball again against the wall.

"I thought you were dead," Laila said.

"I know. You told me."

Laila's voice broke. She had to clear her throat, collect herself. "The man who came to give the news, he was so earnest . . . I believed him, Tariq. I wish I hadn't, but I did. And then I felt so alone and scared. Otherwise, I wouldn't have agreed to marry Rasheed. I wouldn't have . . ."

"You don't have to do this," he said softly, avoiding her eyes. There was no hidden reproach, no recrimination, in the way he had said this. No suggestion of blame.

"But I do. Because there was a bigger reason why I married him. There's something you don't know, Tariq. *Someone.* I have to tell you."

"Did you sit and talk with him too?" Rasheed asked Zalmai.

Zalmai said nothing. Laila saw hesitation and uncertainty in his eyes now, as if he had just realized that what he'd disclosed had turned out to be far bigger than he'd thought.

"I asked you a question, boy."

Zalmai swallowed. His gaze kept shifting. "I was upstairs, playing with Mariam."

"And your mother?"

Zalmai looked at Laila apologetically, on the verge of tears.

"It's all right, Zalmai," Laila said. "Tell the truth."

"She was . . . She was downstairs, talking to that man," he said in a thin voice hardly louder than a whisper.

"I see," said Rasheed. "Teamwork."

As he was leaving, Tariq said, "I want to meet her. I want to see her."

"I'll arrange it," Laila said.

"Aziza. Aziza." He smiled, tasting the word. Whenever Rasheed uttered her daughter's name, it came out sounding unwholesome to Laila, almost vulgar. "Aziza. It's lovely."

"So is she. You'll see."

"I'll count the minutes."

Almost ten years had passed since they had last seen each other. Laila's mind flashed to all the times they'd met in the alley, kissing in secret. She wondered how she must seem to him now. Did he still find her pretty? Or did she seem withered to him, reduced, pitiable, like a fearful, shuffling old woman? Almost ten years. But, for a moment, standing there with Tariq in the sunlight, it was as though those years had never happened. Her parents' deaths, her marriage to Rasheed, the killings, the rockets, the Taliban, the beatings, the hunger, even her children, all of it seemed like a dream, a bizarre detour, a mere interlude between that last afternoon together and this moment.

Then Tariq's face changed, turned grave. She knew this expression. It was the same look he'd had on his face that day, all those years ago when they'd both been children, when he'd unstrapped his leg and gone after Khadim. He reached with one hand now and touched the corner of her lower lip.

"He did this to you," he said coldly.

At his touch, Laila remembered the frenzy of that afternoon again when they'd conceived Aziza. His breath on her neck, the muscles of his hips flexing, his chest pressing against her breasts, their hands interlocked.

"I wish I'd taken you with me," Tariq nearly whispered.

Laila had to lower her gaze, try not to cry.

"I know you're a married woman and a mother now. And here I am, after all these years, after all that's happened, showing up at your doorstep. Probably, it isn't proper, or fair, but I've come such a long way to see you, and . . . Oh, Laila, I wish I'd never left you."

"Don't," she croaked.

"I should have tried harder. I should have married you when I had the chance. Everything would have been different, then."

"Don't talk this way. Please. It hurts."

He nodded, started to take a step toward her, then stopped himself. "I don't want to assume anything. And I don't mean to turn your life upside down, appearing like this out of nowhere. If you want me to leave, if you want me to go back to Pakistan, say the word, Laila. I mean it. Say it and I'll go. I'll never trouble you again. I'll—"

"No!" Laila said more sharply than she'd intended to. She saw that she'd reached for his arm, that she was clutching it. She dropped her hand. "No. Don't leave, Tariq. No. Please stay."

Tariq nodded.

"He works from noon to eight. Come back tomorrow afternoon. I'll take you to Aziza."

"I'm not afraid of him, you know."

"I know. Come back tomorrow afternoon."

"And then?"

"And then . . . I don't know. I have to think. This is . . ."

"I know it is," he said. "I understand. I'm sorry. I'm sorry for a lot of things."

"Don't be. You promised you'd come back. And you did."

His eyes watered. "It's good to see you, Laila."

She watched him walk away, shivering where she stood. She thought, *Volumes,* and another shudder passed through her, a current of something sad and forlorn, but also something eager and recklessly hopeful.

45.

Mariam

I was upstairs, playing with Mariam," Zalmai said.

"And your mother?"

"She was . . . She was downstairs, talking to that man."

"I see," said Rasheed. "Teamwork."

Mariam watched his face relax, loosen. She watched the folds clear from his brow. Suspicion and misgiving winked out of his eyes. He sat up straight, and, for a few brief moments, he appeared merely thoughtful, like a ship captain informed of imminent mutiny taking his time to ponder his next move.

He looked up.

Mariam began to say something, but he raised a hand, and, without looking at her, said, "It's too late, Mariam."

To Zalmai he said coldly, "You're going upstairs, boy."

On Zalmai's face, Mariam saw alarm. Nervously, he looked around at the three of them. He sensed now that his tattletale game had let something serious—adult serious—into the room. He cast a despondent, contrite glance toward Mariam, then his mother.

In a challenging voice, Rasheed said, *"Now!"*

He took Zalmai by the elbow. Zalmai meekly let himself be led upstairs.

They stood frozen, Mariam and Laila, eyes to the ground, as though looking at each other would give credence to the way Rasheed saw things, that while he was opening doors and lugging baggage for people who wouldn't spare him a glance a lewd conspiracy was shaping behind his back, in his home, in his beloved son's presence. Neither one of them said a word. They listened to the footsteps in the hallway above, one heavy and foreboding, the other the pattering of a skittish little animal. They listened to muted words passed, a squeaky plea, a curt retort, a door shut, the rattle of a key as it turned. Then one set of footsteps returning, more impatiently now.

Mariam saw his feet pounding the steps as he came down. She saw him pocketing the key, saw his belt, the perforated end wrapped tightly around his knuckles. The fake brass buckle dragged behind him, bouncing on the steps.

She went to stop him, but he shoved her back and blew by her. Without saying a word, he swung the belt at Laila. He did it with such speed that she had no time to retreat or duck, or even raise a protective arm. Laila touched her fingers to her temple, looked at the blood, looked at Rasheed, with astonishment. It lasted only a moment or two, this look of disbelief, before it was replaced by something hateful.

Rasheed swung the belt again.

This time, Laila shielded herself with a forearm and made a grab at the belt. She missed, and Rasheed brought the belt down again. Laila caught it briefly before Rasheed yanked it free and lashed at her again. Then Laila was dashing around the room, and Mariam was screaming words that ran together and imploring Rasheed, as he

337

chased Laila, as he blocked her way and cracked his belt at her. At one point, Laila ducked and managed to land a punch across his ear, which made him spit a curse and pursue her even more relentlessly. He caught her, threw her up against the wall, and struck her with the belt again and again, the buckle slamming against her chest, her shoulder, her raised arms, her fingers, drawing blood wherever it struck.

Mariam lost count of how many times the belt cracked, how many pleading words she cried out to Rasheed, how many times she circled around the incoherent tangle of teeth and fists and belt, before she saw fingers clawing at Rasheed's face, chipped nails digging into his jowls and pulling at his hair and scratching his forehead. How long before she realized, with both shock and relish, that the fingers were hers.

He let go of Laila and turned on her. At first, he looked at her without seeing her, then his eyes narrowed, appraised Mariam with interest. The look in them shifted from puzzlement to shock, then disapproval, disappointment even, lingering there a moment.

Mariam remembered the first time she had seen his eyes, under the wedding veil, in the mirror, with Jalil looking on, how their gazes had slid across the glass and met, his indifferent, hers docile, conceding, almost apologetic.

Apologetic.

Mariam saw now in those same eyes what a fool she had been.

Had she been a deceitful wife? she asked herself. A complacent wife? A dishonorable woman? Discreditable? Vulgar? What harmful thing had she willfully done to this man to warrant his malice, his continual assaults, the relish with which he tormented her? Had she not looked after him when he was ill? Fed him, and his friends, cleaned up after him dutifully?

Had she not given this man her youth?

Had she ever justly deserved his meanness?

The belt made a thump when Rasheed dropped it to the ground and came for her. Some jobs, that *thump* said, were meant to be done with bare hands.

But just as he was bearing down on her, Mariam saw Laila behind him pick something up from the ground. She watched Laila's hand rise overhead, hold, then come swooping down against the side of his face. Glass shattered. The jagged remains of the drinking glass rained down to the ground. There was blood on Laila's hands, blood flowing from the open gash on Rasheed's cheek, blood down his neck, on his shirt. He turned around, all snarling teeth and blazing eyes.

They crashed to the ground, Rasheed and Laila, thrashing about. He ended up on top, his hands already wrapped around Laila's neck.

Mariam clawed at him. She beat at his chest. She hurled herself against him. She struggled to uncurl his fingers from Laila's neck. She bit them. But they remained tightly clamped around Laila's windpipe, and Mariam saw that he meant to carry this through.

He meant to suffocate her, and there was nothing either of them could do about it.

Mariam backed away and left the room. She was aware of a thumping sound from upstairs, aware that tiny palms were slapping against a locked door. She ran down the hallway. She burst through the front door. Crossed the yard.

In the toolshed, Mariam grabbed the shovel.

Rasheed didn't notice her coming back into the room. He was still on top of Laila, his eyes wide and crazy, his hands wrapped around her neck. Laila's face was turning blue now, and her eyes had rolled back. Mariam saw that she was no longer struggling. *He's going to kill her,* she thought. *He really means to.* And Mariam could not, would not, allow that to happen. He'd taken so much from her in twenty-seven years of marriage. She would not watch him take Laila too.

Mariam steadied her feet and tightened her grip around the shovel's handle. She raised it. She said his name. She wanted him to see.

"Rasheed."

He looked up.

Mariam swung.

She hit him across the temple. The blow knocked him off Laila.

Rasheed touched his head with the palm of his hand. He looked at the blood on his fingertips, then at Mariam. She thought she saw his face soften. She imagined that something had passed between them, that maybe she had quite literally knocked some understanding into his head. Maybe he saw something in her face too, Mariam thought, something that made him hedge. Maybe he saw some trace of all the self-denial, all the sacrifice, all the sheer exertion it had taken her to live with him for all these years, live with his continual condescension and violence, his faultfinding and meanness. Was that respect she saw in his eyes? Regret?

But then his upper lip curled back into a spiteful sneer, and Mariam knew then the futility, maybe even the irresponsibility, of not finishing this. If she let him walk now, how long before he fetched the key from his pocket and went for that gun of his upstairs in the room where he'd locked Zalmai? Had Mariam been certain that he would be satisfied with shooting only her, that there was a chance he would spare Laila, she might have dropped the shovel. But in Rasheed's eyes she saw murder for them both.

And so Mariam raised the shovel high, raised it as high as she could, arching it so it touched the small of her back.

340

She turned it so the sharp edge was vertical, and, as she did, it occurred to her that this was the first time that *she* was deciding the course of her own life.

And, with that, Mariam brought down the shovel. This time, she gave it everything she had.

46.

Laila

Laila was aware of the face over her, all teeth and tobacco and foreboding eyes. She was dimly aware, too, of Mariam, a presence beyond the face, of her fists raining down. Above them was the ceiling, and it was the ceiling Laila was drawn to, the dark markings of mold spreading across it like ink on a dress, the crack in the plaster that was a stolid smile or a frown, depending on which end of the room you looked at it from. Laila thought of all the times she had tied a rag around the end of a broom and cleaned cobwebs from this ceiling. The three times she and Mariam had put coats of white paint on it. The crack wasn't a smile any longer now but a mocking leer. And it was receding. The ceiling was shrinking, lifting, rising away from her and toward some hazy dimness beyond. It rose until it shrank to the size of a postage stamp, white and bright, everything around it blotted out by the shuttered darkness. In the dark, Rasheed's face was like a sunspot.

Brief little bursts of blinding light before her eyes now, like silver stars exploding. Bizarre geometric forms in the light, worms, egg-shaped things, moving up and down, sideways, melting into each other, breaking apart, morphing into something else, then fading, giving way to blackness.

Voices muffled and distant.

Behind the lids of her eyes, her children's faces flared and fizzled. Aziza, alert and burdened, knowing, secretive. Zalmai, looking up at his father with quivering eagerness.

It would end like this, then, Laila thought. What a pitiable end.

But then the darkness began to lift. She had a sensation of rising up, of being hoisted up. The ceiling slowly came back, expanded, and now Laila could make out the crack again, and it was the same old dull smile.

She was being shaken. *Are you all right? Answer me, are you all right?* Mariam's face, engraved with scratches, heavy with worry, hovered over Laila.

Laila tried a breath. It burned her throat. She tried another. It burned even more this time, and not just her throat but her chest too. And then she was coughing, and wheezing. Gasping. But breathing. Her good ear rang.

THE FIRST THING she saw when she sat up was Rasheed. He was lying on his back, staring at nothing with an unblinking, fish-mouthed expression. A bit of foam, lightly pink, had dribbled from his mouth down his cheek. The front of his pants was wet. She saw his forehead.

Then she saw the shovel.

A groan came out of her. "Oh," she said, tremulously, barely able to make a voice, "Oh, Mariam."

LAILA PACED, moaning and banging her hands together, as Mariam sat near Rasheed, her hands in her lap, calm and motionless. Mariam didn't say anything for a long time.

Laila's mouth was dry, and she was stammering her words, trembling all over. She willed herself not to look at Rasheed, at the rictus of his mouth, his open eyes, at the blood congealing in the hollow of his collarbone.

Outside, the light was fading, the shadows deepening. Mariam's face looked thin and drawn in this light, but she did not appear agitated or frightened, merely preoccupied, thoughtful, so self-possessed that when a fly landed on her chin she paid it no attention. She just sat there with her bottom lip stuck out, the way she did when she was absorbed in thought.

At last, she said, "Sit down, Laila jo."

Laila did, obediently.

"We have to move him. Zalmai can't see this."

Mariam fished the bedroom key from Rasheed's pocket before they wrapped him in a bedsheet. Laila took him by the legs, behind the knees, and Mariam grabbed him under the arms. They tried lifting him, but he was too heavy, and they ended up dragging him. As they were passing through the front door and into the yard, Rasheed's foot caught against the doorframe and his leg bent sideways. They had to back up and try again, and then something thumped upstairs and Laila's legs gave out. She dropped Rasheed. She slumped to the ground, sobbing and shaking, and Mariam had to stand over her, hands on hips, and say that she had to get herself together. That what was done was done.

After a time, Laila got up and wiped her face, and they carried Rasheed to the yard without further incident. They took him into the toolshed. They left him behind the workbench, on which sat his saw, some nails, a chisel, a hammer, and a cylindrical block of wood that Rasheed had

344

been meaning to carve into something for Zalmai but had never gotten around to doing.

Then they went back inside. Mariam washed her hands, ran them through her hair, took a deep breath and let it out. "Let me tend to your wounds now. You're all cut up, Laila jo."

MARIAM SAID SHE needed the night to think things over. To get her thoughts together and devise a plan.

"There is a way," she said, "and I just have to find it."

"We have to leave! We can't stay here," Laila said in a broken, husky voice. She thought suddenly of the sound the shovel must have made striking Rasheed's head, and her body pitched forward. Bile surged up her chest.

Mariam waited patiently until Laila felt better. Then she had Laila lie down, and, as she stroked Laila's hair in her lap, Mariam said not to worry, that everything would be fine. She said that they would leave—she, Laila, the children, and Tariq too. They would leave this house, and this unforgiving city. They would leave this despondent country altogether, Mariam said, running her hands through Laila's hair, and go someplace remote and safe where no one would find them, where they could disown their past and find shelter.

"Somewhere with trees," she said. "Yes. Lots of trees."

They would live in a small house on the edge of some town they'd never heard of, Mariam said, or in a remote village where the road was narrow and unpaved but lined with all manner of plants and shrubs. Maybe there would be a path to take, a path that led to a grass field where the children could play, or maybe a graveled road that would take them to a clear blue lake where trout swam and reeds poked through the surface. They would raise sheep and chickens, and they would make bread together and teach the children to read. They would make new lives for themselves—peaceful, solitary lives—and there the weight of all that they'd endured would lift from them, and they would be deserving of all the happiness and simple prosperity they would find.

Laila murmured encouragingly. It would be an existence rife with difficulties, she saw, but of a pleasurable kind, difficulties they could take pride in, possess, value, as one would a family heirloom. Mariam's soft maternal voice went on, brought a degree of comfort to her. *There is a way,* she'd said, and, in the morning, Mariam would tell her what needed to be done and they would do it, and maybe by tomorrow this time they would be on their way to this new life, a life luxuriant with possibility and joy and welcomed difficulties. Laila was grateful that Mariam was in charge, unclouded and sober, able to think this through for both of them. Her own mind was a jittery, muddled mess.

Mariam got up. "You should tend to your son now." On her was the most stricken expression Laila had ever seen on a human face.

LAILA FOUND HIM in the dark, curled up on Rasheed's side of the mattress. She slipped beneath the covers beside him and pulled the blanket over them.

"Are you asleep?"

Without turning around to face her, he said, "Can't sleep yet. Baba jan hasn't said the *Babaloo* prayers with me."

"Maybe I can say them with you tonight."

"You can't say them like he can."

She squeezed his little shoulder. Kissed the nape of his neck. "I can try."

"Where is Baba jan?"

"Baba jan has gone away," Laila said, her throat closing up again.

And there it was, spoken for the first time, the great, damning lie. How many more times would this lie have to be told? Laila wondered miserably. How many more times would Zalmai have to be deceived? She pictured Zalmai, his jubilant, running welcomes when Rasheed came home and Rasheed picking him up by the elbows and swinging him round and round until Zalmai's legs flew straight out, the two of them giggling afterward when Zalmai stumbled around like a drunk. She thought of their disorderly games and their boisterous laughs, their secretive glances.

A pall of shame and grief for her son fell over Laila.

"Where did he go?"

"I don't know, my love."

When was he coming back? Would Baba jan bring a present with him when he returned?

She did the prayers with Zalmai. Twenty-one *Bismallah-e-rahman-e-rahims*—one for each knuckle of seven fingers. She watched him cup his hands before his face and blow into them, then place the back of both hands on his forehead and make a casting-away motion, whispering, Babaloo, *be gone, do not come to Zalmai, he has no business with you.* Babaloo, *be gone.* Then, to finish off, they said *Allah-u-akbar* three times. And later, much later that night, Laila was startled by a muted voice: *Did Baba jan leave because of me? Because of what I said, about you and the man downstairs?*

She leaned over him, meaning to reassure, meaning to say *It had nothing to do with you, Zalmai. No. Nothing is your fault.* But he was asleep, his small chest rising and sinking.

WHEN LAILA WENT to bed, her mind was muffled up, clouded, incapable of sustained rational thought. But when she woke up, to the muezzin's call for morning prayer, much of the dullness had lifted.

She sat up and watched Zalmai sleep for a while, the

ball of his fist under his chin. Laila pictured Mariam sneaking into the room in the middle of the night as she and Zalmai had slept, watching them, making plans in her head.

Laila slipped out of bed. It took effort to stand. She ached everywhere. Her neck, her shoulders, her back, her arms, her thighs, all engraved with the cuts of Rasheed's belt buckle. Wincing, she quietly left the bedroom.

In Mariam's room, the light was a shade darker than gray, the kind of light Laila had always associated with crowing roosters and dew rolling off blades of grass. Mariam was sitting in a corner, on a prayer rug facing the window. Slowly, Laila lowered herself to the ground, sitting down across from her.

"You should go and visit Aziza this morning," Mariam said.

"I know what you mean to do."

"Don't walk. Take the bus, you'll blend in. Taxis are too conspicuous. You're sure to get stopped for riding alone."

"What you promised last night . . ."

Laila could not finish. The trees, the lake, the nameless village. A delusion, she saw. A lovely lie meant to soothe. Like cooing to a distressed child.

"I meant it," Mariam said. "I meant it for *you*, Laila jo."

"I don't want any of it without you," Laila croaked.

Mariam smiled wanly.

"I want it to be just like you said, Mariam, all of us going together, you, me, the children. Tariq has a place in Pakistan. We can hide out there for a while, wait for things to calm down—"

"That's not possible," Mariam said patiently, like a parent to a well-meaning but misguided child.

"We'll take care of each other," Laila said, choking on the words, her eyes wet with tears. "Like you said. No. I'll take care of *you* for a change."

"Oh, Laila jo."

Laila went on a stammering rant. She bargained. She promised. She would do all the cleaning, she said, and all the cooking. "You won't have to do a thing. Ever again. You rest, sleep in, plant a garden. Whatever you want, you ask and I'll get it for you. Don't do this, Mariam. Don't leave me. Don't break Aziza's heart."

"They chop off hands for stealing bread," Mariam said. "What do you think they'll do when they find a dead husband and two missing wives?"

"No one will know," Laila breathed. "No one will find us."

"They will. Sooner or later. They're bloodhounds." Mariam's voice was low, cautioning; it made Laila's promises sound fantastical, trumped-up, foolish.

"Mariam, please—"

"When they do, they'll find you as guilty as me. Tariq too. I won't have the two of you living on the run, like fugitives. What will happen to your children if you're caught?"

Laila's eyes brimming, stinging.

"Who will take care of them then? The Taliban? Think like a mother, Laila jo. Think like a mother. I am."

"I can't."

"You have to."

"It isn't fair," Laila croaked.

"But it *is*. Come here. Come lie here."

Laila crawled to her and again put her head on Mariam's lap. She remembered all the afternoons they'd spent together, braiding each other's hair, Mariam listening patiently to her random thoughts and ordinary stories with an air of gratitude, with the expression of a person to whom a unique and coveted privilege had been extended.

"It *is* fair," Mariam said. "I've killed our husband. I've deprived your son of his father. It isn't right that I run. I *can't*. Even if they never catch us, I'll never . . ." Her lips

349

trembled. "I'll never escape your son's grief. How do I look at him? How do I ever bring myself to look at him, Laila jo?"

Mariam twiddled a strand of Laila's hair, untangled a stubborn curl.

"For me, it ends here. There's nothing more I want. Everything I'd ever wished for as a little girl you've already given me. You and your children have made me so very happy. It's all right, Laila jo. This is all right. Don't be sad."

Laila could find no reasonable answer for anything Mariam said. But she rambled on anyway, incoherently, childishly, about fruit trees that awaited planting and chickens that awaited raising. She went on about small houses in unnamed towns, and walks to trout-filled lakes. And, in the end, when the words dried up, the tears did not, and all Laila could do was surrender and sob like a child overwhelmed by an adult's unassailable logic. All she could do was roll herself up and bury her face one last time in the welcoming warmth of Mariam's lap.

LATER THAT MORNING, Mariam packed Zalmai a small lunch of bread and dried figs. For Aziza too she packed some figs, and a few cookies shaped like animals. She put it all in a paper bag and gave it to Laila.

"Kiss Aziza for me," she said. "Tell her she is the *noor* of my eyes and the sultan of my heart. Will you do that for me?"

Laila nodded, her lips pursed together.

"Take the bus, like I said, and keep your head low."

"When will I see you, Mariam? I want to see you before I testify. I'll tell them how it happened. I'll explain that it wasn't your fault. That you had to do it. They'll understand, won't they, Mariam? They'll understand."

Mariam gave her a soft look.

She hunkered down to eye level with Zalmai. He was

350

wearing a red T-shirt, ragged khakis, and a used pair of cowboy boots Rasheed had bought him from Mandaii. He was holding his new basketball with both hands. Mariam planted a kiss on his cheek.

"You be a good, strong boy, now," she said. "You treat your mother well." She cupped his face. He pulled back but she held on. "I am so sorry, Zalmai jo. Believe me that I'm so very sorry for all your pain and sadness."

Laila held Zalmai's hand as they walked down the road together. Just before they turned the corner, Laila looked back and saw Mariam at the door. Mariam was wearing a white scarf over her head, a dark blue sweater buttoned in the front, and white cotton trousers. A crest of gray hair had fallen loose over her brow. Bars of sunlight slashed across her face and shoulders. Mariam waved amiably.

They turned the corner, and Laila never saw Mariam again.

47.

Mariam

Back in a *kolba*, it seemed, after all these years.

The Walayat women's prison was a drab, square-shaped building in Shar-e-Nau near Chicken Street. It sat in the center of a larger complex that housed male inmates. A padlocked door separated Mariam and the other women from the surrounding men. Mariam counted five working cells. They were unfurnished rooms, with dirty, peeling walls, and small windows that looked into the courtyard. The windows were barred, even though the doors to the cells were unlocked and the women were free to come and go to the courtyard as they pleased. The windows had no glass. There were no curtains either, which meant the Talib guards who roamed the courtyard had an eyeful of the interior of the cells. Some of the women complained that the guards smoked outside the window and leered in, with their inflamed eyes and wolfish smiles, that they muttered indecent jokes to each other about them. Because of this, most of the women wore burqas all day and lifted them only after sundown, after the main gate was locked and the guards had gone to their posts.

At night, the cell Mariam shared with five women and four children was dark. On those nights when there was electrical power, they hoisted Naghma, a short, flat-chested girl with black frizzy hair, up to the ceiling. There was a wire there from which the coating had been stripped. Naghma would hand-wrap the live wire around the base of the lightbulb then to make a circuit.

The toilets were closet-sized, the cement floor cracked. There was a small, rectangular hole in the ground, at the bottom of which was a heap of feces. Flies buzzed in and out of the hole.

In the middle of the prison was an open, rectangular courtyard, and, in the middle of that, a well. The well had no drainage, meaning the courtyard was often a swamp and the water tasted rotten. Laundry lines, loaded with hand-washed socks and diapers, slashed across each other in the courtyard. This was where inmates met visitors, where they boiled the rice their families brought them—the prison provided no food. The courtyard was also the children's playground—Mariam had learned that many of the children had been born in Walayat, had never seen the world outside these walls. Mariam watched them chase each other around, watched their shoeless feet sling mud. All day, they ran around, making up lively games, unaware of the stench of feces and urine that permeated Walayat and their own bodies, unmindful of the Talib guards until one smacked them.

Mariam had no visitors. That was the first and only thing she had asked the Talib officials here. No visitors.

NONE OF THE women in Mariam's cell were serving time for violent crime—they were all there for the common offense of "running away from home." As a result, Mariam gained some notoriety among them, became a kind of celebrity. The women eyed her with a reverent, almost awestruck, expression. They offered her their blankets. They competed to share their food with her.

The most avid was Naghma, who was always hugging her elbows and following Mariam everywhere she went. Naghma was the sort of person who found it entertaining to dispense news of misfortune, whether others' or her own. She said her father had promised her to a tailor some thirty years older than her.

"He smells like *goh,* and has fewer teeth than fingers," Naghma said of the tailor.

She'd tried to elope to Gardez with a young man she'd fallen in love with, the son of a local mullah. They'd barely made it out of Kabul. When they were caught and sent back, the mullah's son was flogged before he repented and said that Naghma had seduced him with her feminine charms. She'd cast a spell on him, he said. He promised he would rededicate himself to the study of the Koran. The mullah's son was freed. Naghma was sentenced to five years.

It was just as well, she said, her being here in prison. Her father had sworn that the day she was released he would take a knife to her throat.

Listening to Naghma, Mariam remembered the dim glimmer of cold stars and the stringy pink clouds streaking over the Safid-koh mountains that long-ago morning when Nana had said to her, *Like a compass needle that points north, a man's accusing finger always finds a woman. Always. You remember that, Mariam.*

MARIAM'S TRIAL HAD taken place the week before. There was no legal council, no public hearing, no cross-examining of evidence, no appeals. Mariam declined her right to witnesses. The entire thing lasted less than fifteen minutes.

The middle judge, a brittle-looking Talib, was the

leader. He was strikingly gaunt, with yellow, leathery skin and a curly red beard. He wore eyeglasses that magnified his eyes and revealed how yellow the whites were. His neck looked too thin to support the intricately wrapped turban on his head.

"You admit to this, *hamshira?*" he asked again in a tired voice.

"I do," Mariam said.

The man nodded. Or maybe he didn't. It was hard to tell; he had a pronounced shaking of his hands and head that reminded Mariam of Mullah Faizullah's tremor. When he sipped tea, he did not reach for his cup. He motioned to the square-shouldered man to his left, who respectfully brought it to his lips. After, the Talib closed his eyes gently, a muted and elegant gesture of gratitude.

Mariam found a disarming quality about him. When he spoke, it was with a tinge of guile and tenderness. His smile was patient. He did not look at Mariam despisingly. He did not address her with spite or accusation but with a soft tone of apology.

"Do you fully understand what you're saying?" the bony-faced Talib to the judge's right, not the tea giver, said. This one was the youngest of the three. He spoke quickly and with emphatic, arrogant confidence. He'd been irritated that Mariam could not speak Pashto. He struck Mariam as the sort of quarrelsome young man who relished his authority, who saw offenses everywhere, thought it his birthright to pass judgment.

"I do understand," Mariam said.

"I wonder," the young Talib said. "God has made us differently, you women and us men. Our brains are different. You are not able to think like we can. Western doctors and their science have proven this. This is why we require only one male witness but two female ones."

"I admit to what I did, brother," Mariam said. "But, if I

hadn't, he would have killed her. He was strangling her."

"So you say. But, then, women swear to all sorts of things all the time."

"It's the truth."

"Do you have witnesses? Other than your *ambagh*?"

"I do not," said Mariam.

"Well, then." He threw up his hands and snickered.

It was the sickly Talib who spoke next.

"I have a doctor in Peshawar," he said. "A fine, young Pakistani fellow. I saw him a month ago, and then again last week. I said, tell me the truth, friend, and he said to me, three months, Mullah sahib, maybe six at most—all God's will, of course."

He nodded discreetly at the square-shouldered man on his left and took another sip of the tea he was offered. He wiped his mouth with the back of his tremulous hand. "It does not frighten me to leave this life that my only son left five years ago, this life that insists we bear sorrow upon sorrow long after we can bear no more. No, I believe I shall gladly take my leave when the time comes.

"What frightens me, *hamshira,* is the day God summons me before Him and asks, *Why did you not do as I said, Mullah? Why did you not obey my laws?* How shall I explain myself to Him, *hamshira?* What will be my defense for not heeding His commands? All I can do, all any of us can do, in the time we are granted, is to go on abiding by the laws He has set for us. The clearer I see my end, *hamshira,* the nearer I am to my day of reckoning, the more determined I grow to carry out His word. However painful it may prove."

He shifted on his cushion and winced.

"I believe you when you say that your husband was a man of disagreeable temperament," he resumed, fixing Mariam with his bespectacled eyes, his gaze both stern and compassionate. "But I cannot help but be disturbed by the brutality of your action, *hamshira*. I am troubled by what you have done; I am troubled that his little boy was crying for him upstairs when you did it.

"I am tired and dying, and I want to be merciful. I want to forgive you. But when God summons me and says, *But it wasn't for you to forgive, Mullah,* what shall I say?"

His companions nodded and looked at him with admiration.

"Something tells me you are not a wicked woman, *hamshira*. But you have done a wicked thing. And you must pay for this thing you have done. *Shari'a* is not vague on this matter. It says I must send you where I will soon join you myself.

"Do you understand, *hamshira?*"

Mariam looked down at her hands. She said she did.

"May Allah forgive you."

Before they led her out, Mariam was given a document, told to sign beneath her statement and the mullah's sentence. As the three Taliban watched, Mariam wrote it out, her name—the *meem*, the *reh*, the *yah*, and the *meem*—remembering the last time she'd signed her name to a document, twenty-seven years before, at Jalil's table, beneath the watchful gaze of another mullah.

MARIAM SPENT TEN DAYS in prison. She sat by the window of the cell, watched the prison life in the courtyard. When the summer winds blew, she watched bits of scrap paper ride the currents in a frenzied, corkscrew motion, as they were hurled this way and that, high above the prison walls. She watched the winds stir mutiny in the dust, whipping it into violent spirals that ripped through the courtyard. Everyone—the guards, the inmates, the children, Mariam—burrowed their faces in the hook of their elbows, but the dust would not be denied. It made homes of ear canals and nostrils, of eyelashes and skin folds, of the space between molars. Only at dusk did the winds die down. And then if a night breeze blew, it did so timidly, as if to atone for the excesses of its daytime sibling.

On Mariam's last day at Walayat, Naghma gave her a tangerine. She put it in Mariam's palm and closed her fingers around it. Then she burst into tears.

"You're the best friend I ever had," she said.

Mariam spent the rest of the day by the barred window watching the inmates below. Someone was cooking a meal, and a stream of cumin-scented smoke and warm air wafted through the window. Mariam could see the children playing a blindfolded game. Two little girls were singing a rhyme, and Mariam remembered it from her childhood, remembered Jalil singing it to her as they'd sat on a rock, fishing in the stream:

Lili lili birdbath,
Sitting on a dirt path,
Minnow sat on the rim and drank,
Slipped, and in the water she sank.

Mariam had disjointed dreams that last night. She dreamed of pebbles, eleven of them, arranged vertically. Jalil, young again, all winning smiles and dimpled chins and sweat patches, coat flung over his shoulder, come at last to take his daughter away for a ride in his shiny black Buick Roadmaster. Mullah Faizullah twirling his rosary beads, walking with her along the stream, their twin shadows gliding on the water and on the grassy banks sprinkled with a blue-lavender wild iris that, in this dream, smelled like cloves. She dreamed of Nana in the doorway of the *kolba*, her voice dim and distant, calling her to dinner, as Mariam played in cool, tangled grass where ants crawled and beetles scurried and grasshoppers skipped amid all the different shades of green. The squeak of a wheelbarrow laboring up a dusty path. Cowbells clanging. Sheep baaing on a hill.

ON THE WAY to Ghazi Stadium, Mariam bounced in the bed of the truck as it skidded around potholes and its wheels spat pebbles. The bouncing hurt her tailbone. A young, armed Talib sat across from her looking at her.

Mariam wondered if he would be the one, this amiable-looking young man with the deep-set bright eyes and slightly pointed face, with the black-nailed index finger drumming the side of the truck.

"Are you hungry, mother?" he said.

Mariam shook her head.

"I have a biscuit. It's good. You can have it if you're hungry. I don't mind."

"No. *Tashakor*, brother."

He nodded, looked at her benignly. "Are you afraid, mother?"

A lump closed off her throat. In a quivering voice, Mariam told him the truth. "Yes. I'm very afraid."

"I have a picture of my father," he said. "I don't remember him. He was a bicycle repairman once, I know that much. But I don't remember how he moved, you know, how he laughed or the sound of his voice." He looked away, then back at Mariam. "My mother used to say that he was the bravest man she knew. Like a lion, she'd say. But she told me he was crying like a child the morning the communists took him. I'm telling you so you know that it's normal to be scared. It's nothing to be ashamed of, mother."

For the first time that day, Mariam cried a little.

THOUSANDS OF EYES bore down on her. In the crowded bleachers, necks were craned for the benefit of a better view. Tongues clucked. A murmuring sound rippled through the stadium when Mariam was helped down from the truck. Mariam imagined heads shaking when the loud-speaker announced her crime. But she did not look up to see whether they were shaking with disapproval or charity, with reproach or pity. Mariam blinded herself to them all.

Earlier that morning, she had been afraid that she would make a fool of herself, that she would turn into a pleading, weeping spectacle. She had feared that she might scream or vomit or even wet herself, that, in her last moments, she would be betrayed by animal instinct or bodily disgrace. But when she was made to descend from the truck, Mariam's legs did not buckle. Her arms did not flail. She did not have to be dragged. And when she did feel herself faltering, she thought of Zalmai, from whom she had taken the love of his life, whose days now would be shaped by the sorrow of his father's disappearance. And then Mariam's stride steadied and she could walk without protest.

An armed man approached her and told her to walk toward the southern goalpost. Mariam could sense the crowd tightening up with anticipation. She did not look up. She kept her eyes to the ground, on her shadow, on her executioner's shadow trailing hers.

Though there had been moments of beauty in it, Mariam knew that life for the most part had been unkind to her. But as she walked the final twenty paces, she could not help but wish for more of it. She wished she could see Laila again, wished to hear the clangor of her laugh, to sit with her once more for a pot of *chai* and leftover *halwa* under a starlit sky. She mourned that she would never see Aziza grow up, would not see the beautiful young woman that she would one day become, would not get to paint her hands with henna and toss *noqul* candy at her wedding. She would never play with Aziza's children. She would have liked that very much, to be old and play with

Aziza's children.

Near the goalpost, the man behind her asked her to stop. Mariam did. Through the crisscrossing grid of the burqa, she saw his shadow arms lift his shadow Kalashnikov.

Mariam wished for so much in those final moments. Yet as she closed her eyes, it was not regret any longer but a sensation of abundant peace that washed over her. She thought of her entry into this world, the *harami* child of a lowly villager, an unintended thing, a pitiable, regrettable accident. A weed. And yet she was leaving the world as a woman who had loved and been loved back. She was leaving it as a friend, a companion, a guardian. A mother. A person of consequence at last. No. It was not so bad, Mariam thought, that she should die this way. Not so bad. This was a legitimate end to a life of illegitimate beginnings.

Mariam's final thoughts were a few words from the Koran, which she muttered under her breath.

He has created the heavens and the earth with the truth; He makes the night cover the day and makes the day overtake the night, and He has made the sun and the moon subservient; each one runs on to an assigned term; now surely He is the Mighty, the Great Forgiver.

"Kneel," the Talib said.

O my Lord! Forgive and have mercy, for you are the best of the merciful ones.

"Kneel here, *hamshira*. And look down."

One last time, Mariam did as she was told.

PART FOUR

48.

Tariq has headaches now.

Some nights, Laila awakens and finds him on the edge of their bed, rocking, his undershirt pulled over his head. The headaches began in Nasir Bagh, he says, then worsened in prison. Sometimes they make him vomit, blind him in one eye. He says it feels like a butcher's knife burrowing in one temple, twisting slowly through his brain, then poking out the other side.

"I can taste the metal, even, when they begin."

Sometimes Laila wets a cloth and lays it on his forehead and that helps a little. The little round white pills Sayeed's doctor gave Tariq help too. But some nights, all Tariq can do is hold his head and moan, his eyes bloodshot, his nose dripping. Laila sits with him when he's in the grip of it like that, rubs the back of his neck, takes his hand in hers, the metal of his wedding band cold against her palm.

They married the day that they arrived in Murree. Sayeed looked relieved when Tariq told him they would. He would not have to broach with Tariq the delicate matter of an unmarried couple living in his hotel. Sayeed is not at all as Laila had pictured him, ruddy-faced and pea-eyed. He has a salt-and-pepper mustache whose ends he rolls to a sharp tip, and a shock of long gray hair combed back from the brow. He is a soft-spoken, mannerly man, with measured speech and graceful movements.

It was Sayeed who summoned a friend and a mullah for the *nikka* that day, Sayeed who pulled Tariq aside and gave him money. Tariq wouldn't take it, but Sayeed insisted. Tariq went to the Mall then and came back with two simple, thin wedding bands. They married later that night, after the children had gone to bed.

In the mirror, beneath the green veil that the mullah draped over their heads, Laila's eyes met Tariq's. There were no tears, no wedding-day smiles, no whispered oaths of long-lasting love. In silence, Laila looked at their reflection, at faces that had aged beyond their years, at the pouches and lines and sags that now marked their once-scrubbed, youthful faces. Tariq opened his mouth and began to say something, but, just as he did, someone pulled the veil, and Laila missed what it was that he was going to say.

That night, they lay in bed as husband and wife, as the children snored below them on sleeping cots. Laila remembered the ease with which they would crowd the air between them with words, she and Tariq, when they were younger, the haywire, brisk flow of their speech, always interrupting each other, tugging each other's collar to emphasize a point, the quickness to laugh, the eagerness to delight. So much had happened since those childhood days, so much that needed to be said. But that first night the enormity of it all stole the words from her. That night, it was blessing enough to be beside him. It was blessing enough to know that he was here, to feel the warmth of him next to her, to lie with him, their heads touching, his right hand laced in her left.

In the middle of the night, when Laila woke up thirsty, she found their hands still clamped together, in the white-knuckle, anxious way of children clutching balloon strings.

LAILA LIKES MURREE'S cool, foggy mornings and its dazzling twilights, the dark brilliance of the sky at night; the green of the pines and the soft brown of the squirrels darting up and down the sturdy tree trunks; the sudden downpours that send shoppers in the Mall scrambling for awning cover. She likes the souvenir shops, and the various hotels that house tourists, even as the locals bemoan the constant construction, the expansion of infrastructure that they say is eating away at Murree's natural beauty. Laila finds it odd that people should lament the *building* of buildings. In Kabul, they would celebrate it.

She likes that they have a bathroom, not an outhouse but an actual bathroom, with a toilet that flushes, a shower, and a sink too, with twin faucets from which she can draw, with a flick of her wrist, water, either hot or cold. She likes waking up to the sound of Alyona bleating in the morning, and the harmlessly cantankerous cook, Adiba, who works marvels in the kitchen.

Sometimes, as Laila watches Tariq sleep, as her children mutter and stir in their own sleep, a great big lump of gratitude catches in her throat, makes her eyes water.

In the mornings, Laila follows Tariq from room to room. Keys jingle from a ring clipped to his waist and a spray bottle of window cleaner dangles from the belt loops of his jeans. Laila brings a pail filled with rags, disinfectant, a toilet brush, and spray wax for the dressers. Aziza tags along, a mop in one hand, the bean-stuffed doll Mariam had made for her in the other. Zalmai trails them reluctantly, sulkily, always a few steps behind.

Laila vacuums, makes the bed, and dusts. Tariq washes

the bathroom sink and tub, scrubs the toilet and mops the linoleum floor. He stocks the shelves with clean towels, miniature shampoo bottles, and bars of almond-scented soap. Aziza has laid claim to the task of spraying and wiping the windows. The doll is never far from where she works.

Laila told Aziza about Tariq a few days after the *nikka*.

It is strange, Laila thinks, almost unsettling, the thing between Aziza and Tariq. Already, Aziza is finishing his sentences and he hers. She hands him things before he asks for them. Private smiles shoot between them across the dinner table as if they are not strangers at all but companions reunited after a lengthy separation.

Aziza looked down thoughtfully at her hands when Laila told her.

"I like him," she said, after a long pause.

"He loves *you*."

"He said that?"

"He doesn't have to, Aziza."

"Tell me the rest, Mammy. Tell me so I know."

And Laila did.

"Your father is a good man. He is the best man I've ever known."

"What if he leaves?" Aziza said.

"He will never leave. Look at me, Aziza. Your father will never hurt you, and he will never leave."

The relief on Aziza's face broke Laila's heart.

TARIQ HAS BOUGHT Zalmai a rocking horse, built him a wagon. From a prison inmate, he learned to make paper animals, and so he has folded, cut, and tucked countless sheets of paper into lions and kangaroos for Zalmai, into horses and brightly plumed birds. But these overtures are dismissed by Zalmai unceremoniously, sometimes venomously.

368

"You're a donkey!" he cries. "I don't want your toys!"

"Zalmai!" Laila gasps.

"It's all right," Tariq says. "Laila, it's all right. Let him."

"You're not my Baba jan! My real Baba jan is away on a trip, and when he gets back he's going to beat you up! And you won't be able to run away, because he has two legs and you only have one!"

At night, Laila holds Zalmai against her chest and recites the *Babaloo* prayers with him. When he asks, she tells him the lie again, tells him his Baba jan has gone away and she doesn't know when he would come back. She abhors this task, abhors herself for lying like this to a child.

Laila knows that this shameful lie will have to be told again and again. It will have to because Zalmai will ask, hopping down from a swing, waking from an afternoon nap, and, later, when he's old enough to tie his own shoes, to walk to school by himself, the lie will have to be delivered again.

At some point, Laila knows, the questions will dry up. Slowly, Zalmai will cease wondering why his father has abandoned him. He will not spot his father any longer at traffic lights, in stooping old men shuffling down the street or sipping tea in open-fronted samovar houses. And one day it will hit him, walking along some meandering river, or gazing out at an untracked snowfield, that his father's disappearance is no longer an open, raw wound. That it has become something else altogether, something more soft-edged and indolent. Like a lore. Something to be revered, mystified by.

Laila is happy here in Murree. But it is not an easy happiness. It is not a happiness without cost.

ON HIS DAYS OFF, Tariq takes Laila and the children to the Mall, along which are shops that sell trinkets and next to which is an Anglican church built in the mid-nineteenth century. Tariq buys them spicy *chapli* kebabs from street vendors. They stroll amid the crowds of locals, the Europeans and their cellular phones and digital cameras, the Punjabis who come here to escape the heat of the plains.

Occasionally, they board a bus to Kashmir Point. From there, Tariq shows them the valley of the Jhelum River, the pine-carpeted slopes, and the lush, densely wooded hills, where he says monkeys can still be spotted hopping from branch to branch. They go to the maple-clad Nathia Gali too, some thirty kilometers from Murree, where Tariq holds Laila's hand as they walk the tree-shaded road to the Governor's House. They stop by the old British cemetery, or take a taxi up a mountain peak for a view of the verdant, fog-shrouded valley below.

Sometimes on these outings, when they pass by a store window, Laila catches their reflections in it. Man, wife, daughter, son. To strangers, she knows, they must appear like the most ordinary of families, free of secrets, lies, and regrets.

AZIZA HAS NIGHTMARES from which she wakes up shrieking. Laila has to lie beside her on the cot, dry her cheeks with her sleeve, soothe her back to sleep.

Laila has her own dreams. In them, she's always back at the house in Kabul, walking the hall, climbing the stairs. She is alone, but behind the doors she hears the rhythmic hiss of an iron, bedsheets snapped, then folded. Sometimes she hears a woman's low-pitched humming of an old Herati song. But when she walks in, the room is empty. There is no one there.

The dreams leave Laila shaken. She wakes from them coated in sweat, her eyes prickling with tears. It is devastating. Every time, it is devastating.

49.

One Sunday that September, Laila is putting Zalmai, who has a cold, down for a nap when Tariq bursts into their bungalow.

"Did you hear?" he says, panting a little. "They killed him. Ahmad Shah Massoud. He's dead."

"What?"

From the doorway, Tariq tells her what he knows.

"They say he gave an interview to a pair of journalists who claimed they were Belgians originally from Morocco. As they're talking, a bomb hidden in the video camera goes off. Kills Massoud and one of the journalists. They shoot the other one as he tries to run. They're saying now the journalists were probably Al-Qaeda men."

Laila remembers the poster of Ahmad Shah Massoud that Mammy had nailed to the wall of her bedroom. Massoud leaning forward, one eyebrow cocked, his face furrowed in concentration, as though he was respectfully listening to someone. Laila remembers how grateful Mammy was that Massoud had said a graveside prayer at her sons' burial, how she told everyone about it. Even after war broke out between his faction and the others, Mammy had refused to blame him. *He's a good man,* she used to say. *He wants peace. He wants to rebuild Afghanistan. But they won't let him. They just won't let him.* For Mammy, even in the end, even after everything went so terribly wrong and Kabul lay in ruins, Massoud was still the Lion of Panjshir.

Laila is not as forgiving. Massoud's violent end brings her no joy, but she remembers too well the neighborhoods razed under his watch, the bodies dragged from the rubble, the hands and feet of children discovered on rooftops or the high branch of some tree days after their funeral. She remembers too clearly the look on Mammy's own face moments before the rocket slammed in and, much as she has tried to forget, Babi's headless torso landing nearby, the bridge tower printed on his T-shirt poking through thick fog and blood.

"There is going to be a funeral," Tariq is saying. "I'm sure of it. Probably in Rawalpindi. It'll be huge."

Zalmai, who was almost asleep, is sitting up now, rubbing his eyes with balled fists.

Two days later, they are cleaning a room when they hear a commotion. Tariq drops the mop and hurries out. Laila tails him.

The noise is coming from the hotel lobby. There is a lounge area to the right of the reception desk, with several chairs and two couches upholstered in beige suede. In the corner, facing the couches, is a television, and Sayeed, the concierge, and several guests are gathered in front of.

Laila and Tariq work their way in.

The TV is tuned to BBC. On the screen is a building, a tower, black smoke billowing from its top floors. Tariq says something to Sayeed and Sayeed is in midreply when a plane appears from the corner of the screen. It crashes into the adjacent tower, exploding into a fireball that dwarfs any ball of fire that Laila has ever seen. A collective yelp rises from everyone in the lobby.

In less than two hours, both towers have collapsed.

Soon all the TV stations are talking about Afghanistan and the Taliban and Osama bin Laden.

"Did you hear what the Taliban said?" Tariq asks. "About bin Laden?"

Aziza is sitting across from him on the bed, considering the board. Tariq has taught her to play chess. She is frowning and tapping her lower lip now, mimicking the body language her father assumes when he's deciding on a move.

Zalmai's cold is a little better. He is asleep, and Laila is rubbing Vicks on his chest.

"I heard," she says.

The Taliban have announced that they won't relinquish bin Laden because he is a *mehman,* a guest, who has found sanctuary in Afghanistan and it is against the *Pashtunwali* code of ethics to turn over a guest. Tariq chuckles bitterly, and Laila hears in his chuckle that he is revolted by this distortion of an honorable Pashtun custom, this misrepresentation of his people's ways.

A few days after the attacks, Laila and Tariq are in the hotel lobby again. On the TV screen, George W. Bush is speaking. There is a big American flag behind him. At one point, his voice wavers, and Laila thinks he is going to weep.

Sayeed, who speaks English, explains to them that Bush has just declared war.

"On whom?" says Tariq.

"On your country, to begin with."

* * *

373

"It may not be such a bad thing," Tariq says.

They have finished making love. He's lying beside her, his head on her chest, his arm draped over her belly. The first few times they tried, there was difficulty. Tariq was all apologies, Laila all reassurances. There are still difficulties, not physical now but logistical. The shack they share with the children is small. The children sleep on cots below them and so there is little privacy. Most times, Laila and Tariq make love in silence, with controlled, muted passion, fully clothed beneath the blanket as a precaution against interruptions by the children. They are forever wary of the rustling sheets, the creaking bedsprings. But for Laila, being with Tariq is worth weathering these apprehensions. When they make love, Laila feels anchored, she feels sheltered. Her anxieties, that their life together is a temporary blessing, that soon it will come loose again in strips and tatters, are allayed. Her fears of separation vanish.

"What do you mean?" she says now.

"What's going on back home. It may not be so bad in the end."

Back home, bombs are falling once again, this time American bombs—Laila has been watching images of the war every day on the television as she changes sheets and vacuums. The Americans have armed the warlords once more, and enlisted the help of the Northern Alliance to drive out the Taliban and find bin Laden.

But it rankles Laila, what Tariq is saying. She pushes his head roughly off her chest.

"Not so bad? People dying? Women, children, old people? Homes destroyed again? Not so bad?"

"*Shh.* You'll wake the children."

"How can you say that, Tariq?" she snaps. "After the so-called blunder in Karam? A hundred innocent people! You saw the bodies for yourself!"

"No," Tariq says. He props himself up on his elbow, looks down at Laila. "You misunderstand. What I meant was—"

"You wouldn't know," Laila says. She is aware that her voice is rising, that they are having their first fight as husband and wife. "You left when the Mujahideen began fighting, remember? I'm the one who stayed behind. Me. I *know* war. I lost my parents to war. My *parents,* Tariq. And now to hear you say that war is not so bad?"

"I'm sorry, Laila. I'm sorry." He cups her face in his hands. "You're right. I'm sorry. Forgive me. What I meant was that maybe there will be hope at the other end of this war, that maybe for the first time in a long time—"

"I don't want to talk about this anymore," Laila says, surprised at how she has lashed out at him. It's unfair, she knows, what she said to him—hadn't war taken his parents too?—and whatever flared in her is softening already. Tariq continues to speak gently, and, when he pulls her to him, she lets him. When he kisses her hand, then her brow, she lets him. She knows that he is probably right. She knows how his comment was intended. Maybe this *is* necessary. Maybe there *will* be hope when Bush's bombs stop falling. But she cannot bring herself to say it, not when what happened to Babi and Mammy is happening to someone now in Afghanistan, not when some unsuspecting girl or boy back home has just been orphaned by a rocket as she was. Laila cannot bring herself to say it. It's hard to rejoice. It seems hypocritical, perverse.

That night, Zalmai wakes up coughing. Before Laila can move, Tariq swings his legs over the side of the bed. He straps on his prosthesis and walks over to Zalmai, lifts him up into his arms. From the bed, Laila watches Tariq's shape moving back and forth in the darkness. She sees the outline of Zalmai's head on his shoulder, the knot of his hands at Tariq's neck, his small feet bouncing by Tariq's hip.

When Tariq comes back to bed, neither of them says anything. Laila reaches over and touches his face. Tariq's cheeks are wet.

50.

For Laila, life in Murree is one of comfort and tranquillity. The work is not cumbersome, and, on their days off, she and Tariq take the children to ride the chairlift to Patriata hill, or go to Pindi Point, where, on a clear day, you can see as far as Islamabad and downtown Rawalpindi. There, they spread a blanket on the grass and eat meatball sandwiches with cucumbers and drink cold ginger ale.

It is a good life, Laila tells herself, a life to be thankful for. It is, in fact, precisely the sort of life she used to dream for herself in her darkest days with Rasheed. Every day, Laila reminds herself of this.

Then one warm night in July 2002, she and Tariq are lying in bed talking in hushed voices about all the changes back home. There have been so many. The coalition forces have driven the Taliban out of every major city, pushed them across the border to Pakistan and to the mountains in the south and east of Afghanistan. ISAF, an international peacekeeping force, has been sent to Kabul. The country has an interim president now, Hamid Karzai.

Laila decides that now is the time to tell Tariq.

A year ago, she would have gladly given an arm to get out of Kabul. But in the last few months, she has found herself missing the city of her childhood. She misses the bustle of Shor Bazaar, the Gardens of Babur, the call of the water carriers lugging their goatskin bags. She misses the garment hagglers at Chicken Street and the melon hawkers in Karteh-Parwan.

But it isn't mere homesickness or nostalgia that has Laila thinking of Kabul so much these days. She has become plagued by restlessness. She hears of schools built in Kabul, roads repaved, women returning to work, and her life here, pleasant as it is, grateful as she is for it, seems . . . insufficient to her. Inconsequential. Worse yet, wasteful. Of late, she has started hearing Babi's voice in her head. *You can be anything you want, Laila,* he says. *I know this about you. And I also know that when this war is over, Afghanistan is going to need you.*

Laila hears Mammy's voice too. She remembers Mammy's response to Babi when he would suggest that they leave Afghanistan. *I want to see my sons' dream come true. I want to be there when it happens, when Afghanistan is free, so the boys see it too. They'll see it through my eyes.* There is a part of Laila now that wants to return to Kabul, for Mammy and Babi, for them to see it through *her* eyes.

And then, most compellingly for Laila, there is Mariam. Did Mariam die for this? Laila asks herself. Did she sacrifice herself so she, Laila, could be a maid in a foreign land? Maybe it wouldn't matter to Mariam what Laila did as long as she and the children were safe and happy. But it matters to Laila. Suddenly, it matters very much.

"I want to go back," she says.

Tariq sits up in bed and looks down at her.

Laila is struck again by how beautiful he is, the perfect curve of his forehead, the slender muscles of his arms, his brooding, intelligent eyes. A year has passed, and still there are times, at moments like this, when Laila cannot believe that they have found each other again, that he is really here, with her, that he is her husband.

"Back? To Kabul?" he asks.

"Only if you want it too."

"Are you unhappy here? You seem happy. The children too."

Laila sits up. Tariq shifts on the bed, makes room for her.

"I *am* happy," Laila says. "Of course I am. But . . . where do we go from here, Tariq? How long do we stay? This isn't home. Kabul is, and back there so much is happening, a lot of it good. I want to be a part of it all. I want to *do* something. I want to contribute. Do you understand?"

Tariq nods slowly. "This is what you want, then? You're sure?"

"I want it, yes, I'm sure. But it's more than that. I feel like I *have* to go back. Staying here, it doesn't feel right anymore."

Tariq looks at his hands, then back up at her.

"But only—only—if you want to go too."

Tariq smiles. The furrows from his brow clear, and for a brief moment he is the old Tariq again, the Tariq who did not get headaches, who had once said that in Siberia snot turned to ice before it hit the ground. It may be her imagination, but Laila believes there are more frequent sightings of this old Tariq these days.

"Me?" he says. "I'll follow you to the end of the world, Laila."

She pulls him close and kisses his lips. She believes she has never loved him more than at this moment. "Thank you," she says, her forehead resting against his.

"Let's go home."

"But first, I want to go to Herat," she says.

"Herat?"

Laila explains.

*　　*　　*

THE CHILDREN NEED reassuring, each in their own way. Laila has to sit down with an agitated Aziza, who still has nightmares, who'd been startled to tears the week before when someone had shot rounds into the sky at a wedding nearby. Laila has to explain to Aziza that when they return to Kabul the Taliban won't be there, that there will not be any fighting, and that she will not be sent back to the orphanage. "We'll all live together. Your father, me, Zalmai. And you, Aziza. You'll never, ever, have to be apart from me again. I promise." She smiles at her daughter. "Until the day *you* want to, that is. When you fall in love with some young man and want to marry him."

On the day they leave Murree, Zalmai is inconsolable. He has wrapped his arms around Alyona's neck and will not let go.

"I can't pry him off of her, Mammy," says Aziza.

"Zalmai. We can't take a goat on the bus," Laila explains again.

It isn't until Tariq kneels down beside him, until he promises Zalmai that he will buy him a goat just like Alyona in Kabul, that Zalmai reluctantly lets go.

There are tearful farewells with Sayeed as well. For good luck, he holds a Koran by the doorway for Tariq, Laila, and the children to kiss three times, then holds it high so they can pass under it. He helps Tariq load the two suitcases into the trunk of his car. It is Sayeed who drives them to the station, who stands on the curb waving goodbye as the bus sputters and pulls away.

As she leans back and watches Sayeed receding in the rear window of the bus, Laila hears the voice of doubt whispering in her head. Are they being foolish, she wonders, leaving behind the safety of Murree? Going back to the land where her parents and brothers perished, where the smoke of bombs is only now settling?

And then, from the darkened spirals of her memory, rise two lines of poetry, Babi's farewell ode to Kabul:

One could not count the moons that shimmer on her roofs,
Or the thousand splendid suns that hide behind her walls.

Laila settles back in her seat, blinking the wetness from her eyes. Kabul is waiting. Needing. This journey home is the right thing to do.

But first there is one last farewell to be said.

THE WARS IN Afghanistan have ravaged the roads connecting Kabul, Herat, and Kandahar. The easiest way to Herat now is through Mashad, in Iran. Laila and her family are there only overnight. They spend the night at a hotel, and, the next morning, they board another bus.

Mashad is a crowded, bustling city. Laila watches as parks, mosques, and *chelo kebab* restaurants pass by. When the bus passes the shrine to Imam Reza, the eighth Shi'a imam, Laila cranes her neck to get a better view of its glistening tiles, the minarets, the magnificent golden dome, all of it immaculately and lovingly preserved. She thinks of the Buddhas in her own country. They are grains of dust now, blowing about the Bamiyan Valley in the wind.

The bus ride to the Iranian-Afghan border takes almost ten hours. The terrain grows more desolate, more barren, as they near Afghanistan. Shortly before they cross the border into Herat, they pass an Afghan refugee camp. To Laila, it is a blur of yellow dust and black tents and scanty structures made of corrugated-steel sheets. She reaches across the seat and takes Tariq's hand.

IN HERAT, most of the streets are paved, lined with fragrant pines. There are municipal parks and libraries in midconstruction, manicured courtyards, freshly painted buildings. The traffic lights work, and, most surprisingly to Laila, electricity is steady. Laila has heard that Herat's feudal-style warlord, Ismail Khan, has helped rebuild the city with the considerable customs revenue that he collects at the Afghan-Iranian border, money that Kabul says belongs not to him but to the central government. There is both a reverential and fearful tone when the taxi driver who takes them to Muwaffaq Hotel mentions Ismail Khan's name.

The two-night stay at the Muwaffaq will cost them nearly a fifth of their savings, but the trip from Mashad has been long and wearying, and the children are exhausted. The elderly clerk at the desk tells Tariq, as he fetches the room key, that the Muwaffaq is popular with journalists and NGO workers.

"Bin Laden slept here once," he boasts.

The room has two beds, and a bathroom with running cold water. There is a painting of the poet Khaja Abdullah Ansary on the wall between the beds. From the window, Laila has a view of the busy street below, and of a park across the street with pastel-colored-brick paths cutting through thick clusters of flowers. The children, who have grown accustomed to television, are disappointed that there isn't one in the room. Soon enough, though, they are asleep. Soon enough, Tariq and Laila too have collapsed. Laila sleeps soundly in Tariq's arms, except for once in the middle of the night when she wakes from a dream she cannot remember.

THE NEXT MORNING, after a breakfast of tea with fresh bread, quince marmalade, and boiled eggs, Tariq finds her a taxi.

"Are you sure you don't want me to come along?" Tariq says. Aziza is holding his hand. Zalmai isn't, but he is standing close to Tariq, leaning one shoulder on Tariq's hip.

"I'm sure."

"I worry."

"I'll be fine," Laila says. "I promise. Take the children to a market. Buy them something."

Zalmai begins to cry when the taxi pulls away, and, when Laila looks back, she sees that he is reaching for Tariq. That he is beginning to accept Tariq both eases and breaks Laila's heart.

"You're not from Herat," the driver says.

He has dark, shoulder-length hair—a common thumbing of the nose at the departed Taliban, Laila has discovered—and some kind of scar interrupting his mustache on the left side. There is a photo taped to the windshield, on his side. It's of a young girl with pink cheeks and hair parted down the middle into twin braids.

Laila tells him that she has been in Pakistan for the last year, that she is returning to Kabul. "Deh-Mazang."

Through the windshield, she sees coppersmiths welding brass handles to jugs, saddlemakers laying out cuts of rawhide to dry in the sun.

"Have you lived here long, brother?" she asks.

"Oh, my whole life. I was born here. I've seen everything. You remember the uprising?"

Laila says she does, but he goes on.

"This was back in March 1979, about nine months before the Soviets invaded. Some angry Heratis killed a few Soviet advisers, so the Soviets sent in tanks and helicopters and pounded this place. For three days, *hamshira,* they fired on the city. They collapsed buildings, destroyed one of the minarets, killed thousands of people. *Thousands.* I lost two sisters in those three days. One of them was twelve years old." He taps the photo on his windshield. "That's her."

"I'm sorry," Laila says, marveling at how every Afghan story is marked by death and loss and unimaginable grief. And yet, she sees, people find a way to survive, to go on. Laila thinks of her own life and all that has happened to her, and she is astonished that she too has survived, that she is alive and sitting in this taxi listening to this man's story.

GUL DAMAN IS a village of a few walled houses rising among flat *kolba*s built with mud and straw. Outside the *kolba*s, Laila sees sunburned women cooking, their faces sweating in steam rising from big blackened pots set on makeshift firewood grills. Mules eat from troughs. Children giving chase to chickens begin chasing the taxi. Laila sees men pushing wheelbarrows filled with stones. They stop and watch the car pass by. The driver takes a turn, and they pass a cemetery with a weather-worn mausoleum in the center of it. The driver tells her that a village Sufi is buried there.

There is a windmill too. In the shadow of its idle, rust-colored vanes, three little boys are squatting, playing with mud. The driver pulls over and leans out of the window. The oldest-looking of the three boys is the one to answer. He points to a house farther up the road. The driver thanks him, puts the car back in gear.

He parks outside the walled, one-story house. Laila sees the tops of fig trees above the walls, some of the branches spilling over the side.

"I won't be long," she says to the driver.

THE MIDDLE-AGED man who opens the door is short, thin, russet-haired. His beard is streaked with parallel stripes of gray. He is wearing a *chapan* over his *pirhan-tumban*.

They exchange *salaam alaykum*s.

"Is this Mullah Faizullah's house?" Laila asks.

"Yes. I am his son, Hamza. Is there something I can do for you, *hamshireh*?"

"I've come here about an old friend of your father's, Mariam."

Hamza blinks. A puzzled look passes across his face. "Mariam . . ."

"Jalil Khan's daughter."

He blinks again. Then he puts a palm to his cheek and his face lights up with a smile that reveals missing and rotting teeth. "Oh!" he says. It comes out sounding like *Ohhhhhh*, like an expelled breath. "Oh! Mariam! Are you her daughter? Is she—" He is twisting his neck now, looking behind her eagerly, searching. "Is she here? It's been so long! Is Mariam here?"

"She has passed on, I'm afraid."

The smile fades from Hamza's face.

For a moment, they stand there, at the doorway, Hamza looking at the ground. A donkey brays somewhere.

"Come in," Hamza says. He swings the door open. "Please come in."

THEY SIT ON the floor in a sparsely furnished room. There is a Herati rug on the floor, beaded cushions to sit on, and a framed photo of Mecca on the wall. They sit by the open window, on either side of an oblong patch of sunlight. Laila hears women's voices whispering from another room. A little barefoot boy places before them a platter of green tea and pistachio *gaaz* nougats. Hamza nods at him.

"My son."

The boy leaves soundlessly.

"So tell me," Hamza says tiredly.

Laila does. She tells him everything. It takes longer than she'd imagined. Toward the end, she struggles to maintain composure. It still isn't easy, one year later, talking about Mariam.

When she's done, Hamza doesn't say anything for a long time. He slowly turns his teacup on its saucer, one way, then the other.

"My father, may he rest in peace, was so very fond of her," he says at last. "He was the one who sang *azan* in her ear when she was born, you know. He visited her every week, never missed. Sometimes he took me with him. He was her tutor, yes, but he was a friend too. He was a charitable man, my father. It nearly broke him when Jalil Khan gave her away."

"I'm sorry to hear about your father. May God forgive him."

Hamza nods his thanks. "He lived to be a very old man. He outlived Jalil Khan, in fact. We buried him in the village cemetery, not far from where Mariam's mother is buried. My father was a dear, dear man, surely heaven-bound."

Laila lowers her cup.

"May I ask you something?"

"Of course."

"Can you show me?" she says. "Where Mariam lived. Can you take me there?"

THE DRIVER AGREES to wait awhile longer.

Hamza and Laila exit the village and walk downhill on the road that connects Gul Daman to Herat. After fifteen minutes or so, he points to a narrow gap in the tall grass that flanks the road on both sides.

"That's how you get there," he says. "There is a path there."

The path is rough, winding, and dim, beneath the vegetation and undergrowth. The wind makes the tall grass slam against Laila's calves as she and Hamza climb the path, take the turns. On either side of them is a kaleido-scope of wildflowers swaying in the wind, some tall with curved petals, others low, fan-leafed. Here and there a few ragged buttercups peep through the low bushes. Laila hears the twitter of swallows overhead and the busy chatter of grasshoppers underfoot.

They walk uphill this way for two hundred yards or more. Then the path levels, and opens into a flatter patch of land. They stop, catch their breath. Laila dabs at her brow with her sleeve and bats at a swarm of mosquitoes hovering in front of her face. Here she sees the low-slung mountains in the horizon, a few cottonwoods, some poplars, various wild bushes that she cannot name.

"There used to be a stream here," Hamza says, a little out of breath. "But it's long dried up now."

He says he will wait here. He tells her to cross the dry streambed, walk toward the mountains.

"I'll wait here," he says, sitting on a rock beneath a poplar. "You go on."

"I won't—"

"Don't worry. Take your time. Go on, *hamshireh*."

Laila thanks him. She crosses the streambed, stepping from one stone to another. She spots broken soda bottles amid the rocks, rusted cans, and a mold-coated metallic container with a zinc lid half buried in the ground.

She heads toward the mountains, toward the weeping willows, which she can see now, the long drooping branches shaking with each gust of wind. In her chest, her heart is drumming. She sees that the willows are arranged as Mariam had said, in a circular grove with a clearing in the middle. Laila walks faster, almost running now. She looks back over her shoulder and sees that Hamza is a tiny figure, his *chapan* a burst of color against the brown of the trees' bark. She trips over a stone and almost falls, then regains her footing. She hurries the rest of the way with the legs of her trousers pulled up. She is panting by the time she reaches the willows.

Mariam's *kolba* is still here.

When she approaches it, Laila sees that the lone windowpane is empty and that the door is gone. Mariam had described a chicken coop and a tandoor, a wooden outhouse too, but Laila sees no sign of them. She pauses at the entrance to the *kolba*. She can hear flies buzzing inside.

To get in, she has to sidestep a large fluttering spiderweb. It's dim inside. Laila has to give her eyes a few moments to adjust. When they do, she sees that the interior is even smaller than she'd imagined. Only half of a single rotting, splintered board remains of the floorboards. The rest, she imagines, have been ripped up for burning as firewood. The floor is carpeted now with dry-edged leaves, broken bottles, discarded chewing gum wrappers, wild mushrooms, old yellowed cigarette butts. But mostly with weeds, some stunted, some springing impudently halfway up the walls.

Fifteen years, Laila thinks. Fifteen years in this place.

Laila sits down, her back to the wall. She listens to the wind filtering through the willows. There are more spiderwebs stretched across the ceiling. Someone has spray-painted something on one of the walls, but much of it has sloughed off, and Laila cannot decipher what it says. Then she realizes the letters are Russian. There is a deserted bird's nest in one corner and a bat hanging upside down in another corner, where the wall meets the low ceiling.

Laila closes her eyes and sits there awhile.

In Pakistan, it was difficult sometimes to remember the details of Mariam's face. There were times when, like a word on the tip of her tongue, Mariam's face eluded her. But now, here in this place, it's easy to summon Mariam behind the lids of her eyes: the soft radiance of her gaze, the long chin, the coarsened skin of her neck, the tight-lipped smile. Here, Laila can lay her cheek on the softness of Mariam's lap again, can feel Mariam swaying back and forth, reciting verses from the Koran, can feel the words vibrating down Mariam's body, to her knees, and into her own ears.

Then, suddenly, the weeds begin to recede, as if something is pulling them by the roots from beneath the ground. They sink lower and lower until the earth in the *kolba* has swallowed the last of their spiny leaves. The spiderwebs magically unspin themselves. The bird's nest self-disassembles, the twigs snapping loose one by one, flying out of the *kolba* end over end. An invisible eraser wipes the Russian graffiti off the wall.

The floorboards are back. Laila sees a pair of sleeping cots now, a wooden table, two chairs, a cast-iron stove in the corner, shelves along the walls, on which sit clay pots and pans, a blackened teakettle, cups and spoons. She hears chickens clucking outside, the distant gurgling of the stream.

A young Mariam is sitting at the table making a doll by the glow of an oil lamp. She's humming something. Her face is smooth and youthful, her hair washed, combed back. She has all her teeth.

Laila watches Mariam glue strands of yarn onto her doll's head. In a few years, this little girl will be a woman who will make small demands on life, who will never burden others, who will never let on that she too has had sorrows, disappointments, dreams that have been ridiculed. A woman who will be like a rock in a riverbed, enduring without complaint, her grace not sullied but *shaped* by the turbulence that washes over her. Already Laila sees something behind this young girl's eyes, something deep in her core, that neither Rasheed nor the Taliban will be able to break. Something as hard and unyielding as a block of limestone. Something that, in the end, will be *her* undoing and Laila's salvation.

The little girl looks up. Puts down the doll. Smiles.

Laila jo?

Laila's eyes snap open. She gasps, and her body pitches forward. She startles the bat, which zips from one end of the *kolba* to the other, its beating wings like the fluttering pages of a book, before it flies out the window.

Laila gets to her feet, beats the dead leaves from the seat of her trousers. She steps out of the *kolba*. Outside, the light has shifted slightly. A wind is blowing, making the grass ripple and the willow branches click.

Before she leaves the clearing, Laila takes one last look at the *kolba* where Mariam had slept, eaten, dreamed, held her breath for Jalil. On sagging walls, the willows cast crooked patterns that shift with each gust of wind. A crow has landed on the flat roof. It pecks at something, squawks, flies off.

"Good-bye, Mariam."

And, with that, unaware that she is weeping, Laila begins to run through the grass.

She finds Hamza still sitting on the rock. When he spots her, he stands up.

"Let's go back," he says. Then, "I have something to give you."

LAILA WAITS FOR Hamza in the garden by the front door. The boy who had served them tea earlier is standing beneath one of the fig trees holding a chicken, watching her impassively. Laila spies two faces, an old woman and a young girl in *hijab*s, observing her demurely from a window.

The door to the house opens and Hamza emerges. He is carrying a box.

He gives it to Laila.

"Jalil Khan gave this to my father a month or so before he died," Hamza says. "He asked my father to safeguard it for Mariam until she came to claim it. My father kept it for two years. Then, just before he passed away, he gave it to me, and asked me to save it for Mariam. But she . . . you know, she never came."

Laila looks down at the oval-shaped tin box. It looks like an old chocolate box. It's olive green, with fading gilt scrolls all around the hinged lid. There is a little rust on the sides, and two tiny dents on the front rim of the lid. Laila tries to open the box, but the latch is locked.

"What's in it?" she asks.

Hamza puts a key in her palm. "My father never unlocked it. Neither did I. I suppose it was God's will that it be you."

BACK AT THE HOTEL, Tariq and the children are not back yet.

Laila sits on the bed, the box on her lap. Part of her wants to leave it unopened, let whatever Jalil had intended remain a secret. But, in the end, the curiosity proves too strong. She slides in the key. It takes some rattling and shaking, but she opens the box.

In it, she finds three things: an envelope, a burlap sack, and a videocassette.

Laila takes the tape and goes down to the reception desk. She learns from the elderly clerk who had greeted them the day before that the hotel has only one VCR, in its biggest suite. The suite is vacant at the moment, and he agrees to take her. He leaves the desk to a mustachioed young man in a suit who is talking on a cellular phone.

The old clerk leads Laila to the second floor, to a door at the end of a long hallway. He works the lock, lets her in. Laila's eyes find the TV in the corner. They register nothing else about the suite.

She turns on the TV, turns on the VCR. Puts the tape in and pushes the PLAY button. The screen is blank for a few moments, and Laila begins to wonder why Jalil had gone to the trouble of passing a blank tape to Mariam. But then there is music, and images begin to play on the screen.

Laila frowns. She keeps watching for a minute or two. Then she pushes STOP, fast-forwards the tape, and pushes PLAY again. It's the same film.

The old man is looking at her quizzically.

The film playing on the screen is Walt Disney's *Pinocchio*. Laila does not understand.

TARIQ AND THE children come back to the hotel just after six o'clock. Aziza runs to Laila and shows her the earrings Tariq has bought for her, silver with an enamel butterfly on each. Zalmai is clutching an inflatable dolphin that squeaks when its snout is squeezed.

"How are you?" Tariq asks, putting his arm around her shoulder.

"I'm fine," Laila says. "I'll tell you later."

They walk to a nearby kebab house to eat. It's a small place, with sticky, vinyl tablecloths, smoky and loud. But the lamb is tender and moist and the bread hot. They walk the streets for a while after. Tariq buys the children rose-water ice cream from a street-side kiosk. They eat, sitting on a bench, the mountains behind them silhouetted against the scarlet red of dusk. The air is warm, rich with the fragrance of cedar.

Laila had opened the envelope earlier when she'd come back to the room after viewing the videotape. In it was a letter, handwritten in blue ink on a yellow, lined sheet of paper.

It read:

May 13, 1987

My dear Mariam:

I pray that this letter finds you in good health.

As you know, I came to Kabul a month ago to speak with you. But you would not see me. I was disappointed but could not blame you. In your place, I might have done the same. I lost the privilege of your good graces a long time ago and for that I only have myself to blame. But if you are reading this letter, then you have read the letter that I left at your door. You have read it and you have come to see Mullah Faizullah, as I had asked that you do. I am grateful that you did, Mariam jo. I am grateful for this chance to say a few words to you.

Where do I begin?

Your father has known so much sorrow since we last spoke, Mariam jo. Your stepmother Afsoon was killed on the first day of the 1979 uprising. A stray bullet killed your sister Niloufar that same day. I can still see her, my little Niloufar, doing headstands to impress guests. Your brother Farhad joined the jihad in 1980. The Soviets killed him in 1982, just outside of Helmand. I never got to see his body. I don't know if you have children of your own, Mariam jo, but if you do I pray that God look after them and spare you the grief that I have known. I still dream of them. I still dream of my dead children.

I have dreams of you too, Mariam jo. I miss you. I miss the sound of your voice, your laughter. I miss reading to you, and all those times we fished together. Do you remember all those times we fished together? You were a good daughter, Mariam jo, and I cannot ever think of you without feeling shame and regret. Regret . . . When it comes to you, Mariam jo, I have oceans of it. I regret that I did not see you the day you came to Herat. I regret that I did not open the door and take you in. I regret that I did not make you a daughter to me, that I let you live in that place for all those years. And for what? Fear of losing face? Of staining my so-called good name? How little those things matter to me now after all the loss, all the terrible things I have seen in this cursed war. But now, of course, it is too late. Perhaps this is just punishment for those who have been heartless, to understand only when nothing can be undone. Now all I can do is say that you were a good daughter, Mariam jo, and that I never deserved you. Now all I can do is ask for your forgiveness. So forgive me, Mariam jo. Forgive me. Forgive me. Forgive me.

I am not the wealthy man you once knew. The communists confiscated so much of my land, and all of my stores as well. But it is petty to complain, for God—for reasons that I do not understand—has still blessed me with far more than most people. Since my return from Kabul, I have managed to sell what little remained of my land. I have enclosed for you your share of the inheritance. You can see that it is far from a fortune, but it is something. It is something. (You will also notice that I have taken the liberty of exchanging the money into dollars. I think it is for the best. God alone knows the fate of our own beleaguered currency.)

I hope you do not think that I am trying to buy your forgiveness. I hope you will credit me with knowing that your forgiveness is not for sale. It never was. I am merely giving you, if belatedly, what was rightfully yours all along. I was not a dutiful father to you in life. Perhaps in death I can be.

Ah, death. I won't burden you with details, but death is within sight for me now. Weak heart, the doctors say. It is a fitting manner of death, I think, for a weak man.

Mariam jo,

I dare, I dare allow myself the hope that, after you read this, you will be more charitable to me than I ever was to *you. That you might find it in your heart to come and see your father. That you will knock on my door one more time and give me the chance to open it this time, to welcome you, to take you in my arms, my daughter, as I should have all those years ago. It is a hope as weak as my heart. This I know. But I will be waiting. I will be listening for your knock. I will be hoping.*

May God grant you a long and prosperous life, my daughter. May God give you many healthy and beautiful children. May you find the happiness, peace, and acceptance that I did not give you. Be well. I leave you in the loving hands of God.

Your undeserving father,
Jalil

That night, after they return to the hotel, after the children have played and gone to bed, Laila tells Tariq about the letter. She shows him the money in the burlap sack. When she begins to cry, he kisses her face and holds her in his arms.

51.

April 2003

The drought has ended. It snowed at last this past winter, knee-deep, and now it has been raining for days. The Kabul River is flowing once again. Its spring floods have washed away Titanic City.

There is mud on the streets now. Shoes squish. Cars get trapped. Donkeys loaded with apples slog heavily, their hooves splattering muck from rain puddles. But no one is complaining about the mud, no one is mourning Titanic City. *We need Kabul to be green again,* people say.

Yesterday, Laila watched her children play in the downpour, hopping from one puddle to another in their backyard beneath a lead-colored sky. She was watching from the kitchen window of the small two-bedroom house that they are renting in Deh-Mazang. There is a pomegranate tree in the yard and a thicket of sweetbriar bushes. Tariq has patched the walls and built the children a slide, a swing set, a little fenced area for Zalmai's new goat. Laila watched the rain slide off Zalmai's scalp—he has asked that he be shaved, like Tariq, who is in charge now of saying the *Babaloo* prayers. The rain flattened Aziza's long hair, turned it into sodden tendrils that sprayed Zalmai when she snapped her head.

Zalmai is almost six. Aziza is ten. They celebrated her birthday last week, took her to Cinema Park, where, at last, *Titanic* was openly screened for the people of Kabul.

"COME ON, CHILDREN, we're going to be late," Laila calls, putting their lunches in a paper bag.

It's eight o'clock in the morning. Laila was up at five. As always, it was Aziza who shook her awake for morning *namaz*. The prayers, Laila knows, are Aziza's way of clinging to Mariam, her way of keeping Mariam close awhile yet before time has its way, before it snatches Mariam from the garden of her memory like a weed pulled by its roots.

After *namaz*, Laila had gone back to bed, and was still asleep when Tariq left the house. She vaguely remembers him kissing her cheek. Tariq has found work with a French NGO that fits land mine survivors and amputees with prosthetic limbs.

Zalmai comes chasing Aziza into the kitchen.

"You have your notebooks, you two? Pencils? Textbooks?"

"Right here," Aziza says, lifting her backpack. Again, Laila notices how her stutter is lessening.

"Let's go, then."

Laila lets the children out of the house, locks the door. They step out into the cool morning. It isn't raining today. The sky is blue, and Laila sees no clumps of clouds in the horizon. Holding hands, the three of them make their way to the bus stop. The streets are busy already, teeming with a steady stream of rickshaws, taxicabs, UN trucks, buses, ISAF jeeps. Sleepy-eyed merchants are unlocking store gates that had been rolled down for the night. Vendors sit behind towers of chewing gum and cigarette packs. Already the widows have claimed their spots at street corners, asking the passersby for coins.

Laila finds it strange to be back in Kabul. The city has changed. Every day now she sees people planting saplings, painting old houses, carrying bricks for new ones. They dig gutters and wells. On windowsills, Laila spots flowers potted in the empty shells of old Mujahideen rockets—rocket flowers, Kabulis call them. Recently, Tariq took Laila and the children to the Gardens of Babur, which are being renovated. For the first time in years, Laila hears music at Kabul's street corners, *rubab* and tabla, *dootar*, harmonium and tamboura, old Ahmad Zahir songs.

Laila wishes Mammy and Babi were alive to see these changes. But, like Jalil's letter, Kabul's penance has arrived too late.

Laila and the children are about to cross the street to the bus stop when suddenly a black Land Cruiser with tinted windows blows by. It swerves at the last instant and misses Laila by less than an arm's length. It splatters tea-colored rainwater all over the children's shirts.

Laila yanks her children back onto the sidewalk, heart somersaulting in her throat.

The Land Cruiser speeds down the street, honks twice, and makes a sharp left.

Laila stands there, trying to catch her breath, her fingers gripped tightly around her children's wrists.

It slays Laila. It slays her that the warlords have been allowed back to Kabul. That her parents' murderers live in posh homes with walled gardens, that they have been appointed minister of this and deputy minister of that, that they ride with impunity in shiny, bulletproof SUVs through neighborhoods that they demolished. It slays her.

But Laila has decided that she will not be crippled by resentment. Mariam wouldn't want it that way. *What's the sense?* she would say with a smile both innocent and wise. *What good is it, Laila jo?* And so Laila has resigned herself to moving on. For her own sake, for Tariq's, for her children's. And for Mariam, who still visits Laila in her dreams, who is never more than a breath or two below her consciousness. Laila has moved on. Because in the end she knows that's all she can do. That and hope.

ZAMAN IS STANDING at the free throw line, his knees bent, bouncing a basketball. He is instructing a group of boys in matching jerseys sitting in a semicircle on the court. Zaman spots Laila, tucks the ball under his arm, and waves. He says something to the boys, who then wave and cry out, *"Salaam, moalim sahib!"*

Laila waves back.

The orphanage playground has a row of apple saplings now along the east-facing wall. Laila is planning to plant some on the south wall as well as soon as it is rebuilt. There is a new swing set, new monkey bars, and a jungle gym.

Laila walks back inside through the screen door.

They have repainted both the exterior and the interior of the orphanage. Tariq and Zaman have repaired all the roof leaks, patched the walls, replaced the windows, carpeted the rooms where the children sleep and play. This past winter, Laila bought a few beds for the children's sleeping quarters, pillows too, and proper wool blankets. She had cast-iron stoves installed for the winter.

Anis, one of Kabul's newspapers, had run a story the month before on the renovation of the orphanage. They'd taken a photo too, of Zaman, Tariq, Laila, and one of the attendants, standing in a row behind the children. When Laila saw the article, she'd thought of her childhood friends Giti and Hasina, and Hasina saying, *By the time we're twenty, Giti and I, we'll have pushed out four, five kids each. But you, Laila, you'll make us two dummies proud. You're going to be somebody. I know one day I'll pick up a newspaper and find your picture on the front page.* The photo hadn't made the front page, but there it was nevertheless, as Hasina had predicted.

Laila takes a turn and makes her way down the same hallway where, two years before, she and Mariam had delivered Aziza to Zaman. Laila still remembers how they had to pry Aziza's fingers from her wrist. She remembers running down this hallway, holding back a howl, Mariam calling after her, Aziza screaming with panic. The hallway's walls are covered now with posters, of dinosaurs, cartoon characters, the Buddhas of Bamiyan, and displays of artwork by the orphans. Many of the drawings depict tanks running over huts, men brandishing AK-47s, refugee camp tents, scenes of jihad.

Laila turns a corner in the hallway and sees the children now, waiting outside the classroom. She is greeted by their scarves, their shaved scalps covered by skullcaps, their small, lean figures, the beauty of their drabness.

When the children spot Laila, they come running. They come running at full tilt. Laila is swarmed. There is a flurry of high-pitched greetings, of shrill voices, of patting, clutching, tugging, groping, of jostling with one another to climb into her arms. There are outstretched little hands and appeals for attention. Some of them call her *Mother*. Laila does not correct them.

It takes Laila some work this morning to calm the children down, to get them to form a proper queue, to usher them into the classroom.

It was Tariq and Zaman who built the classroom by knocking down the wall between two adjacent rooms. The floor is still badly cracked and has missing tiles. For the time being, it is covered with tarpaulin, but Tariq has promised to cement some new tiles and lay down carpeting soon.

Nailed above the classroom doorway is a rectangular board, which Zaman has sanded and painted in gleaming white. On it, with a brush, Zaman has written four lines of poetry, his answer, Laila knows, to those who grumble that the promised aid money to Afghanistan isn't coming, that the rebuilding is going too slowly, that there is corruption, that the Taliban are regrouping already and will come back with a vengeance, that the world will forget once again about Afghanistan. The lines are from his favorite of Hafez's *ghazals*:

Joseph shall return to Canaan, grieve not,
Hovels shall turn to rose gardens, grieve not.
If a flood should arrive, to drown all that's alive,
Noah is your guide in the typhoon's eye, grieve not.

Laila passes beneath the sign and enters the classroom. The children are taking their seats, flipping notebooks open, chattering. Aziza is talking to a girl in the adjacent row. A paper airplane floats across the room in a high arc. Someone tosses it back.

"Open your Farsi books, children," Laila says, dropping her own books on her desk.

To a chorus of flipping pages, Laila makes her way to the curtainless window. Through the glass, she can see the boys in the playground lining up to practice their free throws. Above them, over the mountains, the morning sun is rising. It catches the metallic rim of the basketball hoop, the chain link of the tire swings, the whistle hanging around Zaman's neck, his new, unchipped spectacles. Laila flattens her palms against the warm glass panes. Closes her eyes. She lets the sunlight fall on her cheeks, her eyelids, her brow.

When they first came back to Kabul, it distressed Laila that she didn't know where the Taliban had buried

Mariam. She wished she could visit Mariam's grave, to sit with her awhile, leave a flower or two. But Laila sees now that it doesn't matter. Mariam is never very far. She is here, in these walls they've repainted, in the trees they've planted, in the blankets that keep the children warm, in these pillows and books and pencils. She is in the children's laughter. She is in the verses Aziza recites and in the prayers she mutters when she bows westward. But, mostly, Mariam is in Laila's own heart, where she shines with the bursting radiance of a thousand suns.

Someone has been calling her name, Laila realizes. She turns around, instinctively tilts her head, lifting her good ear just a tad. It's Aziza.

"Mammy? Are you all right?"

The room has become quiet. The children are watching her.

Laila is about to answer when her breath suddenly catches. Her hands shoot down. They pat the spot where, a moment before, she'd felt a wave go through her. She waits. But there is no more movement.

"Mammy?"

"Yes, my love." Laila smiles. "I'm all right. Yes. Very much."

As she walks to her desk at the front of the class, Laila thinks of the naming game they'd played again over dinner the night before. It has become a nightly ritual ever since Laila gave Tariq and the children the news. Back and forth they go, making a case for their own choice. Tariq likes Mohammad. Zalmai, who has recently watched *Superman* on tape, is puzzled as to why an Afghan boy cannot be named Clark. Aziza is campaigning hard for Aman. Laila likes Omar.

But the game involves only male names. Because, if it's a girl, Laila has already named her.

402

AFTERWORD

For almost three decades now, the Afghan refugee crisis has been one of the most severe around the globe. War, hunger, anarchy, and oppression forced millions of people—like Tariq and his family in this tale—to abandon their homes and flee Afghanistan to settle in neighboring Pakistan and Iran. At the height of the exodus, as many as eight million Afghans were living abroad as refugees. Today, more than two million Afghan refugees remain in Pakistan.

Since 2002, nearly five million refugees have returned home with assistance from the UNHCR, the UN Refugee Agency. In September 2007, I visited some of these returnees in northern Afghanistan. I met families who lived on less than a dollar a day. They spent entire winters cooped up in holes dug underground. I visited villages where families routinely lost ten to fifteen children to the elements every winter and every summer. The people I met drank water from muddy rivers and died of easily preventable diseases. They had little shelter and no access to health-care facilities, schools, food, or jobs. I was devastated.

The Khaled Hosseini Foundation was established as a result of this life-altering journey. With this Foundation, we hope to make a meaningful and enduring difference. In 2009, the foundation collaborated with UNHCR and funded the building of shelter homes for 71 homeless families in north-eastern Afghanistan. Plans are underway for the building of more shelters for homeless returnees. We will primarily aim our funding at those projects that benefit refugees, and women and children, two groups that have suffered more than any other in that beleaguered country and are the backbone of Afghanistan's future.

The rebuilding needs of Afghanistan are great, and containing the tide of human suffering there is a task of Herculean proportion. To learn more about this, or The Khaled Hosseini Foundation, please visit: www.khaledhosseinifoundation.org.

Thank you.

Khaled Hosseini
November, 2009

ACKNOWLEDGMENTS

A few clarifications before I give thanks. The village of Gul Daman is a fictional place—as far as I know. Those who are familiar with the city of Herat will notice that I have taken minor liberties describing the geography around it. Last, the title of this novel comes from a poem composed by Saeb-e-Tabrizi, a seventeenth-century Persian poet. Those who know the original Farsi poem will doubtless note that the English translation of the line containing the title of this novel is not a literal one. But it is the generally accepted translation, by Dr. Josephine Davis, and I found it lovely. I am grateful to her.

I would like to thank Qayoum Sarwar, Hekmat Sadat, Elyse Hathaway, Rosemary Stasek, Lawrence Quill, and Haleema Jazmin Quill for their assistance and support.

Very special thanks to my father, Baba, for reading this manuscript, for his feedback, and, as ever, for his love and support. And to my mother, whose selfless, gentle spirit permeates this tale. You are my reason, Mother jo. My thanks go to my in-laws for their generosity and many kindnesses. To the rest of my wonderful family, I remain indebted and grateful to each and every one of you.

I wish to thank my agent, Elaine Koster, for always, always believing, Jody Hotchkiss (Onward!), David Grossman, Helen Heller, and the tireless Chandler Crawford. I am grateful and indebted to every single person at Riverhead Books. In particular, I want to thank Susan Petersen Kennedy and Geoffrey Kloske for their faith in this story. My heartfelt thanks also go to Marilyn Ducksworth, Mih-Ho Cha, Catharine Lynch, Craig D. Burke, Leslie Schwartz, Honi Werner, and Wendy Pearl. Special thanks to my sharp-eyed copy editor, Tony Davis, who misses nothing, and, lastly, to my talented editor, Sarah McGrath, for her patience, foresight, and guidance.

Finally, thank you, Roya. For reading this story, again and again, for weathering my minor crises of confidence (and a couple of major ones), for never doubting. This book would not be without you. I love you.

POSTSCRIPT
BY KHALED HOSSEINI

This extract is taken from a speech given at
Book Expo America on 2 June, 2007.

I began writing like the boy in *The Kite Runner*, Amir. I grew up in Kabul in the 1970s, and I wrote poems and little plays that I would coax my siblings and cousins into staging for our parents at parties. I also wrote short stories, which I recall were dark, intense, even unabashedly, proudly melodramatic and, in their own childish way, dealt with issues of loyalty, friendship and class struggle. They made up for what they lacked in subtlety and style with a big, winning, expansive heart, which are words that some people have used, maybe with some justification, to describe *The Kite Runner*.

The language in which I've written has changed. I began writing in Farsi, then I wrote in French and now I mostly write in English, but one thing remains constant: I've always written for an audience of one. For me, writing has always been the selfish, self-serving act of telling myself a story. You know, something grabs my interest and compels me to sit down and see it through. This is how *The Kite*

Runner was written. I had two boys in mind, one who was conflicted and on very unsure moral ground, the other pure and loyal and rooted in integrity. I knew that their friendship was doomed, that there would be a falling out and that this would impact the lives of those around them in a profound way. The how and why that would happen was the compulsion that led me to sit down and write that novel in March 2001.

I never intended to get the novel published. Even when I was as far as two-thirds of the way through writing, it never crossed my mind that anybody would actually read it although I thought my wife probably would because she loves me. So you can imagine my astonishment at the reception that *The Kite Runner* has received worldwide since its publication. I received letters from India, London, Sydney, Paris, Arkansas, all over the world from readers who expressed a passion to me. Many of them wanted to know how to send money to Afghanistan. Some told me they wanted to adopt an Afghan orphan. In those letters I saw the unique ability that fiction has to connect people who dress differently or practice different religions, and I saw how universal some human experiences are, like friendship, guilt, forgiveness, loss and atonement.

In those letters, I also saw how I had unwittingly placed myself in a daunting position—that of following up *The Kite Runner*, and writing a book that, through no fault of its own, would bear the burden of comparison to *The Kite Runner*, while the ink was still wet on its pages. The reading of every fan letter I received was punctuated by a loud and anxious gulp and a feeling of pity for this as-yet-unwritten novel. I feared for the sanity of my family who would have to bear with me as I set about writing this new book.

I had further complicated matters by deciding on a narrative that demanded not one but two central characters, both of them women. This was a decision that I'd made when I was putting the final edits on *The Kite Runner*—a father and son story set exclusively in the world of men. I wanted to write another love story set in Afghanistan but this time a mother/daughter tale and about the inner lives of two struggling Afghan women. I suppose there were some easier roads I could have gone down, but I chose this one because, both as a writer and as an Afghan, I couldn't think of a more riveting or important or compelling story than the struggle of women in my country. Dramatically speaking, every other topic paled in comparison.

Unfortunately the image of the burqa-wearing woman walking past the stern, glaring face of the Taliban official has become familiar around the world, perhaps even iconic. When I was in Kabul in 2003, I met a man who worked as a bodyguard for a government official. He told me, kind of casually, a story about a woman he had seen beaten by a Taliban official on the street. In telling that story, he used a rather grisly if colorful expression. He said he beat her until her mother's milk leaked out of her bones. In listening to that story it seemed unreal to me that this happened in Kabul. Not long ago, women in Afghanistan were professors at universities, they were doctors and lawyers, worked in hospitals, taught at schools and played an important role in society. They were women like my mother, who was university educated and a teacher of Farsi and history, eventually becoming the vice principal of a very large high school for girls. But that was in Kabul, and Afghanistan is not a nation of urbanized middle-class people. There has always been an ideological gap between liberal reformist Kabul and rural Afghanistan. The sad truth is that the Taliban-style oppression of women in certain regions of Afghanistan existed long before the Taliban was even a twinkle in the loving eye of the Pakistani secret intelligence. Whereas Kabul has been, relatively speaking, a hub for female autonomy, rural Afghanistan, especially south and east along the border with Pakistan, has been traditionally a patriarchal tribal region where men have decided the fates of women. There, women have always lived in confinement. They have always worn the burqa on the street and rarely gone to school beyond the age of twelve so there was rampant illiteracy in those areas. For centuries, women there have been told when they will marry, who they will marry, and, incidentally, for how much. For the most part, rural Afghan women have led quiet, subterranean lives of obedience and service.

This may surprise you but throughout the last century there were multiple attempts to liberate, as it were, the women of Afghanistan, originating in Kabul. There was a king named Amanullah in the 1920s who actually banned the wearing of the burqa in public. He built the first hospital for women and the first school for girls. He brought teachers over from Europe and sent women to Europe to get an education. Amanullah tried to ban forced marriage, raise the minimum marrying age for girls to sixteen and ban the practice of bride price. Unfortunately, largely as a result of these attempts, there was a rebellion and he was run out of town. He ended up dying an old man in exile.

There were other attempts in the 1950s, 60s and 70s, some of which had fruition. In 1964, Afghan women gained the right to vote. But Kabul's reforms have always been met by the patriarchal tribal leaders with mockery, contempt or in some cases mutiny, as in the case of poor King Amanullah.

So, as you can see, life was a struggle for some women in Afghanistan well before the Taliban. But it became all but unbearable with the outbreak of factional war, anarchy and extremism. In many ways, that's when disaster really struck.

Women suffered not only through the bombings and indiscriminate shelling of civilian areas like everyone else, not only were beaten and tortured and humiliated and imprisoned, not only had their fundamental human rights violated over and over again, but in large numbers also suffered from gender-based abuse. They were abducted and sold as slaves, forced into marriage to militia commanders, forced into prostitution, and raped, a crime particularly heinous and unforgivable that was used to intimidate families who were opposed to one faction or another.

Today in post-Taliban, post-9/11 Afghanistan there is talk again of liberating women, as there should be. The gender apartheid that has been forced on Afghan women has been one of the great unresolved injustices of the modern world. In addition, Afghanistan needs its women. The whole project of rebuilding Afghanistan is doomed if the fundamental human rights of its women are not respected and its women are not allowed to participate.

Queen Soraya, wife of King Amanullah, said: "Do not think, however, that our nation needs only men to serve it. Women should also take their part, as women did in the early years of Islam. The valuable services rendered by women are recounted throughout history. And from their examples, we learn that we must all contribute toward a development of our nation." The Queen said those words back in 1926 and it seems to me that her words are as relevant eighty years later, and perhaps even more so than they were back then.

I returned to Kabul in 2003 and met people from all walks of life, and I remember standing at street corners and seeing fully covered women walking along, trailed by four, five, six, seven children. I remember thinking, who is that person inside? What has she seen? What has she endured? What makes her happy? What gives her sorrow?

What are her hopes, her longings, her disappointments? *A Thousand Splendid Suns* is in some ways my attempt at imagining answers to those questions. It's my attempt to explore the inner lives of these two fictional women and look for the very ordinary humanity beneath their veils.

A Thousand Splendid Suns is very, very dear to me. It has been a labor of love, and I hope that it doesn't sound too pretentious if I say that I think of it as my modest tribute to the great courage, endurance and resilience of Afghanistan.

I hope that I will engage you, that I will transport you and that the novel will move you and leave you with some sense of compassion and empathy for Afghan women whose suffering has been matched by very few groups in recent world history.

Khaled Hosseini

READING GUIDE

In brief

Mariam is a *harami*, an illegitimate child, who only sees her adored father once a week. On those precious days they go fishing, he reads to her and gives her beautiful presents, but she can never live with him. She decides to visit his home, a visit he does not acknowledge, and returns to find that her mother has hanged herself. Determined that she will not secure a place in their household, her father's wives marry her off to Rasheed, an elderly widower from Kabul, far enough away for Mariam to be safely forgotten. It is a marriage that soon deteriorates into brutality and misery made worse for Mariam by Rasheed's decision to also marry the orphaned Laila. When Laila disappoints Rasheed by bearing a daughter, she too finds herself the target of his cruelty. But out of this unhappy household grows a friendship which will bind the two women in a union as close as any marriage, and which will endure beyond death. Written in often lyrical prose, Khaled Hosseini's second novel weaves thirty years of turbulent Afghan history through an intensely powerful story of family, friendship and, ultimately, hope.

Background

Khaled Hosseini's reputation as an accomplished story-teller has already been well and truly established with *The Kite Runner*, his celebrated debut novel written in the early hours before setting off for his "day job" as a doctor. Brought up in a tradition of storytelling, Hosseini has described this tradition as first and foremost what writing novels is about. It is a quality central to *A Thousand Splendid Suns* which seamlessly blends the compelling narratives of Mariam and Laila with the deeply troubled history of Afghanistan over the past thirty years. Hosseini has described writing the novel as "an even more satisfying experience for me than the writing of *The Kite Runner*, because it was a more complex and ultimately unexpected journey."

With his first novel Hosseini had wanted to give a Western public assailed with media images of war-torn Afghanistan, firstly during the Soviet occupation and then under the Taliban, a glimpse of the country he remembered from childhood and to dispel some of the misconceptions that some of his adopted countrymen had about it. Many of those misconceptions were about women who had not suffered repression before the Taliban seized power, contrary to popular Western belief. During what many have called the "Golden Years" of the 1960s and 70s, women actively contributed to Afghan society—Hosseini's mother, for example, taught at a girls' school—and their rights had been confirmed in a new constitution in the mid-1970s. It is the role of women that Hosseini has chosen to explore in his second novel and he does so vividly through the stories of Mariam and Laila, two women separated by a generation but united by an unbreakable bond of friendship. These two endure not only the brutality of their husband Rasheed, but also the appalling atrocities of the Taliban, yet remain resilient and true to themselves.

Hosseini's family sought asylum in the United States in 1980 shortly after the Soviet invasion. Hosseini returned to Afghanistan after a twenty-seven year absence, following the fall of the Taliban, partly to satisfy a yearning to see his homeland again but also to find out how it was faring. He came back to the United States with a sense of optimism although not as much as he had hoped for, citing the security situation and the narcotics trade as two causes for grave concern.

About the author

Khaled Hosseini was born in 1965 in Kabul where his father was a diplomat and his mother taught Farsi and history. After the 1978 coup and the subsequent Russian invasion, the family fled Afghanistan for the United States, receiving political asylum in 1980. They settled in San Jose, California where his father found work as a driving instructor. Hosseini is a doctor and lives with his wife and two children in Northern California. *The Kite Runner*, his first novel, has been met with great critical and popular acclaim.

For discussion

● The novel opens with the sentence, "Mariam was five years old the first time she heard the word *harami*." How important is that word in the novel? How does Mariam's illegitimacy shape her life?

● "The next time Mariam signed her name to a document, twenty-seven years later, a mullah would again be present" (page 54). Khaled Hosseini foreshadows events, both domestic and national, at many points throughout *A Thousand Splendid Suns*. What effect does this have?

- "But it was the women who drew Mariam's eyes the most" (page 74). What is it that fascinates Mariam about the women of Kabul, and why does it capture her attention? How are women treated by the various regimes that take control of Afghanistan? How are the main female characters portrayed in the novel? To what extent do these portrayals differ from any preconceptions that you may have had about women in Afghanistan?

- Mariam protests at the idea of marrying Rasheed, begging her father not to force her. What kind of husband does he prove to be? How does she come to feel about him? How does their marriage change? Why do you think Rasheed behaves in the way that he does?

- "And in this fleeting, wordless exchange with Mariam, Laila knew that they were not enemies any longer" (page 244). How is the deep bond between Mariam and Laila forged? How does this bond sustain both of them?

- How does the observation of Islam in Kabul differ from Mariam's hometown of Herat? What part does religion play in her life? How important is it in the novel?

- "To me, it's nonsense – and very dangerous nonsense at that – all this talk of I'm Tajik and you're Pashtun and he's Hazara and she's Uzbek. We're all Afghans, and that's all that should matter" (page 128), Laila's father tells her. How important is this ethnic diversity both in the novel and in what happens to Afghanistan throughout the thirty years the book spans?

- What is the significance of the novel's title? Why do you think Hosseini chose it?

- What do you think of the novel's ending?

- How would you describe Hosseini's writing style? Were there particular passages that impressed you and if so what were they and why?

- How are the West and the Soviet Union portrayed in the novel? What part do they play in Afghanistan's troubles?
- Hosseini is an expatriate Afghan. To what extent do you think this has influenced the writing of *A Thousand Splendid Suns*, and his portrayal of Afghanistan?

Resources
- www.khaledhosseini.com – Khaled Hosseini's website
- www.barnesandnoble.com/writers/writer details.asp?z=y&cid=1145572#interview – interview published on Barnes and Noble's website
- www.afghanmagazine.com/2004_06/profile/khosseini.shtml – conversation with Farhad Ahzad published on afghanmagazine.com
- www.bloomsbury.com/Authors/microsite.asp?id=480&section=1&aid=863 – conversation between Hosseini and Riverhead Books, his American publisher
- http://news.bbc.co.uk/1/hi/world/south_asia/1162108.stm – Afghanistan timeline published at the BBC's website

Suggested further reading
Fiction
Half of a Yellow Sun by Chimamanda Ngozi Adichie
A Married Woman by Manju Kapur
The Woman Who Walked into Doors by Roddy Doyle
Swallows of Kabul by Yasmina Khadra

Non-fiction
The Sewing Circles of Herat by Christina Lamb
The Bookseller of Kabul by Asne Seierstad

Other books by Khaled Hosseini
The Kite Runner

A NOTE ON THE AUTHOR

Khaled Hosseini was born in Kabul, Afghanistan and moved to the United States in 1980. His first novel, *The Kite Runner*, was an international bestseller, published in thirty-four countries. In 2006 he was named a US goodwill envoy to the United Nations Refugee Agency. He lives in Northern California.

ALSO AVAILABLE BY KHALED HOSSEINI

The Kite Runner

Read by over 8 million people, this astonishing
international bestseller won the Penguin/Orange
Readers' Group Prize in both 2006 and 2007.

1970s Afghanistan: Twelve-year-old Amir is desperate to
win the local kite-fighting tournament and his loyal friend
Hassan promises to help him. But neither of the boys can
foresee what will happen to Hassan that afternoon, an
event that is to shatter their lives. After the Russians invade
and the family is forced to flee to America, Amir realises
that one day he must return to an Afghanistan under
Taliban rule to find the one thing that his new world
cannot grant him: redemption.

'Unforgettable . . . extraordinary . . . powerful'
Isabel Allende

'A devastating, masterful and painfully honest story'
Daily Telegraph

'A novel of unusual generosity, honesty and compassion'
Independent

'Rich in warmth and humour . . . full of haunting images
. . . vivid and engaging' *New York Times*

OUT NOW IN ALL GOOD BOOKSHOPS